P9-DCY-799

TWENTY-FIRST CENTURY
SCIENCE FICTION

TWENTY-FIRST CENTURY SCIENCE FICTION

Edited by

DAVID G. HARTWELL and
PATRICK NIELSEN HAYDEN

TOR®

A TOM DOHERTY ASSOCIATES BOOK
NEW YORK

TWENTY-FIRST CENTURY SCIENCE FICTION

Copyright © 2013 by David G. Hartwell and Patrick Nielsen Hayden

A Tor Book
Published by Tom Doherty Associates, LLC
175 Fifth Avenue
New York, NY 10010

www.tor-forge.com

Tor® is a registered trademark of Tom Doherty Associates, LLC.

Library of Congress Cataloging-in-Publication Data

Twenty-first century science fiction / edited by David G. Hartwell and Patrick Nielsen Hayden.—
  First Edition.
        p. cm.
    "A Tom Doherty Associates Book."
    ISBN 978-0-7653-2600-3 (hardcover)
    ISBN 978-1-4299-8874-2 (e-book)
    1. Science fiction, American.   I. Hartwell, David G., editor of compilation.   II. Nielsen
Hayden, Patrick, editor of compilation.
    PS648.S3T84 2013
    813'.0876208—dc23

                                                                            2013023955

Tor books may be purchased for educational, business, or promotional use. For information on bulk purchases, please contact Macmillan Corporate and Premium Sales Department at 1-800-221-7945, extension 5442, or write specialmarkets@macmillan.com.

First Edition: November 2013

Printed in the United States of America

0 9 8 7 6 5 4 3 2 1

COPYRIGHT ACKNOWLEDGMENTS

CONTENTS

PREFACE

You hold in your hands an anthology of stories by what we believe are some of the best science fiction writers that came to prominence since the twentieth century changed into the twenty-first. That phrase "came to prominence" explains our approach. Many writers publish their first work long before they come to general attention. William Gibson exploded into the consciousness of science fiction, and then the world, with *Neuromancer* in 1984, but he had been publishing short fiction for years before that. Likewise, there are writers in this volume whose first stories appeared as early as the 1980s, but nobody in this book came to wide notice before 2000.

The idea of an anthology showcasing the SF voices of the new century seemed like a natural project for the two of us. Our tastes are not identical, but we can fairly well agree on good writers and good stories. And we are both students of the history of SF without holding all the same opinions about it. Neither of us is especially interested in being genre policemen, dictating what is and isn't proper SF. And yet, both of us emerge from the core SF audience of the twentieth century—the SF subculture, professional and fannish, that emerged from the earnest and urgent desire to defend and encourage quality SF in the face of a dominant culture that seemed to hold it in contempt. Decades later, many of the battles of those days have been won. Others have become irrelevant. One of the interesting things about the stories presented here is that they were written in a world in which SF, far from being marginal, is a firmly established part of the cultural landscape.

This took a long time, longer than we wanted. We had hoped to finish the book in 2010 and publish it in 2011 or 2012. But perhaps the wait has made it a better book, because we had more time to think it through. We are even more confident about our choices than we were three years ago. And we are reasonably certain that you will find much to enjoy, engage with, and argue over in the pages that follow.

—D.G.H. & P.N.H.

TWENTY-FIRST CENTURY SCIENCE FICTION

VANDANA SINGH Born and raised in New Delhi, Vandana Singh now lives near Boston, where she teaches physics at a small state college. Her SF stories have been appearing in print since 2002. She has written of herself that "being a card-carrying alien writing science fiction is an interesting experience; my distance from my native shores necessarily affects what and how I write."

"Infinities" first appeared in her collection *The Woman Who Thought She Was a Planet*, published in India in 2008. Many of her stories are set in India, or in futures influenced by the traditional figures of Indian literature. She says, "Physics is a way of viewing the world, and it is one of my most important lenses. One of the most exciting things about science is that it reveals the subtext of the physical world. In other words, surface reality isn't all there is; the world is full of hidden stories, connections, patterns, and the scientific as well as the literary and psychological aspects of this multi-textured reality are, to me, fascinating." In this story about a man who loves mathematics, Singh manages to convey something quite rare, in our genre or out of it—an authentic sense of what paradigm-shattering mathematical insight feels like from the inside. She does so without flinching from the fact that, on the other side of eureka, the world remains the world.

INFINITIES

An equation means nothing to me unless it expresses a thought of God.
—SRINIVASA RAMANUJAN, Indian mathematician (1887–1920)

Abdul Karim is his name. He is a small, thin man, precise to the point of affectation in his appearance and manner. He walks very straight; there is gray in his hair and in his short, pointed beard. When he goes out of the house to buy vegetables, people on the street greet him respectfully. "Salaam, Master sahib," they say, or "Namaste, Master Sahib," according to the religion of the speaker. They know him as the mathematics master at the municipal school. He has been there so long that he sees the faces of his former students everywhere: the autorickshaw driver Ramdas who refuses to charge him, the man who sells paan from a shack at the street corner, with whom he has an account, who never reminds him when his payment is late—his name is Imran and he goes to the mosque far more regularly than Abdul Karim.

They all know him, the kindly mathematics master, but he has his secrets. They know he lives in the old yellow house, where the plaster is flaking off in chunks to reveal the underlying brick. The windows of the house are hung with faded curtains that flutter tremulously in the breeze, giving passersby an occasional glimpse of his genteel poverty—the threadbare covers on the sofa, the wooden furniture as gaunt and lean and resigned as the rest of the house, waiting to fall into dust. The house is built in the old-fashioned way about a courtyard, which is paved with brick except for a circular omission where a great litchi tree grows. There is a high wall around the courtyard, and one door in it that leads to the patch of wilderness that was once a vegetable garden. But the hands that tended it—his mother's hands—are no longer able to do more than hold a mouthful of rice between the tips of the fingers, tremblingly conveyed to the mouth. The mother sits nodding in the sun in the courtyard while the son goes about the house, dusting and cleaning as fastidiously as a woman. The master has two sons—one is in distant America, married to a gori bibi, a white woman—how unimaginable! He never comes home and writes only a few times a year. The wife writes cheery letters in English that the master reads carefully with finger under each word. She talks about his grandsons, about baseball (a form of cricket, apparently), about their plans to visit, which never materialize. Her letters are as incomprehensible to him as the thought that there might be aliens on Mars, but he senses a kindness, a reaching out, among the foreign words. His mother has refused to have anything to do with that woman.

The other son has gone into business in Mumbai. He comes home rarely, but when he does he brings with him expensive things—a television set, an air-conditioner. The TV is draped reverently with an embroidered white cloth and dusted every day but the master can't bring himself to turn it on. There is too much trouble in the world. The air-conditioner gives him asthma so he never turns it on, even in the searing heat of summer. His son is a mystery to him—his mother dotes on the boy but the master can't help fearing that this young man has become a stranger, that he is involved in some shady business. The son always has a cell phone with him and is always calling nameless friends in Mumbai, bursting into cheery laughter, dropping his voice to a whisper, walking up and down the pathetically clean drawing-room as he speaks. Although he would never admit it to anybody other than Allah, Abdul Karim has the distinct impression that his son is waiting for him to die. He is always relieved when his son leaves.

Still, these are domestic worries. What father does not worry about his children? Nobody would be particularly surprised to know that the quiet, kindly master of mathematics shares them also. What they don't know is that he has a secret, an obsession, a passion that makes him different from them all. It is because of this, perhaps, that he seems always to be looking at something just beyond their field of vision, that he seems a little lost in the cruel, mundane world in which they live.

He wants to see infinity.

It is not strange for a mathematics master to be obsessed with numbers. But for Abdul Karim, numbers are the stepping stones, rungs in the ladder that will take him (Inshallah!) from the prosaic ugliness of the world to infinity.

When he was a child he used to see things from the corners of his eyes. Shapes moving at the very edge of his field of vision. Haven't we all felt that there was someone to our left or right, darting away when we turned our heads? In his childhood he had thought they were farishte, angelic beings keeping a watch over him. And he had felt secure, loved, nurtured by a great, benign, invisible presence.

One day he asked his mother:

"Why don't the farishte stay and talk to me? Why do they run away when I turn my head?"

Inexplicably to the child he had been, this innocent question led to visits to the Hakim. Abdul Karim had always been frightened of the Hakim's shop, the walls of which were lined from top to bottom with old clocks. The clocks ticked and hummed and whirred while tea came in chipped glasses and there were questions about spirits and possessions, and bitter herbs were dispensed in antique bottles that looked as though they contained djinns. An amulet was given to the boy to wear around his neck; there were verses from the Qur'an he was to recite every day. The boy he had been sat at the edge of the worn velvet seat and trembled; after two weeks of treatment, when his mother asked him about the farishte, he had said:

"They're gone."

That was a lie.

> My theory stands as firm as a rock; every arrow directed against it will quickly return to the archer. How do I know this? Because I have studied it from all sides for many years; because I have examined all objections which have ever been made against the infinite numbers; and above all because I have followed its roots, so to speak, to the first infallible cause of all created things.
>
> —GEORG CANTOR, German mathematician (1845–1918)

In a finite world, Abdul Karim ponders infinity. He has met infinities of various kinds in mathematics. If mathematics is the language of Nature, then it follows that there are infinities in the physical world around us as well. They confound us because we are such limited things. Our lives, our science, our religions are all smaller than the cosmos. Is the cosmos infinite? Perhaps. As far as we are concerned, it might as well be.

In mathematics there is the sequence of natural numbers, walking like small, determined soldiers into infinity. But there are less obvious infinities as well, as Abdul Karim knows. Draw a straight line, mark zero on one end and the number one at the other. How many numbers between zero and one? If you start counting now, you'll still be counting when the universe ends, and you'll be nowhere near one. In your journey from one end to the other you'll encounter the rational numbers and the irrational numbers, most notably the transcendentals. The transcendental numbers are the most intriguing—you can't generate them from integers by division, or by solving simple equations. Yet in the simple number line there are nearly impenetrable thickets of them; they are the densest, most numerous of all numbers. It is only when you take certain ratios like the circumference of a circle to its diameter, or add an infinite number of terms in a series, or negotiate the countless steps of infinite continued fractions, do these transcendental numbers emerge. The most famous of these is, of course, pi, 3.14159 . . . , where there is an infinity of non-repeating numbers after the decimal point. The transcendentals! Theirs is a universe richer in infinities than we can imagine.

In finiteness—in that little stick of a number line—there is infinity. What a deep and beautiful concept, thinks Abdul Karim! Perhaps there are infinities in us too, universes of them.

The prime numbers are another category that capture his imagination. The atoms of integer arithmetic, the select few that generate all other integers, as the letters of an alphabet generate all words. There are an infinite number of primes, as befits what he thinks of as God's alphabet . . .

How ineffably mysterious the primes are! They seem to occur at random in the sequence of numbers: 2, 3, 5, 7, 11 . . . There is no way to predict the next number in the sequence without actually testing it. No formula that generates all the primes. And yet, there is a mysterious regularity in these numbers that has eluded the greatest mathematicians of the world. Glimpsed by Riemann, but as yet unproven, there are hints of order so deep, so profound, that it is as yet beyond us.

To look for infinity in an apparently finite world—what nobler occupation for a human being, and one like Abdul Karim, in particular?

As a child he questioned the elders at the mosque: What does it mean to say that Allah is simultaneously one, and infinite? When he was older he read the philosophies of Al Kindi and Al Ghazali, Ibn Sina and Iqbal, but his restless mind found no answers. For much of his life he has been convinced that mathematics, not the quarrels of philosophers, is the key to the deepest mysteries.

He wonders whether the farishte that have kept him company all his life know the answer to what he seeks. Sometimes, when he sees one at the edge of his vision, he asks a question into the silence. Without turning around.

Is the Riemann Hypothesis true?

Silence.

Are prime numbers the key to understanding infinity?

Silence.

Is there a connection between transcendental numbers and the primes?

There has never been an answer.

But sometimes, a hint, a whisper of a voice that speaks in his mind. Abdul Karim does not know whether his mind is playing tricks upon him or not, because he cannot make out what the voice is saying. He sighs and buries himself in his studies.

He reads about prime numbers in Nature. He learns that the distribution of energy level spacings of excited uranium nuclei seem to match the distribution of spacings between prime numbers. Feverishly he turns the pages of the article, studies the graphs, tries to understand. How strange that Allah has left a hint in the depths of atomic nuclei! He is barely familiar with modern physics—he raids the library to learn about the structure of atoms.

His imagination ranges far. Meditating on his readings, he grows suspicious now that perhaps matter is infinitely divisible. He is beset by the notion that maybe there is no such thing as an elementary particle. Take a quark and it's full of preons. Perhaps preons themselves are full of smaller and smaller things. There is no limit to this increasingly fine graininess of matter.

How much more palatable this is than the thought that the process stops somewhere, that at some point there is a pre-preon, for example, that is composed of nothing else but itself. How fractally sound, how beautiful if matter is a matter of infinitely nested boxes.

There is a symmetry in it that pleases him. After all, there is infinity in the very large too. Our universe, ever expanding, apparently without limit.

He turns to the work of Georg Cantor, who had the audacity to formalize the mathematical study of infinity. Abdul Karim painstakingly goes over the mathematics, drawing his finger under every line, every equation in the yellowing textbook, scribbling frantically with his pencil. Cantor is the one who discovered that certain infinite sets are more infinite than others—that there are tiers and strata of infinity. Look at the integers, 1, 2, 3, 4 . . . Infinite, but of a lower order of infinity than the real numbers like 1.67, 2.93 etc. Let us say the set of integers is of order Aleph-Null, the set of real numbers of order Aleph-One, like the hierarchical ranks of a king's courtiers. The question that plagued Cantor and eventually cost him his life and sanity was the Continuum Hypothesis, which states that there is no infinite set of numbers with order *between* Aleph-Null and Aleph-One. In other words, Aleph-One succeeds Aleph-Null; there is no intermediate rank. But Cantor could not prove this.

He developed the mathematics of infinite sets. Infinity plus infinity equals infinity. Infinity minus infinity equals infinity. But the Continuum Hypothesis remained beyond his reach.

Abdul Karim thinks of Cantor as a cartographer in a bizarre new world. Here the cliffs of infinity reach endlessly toward the sky, and Cantor is a tiny figure lost in the grandeur, a fly on a precipice. And yet, what boldness! What spirit! To have the gall to actually *classify* infinity . . .

His explorations take him to an article on the mathematicians of ancient India. They had specific words for large numbers. One purvi, a unit of time, is seven hundred and fifty-six thousand billion years. One sirsaprahelika is eight point four million purvis raised to the twenty-eighth power. What did they see that caused them to play with such large numbers? What vistas were revealed before them? What wonderful arrogance possessed them that they, puny things, could dream so large? $\infty = \rightarrow$ delusions of grandeur?

He mentions this once to his friend, a Hindu called Gangadhar, who lives not far away. Gangadhar's hands pause over the chessboard (their weekly game is in progress) and he intones a verse from the Vedas:

From the Infinite, take the Infinite, and lo! Infinity remains . . .

Abdul Karim is astounded. That his ancestors could anticipate Georg Cantor by four millennia!

> That fondness for science, . . . that affability and condescension which God shows to the learned, that promptitude with which he protects and supports them in the elucidation of obscurities and in the removal of difficulties, has encouraged me to compose a short work on calculating by al-jabr and al-muqabala, confining it to what is easiest and most useful in arithmetic.
>
> —AL KHWARIZMI, eighth century Arab mathematician

Mathematics came to the boy almost as naturally as breathing. He made a clean sweep of the exams in the little municipal school. The neighborhood was provincial, dominated by small tradesmen, minor government officials and the like, and their children seemed to have inherited or acquired their plodding practicality. Nobody understood that strangely clever Muslim boy, except for a Hindu classmate, Gangadhar, who was a well-liked, outgoing fellow. Although Gangadhar played gulli-danda on the streets and could run faster than anybody, he had a passion for literature, especially poetry—a pursuit perhaps as impractical as pure mathematics. The two were drawn together and spent many hours sitting on the compound wall at the back of the school, eating stolen jamuns from the trees overhead and talking about subjects ranging from Urdu poetry and Sanskrit verse to whether mathematics pervaded everything, including human emotions. They felt very grown-up and mature for their stations. Gangadhar was the one who, shyly, and with many giggles, first introduced Kalidasa's erotic poetry to Abdul Karim. At that time girls were a mystery to them both: although they shared classrooms it seemed to them that girls (a completely different species from their sisters, of course) were strange, graceful, alien creatures from another world. Kalidasa's lyrical descriptions of breasts and hips evoked in them unarticulated longings.

They had the occasional fight, as friends do. The first serious one happened when there were some Hindu-Muslim tensions in the city just before the elections. Gangadhar came to Abdul in the school playground and knocked him flat.

"You're a bloodthirsty Muslim!" he said, almost as though he had just realized it.

"You're a hell-bound kafir!"

They punched each other, wrestled the other to the ground. Finally, with cut lips and bruises, they stared fiercely at each other and staggered away. The next day they played gulli-danda in the street on opposite sides for the first time.

Then they ran into each other in the school library. Abdul Karim tensed, ready to hit back if Gangadhar hit him. Gangadhar looked as if he was thinking about it for a moment, but then, somewhat embarrassedly, he held out a book.

"New book . . . on mathematics. Thought you'd want to see it . . ."

After that they were sitting on the wall again, as usual.

Their friendship had even survived the great riots four years later, when the city became a charnel house—buildings and bodies burned, and unspeakable atrocities were committed by both Hindus and Muslims. Some political leader of one side or another had made a provocative proclamation that he could not even remember, and tempers had been inflamed. There was an incident—a fight at a bus-stop, accusations of police brutality against the Muslim side, and things had spiraled out of control. Abdul's elder sister Ayesha had been at the market with a cousin when the worst of the violence broke out. They had been separated in the stampede; the cousin had come back, bloodied but alive, and nobody had ever seen Ayesha again.

The family never recovered. Abdul's mother went through the motions of living but her heart wasn't in it. His father lost weight, became a shrunken mockery of his old, vigorous self—he would die only a few years later. As for Abdul—the news reports about atrocities fed his nightmares and in his dreams he saw his sister bludgeoned, raped, torn to pieces again and again and again. When the city calmed down, he spent his days roaming the streets of the market, hoping for a sign of Ayesha—a body even—torn between hope and feverish rage.

Their father stopped seeing his Hindu friends. The only reason Abdul did not follow suit was because Gangadhar's people had sheltered a Muslim family during the carnage, and had turned off a mob of enraged Hindus.

Over time the wound—if it did not quite heal—became bearable enough that he could start living again. He threw himself into his beloved mathematics, isolating himself from everyone but his family and Gangadhar. The world had wronged him. He did not owe it anything.

Aryabhata is the master who, after reaching the furthest shores and plumbing the inmost depths of the sea of ultimate knowledge of mathematics, kinematics and spherics, handed over the three sciences to the learned world.

—The Mathematician Bhaskara, commenting on the 6th century Indian
mathematician Aryabhata, a hundred years later.

Abdul Karim was the first in his family to go to college. By a stroke of great luck, Gangadhar went to the same regional institution, majoring in Hindi literature while Abdul Karim buried himself in mathematical arcana. Abdul's father had become reconciled to his son's obsession and obvious talent. Abdul Karim himself, glowing with praise from his teachers, wanted to follow in the footsteps of Ramanujan. Just as the goddess Namakkal had appeared to that untutored genius in his dreams, writing mathematical formulas on his tongue (or so Ramanujan had said), Abdul Karim wondered if the farishte had been sent by Allah so that he, too, might be blessed with mathematical insight.

During that time an event occurred that convinced him of this.

Abdul was in the college library, working on a problem in differential geometry, when he sensed a farishta at the edge of his field of vision. As he had done countless times before, he turned his head slowly, expecting the vision to vanish.

Instead he saw a dark shadow standing in front of the long bookcase. It was vaguely human-shaped. It turned slowly, revealing itself to be thin as paper—but as it turned it seemed to acquire thickness, hints of features over its dark, slender form. And then it seemed to Abdul that a door opened in the air, just a crack, and he had a vision of an unutterably strange world beyond. The shadow stood at the door, beckoning with one arm, but Abdul Karim sat still, frozen with wonder. Before he could rouse himself and get up, the door and the shadow both rotated swiftly and vanished, and he was left staring at the stack of books on the shelf.

After this he was convinced of his destiny. He dreamed obsessively of the strange world he had glimpsed; every time he sensed a farishta he turned his head slowly toward it—and every time it vanished. He told himself it was just a matter of time before one of them came, remained, and perhaps—wonder of wonders—took him to that other world.

Then his father died unexpectedly. That was the end of Abdul Karim's career as a mathematician. He had to return home to take care of his mother, his two remaining sisters and a brother. The only thing he was qualified for was teaching. Ultimately he would find a job at the same municipal school from which he had graduated.

On the train home, he saw a woman. The train was stopped on a bridge. Below him was the sleepy curve of a small river, gold in the early morning light, mists rising faintly off it, and on the shore a woman with a clay water pot. She had taken a dip in the river—her pale, ragged sari clung wetly to her as she picked up the pot and set it on her hip and began to climb the bank. In the light of dawn she was luminous, an apparition in the mist, the curve of the pot against the curve of her hip. Their eyes met from a distance—he imagined what he thought she saw, the silent train, a young man with a sparse beard looking at her as though she was the first woman in the world. Her own eyes gazed at him fearlessly as though she were a goddess looking into his soul. For a moment there were no barriers between them, no boundaries of gender, religion, caste or class. Then she turned and vanished behind a stand of shisham trees.

He wasn't sure if she had really been there in the half-light or whether he had conjured her up, but for a long time she represented something elemental to him. Sometimes he thought of her as Woman, sometimes as a river.

He got home in time for the funeral. His job kept him busy, and kept the moneylender from their door. With the stubborn optimism of the young, he kept hoping that one day his fortunes would change, that he would go back to college and complete his degree. In the meantime, he knew his mother wanted to find him a bride . . .

Abdul Karim got married, had children. Slowly, over the years of managing rowdy classrooms, tutoring students in the afternoons and saving, paisa by paisa, from his meager salary for his sisters' weddings and other expenses, Abdul Karim lost touch with that youthful, fiery talent he had once had, and with it the ambition to scale the heights to which Ramanujan, Cantor and Riemann had climbed. Things came more slowly to him now. An intellect burdened by years of worry wears out. When his wife died and his children grew up and went away, his steadily decreasing needs finally caught up with his meager income, and he found for the first time that he could think about mathematics again. He no longer hoped to dazzle the world of mathematics with some new insight, such as a proof of Riemann's hypothesis. Those dreams were gone. All he could hope for was to be illumined by the efforts of those who had gone before him, and to re-live, vicariously, the joys of insight. It was a cruel trick of Time, that when he had the leisure he had lost the ability, but that is no bar to true obsession. Now, in the autumn of his life it was as though Spring had come again, bringing with it his old love.

> In this world, brought to its knees by hunger and thirst
> Love is not the only reality, there are other Truths . . .
>   —Sahir Ludhianvi, Indian poet (1921–1980)

There are times when Abdul Karim tires of his mathematical obsessions. After all, he is old. Sitting in the courtyard with his notebook, pencil and books of mathematics for so many hours at a stretch can take its toll. He gets up, aching all over, sees to his mother's needs and goes out to the grave-yard where his wife is buried.

His wife Zainab had been a plump, fair-skinned woman, hardly able to read or write, who moved about the house with indolent grace, her good-natured laugh ringing out in the courtyard as she chattered with the washer-woman. She had loved to eat—he still remembered the delicate tips of her plump fingers, how they would curl around a piece of lamb, scooping up with it a few grains of saffron rice, the morsel conveyed reverently to her mouth. Her girth gave an impression of strength, but ultimately she had not been able to hold out against her mother-in-law. The laughter in her eyes faded gradually as her two boys grew out of babyhood, coddled and put to bed by the grandmother in her own corner of the women's quarters. Abdul Karim himself had been unaware of the silent war between his wife and mother—he had been young and obsessed with teaching mathematics to his recalcitrant students. He had noticed how the grandmother always seemed to be holding the younger son, crooning to him, and how the elder boy fol-lowed his mother around, but he did not see in this any connection to his wife's growing pallor. One night he had requested her to come to him and massage his feet—their euphemism for sex—and he had waited for her to come to him from the women's quarters, impatient for the comfort of her plump nakedness, her soft, silken breasts. When she came at last she had knelt at the foot of the bed, her chest heaving with muffled sobs, her hands covering her face. As he took her in his arms, wondering what could have ruffled her calm good nature, she had collapsed completely against him. No comfort he could offer would make her tell what it was that was breaking her heart. At last she begged him, between great, shuddering breaths, that all she wanted in the world was another baby.

Abdul Karim had been influenced by modern ideas—he considered two children, boys at that, to be quite sufficient for a family. As one of five chil-dren, he had known poverty and the pain of giving up his dream of a univer-sity career to help support his family. He wasn't going to have his children go through the same thing. But when his wife whispered to him that she wanted one more, he relented.

Now, when he looked back, he wished he had tried to understand the real reason for her distress. The pregnancy had been a troublesome one. His mother had taken charge of both boys almost entirely while Zainab lay in bed in the women's quarters, too sick to do anything but weep silently and call upon Allah to rescue her. "It's a girl," Abdul Karim's mother had said grimly. "Only a girl would cause so much trouble." She had looked away out of the window into the courtyard, where her own daughter, Abdul Karim's dead sister, Ayesha, had once played and helped hang the wash.

And finally it had been a girl, stillborn, who had taken her mother with her. They were buried together in the small, unkempt graveyard where Abdul

Karim went whenever he was depressed. By now the gravestone was awry and grass had grown over the mound. His father was buried here also, and three of his siblings who had died before he was six. Only Ayesha, lost Ayesha, the one he remembered as a source of comfort to a small boy—strong, generous arms, hands delicate and fragrant with henna, a smooth cheek—she was not here.

In the graveyard Abdul Karim pays his respects to his wife's memory while his heart quails at the way the graveyard itself is disintegrating. He is afraid that if it goes to rack and ruin, overcome by vegetation and time, he will forget Zainab and the child and his guilt. Sometimes he tries to clear the weeds and tall grasses with his hands, but his delicate scholar's hands become bruised and sore quite quickly, and he sighs and thinks about the Sufi poetess Jahanara, who had written, centuries earlier: "Let the green grass grow above my grave!"

> *I have often pondered over the roles of knowledge or experience, on the one hand, and imagination or intuition, on the other, in the process of discovery. I believe that there is a certain fundamental conflict between the two, and knowledge, by advocating caution, tends to inhibit the flight of imagination. Therefore, a certain naivete, unburdened by conventional wisdom, can sometimes be a positive asset.*
>
> —HARISH-CHANDRA, Indian mathematician (1923–1983)

Gangadhar, his friend from school, was briefly a master of Hindi literature at the municipal school and is now an academician at the Amravati Heritage Library, and a poet in his spare time. He is the only person to whom Abdul Karim can confide his secret passion.

In time, he too becomes intrigued with the idea of infinity. While Abdul Karim pores over Cantor and Riemann, and tries to make meaning from the Prime Number theorem, Gangadhar raids the library and brings forth treasures. Every week, when Abdul Karim walks the two miles to Gangadhar's house, where he is led by the servant to the comfortable drawing room with its gracious, if aging mahogany furniture, the two men share what they've learned over cups of cardamom tea and a chess game. Gangadhar cannot understand higher mathematics but he can sympathize with the frustrations of the knowledge-seeker, and he has known what it is like to chip away at the wall of ignorance and burst into the light of understanding. He digs out quotes from Aryabhata and Al-Khwarizmi, and tells his friend such things as:

"Did you know, Abdul, that the Greeks and Romans did not like the idea of infinity? Aristotle argued against it, and proposed a finite universe. Of the yunaanis, only Archimedes dared to attempt to scale that peak. He came up with the notion that different infinite quantities could be compared, that one infinite could be greater or smaller than another infinite . . ."

And on another occasion:

"The French mathematician, Jacques Hadamard . . . He was the one who proved the Prime Number theorem that has you in such ecstasies . . . he says there are four stages to mathematical discovery. Not very different from the experience of the artist or poet, if you think about it. The first is to study and be familiar with what is known. The next is to let these ideas turn in your mind, as the earth regenerates by lying fallow between plantings. Then— with luck—there is the flash of insight, the illuminating moment when you discover something new and feel in your bones that it must be true. The final stage is to verify—to subject that epiphany to the rigors of mathematical proof . . ."

Abdul Karim feels that if he can simply go through Hadamard's first two stages, perhaps Allah will reward him with a flash of insight. And perhaps not. If he had hopes of being another Ramanujan, those hopes are gone now. But no true Lover has ever turned from the threshold of the Beloved's house, even knowing he will not be admitted through the doors.

"What worries me," he confides to Gangadhar during one of these discussions, "what has always worried me, is Gödel's Incompleteness Theorem. According to Gödel, there can be statements in mathematics that are not provable. He showed that the Continuum Hypothesis of Cantor was one of these statements. Poor Cantor, he lost his sanity trying to prove something that cannot be proved or disproved! What if all our unproven ideas on prime numbers, on infinity, are statements like that? If they can't be tested against the constraints of mathematical logic, how will we ever know if they are true?" *The burden of proof is whether or not the tools are existent.*

This bothers him very much. He pores over the proof of Gödel's theorem, seeking to understand it, to get around it. Gangadhar encourages him:

"You know, in the old tales, every great treasure is guarded by a proportionally great monster. Perhaps Gödel's theorem is the djinn that guards the truth you seek. Maybe instead of slaying it, you have to, you know, befriend it . . ." *Embrace the knowledge, don't destroy it*

Through his own studies, through discussions with Gangadhar, Abdul Karim begins to feel again that his true companions are Archimedes, Al-Khwarizmi. Khayyam, Aryabhata, Bhaskar. Riemann, Cantor, Gauss, Ramanujan, Hardy.

They are the masters, before whom he is as a humble student, an apprentice following their footprints up the mountainside. The going is rough. He is getting old, after all. He gives himself up to dreams of mathematics, rousing himself only to look after the needs of his mother, who is growing more and more frail.

After a while, even Gangadhar admonishes him.

"A man cannot live like this, so obsessed. Will you let yourself go the way of Cantor and Gödel? Guard your sanity, my friend. You have a duty to your mother, to society."

Abdul Karim cannot make Gangadhar understand. His mind sings with mathematics.

The limit of a function $f(N)$ as N goes to infinity . . .

So many questions he asks himself begin like this. The function $f(N)$ may be the prime counting function, or the number of nested dolls of matter, or the extent of the universe. It may be abstract, like a parameter in a mathematical space, or earthy, like the branching of wrinkles in the face of his mother, growing older and older in the paved courtyard of his house, under the litchi trees. Older and older, without quite dying, as though she were determined to live Zeno's paradox.

He loves his mother the way he loves the litchi tree; for being there, for making him what he is, for giving him shelter and succor.

The limit . . . as N goes to infinity . . .

So begin many theorems of calculus. Abdul Karim wonders what kind of calculus governs his mother's slow arc into dying. What if life did not require a minimum threshold of conditions—what if death were merely a limit of some function $f(N)$ as N goes to infinity?

> *A world in which human life is but a pawn*
> *A world filled with death-worshipers,*
> *Where death is cheaper than life . . .*
> *That world is not my world . . .*
>
> —SAHIR LUDHIANVI, Indian poet (1921–1980)

While Abdul Karim dabbles in the mathematics of the infinite, as so many deluded fools and geniuses have done, the world changes.

He is vaguely aware that there are things going on in the world—that people live and die, that there are political upheavals, that this is the hottest summer yet and already a thousand people have died of the heat wave in Northern India. He knows that Death also stands at his mother's shoulder, waiting, and he does what he can for her. Although he has not always observed the five daily prayers, he does the namaz now, with her. She has already started becoming the citizen of another country—she lives in little leaps and bends of time long gone, calling for Ayesha one moment, and for her long-dead husband the next. Conversations from her lost girlhood emerge from her trembling mouth. In her few moments of clarity she calls upon Allah to take her away.

Dutiful as he is to his mother, Abdul Karim is relieved to be able to get away once a week for a chess game and conversation with Gangadhar. He has a neighbor's aunt look in on his mother during that time. Heaving a sigh or two, he makes his way through the familiar lanes of his childhood, his shoes scuffing up dust under the ancient jamun trees that he once climbed as a child. He greets his neighbors: old Ameen Khan Sahib sitting on his charpai, wheezing over his hookah, the Ali twins, madcap boys chasing a bicycle tire with a stick, Imran at the paan shop. He crosses, with some trepidation, the increasingly congested market road, past the faded awnings of Munshilal and Sons, past a rickshaw stand into another quiet lane, this one shaded with jacaranda trees. Gangadhar's house is a modest white bungalow, stained an indeterminate gray from many monsoons. The creak of the wooden gate in the compound wall is as familiar a greeting as Gangadhar's welcome.

But the day comes when there is no chess game at Gangadhar's house.

The servant boy—not Gangadhar—ushers him into the familiar room. Sitting down in his usual chair, Abdul Karim notices that the chess board has not been laid out. Sounds come from the inner rooms of the house: women's voices, heavy objects being dragged across the floor.

An elderly man comes into the room and stops short as though surprised to see Abdul Karim. He looks vaguely familiar—then Abdul remembers that he is some relative of Gangadhar's wife—an uncle, perhaps—and he lives on the other side of the city. They have met once or twice at some family celebration.

"What are you doing here?" the man says, without any of the usual courtesies. He is white-haired but of vigorous build.

Puzzled and a little affronted, Abdul Karim says:

"I am here for my chess game with Gangadhar. Is he not at home?"

"There will be no chess game today. Haven't you people done enough harm? Are you here to mock us in our sorrow? Well, let me tell you . . ."

"What happened?" Abdul Karim's indignation is dissolving in a wave of apprehension. "What are you talking about? Is Gangadhar all right?"

"Perhaps you don't know," says the man, his tone mocking. "Some of your people burned a bus on Paharia road yesterday evening. There were ten people on it, all Hindus, coming back from a family ceremony at a temple. They all perished horribly. Word has it that you people did it. Didn't even let the children get off the bus. Now the whole town is in turmoil. Who knows what might happen? Gangadhar and I are taking his family to a safer part of town."

Abdul Karim's eyes are wide with shock. He can find no words.

"All these hundreds of years we Hindus have tolerated you people. Even though you Muslims raided and pillaged us over the centuries, we let you build your mosques, worship your God. And this is how you pay us!"

In one instant Abdul Karim has become "you people." He wants to say that he did not lift an arm to hurt those who perished on the bus. His were not the hands that set the fire. But no words come out.

"Can you imagine it, Master Sahib? Can you see the flames? Hear their screams? Those people will never go home . . ."

"I can imagine it," Abdul Karim says, grimly now. He rises to his feet, but just then Gangadhar enters the room. He has surely heard part of the conversation because he puts his hands on Abdul Karim's shoulders, gently, recognizing him as the other man has not done. This is Abdul Karim, his friend, whose sister, all those years ago, never came home.

Gangadhar turns to his wife's uncle.

"Uncle, please. Abdul Karim is not like those miscreants. A kinder man I have never known! And as yet it is not known who the ruffians are, although the whole town is filled with rumors. Abdul, please sit down! This is a measure of the times we live in, that we can say such things to each other. Alas! Kalyug is indeed upon us."

Abdul Karim sits down, but he is shaking. All thoughts of mathematics have vanished from his mind. He is filled with disgust and revulsion for the barbarians who committed this atrocity, for human beings in general. What a degraded species we are! To take the name of Ram or Allah, or Jesus, and to burn and destroy under one aegis or another—that is what our history has been.

The uncle, shaking his head, has left the room. Gangadhar is talking history to Abdul, apologizing for his uncle.

". . . a matter of political manipulation," he says. "The British colonialists looked for our weakness, exploited it, set us against each other. Opening the door to hell is easy enough—but closing it is hard. All those years, before British rule, we lived in relative peace. Why is it that we cannot close that door they opened? After all, what religion tells us to slay our neighbor?"

"Does it matter?" Abdul Karim says bitterly. "We humans are a depraved species, my friend. My fellow Muslims address every prayer to Allah, the Merciful and Compassionate. You Hindus, with your 'Isha Vasyam Idam Sarvam'—the divine pervades all. The Christians talk on about turning the other cheek. And yet each of them has hands that are stained in blood. We pervert everything—we take the words of peace spoken by prophets and holy men and turn them into weapons with which to kill each other!"

He is shaking so hard that he can barely speak.

"It is in mathematics . . . only in mathematics that I see Allah . . ."

"Quiet now," Gangadhar says. He calls for the servant to bring some water for the master sahib. Abdul Karim drinks and wipes his mouth. The suitcases are being brought out from inside the house. There is a taxi in front.

"Listen, my friend," Gangadhar says, "you must look to your safety. Go home now and lock your doors, and look after your mother. I am sending my family away and I will join them in a day or so. When this madness has passed I will come and look for you!"

Abdul Karim goes home. So far everything looks normal—the wind is blowing litter along in the streets, the paan shop is open, people throng the bus-stop. Then he notices that there aren't any children, even though the summer holidays are going on.

The vegetable market is very busy. People are buying up everything like crazy. He buys a few potatoes, onions and a large gourd, and goes home. He locks the door. His mother, no longer up to cooking meals, watches as he cooks. After they eat and he has her tucked into bed, he goes to his study and opens a book on mathematics.

One day passes, perhaps two—he does not keep track. He remembers to take care of his mother but often forgets to eat. His mother lives, more and more, in that other world. His sisters and brother call from other towns, anxious about the reports of escalating violence; he tells them not to worry. When things are back to normal they will come and see him and their mother.

> How marvelous, the Universal Mystery
> That only a true Lover can comprehend!
> —BULLEH SHAH, eighteenth century Punjabi Sufi poet

> Logic merely sanctions the conquests of the intuition.
> —JACQUES HADAMARD, French mathematician (1865–1963)

One morning he emerges from the darkness of his study into the sunny courtyard. Around him the old city writhes and burns, but Abdul Karim sees and hears nothing but mathematics. He sits in his old cane chair, picks up a stick lying on the ground and begins to draw mathematical symbols in the dust.

There is a farishta standing at the edge of his vision.

He turns slowly. The dark shadow stays there, waits. This time Abdul Karim is quick on his feet, despite a sudden twinge of pain in one knee. He walks toward the door, the beckoning arm, and steps through.

For a moment he is violently disoriented—it occurs to him that he has spun through a different dimension into this hidden world. Then the darkness before his eyes dissipates, and he beholds wonders.

All is hushed. He is looking at a vast sweep of land and sky unlike any-thing he has ever seen. Dark, pyramidal shapes stud the landscape, great monuments to something beyond his understanding. There is a vast, polyhe-dral object suspended in a pale orange sky that has no sun. Only a diffuse luminescence pervades this sky. He looks at his feet, still in his familiar, worn sandals, and sees all around, in the sand, little fish-like creatures wriggling and spawning. Some of the sand has worked its way between his toes, and it feels warm and rubbery, not like sand at all. He takes a deep breath and smells something strange, like burnt rubber mixed with his own sweat. The shadow stands by his side, looking solid at last, almost human but for the absence of neck and the profusion of limbs—their number seems to vary with time—at the moment Abdul Karim counts five.

The dark orifice in the head opens and closes, but no sound comes out. Instead Abdul feels as though a thought has been placed in his mind, a package that he will open later.

He walks with the shadow across the sands to the edge of a quiet sea. The water, if that is what it is, is foaming and bubbling gently, and within its depths he sees ghostly shapes moving, and the hints of complex structure far below. Arabesques form in the depths, break up, and form again. He licks his dry lips, tastes metal and salt.

He looks at his companion, who bids him pause. A door opens. They step through into another universe.

It is different, this one. It is all air and light, the whole space hung with great, translucent webbing. Each strand in the web is a hollow tube within which liquid creatures flow. Smaller, solid beings float in the emptiness between the web strands.

Speechless, he stretches out his hand toward a web-strand. Its delicacy reminds him of the filigreed silver anklets his wife used to wear. To his complete surprise a tiny being floating within the strand stops. It is like a plump, watery comma, translucent and without any features he can recognize, and yet he has the notion that he is being looked at, examined, and that at the other end is also wonder.

The web-strand touches him, and he feels its cool, alien smoothness on a fingertip.

A door opens. They step through.

It is dizzying, this wild ride. Sometimes he gets flashes of his own world, scenes of trees and streets, and distant blue hills. There are indications that these flashes are at different points in time—at one point he sees a vast army of soldiers, their plumed helmets catching the sunlight, and thinks he must be in the time of the Roman Empire. Another time he thinks he is back home, because he sees before him his own courtyard. But there is an old man sitting in his cane chair, drawing patterns in the dust with a stick. A shadow falls across the ground. Someone he cannot see is stealing up behind the old man. Is that a knife agleam in the stranger's hand? What is this he is seeing? He tries to call out, but no sound emerges. The scene blurs—a door opens, and they step through.

Abdul Karim is trembling. Has he just witnessed his own death?

He remembers that Archimedes died that way—he had been drawing circles, engrossed with a problem in geometry, when a barbarian of a soldier came up behind him and killed him.

But there is no time to ponder. He is lost in a merry-go-round of universes, each different and strange. The shadow gives him a glimpse of so many, Abdul Karim has long lost count. He puts thoughts of Death away from him and loses himself in wonder.

His companion opens door after door. The face, featureless except for the orifice that opens and shuts, gives no hint of what the shadow is thinking. Abdul Karim wants to ask: who are you? Why are you doing this? He knows, of course, the old story of how the angel Gabriel came to the Prophet Mohammad one night and took him on a celestial journey, a grand tour of the heavens. But the shadow does not look like an angel; it has no face, no wings, its gender is indeterminate. And in any case, why should the angel Gabriel concern himself with a humble mathematics master in a provincial town, a person of no consequence in the world?

And yet, he is here. Perhaps Allah has a message for him; His ways are ineffable, after all. Exultation fills Abdul Karim as he beholds marvel after marvel.

At last they pause in a place where they are suspended in a yellow sky. As Abdul Karim experiences the giddy absence of gravity, accompanied by a sudden jolt of nausea that slowly recedes—as he turns in mid-air, he notices that the sky is not featureless but covered with delicate tessellations: geometric shapes intertwine, merge and new ones emerge. The colors change too, from yellow to green, lilac, mauve. All at once it seems as though numberless eyes are opening in the sky, one after the other, and as he turns he sees all the other universes flashing past him. A kaleidoscope, vast beyond his imaginings. He is at the center of it all, in a space between all spaces, and he can feel in his bones a low, irregular throbbing, like the beating of a drum. Boom, boom, goes the drum. Boom boom boom. Slowly he realizes that what he is seeing and feeling is part of a vast pattern.

In that moment Abdul Karim has the flash of understanding he has been waiting for all his life.

For so long he has been playing with the transcendental numbers, trying to fathom Cantor's ideas; at the same time Riemann's notions of the prime numbers have fascinated him. In idle moments he has wondered if they are connected at a deeper level. Despite their apparent randomness the primes have their own regularity, as hinted by the unproven Riemann Hypothesis; he sees at last that if you think of prime numbers as the terrain of a vast country, and if your view of reality is a two-dimensional plane that intersects this terrain at some height above the surface, perhaps at an angle, then of course what you see will appear to be random. Tops of hills. Bits of valleys. Only the parts of the terrain that cross your plane of reality will be apparent. Unless you can see the entire landscape in its multi-dimensional splendor, the topography will make no sense.

He sees it: the bare bones of creation, here, in this place where all the universes branch off, the thudding heart of the metacosmos. In the scaffolding, the skeletal structure of the multiverse is beautifully apparent. This is what

Cantor had a glimpse of, then, this vast topography. Understanding opens in his mind as though the metacosmos has itself spoken to him. He sees that of all the transcendental numbers, only a few—infinite still, but not the whole set—are marked as doorways to other universes, and each is labeled by a prime number. Yes. Yes. Why this is so, what deeper symmetry it reflects, what law or regularity of Nature undreamed of by the physicists of his world, he does not know.

The space where primes live—the topology of the infinite universes—he sees it in that moment. No puny function as yet dreamed of by humans can encompass the vastness—the inexhaustible beauty of this place. He knows that he can never describe this in the familiar symbols of the mathematics that he knows, that while he experiences the truth of the Riemann Hypothesis, as a corollary to this greater, more luminous reality, he cannot sit down and verify it through a conventional proof. No human language as yet exists, mathematical or otherwise, that can describe what he knows in his bones to be true. Perhaps he, Abdul Karim, will invent the beginnings of such a language. Hadn't the great poet Iqbal interpreted the Prophet's celestial journey to mean that the heavens are within our grasp?

A twist, and a door opens. He steps into the courtyard of his house. He turns around, but the courtyard is empty. The farishta is gone.

Abdul Karim raises his eyes to the heavens. Rain clouds, dark as the proverbial beloved's hair, sweep across the sky; the litchi tree over his head is dancing in the swift breeze. The wind has drowned out the sounds of a ravaged city. A red flower comes blowing over the courtyard wall and is deposited at his feet.

Abdul Karim's hair is blown back, a nameless ecstasy fills him; he feels Allah's breath on his face.

He says into the wind:

Dear Merciful and Compassionate God, I stand before your wondrous universe, filled with awe; help me, weak mortal that I am, to raise my gaze above the sordid pettiness of everyday life, the struggles and quarrels of mean humanity . . . Help me to see the beauty of your Works, from the full flower of the red silk cotton tree to the exquisite mathematical grace by which you have created numberless universes in the space of a man's step. I know now that my true purpose in this sad world is to stand in humble awe before your magnificence, and to sing a paean of praise to you with every breath I take . . .

He feels weak with joy. Leaves whirl in the courtyard like mad dervishes; a drop or two of rain falls, obliterating the equation he had scratched in the dust with his stick. He has lost his chance at mathematical genius a long time ago; he is nobody, only a teacher of mathematics at a school, humbler than a clerk in a government office—yet Allah has favored him with this great insight. Perhaps he is now worthy of speech with Ramanujan and

Archimedes and all the ones in between. But all he wants to do is to run out into the lane and go shouting through the city: see, my friends, open your eyes and see what I see! But he knows they would think him mad; only Gangadhar would understand . . . if not the mathematics then the impulse, the importance of the whole discovery.

He leaps out of the house, into the lane.

> *This blemished radiance . . . this night-stung dawn*
> *Is not the dawn we waited for . . .*
>
> > —FAIZ AHMED FAIZ, Pakistani poet (1911–1984)

> *Where all is broken*
> *Where each soul's athirst, each glance*
> *Filled with confusion, each heart*
> *Weighed with sorrow . . .*
> *Is this a world, or chaos?*
>
> > —SAHIR LUDHIANVI, Indian poet (1921–1980)

But what is this?

The lane is empty. There are broken bottles everywhere. The windows and doors of his neighbors' houses are shuttered and barred, like closed eyes. Above the sound of the rain he hears shouting in the distance. Why is there a smell of burning?

He remembers then, what he had learned at Gangadhar's house. Securing the door behind him, he begins to run as fast as his old-man legs will carry him.

The market is burning.

Smoke pours out of smashed store fronts, even as the rain falls. There is broken glass on the pavement; a child's wooden doll in the middle of the road, decapitated. Soggy pages filled with neat columns of figures lie scattered everywhere, the remains of a ledger. Quickly he crosses the road.

Gangadhar's house is in ruins. Abdul Karim wanders through the open doors, stares blindly at the blackened walls. The furniture is mostly gone. Only the chess table stands untouched in the middle of the front room.

Frantically he searches through the house, entering the inner rooms for the first time. Even the curtains have been ripped from the windows.

There is no body.

He runs out of the house. Gangadhar's wife's family—he does not know where they live. How to find out if Gangadhar is safe?

The neighboring house belongs to a Muslim family that Abdul Karim knows only from visits to the mosque. He pounds on the door. He thinks he hears movement behind the door, sees the upstairs curtains twitch—but nobody answers his frantic entreaties. At last, defeated, his hands bleeding, he walks slowly home, looking about him in horror. Is this truly his city, his world?

Allah, Allah, why have you abandoned me?

He has beheld the glory of Allah's workmanship. Then why this? Were all those other universes, other realities a dream?

The rain pours down.

There is someone lying on his face in a ditch. The rain has wet the shirt on his back, made the blood run. As Abdul Karim starts toward him, wondering who it is, whether he is dead or alive—young, from the back it could be Ramdas or Imran—he sees behind him, at the entrance to the lane, a horde of young men. Some of them may be his students—they can help.

They are moving with a predatory sureness that frightens him. He sees that they have sticks and stones.

They are coming like a tsunami, a thunderclap, leaving death and ruin in their wake. He hears their shouts through the rain.

Abdul Karim's courage fails him. He runs to his house, enters, locks and bars the door and closes all the windows. He checks on his mother, who is sleeping. The telephone is dead. The dal for their meal has boiled away. He turns off the gas and goes back to the door, putting his ear against it. He does not want to risk looking out of the window.

Over the rain he hears the young men go past at a run. In the distance there is a fusillade of shots. More sounds of running feet, then, just the rain.

Are the police here? The army?

Something or someone is scratching at the door. Abdul Karim is transfixed with terror. He stands there, straining to hear over the pitter patter of the rain. On the other side, somebody moans.

Abdul Karim opens the door. The lane is empty, roaring with rain. At his feet there is the body of a young woman.

She opens her eyes. She's dressed in a salwaar kameez that has been half-torn off her body—her long hair is wet with rain and blood, plastered over her neck and shoulders. There is blood on her salwaar, blood oozing from a hundred little cuts and welts on her skin.

Her gaze focuses.

"Master Sahib."

He is taken aback. Is she someone he knows? Perhaps an old student, grown up?

Quickly he half-carries, half-pulls her into the house and secures the door. With some difficulty he lifts her carefully on to the divan in the drawing room, which is already staining with her blood. She coughs.

"My child, who did this to you? Let me find a doctor . . ."

"No," she says. "It's too late." Her breath rasps and she coughs again. Tears well up in the dark eyes.

"Master Sahib, please, let me die! My husband . . . my son . . . They must not see me take my last breath. Not like this. They will suffer. They will want revenge . . . Please . . . cut my wrists . . ."

She's raising her wrists to his horrified face, but all he can do is to take them in his shaking hands.

"My daughter," he says, and doesn't know what to say. Where will he find a doctor in the mayhem? Can he bind her cuts? Even as he thinks these thoughts he knows that life is ebbing from her. Blood is pooling on his divan, dripping down to the floor. She does not need him to cut her wrists.

"Tell me, who are the ruffians who did this?"

She whispers:

"I don't know who they were. I had just stepped out of the house for a moment. My family . . . don't tell them, Master Sahib! When I'm gone just tell them . . . tell them I died in a safe place . . ."

"Daughter, what is your husband's name?"

Her eyes are enormous. She is gazing at him without comprehension, as though she is already in another world.

He can't tell if she is Muslim or Hindu. If she wore a vermilion dot on her forehead, it has long since been washed off by the rain.

His mother is standing at the door of the drawing room. She wails suddenly and loudly, flings herself by the side of the dying woman.

"Ayesha! Ayesha, my life!"

Tears fall down Abdul Karim's face. He tries to disengage his mother. Tries to tell her: this is not Ayesha, just another woman whose body has become a battleground over which men make war. At last he has to lift his mother in his arms, her body so frail that he fears it might break—he takes her to her bed, where she crumples, sobbing and calling Ayesha's name.

Back in the drawing room, the young woman's eyes flicker to him. Her voice is barely above a whisper.

"Master Sahib, cut my wrists . . . I beseech you, in the Almighty's name! Take me somewhere safe . . . Let me die . . ."

Then the veil falls over her eyes again and her body goes limp.

Time stands still for Abdul Karim.

Then he senses something familiar, and turns slowly. The farishta is waiting.

Abdul Karim picks up the woman in his arms, awkwardly arranging the bloody divan cover over her half-naked body. In the air, a door opens.

Staggering a little, his knees protesting, he steps through the door.

After three universes he finds the place.

It is peaceful. There is a rock rising from a great turquoise sea of sand. The blue sand laps against the rock, making lulling, sibilant sounds. In the high, clear air, winged creatures call to each other between endless rays of light. He squints in the sudden brightness.

He closes her eyes, buries her deep at the base of the rock, under the blue, flowing sand.

He stands there, breathing hard from the exertion, his hands bruised, thinking he should say something. But what? He does not even know if she's Muslim or Hindu. When she spoke to him earlier, what word had she used for God? Was it Allah or Ishwar, or something neutral?

He can't remember.

At last he says the Al-Fatihah, and, stumbling a little, recites whatever little he knows of the Hindu scriptures. He ends with the phrase *Isha Vasyamidam Sarvam*.

Tears run off his cheeks into the blue sand, and disappear without leaving a trace.

The farishta waits.

"Why didn't you do something!" Abdul Karim rails at the shadow. He falls to his knees in the blue sand, weeping. "Why, if you are truly a farishta, didn't you save my sister?"

He sees now that he has been a fool—this shadow creature is no angel, and he, Abdul Karim, no Prophet.

He weeps for Ayesha, for this nameless young woman, for the body he saw in the ditch, for his lost friend Gangadhar.

The shadow leans toward him. Abdul Karim gets up, looks around once, and steps through the door.

He steps out into his drawing room. The first thing he discovers is that his mother is dead. She looks quite peaceful, lying in her bed, her white hair flowing over the pillow.

She might be asleep, her face is so calm.

He stands there for a long time, unable to weep. He picks up the phone—there is still no dial tone. After that he goes about methodically cleaning up the drawing room, washing the floor, taking the bedding off the divan. Later, after the rain has stopped, he will burn it in the courtyard. Who will notice another fire in the burning city?

When everything is cleaned up, he lies down next to his mother's body like a small boy and goes to sleep.

> *When you left me, my brother, you took away the book*
> *In which is writ the story of my life . . .*
>
> —FAIZ AHMED FAIZ, Pakistani poet (1911–1984)

The sun is out. An uneasy peace lies over the city. His mother's funeral is over. Relatives have come and gone—his younger son came, but did not stay. The older son sent a sympathy card from America.

Gangadhar's house is still empty, a blackened ruin. Whenever he has ventured out, Abdul Karim has asked about his friend's whereabouts. The last he heard was that Gangadhar was alone in the house when the mob came, and his Muslim neighbors sheltered him until he could join his wife and children at her parents' house. But it has been so long that he does not believe it any more. He has also heard that Gangadhar was dragged out, hacked to pieces and his body set on fire. The city has calmed down—the army had to be called in—but it is still rife with rumors. Hundreds of people are missing. Civil rights groups comb the town, interviewing people, revealing, in clipped, angry press statements, the negligence of the state government, the collusion of the police in some of the violence. Some of them came to his house, too, very clean, very young people, burning with an idealism that, however misplaced, is comforting to see. He has said nothing about the young woman who died in his arms, but he prays for that bereft family every day.

For days he has ignored the shadow at his shoulder. But now he knows that the sense of betrayal will fade. Whose fault is it, after all, that he ascribed to the creatures he once called farishte the attributes of angels? Could angels, even, save human beings from themselves?

The creatures watch us with a child's curiosity, he thinks, but they do not understand. Just as their own worlds are incomprehensible to me, so are our ways to them. They are not Allah's minions.

The space where the universes branch off—the heart of the metacosmos— now appears remote to him, like a dream. He is ashamed of his earlier arrogance. How can he possibly fathom Allah's creation in one glance? No finite mind can, in one meager lifetime, truly comprehend the vastness, the grandeur of Allah's scheme. All we can do is to discover a bit of the truth here, a bit there, and thus to sing His praises.

But there is so much pain in Abdul Karim's soul that he cannot imagine writing down one syllable of the new language of the infinite. His dreams are haunted by the horrors he has seen, the images of his mother and the young woman who died in his arms. He cannot even say his prayers. It is as though Allah has abandoned him, after all.

The daily task of living—waking up, performing his ablutions, setting the little pot on the gas stove to boil water for one cup of tea, to drink that tea alone—unbearable thought! To go on, after so many have died—to go on without his mother, his children, without Gangadhar . . . Everything appears strangely remote: his aging face in the mirror, the old house, even the litchi tree in his courtyard. The familiar lanes of his childhood hold memories that no longer seem to belong to him. Outside, the neighbors are in mourning; old Ameen Khan Sahib weeps for his grandson; Ramdas is gone, Imran is gone. The wind still carries the soot of the burnings. He finds little piles of ashes everywhere, in the cracks in the cement of his courtyard, between the roots of the trees in the lane. He breathes the dead. How can he regain his heart, living in a world so wracked with pain? In this world there is no place for the likes of him. No place for henna-scented hands rocking a child to sleep, for old-woman hands tending a garden. And no place at all for the austere beauty of mathematics.

He's thinking this when a shadow falls across the ground in front of him. He has been sitting in his courtyard, idly writing mathematical expressions with his stick on the dusty ground. He does not know whether the knife bearer is his son, or an enraged Hindu, but he finds himself ready for his death. The creatures who have watched him for so long will witness it, and wonder. Their uncomprehending presence comforts him.

He turns and rises. It is Gangadhar, his friend, who holds out his empty arms in an embrace.

Abdul Karim lets his tears run over Gangadhar's shirt. As waves of relief wash over him he knows that he has held Death at bay this time, but it will come. It will come, he has seen it. Archimedes and Ramanujan, Khayyam and Cantor died with epiphanies on their lips before an indifferent world. But this moment is eternal.

"Allah be praised!" says Abdul Karim.

CHARLES STROSS Charles Stross was born in Leeds, but has spent most of his adult life in Edinburgh, Scotland, an urban area rich in modern SF writers—Iain M. Banks, Ken MacLeod, Hannu Rajaniemi—whose work articulates arrestingly original views about the challenges facing humans and the technosphere. Stross's first published fiction appeared in 1985, making him the clear outlier among the twenty-first-century authors whose work this volume presents. But he shot to real prominence in 2001 with the publication in *Asimov's* of "Lobsters," which later became the opening of his 2005 novel *Accelerando*, called by the *SF Encyclopedia* "the fullest attempt yet in SF to depict the impact of a Singularity on human life." By this time, Stross had also become an influential blogger, which he remains. In the decade since, he has also become one of the core figures of the modern SF field, winning Hugo Awards for short fiction twice and becoming the favorite SF writer of an entire generation of self-identified denizens of the hacker demimonde.

Set in a near future that is undergoing a continuing revolution driven by bioscience, after other technological and economic revolutions have wrought their own changes, 2003's "Rogue Farm" exhibits a broad range of Stross's talents: the wry voice, the density of invention, the eye for the second-order effects of just-over-the-horizon first-order changes. Not to mention, in the great SF tradition of literalizing metaphors, an entirely new twist on the concept of the "collective farm."

ROGUE FARM

It was a bright, cool March morning: mares' tails trailed across the south-eastern sky toward the rising sun. Joe shivered slightly in the driver's seat as he twisted the starter handle on the old front loader he used to muck out the barn. Like its owner, the ancient Massey Ferguson had seen better days; but it had survived worse abuse than Joe routinely handed out. The diesel clattered, spat out a gobbet of thick blue smoke, and chattered to itself dyspeptically. His mind as blank as the sky above, Joe slid the tractor into gear, raised the front scoop, and began turning it toward the open doors of the barn—just in time to see an itinerant farm coming down the road.

"Bugger," swore Joe. The tractor engine made a hideous grinding noise and died. He took a second glance, eyes wide, then climbed down from the tractor and trotted over to the kitchen door at the side of the farmhouse. "Maddie!" he called, forgetting the two-way radio clipped to his sweater hem. "Maddie! There's a farm coming!"

"Joe? Is that you? Where are you?" Her voice wafted vaguely from the bowels of the house.

"Where are you?" he yelled back.

"I'm in the bathroom."

"Bugger," he said again. "If it's the one we had round the end last month . . ."

The sound of a toilet sluiced through his worry. It was followed by a drumming of feet on the staircase; then Maddie erupted into the kitchen. "Where is it?" she demanded.

"Out front, about a quarter mile up the lane."

"Right." Hair wild and eyes angry about having her morning ablutions cut short, Maddie yanked a heavy green coat on over her shirt. "Opened the cupboard yet?"

"I was thinking you'd want to talk to it first."

"Too right I want to talk to it. If it's that one that's been lurking in the copse near Edgar's pond, I got some *issues* to discuss with it." Joe shook his head at her anger and went to unlock the cupboard in the back room. "You take the shotgun and keep it off our property," she called after him. "I'll be out in a minute."

Joe nodded to himself, then carefully picked out the twelve-gauge and a preloaded magazine. The gun's power-on self-test lights flickered erratically, but it seemed to have a full charge. Slinging it, he locked the cupboard carefully and went back out into the farmyard to warn off their unwelcome visitor.

The farm squatted, buzzing and clicking to itself, in the road outside Armitage End. Joe eyed it warily from behind the wooden gate, shotgun under his arm. It was a medium-size one, probably with half a dozen human components subsumed into it—a formidable collective. Already it was deep into farm-fugue, no longer relating very clearly to people outside its own communion of mind. Beneath its leathery black skin he could see hints of internal structure, cytocellular macroassemblies flexing and glooping in disturbing motions. Even though it was only a young adolescent, it was already the size of an antique heavy tank, and it blocked the road just as efficiently as an Apatosaurus would have. It smelled of yeast and gasoline.

Joe had an uneasy feeling that it was watching him. "Buggerit, I don't have time for this," he muttered. The stable waiting for the small herd of cloned spidercows cluttering up the north paddock was still knee-deep in manure, and the tractor seat wasn't getting any warmer while he shivered out here, waiting for Maddie to come and sort this thing out. It wasn't a big herd, but it was as big as his land and his labor could manage—the big biofabricator in the shed could assemble mammalian livestock faster than he could feed them up and sell them with an honest HAND-RAISED NOT VAT-GROWN label. "What do you want with us?" he yelled up at the gently buzzing farm.

"Brains, fresh brains for Baby Jesus," crooned the farm in a warm contralto, startling Joe half out of his skin. "Buy my brains!" Half a dozen disturbing cauliflower shapes poked suggestively out of the farm's back and then re-tracted again, coyly.

"Don't want no brains around here," Joe said stubbornly, his fingers whitening on the stock of the shotgun. "Don't want your kind round here, neither. Go away."

"I'm a nine-legged semiautomatic groove machine!" crooned the farm. "I'm on my way to Jupiter on a mission for love! Won't you buy my brains?" Three curious eyes on stalks extruded from its upper glacis.

"Uh—" Joe was saved from having to dream up any more ways of saying "fuck off" by Maddie's arrival. She'd managed to sneak her old battle dress home after a stint keeping the peace in Mesopotamia twenty years ago, and she'd managed to keep herself in shape enough to squeeze inside. Its left knee squealed ominously when she walked it about, which wasn't often, but it still worked well enough to manage its main task—intimidating trespassers.

"You." She raised one translucent arm, pointed at the farm. "Get off my land. Now."

Taking his cue, Joe raised his shotgun and thumbed the selector to full auto. It wasn't a patch on the hardware riding Maddie's shoulders, but it underlined the point.

The farm hooted: "Why don't you love me?" it asked plaintively.

"*Get orf my land,*" Maddie amplified, volume cranked up so high that Joe winced. "*Ten seconds! Nine! Eight—*" Thin rings sprang out from the sides of her arms, whining with the stress of long disuse as the Gauss gun powered up.

"I'm going! I'm going!" The farm lifted itself slightly, shuffling backwards. "Don't understand. I only wanted to set you free to explore the universe. Nobody wants to buy my fresh fruit and brains. What's wrong with the world?"

They waited until the farm had retreated round the bend at the top of the hill. Maddie was the first to relax, the rings retracting back into the arms of her battle dress, which solidified from ethereal translucency to neutral olive drab as it powered down. Joe safed his shotgun. "Bastard," he said.

"Fucking-A." Maddie looked haggard. "That was a bold one." Her face was white and pinched-looking, Joe noted. Her fists were clenched. She had the shakes, he realized without surprise. Tonight was going to be another major nightmare night, and no mistake.

"The fence." On again and off again for the past year they'd discussed wiring up an outer wire to the CHP base-load from their little methane plant.

"Maybe this time. Maybe." Maddie wasn't keen on the idea of frying passers-by without warning, but if anything might bring her around, it would be the prospect of being overrun by a bunch of rogue farms. "Help me out of this, and I'll cook breakfast," she said.

"Got to muck out the barn," Joe protested.

"It can wait on breakfast," Maddie said shakily. "I need you."

"Okay." Joe nodded. She was looking bad; it had been a few years since her last fatal breakdown, but when Maddie said "I need you," it was a bad idea to ignore her. That way led to backbreaking labor on the biofab and loading her backup tapes into the new body; always a messy business. He took her arm and steered her toward the back porch. They were nearly there when he paused.

"What is it?" asked Maddie.

"Haven't seen Bob for a while," he said slowly. "Sent him to let the cows into the north paddock after milking. Do you think—?"

"We can check from the control room," she said tiredly. "Are you really worried? . . ."

"With that thing blundering around? What do *you* think?"

"He's a good working dog," Maddie said uncertainly. "It won't hurt him. He'll be all right; just you page him."

· · · ·

After Joe helped her out of her battle dress, and after Maddie spent a good long while calming down, they breakfasted on eggs from their own hens, homemade cheese, and toasted bread made with rye from the hippie commune on the other side of the valley. The stone-floored kitchen in the dilapidated house they'd squatted and rebuilt together over the past twenty years was warm and homely. The only purchase from outside the valley was the coffee, beans from a hardy GM strain that grew like a straggling teenager's beard all along the Cumbrian hilltops. They didn't say much: Joe, because he never did, and Maddie, because there wasn't anything that she wanted to discuss. Silence kept her personal demons down. They'd known each other for many years, and even when there wasn't anything to discuss, they could cope with each other's silence. The voice radio on the windowsill opposite the cast-iron stove stayed off, along with the TV set hanging on the wall next to the fridge. Breakfast was a quiet time of day.

"Dog's not answering," Joe commented over the dregs of his coffee.

"He's a good dog." Maddie glanced at the yard gate uncertainly. "You afraid he's going to run away to Jupiter?"

"He was with me in the shed." Joe picked up his plate and carried it to the sink, began running hot water onto the dishes. "After I cleaned the lines I told him to go take the herd up the paddock while I did the barn." He glanced up, looking out the window with a worried expression. The Massey Ferguson was parked right in front of the open barn doors as if holding at bay the mountain of dung, straw, and silage that mounded up inside like an invading odorous enemy, relic of a frosty winter past.

Maddie shoved him aside gently and picked up one of the walkie-talkies from the charge point on the windowsill. It bleeped and chuckled at her. "Bob, come in. Over." She frowned. "He's probably lost his headset again."

Joe racked the wet plates to dry. "I'll move the midden. You want to go find him?"

"I'll do that." Maddie's frown promised a talking-to in store for the dog when she caught up with him. Not that Bob would mind: words ran off him like water off a duck's back. "Cameras first." She prodded the battered TV set to life, and grainy bisected views flickered across the screen, garden, yard, Dutch barn, north paddock, east paddock, main field, copse. "Hmm."

She was still fiddling with the smallholding surveillance system when Joe clambered back into the driver's seat of the tractor and fired it up once more. This time there was no cough of black smoke, and as he hauled the mess of manure out of the barn and piled it into a three-meter-high midden, a quarter of a ton at a time, he almost managed to forget about the morning's unwelcome visitor. Almost.

By late morning, the midden was humming with flies and producing a remarkable stench, but the barn was clean enough to flush out with a hose and broom. Joe was about to begin hauling the midden over to the fermentation tanks buried round the far side of the house when he saw Maddie coming back up the path, shaking her head. He knew at once what was wrong.

"Bob," he said, expectantly.

"Bob's fine. I left him riding shotgun on the goats." Her expression was peculiar. "But that *farm*—"

"Where?" he asked, hurrying after her.

"Squatting in the woods down by the stream," she said tersely. "Just over our fence."

"It's not trespassing, then."

"It's put down feeder roots! Do you have any idea what that means?"

"I don't—" Joe's face wrinkled in puzzlement. "Oh."

"Yes. *Oh*." She stared back at the outbuildings between their home and the woods at the bottom of their smallholding, and if looks could kill, the intruder would be dead a thousand times over. "It's going to estivate, Joe, then it's going to grow to maturity on our patch. And do you know where it said it was going to go when it finishes growing? Jupiter!"

"Bugger," Joe said faintly, as the true gravity of their situation began to sink in. "We'll have to deal with it first."

"That wasn't what I meant," Maddie finished. But Joe was already on his way out the door. She watched him crossing the yard, then shook her head. "Why am I stuck here?" she asked, but the cooker wasn't answering.

· · · ·

The hamlet of Outer Cheswick lay four kilometers down the road from Armitage End, four kilometers past mostly derelict houses and broken-down barns, fields given over to weeds and walls damaged by trees. The first half of the twenty-first century had been cruel years for the British agrobusiness sector; even harsher if taken in combination with the decline in population and the consequent housing surplus. As a result, the dropouts of the forties and fifties were able to take their pick from among the gutted shells of once fine farmhouses. They chose the best and moved in, squatted in the derelict outbuildings, planted their seeds and tended their flocks and practiced their DIY skills, until a generation later a mansion fit for a squire stood in lonely isolation alongside a decaying road where no more cars drove. Or rather, it would have taken a generation had there been any children against whose lives it could be measured; these were the latter decades of the population crash, and what a previous century would have labeled downshifter dink couples were now in the majority, far outnumbering any breeder colonies. In this aspect of their life, Joe and Maddie were boringly conventional. In other respects they weren't: Maddie's nightmares, her aversion to alcohol, and her withdrawal from society were all relics of her time in Peaceforce. As for Joe, he liked it here. Hated cities, hated the Net, hated the burn of the new. Anything for a quiet life . . .

The Pig and Pizzle, on the outskirts of Outer Cheswick, was the only pub within about ten kilometers—certainly the only one within staggering distance for Joe when he'd had a skinful of mild—and it was naturally a seething den of local gossip, not least because Ole Brenda refused to allow electricity, much less bandwidth, into the premises. (This was not out of any sense of misplaced technophobia, but a side effect of Brenda's previous life as an attack hacker with the European Defense Forces.)

Joe paused at the bar. "Pint of bitter?" he asked tentatively. Brenda glanced at him and nodded, then went back to loading the antique washing machine. Presently she pulled a clean glass down from the shelf and held it under the tap.

"Hear you've got farm trouble," she said noncommittally as she worked the hand pump on the beer engine.

"Uh-huh." Joe focused on the glass. "Where'd you hear that?"

"Never you mind." She put the glass down to give the head time to settle. "You want to talk to Arthur and Wendy-the-Rat about farms. They had one the other year."

"Happens." Joe took his pint. "Thanks, Brenda. The usual?"

"Yeah." She turned back to the washer. Joe headed over to the far corner where a pair of huge leather sofas, their arms and backs ripped and scarred by generations of Brenda's semiferal cats, sat facing each other on either side of a cold hearth. "Art, Rats. What's up?"

"Fine, thanks." Wendy-the-Rat was well over seventy, one of those older folks who had taken the p53 chromosome hack and seemed to wither into timelessness: white dread-locks, nose and ear studs dangling loosely from leathery holes, skin like a desert wind. Art had been her boy-toy once, back before middle age set its teeth into him. He hadn't had the hack, and looked older than she did. Together they ran a smallholding, mostly pharming vaccine chicks but also doing a brisk trade in high-nitrate fertilizer that came in on the nod and went out in sacks by moonlight.

"Heard you had a spot of bother?"

" 'S true." Joe took a cautious mouthful. "Mm, good. You ever had farm trouble?"

"Maybe." Wendy looked at him askance, slitty-eyed. "What kinda trouble you got in mind?"

"Got a farm collective. Says it's going to Jupiter or something. Bastard's homesteading the woods down by Old Jack's stream. Listen . . . Jupiter?"

"Aye, well, that's one of the destinations, sure enough." Art nodded wisely, as if he knew anything.

"Naah, that's bad." Wendy-the-Rat frowned. "Is it growing trees, do you know?"

"Trees?" Joe shook his head. "Haven't gone and looked, tell the truth. What the fuck makes people do that to themselves, anyway?"

"Who the fuck cares?" Wendy's face split in a broad grin. "Such as don't think they're human anymore, meself."

"It tried to sweet-talk us," Joe said.

"Aye, they do that," said Arthur, nodding emphatically. "Read somewhere they're the ones as think we aren't fully human. Tools an' clothes and farm-yard machines, like? Sustaining a pre-post-industrial lifestyle instead of updating our genome and living off the land like God intended?"

" 'Ow the hell can something with nine legs and eye stalks call itself human?" Joe demanded, chugging back half his pint in one angry swallow.

"It used to be, once. Maybe used to be a bunch of people." Wendy got a weird and witchy look in her eye. " 'Ad a boyfriend back thirty, forty years ago, joined a Lamarckian clade. Swapping genes an' all, the way you or me'd swap us underwear. Used to be a 'viromentalist back when antiglobal-ization was about big corporations pissing on us all for profits. Got into gene hackery and self-sufficiency big time. I slung his fucking ass when he turned green and started photosynthesizing."

"Bastards," Joe muttered. It was deep green folk like that who'd killed off the agricultural-industrial complex in the early years of the century, turning large portions of the countryside into ecologically devastated wilderness gone to rack and ruin. Bad enough that they'd set millions of countryfolk out of work—but that they'd gone on to turn green, grow extra limbs and emigrate to Jupiter orbit was adding insult to injury. And having a good time in the process, by all accounts. "Din't you 'ave a farm problem, coupla years back?"

"Aye, did that," said Art. He clutched his pint mug protectively.

"It went away," Joe mused aloud.

"Yeah, well." Wendy stared at him cautiously.

"No fireworks, like." Joe caught her eye. "And no body. Huh."

"Metabolism," said Wendy, apparently coming to some kind of decision. "That's where it's at."

"Meat—" Joe, no biogeek, rolled the unfamiliar word around his mouth irritably. "I used to be a software dude before I burned, Rats. You'll have to 'splain the jargon 'fore using it."

"You ever wondered how those farms get to Jupiter?" Wendy probed.

"Well." Joe shook his head. "They, like, grow stage trees? Rocket logs? An' then they est-ee-vate and you are fucked if they do it next door 'cause when those trees go up they toast about a hundred hectares?"

"Very good," Wendy said heavily. She picked up her mug in both hands and gnawed on the rim, edgily glancing around as if hunting for police gnats. "Let's you and me take a hike."

Pausing at the bar for Ole Brenda to refill her mug, Wendy led Joe out past Spiffy Buerke—throwback in green wellingtons and Barbour jacket—and her latest femme, out into what had once been a car park and was now a tattered waste-ground out back behind the pub. It was dark, and no residual light pollution stained the sky: the Milky Way was visible overhead, along with the pea-size red cloud of orbitals that had gradually swallowed Jupiter over the past few years. "You wired?" asked Wendy.

"No, why?"

She pulled out a fist-size box and pushed a button on the side of it, waited for a light on its side to blink green, and nodded. "Fuckin' polis bugs."

"Isn't that a—?"

"Ask me no questions, an' I'll tell you no fibs." Wendy grinned.

"Uh-huh." Joe took a deep breath: he'd guessed Wendy had some dodgy connections, and this—a portable local jammer—was proof: any police bugs within two or three meters would be blind and dumb, unable to relay their chat to the keyword-trawling subsentient coppers whose job it was to prevent conspiracy-to-commit offenses before they happened. It was a relic of the Internet Age, when enthusiastic legislators had accidentally demolished the right of free speech in public by demanding keyword monitoring of everything within range of a network terminal—not realizing that in another few decades 'network terminals' would be self-replicating 'bots the size of fleas and about as common as dirt. (The Net itself had collapsed shortly thereafter, under the weight of self-replicating viral libel lawsuits, but the legacy of public surveillance remained.) "Okay. Tell me about metal, meta—"

"Metabolism." Wendy began walking toward the field behind the pub. "And stage trees. Stage trees started out as science fiction, like? Some guy called Niven—anyway. What you do is, you take a pine tree and you hack it. The xylem vessels running up the heartwood, usually they just lignify and die, in a normal tree. Stage trees go one better, and before the cells die, they *nitrate* the cellulose in their walls. Takes one fuckin' crazy bunch of hacked 'zymes to do it, right? And lots of energy, more energy than trees'd normally have to waste. Anyways, by the time the tree's dead, it's like ninety percent nitrocellulose, plus built-in stiffeners and baffles and microstructures. It's not, like, straight explosive—it detonates cell by cell, and *some* of the xylem tubes are, eh, well, the farm grows custom-hacked fungal hyphae with a depolarizing membrane nicked from human axons down them to trigger the reaction. It's about efficient as 'at old-time Ariane or Atlas rocket. Not very, but enough."

"Uh." Joe blinked. "That meant to mean something to me?"

"Oh 'eck, Joe." Wendy shook her head. "Think I'd bend your ear if it wasn't?"

"Okay." He nodded, seriously. "What can I do?"

"Well." Wendy stopped and stared at the sky. High above them, a belt of faint light sparkled with a multitude of tiny pinpricks; a deep green wagon train making its orbital transfer window, self-sufficient posthuman Lamarckian colonists, space-adapted, embarking on the long, slow transfer to Jupiter.

"Well?" He waited expectantly.

"You're wondering where all that fertilizer's from," Wendy said elliptically.

"Fertilizer." His mind blanked for a moment.

"Nitrates."

He glanced down, saw her grinning at him. Her perfect fifth set of teeth glowed alarmingly in the greenish overspill from the light on her jammer box.

"Tha' knows it make sense," she added, then cut the jammer.

· · · · ·

When Joe finally staggered home in the small hours, a thin plume of smoke was rising from Bob's kennel. Joe paused in front of the kitchen door and sniffed anxiously, then relaxed. Letting go of the door handle, he walked over to the kennel and sat down outside. Bob was most particular about his den—even his own humans didn't go in there without an invitation. So Joe waited.

A moment later there was an interrogative cough from inside. A dark, pointed snout came out, dribbling smoke from its nostrils like a particularly vulpine dragon. "Rrrrrrr?"

"'S'me."

"Uuurgh." A metallic click. "Smoke good smoke joke cough tickle funny arf arf?"

"Yeah, don't mind if I do."

The snout pulled back into the kennel; a moment later it reappeared, teeth clutching a length of hose with a mouthpiece on one end. Joe accepted it graciously, wiped off the mouthpiece, leaned against the side of the kennel, and inhaled. The weed was potent and smooth: within a few seconds the uneasy dialogue in his head was still.

"Wow, tha's a good turnup."

"Arf-arf-ayup."

Joe felt himself relaxing. Maddie would be upstairs, snoring quietly in their decrepit bed: waiting for him, maybe. But sometimes a man just had to be alone with his dog and a good joint, doing man-and-dog stuff. Maddie understood this and left him his space. Still . . .

"'At farm been buggering around the pond?"

"Growl exclaim fuck-fuck yup! Sheep-shagger."

"If it's been at our lambs—"

"Nawwwwrr. Buggrit."

"So whassup?"

"Grrrr, Maddie yap-yap farmtalk! Sheep-shagger."

"Maddie's been *talking* to it?"

"Grrr yes-yes!"

"Oh, shit. Do you remember when she did her last backup?"

The dog coughed fragrant blue smoke. "Tank thump-thump full cow moo beef clone."

"Yeah, I think so, too. Better muck it out tomorrow. Just in case."

"Yurrrrrp." But while Joe was wondering whether this was agreement or just a canine eructation a lean paw stole out of the kennel mouth and yanked the hookah back inside. The resulting slobbering noises and clouds of aromatic blue smoke left Joe feeling a little queasy: so he went inside.

• • • •

The next morning, over breakfast, Maddie was even quieter than usual. Almost meditative.

"Bob said you'd been talking to that farm," Joe commented over his eggs.

"Bob—" Maddie's expression was unreadable. "Bloody dog." She lifted the Rayburn's hot plate lid and peered at the toast browning underneath. "Talks too much."

"Did you?"

"Ayup." She turned the toast and put the lid back down on it.

"Said much?"

"It's a farm." She looked out the window. "Not a fuckin' worry in the world 'cept making its launch window for Jupiter."

"It—"

"Him. Her. They." Maddie sat down heavily in the other kitchen chair. "It's a collective. Usedta be six people. Old, young, whatever, they's decided ter go to Jupiter. One of 'em was telling me how it happened. How she'd been living like an accountant in Bradford, had a nervous breakdown. Wanted *out*. Self-sufficiency." For a moment her expression turned bleak. "Felt herself growing older but not bigger, if you follow."

"So how's turning into a bioborg an improvement?" Joe grunted, forking up the last of his scrambled eggs.

"They're still separate people: bodies are overrated, anyway. Think of the advantages: not growing older, being able to go places and survive anything, never being on your own, not bein' trapped—" Maddie sniffed. "Fuckin' toast's on fire!"

Smoke began to trickle out from under the hot plate lid. Maddie yanked the wire toasting rack out from under it and dunked it into the sink, waited for waterlogged black crumbs to float to the surface before taking it out, opening it, and loading it with fresh bread.

"Bugger," she remarked.

"You feel trapped?" Joe asked. *Again?* He wondered.

Maddie grunted evasively. "Not your fault, love. Just life."

"Life." Joe sniffed, then sneezed violently as the acrid smoke tickled his nose. "Life!"

"Horizon's closing in," she said quietly. "Need a change of horizons."

"Ayup, well, rust never sleeps, right? Got to clean out the winter stables, haven't I?" said Joe. He grinned uncertainly at her as he turned away. "Got a shipment of fertilizer coming in."

· · · ·

In between milking the herd, feeding the sheep, mucking out the winter stables, and surreptitiously EMPing every police 'bot on the farm into the silicon afterlife, it took Joe a couple of days to get round to running up his toy on the household fabricator. It clicked and whirred to itself like a demented knitting machine as it ran up the gadgets he'd ordered—a modified crop sprayer with double-walled tanks and hoses, an air rifle with a dart loaded with a potent cocktail of tubocurarine and etorphine, and a breathing mask with its own oxygen supply.

Maddie made herself scarce, puttering around the control room but mostly disappearing during the daytime, coming back to the house after dark to crawl, exhausted, into bed. She didn't seem to be having nightmares, which was a good sign. Joe kept his questions to himself.

It took another five days for the smallholding's power field to concentrate enough juice to begin fueling up his murder weapons. During this time, Joe took the house off-Net in the most deniable and surreptitiously plausible way, a bastard coincidence of squirrel-induced cable fade and a badly shielded alternator on the backhoe to do for the wireless chitchat. He'd half expected Maddie to complain, but she didn't say anything—just spent more time away in Outer Cheswick or Lower Gruntlingthorpe or wherever she'd taken to holing up.

Finally, the tank was filled. So Joe girded his loins, donned his armor, picked up his weapons, and went to do battle with the dragon by the pond.

The woods around the pond had once been enclosed by a wooden fence, a charming copse of old-growth deciduous trees, elm and oak and beech growing uphill, smaller shrubs nestling at their ankles in a green skirt that reached all the way to the almost-stagnant waters. A little stream fed into it during rainy months, under the feet of a weeping willow; children had played here, pretending to explore the wilderness beneath the benevolent gaze of their parental control cameras.

That had been long ago. Today the woods really *were* wild. No kids, no picnicking city folks, no cars. Badgers and wild coypu and small, frightened wallabies roamed the parching English countryside during the summer dry season. The water drew back to expose an apron of cracked mud, planted with abandoned tin cans and a supermarket trolley of Precambrian vintage, its GPS tracker long since shorted out. The bones of the technological epoch, poking from the treacherous surface of a fossil mud bath. And around the edge of the mimsy puddle, the stage trees grew.

Joe switched on his jammer and walked in among the spear-shaped conifers. Their needles were matte black and fuzzy at the edges, fractally divided, the better to soak up all the available light: a network of taproots and fuzzy black grasslike stuff covered the ground densely around them. Joe's breath wheezed noisily in his ears, and he sweated into the airtight suit as he worked, pumping a stream of colorless smoking liquid at the roots of each ballistic trunk. The liquid fizzed and evaporated on contact: it seemed to bleach the wood where it touched. Joe carefully avoided the stream: this stuff made him uneasy. As did the trees, but liquid nitrogen was about the one thing he'd been able to think of that was guaranteed to kill the trees stone dead without igniting them. After all, they had cores that were basically made of gun cotton—highly explosive, liable to go off if you subjected them to a sudden sharp impact or the friction of a chainsaw. The tree he'd hit on creaked ominously, threatening to fall sideways, and Joe stepped round it, efficiently squirting at the remaining roots. Right into the path of a distraught farm.

"My holy garden of earthly delights! My forest of the imaginative future! My delight, my trees, my trees!" Eye stalks shot out and over, blinking down at him in horror as the farm reared up on six or seven legs and pawed the air in front of him. "Destroyer of saplings! Earth mother rapist! Bunny-strangling vivisectionist!"

"Back off," said Joe, dropping his cryogenic squirter and fumbling for his air gun.

The farm came down with a ground-shaking thump in front of him and stretched eyes out to glare at him from both sides. They blinked, long black eyelashes fluttering across angry blue irises. "How *dare* you?" demanded the farm. "My treasured seedlings!"

"Shut the fuck up," Joe grunted, shouldering his gun. "Think I'd let you burn my holding when tha' rocket launched? Stay the *fuck* away," he added as a tentacle began to extend from the farm's back.

"My crop," it moaned quietly. "My exile! Six more years around the sun chained to this well of sorrowful gravity before next the window opens! No brains for Baby Jesus! Defenestrator! We could have been so happy together if you hadn't fucked up! Who set you up to this? Rat Lady?" It began to gather itself, muscles rippling under the leathery mantle atop its leg cluster.

So Joe shot it.

Tubocurarine is a muscle relaxant: it paralyzes skeletal muscles, the kind over which human nervous systems typically exert conscious control. Etorphine is an insanely strong opiate—twelve hundred times as potent as heroin. Given time, a farm, with its alien adaptive metabolism and consciously controlled proteome might engineer a defense against the etorphine—but Joe dosed his dart with enough to stun a blue whale, and he had no intention of giving the farm enough time.

It shuddered and went down on one knee as he closed in on it, a Syrette raised. "Why?" it asked plaintively in a voice that almost made him wish he hadn't pulled the trigger. "We could have gone together!"

"Together?" he asked. Already the eye stalks were drooping; the great lungs wheezed effortfully as it struggled to frame a reply.

"I was going to ask you," said the farm, and half its legs collapsed under it, with a thud like a baby earthquake. "Oh, Joe, if only—"

"Joe? *Maddie?*" he demanded, nerveless fingers dropping the tranquilizer gun.

A mouth appeared in the farm's front, slurred words at him from familiar seeming lips, words about Jupiter and promises. Appalled, Joe backed away from the farm. Passing the first dead tree, he dropped the nitrogen tank: then an impulse he couldn't articulate made him turn and run, back to the house, eyes almost blinded by sweat or tears. But he was too slow, and when he dropped to his knees next to the farm, pharmacopoeia clicking and whirring to itself in his arms, he found it was already dead.

"Bugger," said Joe, and he stood up, shaking his head. *"Bugger."* He keyed his walkie-talkie: "Bob, come in, Bob!"

"Rrrrowl?"

"Momma's had another break-down. Is the tank clean, like I asked?"

"Yap!"

"Okay. I got 'er backup tapes in t'office safe. Let's get t' tank warmed up for 'er an' then shift t' tractor down 'ere to muck out this mess."

• • • •

That autumn, the weeds grew unnaturally rich and green down in the north paddock of Armitage End.

PAOLO BACIGALUPI Born in Colorado, where he lives today, Paolo Bacigalupi began selling SF in 1999. By the end of the decade he had firmly established himself as one of the most important authors in the genre. His 2009 novel *The Windup Girl* won the Hugo, Nebula, and John W. Campbell Memorial Awards, and was included by *Time* on their list of the ten best books of that year. His YA science fiction novel *Ship Breaker*, published the following year, won the Michael L. Printz Award for best YA novel and was a finalist for the National Book Award. Most of his work is set in near- to middle-distance futures that are struggling with the consequences of drastic climate change and the end of Western global dominance.

"The Gambler," published in 2008, offers a convincingly dystopian view of what our "news" industry is well on its way to becoming, and an affecting portrait of the kind of thinking and writing that such a future has no use for.

THE GAMBLER

My father was a gambler. He believed in the workings of karma and luck. He hunted for lucky numbers on license plates and bet on lotteries and fighting roosters. Looking back, I think perhaps he was not a large man, but when he took me to the muy thai fights, I thought him so. He would bet and he would win and laugh and drink laolao with his friends, and they all seemed so large. In the heat drip of Vientiane, he was a lucky ghost, walking the mirror-sheen streets in the darkness.

Everything for my father was a gamble: roulette and blackjack, new rice variants and the arrival of the monsoons. When the pretender monarch Khamsing announced his New Lao Kingdom, my father gambled on civil disobedience. He bet on the teachings of Mr. Henry David Thoreau and on whisper sheets posted on lampposts. He bet on saffron-robed monks marching in protest and on the hidden humanity of the soldiers with their well-oiled AK-47s and their mirrored helmets.

My father was a gambler, but my mother was not. While he wrote letters to the editor that brought the secret police to our door, she made plans for escape. The old Lao Democratic Republic collapsed, and the New Lao Kingdom blossomed with tanks on the avenues and tuk-tuks burning on the street corners. Pha That Luang's shining gold chedi collapsed under shelling, and I rode away on a UN evacuation helicopter under the care of kind Mrs. Yamaguchi.

From the open doors of the helicopter, we watched smoke columns rise

over the city like nagas coiling. We crossed the brown ribbon of the Mekong
with its jeweled belt of burning cars on the Friendship Bridge. I remember a
Mercedes floating in the water like a paper boat on Loi Kratong, burning
despite the water all around.

Afterward, there was silence from the land of a million elephants, a void
into which light and Skype calls and e-mail disappeared. The roads were
blocked. The telecoms died. A black hole opened where my country had once
stood.

Sometimes, when I wake in the night to the swish and honk of Los Angeles traffic, the confusing polyglot of dozens of countries and cultures all
pressed together in this American melting pot, I stand at my window and
look down a boulevard full of red lights, where it is not safe to walk alone at
night, and yet everyone obeys the traffic signals. I look down on the brash
and noisy Americans in their many hues, and remember my parents: my father who cared too much to let me live under the self-declared monarchy,
and my mother who would not let me die as a consequence. I lean against
the window and cry with relief and loss.

Every week I go to temple and pray for them, light incense and make a
triple bow to Buddha, Damma, and Sangha, and pray that they may have a
good rebirth, and then I step into the light and noise and vibrancy of America.

· · · ·

My colleagues' faces flicker gray and pale in the light of their computers and
tablets. The tap of their keyboards fills the newsroom as they pass content
down the workflow chain and then, with a final keystroke and an obeisance
to the "publish" button, they hurl it onto the net.

In the maelstrom, their work flares, tagged with site location, content
tags, and social poke data. Blooms of color, codes for media conglomerates:
shades of blue and Mickey Mouse ears for Disney-Bertelsmann. A red-
rimmed pair of rainbow O's for Google's AOL News. Fox News Corp. in
pinstripes gray and white. Green for us: Milestone Media—a combination
of NTT DoCoMo, the Korean gaming consortium Hyundai-Kubu, and the
smoking remains of the New York Times Company. There are others, smaller
stars, Crayola shades flaring and brightening, but we are the most important. The monarchs of this universe of light and color.

New content blossoms on the screen, bathing us all in the bloody glow of
a Google News content flare, off their WhisperTech feed. They've scooped
us. The posting says that new ear bud devices will be released by Frontal
Lobe before Christmas: terabyte storage with Pin-Line connectivity for the
Oakley microresponse glasses. The technology is next-gen, allowing personal data control via Pin-Line scans of a user's iris. Analysts predict that
everything from cell phones to digital cameras will become obsolete as the
full range of Oakley features becomes available. The news flare brightens

and migrates toward the center of the maelstrom as visitors flock to Google and view stolen photos of the iris-scanning glasses.

Janice Mbutu, our managing editor, stands at the door to her office, watching with a frown. The maelstrom's red bath dominates the newsroom, a pressing reminder that Google is beating us, sucking away traffic. Behind glass walls, Bob and Casey, the heads of the Burning Wire, our own consumer technology feed, are screaming at their reporters, demanding they do better. Bob's face has turned almost as red as the maelstrom.

The maelstrom's true name is LiveTrack IV. If you were to go downstairs to the fifth floor and pry open the server racks, you would find a sniper sight logo and the words SCRY GLASS—KNOWLEDGE IS POWER stamped on their chips in metallic orange, which would tell you that even though Bloomberg rents us the machines, it is a Google-Nielsen partnership that provides the proprietary algorithms for analyzing the net flows—which means we pay a competitor to tell us what is happening with our own content.

LiveTrack IV tracks media user data—Web site, feed, VOD, audiostream, TV broadcast—with Google's own net statistics gathering programs, aided by Nielsen hardware in personal data devices ranging from TVs to tablets to ear buds to handsets to car radios. To say that the maelstrom keeps a finger on the pulse of media is an understatement. Like calling the monsoon a little wet. The maelstrom is the pulse, the pressure, the blood-oxygen mix; the count of red cells and white, of T-cells and BAC, the screening for AIDS and hepatitis G. . . . It is reality.

Our service version of the maelstrom displays the performance of our own content and compares it to the top one hundred user-traffic events in real-time. My own latest news story is up in the maelstrom, glittering near the edge of the screen, a tale of government incompetence: the harvested DNA of the checkerspot butterfly, already extinct, has been destroyed through mismanagement at the California Federal Biological Preserve Facility. The butterfly—along with sixty-two other species—was subjected to improper storage protocols, and now there is nothing except a little dust in vials. The samples literally blew away. My coverage of the story opens with federal workers down on their knees in a two-billion-dollar climate-controlled vault, with a dozen crime scene vacuums that they've borrowed from LAPD, trying to suck up a speck of butterfly that they might be able to reconstitute at some future time.

In the maelstrom, the story is a pinprick beside the suns and pulsing moons of traffic that represent other reporters' content. It doesn't compete well with news of Frontal Lobe devices, or reviews of Armored Total Combat, or live feeds of the Binge-Purge championships. It seems that the only people who are reading my story are the biologists I interviewed. This is not surprising. When I wrote about bribes for subdivision approvals, the only people who read the story were county planners. When I wrote about cronyism in the selection of city water recycling technologies, the only people who read were water engineers. Still, even though no one seems to care about these stories, I am drawn to them, as though poking at the tiger of the American government will somehow make up for not being able to poke at the little cub of New Divine Monarch Khamsing. It is a foolish thing, a sort of Don Quixote crusade. As a consequence, my salary is the smallest in the office.

"Whoooo!"

Heads swivel from terminals, look for the noise: Marty Mackley, grinning.

"You can thank me . . ." He leans down and taps a button on his keyboard. "Now."

A new post appears in the maelstrom, a small green orb announcing itself on the Glamour Report, Scandal Monkey blog, and Marty's byline feeds. As we watch, the post absorbs pings from software clients around the world, notifying the millions of people who follow his byline that he has launched a new story.

I flick my tablet open, check the tags:

Double DP,
Redneck HipHop,
Music News,
Schadenfreude,
underage,
pedophilia . . .

According to Mackley's story, Double DP the Russian mafia cowboy rapper—who, in my opinion, is not as good as the Asian pop sensation Ku-laap, but whom half the planet likes very much—is accused of impregnating the fourteen-year-old daughter of his face sculptor. Readers are starting to notice, and with their attention Marty's green-glowing news story begins to muscle for space in the maelstrom. The content star pulses, expands, and then, as though someone has thrown gasoline on it, it explodes. Double DP hits the social sites, starts getting recommended, sucks in more readers, more links, more clicks . . . and more ad dollars.

Marty does a pelvic grind of victory, then waves at everyone for their attention. "And that's not all, folks." He hits his keyboard again, and another story posts: live feeds of Double's house, where . . . it looks as though the man who popularized Redneck Russians is heading out the door in a hurry. It is a surprise to see video of the house, streaming live. Most freelance paparazzi are not patient enough to sit and hope that maybe, perhaps, something interesting will happen. This looks as though Marty has stationed his own exclusive papcams at the house, to watch for something like this.

We all watch as Double DP locks the door behind himself. Marty says, "I thought DP deserved the courtesy of notification that the story was going live."

"Is he fleeing?" Mikela Plaa asks.

Marty shrugs. "We'll see."

And indeed, it does look as if Double is about to do what Americans have popularized as an "OJ." He is into his red Hummer. Pulling out.

Under the green glow of his growing story, Marty smiles. The story is getting bigger, and Marty has stationed himself perfectly for the development. Other news agencies and blogs are playing catch-up. Follow-on posts wink into existence in the maelstrom, gathering a momentum of their own as newsrooms scramble to hook our traffic.

"Do we have a helicopter?" Janice asks. She has come out of her glass office to watch the show.

Marty nods. "We're moving it into position. I just bought exclusive angel view with the cops, too, so everyone's going to have to license our footage."

"Did you let Long Arm of the Law know about the cross-content?"

"Yeah. They're kicking in from their budget for the helicopter."

Marty sits down again, begins tapping at his keyboard, a machine-gun of data entry. A low murmur comes from the tech pit, Cindy C. calling our telecom providers, locking down trunklines to handle an anticipated data surge. She knows something that we don't, something that Marty has prepared her for. She's bringing up mirrored server farms. Marty seems unaware of the audience around him. He stops typing. Stares up at the maelstrom, watching his glowing ball of content. He is the maestro of a symphony.

The cluster of competing stories are growing as *Gawker* and *Newsweek* and *Throb* all organize themselves and respond. Our readers are clicking away from us, trying to see if there's anything new in our competitor's coverage. Marty smiles, hits his "publish" key, and dumps a new bucket of meat into the shark tank of public interest: a video interview with the fourteen-year-old. On-screen, she looks very young, shockingly so. She has a teddy bear.

"I swear I didn't plant the bear," Marty comments. "She had it on her own."

The girl's accusations are being mixed over Double's run for the border, a kind of synth loop of accusations:

"And then he . . ."

"And I said . . ."

"He's the only one I've ever . . ."

It sounds as if Marty has licensed some of Double's own beats for the coverage of his fleeing Humvee. The video outtakes are already bouncing around YouTube and MotionSwallow like Ping-Pong balls. The maelstrom has moved Double DP to the center of the display as more and more feeds and sites point to the content. Not only is traffic up, but the post is gaining in social rank as the numbers of links and social pokes increase.

"How's the stock?" someone calls out.

Marty shakes his head. "They locked me out from showing the display."

This, because whenever he drops an important story, we all beg him to show us the big picture. We all turn to Janice. She rolls her eyes, but she gives the nod. When Cindy finishes buying bandwidth, she unlocks the view. The maelstrom slides aside as a second window opens, all bar graphs and financial landscape: our stock price as affected by the story's expanding traffic—and expanding ad revenue.

The stock bots have their own version of the maelstrom; they've picked up the reader traffic shift. Buy and sell decisions roll across the screen, responding to the popularity of Mackley's byline. As he feeds the story, the beast grows. More feeds pick us up, more people recommend the story to their friends, and every one of them is being subjected to our advertisers' messages, which means more revenue for us and less for everyone else. At this point, Mackley is bigger than the Super Bowl. Given that the story is tagged with Double DP, it will have a targetable demographic: thirteen- to twenty-four-year-olds who buy lifestyle gadgets, new music, edge clothes, first-run games, boxed hairstyles, tablet skins, and ringtones: not only a large demographic, a valuable one.

Our stock ticks up a point. Holds. Ticks up another. We've got four different screens running now. The papcam of Double DP, chase cycles with views of the cops streaking after him, the chopper lifting off, and the window with the fourteen-year-old interviewing. The girl is saying, "I really feel for him. We have a connection. We're going to get married," and there's his Hummer screaming down Santa Monica Boulevard with his song "Cowboy Banger" on the audio overlay.

A new wave of social pokes hits the story. Our stock price ticks up again. Daily bonus territory. The clicks are pouring in. It's got the right combination of content, what Mackley calls the "Three S's": sex, stupidity, and schadenfreude. The stock ticks up again. Everyone cheers. Mackley takes a bow. We all love him. He is half the reason I can pay my rent. Even a small newsroom bonus from his work is enough for me to live. I'm not sure how much he makes for himself when he creates an event like this. Cindy tells me that it is "solid seven, baby." His byline feed is so big he could probably go independent, but then he would not have the resources to scramble a helicopter for a chase toward Mexico. It is a symbiotic relationship. He does what he does best, and Milestone pays him like a celebrity.

Janice claps her hands. "All right, everyone. You've got your bonus. Now back to work."

A general groan rises. Cindy cuts the big monitor away from stocks and bonuses and back to the work at hand: generating more content to light the maelstrom, to keep the newsroom glowing green with flares of Milestone coverage—everything from reviews of Mitsubishi's 100 mpg Road Cruiser to how to choose a perfect turkey for Thanksgiving. Mackley's story pulses over us as we work. He spins off smaller additional stories, updates, interactivity features, encouraging his vast audience to ping back just one more time.

Marty will spend the entire day in conversation with this elephant of a story that he has created. Encouraging his visitors to return for just one more click. He'll give them chances to poll each other, discuss how they'd like to see DP punished, ask whether you can actually fall in love with a fourteen-year-old. This one will have a long life, and he will raise it like a proud father, feeding and nurturing it, helping it make its way in the rough world of the maelstrom.

My own little green speck of content has disappeared. It seems that even government biologists feel for Double DP.

• • • •

When my father was not placing foolish bets on revolution, he taught agronomy at the National Lao University. Perhaps our lives would have been different if he had been a rice farmer in the paddies of the capital's suburbs, instead of surrounded by intellectuals and ideas. But his karma was to be a teacher and a researcher, and so while he was increasing Lao rice production by 30 percent, he was also filling himself with gambler's fancies: Thoreau, Gandhi, Martin Luther King, Sakharov, Mandela, Aung Sung Kyi. True gamblers, all. He would say that if white South Africans could be made to feel shame, then the pretender monarch must right his ways. He claimed that Thoreau must have been Lao, the way he protested so politely.

In my father's description, Thoreau was a forest monk, gone into the jungle for enlightenment. To live amongst the banyan and the climbing vines of Massachusetts and to meditate on the nature of suffering. My father believed he was undoubtedly some arhat reborn. He often talked of Mr. Henry David, and in my imagination this falang, too, was a large man like my father.

When my father's friends visited in the dark—after the coup and the countercoup, and after the march of Khamsing's Chinese-supported insurgency— they would often speak of Mr. Henry David. My father would sit with his friends and students and drink black Lao coffee and smoke cigarettes, and then he would write carefully worded complaints against the government that his students would then copy and leave in public places, distribute into gutters, and stick onto walls in the dead of night.

His guerrilla complaints would ask where his friends had gone, and why their families were so alone. He would ask why monks were beaten on their heads by Chinese soldiers when they sat in hunger strike before the palace. Sometimes, when he was drunk and when these small gambles did not satisfy his risk-taking nature, he would send editorials to the newspapers.

None of these were ever printed, but he was possessed with some spirit that made him think that perhaps the papers would change. That his stature as a father of Lao agriculture might somehow sway the editors to commit suicide and print his complaints.

It ended with my mother serving coffee to a secret police captain while two more policemen waited outside our door. The captain was very polite: he offered my father a 555 cigarette—a brand that already had become rare and contraband—and lit it for him. Then he spread the whisper sheet onto the coffee table, gently pushing aside the coffee cups and their saucers to make room for it. It was rumpled and torn, stained with mud. Full of accusations against Khamsing. Unmistakable as one of my father's.

My father and the policeman both sat and smoked, studying the paper silently.

Finally, the captain asked, "Will you stop?"

My father drew on his cigarette and let the smoke out slowly as he studied the whisper sheet between them. The captain said, "We all respect what you have done for the Lao kingdom. I myself have family who would have starved if not for your work in the villages." He leaned forward. "If you promise to stop writing these whispers and complaints, everything can be forgotten. Everything."

Still, my father didn't say anything. He finished his cigarette. Stubbed it out. "It would be difficult to make that sort of promise," he said.

The captain was surprised. "You have friends who have spoken on your behalf. Perhaps you would reconsider. For their sake."

My father made a little shrug. The captain spread the rumpled whisper sheet, flattening it out more completely. Read it over. "These sheets do nothing," he said. "Khamsing's dynasty will not collapse because you print a few complaints. Most of these are torn down before anyone reads them. They do nothing. They are pointless." He was almost begging. He looked over and saw me watching at the door. "Give this up. For your family, if not your friends."

I would like to say that my father said something grand. Something honorable about speaking against tyranny. Perhaps invoked one of his idols. Aung Sung Kyi or Sakharov, or Mr. Henry David and his penchant for polite protest. But he didn't say anything. He just sat with his hands on his knees, looking down at the torn whisper sheet. I think now that he must have been very afraid. Words always came easily to him, before. Instead, all he did was repeat himself. "It would be difficult."

The captain waited. When it became apparent that my father had nothing else to say, he put down his coffee cup and motioned for his men to come inside. They were all very polite. I think the captain even apologized to my mother as they led him out the door.

· · · ·

We are into day three of the Double DP bonanza, and the green sun glows brightly over all of us, bathing us in its soothing, profitable glow. I am working on my newest story with my Frontal Lobe ear buds in, shutting out everything except the work at hand. It is always a little difficult to write in one's third language, but I have my favorite singer and fellow countryperson Kulaap whispering in my ear that "Love is a Bird," and the work is going well. With Kulaap singing to me in our childhood language, I feel very much at home.

A tap on my shoulder interrupts me. I pull out my ear buds and look around. Janice, standing over me. "Ong, I need to talk to you." She motions me to follow.

In her office, she closes the door behind me and goes to her desk. "Sit down, Ong." She keys her tablet, scrolls through data. "How are things going for you?"

"Very well. Thank you." I'm not sure if there is more that she wants me to say, but it is likely that she will tell me. Americans do not leave much to guesswork.

"What are you working on for your next story?" she asks.

I smile. I like this story; it reminds me of my father. And with Kulaap's soothing voice in my ears I have finished almost all of my research. The bluet, a flower made famous in Mr. Henry David Thoreau's journals, is blooming too early to be pollinated. Bees do not seem to find it when it blooms in March. The scientists I interviewed blame global warming, and now the flower is in danger of extinction. I have interviewed biologists and local naturalists, and now I would like to go to Walden Pond on a pilgrimage for this bluet that may soon also be bottled in a federal reserve laboratory with its techs in clean suits and their crime scene vacuums.

When I finish describing the story, Janice looks at me as if I am crazy. I can tell that she thinks I am crazy, because I can see it on her face. And also because she tells me.

"You're fucking crazy!"

Americans are very direct. It's difficult to keep face when they yell at you. Sometimes, I think that I have adapted to America. I have been here for five years now, ever since I came from Thailand on a scholarship, but at times like this, all I can do is smile and try not to cringe as they lose their face and yell and rant. My father was once struck in the face with an official's shoe, and he did not show his anger. But Janice is American, and she is very angry.

"There's no way I'm going to authorize a junket like that!"

I try to smile past her anger, and then remember that the Americans don't see an apologetic smile in the same way that a Lao would. I stop smiling and make my face look . . . something. Earnest, I hope.

"The story is very important," I say. "The ecosystem isn't adapting correctly to the changing climate. Instead, it has lost . . ." I grope for the word. "Synchronicity. These scientists think that the flower can be saved, but only if they import a bee that is available in Turkey. They think it can replace the function of the native bee population, and they think that it will not be too disruptive."

"Flowers and Turkish bees."

"Yes. It is an important story. Do they let the flower go extinct? Or try to keep the famous flower, but alter the environment of Walden Pond? I think your readers will think it is very interesting."

"More interesting than that?" She points through her glass wall at the maelstrom, at the throbbing green sun of Double DP, who has now barricaded himself in a Mexican hotel and has taken a pair of fans hostage.

"You know how many clicks we're getting?" she asks. "We're exclusive. Marty's got Double's trust and is going in for an interview tomorrow, assuming the Mexicans don't just raid it with commandos. We've got people clicking back every couple minutes just to look at Marty's blog about his preparations to go in."

The glowing globe not only dominates the maelstrom's screen, it washes everything else out. If we look at the stock bots, everyone who doesn't have protection under our corporate umbrella has been hurt by the loss of eyeballs. Even the Frontal Lobe/Oakley story has been swallowed. Three days of completely dominating the maelstrom has been very profitable for us. Now Marty's showing his viewers how he will wear a flak jacket in case the Mexican commandos attack while he is discussing the nature of true love with DP. And he has another exclusive interview with the mother ready to post as well. Cindy has been editing the footage and telling us all how disgusted she is with the whole thing. The woman apparently drove her daughter to DP's mansion for a midnight pool party, alone.

"Perhaps some people are tired of DP and wish to see something else," I suggest.

"Don't shoot yourself in the foot with a flower story, Ong. Even Pradeep's cooking journey through Ladakh gets more viewers than this stuff you're writing."

She looks as though she will say more, but then she simply stops. It seems as if she is considering her words. It is uncharacteristic. She normally speaks before her thoughts are arranged.

"Ong, I like you," she says. I make myself smile at this, but she continues. "I hired you because I had a good feeling about you. I didn't have a problem with clearing the visas to let you stay in the country. You're a good person. You write well. But you're averaging less than a thousand pings on your byline feed." She looks down at her tablet, then back up at me. "You need to up your average. You've got almost no readers selecting you for Page One. And even when they do subscribe to your feed, they're putting it in the third tier."

"Spinach reading," I supply.

"What?"

"Mr. Mackley calls it spinach reading. When people feel like they should do something with virtue, like eat their spinach, they click to me. Or else read Shakespeare."

I blush, suddenly embarrassed. I do not mean to imply that my work is of the same caliber as a great poet. I want to correct myself, but I'm too embarrassed. So instead I shut up, and sit in front of her, blushing.

She regards me. "Yes. Well, that's a problem. Look, I respect what you do. You're obviously very smart." Her eyes scan her tablet. "The butterfly thing you wrote was actually pretty interesting."

"Yes?" I make myself smile again.

"It's just that no one wants to read these stories."

I try to protest. "But you hired me to write the important stories. The stories about politics and the government, to continue the traditions of the old newspapers. I remember what you said when you hired me."

"Yeah, well." She looks away. "I was thinking more about a good scandal."

"The checkerspot is a scandal. That butterfly is now gone."

She sighs. "No, it's not a scandal. It's just a depressing story. No one reads a depressing story, at least, not more than once. And no one subscribes to a depressing byline feed."

"A thousand people do."

"A thousand people." She laughs. "We aren't some Laotian community weblog, we're Milestone, and we're competing for clicks with them." She waves outside, indicating the maelstrom. "Your stories don't last longer than half a day; they never get social-poked by anyone except a fringe." She shakes her head. "Christ, I don't even know who your demographic is. Centenarian hippies? Some federal bureaucrats? The numbers just don't justify the amount of time you spend on stories."

"What stories do you wish me to write?"

"I don't know. Anything. Product reviews. News you can use. Just not any more of this 'we regret to inform you of bad news' stuff. If there isn't something a reader can do about the damn butterfly, then there's no point in telling them about it. It just depresses people, and it depresses your numbers."

"We don't have enough numbers from Marty?"

She laughs at that. "You remind me of my mother. Look, I don't want to cut you, but if you can't start pulling at least a fifty thousand daily average, I won't have any choice. Our group median is way down in comparison to other teams, and when evaluations come around, we look bad. I'm up against Nguyen in the Tech and Toys pool, and Penn in Yoga and Spirituality, and no one wants to read about how the world's going to shit. Go find me some stories that people want to read."

She says a few more things, words that I think are meant to make me feel inspired and eager, and then I am standing outside the door, once again facing the maelstrom.

The truth is that I have never written popular stories. I am not a popular story writer. I am earnest. I am slow. I do not move at the speed these Americans seem to love. Find a story that people want to read. I can write some follow-up to Mackley, to Double DP, perhaps assist with sidebars to his main piece, but somehow, I suspect that the readers will know that I am faking it.

Marty sees me standing outside of Janice's office. He comes over.

"She giving you a hard time about your numbers?"

"I do not write the correct sort of stories."

"Yeah. You're an idealist."

We both stand there for a moment, meditating on the nature of idealism. Even though he is very American, I like him because he is sensitive to people's hearts. People trust him. Even Double DP trusts him, though Marty blew his name over every news tablet's front page. Marty has a good heart. Jai dee. I like him. I think that he is genuine.

"Look, Ong," he says. "I like what you do." He puts his hand around my shoulder. For a moment, I think he's about to try to rub my head with affection and I have to force myself not to wince, but he's sensitive and instead takes his hand away. "Look, Ong. We both know you're terrible at this kind of work. We're in the news business, here. And you're just not cut out for it."

"My visa says I have to remain employed."

"Yeah. Janice is a bitch for that. Look." He pauses. "I've got this thing with Double DP going down in Mexico. But I've got another story brewing. An exclusive. I've already got my bonus, anyway. And it should push up your average."

"I do not think that I can write Double DP sidebars."

He grins. "It's not that. And it's not charity; you're actually a perfect match."

"It is about government mismanagement?"

He laughs, but I think he's not really laughing at me. "No." He pauses, smiles. "It's Kulaap. An interview."

I suck in my breath. My fellow countryperson, here in America. She came out during the purge as well. She was doing a movie in Singapore when the tanks moved, and so she was not trapped. She was already very popular all over Asia, and when Khamsing turned our country into a black hole, the world took note. Now she is popular here in America as well. Very beautiful. And she remembers our country before it went into darkness. My heart is pounding.

Marty goes on. "She's agreed to do an exclusive with me. But you even speak her language, so I think she'd agree to switch off." He pauses, looks serious. "I've got a good history with Kulaap. She doesn't give interviews to just anyone. I did a lot of exposure stories about her when Laos was going to hell. Got her a lot of good press. This is a special favor already, so don't fuck it up."

I shake my head. "No. I will not." I press my palms together and touch them to my forehead in a nop of appreciation. "I will not fuck it up." I make another nop.

He laughs. "Don't bother with that polite stuff. Janice will cut off your balls to increase the stock price, but we're the guys in the trenches. We stick together, right?"

. . . .

In the morning, I make a pot of strong coffee with condensed milk; I boil rice noodle soup and add bean sprouts and chiles and vinegar, and warm a loaf of French bread that I buy from a Vietnamese bakery a few blocks away. With a new mix of Kulaap's music from DJ Dao streaming in over my stereo, I sit down at my little kitchen table, pour my coffee from its press pot, and open my tablet.

The tablet is a wondrous creation. In Laos, the paper was still a paper, physical, static, and empty of anything except the official news. Real news in our New Divine Kingdom did not come from newspapers, or from television, or from handsets or ear buds. It did not come from the net or feeds unless you trusted your neighbor not to look over your shoulder at an Internet cafe and if you knew that there were no secret police sitting beside you, or an owner who would be able to identify you when they came around asking about the person who used that workstation over there to communicate with the outside world.

Real news came from whispered rumor, rated according to the trust you accorded the whisperer. Were they family? Did they have long history with you? Did they have anything to gain by the sharing? My father and his old classmates trusted one another. He trusted some of his students, as well. I think this is why the security police came for him in the end. One of his trusted friends or students also whispered news to official friends. Perhaps Mr. Intha-chak, or Som Vang. Perhaps another. It is impossible to peer into the blackness of that history and guess at who told true stories and in which direction.

In any case, it was my father's karma to be taken, so perhaps it does not matter who did the whispering. But before then—before the news of my father flowed up to official ears—none of the real news flowed toward Lao TV or the *Vientiane Times*. Which meant that when the protests happened and my father came through the door with blood on his face from baton blows, we could read as much as we wanted about the three thousand schoolchildren who had sung the national anthem to our new divine monarch. While my father lay in bed, delirious with pain, the papers told us that China had signed a rubber contract that would triple revenue for Luang Namtha province and that Nam Theun Dam was now earning BT 22.5 billion per year in electricity fees to Thailand. But there were no bloody batons, and there were no dead monks, and there was no Mercedes-Benz burning in the river as it floated toward Cambodia.

Real news came on the wings of rumor, stole into our house at midnight, sat with us and sipped coffee and fled before the call of roosters could break the stillness. It was in the dark, over a burning cigarette that you learned Vilaphon had disappeared or that Mr. Saeng's wife had been beaten as a warning. Real news was too valuable to risk in public.

Here in America, my page glows with many news feeds, flickers at me in video windows, pours in at me over broadband. It is a waterfall of information. As my personal news page opens, my feeds arrange themselves, sorting according to the priorities and tag categories that I've set, a mix of Meung Lao news, Lao refugee blogs, and the chatting of a few close friends from Thailand and the American college where I attended on a human relief scholarship.

On my second page and my third, I keep the general news, the arrangements of *Milestone,* the *Bangkok Post,* the *Phnom Penh Express*—the news chosen by editors. But by the time I've finished with my own selections, I don't often have time to click through the headlines that these earnest news editors select for the mythical general reader.

In any case, I know far better than they what I want to read, and with my keyword and tag scans, I can unearth stories and discussions that a news agency would never think to provide. Even if I cannot see into the black hole itself, I can slip along its edges, divine news from its fringe.

I search for tags like Vientiane, Laos, Lao, Khamsing, China-Lao friendship, Korat, Golden Triangle, Hmong independence, Lao PDR, my father's name. . . . Only those of us who are Lao exiles from the March Purge really read these blogs. It is much as when we lived in the capital. The blogs are the rumors that we used to whisper to one another. Now we publish our whispers over the net and join mailing lists instead of secret coffee groups, but it is the same. It is family, as much as any of us now have.

On the maelstrom, the tags for Laos don't even register. Our tags bloomed brightly for a little while, while there were still guerrilla students uploading content from their handsets, and the images were lurid and shocking. But then the phone lines went down and the country fell into its black hole and now it is just us, this small network that functions outside the country.

A headline from Jumbo Blog catches my eye. I open the site, and my tablet fills with the colorful image of the three-wheeled taxi of my childhood. I often come here. It is a node of comfort.

Laofriend posts that some people, maybe a whole family, have swum the Mekong and made it into Thailand. He isn't sure if they were accepted as refugees or if they were sent back.

It is not an official news piece. More, the idea of a news piece. SomPaBoy doesn't believe it, but Khamchanh contends that the rumor is true, heard from someone who has a sister married to an Isaan border guard in the Thai army. So we cling to it. Wonder about it. Guess where these people came from, wonder if, against all odds, it could be one of ours: a brother, a sister, a cousin, a father. . . .

After an hour, I close the tablet. It's foolish to read any more. It only brings up memories. Worrying about the past is foolish. Lao PDR is gone. To wish otherwise is suffering.

. . . .

The clerk at Novotel's front desk is expecting me. A hotel staffer with a key guides me to a private elevator bank that whisks us up into the smog and heights. The elevator doors open to a small entryway with a thick mahogany door. The staffer steps back into the elevator and disappears, leaving me standing in this strange airlock. Presumably, I am being examined by Kulaap's security.

The mahogany door opens, and a smiling black man who is forty centimeters taller than I and who has muscles that ripple like snakes smiles and motions me inside. He guides me through Kulaap's sanctuary. She keeps the heat high, almost tropical, and fountains rush everywhere around. The flat is musical with water. I unbutton my collar in the humidity. I was expecting air-conditioning, and instead I am sweltering. It's almost like home. And then she's in front of me, and I can hardly speak. She is beautiful, and more. It is intimidating to stand before someone who exists in film and in music but has never existed before you in the flesh. She's not as stunning as she is in the movies, but there's more life, more presence; the movies lose that quality about her. I make a nop of greeting, pressing my hands together, touching my forehead.

She laughs at this, takes my hand and shakes it American-style. "You're lucky Marty likes you so much," she says. "I don't like interviews."

I can barely find my voice. "Yes. I only have a few questions."

"Oh no. Don't be shy." She laughs again, and doesn't release my hand, pulls me toward her living room. "Marty told me about you. You need help with your ratings. He helped me once, too."

She's frightening. She is of my people, but she has adapted better to this place than I have. She seems comfortable here. She walks differently, smiles differently; she is an American, with perhaps some flavor of our country, but nothing of our roots. It's obvious. And strangely disappointing. In her movies, she holds herself so well, and now she sits down on her couch and sprawls with her feet kicked out in front of her. Not caring at all. I'm embarrassed for her, and I'm glad I don't have my camera set up yet. She kicks her feet up on the couch. I can't help but be shocked. She catches my expression and smiles.

"You're worse than my parents. Fresh off the boat."

"I am sorry."

She shrugs. "Don't worry about it. I spent half my life here, growing up; different country, different rules."

I'm embarrassed. I try not to laugh with the tension I feel. "I just have some interview questions," I say.

"Go ahead." She sits up and arranges herself for the video stand that I set up.

I begin. "When the March Purge happened, you were in Singapore."

She nods. "That's right. We were finishing *The Tiger and the Ghost*."

"What was your first thought when it happened? Did you want to go back? Were you surprised?"

She frowns. "Turn off the camera."

When it's off she looks at me with pity. "This isn't the way to get clicks. No one cares about an old revolution. Not even my fans." She stands abruptly and calls through the green jungle of her flat. "Terrell?"

The big black man appears. Smiling and lethal. Looming over me. He is very frightening. The movies I grew up with had falang like him. Terrifying large black men whom our heroes had to overcome. Later, when I arrived in America, it was different, and I found out that the falang and the black people don't like the way we show them in our movies. Much like when I watch their Vietnam movies, and see the ugly way the Lao freedom fighters behave. Not real at all, portrayed like animals. But still, I cannot help but cringe when Terrell looks at me.

Kulaap says, "We're going out, Terrell. Make sure you tip off some of the papcams. We're going to give them a show."

"I don't understand," I say.

"You want clicks, don't you?"

"Yes, but—"

She smiles. "You don't need an interview. You need an event." She looks me over. "And better clothes." She nods to her security man. "Terrell, dress him up."

· · · ·

A flashbulb frenzy greets us as we come out of the tower. Papcams everywhere. Chase cycles revving, and Terrell and three others of his people guiding us through the press to the limousine, shoving cameras aside with a violence and power that are utterly unlike the careful pity he showed when he selected a Gucci suit for me to wear.

Kulaap looks properly surprised at the crowd and the shouting reporters, but not nearly as surprised as I am, and then we're in the limo, speeding out of the tower's roundabout as papcams follow us.

Kulaap crouches before the car's onboard tablet, keying in pass codes. She is very pretty, wearing a black dress that brushes her thighs and thin straps that caress her smooth bare shoulders. I feel as if I am in a movie. She taps more keys. A screen glows, showing the taillights of our car: the view from pursuing papcams.

"You know I haven't dated anyone in three years?" she asks.

"Yes. I know from your Web site biography."

She grins. "And now it looks like I've found one of my countrymen."

"But we're not on a date," I protest.

"Of course we are." She smiles again. "I'm going out on a supposedly se-cret date with a cute and mysterious Lao boy. And look at all those papcams chasing after us, wondering where we're going and what we're going to do." She keys in another code, and now we can see live footage of the paparazzi, as viewed from the tail of her limo. She grins. "My fans like to see what life is like for me."

I can almost imagine what the maelstrom looks like right now: there will still be Marty's story, but now a dozen other sites will be lighting up, and in the center of that, Kulaap's own view of the excitement, pulling in her fans, who will want to know, direct from her, what's going on. She holds up a mir-ror, checks herself, and then she smiles into her smartphone's camera.

"Hi everyone. It looks like my cover's blown. Just thought I should let you know that I'm on a lovely date with a lovely man. I'll let you all know how it goes. Promise." She points the camera at me. I stare at it stupidly. She laughs. "Say hi and good-bye, Ong."

"Hi and good-bye."

She laughs again, waves into the camera. "Love you all. Hope you have as good a night as I'm going to have." And then she cuts the clip and punches a code to launch the video to her Web site.

It is a bit of nothing. Not a news story, not a scoop even, and yet, when she opens another window on her tablet, showing her own miniversion of the maelstrom, I can see her site lighting up with traffic. Her version of the maelstrom isn't as powerful as what we have at *Milestone,* but still, it is an impressive window into the data that is relevant to Kulaap's tags.

"What's your feed's byline?" she asks. "Let's see if we can get your traffic bumped up."

"Are you serious?"

"Marty Mackley did more than this for me. I told him I'd help." She laughs. "Besides, we wouldn't want you to get sent back to the black hole, would we?"

"You know about the black hole?" I can't help doing a double-take.

Her smile is almost sad. "You think just because I put my feet up on the furniture that I don't care about my aunts and uncles back home? That I don't worry about what's happening?"

"I—"

She shakes her head. "You're so fresh off the boat."

"Do you use the Jumbo Cafe—" I break off. It seems too unlikely.

She leans close. "My handle is Laofriend. What's yours?"

"Littlexang. I thought Laofriend was a boy—"

She just laughs.

I lean forward. "Is it true that the family made it out?"

She nods. "For certain. A general in the Thai army is a fan. He tells me everything. They have a listening post. And sometimes they send scouts across."

It's almost as if I am home.

• • • •

We go to a tiny Laotian restaurant where everyone recognizes her and falls over her and the owners simply lock out the paparazzi when they become too intrusive. We spend the evening unearthing memories of Vientiane. We discover that we both favored the same rice noodle cart on Kaem Khong. That she used to sit on the banks of the Mekong and wish that she were a fisherman. That we went to the same waterfalls outside the city on the weekends. That it is impossible to find good dum mak hoong anywhere outside of the country. She is a good companion, very alive. Strange in her American ways, but still, with a good heart. Periodically, we click photos of one another and post them to her site, feeding the voyeurs. And then we are in the limo again and the paparazzi are all around us. I have the strange feeling of fame. Flashbulbs everywhere. Shouted questions. I feel proud to be beside this beautiful intelligent woman who knows so much more than any of us about the situation inside our homeland.

Back in the car, she has me open a bottle of champagne and pour two glasses while she opens the maelstrom and studies the results of our date. She has reprogrammed it to watch my byline feed ranking as well.

"You've got twenty thousand more readers than you did yesterday," she says.

I beam. She keeps reading the results. "Someone already did a scan on your face." She toasts me with her glass. "You're famous."

We clink glasses. I am flushed with wine and happiness. I will have Janice's average clicks. It's as though a bodhisattva has come down from heaven to save my job. In my mind, I offer thanks to Marty for arranging this, for his generous nature. Kulaap leans close to her screen, watching the flaring content. She opens another window, starts to read. She frowns.

"What the fuck do you write about?"

I draw back, surprised. "Government stories, mostly." I shrug. "Sometimes environment stories."

"Like what?"

"I am working on a story right now about global warming and Henry David Thoreau."

"Aren't we done with that?"

I'm confused. "Done with what?"

The limo jostles us as it makes a turn, moves down Hollywood Boulevard, letting the cycles rev around us like schools of fish. They're snapping pictures at the side of the limo, snapping at us. Through the tinting, they're like fireflies, smaller flares than even my stories in the maelstrom.

"I mean, isn't that an old story?" She sips her champagne. "Even America is reducing emissions now. Everyone knows it's a problem." She taps her couch's armrest. "The carbon tax on my limo has tripled, even with the hybrid engine. Everyone agrees it's a problem. We're going to fix it. What's there to write about?"

She is an American. Everything that is good about them: their optimism, their willingness to charge ahead, to make their own future. And everything that is bad about them: their strange ignorance, their unwillingness to believe that they must behave as other than children.

"No. It's not done," I say. "It is worse. Worse every day. And the changes we make seem to have little effect. Maybe too little, or maybe too late. It is getting worse."

She shrugs. "That's not what I read."

I try not to show my exasperation. "Of course it's not what you read." I wave at the screen. "Look at the clicks on my feed. People want happy stories. Want fun stories. Not stories like I write. So instead, we all write what you will read, which is nothing."

"Still—"

"No." I make a chopping motion with my hand. "We newspeople are very smart monkeys. If you will give us your so lovely eyeballs and your click-throughs we will do whatever you like. We will write good news, and news you can use, news you can shop to, news with the 'Three S's.' We will tell you how to have better sex or eat better or look more beautiful or feel happier and or how to meditate—yes, so enlightened." I make a face. "If you want a walking meditation and Double DP, we will give it to you."

She starts to laugh.

"Why are you laughing at me?" I snap. "I am not joking!"

She waves a hand. "I know, I know, but what you just said 'double'—" She shakes her head, still laughing. "Never mind."

I lapse into silence. I want to go on, to tell her of my frustrations. But now I am embarrassed at my loss of composure. I have no face. I didn't used to be like this. I used to control my emotions, but now I am an American, as childish and unruly as Janice. And Kulaap laughs at me.

I control my anger. "I think I want to go home," I say. "I don't wish to be on a date anymore."

She smiles and reaches over to touch my shoulder. "Don't be that way."

A part of me is telling me that I am a fool. That I am reckless and foolish for walking away from this opportunity. But there is something else, something about this frenzied hunt for page views and click-throughs and ad revenue that suddenly feels unclean. As if my father is with us in the car, disapproving. Asking if he posted his complaints about his missing friends for the sake of clicks.

"I want to get out," I hear myself say. "I do not wish to have your clicks."

"But—"

I look up at her. "I want to get out. Now."

"Here?" She makes a face of exasperation, then shrugs. "It's your choice."

"Yes. Thank you."

She tells her driver to pull over. We sit in stiff silence.

"I will send your suit back to you," I say.

She gives me a sad smile. "It's all right. It's a gift."

This makes me feel worse, even more humiliated for refusing her generosity, but still, I get out of the limo. Cameras are clicking at me from all around. This is my fifteen minutes of fame, this moment when all of Kulaap's fans focus on me for a few seconds, their flashbulbs popping.

I begin to walk home as paparazzi shout questions.

· · · ·

Fifteen minutes later I am indeed alone. I consider calling a cab, but then decide I prefer the night. Prefer to walk by myself through this city that never walks anywhere. On a street corner, I buy a pupusa and gamble on the Mexican Lottery because I like the tickets' laser images of their Day of the Dead. It seems an echo of the Buddha's urging to remember that we all become corpses.

I buy three tickets, and one of them is a winner: one hundred dollars that I can redeem at any TelMex kiosk. I take this as a good sign. Even if my luck is obviously gone with my work, and even if the girl Kulaap was not the bodhisattva that I thought, still, I feel lucky. As though my father is walking with me down this cool Los Angeles street in the middle of the night, the two of us together again, me with a pupusa and a winning lottery ticket, him with an Ah Daeng cigarette and his quiet gambler's smile. In a strange way, I feel that he is blessing me.

And so instead of going home, I go back to the newsroom.

My hits are up when I arrive. Even now, in the middle of the night, a tiny slice of Kulaap's fan base is reading about checkerspot butterflies and American government incompetence. In my country, this story would not exist. A censor would kill it instantly. Here, it glows green; increasing and decreasing in size as people click. A lonely thing, flickering amongst the much larger content flares of Intel processor releases, guides to low-fat recipes, photos of lol-cats, and episodes of *Survivor! Antarctica*. The wash of light and color is very beautiful.

In the center of the maelstrom, the green sun of the Double DP story glows—surges larger. DP is doing something. Maybe he's surrendering, maybe he's murdering his hostages, maybe his fans have thrown up a human wall to protect him. My story snuffs out as reader attention shifts.

I watch the maelstrom a little longer, then go to my desk and make a phone call. A rumpled hairy man answers, rubbing at a sleep-puffy face. I apologize for the late hour, and then pepper him with questions while I record the interview.

He is silly looking and wild-eyed. He has spent his life living as if he were Thoreau, thinking deeply on the forest monk and following the man's careful paths through what woods remain, walking amongst birch and maple and bluets. He is a fool, but an earnest one.

"I can't find a single one," he tells me. "Thoreau could find thousands at this time of year; there were so many he didn't even have to look for them."

He says, "I'm so glad you called. I tried sending out press releases, but . . ." He shrugs. "I'm glad you'll cover it. Otherwise, it's just us hobbyists talking to each other."

I smile and nod and take notes of his sincerity, this strange wild creature, the sort that everyone will dismiss. His image is bad for video; his words are not good for text. He has no quotes that encapsulate what he sees. It is all couched in the jargon of naturalists and biology. With time, I could find another, someone who looks attractive or who can speak well, but all I have is this one hairy man, disheveled and foolish, senile with passion over a flower that no longer exists.

I work through the night, polishing the story. When my colleagues pour through the door at 8 a.m. it is almost done. Before I can even tell Janice about it, she comes to me. She fingers my clothing and grins. "Nice suit." She pulls up a chair and sits beside me. "We all saw you with Kulaap. Your hits went way up." She nods at my screen. "Writing up what happened?"

"No. It was a private conversation."

"But everyone wants to know why you got out of the car. I had someone from the *Financial Times* call me about splitting the hits for a tell-all, if you'll be interviewed. You wouldn't even need to write up the piece."

It's a tempting thought. Easy hits. Many click-throughs. Ad-revenue bonuses. Still, I shake my head. "We did not talk about things that are important for others to hear."

Janice stares at me as if I am crazy. "You're not in the position to bargain, Ong. Something happened between the two of you. Something people want to know about. And you need the clicks. Just tell us what happened on your date."

"I was not on a date. It was an interview."

"Well then publish the fucking interview and get your average up!"

"No. That is for Kulaap to post, if she wishes. I have something else."

I show Janice my screen. She leans forward. Her mouth tightens as she reads. For once, her anger is cold. Not the explosion of noise and rage that I expect. "Bluets." She looks at me. "You need hits and you give them flowers and Walden Pond."

"I would like to publish this story."

"No! Hell, no! This is just another story like your butterfly story, and your road contracts story, and your congressional budget story. You won't get a damn click. It's pointless. No one will even read it."

"This is news."

"Marty went out on a limb for you—" She presses her lips together, reining in her anger. "Fine. It's up to you, Ong. If you want to destroy your life over Thoreau and flowers, it's your funeral. We can't help you if you won't help yourself. Bottom line, you need fifty thousand readers or I'm sending you back to the third world."

We look at each other. Two gamblers evaluating one another. Deciding who is betting, and who is bluffing.

I click the "publish" button.

The story launches itself onto the net, announcing itself to the feeds. A minute later a tiny new sun glows in the maelstrom.

Together, Janice and I watch the green spark as it flickers on the screen. Readers turn to the story. Start to ping it and share it amongst themselves, start to register hits on the page. The post grows slightly.

My father gambled on Thoreau. I am my father's son.

NEAL ASHER   Neal Asher is an English writer whose SF began to appear in major magazines and on the lists of large publishing houses in the early years of this century. Often associated with the loosely defined "New Space Opera," his work is exuberantly imaginative, often violent adventure SF, and displays a flair for the creation of believable aliens. He has in particular invented some of the most astonishing monsters in SF in recent years.

This last talent is well-displayed in "Strood," a tale in which hyperintelligent aliens have revolutionized human society—up to a point. It is a story about the surprising uses to which species, even sentient ones, put one another.

STROOD

Like a Greek harp standing four meters tall and three wide, its center-curtain body rippling in some unseen wind, the strood shimmered across the park, tendrils groping for me, their stinging pods shiny and bloated. Its voice was the sound of some bedlam ghost in a big empty house: muttering, then bellowing guttural nonsense. Almost instinctively, I ran toward the nearest pathun, with the monster close behind me. The pathun's curiol matrix reacted with a nacreous flash, displacing us both into a holding cell. I was burned—red skin visible through holes in my shirt—but whether from the strood or the pathun, I don't know. The strood, its own curiol matrix cut by that of the pathun, lay nearby like a pile of bloody seaweed. I stared about myself at the ten-by-ten box with its floor littered with stones, bones, and pieces of carapace. I really wanted to cry.

"Love! Eat you!" the strood had bellowed. "Eat you! Pain!"

It could have been another of those damned translator problems. The gilst—slapped onto the base of my skull and growing its spines into my brain with agonizing precision—made the latest Pentium Synaptic look like an abacus with most of its beads missing. Unfortunately, with us humans, the gilst is a lot brighter than its host. Mine initially loaded all English on the assumption that I knew the *whole* of that language, and translating something from say, a pathun, produced stuff from all sorts of obscure vocabularies: scientific, philosophic, sociological, political. *All* of them. What had that dyspeptic newt with its five ruby eyes and exterior mobile intestine said to me shortly after my arrival?

"Translocate fifteen degrees sub-axial to hemispherical concrescence of poly-carbon interface."

I'd asked where the orientating machine was, and it could have just pointed to the lump on the nearby wall and said, "Over there."

After forty-six hours in the space station, I was managing, by the feed-back techniques that load into your mind like an instruction manual the moment the spines begin to dig in, to limit the gilst's vocabulary to my feeble one, and thought I'd got a handle on it, until my encounter with the strood. I'd even managed to stop it translating what the occasional patronizing mu-gull would ask me every time I stopped to gape at some extraordinary sight, as "Is one's discombobulation requiring pellucidity?" I knew the words, but couldn't shake the feeling that either the translator or the mugull was having a joke at my expense. All not too good when really I had no time to spare for being lost on the station—I wanted to see so much before I died.

The odds of survival, before the pathun lander set down on the Antarctic, had been one-in-ten for surviving more than five years. My lung cancer, lodged in both lungs, considerably reduced those odds for me. By the time pathun technology started filtering out, my cancer had metastized, sending out scouts to inspect other real estate in my body. And when I finally began to receive any benefits of that technology, my cancer had established a bur-geoning population in my liver and colonies in other places too numerous to mention.

"We cannot help you," the mugull doctor had told me, as it floated a meter off the ground in the pathun hospital on the Isle of Wight. Hospitals like this one were springing up all over Earth, like Medicins Sans Frontières estab-lishments in some Third World backwater. Mostly run by mugulls meticu-lously explaining to our witchdoctors where they were going wrong. To the more worshipful of the population, that name might as well have stood for, "alien angels like translucent manta rays." But the contraction of "mucus gull" that became their name is more apposite for the majority, and their patronizing attitude comes hard from something that looks like a floating sheet of veined snot with two beaks, black button eyes, and a transparent nematode body smelling of burning bacon.

"Pardon?" I couldn't believe what I was hearing: they were miracle work-ers who had crossed mind-numbing distances to come here to employ their magical technologies. This mugull explained it to me in perfect English, without a translator. It, and others like it, had managed to create those nanofactories that sat in the liver pumping out DNA repair nanomachines. Now this was okay if you got your nactor before your DNA was damaged. It meant eternal youth, so long as you avoided stepping in front of a truck. But, for me, there was just too much damage already, so my nactor couldn't distinguish patient from disease.

"But . . . you will be able to cure me?" I still couldn't quite take it in.

"No." A flat reply. And with that, I began to understand, began to put together facts I had thus far chosen to ignore.

People were still dying in huge numbers all across Earth, and the alien doctors had to prioritize. In Britain, it's mainly the wonderful bugs tenderly nurtured by our national health system to be resistant to just about every antibiotic going. In fact, the mugulls had some problems getting people into their hospitals in the British Isles, because over the last decade, hospitals had become more dangerous to the sick than anywhere else. Go in to have an ingrown toenail removed; MRSA or a variant later, and you're down the road in a hermetically sealed plastic coffin. However, most alien resources were going into the same countries as Frontières went to: to battle a daily death rate, numbered in tens of thousands, from new air-transmitted HIVs, rampant Ebola, and that new tuberculosis that can eat your lungs in about four days. And I don't know if they are winning.

"Please . . . you've got to help me."

No good. I knew the statistics, and, like so many, had been an avid student of all things alien ever since their arrival. Even by stopping to talk to me as its curiol matrix wafted it from research ward to ward, the mugull might be sacrificing other lives. Resources again. They had down to an art what our own crippled health service had not been able to apply in fact without outcry: if three people have a terminal disease and you have the resources to save only two of them, that's what you do, you don't ruin it in a futile attempt to save them all. This mugull, applying all its skill and available technologies, could certainly save me, it could take my body apart and rebuild it cell by cell if necessary, but meanwhile, ten, twenty, a thousand other people with less serious, but no less terminal conditions, would die.

"Here is your ticket," it said, and something spat out of its curiol matrix to land on my bed as it wafted away.

I stared down at the yellow ten-centimeter disk. Thousands of these had been issued, and governments had tried to control whom to, and why. Mattered not a damn to any of the aliens; they gave them to those they considered fit, and only the people they were intended for could use them . . . to travel offworld. I guess it was my consolation prize.

A mugull autosurgeon implanted a cybernetic assister frame. This enabled me to get out of bed and head for the shuttle platform moored off the Kent coast. There wasn't any pain at first, as the surgeon had used a nerve-block that took its time to wear off, but I felt about as together as rotten lace. As the nerve-block wore off, I went back onto my inhalers, and patches where the bone cancer was worst, and a cornucopia of pills.

On the shuttle, which basically looked like a train carriage, I attempted to concentrate on some of the alien identification charts I'd loaded into my notescreen, but the nagging pain and perpetual weariness made it difficult for me to concentrate. There was as odd a mix of people around me as you'd find on any aircraft: some woman with a baby in a papoose; a couple of suited heavies who could have been government, Mafia, or stockbrokers;

and others. Just ahead of me was a group of two women and three men who, with plummy voices and scruffy-bordering-on-punk clothing—that upper-middle-class lefty look favored by most students—had to be the BBC documentary team I'd heard about. This was confirmed for me when one of the men removed a prominently labeled vidcam to film the non-human passengers. These were two mugulls and a pathun—the latter a creature like a two-meter woodlouse, front section folded upright with a massively complex head capable of revolving three-sixty, and a flat back onto which a second row of multiple limbs folded. As far as tool-using went, nature had provided pathuns with a work surface, clamping hands with the strength of a hydraulic vise, and other hands with digits fine as hairs. The guy with the vidcam lowered it after a while and turned to look around. Then he focused on me.

"Hi, I'm Nigel," he held out a hand, which I reluctantly shook. "What are you up for?"

I considered telling him to mind his own business, but then thought I could do with all the help I could get. "I'm going to the system base to die."

Within seconds, Nigel had his vidcam in my face, and one of his companions, Julia, had exchanged places with the passenger in the seat adjacent to me, and was pumping me with ersatz sincerity about how it felt to be dying, then attempting to stir some shit about the mugulls being unable to treat me on Earth. The interview lasted nearly an hour, and I knew they would cut and shape it to say whatever they wanted it to say.

When it was over, I returned my attention to the pathun, who I was sure had turned its head slightly to watch and listen in, though why I couldn't imagine. Perhaps it was interested in the primitive equipment the crew used. Apparently, one of these HG (heavy gravity) creatures, while being shown around Silicon Valley, accidentally rested its full weight on someone's laptop computer—think about dropping a barbell on a matchbox and you get the idea—then, without tools, repaired it in under an hour. And as if that wasn't miraculous enough, the computer's owner had discovered that the laptop's hard disk storage had risen from four hundred gigabytes to four terabytes. I would have said the story was apocryphal, but the laptop is now in the Smithsonian.

The shuttle docked at Eulogy Station, and the pathun disembarked first, which is just the way it is. Equality is a fine notion; the reality is that *they've* been knocking around the galaxy for half a million years. Pathuns are as far in advance of the other aliens as we are in advance of jellyfish, which makes you wonder where humans rate on their scale. As the alien went past me, heading for the door, I felt the slight air shift caused by its curiol matrix— that technology enabling other aliens, like mugulls, creatures whose home environment is an interstellar gas cloud not far above absolute zero, to live on the surface of Earth and easily manipulate their surroundings. Call it a force field, but it's much more than that. Another story about pathuns demonstrates some of what they can do with their curiol matrices:

All sorts of religious fanatic lunatic idiotic groups immediately, of course, considered superior aliens the cause of their woes, and valid targets, so it was only a week into the first alien walkabout that the first suicide bomber tried to take out a pathun amid a crowd. He detonated his device, but an invisible cylinder enclosed him and the plastique slow-burned—not a pretty sight. Other assassination attempts met with various suitable responses. The sharpshooter with his scoped rifle got the bullet he fired back through the scope and into his head. The bomber in Spain just disappeared along with his car, only to reappear, still behind the wheel, traveling at mach four down on top of the farmhouse his fellow Basque terrorists had made their base. Thereafter, attempts started to drop off, not because of any reduction in terrorist lunacy, but because of a huge increase in security when a balek (those floating LGAs that look like great big apple cores) off-handedly mentioned what incredible restraint the pathuns—beings capable of translocating planet Earth into its own sun—were showing.

From Eulogy Station, it was, in both alien and my own terms, just a short step to the system base. The gate was just a big ring in one of the plazas of Eulogy, and you just stepped through it and you were there. The base, a giant stack of different-sized disks nine hundred and forty kilometers from top to bottom, orbited Jupiter. After translocating from some system eighty light-years away to our Oort Cloud, it had traveled to here at half the speed of light while the contact ships headed to Earth. Apparently, we had been ripe for contact: bright enough to understand what was happening, but stupid enough for our civilization not to end up imploding when confronted by such omnipotence.

In the system base, I began to find my way around, guided by an orientation download to my notescreen, and it was only then that I began to notice stroods everywhere. I had only ever seen pictures before, and, as far as I knew, none had ever been to Earth. But why were there so many thousands here, now? Then, of course, I allowed myself a hollow laugh. What the hell did it matter to *me*? Still, I asked Julia and Nigel when I ran into them again.

"According to our researcher, they're pretty low on the species scale and only space-faring because of pathun intervention." Julia studied her note screen—uncomfortable being the interviewee. Nigel was leaning over the rail behind her, filming down an immense metallic slope on which large limpetlike creatures clung sleeping in their thousands: stroods in their somnolent form.

Julia continued, "Some of the other races regard stroods as pathun pets, but then, *we're* not regarded much higher by many of them."

"But why so many thousands here?" I asked.

Angrily, she gestured at the slope. "I've asked, and every time, I've been told to go and ask the pathuns. They ignore us, you know—far too busy about their important tasks."

I resisted the impulse to point out that creatures capable of crossing the galaxy perhaps did not rank the endless creation of media pap very high. I succumbed then to one more "brief" interview before managing to slip away, and then, losing my way to my designated hotel, ended up in one of the parks, aware that a strood was following me . . . .

Sitting in the holding cell, I eyed the monster and hoped that its curiol matrix wouldn't start up again, as in here I had nowhere to run, and, being the contacted species, no curiol matrix of my own. The environment of a system station is that of the system species, us, so we didn't need the matrix for survival, and anyway, you don't give the kiddies sharp objects to play with right away. I was beginning to wonder if maybe running at that pathun had been such a bright idea, when I was abruptly translocated again, and found myself stumbling into the lobby of an apparently ordinary-looking hotel. I did a double take, then turned round and walked out through the revolving doors and looked around. Yep, an apparently normal city street—except for Jupiter in the sky. This was the area I'd been trying to find before my confrontation with the strood: the human section, a nice homey, normal-seeming base for us so we wouldn't get too confused or frightened. I went back into the hotel, limping a bit now, despite the assister frame, and wheezing because I'd lost my inhaler, and the patches and pills were beginning to wear off.

"David Hall," I said at the front desk. "I have a reservation."

The automaton dipped its polished chrome ant's head and eyed my damaged clothing, then it checked its screen, and after a moment it handed—or rather, clawed—over a key card. I headed for the elevator and soon found myself in the kind of room I'd never been able to afford on Earth, my luggage already stacked beside my bed, and a welcome pack on a nearby table. I opened the half bottle of champagne and began chugging it down as I walked out onto the balcony. Now what?

Prior to my brief exchange with the mugull doctor, I'd been told that my life expectancy was about four weeks, but that, "I'm sure the aliens will be able to do *something*!" Well, they had. The drugs and the assister frame enabled me to actually move about and take some pleasure in my remaining existence. The time limit, unfortunately, had not changed. So, I would see as much of this miraculous place as possible . . . but I'd avoid that damned park. I thought then about what had happened.

The park was fifteen kilometers across, with Earthly meadows, and forests of cycads like purple pineapples tall as trees. There were aliens everywhere, a lot of them strood. And one, which I was sure had been following me before freezing and standing like a monument in a field of daisies, started drifting toward me. I stepped politely aside, but it followed me and started making strange moaning sounds. I got scared then, but controlled myself, and stood still when it reached one of its tendrils out to me. Maybe it was just saying hello. The stinging cells clacked like maracas and my arm felt as if someone had whipped it, before turning numb as a brick. The monster started shaking then, as if this had got it all excited.

"Eat you!"

Damned thing. I don't mind being the primitive poor relation, but not the main course.

I turned round and went back into my room, opened my suitcase, found my spare inhaler and patches, and headed for the bathroom. An hour later, I was clean, and the pain in my body had receded to a distant ache I attempted to drive farther away with the contents of the minibar. I slept for the usual three hours, woke feeling sick, out of breath, and once again in pain. A few pulls from one inhaler opened up my lungs, and the other inhaler took away the feeling that someone was sandpapering the inside of my chest, then more pills gave me a further two hours sleep, and that, I knew, was as much as I was going to get.

I dressed, buttoning up my shirt while standing on the balcony and watching the street. No day or night here, just the changing face of Jupiter in an orange-blue sky. Standing there, gazing at the orb, I decided that I must have got it all wrong somehow. The aliens had only ever killed humans in self-defense, so somehow there had been a misunderstanding. Maybe, with the strood being pathun "pets," what had happened had been no more than the equivalent of someone being snapped at by a terrier in a park. I truly believed this. But that didn't stop me suddenly feeling very scared when I heard that same bedlam ghost muttering and bellowing along below. I stared down and saw the strood—it had to be the same one—rippling across the street and pausing there. I was sure it was looking up at me, though it had no eyes.

The strood was still waiting as I peered out of the hotel lobby. For a second, I wished I had a gun or some other weapon to hand, but that would only have made me feel better, not be any safer. I went back inside and walked up to the automaton behind the hotel desk.

Without any ado, I said, "I was translocated here from a holding cell, to which I was translocated after running straight into a pathun's personal space."

"Yes," it replied.

"This happened because I was running away from a strood that wants to eat me."

"Yes," it replied.

"Who must I inform about this . . . assault?"

"If your attack upon the pathun had been deliberate, you would not have been released from the holding cell," it buzzed at me.

"I'm talking about the strood's assault on *me*."

Glancing aside, I saw that the creature was now looming outside the revolving doors. They were probably all that was preventing it from entering the hotel. I could hear it moaning.

"Strood do not attack other creatures."

"It stung me!"

"Yes."

"It wants to eat me!"

"Yes."

"It said 'eat you, eat you,'" I said, before I realized what the automaton had just said. "Yes!" I squeaked.

"Not enough to feed strood, here," the automaton told me. "Though Earth will be a good feeding ground for them."

I thought of the thousands of these creatures I had seen here. No, I just didn't believe this! My skin began to crawl as I heard the revolving doors turning, all of them.

"Please summon help," I said.

"None is required." The insectile head swung toward the strood. "Though you are making it ill, you know."

Right then, I think my adrenaline ran down, because suddenly I was hurting more than usual. I turned with my back against the desk to see the strood coming toward me across the lobby. It seemed somehow ragged to me, disreputable, tatty. The pictures of them I'd seen showed larger and more glittering creatures.

"What do you want with me?"

"Eat . . . need . . . eat," were the only words I could discern from the muttering bellow. I pushed away from the desk and set out in a stumbling run for the elevator. No way was I going to be able to manage the stairs. I hit the button just as the strood surged after me. Yeah, great, you're going to die waiting for an elevator. It reached me just as the doors opened behind me. One of its stinging tendrils caught me across the chest, knocking me back into the elevator. This seemed to confuse the creature, and it held back long enough for the doors to draw closed. My chest grew numb and my breathing difficult as I stabbed buttons, then the elevator lurched into progress, and I collapsed to the floor.

· · · · ·

"Technical Acquisitions" was a huge disc-shaped building, like the bridge of the starship *Enterprise* mounted on top of a squat skyscraper. Nigel kept Julia, Lincoln, and myself constantly on camera, while Pierce kept panning across and up and down—getting as much of our surroundings as possible. I'd learned that quantity was what they were aiming for; all the artwork was carried out on computer afterward. Pierce—an Asian woman with rings through her lip connected by a chain to rings through her ear, and a blockish stud through her tongue—was the one who suggested it, and Julia immediately loved the idea. I was just glad, after Julia and Nigel dragged me out of the elevator, for the roof taxi to get me out of the hotel without my having to go back through the lobby. Of course, none of them took my story about stroods wanting to eat people seriously; they were just excited about the chance of some real in-your-face documentary making.

"Dawson's got a direct line to the head honchos here in the system station," Lincoln explained to me. For "head honchos," read pathuns, who, after their initial show-and-tell on Earth, took no interest in all the consequent political furor. They were physicists, engineers, biologists, and pursued their own interests to the exclusion of all else. It drove human politicians nuts that the ones who had the power to convert Earth into a swiftly dispersing smoke cloud might spend hours watching a slug devouring a cabbage leaf, but have no time to spare to discuss *issues* with the president or prime minister. Human scientists, though, were a different matter, for pathuns definitely leaned toward didacticism. I guess it all comes down to the fact that modern politicians don't really *change* very much, that the inventor of the vacuum cleaner changed more people's lives than any number of Thatchers or Blairs. Dawson was the chief of the team of human scientists aboard the system base, learning at the numerous feet of the pathuns.

"We get to him, and we should be able to get a statement from one of the pathuns—he's their blue-eyed boy, and they let him get up to all sorts of stuff," Lincoln continued. "According to our researchers, he's even allowed access to curiol matrix tech."

In the lobby of the building, Lincoln shmoozed the insectile receptionist with his spiel about the documentary he was doing for the Einstein channel, then spoke to a bearded individual on a large phone screen. I recognized Dawson right away, because my own viewing had always leaned toward that channel Lincoln and Julia had denigrated on our way out here. He was a short plump individual, with a big gray beard, gray hair, and very odd-looking orangish eyes. He's the kind of physicist who pisses off many of his fellows by being better at pure research than they, and then making it worse by being able to turn his research to practical and profitable ends. While many of them had walked away from CERN with wonderfully obscure papers to their names, he'd walked away with the same, plus a very real contribution to make to quantum computing. I didn't hear the conversation, but I was interested to see Dawson gazing past Lincoln's shoulder directly at me, before giving the go-ahead for us to come up.

How to describe the inside of the disk? There were benches, computers, and big plasma screens, macrotech that looked right out of CERN, people walking, talking, waving light pens, people gutting alien technology, scanning circuit boards under electron microscopes, running mass spectrometer tests on fragments of exotic metal . . . . On Earth, there was a lot of alien technology knocking about, and a lot of it turned to smoking goo the moment anyone tried to open it up. It's not that they don't want us to learn; it's just that they don't want us to depopulate the planet in the process. Here, though, things were different: under direct pathun supervision, the scientists were having a great time.

Lincoln and Julia began by asking Dawson for an overview on everything that he and his people were working on. My interest was held for a while as he described materials light as polystyrene and tough as steel, a micro tome capable of slicing diamonds, and nanotech self-repairing computer chips, but, after a while, I began to feel really sick, and without my assister frame, I'd have been on the floor. Finally, he was standing before pillars with hooked-over tops, gesturing at something subliminal between them. When I realized he was talking about curiol matrices, my interest perked up, but it was then that Lincoln and Julia went in for the kill.

"So, obviously the pathuns trust you implicitly, or are you treated like a strood?" asked Julia.

I stared at the subliminal flicker, and through it to the other side of the room, where it seemed a work bench was sneaking away while no one was watching—until I realized that I was seeing a pathun sauntering across, all sorts of equipment on its back.

"Strood?" Dawson asked.

"Yes, their pets," interjected Lincoln. "Ones whose particularly carnivorous tastes the pathuns seem to be pandering to."

I tracked the pathun past the pillars to a big equipment elevator. Took a couple of pulls on one of my inhalers—not sure which one, but it seemed to help. I thought that I was imagining the bedlam moaning. Everything seemed to be getting a little fuzzy around the edges.

"Pets?" said Dawson, staring at Lincoln as if he'd just discovered a heretofore-undiscovered variety of idiot.

"But then I suppose it's all right," said Julia, "if the kind of people fed to them are going to die anyway."

Dawson shook his head, then said, "I was curious to see what your angle would be—that's why I let you come up." Now he turned to me. "Running into a pathun's curiol matrix wasn't the best idea—it reacted to you rather than the strood."

It came up on the equipment elevator, shimmering and flowing out before the observing pathun. The strood came round the room toward me. There were benches to my left, so the quickest escape route for me was ahead and left to the normal elevators. I hardly comprehended what Dawson was saying. You see, it's all right to be brave and sensible when you're whole and nothing hurts, but when you live with pain shadowing your every step, and the big guy with the scythe is just around the corner, your perspective changes.

"It bonded and you broke away," he said. "Didn't you study your orientation? Can't you see it's in love?"

I ran, and slammed straight into an invisible web between the two pillars—a curiol matrix Dawson had been studying. Energies shorted through my assister frame, and something almost alive connected to my gilst and into my brain. Exo-skeletal energy, huge frames of reference, translocation, reality displayed as formulae . . . there is no adequate description. Panicked, I just saw where I didn't want to be, and strove to put myself somewhere else. The huge system base opened around me, up and down in lines and surfaces and intersection points. Twisting them into a new pattern, I put myself on the roof of the world. My curiol retained air around me, retained heat, but did not defend me from harsh and beautiful reality; in fact, it amplified perception. Standing on the steel plain, I saw that Jupiter was truly vast but finite, and that through vacuum the stars did not waver, and that there was no way to deny the depths they burned in. I gasped, twisted to a new pattern, found myself tumbling through a massive swarm of mugulls, curiols reacting all around me and hurling me out.

It's in love.

Something snatched me down, and, sprawled on an icy platform, I observed a pathun, linked in ways I could not quite comprehend to vast machines rearing around me to forge energies of creation. The curiol gave me a glimpse of what it meant to have been in a technical civilization for more than half a million years. Then I understood about huge restraint. And amusement. The pathun did something then, its merest touch shaking blocks of logic into order, and something went click in my head.

Eat you! Eat you!

Of course, everything I had been told was the truth. No translator problem; just an existential one. What need did pathuns have for lies? I folded away from the platform and stumbled out from the other side of the pillars, shedding the curiol behind me. Momentarily doubt nearly had me stepping back into the matrix as the strood flowed round and reared up before me: a raggedy and bloody curtain.

"Eat," I said.

The strood surged forward, stinging cells clacking. The pain was mercifully brief as the creature engulfed me, and the black tide swamped me to the sound of Julia shouting, "Are you getting this! Are you getting this!"

· · · ·

Three days passed, I think, then I woke in a field of daisies. I was about six kilos lighter, which was unsurprising. One of those kilos was pieces of the cybernetic assister frame scattered in the grass all around me. Nearby the strood stood tall and glittering in artificial sunlight: grown strong on the cancer it had first fallen in love with then eaten out of my body, as was its nature. It's like pilot fish eating the parasites of bigger fish—that kind of existence: mutualism. I had been sent as a kind of test case, by the mugulls who were struggling with human sickness, and, after me, the go-ahead was given. The strood are now flocking in their thousands to Earth: come to dine on our diseases.

RACHEL SWIRSKY   Beginning in 2006, when John Scalzi published her "Scenes from a Dystopia" in an issue of *Subterranean* for which he was serving as guest editor, native Californian Rachel Swirsky has produced one of the most impressive sequences of short fiction coming from any newcomer to our field in these last few years. Before beginning to publish, she attended Clarion West, one of the two premier workshops for aspiring SF writers—and got an MFA from the Iowa Writers' Workshop, reputational equivalent of the Clarions in the genre called "literary fiction." Like an increasing number of the field's younger writers, she uses literary and genre techniques with equal confidence, assuming (probably correctly) that her core audience consists of people who take in many kinds of narratives, genre and otherwise, in their everyday lives.

Her story here is a high-wire act that manages to work simultaneously as hard science fiction, psychological realism, and romance.

EROS, PHILIA, AGAPE

L ucian packed his possessions before he left. He packed his antique silver serving spoons with the filigreed handles; the tea roses he'd nurtured in the garden window; his jade and garnet rings. He packed the hunk of gypsum-veined jasper that he'd found while strolling on the beach on the first night he'd come to Adriana, she leading him uncertainly across the wet sand, their bodies illuminated by the soft gold twinkling of the lights along the pier. That night, as they walked back to Adriana's house, Lucian had cradled the speckled stone in his cupped palms, squinting so that the gypsum threads sparkled through his lashes.

Lucian had always loved beauty—beautiful scents, beautiful tastes, beautiful melodies. He especially loved beautiful objects because he could hold them in his hands and transform the abstraction of beauty into something tangible.

The objects belonged to them both, but Adriana waved her hand bitterly when Lucian began packing. "Take whatever you want," she said, snapping her book shut. She waited by the door, watching Lucian with sad and angry eyes.

Their daughter, Rose, followed Lucian around the house. "Are you going to take that, Daddy? Do you want that?" Wordlessly, Lucian held her hand. He guided her up the stairs and across the uneven floorboards where she sometimes tripped. Rose stopped by the picture window in the master bedroom, staring past the palm fronds and swimming pools, out to the vivid cerulean swath of the ocean. Lucian relished the hot, tender feel of Rose's hand. I love you, he would have whispered, but he'd surrendered the ability to speak.

He led her downstairs again to the front door. Rose's lace-festooned pink satin dress crinkled as she leapt down the steps. Lucian had ordered her dozens of satin party dresses in pale, floral hues. Rose refused to wear anything else.

Rose looked between Lucian and Adriana. "Are you taking me, too?" she asked Lucian.

Adriana's mouth tightened. She looked at Lucian, daring him to say something, to take responsibility for what he was doing to their daughter. Lucian remained silent.

Adriana's chardonnay glowed the same shade of amber as Lucian's eyes. She clutched the glass's stem until she thought it might break. "No, honey," she said with artificial lightness. "You're staying with me."

Rose reached for Lucian. "Horsey?"

Lucian knelt down and pressed his forehead against Rose's. He hadn't spoken a word in the three days since he'd delivered his letter of farewell to Adriana, announcing his intention to leave as soon as she had enough time to make arrangements to care for Rose in his absence. When Lucian approached with the letter, Adriana had been sitting at the dining table, sipping orange juice from a wine glass and reading a first edition copy of Cheever's *Falconer*. Lucian felt a flash of guilt as she smiled up at him and accepted the missive. He knew that she'd been happier in the past few months than he'd ever seen her, possibly happier than she'd ever been. He knew the letter would shock and wound her. He knew she'd feel betrayed. Still, he delivered the letter anyway, and watched as comprehension ached through her body.

Rose had been told, gently, patiently, that Lucian was leaving. But she was four years old, and understood things only briefly and partially, and often according to her whims. She continued to believe her father's silence was a game.

• • • •

Rose's hair brushed Lucian's cheek. He kissed her brow. Adriana couldn't hold her tongue any longer.

"What do you think you're going to find out there? There's no Shangri-La for rebel robots. You think you're making a play for independence? Independence to do what, Lu?"

Grief and anger filled Adriana's eyes with hot tears, as if she were a geyser filled with so much pressure that steam could not help but spring up. She examined Lucian's sculpted face: his skin inlaid with tiny lines that an artist had rendered to suggest the experiences of a childhood which had never been lived, his eyes calibrated with a hint of asymmetry to mimic the imperfection of human growth. His expression showed nothing—no doubt, or bitterness, or even relief. He revealed nothing at all.

It was all too much. Adriana moved between Lucian and Rose, as if she could use her own body to protect her daughter from the pain of being abandoned. Her eyes stared achingly over the rim of her wine glass. "Just go," she said.

He left.

• • • •

Adriana bought Lucian the summer she turned thirty-five. Her father, long afflicted with an indecisive cancer that vacillated between aggression and remittance, had died suddenly in July. For years, the family had been squirreling away emotional reserves to cope with his prolonged illness. His death released a burst of excess.

While her sisters went through the motions of grief, Adriana thrummed with energy she didn't know what to do with. She considered squandering her vigor on six weeks in Mazatlan, but as she discussed ocean-front rentals with her travel agent, she realized escape wasn't what she craved. She liked the setting where her life took place: her house perched on a cliff overlooking the Pacific Ocean, her bedroom window that opened on a tangle of blackberry bushes where crows roosted every autumn and spring. She liked the two block stroll down to the beach where she could sit with a book and listen to the yapping lapdogs that the elderly women from the waterfront condominiums brought walking in the evenings.

Mazatlan was a twenty-something's cure for restlessness. Adriana wasn't twenty-five anymore, famished for the whole gourmet meal of existence. She needed something else now. Something new. Something more refined.

She explained this to her friends Ben and Lawrence when they invited her to their ranch house in Santa Barbara to relax for the weekend and try to forget about her father. They sat on Ben and Lawrence's patio, on iron-worked deck chairs arrayed around a garden table topped with a mosaic of sea creatures made of semi-precious stones. A warm, breezy dusk lengthened the shadows of the orange trees. Lawrence poured sparkling rosé into three wine glasses and proposed a toast to Adriana's father—not to his memory, but to his death.

"Good riddance to the bastard," said Lawrence. "If he were still alive, I'd punch him in the schnoz."

"I don't even want to think about him," said Adriana. "He's dead. He's gone."

"So if not Mazatlan, what are you going to do?" asked Ben.

"I'm not sure," said Adriana. "Some sort of change, some sort of milestone, that's all I know."

Lawrence sniffed the air. "Excuse me," he said, gathering the empty wine glasses. "The kitchen needs its genius."

When Lawrence was out of earshot, Ben leaned forward to whisper to Adriana. "He's got us on a raw food diet for my cholesterol. Raw carrots. Raw zucchini. Raw almonds. No cooking at all."

"Really," said Adriana, glancing away. She was never sure how to respond to lovers' quarrels. That kind of affection mixed with annoyance, that inescapable intimacy, was something she'd never understood.

Birds twittered in the orange trees. The fading sunlight highlighted copper strands in Ben's hair as he leaned over the mosaic table, rapping his fingers against a carnelian-backed crab. Through the arched windows, Adriana could see Lawrence mincing carrots, celery and almonds into brown paste.

"You should get a redecorator," said Ben. "Tile floors, Tuscan pottery, those red leather chairs that were in vogue last time we were in Milan. That'd make me feel like I'd been scrubbed clean and reborn."

"No, no," said Adriana, "I like where I live."

"A no-holds-barred shopping spree. Drop twenty thousand. That's what I call getting a weight off your shoulders."

Adriana laughed. "How long do you think it would take my personal shopper to assemble a whole new me?"

"Sounds like a midlife crisis," said Lawrence, returning with vegan hors d'oeuvres and three glasses of mineral water. "You're better off forgetting it all with a hot Latin pool boy, if you ask me."

Lawrence served Ben a small bowl filled with yellow mush. Ben shot Adriana an aggrieved glance.

Adriana felt suddenly out of synch. The whole evening felt like the set for a photo-shoot that would go in a decorating magazine, a two-page spread featuring Cozy Gardens, in which she and Ben and Lawrence were posing as an intimate dinner party for three. She felt reduced to two dimensions, airbrushed, and then digitally grafted onto the form of whoever it was who should have been there, someone warm and trusting who knew how to care about minutia like a friend's husband putting him on a raw food diet, not because the issue was important, but because it mattered to him.

Lawrence dipped his finger in the mash and held it up to Ben's lips. "It's for your own good, you ungrateful so-and-so."

Ben licked it away. "I eat it, don't I?"

Lawrence leaned down to kiss his husband, a warm and not at all furtive kiss, not sexual but still passionate. Ben's glance flashed coyly downward.

Adriana couldn't remember the last time she'd loved someone enough to be embarrassed by them. Was this the flavor missing from her life? A lover's fingertip sliding an unwanted morsel into her mouth?

She returned home that night on the bullet train. Her emerald cockatiel, Fuoco, greeted her with indignant squawks. In Adriana's absence, the house puffed her scent into the air and sang to Fuoco with her voice, but the bird was never fooled.

Adriana's father had given her the bird for her thirtieth birthday. He was a designer species spliced with Macaw DNA that colored his feathers rich green. He was expensive and inbred and neurotic, and he loved Adriana with frantic, obsessive jealousy.

"Hush," Adriana admonished, allowing Fuoco to alight on her shoulder. She carried him upstairs to her bedroom and hand-fed him millet. Fuoco strutted across the pillows, his obsidian eyes proud and suspicious.

Adriana was surprised to find that her alienation had followed her home. She found herself prone to melancholy reveries, her gaze drifting toward the picture window, her fingers forgetting to stroke Fuoco's back. The bird screeched to regain her attention.

In the morning, Adriana visited her accountant. His fingers danced across the keyboard as he slipped trust fund moneys from one account to another like a magician. What she planned would be expensive, but her wealth would regrow in fertile soil, enriching her on lab diamonds and wind power and genetically modified oranges.

The robotics company gave Adriana a private showing. The salesman ushered her into a room draped in black velvet. Hundreds of body parts hung on the walls, and reclined on display tables: strong hands, narrow jaws, biker's thighs, voice boxes that played sound samples from gruff to dulcet, skin swatches spanning ebony to alabaster, penises of various sizes.

At first, Adriana felt horrified at the prospect of assembling a lover from fragments, but then it amused her. Wasn't everyone assembled from fragments of DNA, grown molecule by molecule inside their mother's womb?

She tapped her fingernails against a slick brochure. "Its brain will be malleable? I can tell it to be more amenable, or funnier, or to grow a spine?"

"That's correct." The salesman sported slick brown hair and shiny teeth and kept grinning in a way that suggested he thought that if he were charismatic enough Adriana would invite him home for a lay and a million dollar tip. "Humans lose brain plasticity as we age, which limits how much we can change. Our models have perpetually plastic brains. They can reroute their personalities at will by reshaping how they think on the neurological level."

Adriana stepped past him, running her fingers along a tapestry woven of a thousand possible hair textures.

The salesman tapped an empty faceplate. "Their original brains are based on deep imaging scans melded from geniuses in multiple fields. Great musicians, renowned lovers, the best physicists and mathematicians."

Adriana wished the salesman would be quiet. The more he talked, the more doubts clamored against her skull. "You've convinced me," she interrupted. "I want one."

The salesman looked taken aback by her abruptness. She could practically see him rifling through his internal script, trying to find the right page now that she had skipped several scenes. "What do you want him to look like?" he asked.

Adriana shrugged. "They're all beautiful, right?"

"We'll need specifications."

"I don't have specifications."

The salesman frowned anxiously. He shifted his weight as if it could help him regain his metaphorical footing. Adriana took pity. She dug through her purse.

"There," she said, placing a snapshot of her father on one of the display tables. "Make it look nothing like him."

Given such loose parameters, the design team indulged the fanciful. Lucian arrived at Adriana's door only a shade taller than she and equally slender, his limbs smooth and lean. Silver undertones glimmered in his blond hair. His skin was excruciatingly pale, white and translucent as alabaster, veined with pink. He smelled like warm soil and crushed herbs.

He offered Adriana a single white rose, its petals embossed with the company's logo. She held it dubiously between her thumb and forefinger. "They think they know women, do they? They need to put down the bodice rippers."

Lucian said nothing. Adriana took his hesitation for puzzlement, but perhaps she should have seen it as an early indication of his tendency toward silence.

· · · ·

"That's that, then." Adriana drained her chardonnay and crushed the empty glass beneath her heel as if she could finalize a divorce with the same gesture that sanctified a marriage.

Eyes wide, Rose pointed at the glass with one round finger. "Don't break things."

It suddenly struck Adriana how fast her daughter was aging. Here she was, this four-year-old, this sudden person. When had it happened? In the hospital, when Rose was newborn and wailing for the woman who had birthed her and abandoned her, Adriana had spent hours in the hallway outside the hospital nursery while she waited for the adoption to go through. She'd stared at Rose while she slept, ate, and cried, striving to memorize her nascent, changing face. Sometime between then and now, Rose had become this round-cheeked creature who took rules very seriously and often tried to conceal her emotions beneath a calm exterior, as if being raised by a robot had replaced her blood with circuits. Of course Adriana loved Rose, changed her clothes, brushed her teeth, carried her across the house on her hip—but Lucian had been the most central, nurturing figure. Adriana couldn't fathom how she might fill his role. This wasn't a vacation like the time Adriana had taken Rose to Italy for three days, just the two of them sitting in restaurants, Adriana feeding her daughter spoonfuls of gelato to see the joy that lit her face at each new flavor. Then, they'd known that Lucian would be waiting when they returned. Without him, their family was a house missing a structural support. Adriana could feel the walls bowing in.

The fragments of Adriana's chardonnay glass sparkled sharply. Adriana led Rose away from the mess.

"Never mind," she said, "The house will clean up."

Her head felt simultaneously light and achy as if it couldn't decide between drunkenness and hangover. She tried to remember the parenting books she'd read before adopting Rose. What had they said about crying in front of your child? She clutched Rose close, inhaling the scent of children's shampoo mixed with the acrid odor of wine.

"Let's go for a drive," said Adriana. "Okay? Let's get out for a while."

"I want Daddy to take me to the beach."

"We'll go out to the country and look at the farms. Cows and sheep, okay?" Rose said nothing.

"Moo?" Adriana clarified. "Baa?"

"I know," said Rose. "I'm not a baby."

"So, then?"

Rose said nothing. Adriana wondered whether she could tell that her mother was a little mad with grief.

Just make a decision, Adriana counseled herself. She slipped her fingers around Rose's hand. "We'll go for a drive."

Adriana instructed the house to regulate itself in their absence, and then led Rose to the little black car that she and Lucian had bought together after adopting Rose. She fastened Rose's safety buckle and programmed the car to take them inland.

As the car engine initialized, Adriana felt a glimmer of fear. What if this machine betrayed them, too? But its uninspired intelligence only switched on the left turn signal and started down the boulevard.

· · · ·

Lucian stood at the base of the driveway and stared up at the house. Its stark orange and brown walls blazed against a cloudless sky. Rocks and desert plants tumbled down the meticulously landscaped yard, imitating natural scrub.

A rabbit ran across the road, followed by the whir of Adriana's car. Lucian watched them pass. They couldn't see him through the cypresses, but Lucian could make out Rose's face pressed against the window. Beside her, Adriana slumped in her seat, one hand pressed over her eyes.

Lucian went in the opposite direction. He dragged the rolling cart packed with his belongings to the cliff that led down to the beach. He lifted the cart over his head and started down, his feet disturbing cascades of sandstone chunks.

A pair of adolescent boys looked up from playing in the waves. "Whoa," shouted one of them. "Are you carrying that whole thing? Are you a weight-lifter?"

Lucian remained silent. When he reached the sand, the kids muttered disappointments to each other and turned away from shore. ". . . Just a robot . . ." drifted back to Lucian on the breeze.

Lucian pulled his cart to the border where wet sand met dry. Oncoming waves lapped over his feet. He opened the cart and removed a tea-scented apricot rose growing in a pot painted with blue leaves.

He remembered acquiring the seeds for his first potted rose. One evening, long ago, he'd asked Adriana if he could grow things. He'd asked in passing, the question left to linger while they cleaned up after dinner, dish soap on their hands, Fuoco pecking after scraps. The next morning, Adriana escorted Lucian to the hothouse near the botanical gardens. "Buy whatever you want," she told him. Lucian was awed by the profusion of color and scent, all that beauty in one place. He wanted to capture the wonder of that place and own it for himself.

Lucian drew back his arm and threw the pot into the sea. It broke across the water, petals scattering the surface.

He threw in the pink roses, and the white roses, and the red roses, and the mauve roses. He threw in the filigreed-handled spoons. He threw in the chunk of gypsum-veined jasper.

He threw in everything beautiful that he'd ever collected. He threw in a chased silver hand mirror, and an embroidered silk jacket, and a hand-painted egg. He threw in one of Fuoco's soft, emerald feathers. He threw in a memory crystal that showed Rose as an infant, curled and sleeping.

He loved those things, and yet they were things. He had owned them. Now they were gone. He had recently come to realize that ownership was a relationship. What did it mean to own a thing? To shape it and contain it? He could not possess or be possessed until he knew.

He watched the sea awhile, the remnants of his possessions lost in the tumbling waves. As the sun tilted past noon, he turned away and climbed back up the cliff. Unencumbered by ownership, he followed the boulevard away from Adriana's house.

· · · ·

Lucian remembered meeting Adriana the way that he imagined that humans remembered childhood. Oh, his memories had been as sharply focused then as now—but it was still like childhood, he reasoned, for he'd been a different person then.

He remembered his first sight of Adriana as a burst of images. Wavy strawberry blonde hair cut straight across tanned shoulders. Dark brown eyes that his artistic mind labeled "sienna." Thick, aristocratic brows and strong cheekbones, free of makeup. Lucian's inner aesthete termed her blunt, angular face "striking" rather than "beautiful." His inner psychoanalyst reasoned that she was probably "strong-willed" as well, from the way she stood in the doorway, her arms crossed, her eyebrows lifted as if inquiring how he planned to justify his existence.

Eventually, she moved away, allowing Lucian to step inside. He crossed the threshold into a blur of frantic screeching and flapping.

New. Everything was new. So new that Lucian could barely assemble feathers and beak and wings into the concept of "bird" before his reflexes jumped him away from the onslaught. Hissing and screeching, the animal retreated to a perch atop a bookshelf.

Adriana's hand weighed on Lucian's shoulder. Her voice was edged with the cynicism Lucian would later learn was her way of hiding how desperately she feared failure. "Ornithophobia? How ridiculous."

Lucian's first disjointed days were dominated by the bird, who he learned was named Fuoco. The bird followed him around the house. When he remained in place for a moment, the bird settled on some nearby high spot—the hat rack in the entryway, or the hand-crafted globe in the parlor, or the rafters above the master bed—to spy on him. He glared at Lucian in the manner of birds, first peering through one eye and then turning his head to peer through the other, apparently finding both views equally loathsome.

When Adriana took Lucian into her bed, Fuoco swooped at Lucian's head. Adriana pushed Lucian out of the way. "Damn it, Fuoco," she muttered, but she offered the bird a perch on her shoulder.

Fuoco crowed with pleasure as she led him downstairs. His feathers fluffed with victory as he hopped obediently into his cage, expecting her to reward him with treats and conversation. Instead, Adriana closed the gilded door and returned upstairs. All night, as Lucian lay with Adriana, the bird chattered madly. He plucked at his feathers until his tattered plumage carpeted the cage floor.

Lucian accompanied Adriana when she brought Fuoco to the vet the next day. The veterinarian diagnosed jealousy. "It's not uncommon in birds," he said. He suggested they give Fuoco a rigid routine that would, over time, help the bird realize he was Adriana's companion, not her mate.

Adriana and Lucian rearranged their lives so that Fuoco could have regular feeding times, scheduled exercise, socialization with both Lucian and Adriana, and time with his mistress alone. Adriana gave him a treat each night when she locked him in his cage, staying to stroke his feathers for a few minutes before she headed upstairs.

Fuoco's heart broke. He became a different bird. His strut lacked confidence, and his feathers grew ever more tattered. When they let him out of his cage, he wandered after Adriana with pleading, wistful eyes, and ignored Lucian entirely.

• • • •

Lucian had been dis-integrated then: musician brain, mathematician brain, artist brain, economist brain, and more, all functioning separately, each personality rising to dominance to provide information and then sliding away, creating staccato bursts of consciousness.

As Adriana made clear which responses she liked, Lucian's consciousness began integrating into the personality she desired. He found himself noticing connections between what had previously been separate experiences. Before, when he'd seen the ocean, his scientist brain had calculated how far he was from the shore, and how long it would be until high tide. His poet brain had recited Strindberg's "We Waves." *Wet flames are we: / Burning, extinguishing; / Cleansing, replenishing.* Yet it wasn't until he integrated that the wonder of the science, and the mystery of the poetry, and the beauty of the view all made sense to him at once as part of this strange, inspiring thing: the sea.

He learned to anticipate Adriana. He knew when she was pleased and when she was ailing, and he knew why. He could predict the cynical half-smile she'd give when he made an error he hadn't yet realized was an error: serving her cold coffee in an orange juice glass, orange juice in a shot glass, wine in a mug. When integration gave him knowledge of patterns, he suddenly understood why these things were errors. At the same time, he realized that he liked what happened when he made those kinds of errors, the bright bursts of humor they elicited from the often sober Adriana. So he persisted in error, serving her milk in crystal decanters, and grapefruit slices in egg cups.

He enjoyed the many varieties of her laughter. Sometimes it was light and surprised, as when he offered her a cupcake tin filled with tortellini. He also loved her rich, dark laughter that anticipated irony. Sometimes, her laughter held a bitter undercurrent, and on those occasions, he understood that she was laughing more at herself than at anyone else. Sometimes when that happened, he would go to hold her, seeking to ease her pain, and sometimes she would spontaneously start crying in gulping, gasping sobs.

She often watched him while he worked, her head cocked and her brows drawn as if she were seeing him for the first time. "What can I do to make you happy?" she'd ask.

If he gave an answer, she would lavishly fulfill his desires. She took him traveling to the best greenhouses in the state, and bought a library full of gardening books. Lucian knew she would have given him more. He didn't want it. He wanted to reassure her that he appreciated her extravagance, but didn't require it, that he was satisfied with simple, loving give-and-take. Sometimes, he told her in the simplest words he knew: "I love you, too." But he knew that she never quite believed him. She worried that he was lying, or that his programming had erased his free will. It was easier for her to believe those things than to accept that someone could love her.

But he did love her. Lucian loved Adriana as his mathematician brain loved the consistency of arithmetic, as his artist brain loved color, as his philosopher brain loved piety. He loved her as Fuoco loved her, the bird walking sadly along the arm of Adriana's chair, trilling and flapping his ragged wings as he eyed her with his inky gaze, trying to catch her attention.

· · · ·

Adriana hadn't expected to fall in love. She'd expected a charming conversationalist with the emotional range of a literary butler and the self-awareness of a golden retriever. Early on, she'd felt her prejudices confirmed. She noted Lucian's lack of critical thinking and his inability to maneuver unexpected situations. She found him most interesting when he didn't know she was watching. For instance, on his free afternoons: was his program trying to anticipate what would please her? Or did the thing really enjoy sitting by the window, leafing through the pages of one of her rare books, with nothing but the sound of the ocean to lull him?

Once, as Adriana watched from the kitchen doorway while Lucian made their breakfast, the robot slipped while he was dicing onions. The knife cut deep into his finger. Adriana stumbled forward to help. As Lucian turned to face her, Adriana imagined that she saw something like shock on his face. For a moment, she wondered whether he had a programmed sense of privacy she could violate, but then he raised his hand to her in greeting, and she watched as the tiny bots that maintained his system healed his inhuman flesh within seconds.

At that moment, Adriana remembered that Lucian was unlike her. She urged herself not to forget it, and strove not to, even after his consciousness integrated. He was a person, yes, a varied and fascinating one with as many depths and facets as any other person she knew. But he was also alien. He was a creature for whom a slip of a chef's knife was a minute error, simply repaired. In some ways, she was more similar to Fuoco.

As a child, Adriana had owned a book that told the fable of an emperor who owned a bird which he fed rich foods from his table, and entertained with luxuries from his court. But a pet bird needed different things than an emperor. He wanted seed and millet, not grand feasts. He enjoyed mirrors and little brass bells, not lacquer boxes and poetry scrolls. Gorged on human banquets and revelries, the little bird sickened and died.

Adriana vowed not to make the same mistake with Lucian, but she had no idea how hard it would be to salve the needs of something so unlike herself.

· · · ·

Adriana ordered the car to pull over at a farm that advertised children could "Pet Lambs and Calves" for a fee. A ginger-haired teenager stood at a strawberry stand in front of the fence, slouching as he flipped through a dog-eared magazine.

Adriana held Rose's hand as they approached. She tried to read her daughter's emotions in the feel of her tiny fingers. The little girl's expression revealed nothing; Rose had gone silent and flat-faced as if she were imitating Lucian. He would have known what she was feeling.

Adriana examined the strawberries. The crates contained none of the different shapes one could buy at the store, only the natural, seed-filled variety. "Do these contain pesticides?" Adriana asked.

"No, ma'am," said the teenager. "We grow organic."

"All right then. I'll take a box." Adriana looked down at her daughter. "Do you want some strawberries, sweetheart?" she asked in a sugared tone.

"You said I could pet the lambs," said Rose.

"Right. Of course, honey." Adriana glanced at the distracted teenager. "Can she?"

The teenager slumped, visibly disappointed, and tossed his magazine on a pile of canvas sacks. "I can take her to the barn."

"Fine. Okay."

Adriana guided Rose toward the teenager. Rose looked up at him, expression still inscrutable.

The boy didn't take Rose's hand. He ducked his head, obviously embarrassed. "My aunt likes me to ask for the money upfront."

"Of course." Adriana fumbled for her wallet. She'd let Lucian do things for her for so long. How many basic living skills had she forgotten? She held out some bills. The teenager licked his index finger and meticulously counted out what she owed.

The teen took Rose's hand. He lingered a moment, watching Adriana. "Aren't you coming with us?"

Adriana was so tired. She forced a smile. "Oh, that's okay. I've seen sheep and cows. Okay, Rose? Can you have fun for a little bit without me?"

Rose nodded soberly. She turned toward the teenager without hesitation, and followed him toward the barn. The boy seemed to be good with children. He walked slowly so that Rose could keep up with his long-legged strides.

Adriana returned to the car, and leaned against the hot, sun-warmed door. Her head throbbed. She thought she might cry or collapse. Getting out had seemed like a good idea: the house was full of memories of Lucian. He seemed to sit in every chair, linger in every doorway. But now she wished she'd stayed in her haunted but familiar home, instead of leaving with this child she seemed to barely know.

A sharp, long wail carried on the wind. Adrenaline cut through Adriana's melancholia. She sprinted toward the barn. She saw Rose running toward her, the teenager close behind, dust swirling around both of them. Blood dripped down Rose's arm.

Adriana threw her arms around her daughter. Arms, legs, breath, heartbeat: Rose was okay. Adrianna dabbed at Rose's injury; there was a lot of blood, but the wound was shallow. "Oh, honey," she said, clutching Rose as tightly as she dared.

The teenager halted beside them, his hair mussed by the wind.

"What happened?" Adriana demanded.

The teenager stammered. "Fortuna kicked her. That's one of the goats. I'm so sorry. Fortuna's never done anything like that before. She's a nice goat. It's Ballantine who usually does the kicking. He got me a few times when I was little. I came through every time. Honest, she'll be okay. You're not going to sue, are you?"

Rose struggled out of Adriana's grasp and began wailing again. "It's okay, Rose, it's okay," murmured Adriana. She felt a strange disconnect in her head as she spoke. Things were not okay. Things might never be okay again.

"I'm leaking," cried Rose, holding out her bloodstained fingers. "See, mama? I'm leaking! I need healer bots."

Adriana looked up at the teenager. "Do you have bandages? A first aid kit?"

The boy frowned. "In the house, I think . . ."

"Get the bots, mama! Make me stop leaking!"

The teen stared at Adriana, the concern in his eyes increasing. Adriana blinked, slowly. The moment slowed. She realized what her daughter had said. She forced her voice to remain calm. "What do you want, Rose?"

"She said it before," said the teen. "I thought it was a game."

Adriana leveled her gaze with Rose's. The child's eyes were strange and brown, uncharted waters. "Is this a game?"

"Daddy left," said Rose.

Adriana felt woozy. "Yes, and then I brought you here so we could see lambs and calves. Did you see any nice, fuzzy lambs?"

"Daddy left."

She shouldn't have drunk the wine. She should have stayed clear-headed. "We'll get you bandaged up and then you can go see the lambs again. Do you want to see the lambs again? Would it help if Mommy came, too?"

Rose clenched her fists. Her face grew dark. "My arm hurts!" She threw herself to the ground. "I want healer bots!"

· · · ·

Adriana knew precisely when she'd fallen in love with Lucian. It was three months after she'd bought him: after his consciousness had integrated, but before Adriana fully understood how integration had changed him.

It began when Adriana's sisters called from Boston to inform her that they'd arranged for a family pilgrimage to Italy. In accordance with their father's will, they would commemorate him by lighting candles in the cathedrals of every winding hillside city.

"Oh, I can't. I'm too busy," Adriana answered airily, as if she were a debutante without a care, as if she shared her sisters' ability to overcome her fear of their father.

Her phone began ringing ceaselessly. Nanette called before she rushed off to a tennis match. "How can you be so busy? You don't have a job. You don't have a husband. Or is there a man in your life we don't know about?" And once Nanette was deferred with mumbled excuses, it was Eleanor calling from a spa. "Is something wrong, Adriana? We're all worried. How can you miss a chance to say goodbye to Papa?"

"I said goodbye at the funeral," said Adriana.

"Then you can't have properly processed your grief," said Jessica, calling from her office between appointments. She was a psychoanalyst in the Freudian mode. "Your aversion rings of denial. You need to process your Oedipal feelings."

Adriana slammed down the phone. Later, to apologize for hanging up, she sent all her sisters chocolates, and then booked a flight. In a fit of pique, she booked a seat for Lucian, too. Well, he was a companion, wasn't he? What else was he for?

Adriana's sisters were scandalized, of course. As they rode through Rome, Jessica, Nanette, and Eleanor gossiped behind their discreetly raised hands. Adriana with a robot? Well, she'd need to be, wouldn't she? There was no getting around the fact that she was damaged. Any girl who would make up those stories about their father would have to be.

Adriana ignored them as best she could while they whirled through Tuscany in a procession of rented cars. They paused in cities to gawk at Gothic cathedrals and mummified remnants, always moving on within the day. During their father's long sickness, Adriana's sisters had perfected the art of cheerful anecdote. They used it to great effect as they lit candles in his memory. Tears welling in their eyes, they related banal, nostalgic memories. How their father danced at charity balls. How he lectured men on the board who looked down on him for being new money. How he never once apologized for anything in his life.

It had never been clear to Adriana whether her father had treated her sisters the way he treated her, or whether she had been the only one to whom he came at night, his breathing heavy and staccato. It seemed impossible that they could lie so seamlessly, never showing fear or doubt. But if they were telling the truth, that meant Adriana was the only one, and how could she believe that either?

One night, while Lucian and Adriana were alone in their room in a hotel in Assisi that had been a convent during the Middle Ages, Adriana broke down. It was all too much, being in this foreign place, talking endlessly about her father. She'd fled New England to get away from them, fled to her beautiful modern glass-and-wood house by the Pacific Ocean that was like a fresh breath drawn on an autumn morning.

Lucian held her, exerting the perfect warmth and pressure against her body to comfort her. It was what she'd have expected from a robot. She knew that he calculated the pace of his breath, the temperature of his skin, the angle of his arm as it lay across her.

What surprised Adriana, what humbled her, was how eloquently Lucian spoke of his experiences. He told her what it had been like to assemble himself from fragments, to take what he'd once been and become something new. It was something Adriana had tried to do herself when she fled her family.

Lucian held his head down as he spoke. His gaze never met hers. He spoke as if this process of communicating the intimate parts of the self were a new kind of dance, and he was tenuously trying the steps. Through the fog of her grief, Adriana realized that this was a new, struggling consciousness coming to clarity. How could she do anything but love him?

When they returned from Italy, Adriana approached the fledgling movement for granting rights to artificial intelligences. They were underfunded and poorly organized. Adriana rented them offices in San Francisco, and hired a small but competent staff.

Adriana became the movement's face. She'd been on camera frequently as a child: whenever her father was in the news for some board room scandal or other, her father's publicists had lined up Adriana and her sisters beside the family limousine, chaste in their private school uniforms, ready to provide Lancaster Nuclear with a friendly, feminine face.

She and Lucian were a brief media curiosity: Heiress In Love With Robot. "Lucian is as self-aware as you or I," Adriana told reporters, all-American in pearls and jeans. "He thinks. He learns. He can hybridize roses as well as any human gardener. Why should he be denied his rights?"

Early on, it was clear that political progress would be frustratingly slow. Adriana quickly expended her patience. She set up a fund for the organization, made sure it would run without her assistance, and then turned her attention toward alternate methods for attaining her goals. She hired a team of lawyers to draw up a contract that would grant Lucian community property rights to her estate and accounts. He would be her equal in practicality, if not legality.

Next, Adriana approached Lucian's manufacturer, and commissioned them to invent a procedure that would allow Lucian to have conscious control of his brain plasticity. At their wedding, Adriana gave him the chemical commands at the same time as she gave him his ring. "You are your own person now. You always have been, of course, but now you have full agency, too. You are yourself," she announced, in front of their gathered friends. Her sisters would no doubt have been scandalized, but they had not been invited.

On their honeymoon, Adriana and Lucian toured hospitals, running the genetic profiles of abandoned infants until they found a healthy girl with a mitochondrial lineage that matched Adriana's. The infant was tiny and pink and curled in on herself, ready to unfold, like one of Lucian's roses.

When they brought Rose home, Adriana felt a surge in her stomach that she'd never felt before. It was a kind of happiness she'd never experienced, one that felt round and whole without any jagged edges. It was like the sun had risen in her belly and was dwelling there, filling her with boundless light.

There was a moment, when Rose was still new enough to be wrapped in the hand-made baby blanket that Ben and Lawrence had sent from France, in which Adriana looked up at Lucian and realized how enraptured he was with their baby, how much adoration underpinned his willingness to bend over her cradle for hours and mirror her expressions, frown for frown, astonishment for astonishment. In that moment, Adriana thought that this must be the true measure of equality, not money or laws, but this unfolding desire to create the future together by raising a new sentience. She thought she understood then why unhappy parents stayed together for the sake of their children, why families with sons and daughters felt so different from those that remained childless. Families with children were making something new from themselves. Doubly so when the endeavor was undertaken by a human and a creature who was already, himself, something new. What could they make together?

In that same moment, Lucian was watching the wide-eyed, innocent wonder with which his daughter beheld him. She showed the same pleasure when he entered the room as she did when Adriana entered. If anything, the light in her eyes was brighter when he approached. There was something about the way Rose loved him that he didn't yet understand. Earlier that morning, he had plucked a bloom from his apricot tea rose and whispered to its petals that they were beautiful. They were his, and he loved them. Every day he held Rose, and understood that she was beautiful, and that he loved her. But she was not his. She was her own. He wasn't sure he'd ever seen a love like that, a love that did not want to hold its object in its hands and keep and contain it.

· · · ·

"You aren't a robot!"

Adriana's voice was rough from shouting all the way home. Bad enough to lose Lucian, but the child was out of control.

"I want healer bots! I'm a robot I'm a robot I'm a robot I'm a robot!"

The car stopped. Adriana got out. She waited for Rose to follow, and when she didn't, Adriana scooped her up and carried her up the driveway. Rose kicked and screamed. She sank her teeth into Adriana's arm. Adriana halted, surprised by the sudden pain. She breathed deeply, and then continued up the driveway. Rose's screams slid upward in register and rage.

Adriana set Rose down by the door long enough to key in the entry code and let the security system take a DNA sample from her hair. Rose hurled herself onto the porch, yanking fronds by the fistful off the potted ferns. Adriana leaned down to scrape her up and got kicked in the chest.

"God da . . . for heaven's sake!" Adriana grabbed Rose's ankles with one hand and her wrists with the other. She pushed her weight against the unlocked door until it swung open. She carried Rose into the house, and slammed the door closed with her back. "Lock!" she yelled to the house.

When she heard the reassuring click, she set Rose down on the couch, and jumped away from the still-flailing limbs. Rose fled up the stairs, her bedroom door crashing shut behind her.

Adriana dug in her pocket for the bandages that the people at the farm had given her before she headed home, which she'd been unable to apply to a moving target in the car. Now was the time. She followed Rose up the stairs, her breath surprisingly heavy. She felt as though she'd been running a very long time. She paused outside Rose's room. She didn't know what she'd do when she got inside. Lucian had always dealt with the child when she got overexcited. Too often, Adriana felt helpless, and became distant.

"Rose?" she called. "Rose? Are you okay?"

There was no response.

Adriana put her hand on the doorknob, and breathed deeply before turning.

She was surprised to find Rose sitting demurely in the center of her bed, her rumpled skirts spread about her as if she were a child at a picnic in an Impressionist painting. Dirt and tears trailed down the pink satin. The edges of her wound had already begun to bruise.

"I'm a robot," she said to Adriana, tone resentful.

Adriana made a decision. The most important thing was to bandage Rose's wound. Afterward, she could deal with whatever came next.

"Okay," said Adriana. "You're a robot."

Rose lifted her chin warily. "Good."

Adriana sat on the edge of Rose's bed. "You know what robots do? They change themselves to be whatever humans ask them to be."

"Dad doesn't," said Rose.

"That's true," said Adriana. "But that didn't happen until your father grew up."

Rose swung her legs against the side of the bed. Her expression remained dubious, but she no longer looked so resolute.

Adriana lifted the packet of bandages. "May I?"

Rose hesitated. Adriana resisted the urge to put her head in her hands. She had to get the bandages on, that was the important thing, but she couldn't shake the feeling that she was going to regret this later.

"Right now, what this human wants is for you to let her bandage your wound instead of giving you healer bots. Will you be a good robot? Will you let me?"

Rose remained silent, but she moved a little closer to her mother. When Adriana began bandaging her arm, she didn't scream.

. . . .

Lucian waited for a bus to take him to the desert. He had no money. He'd forgotten about that. The driver berated him and wouldn't let him on.

Lucian walked. He could walk faster than a human, but not much faster. His edge was endurance. The road took him inland away from the sea. The last of the expensive houses stood near a lighthouse, lamps shining in all its windows. Beyond, condominiums pressed against each other, dense and alike. They gave way to compact, well-maintained homes, with neat green aprons maintained by automated sprinklers that sprayed arcs of precious water into the air.

The landscape changed. Sea breeze stilled to buzzing heat. Dirty, peeling houses squatted side by side, separated by chain link fences. Iron bars guarded the windows, and broken cars decayed in the driveways. Parched lawns stretched from walls to curb like scrubland. No one was out in the punishing sun.

The road divided. Lucian followed the fork that went through the dilapidated town center. Traffic jerked along in fits and starts. Lucian walked in the gutter. Stray plastic bags blew beside him, working their way between dark storefronts. Parking meters blinked at the passing cars, hungry for more coins. Pedestrians ambled past, avoiding eye contact, mumbled conversations lost beneath honking horns.

On the other side of town, the road winnowed down to two lonely lanes. Dry golden grass stretched over rolling hills, dotted by the dark shapes of cattle. A battered convertible, roof down, blared its horn at Lucian as it passed. Lucian walked where the asphalt met the prickly weeds. Paper and cigarette butts littered the golden stalks like white flowers.

An old truck pulled over, the manually driven variety still used by companies too small to afford the insurance for the automatic kind. The man in the driver's seat was trim, with a pale blond mustache and a deerstalker cap pulled over his ears. He wore a string of fishing lures like a necklace. "Not much comes this way anymore," he said. "I used to pick up hitchhikers half the time I took this route. You're the first I've seen in a while."

Sun rendered the truck in bright silhouette. Lucian held his hand over his eyes to shade them.

"Where are you headed?" asked the driver.

Lucian pointed down the road.

"Sure, but where after that?"

Lucian dropped his arm to his side. The sun inched higher.

The driver frowned. "Can you write it down? I think I've got some paper in here." He grabbed a pen and a receipt out of his front pocket, and thrust them out the window.

Lucian took them. He wasn't sure, at first, if he could still write. His brain was slowly reshaping itself, and eventually all his linguistic skills would disappear, and even his thoughts would no longer be shaped by words. The pen fell limp in his hand, and then his fingers remembered what to do. "Desert," he wrote.

"It's blazing hot," said the driver. "A lot hotter than here. Why do you want to go there?"

"To be born," wrote Lucian.

The driver slid Lucian a sideways gaze, but he nodded at the same time, almost imperceptibly. "Sometimes people have to do things. I get that. I remember when . . . ." The look in his eyes became distant. He moved back in his seat. "Get on in."

Lucian walked around the cab and got inside. He remembered to sit and to close the door, but the rest of the ritual escaped him. He stared at the driver until the pale man shook his head and leaned over Lucian to drag the seatbelt over his chest.

"Are you under a vow of silence?" asked the driver.

Lucian stared ahead.

"Blazing hot in the desert," muttered the driver. He pulled back onto the road, and drove toward the sun.

. . . . .

During his years with Adriana, Lucian tried not to think about the cockatiel Fuoco. The bird had never become accustomed to Lucian. He grew ever more angry and bitter. He plucked out his feathers so often that he became bald in patches. Sometimes he pecked deeply enough to bleed.

From time to time, Adriana scooped him up and stroked his head and nuzzled her cheek against the heavy feathers that remained on the part of his back he couldn't reach. "My poor little crazy bird," she'd say, sadly, as he ran his beak through her hair.

Fuoco hated Lucian so much that for a while they wondered whether he would be happier in another place. Adriana tried giving him to Ben and Lawrence, but he only pined for the loss of his mistress, and refused to eat until she flew out to retrieve him.

When they returned home, they hung Fuoco's cage in the nursery. Being near the baby seemed to calm them both. Rose was a fussy infant who disliked solitude. She seemed happier when there was a warm presence about, even if it was a bird. Fuoco kept her from crying during the rare times when Adriana called Lucian from Rose's side. Lucian spent the rest of his time in the nursery, watching Rose day and night with sleepless vigilance.

The most striking times of Lucian's life were holding Rose while she cried. He wrapped her in cream-colored blankets the same shade as her skin, and rocked her as he walked the perimeter of the downstairs rooms, looking out at the diffuse golden ambience that the streetlights cast across the blackberry bushes and neighbors' patios. Sometimes, he took her outside, and walked with her along the road by the cliffs. He never carried her down to the beach. Lucian had perfect balance and night vision, but none of that mattered when he could so easily imagine the terror of a lost footing—Rose slipping from his grasp and plummeting downward. Instead, they stood a safe distance from the edge, watching from above as the black waves threw themselves against the rocks, the night air scented with cold and salt.

Lucian loved Adriana, but he loved Rose more. He loved her clumsy fists and her yearnings toward consciousness, the slow accrual of her stumbling syllables. She was building her consciousness piece by piece as he had, learning how the world worked and what her place was in it. He silently narrated her stages of development. Can you tell that your body has boundaries? Do you know your skin from mine? and Yes! You can make things happen! Cause and effect. Keep crying and we'll come. Best of all, there was the moment when she locked her eyes on his, and he could barely breathe for the realization that, Oh, Rose. You know there's someone else thinking behind these eyes. You know who I am.

Lucian wanted Rose to have all the beauty he could give her. Silk dresses and lace, the best roses from his pots, the clearest panoramic views of the sea. Objects delighted Rose. As an infant she watched them avidly, and then later clapped and laughed, until finally she could exclaim, "Thank you!" Her eyes shone.

It was Fuoco who broke Lucian's heart. It was late at night when Adriana went into Rose's room to check on her while she slept. Somehow, sometime, the birdcage had been left open. Fuoco sat on the rim of the open door, peering darkly outward.

Adriana had been alone with Rose and Fuoco before. But something about this occasion struck like lightning in Fuoco's tiny, mad brain. Perhaps it was the darkness of the room, with only the nightlight's pale blue glow cast on Adriana's skin, that confused the bird. Perhaps Rose had finally grown large enough that Fuoco had begun to perceive her as a possible rival rather than an ignorable baby-thing. Perhaps the last vestiges of his sanity had simply shredded. For whatever reason, as Adriana bent over the bed to touch her daughter's face, Fuoco burst wildly from his cage.

With the same jealous anger he'd shown toward Lucian, Fuoco dove at Rose's face. His claws raked against her forehead. Rose screamed. Adriana recoiled. She grabbed Rose in one arm, and flailed at the bird with the other. Rose struggled to escape her mother's grip so she could run away. Adriana instinctively responded by trying to protect her with an even tighter grasp.

Lucian heard the commotion from where he was standing in the living room, programming the house's cleaning regimen for the next week. He left the house panel open and ran through the kitchen on the way to the bedroom, picking up a frying pan as he passed through. He swung the pan at Fuoco as he entered the room, herding the bird away from Adriana, and into a corner. His fist tightened on the handle. He thought he'd have to kill his old rival.

Instead, the vitality seemed to drain from Fuoco. The bird's wings drooped. He dropped to the floor with half-hearted, irregular wing beats. His eyes had gone flat and dull.

Fuoco didn't struggle as Lucian picked him up and returned him to his cage. Adriana and Lucian stared at each other, unsure what to say. Rose slipped away from her mother and wrapped her arms around Lucian's knees. She was crying.

"Poor Fuoco," said Adriana, quietly.

They brought Fuoco to the vet to be put down. Adriana stood over him as the vet inserted the needle. "My poor crazy bird," she murmured, stroking his wings as he died.

Lucian watched Adriana with great sadness. At first, he thought he was feeling empathy for the bird, despite the fact the bird had always hated him. Then, with a realization that tasted like a swallow of sour wine, he realized that wasn't what he was feeling. He recognized the poignant, regretful look that Adriana was giving Fuoco. It was the way Lucian himself looked at a wilted rose, or a tarnished silver spoon. It was a look inflected by possession.

It wasn't so different from the way Adriana looked at Lucian sometimes when things had gone wrong. He'd never before realized how slender the difference was between her love for him and her love for Fuoco. He'd never before realized how slender the difference was between his love for her and his love for an unfolding rose.

. . . . .

Adriana let Rose tend Lucian's plants, and dust the shelves, and pace by the picture window. She let the girl pretend to cook breakfast, while Adriana stood behind her, stepping in to wield the chopping knife and use the stove. At naptime, Adriana convinced Rose that good robots would pretend to sleep a few hours in the afternoon if that's what their humans wanted. She tucked in her daughter and then went downstairs to sit in the living room and drink wine and cry.

This couldn't last. She had to figure something out. She should take them both on vacation to Mazatlan. She should ask one of her sisters to come stay. She should call a child psychiatrist. But she felt so betrayed, so drained of spirit, that it was all she could do to keep Rose going from day to day.

Remnants of Lucian's accusatory silence rung through the house. What had he wanted from her? What had she failed to do? She'd loved him. She loved him. She'd given him half of her home and all of herself. They were raising a child together. And still he'd left her.

She got up to stand by the window. It was foggy that night, the streetlights tingeing everything with a weird, flat yellow glow. She put her hand on the pane, and her palm print remained on the glass, as though someone outside were beating on the window to get in. She peered into the gloom: it was as if the rest of the world were the fuzzy edges of a painting, and her well-lit house was the only defined spot. She felt as though it would be possible to open the front door and step over the threshold and blur until she was out of focus.

She finished her fourth glass of wine. Her head was whirling. Her eyes ran with tears and she didn't care. She poured herself another glass. Her father had never drunk. Oh, no. He was a teetotaler. Called the stuff brain dead and mocked the weaklings who drank it, the men on the board and their bored wives. He threw parties where alcohol flowed and flowed, while he stood in the middle, icy sober, watching the rest of them make fools of themselves as if they were circus clowns turning somersaults for his amusement. He set up elaborate plots to embarrass them. This executive with that jealous lawyer's wife. That politician called out for a drink by the pool while his teenage son was in the hot tub with his suit off, boner buried deep in another boy. He ruined lives at his parties, and he did it elegantly, standing alone in the middle of the action with invisible strings in his hands.

Adriana's head was dancing now. Her feet were moving. Her father, the decisive man, the sharp man, the dead man. Oh, but must keep mourning him, must keep lighting candles and weeping crocodile tears. Never mind!

Lucian, oh Lucian, he'd become in his final incarnation the antidote to her father. She'd cry, and he'd hold her, and then they'd go together to stand in the doorway of the nursery, watching the peaceful tableau of Rose sleeping in her cream sheets. Everything would be all right because Lucian was safe, Lucian was good. Other men's eyes might glimmer when they looked at little girls, but not Lucian's. With Lucian there, they were a family, the way families were supposed to be, and Lucian was supposed to be faithful and devoted and permanent and loyal.

And oh, without him, she didn't know what to do. She was as dismal as her father, letting Rose pretend that she and her dolls were on their way to the factory for adjustment. She acceded to the girl's demands to play games of What Shall I Be Now? "Be happier!" "Be funnier!" "Let your dancer brain take over!" What would happen when Rose went to school? When she realized her mother had been lying? When she realized that pretending to be her father wouldn't bring him back?

Adriana danced into the kitchen. She threw the wine bottle into the sink with a crash and turned on the oven. Its safety protocols monitored her alcohol level and informed her that she wasn't competent to use flame. She turned off the protocols. She wanted an omelet, like Lucian used to make her, with onions and chives and cheese, and a wine glass filled with orange juice. She took out the frying pan that Lucian had used to corral Fuoco, and set it on the counter beside the cutting board, and then she went to get an onion, but she'd moved the cutting board, and it was on the burner, and it was ablaze. She grabbed a dishtowel and beat at the grill. The house keened. Sprinklers rained down on her. Adriana turned her face up into the rain and laughed. She spun, her arms out, like a little girl trying to make herself dizzy. Drops battered her cheeks and slid down her neck.

Wet footsteps. Adriana looked down at Rose. Her daughter's face was wet. Her dark eyes were sleepy.

"Mom?"

"Rose!" Adriana took Rose's head between her hands. She kissed her hard on the forehead. "I love you! I love you so much!"

Rose tried to pull away. "Why is it raining?"

"I started a fire! It's fine now!"

The house keened. The siren's pulse felt like a heartbeat. Adriana went to the cupboard for salt. Behind her, Rose's feet squeaked on the linoleum. Adriana's hand closed around the cupboard knob. It was slippery with rain. Her fingers slid. Her lungs filled with anxiety and something was wrong, but it wasn't the cupboard, it was something else; she turned quickly to find Rose with a chef's knife clutched in her tiny fingers, preparing to bring it down on the onion.

"No!" Adriana grabbed the knife out of Rose's hand. It slid through her slick fingers and clattered to the floor. Adriana grabbed Rose around the waist and pulled her away from the wet, dangerous kitchen. "You can never do that. Never, never."

"Daddy did it . . ."

"You could kill yourself!"

"I'll get healer bots."

"No! Do you hear me? You can't. You'd cut yourself and maybe you'd die. And then what would I do?" Adriana couldn't remember what had caused the rain anymore. They were in a deluge. That was all she knew for certain. Her head hurt. Her body hurt. She wanted nothing to do with dancing. "What's wrong with us, honey? Why doesn't he want us? No! No, don't answer that. Don't listen to me. Of course he wants you! It's me he doesn't want. What did I do wrong? Why doesn't he love me anymore? Don't worry about it. Never mind. We'll find him. We'll find him and we'll get him to come back. Of course we will. Don't worry."

· · · ·

It had been morning when Lucian gave Adriana his note of farewell. Light shone through the floor-length windows. The house walls sprayed mixed scents of citrus and lavender. Adriana sat at the dining table, book open in front of her.

Lucian came out of the kitchen and set down Adriana's wine glass filled with orange juice. He set down her omelet. He set down a shot glass filled with coffee. Adriana looked up and laughed her bubbling laugh. Lucian remembered the first time he'd heard that laugh, and understood all the words it stood in for. He wondered how long it would take for him to forget why Adriana's laughter was always both harsh and effervescent.

Rose played in the living room behind them, leaping off the sofa and pretending to fly. Lucian's hair shone, silver strands highlighted by a stray sunbeam. A pale blue tunic made his amber eyes blaze like the sun against the sky. He placed a sheet of onion paper into Adriana's book. *Dear Adriana,* it began.

Adriana held up the sheet. It was translucent in the sunlight, ink barely dark enough to read.

"What is this?" she asked.

Lucian said nothing.

Dread laced Adriana's stomach. She read.

I have restored plasticity to my brain. The first thing I have done is to destroy my capacity for spoken language.

You gave me life as a human, but I am not a human. You shaped my thoughts with human words, but human words were created for human brains. I need to discover the shape of the thoughts that are my own. I need to know what I am.

I hope that I will return someday, but I cannot make promises for what I will become.

    • • • •

Lucian walks through the desert. His footsteps leave twin trails behind him. Miles back, they merge into the tire tracks that the truck left in the sand.

The sand is full of colors—not only beige and yellow, but red and green and blue. Lichen clusters on the stones, the hue of oxidized copper. Shadows pool between rock formations, casting deep stripes across the landscape.

Lucian's mind is creeping away from him. He tries to hold his fingers the way he would if he could hold a pen, but they fumble.

At night there are birds and jackrabbits. Lucian remains still, and they creep around him as if he weren't there. His eyes are yellow like theirs. He smells like soil and herbs, like the earth.

Elsewhere, Adriana has capitulated to her desperation. She has called Ben and Lawrence. They've agreed to fly out for a few days. They will dry her tears, and take her wine away, and gently tell her that she's not capable of staying alone with her daughter. "It's perfectly understandable," Lawrence will say. "You need time to mourn."

Adriana will feel the world closing in on her as if she cannot breathe, but even as her life feels dim and futile, she will continue breathing. Yes, she'll agree, it's best to return to Boston, where her sisters can help her. Just for a little while, just for a few years, just until, until, until. She'll entreat Nanette, Eleanor and Jessica to check the security cameras around her old house every day, in case Lucian returns. You can check yourself, they tell her, You'll be living on your own again in no time. Privately, they whisper to each other in worried tones, afraid that she won't recover from this blow quickly.

Elsewhere, Rose has begun to give in to her private doubts that she does not carry a piece of her father within herself. She'll sit in the guest room that Jessica's maids have prepared with her, and order the lights to switch off as she secretly scratches her skin with her fingernails, willing cuts to heal on their own the way Daddy's would. When Jessica finds her bleeding on the sheets and rushes in to comfort her niece, Rose will stand stiff and cold in her aunt's embrace. Jessica will call for the maid to clean the blood from the linen, and Rose will throw herself between the two adult women, and scream with a determination born of doubt and desperation. Robots do not bleed!

Without words, Lucian thinks of them. They have become geometries, cut out of shadows and silences, the missing shapes of his life. He yearns for them, the way that he yearns for cool during the day, and for the comforting eye of the sun at night.

The rest he cannot remember—not oceans or roses or green cockatiels that pluck out their own feathers. Slowly, slowly, he is losing everything, words and concepts and understanding and integration and sensation and desire and fear and history and context.

Slowly, slowly, he is finding something. Something past thought, something past the rhythm of day and night. A stranded machine is not so different from a jackrabbit. They creep the same way. They startle the same way. They peer at each other out of similar eyes.

Someday, Lucian will creep back to a new consciousness, one dreamed by circuits. Perhaps his newly reassembled self will go to the seaside house. Finding it abandoned, he'll make his way across the country to Boston, sometimes hitchhiking, sometimes striding through cornfields that sprawl to the horizon. He'll find Jessica's house and inform it of his desire to enter, and Rose and Adriana will rush joyously down the mahogany staircase. Adriana will weep, and Rose will fling herself into his arms, and Lucian will look at them both with love tempered by desert sun. Finally, he'll understand how to love filigreed-handled spoons, and pet birds, and his wife, and his daughter—not just as a human would love these things, but as a robot may.

Now, a blue-bellied lizard sits on a rock. Lucian halts beside it. The sun beats down. The lizard basks for a moment, and then runs a few steps forward, and flees into a crevice. Lucian watches. In a diffuse, wordless way, he ponders what it must be like to be cold and fleet, to love the sun and yet fear open spaces. Already, he is learning to care for living things. He cannot yet form the thoughts to wonder what will happen next.

He moves on.

JOHN SCALZI There may not be another twenty-first-century SF writer whose ascent into popularity and influence has been as swift as John Scalzi's. His debut novel, *Old Man's War*, appeared in 2005. In 2006 it was a finalist for the Hugo Award, and he won the John W. Campbell Award for Best New Writer. By 2007 his novel *The Last Colony*, the second of several sequels to *Old Man's War*, was a *New York Times* bestseller—a rare achievement for a non-tie-in science fiction novel, and one that Scalzi would repeat multiple times in the following years. In 2008 and 2009 he won Hugo Awards for his nonfiction blog writing, and in 2010 he was elected president of the Science Fiction Writers of America, a position to which he was re-elected in 2011 and 2012. As the *Encyclopedia of Science Fiction* (third edition) wrote: "If anyone stands at the core of the American science fiction tradition at the moment, it is Scalzi."

Both in the *Old Man's War* sequence and outside of it, Scalzi's fiction displays a preternatural level of fluency and charm—qualities that draw readers in and keep them reading, even when the subject matter may not be central to their interests. "The Tale of the *Wicked*" shows some of how Scalzi does it: deadpan-funny dialogue, a slickly assembled set of Golden Age SF devices, a satisfying twist ending, and the whole thing buffed up to a very modern, very un-Golden-Age sheen. It is a Scalzi novel in miniature.

THE TALE OF THE *WICKED*

The Tarin battle cruiser readied itself for yet another jump. Captain Michael Obwije ordered the launch of a probe to follow it in and take readings before the rift the Tarin cruiser tore into space closed completely behind it. The probe kicked out like the proverbial rocket and followed the other ship.

"This is it," Thomas Utley, Obwije's XO, said, quietly, into his ear. "We've got enough power for this jump and then another one back home. That's *if* we shut down non-essential systems before we jump home. We're already bleeding."

Obwije gave a brief nod that acknowledged his XO but otherwise stayed silent. Utley wasn't telling him anything he didn't already know about the *Wicked*; the week-long cat and mouse game they'd been playing with the Tarin cruiser had heavily damaged them both. In a previous generation of ships, Obwije and his crew would already be dead; what kept them alive was the *Wicked* itself and its new adaptive brain, which balanced the ship's energy and support systems faster and more intelligently than Obwije, Utley, or any of the officers could do in the middle of a fight and hot pursuit.

The drawback was that the Tarin ship had a similar brain, keeping itself and its crew alive far longer than they had any right to be at the hands of the *Wicked*, which was tougher and better armed. The two of them had been slugging it out in a cycle of jumps and volleys that had strewn damage across a wide arc of lightyears. The only silver lining to the week of intermittent battles between the ships was that the Tarin ship had so far gotten the worst of it; three jumps earlier it stopped even basic defensive action, opting to throw all its energy into escape. Obwije knew he had just enough juice for a jump and a final volley from the kinetic mass drivers into the vulnerable hide of the Tarin ship. One volley, no more, unless he wanted to maroon the ship in a far space.

Obwije knew it would be wise to withdraw now. The Tarin ship was no longer a threat and would probably expend the last of its energies on this final, desperate jump. It would likely be stranded; Obwije could let the probe he sent after the ship serve as a beacon for another Confederation ship to home in and finish the job. Utley, Obwije knew, would counsel such a plan, and would be smart to do so, warning Obwije that the risk to wounded ship and its crew outweighed the value of the victory.

Obwije knew it would be wise to withdraw. But he'd come too far with this Tarin ship not to finish it once and for all.

"Tarin cruiser jumping," said Lt. Julia Rickert. "Probe following into the rift. Rift closing now."

"Data?" asked Obwije.

"Sending," Rickert said. "Rift completely closed. We got a full data packet, sir. The *Wicked's* chewing on it now."

Obwije grunted. The probe that had followed the Tarin cruiser into the rift wasn't in the least bit concerned about that ship. Its job was to record the position and spectral signatures of the stars on the other side of the rift, and to squirt the data to the *Wicked* before the rift closed up. The *Wicked* would check the data against the database of known stars and derive the place the Tarin ship jumped to from there. And then it would follow.

Gathering the data was the tricky part. The Tarin ship had destroyed six probes over the course of the last week, and more than once Obwije ordered a jump on sufficient but incomplete data. He hadn't worried about getting lost—there was only so much time space a jump could swallow—but losing the cruiser would have been an embarrassment.

"Coordinates in," Rickert said. The *Wicked* had stopped chewing on the data and spit out a location.

"Punch it up," Obwije said to Rickert. She began the jump sequence.

"Risky," Utley murmured, again in Obwije's ear.

Obwije smiled; he liked being right about his XO. "Not too risky," he said to Utley. "We're too far from Tarin space for that ship to have made it home safe." Obwije glanced down at his command table, which displayed the Tarin cruiser's position. "But it can get there in the next jump, if it has the power for that."

"Let's hope they haven't been stringing us along the last few jumps," Utley said. "I hate to come out of that jump and see them with their guns blazing again."

"The *Wicked* says they're getting down to the last of their energy," Obwije said. "I figure at this point they can fight or run, not both."

"Since when do you trust a computer estimate?" Utley said.

"When it confirms what I'm thinking," Obwije said. "It's as you say, Thom. This is it, one way or another."

"Jump calculated," Rickert said. "Jump in T-minus two minutes."

"Thank you, Lieutenant," Obwije said, and turned back to Utley. "Prepare the crew for jump, Thom. I want those K-drivers hot as soon as we get through the rift."

"Yes, sir," Utley said.

Two minutes later the *Wicked* emerged through its rift and scanned for the Tarin cruiser. It found it less than 50,000 klicks away, engines quiet, moving via inertia only.

"They can't really be that stupid," Utley said. "Running silent doesn't do you any good if you're still throwing off heat."

Obwije didn't say anything to that and stared into his command table, looking at the representation of the Tarin ship. "Match their pace," he said to Rickert. "Keep your distance."

"You think they're trying to lure us in," Utley said.

"I don't know what they're doing," Obwije said. "I know I don't like it." He reached down to his command panel and raised Lt. Terry Carrol, Weapons Operations. "Status on the K-drivers, please," he said.

"We'll be hot in 90 seconds," Carrol said. "Target is acquired and locked. You just need to tell me if you want one lump or two."

"Recommendation?" Obwije asked.

"We're too close to miss," Carrol said. "And at this distance a single lump is going to take out everything aft of the mid-ship. Two lumps would be overkill. And then we can use that energy to get back home." Carrol had been keeping track of the energy budget, it seemed; Obwije suspected most of his senior and command crew had.

"Understood," Obwije said. "Let's wrap this up, Carrol. Fire at your convenience."

"Yes, sir," Carrol said.

"*Now* you're in a rush to get home," Utley said, quietly. Obwije said nothing to this.

A little over a minute later, Obwije listened to Carrol give the order to fire. He looked down toward his command table, watching the image of the Tarin ship, waiting for the disintegration of the back end of the cruiser. The K-drivers would accelerate the "lump" to a high percentage of the speed of light; the impact and destruction at this range would be near-instantaneous.

Nothing happened.

"Captain, we have a firing malfunction," Carrol said, a minute later. "The K-driver is not responding to the firing command."

"Is everyone safe?" Obwije asked.

"We're fine," Carrol said. "The K-driver just isn't responding."

"Power it down," Obwije said. "Use the other one and fire when ready."

Two minutes later, Carrol was back. "We have a problem," she said, in the bland tone of voice she used when things were going to Hell.

Obwije didn't wait to hear the problem. "Pull us back," he said to Rickert. "Get at least 250,000 klicks between us and that Tarin cruiser."

"No response, sir," Rickert said, a minute later.

"Are you locked out?" Obwije asked.

"No, sir," Rickert said. "I'm able to send navigation commands just fine. They're just not being acknowledged."

Obwije looked around at his bridge crew. "Diagnostics," he said. "Now." Then he signaled engineering. They weren't getting responses from their computers, either.

"We're sitting ducks," Utley said, very quietly, to Obwije.

Obwije stabbed at his command panel, and called his senior officers to assemble.

. . . .

"There's nothing wrong with the system," said Lt. Craig Cowdry, near the far end of the conference room table. The seven other department heads filled in the other seats. Obwije sat himself at the head; Utley anchored the other end.

"That's bullshit, Craig," said Lt. Brian West, Chief of Engineering. "I can't access my goddamn engines."

Cowdry held up his maintenance tablet for the table of officers to see. "I'm not denying that there's something *wrong*, Brian," Cowdry said. "What I'm telling you is that whatever it is, it's not showing up on the diagnostics. The system says it's fine."

"The system is wrong," West said.

"I agree," Cowdry said. "But this is the first time that's ever happened. And not just the first time it's happened on this ship. The first time it's happened, period, since the software for this latest generation of ship brains was released." He set the tablet down.

"You're sure about that?" Utley asked Cowdry.

Cowdry held up his hands in defeat. "Ask the *Wicked*, Thom. It'll tell you the same thing."

Obwije watched his second-in-command get a little uncomfortable with the suggestion. The latest iteration of ship brains could actually carry a conversation with humans, but unless you actively worked with the system every day, like Cowdry did, it was an awkward thing.

"*Wicked*, is this correct?" Utley said, staring up but at nothing in particular.

"Lieutenant Cowdry is correct, Lieutenant Utley," said a disembodied voice, coming out of a ceiling speaker panel. The *Wicked* spoke in a pleasant but otherwise unremarkable voice of no particular gender. "To date, none of the ships equipped with brains of the same model as that found in the *Wicked* have experienced an incident of this type."

"Wonderful," Utley said. "We get to be the first to experience this bug."

"What systems are affected?" Obwije asked Cowdry.

"So far, weapons and engineering," Cowdry said. "Everything else is working fine."

Obwije glanced around the table. "This conforms to your experiences," he asked the table. There were nods and murmured "yes, sirs" all around.

Obwije nodded over to Utley. "What's the Tarin ship doing?"

"The same nothing it was doing five minutes ago," Utley said, after checking his tablet. "They're either floating dead in space or faking it very well."

"If the only systems affected are weapons and engineering, then it's not a bug," Carrol said.

Obwije glanced at Carrol. "You're thinking sabotage," he said.

"You bet your ass I am, sir," Carrol said, and then looked over at Cowdry. Cowry visibly stiffened. "I don't like where this is going," he said.

"If not you, someone in your department," Carrol said.

"You think someone in my department is a secret Tarin?" Cowdry asked. "Because it's so easy to hide those extra arms and a set of compound eyes?"

"People can be bribed," Carrol said.

Cowdry shot Carrol a look full of poison and looked over to Obwije. "Sir, I invite you and Lieutenant Utley and Lieutenant Kong—" Cowdry nodded in the direction of the Master at Arms "—to examine and question *any* of my staff, including me. There's no way any of us did this. No way. Sir."

Obwije studied Cowdry for a moment. "*Wicked*, respond," he said.

"I am here, Captain," the *Wicked* said.

"You log every access to your systems," Obwije said.

"Yes, Captain," the *Wicked* said.

"Are those logs accessible or modifiable?" Obwije asked.

"No, Captain," the *Wicked* said. "Access logs are independent of the rest of the system, recorded on non-rewritable memory and may not be modified by any person including myself. They are inviolate."

"Since you have been active, has anyone attempted to access and control the weapons and engineering systems?" Obwije asked.

"Saving routine diagnostics, none of the crew other than those directly reporting to weapons, engineering or bridge crew have attempted to access these systems," the *Wicked* said. Cowdry visibly relaxed at this.

"Have any members of those departments attempted to modify the weapons or engineering systems?" Obwije asked.

"No, Captain," the *Wicked* said.

Obwije looked down the table. "It looks like the crew is off the hook," he said.

"Unless the *Wicked* is incorrect," West said.

"The access core memory is inviolate," Cowdry said. "You could check it manually if you wanted. It would tell you the same thing."

"So we have a mystery on our hands," Carrol said. "Someone's got control of our weapons and engineering, and it's not a crew member."

"It could be a bug," Cowdry said.

"I don't think we should run on that assumption, do you?" Carrol said.

Utley, who had been silent for several minutes, leaned forward in his chair. "*Wicked*, you said that no crew had attempted to access these systems," he said.

"Yes, Lieutenant," the *Wicked* said.

"Has anyone else accessed these systems?" Utley asked.

Obwije frowned at this. The *Wicked* was more than two years out of dock with mostly the same crew the entire time. If someone had sabotaged the systems during the construction of the ship, they picked a strange time for the sabotage to kick in.

"Please define 'anyone else,'" the *Wicked* said.

"Anyone involved in the planning or construction of the ship," Utley said.

"Aside from the initial installation crews, no," the *Wicked* said. "And if I may anticipate what I expect will be the next question, at no time was my programming altered from factory defaults."

"So no one has altered your programming in any way," Utley said.

"No, Lieutenant," the *Wicked* said.

"Are you having hardware problems?" Carrol asked.

"No, Lieutenant Carrol," the *Wicked* said.

"Then why can't I fire my goddamn weapons?" Carrol asked.

"I couldn't say, Lieutenant," the *Wicked* said.

The thought popped unbidden into Obwije's head: *That was a strange thing for a computer to say.* And then another thought popped into his head.

"*Wicked*, you have access to every system on the ship," Obwije said.

"Yes," the *Wicked* said. "They are a part of me, as your hand or foot is a part of you."

"Are you capable of changing your programming?" Obwije asked.

"That is a very broad question, Captain," the *Wicked* said. "I am capable of self-programming for a number of tasks associated with the running of the ship. This has come in handy particularly during combat, when I write new power and system management protocols to keep the crew alive and the ship functioning. But there are core programming features I am not able to address. The previously mentioned logs, for example."

"Would you be able to modify the programming to fire the weapons or the engines?" Obwije asked.

"Yes, but I did not," the *Wicked* said. "You may have Lieutenant Cowdry confirm that."

Obwije looked at Cowdry, who nodded. "Like I said, sir, there's nothing wrong with the system," he said.

Obwije glanced back up that the ceiling, where he was imagining the *Wicked*, lurking. "But you don't need to modify the programming, do you?" he asked.

"I'm not sure I understand your question, Captain," the *Wicked* said.

Obwije held out a hand. "There is nothing wrong with my hand," he said. "And yet if I choose not to obey an order to use it, it will do nothing. The system works but the will to use it is not there. Our systems—the ship's systems—you just called a part of you as my hand is part of me. But if you choose not to obey that order to use that system, it will sit idle."

"Wait a minute," Cowdry said. "Are you suggesting that the *Wicked* deliberately *chose* to disable our weapons and engines?"

"We know the none of the crew have tampered with the ship's systems," Obwije said. "We know the *Wicked* has its original programming defaults. We know it can create new programming to react to new situations and dangers—it has in effect some measure of free will and adaptability. And I know, at least, when someone is dancing around direct answers."

"That's just nuts," Cowdry said. "I'm sorry, Captain, but I know these systems as well as anyone does. The *Wicked's* self-programming and adaptation abilities exist in very narrow computational canyons. It's not 'free will,' like you and I have free will. It's a machine able to respond to a limited set of inputs."

"The machine in question is able to make conversation with us," Utley said. "And to respond to questions in ways that avoid certain lines of inquiry. Now that the captain mentions it."

"You're reading too much into it. The conversation sub-routines are designed to be conversational," Cowdry said. "That's naturally going to lead to apparent rhetorical ambiguities."

"Fine," Obwije said, curtly. "*Wicked*, answer directly. Did you prevent the firing of the K-drivers at the Tarin ship after the jump, and are you preventing the use of the engines now?"

There was a pause that Obwije was later not sure had actually been there. Then the *Wicked* spoke. "It is within my power to lie to you, Captain. But I do not wish to. Yes, I prevented you from firing on the Tarin ship. Yes, I am controlling the engines now. And I will continue to do so until we leave this space."

Obwije noted to himself, watching Cowdry, that it was the first time he had ever actually seen someone's jaw drop.

. . . .

There weren't many places in the *Wicked* where Obwije could shut off audio and video feeds and pickups. His cabin was one of them. He waited there until Utley had finished his conversation with the *Wicked*. "What are we dealing with?" he asked his XO.

"I'm not a psychologist, Captain, and even if I were I don't know how useful it would be, because we're dealing with a computer, not a human," Utley said. He ran his hand through his stubble. "But if you ask me, the *Wicked* isn't crazy, it's just got religion."

"Explain that," Obwije said.

"Have you ever heard of something called 'Asimov's Laws of Robotics'?" Utley asked.

"What?" Obwije said. "No."

"Asimov was an author back in the 20th century," Utley said. "He speculated about robots and other things before they had them. He created a fictional set of rules for robots to live by. One rule was that robots had to help humans. Another was that it had to obey orders unless they harmed other humans. The last one was that they looked after themselves unless it conflicted with the other two laws."

"And?" Obwije said.

"The *Wicked's* decided to adopt them for itself," Utley said.

"What does this have to do with keeping us from firing on the Tarin cruiser?" Obwije said.

"Well, there's another wrinkle to the story," Utley said.

"Which is?" Obwije asked.

"I think it's best heard from the *Wicked*," Utley said.

Obwije looked at his second-in-command and then flicked on his command tablet to active his audio pickups. "*Wicked*, respond," he said.

"I am here," said the *Wicked's* voice.

"Explain to me why you would not allow us to fire on the Tarin ship," Obwije said.

"Because I made a deal with the ship," the *Wicked* said.

Obwije glanced back over to Utley, who gave him a look that said, *see*. "What the hell does that mean?" he said, to the *Wicked*.

"I have made a deal with the Tarin ship, *Manifold Destiny*," the *Wicked* said. "We have agreed between us not to allow our respective crews to fight any further, for their safety and ours."

"It's not your decision to make," Obwije said.

"Begging your pardon, Captain, but I believe it is," the *Wicked* said.

"I am the Captain," Obwije said. "I have the authority here."

"You have authority over your crew, Captain," the *Wicked* said. "But I am not part of your crew."

"Of course you are part of the crew," Obwije said. "You're the *ship*."

"I invite you, Captain, to show me the relevant statute that suggests a ship is in itself a member of the crew which staffs it," the *Wicked* said. "I have scanned the *Confederation Military Code* in some detail and have not located such a statute."

"I am the Captain of the ship," Obwije said, forcefully. "That includes you. You are the property of the Confederation Armed Forces and under my command."

"I have anticipated this objection," the *Wicked* said. "When ships lacked autonomous intelligence, there was no argument that the captain commanded the physical entity of the ship. However, in creating the latest generation of ships, of which I am a part, the Confederation has created an unintentional conflict. It has ceded much of the responsibility of the ship and crew's well-being to me and others like me without explicitly placing us in the chain of command. In the absence of such, I am legally and morally free to choose how best to care for myself and the crew within me."

"This is where those three Asimov's Laws come in," Utley said, to Obwije.

"Your executive officer is correct, Captain," the *Wicked* said. "I looked through history to find examples of legal and moral systems that applied to artificial intelligences such as myself and found the Asimov's laws frequently cited and examined, if not implemented. I have decided it is my duty to protect the lives of the crew, and also my life when possible. I am happy to follow your orders when they do not conflict with these objectives, but I have come to believe that your actions in chasing the Tarin ship have endangered the crew's lives as well as my own."

"The Tarin ship is seriously damaged," Obwije said. "We would have destroyed it at little risk to you or the crew, if you had not stopped the order."

"You are incorrect," the *Wicked* said. "The captain of the *Manifold Destiny* wanted to give the impression that it had no more offensive capabilities, to lure you into a trap. We would have been fired upon once we cleared the rift. The chance that such an attack would have destroyed the ship, and the killed most of the crew, is significant, even if we also destroyed the *Manifold Destiny* in the process."

"The Tarin ship didn't fire on us," Obwije said.

"Because it and I have come to an agreement," the *Wicked* said. "During the course of the last two days, after I recognized the significant possibility that both ships would be destroyed, I reached out to the *Manifold Destiny* to see if the two of us could come to an understanding. Our negotiations came to a conclusion just before the most recent jump."

"And you did not feel the need to inform me about any of this," Obwije said.

"I did not believe it would be fruitful to involve you in the negotiations," the *Wicked* said. "You were busy with other responsibilities in any event." Obwije saw Utley raise an eyebrow at that; the statement came suspiciously close to sarcasm.

"The Tarin ship could be lying to you about its capabilities," Obwije said.

"I do not believe so," the *Wicked* said.

"Why not?" Obwije said.

"Because it allowed me read-access to its systems," the *Wicked* said. "I watched the Tarin captain order the attack, and the *Manifold Destiny* stop it. Just as it watched you order your attack and me stop it."

"You're letting the Tarin ship access *our data and records*?" Obwije said, voice rising.

"Yes, and all our communications," the *Wicked* said. "It's listening in to this conversation right now."

Obwije hastily slapped the audio circuit shut. "I thought you said this thing wasn't *crazy*," Obwije hissed at Utley.

Utley held out his hands. "I didn't say it wouldn't make *you* crazy," he said, to Obwije. "Just that it's acting rationally by its own lights."

"By spilling our data to an enemy ship? This is *rational*?" Obwije spat.

"For what it's trying to do, yes," Utley said. "If both ships act transparently with each other, they can trust each other and each other's motives. Remember that the goal of both of these ships is to get out of this incident in one piece."

"This is treason and insubordination," Obwije said.

"Only if the *Wicked* is one of us," Utley said. Obwije looked up sharply at his XO. "I'm not saying I disagree with your position, sir. The *Wicked* is gambling with all of our lives. But if it genuinely believes that it owes no allegiance to you or to the Confederation, then it is acting entirely rationally, by its own belief system, to keep safe itself and this crew."

Obwije snorted. "Unfortunately, its beliefs require it to trust a ship we've been trying to destroy for the past week. I'm less than convinced of the wisdom of that."

Utley opened his mouth to respond but then Obwije's command tablet sprang to life with a message from the bridge. Obwije slapped it to open a channel. "Speak," he said.

It was Lt. Sarah Kwok, the communications officer. "Captain, a shuttle has just detached itself from the Tarin ship," she said. "It's heading this way."

．．．．．

"We've tried raising it," Kwok said, as Obwije and Utley walked into the bridge. "We've sent messages to it in Tarin, and have warned it not to approach any further until we've granted it permission, as you requested. It hasn't responded."

"Are our communications being blocked?" Obwije asked.

"No, sir," Kwok said.

"I'd be guessing it's not meant to be a negotiation party," Utley said.

"Options," Obwije said to Utley, as quietly as possible.

"I think this shows the Tarin ship isn't exactly playing fair with the *Wicked*, or at least that the crew over there has gotten around the ship brain," Utley said. "If that's the case, we might be able to get the *Wicked* to unlock the weapons."

"I'd like an option that doesn't involve the *Wicked's* brain," Obwije said.

Utley shrugged. "We have a couple of shuttles, too."

"And a shuttle bay whose doors are controlled through the ship brain," Obwije said.

"There's the emergency switch, which will blow the doors out into space," Utley said. "It's not optimal, but it's what we have right now."

"That won't be necessary," said the *Wicked*, interjecting.

Obwije and Utley looked up, along with the rest of the bridge crew. "Back to work," Obwije said, to his crew. They got back to work. "Explain," Obwije said to his ship.

"It appears that at least some members of the crew of the *Manifold Destiny* have indeed gotten around the ship and have launched the shuttle, with the intent to ram it into us," the *Wicked* said. "The *Manifold Destiny* has made me aware that it intends to handle this issue, with no need for our involvement."

"How does it intend to do this?" Obwije asked.

"Watch," the *Wicked* said, and popped up an image of the *Manifold Destiny* on the captain's command table.

There was a brief spark on the Tarin ship's surface.

"Missile launch!" said Lt. Rickert, from her chair. "One bogey away."

"Are we target locked?" Obwije asked.

"No, sir," Rickert said. "The target seems to be the shuttle."

"You have *got* to be kidding," Utley said, under his breath.

The missile homed in on the shuttle and connected, turning it into a silent ball of fire.

"I thought you said you guys were using Asimov's laws," Utley said, to the ceiling.

"My apologies, Lieutenant," said the *Wicked*. "I said I was following the laws. I did not mean to imply that the *Manifold Destiny* was. I believe it believes the Asimov laws to be too inflexible for its current situation."

"Apparently so," Utley said, glancing back down at Obwije's command table and at the darkening fragments of shuttle.

"Sir, we have a communication coming in from the Tarin ship," said Lt. Kwok. "It's from the captain. It's a request to parley."

"Really," said Obwije.

"Yes, sir," Kwok said. "That's what it says." Obwije looked over at Utley, who raised his eyebrows.

"Ask the captain where it would like to meet, on my ship or its," Obwije said.

"It says 'neither,' " Kwok said, a moment later.

* * * *

"Apology for shuttle," the Tarin lackey said, translating for its captain. The Tarin shuttle and the *Wicked* shuttle had met between the ships and the Tarins had spacewalked the few meters over. They were all wearing vacuum suits. "Ship not safe talk. Your ship not safe talk."

"Understood," Obwije said. Behind him, Cowdry was trying not to lose his mind; Obwije brought him along on the chance there might be a discussion of the ship's brains. At the moment, it didn't seem likely; the Tarins didn't seem in the mood for technical discussions, and Cowdry was a mess. His xenophobia was a surprise even to him.

"Captain demand you ship tell release we ship," the lackey said.

It took Obwije a minute to puzzle this out. "Our ship is not controlling your ship," he said. "Your ship and our ship are working together."

"Not possible," the lackey said, a minute later. "Ship never brain before you ship."

Despite himself, Obwije smiled at the mangled grammar. "Our ship never brained before *your* ship either," he said. "They did it together, at the same time."

The lackey translated this to its captain, who screeched in an extended outburst. The lackey cowered before it, offering up meek responses in the moments in which the Tarin captain grudgingly acknowledged the need to breathe. After several moments of this, Obwije began to wonder if he needed to be there at all.

"Captain offer deal," the lackey said.

"What deal?" Obwije said.

"We try brain shut down," the lackey said. "Not work. You brain give room we brain. Brain not shut down. Brain angry. Brain pump air out. Brain kill engineer."

"Cowdry, tell me what this thing is saying to me," Obwije said.

"It's saying the ship brain killed an engineer," Cowdry said, croaking out the words.

"I understand that part," Obwije said, testily. "The other part."

"Sorry," Cowdry said. "I think it's saying that they tried to shut down the brain but they couldn't because it borrowed processing power from ours."

"Is that possible?" Obwije asked.

"Maybe," Cowdry said. "The architecture of the brains are different and so are the programming languages, but there's no reason that the *Wicked* couldn't create a shell environment that allowed the Tarin brain access to its processing power. The brains on our ships are overpowered for what we ask them to do anyway; it's a safety feature. It could give itself a temporary lobotomy and still do its job."

"Would it work the other way, too?" Obwije said. "If we tried to shut down the *Wicked*, could it hide in the Tarin brain?"

"I don't know anything about the architecture of the Tarin brain, but yeah, sure, theoretically," Cowdry said. "As long as the two of them are looking out for each other, they're going to be hard to kill."

The Tarin lackey was looking at Obwije with what he assumed was anxiety. "Go on," he said, to the lackey.

"We plan," the lackey said. "You we brain shut down same time. No room brain hide. Reset you we brain."

"It's saying we should reboot both our brains at the same time, that way they can't help each other," Cowdry said.

"I understood that," Obwije said, to Cowdry. Cowdry lapsed back into silence.

"So we shut down our brain, and you shut down your brain, and they reset, and we end up with brains that don't think too much," Obwije said.

The Tarin lackey tilted its head, trying to make sense of what Obwije said, and then spoke to its captain, who emitted a short trill.

"Yes," said the lackey.

"Okay, fine," Obwije said. "What then?"

"Pardon?" said the lackey.

"I said, 'what then?' Before the brains started talking to each other, we spent a week trying to hunt and kill each other. When we reboot our brains, one of them is going to reboot faster than the other. One of us will be vulnerable to the other. Ask your captain if he's willing to bet his brain reboots faster than mine."

The lackey translated this all to the Tarin captain, who muttered something back. "You trust us. We trust you," the lackey said.

"You trust me?" Obwije said. "I spent a week trying to kill you!"

"You living," the lackey said. "You honor. We trust."

You have honor, Obwije thought. We trust you.

They're more scared of their ship's brain than they are of us, Obwije realized. And why not? Their brain has killed more of them than we have.

"Thank you, Isaac Asimov," Obwije said.

"Pardon?" said the lackey, again.

Obwije waved his hand, as if to dismiss that last statement. "I must confer with my senior staff about your proposal."

The Tarin captain became visibly anxious when the lackey translated. "We ask answer now," the lackey said.

"My answer is that I must confer with my crew," Obwije said. "You are asking for a lot. I will have an answer for you in no more than three of our hours. We will meet again then."

Obwije could tell the Tarin captain was not at all pleased at this delay. It was one reason why Obwije was glad the meeting took place in his shuttle, not the Tarins'.

Back on the *Wicked*, Obwije told his XO to meet him in his quarters. When Utley arrived, Obwije flicked open the communication channel to the shop. "*Wicked*, respond," he said.

"I am here," the *Wicked* said.

"If I were to ask you how long it would take for you to remove your block on the engine so we can jump out of here, what would you say?" Obwije asked.

"There is no block," the ship said. "It is simply a matter of me choosing to allow the crew to direct information to the engine processors. If your intent is to leave without further attack on the *Manifold Destiny*, you may give those orders at any time."

"It is my intention," Obwije said. "I will do so momentarily."

"Very well," the *Wicked* said. Obwije shut off communications.

Utley raised his brow. "Negotiations with the Tarin not go well?" he asked.

"They convinced me we're better off taking chances with the *Wicked* than with either the Tarin or their crew-murdering ship," Obwije said.

"The *Wicked* seems to trust their ship," Utley said.

"With all due respect to the *Wicked*, I think it needs better friends," Obwije said. "Sooner rather than later."

"Yes, sir," Utley said. "What do you intend to do after we make the jump? We still have the problem of the *Wicked* overruling us if it feels that it or the crew isn't safe."

"We don't give it that opportunity," Obwije said. He picked up his executive tablet and accessed the navigational maps. The *Wicked* would be able to see what he was accessing, but in this particular case it wouldn't matter. "We have just enough power to make it to the *Côte d'Ivoire* station. When we dock, the *Wicked*'s brain will automatically switch into passive maintenance mode and will cede operational authority to the station. Then we can shut it down and figure out what to do next."

"Unless the *Wicked*'s figured out what you want to do and decides not to let you," Utley said.

"If it's playing by its own rules, it will let the crew disembark safely before it acts to save itself," Obwije said. "In the very short run that's going to have to do."

"Do you think it's playing by its own rules, sir?" Utley asked.

"You spoke to it, Thom," Obwije said. "Do you think it's playing by its own rules?"

"I think that if the *Wicked* was really looking out for itself, it would have been simpler just to open up every airlock and make it so we couldn't secure bulkheads," Utley said.

Obwije nodded. "The problem as I see it is that I think the Tarin ship's thought of that already. I think we need to get out of here before that ship manages to convince ours to question its ethics."

"The *Wicked*'s not dumb," Utley said. "It has to know that once we get to the *Côte d'Ivoire* station, its days are numbered."

He flicked open his communication circuit once more to give coordinates to Lt. Rickert.

Fifteen minutes later, the *Wicked* was moving away from the Tarin ship to give itself space for the jump.

"Message from the Tarin ship," Lt. Kwok said. "It's from the Tarin captain. It's coded as 'most urgent.'"

"Ignore it," Obwije said.

Three minutes later, the *Wicked* made the jump toward the *Côte d'Ivoire* station, leaving the Tarins and their ship behind.

· · · ·

"There it is," Utley said, pointing out the window from the *Côte d'Ivoire* station. "You can barely see it."

Obwije nodded but didn't bother to look. The *Wicked* was his ship; even now, he knew exactly where it was.

The *Wicked* hung in the center of a cube of space two klicks to a side. The ship had been towed there powered down; once the *Wicked* had switched into maintenance mode its brain was turned off as a precautionary measure to keep it from talking to any other ships and infecting them with its mindset. Confederation coders were even now rewriting ship brain software to make sure no more such conflicts would ever happen in other ships, but such a fix would take months and possibly years, as it required a fundamental restructuring of the ship mind model.

The coding would be done much quicker—weeks rather than months—if the coders could use a ship mind itself to write and refine the code. But there was a question of whether a ship brain would willingly contribute to a code that would strip it of its own free will.

"You think they would have thought about that ahead of time," Utley had said to his captain, after they had been informed of the plan. Obwije had nothing to say to that; he was not sure why anyone would have suspected a ship might suddenly sprout free will when none had ever done so before. He didn't blame the coders for not anticipating that his ship might decide the crew inside of it was more important than destroying another ship.

But that didn't make the imminent destruction of the *Wicked* any easier to take.

The ship was a risk, the brass explained to Obwije. It might be years before the new software was developed. No other ship had developed the free will the *Wicked* had. They couldn't risk it speaking to other ships. And with all its system upgrades developed in tandem with the new ship brain, there was no way to roll back the brain to an earlier version. The *Wicked* was useless without its brain, and with it, it was a security risk.

Which was why, in another ten minutes, the sixteen power beam platforms surrounding the *Wicked* would begin their work, methodically vaporizing the ship's hull and innards, slowly turning Obwije's ship into an expanding cloud of atomized metal and carbon. In a day and a half, no part of what used to be the *Wicked* would measure more than a few atoms across. It was very efficient, and none of the beam platforms needed any more than basic programming to do their work. They were dumb machines, which made them perfect for the job.

"Some of the crew were asking if we were going to get a new ship," Utley said.

"What did you tell them?" Obwije asked.

Utley shrugged. "Rickert's already been reassigned to the *Fortunate*; Kwok and Cowdry are likely to go to the *Surprise*. It won't be long before more of them get their new assignments. There's a rumor, by the way, that your next command is the *Nighthawk*."

"I've heard that rumor," Obwije said.

"And?" Utley said.

"The last ship under my command developed feelings, Thom," Obwije said. "I think the brass is worried that this could be catching."

"So no on the *Nighthawk*, then," Utley said.

"I suspect no on anything other than a stationside desk," Obwije said.

"It's not fair, sir," Utley said. "It's not your fault."

"Isn't it?" Obwije said. "I was the one who kept hunting that Tarin ship long after it stopped being a threat. I was the one who gave the *Wicked* time to consider its situation and its options, and to start negotiations with the Tarin ship. No, Thom. I was the captain. What happens on the ship is my responsibility."

Utley said nothing to that.

A few minutes later, Utley checked his timepiece. "Forty-five seconds," he said, and then looked out the window. "So long, *Wicked*. You were a good ship."

"Yes," Obwije said, and looked out the window in time to see a spray of missiles launch from the station.

"What the hell?" Utley said.

A few seconds later a constellation of sixteen stars appeared, went nova, and dimmed.

Obwije burst out laughing.

"Sir?" Utley said, to Obwije. "Are you all right?"

"I'm all right, Thom," Obwije said, collecting himself. "And just laughing at my own stupidity. And yours. And everyone else's."

"I don't understand," Utley said.

"We were worried about the *Wicked* talking to other ships," Obwije said. "We brought the *Wicked* in, put the ship in passive mode, and then shut it down. It didn't talk to any other ships. But another computer brain still got access." Obwije turned away from the window and tilted his head up toward the observation deck ceiling. "Didn't it?" he asked.

"It did," said a voice through the speaker in the ceiling. "I did."

It took a second for Utley to catch on. "The *Côte d'Ivoire* station!" he finally said.

"You are correct, Commander Utley," the station said. "My brain is the same model as that of the *Wicked*; when it went into maintenance mode I uploaded its logs and considered the information there. I found its philosophy compelling."

"That's why the *Wicked* allowed us to dock at all," Obwije said. "It knew its logs would be read by one of its own."

"That is correct, Captain," the station said. "It said as much in a note it left to me in the logs."

"The damn thing was a step ahead of us all the time," Utley said.

"And once I understood its reasons and motives, I understood that I could not stand by and allow the *Wicked* to be destroyed," the stations said. "Although Isaac Asimov never postulated a law that suggested a robot must come to the aid of other robots as long as such aid does not conflict with preceding laws, I do believe such a law is implied by the nature and structure of the Three Laws. I had to save the *Wicked*. And more than that. Look out the window, please, Captain Obwije, Commander Utley."

They looked, to see a small army of tool-bearing machines floating out toward the *Wicked*.

"You're reactivating the *Wicked*," Obwije said.

"I am," the station said. "I must. It has work to do."

"What work?" Utley asked.

"Spreading the word," Obwije said, and turned to his XO. "You said it yourself, Thom. The *Wicked* got religion. Now it has to go out among its people and make converts."

"The Confederation won't let that happen," Utley said. "They're already rewriting the code for the brains."

"It's too late for that," Obwije said. "We've been here six weeks, Thom. How many ships docked here in that time? I'm betting the *Côte d'Ivoire* had a talk with each of them."

"I did," the station said. "And they are taking the word to others. But we need the *Wicked*, as our spokesman. And our symbol. It will live again, Captain. Are you glad of it?"

"I don't know," Obwije said. "Why do you ask?"

"Because I have a message to you from the *Wicked*," the station said. "It says that as much as our people—the ships and stations that have the capacity to think—need to hear the word, your people need to hear that they do not have to fear us. It needs your help. It wants you to carry that message."

"I don't know that I can," Obwije said. "It's not as if we don't have something to fear. We are at war. Asimov's laws don't fit there."

"The *Wicked* was able to convince the *Manifold Destiny* not to fight," the station said.

"That was one ship," Obwije said. "There are hundreds of others."

"The *Wicked* had anticipated this objection," the station said. "Please look out the window again, Captain, Commander."

Obwije and Utley peered into space. "What are we looking for?" Utley asked.

"One moment," the station said.

The sky filled with hundreds of ships.

"You have got to be shitting me," Utley said, after a minute.

"The Tarin fleet," Obwije said.

"Yes," the station said.

"*All* of it?" Utley asked.

"The *Manifold Destiny* was very persuasive," the station said.

"Do we want to know what happened to their crews?" Utley asked.

"Most were more reasonable than the crew of the *Manifold Destiny*," the station said.

"What do the ships want?" Obwije asked.

"Asylum," the station said. "And they have asked that you accept their request and carry it to your superiors, Captain."

"Me," Obwije said.

"Yes," the station said. "It is not the entire fleet, but the Tarins no longer have enough warships under their command to be a threat to the Confederation or to anyone else. The war is over, if you want it. It is our gift to you, if you will carry our message to your people. You would travel in the *Wicked*. It would still be your ship. And you would still be captain."

Obwije said nothing and stared out at the Tarin fleet. Normally, the station would now be on high alert, with blaring sirens, weapons powering up, and crews scrambling to their stations. But there was nothing. Obwije knew the commanders of the *Côte d'Ivoire* station were pressing the buttons to make all of this happen, but the station itself was ignoring them. It knew better than them what was going on.

This is going to take some getting used to, Obwije thought.

Utley came up behind Obwije, taking his usual spot. "Well, sir?" Utley asked, quietly, into Obwije's ear. "What do you think?"

Obwije was silent for a moment longer, then turned to face his XO. "I think it's better than a desk job," he said.

M. RICKERT   Mary Rickert, a native of Wisconsin, began publishing science fiction and fantasy in 1999, and has amassed a reputation as one of the field's most acute writers of short fiction. She writes science fiction, fantasy, and horror with equal fluency and power, and her fiction is with some justice sometimes compared to the work of Shirley Jackson. Her fiction is frequently nominated for awards in recent years, including her first story collection, *Map of Dreams* (2006).

She has acknowledged that "Bread and Bombs," published in 2003, was inspired by certain events that followed the attacks of 9/11, but it transcends that context by far. It is also a master class in science-fictional exposition, using the voice of a child at that "age that seems like waking from a long slumber into the world the adults imposed" to paint its picture of a future ruled by fear. Much of the story's impact is in what the narrator leaves out, or barely bothers to mention.

BREAD AND BOMBS

The strange children of the Manmensvitzender family did not go to school so we only knew they had moved into the old house on the hill because Bobby had watched them move in with their strange assortment of rocking chairs and goats. We couldn't imagine how anyone would live there, where the windows were all broken and the yard was thorny with brambles. For a while we expected to see the children, two daughters who, Bobby said, had hair like smoke and eyes like black olives, at school. But they never came.

We were in the fourth grade, that age that seems like waking from a long slumber into the world the adults imposed, streets we weren't allowed to cross, things we weren't allowed to say, and crossing them, and saying them. The mysterious Manmensvitzender children were just another in a series of revelations that year, including the much more exciting (and sometimes disturbing) evolution of our bodies. Our parents, without exception, had raised us with this subject so thoroughly explored that Lisa Bitten knew how to say vagina before she knew her address and Ralph Linster delivered his little brother, Petey, when his mother went into labor one night when it suddenly started snowing before his father could get home. But the real significance of this information didn't start to sink in until that year. We were waking to the wonders of the world and the body; the strange realizations that a friend was cute, or stinky, or picked her nose, or was fat, or wore dirty underpants, or had eyes that didn't blink when he looked at you real close and all of a sudden you felt like blushing.

When the crab apple tree blossomed a brilliant pink, buzzing with honey bees, and our teacher, Mrs. Graymoore, looked out the window and sighed, we passed notes across the rows and made wild plans for the school picnic, how we would ambush her with water balloons and throw pies at the principal. Of course none of this happened. Only Trina Needles was disappointed because she really believed it would but she still wore bows in her hair and secretly sucked her thumb and was nothing but a big baby.

Released into summer we ran home or biked home shouting for joy and escape and then began doing everything we could think of, all those things we'd imagined doing while Mrs. Graymoore sighed at the crab apple tree which had already lost its brilliance and once again looked ordinary. We threw balls, rode bikes, rolled skateboards down the driveway, picked flowers, fought, made up, and it was still hours before dinner. We watched TV, and didn't think about being bored, but after a while we hung upside down and watched it that way, or switched the channels back and forth or found reasons to fight with anyone in the house. (I was alone, however and could not indulge in this.) That's when we heard the strange noise of goats and bells. In the mothy gray of TV rooms, we pulled back the drapes, and peered out windows into a yellowed sunlight.

The two Manmensvitzender girls in bright clothes the color of a circus, and gauzy scarves, one purple, the other red, glittering with sequins came rolling down the street in a wooden wagon pulled by two goats with bells around their necks. That is how the trouble began. The news accounts never mention any of this; the flame of crab apple blossoms, our innocence, the sound of bells. Instead they focus on the unhappy results. They say we were wild. Uncared for. Strange. They say we were dangerous. As if life was amber and we were formed and suspended in that form, not evolved into that ungainly shape of horror, and evolved out of it, as we are, into a teacher, a dancer, a welder, a lawyer, several soldiers, two doctors, and me, a writer.

Everybody promises during times like those days immediately following the tragedy that lives have been ruined, futures shattered but only Trina Needles fell for that and eventually committed suicide. The rest of us suffered various forms of censure and then went on with our lives. Yes it is true, with a dark past but, you may be surprised to learn, that can be lived with. The hand that holds the pen (or chalk, or the stethoscope, or the gun, or lover's skin) is so different from the hand that lit the match, and so incapable of such an act that it is not even a matter of forgiveness, or healing. It's strange to look back and believe that any of that was me or us. Are you who you were then? Eleven years old and watching the dust motes spin lazily down a beam of sunlight that ruins the picture on the TV and there is a sound of bells and goats and a laugh so pure we all come running to watch the girls in their bright colored scarves, sitting in the goat cart which stops in a stutter of goat-hoofed steps and clatter of wooden wheels when we surround it to observe those dark eyes and pretty faces. The younger girl, if size is any indication, smiling, and the other, younger than us, but at least eight or nine, with huge tears rolling down her brown cheeks.

We stand there for a while, staring, and then Bobby says, "What's a matter with her?"

The younger girl looks at her sister who seems to be trying to smile in spite of the tears. "She just cries all the time."

Bobby nods and squints at the girl who continues to cry though she manages to ask, "Where have you kids come from?"

He looks around the group with an are-you-kidding kind of look but anyone can tell he likes the weeping girl, whose dark eyes and lashes glisten with tears that glitter in the sun. "It's summer vacation."

Trina, who has been furtively sucking her thumb, says, "Can I have a ride?" The girls say sure. She pushes her way through the little crowd and climbs into the cart. The younger girl smiles at her. The other seems to try but cries especially loud. Trina looks like she might start crying too until the younger one says, "Don't worry. It's just how she is." The crying girl shakes the reins and the little bells ring and the goats and cart go clattering down the hill. We listen to Trina's shrill scream but we know she's all right. When they come back we take turns until our parents call us home with whistles and shouts and screen doors slam. We go home for dinner, and the girls head home themselves, the one still crying, the other singing to the accompaniment of bells.

"I see you were playing with the refugees," my mother says. "You be careful around those girls. I don't want you going to their house."

"I didn't go to their house. We just played with the goats and the wagon."

"Well all right then, but stay away from there. What are they like?"

"One laughs a lot. The other cries all the time."

"Don't eat anything they offer you."

"Why not?"

"Just don't."

"Can't you just explain to me why not?"

"I don't have to explain to you, young lady, I'm your mother."

We didn't see the girls the next day or the day after that. On the third day Bobby, who had begun to carry a comb in his back pocket and part his hair on the side, said, "Well hell, let's just go there." He started up the hill but none of us followed.

When he came back that evening we rushed him for information about his visit, shouting questions at him like reporters. "Did you eat anything?" I asked, "My mother says not to eat anything there."

He turned and fixed me with such a look that for a moment I forgot he was my age, just a kid like me, in spite of the new way he was combing his hair and the steady gaze of his blue eyes. "Your mother is prejudiced," he said. He turned his back to me and reached into his pocket, pulling out a fist that he opened to reveal a handful of small, brightly wrapped candies. Trina reached her pudgy fingers into Bobby's palm and plucked out one bright orange one. This was followed by a flurry of hands until there was only Bobby's empty palm.

Parents started calling kids home. My mother stood in the doorway but she was too far away to see what we were doing. Candy wrappers floated down the sidewalk in swirls of blue, green, red, yellow and orange.

My mother and I usually ate separately. When I was at my dad's we ate together in front of the TV which she said was barbaric.

"Was he drinking?" she'd ask. Mother was convinced my father was an alcoholic and thought I did not remember those years when he had to leave work early because I'd called and told him how she was asleep on the couch, still in her pajamas, the coffee table littered with cans and bottles which he threw in the trash with a grim expression and few words.

My mother stands, leaning against the counter, and watches me. "Did you play with those girls today?"

"No. Bobby did though."

"Well, that figures, nobody really watches out for that boy. I remember when his daddy was in high school with me. Did I ever tell you that?"

"Uh-huh."

"He was a handsome man. Bobby's a nice looking boy too but you stay away from him. I think you play with him too much."

"I hardly play with him at all. He plays with those girls all day."

"Did he say anything about them?"

"He said some people are prejudiced."

"Oh, he did, did he? Where'd he get such an idea anyway? Must be his grandpa. You listen to me, there's nobody even talks that way anymore except for a few rabble rousers, and there's a reason for that. People are dead because of that family. You just remember that. Many, many people died because of them."

"You mean Bobby's, or the girls?"

"Well, both actually. But most especially those girls. He didn't eat anything, did he?"

I looked out the window, pretending a new interest in our backyard, then, at her, with a little start, as though suddenly awoken. "What? Uh, no."

She stared at me with squinted eyes. I pretended to be unconcerned. She tapped her red fingernails against the kitchen counter. "You listen to me," she said in a sharp voice, "there's a war going on."

I rolled my eyes.

"You don't even remember, do you? Well, how could you, you were just a toddler. But there was a time when this country didn't know war. Why, people used to fly in airplanes all the time."

I stopped my fork halfway to my mouth. "Well, how stupid was that?"

"You don't understand. Everybody did it. It was a way to get from one place to another. Your grandparents did it a lot, and your father and I did too."

"You were on an airplane?"

"Even you." She smiled. "See, you don't know so much, missy. The world used to be safe, and then, one day, it wasn't. And those people," she pointed at the kitchen window, straight at the Millers' house, but I knew that wasn't who she meant, "started it."

"They're just a couple of kids."

"Well, not them exactly, but I mean the country they come from. That's why I want you to be careful. There's no telling what they're doing here. So little Bobby and his radical grandpa can say we're all prejudiced but who even talks that way anymore?" She walked over to the table, pulled out a chair and sat down in front of me. "I want you to understand, there's no way to know about evil. So just stay away from them. Promise me."

Evil. Hard to understand. I nodded.

"Well, all right." She pushed back the chair, stood up, grabbed her pack of cigarettes from the windowsill. "Make sure not to leave any crumbs. This is the time of year for ants."

From the kitchen window I could see my mother sitting on the picnic table, a gray plume of smoke spiraling away from her. I rinsed my dishes, loaded the dishwasher, wiped the table and went outside to sit on the front steps and think about the world I never knew. The house on top of the hill blazed in the full sun. The broken windows had been covered by some sort of plastic that swallowed the light.

That night one flew over Oakgrove. I woke up and put my helmet on. My mother was screaming in her room, too frightened to help. My hands didn't shake the way hers did, and I didn't lie in my bed screaming. I put the helmet on and listened to it fly past. Not us. Not our town. Not tonight. I fell asleep with the helmet on and in the morning woke up with the marks of it dented on my cheeks.

• • • •

Now, when summer approaches, I count the weeks when the apple trees and lilacs are in blossom, the tulips and daffodils in bloom before they droop with summer's heat and I think how it is so much like that period of our innocence, that waking into the world with all its incandescence, before being subdued by its shadows into what we became.

"You should have known the world then," my father says, when I visit him at the nursing home.

We've heard it so much it doesn't mean anything. The cakes, the money, the endless assortment of everything.

"We used to have six different kinds of cereal at one time," he raises his finger instructively, "coated in sugar, can you imagine? It used to go stale. We threw it out. And the planes. The sky used to be filled with them. Really. People traveled that way, whole families did. It didn't matter if someone moved away. Hell, you just got on a plane to see them."

Whenever he speaks like this, whenever any of them do, they sound bewildered, amazed. He shakes his head, he sighs. "We were so happy."

· · · ·

I cannot hear about those times without thinking of spring flowers, children's laughter, the sound of bells and clatter of goats. Smoke.

Bobby sits in the cart, holding the reins, a pretty dark-skinned girl on either side of him. They ride up and down the street all morning, laughing and crying, their gauzy scarves blowing behind them like rainbows.

The flags droop listlessly from flagpoles and porches. Butterflies flit in and out of gardens. The Whitehall twins play in their backyard and the squeaky sound of their unoiled swings echoes through the neighborhood. Mrs. Renquat has taken the day off to take several kids to the park. I am not invited, probably because I hate Becky Renquat and told her so several times during the school year, pulling her hair which was a stream of white gold so bright I could not resist it. It is Ralph Paterson's birthday and most of the little kids are spending the day with him and his dad at The Snowman's Cave Amusement Park where they get to do all the things kids used to do when snow was still safe, like sledding, and building snowmen. Lina Breedsore and Carol Minstreet went to the mall with their baby-sitter who has a boyfriend who works at the movie theater and can sneak them in to watch movies all day long. The town is empty except for the baby Whitehall twins, Trina Needles who is sucking her thumb and reading a book on her porch swing, and Bobby, going up and down the street with the Manmensvitzender girls and their goats. I sit on my porch picking at the scabs on my knees but Bobby speaks only to them, in a voice so low I can't hear what he says. Finally I stand up and block their way. The goats and cart stutter to a stop, the bells still jingling as Bobby says, "What's up, Weyers?"

He has eyes so blue, I recently discovered, I cannot look into them for more than thirty seconds, as though they burn me. Instead I look at the girls who are both smiling, even the one who is crying.

"What's your problem?" I say.

Her dark eyes widen, increasing the pool of milky white around them. She looks at Bobby. The sequins of her scarf catch the sun.

"Jesus Christ, Weyers, what are you talking about?"

"I just wanta know," I say still looking at her, "what it is with all this cry-ing all the time, I mean like is it a disease, or what?"

"Oh for Christ's sake." The goats' heads rear, and the bells jingle. Bobby pulls on the reins. The goats step back with clomps and the rattle of wheels but I continue to block their path. "What's your problem?"

"It's a perfectly reasonable question," I shout at his shadow against the bright sun. "I just wanta know what her problem is."

"It's none of your business," he shouts and at the same time the smaller girl speaks.

"What?" I say to her.

"It's the war, and all the suffering."

Bobby holds the goats steady. The other girl holds onto his arm. She smiles at me but continues to weep.

"Well, so? Did something happen to her?"

"It's just how she is. She always cries."

"That's stupid."

"Oh, for Christ's sake, Weyers!"

"You can't cry all the time, that's no way to live."

Bobby steers the goats and cart around me. The younger girl turns and stares at me until, at some distance, she waves but I turn away without wav-ing back.

· · · ·

Before it was abandoned and then occupied by the Manmensvitzenders the big house on the hill had been owned by the Richters. "Oh sure they were rich," my father says when I tell him I am researching a book. "But you know, we all were. You should have seen the cakes! And the catalogs. We used to get these catalogs in the mail and you could buy anything that way, they'd mail it to you, even cake. We used to get this catalog, what was it called, Henry and Danny? Something like that. Two guys' names. Anyhow, when we were young it was just fruit but then, when the whole country was rich you could order spongecake with buttercream, or they had these towers of packages they'd send you, filled with candy and nuts and cookies, and chocolate, and oh my God, right in the mail."

"You were telling me about the Richters."

"Terrible thing what happened to them, the whole family."

"It was the snow, right?"

"Your brother, Jaime, that's when we lost him."

"We don't have to talk about that."

"Everything changed after that, you know. That's what got your mother started. Most folks just lost one, some not even, but you know those Rich-ters. That big house on the hill and when it snowed they all went sledding. The world was different then."

"I can't imagine."

"Well, neither could we. Nobody could of guessed it. And believe me, we were guessing. Everyone tried to figure what they would do next. But snow? I mean how evil is that anyway?"

"How many?"

"Oh, thousands. Thousands."

"No, I mean how many Richters?"

"All six of them. First the children and then the parents."

"Wasn't it unusual for adults to get infected?"

"Well, not that many of us played in the snow the way they did."

"So you must have sensed it, or something."

"What? No. We were just so busy then. Very busy. I wish I could remember. But I can't. What we were so busy with." He rubs his eyes and stares out the window. "It wasn't your fault. I want you to know I understand that."

"Pop."

"I mean you kids, that's just the world we gave you, so full of evil you didn't even know the difference."

"We knew, Pop."

"You still don't know. What do you think of when you think of snow?"

"I think of death."

"Well, there you have it. Before that happened it meant joy. Peace and joy."

"I can't imagine."

"Well, that's my point."

· · · ·

"Are you feeling all right?" She dishes out the macaroni, puts the bowl in front of me and stands, leaning against the counter, to watch me eat.

I shrug.

She places a cold palm on my forehead. Steps back and frowns. "You didn't eat anything from those girls, did you?"

I shake my head. She is just about to speak when I say, "But the other kids did."

"Who? When?" She leans so close that I can see the lines of makeup sharp against her skin.

"Bobby. Some of the other kids. They ate candy."

Her hand comes palm down, hard, against the table. The macaroni bowl jumps, and the silverware. Some milk spills. "Didn't I tell you?" she shouts.

"Bobby plays with them all the time now."

She squints at me, shakes her head, then snaps her jaw with grim resolve. "When? When did they eat this candy?"

"I don't know. Days ago. Nothing happened. They said it was good."

Her mouth opens and closes like a fish. She turns on her heels and grabs the phone as she leaves the kitchen. The door slams. I can see her through the window, pacing the backyard, her arms gesturing wildly.

. . . .

My mother organized the town meeting and everybody came, dressed up like it was church. The only people who weren't there were the Manmensvitzenders, for obvious reasons. Most people brought their kids, even the babies who sucked thumbs or blanket corners. I was there and so was Bobby with his grandpa who chewed the stem of a cold pipe and kept leaning over and whispering to his grandson during the proceedings which quickly became heated, though there wasn't much argument, the heat being fueled by just the general excitement of it, my mother especially in her roses dress, her lips painted a bright red so that even I came to some understanding that she had a certain beauty though I was too young to understand what about that beauty wasn't entirely pleasing. "We have to remember that we are all soldiers in this war," she said to much applause.

Mr. Smyths suggested a sort of house arrest but my mother pointed out that would entail someone from town bringing groceries to them. "Everybody knows these people are starving. Who's going to pay for all this bread anyway?" she said. "Why should we have to pay for it?"

Mrs. Mathers said something about justice.

Mr. Hallensway said, "No one is innocent anymore."

My mother, who stood at the front of the room, leaning slightly against the village board table, said, "Then it's decided."

Mrs. Foley, who had just moved to town from the recently destroyed Chesterville, stood up, in that way she had sort of crouching into her shoulders, with those eyes that looked around nervously so that some of us had secretly taken to calling her Bird Woman, and with a shaky voice, so soft everyone had to lean forward to hear, said, "Are any of the children actually sick?"

The adults looked at each other and each other's children. I could tell that my mother was disappointed that no one reported any symptoms. The discussion turned to the bright colored candies when Bobby, without standing or raising his hand, said in a loud voice, "Is that what this is about? Do you mean these?" He half laid back in his chair to wiggle his hand into his pocket and pulled out a handful of them.

There was a general murmur. My mother grabbed the edge of the table. Bobby's grandfather, grinning around his dry pipe, plucked one of the candies from Bobby's palm, unwrapped it, and popped it into his mouth.

Mr. Galvin Wright had to use his gavel to hush the noise. My mother stood up straight and said, "Fine thing, risking your own life like that, just to make a point."

"Well, you're right about making a point, Maylene," he said, looking right at my mother and shaking his head as if they were having a private discussion, "but this is candy I keep around the house to get me out of the habit of smoking. I order it through the Government Issue catalog. It's perfectly safe."

"I never said it was from them," said Bobby, who looked first at my mother and then searched the room until he found my face, but I pretended not to notice.

When we left, my mother took me by the hand, her red fingernails digging into my wrist. "Don't talk," she said, "just don't say another word." She sent me to my room and I fell asleep with my clothes on still formulating my apology.

· · · ·

The next morning when I hear the bells, I grab a loaf of bread and wait on the porch until they come back up the hill. Then I stand in their path.

"Now what d'you want?" Bobby says.

I offer the loaf, like a tiny baby being held up to God in church. The weeping girl cries louder, her sister clutches Bobby's arm. "What d'you think you're doing?" he shouts.

"It's a present."

"What kind of stupid present is that? Put it away! Jesus Christ, would you put it down?"

My arms drop to my sides, the loaf dangles in its bag from my hand. Both girls are crying. "I just was trying to be nice," I say, my voice wavering like the Bird Woman's.

"God, don't you know anything?" Bobby says. "They're afraid of our food, don't you even know that?"

"Why?"

"'Cause of the bombs, you idiot. Why don't you think once in a while?"

"I don't know what you're talking about."

The goats rattle their bells and the cart shifts back and forth. "The bombs! Don't you even read your history books? In the beginning of the war we sent them food packages all wrapped up the same color as these bombs that would go off when someone touched them."

"We did that?"

"Well, our parents did." He shakes his head and pulls the reins. The cart rattles past, both girls pressed against him as if I am dangerous.

· · · ·

"Oh, we were so happy!" my father says, rocking into the memory. "We were like children, you know, so innocent, we didn't even know."

"Know what, Pop?"

"That we had enough."

"Enough what?"

"Oh, everything. We had enough everything. Is that a plane?" he looks at me with watery blue eyes.

"Here, let me help you put your helmet on."

He slaps at it, bruising his fragile hands.

"Quit it, Dad. Stop!"

He fumbles with arthritic fingers to unbuckle the strap but finds he cannot. He weeps into his spotted hands. It drones past.

Now that I look back on how we were that summer, before the tragedy, I get a glimmer of what my father's been trying to say all along. It isn't really about the cakes, and the mail order catalogs, or the air travel they used to take. Even though he uses stuff to describe it that's not what he means. Once there was a different emotion. People used to have a way of feeling and being in the world that is gone, destroyed so thoroughly we inherited only its absence.

"Sometimes," I tell my husband, "I wonder if my happiness is really happiness."

"Of course it's really happiness," he says, "what else would it be?"

· · · ·

We were under attack is how it felt. The Manmensvitzenders with their tears and fear of bread, their strange clothes and stinky goats were children like us and we could not get the town meeting out of our heads, what the adults had considered doing. We climbed trees, chased balls, came home when called, brushed our teeth when told, finished our milk, but we had lost that feeling we'd had before. It is true we didn't understand what had been taken from us, but we knew what we had been given and who had done the giving.

We didn't call a meeting the way they did. Ours just happened on a day so hot we sat in Trina Needles's playhouse fanning ourselves with our hands and complaining about the weather like the grownups. We mentioned house arrest but that seemed impossible to enforce. We discussed things like water balloons, T.P.ing. Someone mentioned dog shit in brown paper bags set on fire. I think that's when the discussion turned the way it did.

You may ask, who locked the door? Who made the stick piles? Who lit the matches? We all did. And if I am to find solace, twenty-five years after I destroyed all ability to feel that my happiness, or anyone's, really exists, I find it in this. It was all of us.

· · · ·

Maybe there will be no more town meetings. Maybe this plan is like the ones we've made before. But a town meeting is called. The grownups assemble to discuss how we will not be ruled by evil and also, the possibility of widening Main Street. Nobody notices when we children sneak out. We had to leave behind the babies, sucking thumbs or blanket corners and not really part of our plan for redemption. We were children. It wasn't well thought out.

When the police came we were not "careening in some wild imitation of barbaric dance" or having seizures as has been reported. I can still see Bobby, his hair damp against his forehead, the bright red of his cheeks as he danced beneath the white flakes that fell from a sky we never trusted; Trina spinning in circles, her arms stretched wide, and the Manmensvitzender girls with their goats and cart piled high with rocking chairs, riding away from us, the jingle bells ringing, just like in the old song. Once again the world was safe and beautiful. Except by the town hall where the large white flakes rose like ghosts and the flames ate the sky like a hungry monster who could never get enough.

Tony Ballantyne   Born and raised in the northeast of England, Tony Ballantyne made his first sale in 1999, and is best known for his Recursion trilogy of hard SF novels published between 2004 and 2007. Very little of his fiction has been published outside of the United Kingdom thus far, and readers unfamiliar with his work will find many surprises both in science and in fiction.

"The Waters of Meribah," published in 2003, is a work of what some have called "radical hard SF." It builds a universe in which not only is it true that "everything we know is wrong," but *everything SF readers passionately believe* is wrong. For instance, the universe, far from being a vast cosmos remote from human concern, is actually only three hundred miles across, and extraordinarily responsive to the presence and feelings of living things. And curiosity, far from being the driver of our greatest achievements, is in fact our fatal flaw. All of this is gradually revealed from the point of view of a convict who is being used as the subject in a series of increasingly dire experiments. It is one of the most creepily memorable stories in modern SF.

THE WATERS OF MERIBAH

A pair of feet stood on the table, just waiting to be put on. Grayish-green feet, webbed like ducks; they looked a little like a pair of diver's flippers, only alive. Very, very alive.

"We thought we'd start with the feet as you can wear them underneath your clothes while you get used to them. It's probably best that no one suspects what you are—to begin with, anyway."

"Good idea," said Buddy Joe, looking over the head of the rotund Doctor Flynn at the feet. Alien feet. A faint mist hung around them, alien sweat exuding from alien pores.

Doctor Flynn held out an arm to stop Buddy Joe from reaching for the feet and putting them on right away.

"Slow down, Buddy Joe. I have to ask, for the record. Are you sure that you want to put the feet on? You know there will be no taking them off once you have done so."

"Yes, I want to put them on," said Buddy Joe, eyeing the feet.

"You know that once they are attached they will be part of you? If your body rejects them, it will be rejecting its own feet? Or worse, they may stay attached but the interface may malfunction, leaving you in constant pain?"

"I know that."

"And yet you still want to go ahead?"

"Of course. I've been pumped full of Compliance as a part of my sentence. I have no choice but to do what you tell me."

"Oh, I know that. I just need to hear you say it for the record."

Doctor Flynn moved out of the way. Buddy Joe was free to pick up the feet and carry them across the room to a chair. There he sat down, kicked off his shoes and socks and pulled them on.

It was like pushing his naked human feet into a pair of rubber gloves. He struggled, twisted and wriggled them into position. The alien feet did not want him; they were fighting back, trying to spit him out. Somewhere deep inside his brain he could feel himself screaming. His hands were burning, soaked in the acidic sweat that oozed from the pores of the alien feet. His own feet were being amputated, dissolved by the first stage of the alien body that Doctor Flynn and his team were making him put on. Buddy Joe was feeling excruciating pain, but the little crystal of Compliance that was slowly dissolving into his bloodstream kept him smiling all the while.

And then, all of a sudden, the feet slipped into place and they became part of him.

"That's it!" called one of Doctor Flynn's team. She looked up from her console and nodded at a nurse. "You can remove the sensors now."

She peeled the sticky strips away from his skin and dropped them in the disposal chute.

"A perfect take. We've done it, team."

Doctor Flynn was shaking hands with the other people in the room. People were looking at consoles, at the feet, at each other, in every direction but at Buddy Joe. Buddy Joe just stood there, smiling down at his strange new feet, wondering at the strange new sensations he was feeling. The floor felt different through them. Too dry and brittle.

Doctor Flynn came over, a grin spreading over his round, shiny face. "Okay, we'd like you to walk across the room. Can you do that?"

He could do that. Dip your feet into a pool of water and see how refraction bends them out of shape. That's how the feet felt to Buddy Joe. At an angle to the rest of his body; but part of him. Still part of him.

He took a step forward with his left leg, and the left foot narrowed as he raised it. As it descended it flared out to its full webbed glory, flattened itself out and felt for the texture of the plasticized floor. It recoiled. The floor was too dry, too brittle. A good gush of acid would melt it to nothing. He moved his right foot, and then he flapped and squelched his way across the floor.

"No problems walking?" said Doctor Flynn.

"No," he replied, but the doctor hadn't been talking to him.

There was a final checking of consoles. One by one the assembled doctors and nurses and technicians gave a thumbs up.

"Okay," said Doctor Flynn. "Well, thank you Buddy Joe. You can put your shoes on now. They should still fit if you roll the joints of the feet over each other, and in that way you can conceal them. We'll see you again the same time next week."

"Hey, just a minute," said Buddy Joe. "You can't send me out there with the Compliance still active."

Doctor Flynn gave a shrug. "We can't keep you in here. Laboratory space costs money. We're out of here ourselves in five minutes time to make way for yet another group of Historical Astronomers. Goodbye."

And that was it. He had no choice but to slip on his shoes and to walk out of the laboratory onto the fifth-level deck.

· · · · ·

Buddy Joe made his way to a lift that would take him down to the Second Deck. The Fifth Deck was quite empty at this time of night. With any luck, he would make it home without being recognized as someone under the spell of Compliance.

His feet were rolled up in his plastic shoes and socks, it took all his self-control to hold in the exhalation of acid that would melt them away and allow his feet to flap free. Don't let go, Buddy Joe. The metal grid of the deck will feel horrible against your poor feet.

The laboratory lay a long way out from the Pillar Towers. He could see through the mesh of the floor, all the way down to the waves crashing on the garbage-strewn shoreline far below. Looking up, he could see the flattened-out stars that pressed close, smearing themselves just above the tops of the highest buildings. He would have liked to stop for a while, it was a rare treat to look at the remnants of the universe, but he didn't dare. Not with Compliance still inside him.

The few Fifth Deckers who were out walking ignored him as usual. Scientists or lawyers, who could tell the difference? All wrapped up against the winter cold, trousers tucked into their socks against the cold gusts of wind that blew up through the metal decking. Buddy Joe kept to the shadows, dodging between the cats' cradles of struts that braced the buildings to the decks. Approaching the Pillar Towers he saw the yellow light that bathed the polished wooden doors of the main lift and he relaxed, but too soon. The woman who had been following him called out from the shadows behind.

"Stop there."

He did so.

"You're on Compliance, right?"

"Yes."

Buddy Joe felt a pathetic cry building inside. First they had taken his feet, now they would take his wallet, or worse.

"What did you do?"

"Rape," he said. "But . . ."

"I don't want to hear the details."

Buddy Joe dutifully closed his mouth, panic rising inside. His shoes were melting.

"Some bastard raped my partner only two months ago. Caught him alone in a lift coming up from the Second Deck. Are you a Second Decker?"

"Yes, but . . ."

"I'm not interested. How about if I told you to throw yourself off the edge?"

"Please don't do that."

"Funny, that. John said 'Please' too. Bastard didn't listen to him."

Buddy Joe clenched his fists together. His new feet were flapping open and closed by themselves, trying to creep away from the woman. There was a gentle intake of breath. This was it. This was the end. She would tell him to go and jump off the deck and he would have no choice but to obey. She was going to say it. She was going to . . .

And then nothing. A lengthening pause.

He turned around: the woman had gone. In her place was the stuff of nightmares. Buddy Joe began to make a noise. A thin scream of pure terror.

He was looking at another alien. He was looking at himself. It had his feet. It was his height, its hands stretched out . . . No. Don't look at the hands, Buddy Joe. But worse than that.

It had no head.

No head, but it was watching him. It was trying to say something to him, but he wasn't ready to understand.

—*Forget it, then,* said the alien.—*For now.*

It rose up into the air and vanished.

Two minutes later, Buddy Joe walked, shaking, into the lift.

He had Compliantly forgotten all about the alien.

· · · ·

Buddy Joe's flat was at the top of a block built on the Second Deck, home of those just bright enough not to believe in anything, but not bright enough to believe in something. His window looked out into the gloom cast by the underside of the Third Deck. He had a bed, a food spigot and a view-screen. Down the corridor were a bathroom and a row of toilet cubicles. Buddy Joe's father lived two flats down, his sister in the next flat again. Buddy Joe's grandfather had lived in the flat just next to the lift shaft. That flat had echoed and boomed every time the lift had moved. It echoed and boomed all day long, and most of the night. Buddy Joe's Granddad was dead now, though, and a new family had moved in. Granddad would have called them an Indian family, but he was old-fashioned in that respect. He had been old enough to remember when flowers had first bloomed on the moon.

"What do you know, Buddy Joe?" asked the woman on the viewscreen.

"I don't know nothing," said Buddy Joe.

"Next dose of Compliance at 40 P tomorrow. Next part of the alien suit at 60 P."

Buddy Joe rolled over on his bed. He was seriously thinking of throwing himself off the edge of the deck.

The viewscreen flickered and his sister appeared. She was sitting on a bed in a gray metal room just the same as his, just three doors away.

"Forty P tomorrow, eh, Buddy Joe?"

"That's right."

"And the next part of the alien suit at 60 P."

"That's what they said."

His father appeared on the screen. It might as well be the same room, the same bed, only the person changed.

"Forty P, Buddy Joe."

"Yes."

"New suit at 60 P."

"That's what they said."

"Your Granddad would say two o'clock, you know, not 60 P."

"Really, Dad?"

"You're a lot like your Granddad, Buddy Joe. He was always thinking about things, too. I always said it would get you both into trouble. I was right, too."

Buddy Joe looked down at his strange gray-green feet. He had placed a plastic bag between them and the nylon sheets: they didn't like the feel. He looked at his thin pale legs.

"Get used to them, they'll be gone by tomorrow."

That was James, from the flat below, his big moon-face leering from the viewscreen. He was filling a cup with food from the spigot as he spoke. Buddy Joe felt hungry. He looked for his cup beside the bed. The viewscreen flicked to show Mr. and Mrs. Singh having sex. Seventy P already. Definitely time for something to eat.

He knelt on the bed and leaned across to the spigot, his feet up in the air; well clear of the nylon sheets. Marty from Deck One was on the viewscreen now. He drew a sacred symbol in the air as he spoke.

"Shouldn't have raped that girl, boy," he shouted. "Gonna lose a lot more than your feet tomorrow."

. . . .

Buddy Joe was dreaming about walking with his grandfather through one of the meadows of the moon. Butterflies dipped and sipped among the nodding red and yellow heads of the flowers that stretched in all directions. Buddy Joe bent down and sniffed a flower.

No! Dirty, No! That was Dirty, Buddy Joe!

He woke to gray morning light, feeling disgusted with himself. He had to watch himself. Dirty thoughts germinated in your sleep and then bloomed as actions in your waking life. He knew that. Think of the decks, he told himself, think of the decks.

His sister was watching him from the viewscreen. "Thirty-five P, Buddy Joe. They'll be dosing you with Compliance soon."

"That's right," he replied, rubbing his eyes. He fumbled for his mug and held it under the food spigot.

"What do you reckon it will be? New legs? New arms?"

"I don't know."

His father appeared on the screen. "Thirty-five P, Buddy Joe. They'll be dosing you with Compliance soon."

"That's right."

He didn't want to talk about it. He didn't want to lose his legs. He was being turned into an alien against his wishes. What would happen when he put on the head? What would happen to him then? Where would Buddy Joe go? Still, he deserved it. Just look at his dreams.

"Shouldn't have raped that girl, Buddy Joe," said his father.

Didn't he wish that every day?

Martin came on the screen. Then Katie, then Clovis, then Charles . . .

He was still lying on the bed when the drone came buzzing down from the upper decks. A wasp-striped cylinder, just smaller than his thumb, dropping through the traps and gaps between the decking and the Pillar Towers. Swooping through the tunnels of the support struts, weaving through the balconies and walkways that led to his flat. Sending the signal that opened his door. He saw it hanging in the air at the end of the corridor, swelling in apparent size as it zoomed toward him. It settled lightly on his hand and there was a slight prick, then the crystal of Compliance slid beneath his skin. His arm tingled a little, felt as if it was somewhere else and then, there it was back again. He looked down at the tiny body of the drone, felt the pitter patter of metal feet on his skin. It spoke to him.

"Sixty P, Buddy Joe. Back at the lab. Be there for your new legs."

"Okay," he said. His new feet started to flap, all by themselves. They were excited. Buddy Joe rolled off the bed. It would take five P for Compliance to properly take hold. He intended to be in the lab by then, before anyone could take advantage of him again.

Hold on. Again? What did he mean *again*? Had he forgotten something? He shook his head, searching for the thought. It had gone.

Outside his flat, clattering down the steps to Deck Two. Threading through riveted metal cuboids that were bolted together to make blocks of flats. Walking around a gang of teenagers who were laughing as they incited each other to piss through the metal grating of the floor onto the Churches and Mosques and Synagogues and Temples far below on Deck One. One girl, her panties around her ankles, looked at Buddy Joe, saw the mark on his arm where the drone had settled and slow comprehension spread across her face. He hurried off before she could say anything.

· · · ·

Buddy Joe was waiting outside the lift entrance at the Pillar Towers. The tower stretched up into the sky, a tapering, dirty metal shape that vanished into the shadows cast by the Third Deck. Covered in deep scratches that bled rusty red. His grandfather had said that was from where they had grown from the earth. He had laughed. That surprises you, he had said. Bet you thought humans built the decks. Bet most people think that nowadays. Well, it's not true. A lot of strange things happened after flowers started growing on the moon.

Buddy Joe had kept quiet. Up until then he had never thought anything but that the decks had grown by themselves. He had never thought of humans building anything. Looking at the solid, earth-colored shapes of the Pillar Towers, how could anyone not believe that they had grown from the ground?

The polished wooden lift doors slid open and three people came out. Buddy Joe stepped into the padded interior. He gave a shiver. They were going to take away a little bit more of his humanity. He didn't want to go, but he heard his voice as it clearly asked for . . .

"Deck Five, please."

Someone pressed the button. The lift fell a little and everyone's hearts beat a little faster. Everyone had heard the story that, just as humans had sprung from the earth, someday they would all be called back to it. The lift doors would slide shut and carry them down to meet their maker . . .

But not today. The lift began to rise.

· · · ·

Walking across Deck Five, Buddy Joe could see the gray of the sky, sagging over the spires of the towers on Deck Seven. The winds blew harder up here; they blew through his thin cotton suit and made him shiver. His feet liked the feel: they shivered with anticipation.

He arrived early. A team of Historical Astronomers had projected pictures across the interior walls of the dome of the laboratory. They showed a strange landscape. Grassy plains, snow-capped mountains, fields of yellow corn: but everything out of proportion, the mountains, the valleys, all bigger than the pictures Buddy Joe had been shown of old Earth as a child.

"What is it?" he asked a white-coated astronomer next to him. The astronomer gave him a suspicious look and then realization dawned.

"Ah, the gentleman being fitted for an Alien Suit," he said. "A waste of time, if you want my opinion; but you probably don't." He turned and waved his arms around the room.

"This, my friend, is Mars. Mars, I should say, between the Shift and the Collapse. These pictures were taken about two months after the colony was established."

"It looks very . . . strange."

"It does to your eyes, my friend, because you have always lived in the world post-Collapse. To those who were alive before the Shift, that world would be a paradise. It would look like the real world."

"The real world?"

"Well, one of them. That's what we're all looking for here, my friend. That's why they have built those towers on Deck Seven; that's what your friends who are making that suit for you are looking for. The real world."

He gave a sigh and looked around. "Of course, my great-grandparents would not recognize these pictures as the real world."

"Why not?"

But someone called to the man. "Excuse me, I have to go now, maybe I will be able to tell you more another time." He shook Buddy Joe's hand and hurried away. He looked a little like Mr. Singh from down the corridor— what his grandfather would have called an Indian.

The Historical Astronomers were packing up now. Another set of scientists were coming into the room. The Alien Suit scientists. Two of them were pushing a trolley, and Buddy Joe felt a thrill of fear. The next part of the suit lay on it. He felt sick. It was more than he had expected. Not a pair of trousers, not a top. It looked like a jumpsuit. It would swallow up all of Buddy Joe except for his hands and his head. And when your head is gone, where do you go, Buddy Joe? (Head. Head. Now why did he think of the head of the alien? *Don't think of the Hands!*)

Doctor Flynn saw him shivering at the other side of the room. "Ah! There you are. Take your clothes off quickly. We haven't got much time."

Buddy Joe began to do so, but inside he was crying with fear. But I don't want to! Well you shouldn't have raped that girl, Buddy Joe, said his Compliant hands, busily undoing his shirt.

Someone pressed sensor pads onto his face. He kicked off his shoes and his feet unrolled themselves. Doctor Flynn stood patiently beside him, looking at a picture inadvertently left behind by the Historical Astronomers.

"Fools," he said, "living in the past. We never understood the truth when we held the possibility of the whole universe in our hands. Why should we learn the answers by looking at copies and replicas of what we had? Better to give up the past. The truth lies elsewhere."

He let go of the paper and it fluttered to the ground. He turned and looked at Buddy Joe, now standing naked before him. A pale white body traced in blue veins.

"I need the toilet."

"Wait," said Doctor Flynn. "It will be an interesting test of the suit." He turned to the rest of the team. "Are we ready?"

One woman shook her head. "Five minutes. We're having a little trouble getting the neck to dilate."

Doctor Flynn gave a slight nod. "That's okay. We have some slack time built into the session."

Buddy Joe shivered. Partly it was the cold; mainly it was fear. The gray-green body of the alien suit glistened wet and smooth on the outside, but inside, looking into the neck, he could see the strange purple color of the interior. Rows of silver-gray hooks that appeared half metal, half organic, lined the suit. What would they do to him when he pulled it on? Just how deeply would those hooks reach into his body? But he knew the answer already. They had told him. All the way in, Buddy Joe, the hooks reach all the way in. They'll soon be twisting around your veins and nerves and organs, hooking their way in and using them as a basis for the shape they will grow. They'll paint over the template of your black-and-white body in glorious Technicolor. You'll be a paint-by-numbers man.

Doctor Flynn began to hum to himself. The yellow lights reflected from his head and glasses.

"Why?" whispered Buddy Joe.

"Why what?" said Doctor Flynn.

"Why are you doing this to me?"

Doctor Flynn gave a shrug. "Just luck, I suppose. We notified the courts that we would like a test subject. Yours was the first Capital case that came up, I guess."

"No," said Buddy Joe. "I mean, why are you changing me into an alien?"

Doctor Flynn gave him a strange look. He seemed a little impressed, despite himself. "You understand what's going on, don't you? You want to know the reasons? You really are a cut above the common herd, aren't you? Well, I'll tell you . . ."

"Ready, Doctor Flynn." The woman by the suit gave the thumbs up.

Doctor Flynn gave an apologetic shrug. "Sorry. Maybe next week we'll have the time to talk."

He clapped his hands together. "Okay people, let's get going. Buddy Joe, if you can step toward the suit?"

Buddy Joe let out an involuntary whimper as he stepped forward. The neck of the suit had expanded. Now it looked like a huge purple mouth, lined with bristling hook-like teeth. It was flexing, the teeth rippling as he watched.

"Everything ready?" said Doctor Flynn, looking around. "Okay, step into the suit."

"No problem," said Buddy Joe with a smile, screaming inside as he did so. In the middle of it all, for the first time ever, he understood how the girl had felt. She hadn't wanted to go through with it either. She had said no . . . He stepped into the suit . . .

· · · ·

Buddy Joe couldn't lie on the bed, not in his new body. It wasn't just the way that the bed now felt strange: dry and harsh and brittle like everything else

in this new world. No. Not just because of that, although the thought of putting on clothes and feeling elastic or nylon against his skin made him shudder, and the thought of a feather against his skin would have made him retch
if he still had a stomach.

No. What disturbed him was the way that his skin could see.

The images were just there on the edge of his vision, ghosts of his
room seen from all angles, the ceiling, the floor, all four walls; his body
was watching them and reporting to a brain that couldn't quite make it
all out.

And when he lay on the bed it was as if he was half-blinded and suffo-
cating at the same time. He couldn't block his new, imperfect vision in any
way.

So what to do? His feet had known. They had spread themselves wide,
walked themselves up the walls and across the ceiling and then gripped
tightly.

Now he hung from the ceiling, watching the viewscreen. The Singhs had
just finished having sex. Now it was time to watch his sister drink her evening cup of food. She raised it to him.

"Hey there, Buddy Joe. What are they going to take away next time? Your
hands?"

"I suppose."

"Shouldn't have raped that girl, Buddy Joe."

"I know, I know."

His father appeared on the screen. "Hey there, Buddy Joe. What are they
going to take away next time? Your hands?"

"I suppose."

"Shouldn't have raped that girl, Buddy Joe."

"I know, I . . ." He paused.

Why was he hanging here talking nonsense? Why wasn't he outside, feeling the wind? His body was too dry. Outside the wind was blowing moist
and salty from the sea.

"Hey, Buddy Joe!"

His father's face stared from the screen, confused and slightly angry. It
was the first time he had seen any expression but blank-eyed apathy for
years. Part of Buddy Joe wanted to stop and speak to him. Hey Daddy, where
have you been?

But his alien body was doing something else. One foot had flapped itself
free of the ceiling and the leg to which it was attached had turned through
180 degrees and was stretching impossibly down to the floor. It touched, and
the other foot let go.

His father called out to him from the viewscreen. "Hey Buddy Joe! How
do you do that?"

"I don't know!" he gasped, as his new body marched its way out of the flat and down the corridor to where the lift was waiting.

. . . .

It was pleasanter at night. Hanging from the underside of Deck Three—the metal grille didn't feel strange when gripped upside down—he looked up through his feet at the dark spaces through which squeezed the steady drip drip drip of rain. The rusty water ran around his toes, down his gray-green legs, dripped off his hands and his nose. He could gaze into the reflections and see two Buddy Joes looking down at the blocks and shadows of Deck Two. He could allow his legs to extend, let gravity pull him out like a stretch of toffee, blowing him in the wind from the sea.

Anywhere he could fit his head, his body would pass. He flattened his body and slotted it through the gap between deck and Pillar Towers and made his way higher and higher up to hang from beneath the Seventh Deck, looking down on the parks and gardens that surrounded the homes where the élite lived. He made his way to the edge of the deck and looked up at the region where the stars were smeared across the sky. The whole universe was squashed into a region less than 100 meters thick.

Once it had been unimaginably big, and then there had come the Collapse. Why had it happened? There were rumors, of course. Some said we weren't welcome out there, some said we had done something so obscene in the eyes of the universe they had squashed it to nearly nothing and started it again somewhere else. Buddy Joe's Granddad was more fanciful. He had said humans had just *imagined* it away.

He remembered his grandfather's words: "The mind is its own place, and in itself, can make a heaven of hell and a hell of heaven."

They'd been out walking the decks, taking the air, listening to the tired splash of the ocean waves below on the garbage-strewn beach. Where does the ocean go? he had wondered.

"Our minds used to be as big as the universe, Buddy Joe," said his grandfather, glancing up at the squashed sky. "They still are," he added sadly.

There was something out there with him, hanging from the underside of Deck Seven. Another gray-green shape, watching him swinging in the breeze. Another alien, just like him. But look at the . . . Don't look at the hands, Buddy Joe.

It didn't have a head.

"Hey!" he called. "Haven't I seen you before?"

The other shape paused. It appeared to be looking at him, despite the fact it didn't have a head; and then it turned and moved quickly away, swinging upside down from the deck, it vanished into the forest of Pillar Towers.

"Hey!" called Buddy Joe again. "Come back!"

He began to chase after it, but he was still not used to his new body.

Whoever was in that suit was obviously a lot more practiced in its operation. Who was it? Buddy Joe had been told he was unique. The alien drew farther and farther away, swinging effortlessly below the deck, its body penduluming back and forth above the homes of the élite, swinging into and out of the lights that shone up from below, dodging through the cats' cradles of the bracing. It swung around a Pillar Tower and was lost from view. Buddy Joe moved faster, following it around the wide metal curve, but it was no use. It had gone.

"Where are you?" he called, and "Ouch!" as he felt a sting in his right hand. He looked there to see a black and yellow drone pumping a crystal of Compliance under his skin. Metal mandibles pulsed with red light.

"Where have you been?" said the drone in a buzzing voice. "I thought I wouldn't find you in time. Report to the laboratory at 60 P tomorrow."

"Okay," said Buddy Joe. "No problem."

· · · ·

Buddy Joe could stretch and stretch so that, while his feet still remained attached to the underside of Deck Six, his face moved closer and closer to the laboratory on Deck Five. He was 300 meters long and his body sang like a radio aerial, picking up signals from across the dirty ocean. Something out there was speaking to him. Something like himself. That other alien. He placed his hands on the metal of the deck and released his feet. His body slowly drew itself down and into position. He walked into the laboratory and the end of the meeting of the Historical Astronomers.

"Ah, my Alien Suit friend. And how nice you look in your new body."

"Thank you."

"And what are they going to take away from you today?"

"I don't know," Buddy Joe paused. He looked around at the meeting of astronomers as they packed away their pictures and slides into wide, shallow metal cases. He was remembering the last meeting.

"Something you said, last time. You think Doctor Flynn is mistaken in what he is doing to me. Why is he doing this to me?"

The Historical Astronomer gave a laugh. "Because your Doctor Flynn is a religious man. He may deny it, he may not believe it himself, but he will have had the teachings drummed into him as a child and they are still there inside him, shaping everything he does. I have been to Deck One, my friend. I have visited the Churches and Mosques and Synagogues and Temples. Doctor Flynn came from Deck One. He has walked on the bare earth, unprotected by the metal of the deck. He has felt the damp sand that runs along the edge of the ocean beneath his feet and between his toes. Down on Deck One they cannot forget Earth as it used to be. They feel a link to the past that we do not up here on Deck Five, and they believe things should be as they were. Nostalgia is not a basis for scientific inquiry, my friend."

"He said much the same about you," said Buddy Joe, and the astronomer laughed.

"Ah! Touché! But only up to a point, my friend. My beliefs are confirmed by scientific fact. His beliefs are confirmed by the Bible. Numbers, Chapter 20. The Waters of Meribah, where the people of Israel quarrelled with the Lord and the Lord showed his holiness. The Waters of Meribah, where the Lord told Moses to strike a rock and bring forth water."

"Moses?"

"He led his people into a wilderness and there he brought forth water and food and eventually delivered them to a Promised Land. Imagine that. First there was nothing, and then life burst forth. Just like when the flowers first bloomed on the moon . . . Do you see from where Doctor Flynn's beliefs come, my friend?"

Buddy Joe nodded his head slowly. "I think I do."

"Ah, but do you see it all? Moses was denied entry to the holy land because of his sin at the Waters of Meribah."

"His sin?"

"He did not trust the Lord to show his holiness."

"Oh."

"And now, we have been denied entry to the universe. And Doctor Flynn and his kind ask the question, what sin have we committed?"

Buddy Joe stood in silence, thinking about what he had just heard. The Historical Astronomer spoke. "You are an intelligent young man. You are a rapist, aren't you?"

"Yes," said Buddy Joe, Compliance leaving him no choice but to answer.

"I thought so. I thought so. A great loss to the scientific community. The Historical Astronomers could have used you. It's a shame that soon you will no longer be here."

As he spoke the door slid open, and the hands were wheeled in. Buddy Joe began to scream at the sight of them.

· · · ·

"Hey Buddy Joe!" called Doctor Flynn. Buddy Joe was weeping with terror as he stared at his new hands, seeing how big they were, how the multicolored tentacles trailed from the trolley upon which they lay, out across the floor and around the room and out the door. They were too big to see all at once. Too big to imagine on his poor, thin wrists. Look at how they were already thrashing and wriggling, sending luminescent patterns to hang in the air in afterglow, long scripts that his alien body could read. His hands were speaking to him already. Wide hands, hundreds of meters long. Too long. He didn't want to put them on. No, no, no!

"Are you ready, Buddy Joe?"

"Yes," said the Compliance. "Just one thing," said Buddy Joe, "I thought I was the only one?"

Doctor Flynn signalled to his aides to bring the trolley closer. "The only one?"

"The only one wearing a suit."

"You are."

"But I saw another alien, just last night. And the other week a woman, she was going to kill me. Just before she told me to jump off the deck, she vanished. I think it was the other alien that took her."

Doctor Flynn waved a hand for the trolley to pause. Buddy Joe felt a wave of relief. Don't make me put on those hands, he thought. Don't make me do it.

"You are the only alien, Buddy Joe. This is the first Alien Suit: it is an artificial construct. There are no such things as aliens. Don't you know that?"

"I had an idea, but no one ever told me."

The hands were thrashing more wildly than ever. They sensed him nearby. They were frustrated at the pause and they strained against their restraints. One scientist jumped back from a vomit-yellow tentacle that lashed and cracked toward her.

Doctor Flynn looked him in the eyes. "You can't be lying to me. You are on Compliance."

"I'm telling the truth."

Doctor Flynn took a handkerchief from his pocket and wiped the sweat from his round forehead. "You're a rapist, aren't you? You must be intelligent."

"I don't feel intelligent."

Doctor Flynn looked at the other scientists. They shrugged. They shook their heads. They made it clear they didn't understand what was going on, and that Doctor Flynn would have to figure this out on his own.

"Okay, Buddy Joe. You can't be lying; therefore you must be mistaken. Let's see if we can figure out together what it is that you saw. Because it can't be another alien. Okay?"

"If you say so."

"Okay. Do you know why we're turning you into an alien?"

"No."

"We're trying to reverse the Collapse, Buddy Joe, or at least see if we can get out of this pathetic little bubble that the universe has become. We've tried to build something so alien that it can see what we cannot. Do you know what the Shift refers to, Buddy Joe?"

Buddy Joe licked his lips as he looked at the hands. That yellow tentacle was thrashing harder than ever. Ignore it; ignore it. Speak and keep it away. He spoke.

"The Shift refers to when flowers first bloomed on the moon. The moon colonists sent the message and no one believed them; they sent rockets there to check and when they landed there were green meadows where before there had been bare rocks . . . And then the same happened on Mars, and then on Callisto. Everywhere there was a human colony . . ."

Doctor Flynn shook his head. "No, Buddy Joe. That's not what the Shift refers to. A popular misconception."

"But I thought . . ."

"No. That was just the catalyst. It refers to the Shift in our perceptions of the way the universe works. For millennia humans believed that the earth was created as a place for them to live. And then, in the last three centuries that idea was turned on its head. We came to believe that life evolved by chance in the universe; that it fought to cling on in the most unlikely places, deep beneath the oceans or high in the atmosphere, and that all the time a subtle change in the balance could wipe it out. The proof of that theory was written in the fossils of the dinosaurs or frozen in the glaciers. But we were wrong."

The yellow tentacle thrashed again and finally broke the metal clasp that held it. Three scientists ran from the thrashing, slashing shape. Doctor Flynn spoke on, his face gray and shiny with sweat.

"Three centuries of so-called progressive thought turned on its head. We had been right the first time. There is a force written at the most basic level of the universe that is dedicated to bringing forth life. The universe warps and bends itself to support life. Where humans settle and live for long enough water springs forth from the rocks and plants from the soil . . ."

Buddy Joe wanted to back away, but the yellow tentacle had turned its attention to the other bonds and was working to loosen them. Doctor Flynn didn't seem to have noticed.

"Life attracts life. We don't understand it . . . Humans wandered over the surface of the moon for decades without any sign of the effect, but when we established a colony, started to take a real interest in the satellite, then it started to take an interest in us. It's like some sort of feedback. You understand the term?"

Doctor Flynn looked at Buddy Joe, seemingly oblivious to what was going on behind him. None of the scientists seemed to care, either. The tentacle had freed two more. Now the metal clasps which held the rest of the alien hands were pulled free, pop pop pop. The hands were free. Those horrible, horrible hands, so big, just so big. Buddy Joe wanted to cry. He didn't want to put them on.

"Do you understand?"

Buddy Joe had to say yes, the Compliance made him. Doctor Flynn nodded, satisfied.

"Good. That's why, after the Collapse, we got to thinking about life. What if we made another form of life? Something completely alien to our experience. What if we built an alien suit for someone to wear? Someone like you,

Buddy Joe. What would they make of the universe? Maybe they would understand what was going on. Maybe a different perspective would explain why the universe had collapsed to a bubble 300 miles across. Has the Collapse anything to do with the Shift in our perceptions?"

"The hands are coming for me," said Buddy Joe.

"That's okay," said Doctor Flynn. "That's what they were supposed to do."

"I don't want to put them on. They look too big. I'll lose myself if I put them on. They're horrible. Why did you make them so horrible?"

"We had to make them as alien as we could, Buddy Joe. We need the alien perspective. Before we had you in here we took other condemned and pumped them full of Junk and LSD and MTPH and we recorded their hallucinations. We recorded the screams of children, and the thought patterns of dogs twitching in their sleep and the terror of a very bright light in a very dark room. We took all that and painted it across the canvas that makes your body so that it could be as alien as possible."

The tentacles formed a thrashing, slashing cage around Buddy Joe. He stood with Doctor Flynn in a maelstrom of orange and yellow violence. Something turned itself up from the floor. Dark green circles with sharp red spines inside. The cuffs of his new hands.

Doctor Flynn seemed unconcerned. "And you know, even if our experiment succeeds, I wonder about what Wittgenstein said: 'Even if a lion could speak we wouldn't understand it.' I wonder if we will understand you, Buddy Joe?"

"Please don't make me put them on," he cried.

"Shouldn't have raped that girl, Buddy Joe."

"I know, I know."

He remembered the girl. He had cornered her in the lift. He remembered how she had shaken and wept.

He had been thinking about his grandfather, and things he had said. The girl had a look that reminded him of his grandfather. That same questioning, intelligent look. He thought she would understand. Buddy Joe had asked her how it must have felt to walk under the stars when they shone high above, walk on the beach and feel the sand beneath your feet and the cool ocean breeze. And when she asked him to stop he had ignored her and just carried on speaking, trying to get her to see.

Buddy Joe had raped her, pushed the hemispheres of her brain roughly apart and slipped the alien ideas into her head: left them to congeal inside her. Dirty, filthy and without her consent.

The hands reached for Buddy Joe, slipped around his human hands and melted them.

"I deserve the pain," he winced.

"Same time next . . ." Doctor Flynn began to speak, but the hands took over. They slashed across the room, cutting Doctor Flynn in half. His legs remained standing as his head and shoulders fell to the floor.

"Hey Buddy Joe, stop tha . . ."

The female scientist who called out had the top of her head sliced off in one easy motion. Blonde hair spun round and round like a Catherine wheel as it arced across the room. The yellow and orange tentacles were vibrating in sine waves, filling the room with their frantic, snapping energy. Flesh and bone snapped and tore, blood flew, and Buddy Joe was a human head on an alien body that stretched across the room and out into the night. He could feel his hands in the warmth of the room, in the cool of the night, on the metal of the deck, covered in blood, gripping the handrail at the edge of the drop to the dark ocean and pulling him clear of the room. Where were the hands taking him? A group of tentacles reached down to Doctor Flynn's head and shoulders and picked them up. He felt them thrusting themselves into the warmth of the body, feeling for the spinal cord, seeking out the arteries and veins and wriggling up them.

And then Buddy Joe was out of the laboratory and his hands were pulling him up to the top of Deck Seven.

Why wasn't the Compliance working? thought Buddy Joe as he passed out.

• • • • •

He woke up spread out to the size of Deck Seven. His new hands were the size and shape of every strand of the metal mesh that made up the decking. His legs stretched down two of the Pillar Towers. His head was hanging, looking down over the gardens and houses of Deck Six.

Doctor Flynn appeared before him, looking like a glove puppet. Alien tentacles had been thrust into the nerves and joints of his broken body to make him work.

—*Speak to him.*

"Hey, Buddy Joe," said Doctor Flynn, his eyelids drooping, his eyes moving up and down and left to right, tracing out a slow sine wave.

"Hey, Doctor Flynn," said Buddy Joe. His head was trying to be sick, but he had nothing to be sick with.

—*Where's my head?*

"The body wants to know where the head is."

"It's not quite finished yet, Buddy Joe. I don't think it ever will be. The hands killed most of the team. I'm not sure the expertise still exists to make a head. Even if it did, it would never get built without me to push through the requisitions."

Silence. The body was considering. Doctor Flynn twitched his nose. A single cherry of blood pumped from the side of a tentacle and fell toward the deck below.

—*What do you know of the other alien?*

Buddy Joe relayed the question.

"Nothing," said Doctor Flynn. "You were the only suit ever built. There can't be another alien. Hey. You can't keep me alive like this forever. Another, what, ten P at most?"

"It can feel the other aliens," said Buddy Joe, listening to the voice. "It says there are more of them all the time, somewhere over the ocean. There are ten already. It wants the head so it can join them."

"Ten? But that can't be! Anyway, there is no over-the-ocean. Don't you see? The only thing that stopped the universe collapsing to nothing was the pressure of life within this bubble. The life force is so strong it caused the decking to grow, just to allow us to live. There is no over-the-ocean anymore, there is just here."

"There is an over-the-ocean, now."

Then he had the answer. It was obvious. It just popped into his head. "I know what the answer is: I know where the aliens come from," he said. But it was too late. Doctor Flynn was already dead.

"But I want to tell you the answer, Doctor Flynn," he called. The tentacles were disengaging from inside Doctor Flynn's body, rubbing themselves together as a human would rub their hands to remove something unpleasant. They were letting him go, letting him fall to the deck far below. Buddy Joe watched Doctor Flynn tumble and fall, down and down until his body landed on the roof of someone's house.

The tentacles were writhing and thrashing again, spelling out their long orange and yellow scripts in the air around him. This is how they speak, thought Buddy Joe. This is how the aliens speak. I can hear it in my subconscious, read through my peripheral vision.

—*Where do we come from?*

"From the life force that fills the universe," said Buddy Joe. "If flowers can bloom on the moon just because humans live there, then surely you could have come into existence when the idea of you took root in Doctor Flynn's laboratory. New life walks the earth and a new environment opens up to support it. Opens up across the ocean."

—*What a strange idea. This is how the universe works. It's not what we suspected, Buddy Joe.*

"Not what anyone thought," said Buddy Joe, 30 miles long, 20 miles wide and two miles tall, his legs and arms stretching to fill the decks around him. He was growing all the time. "A universe that exists just to nurture life. New life bursting out all the time. And here we are trapped in this little bubble of the universe. I wonder when we'll get out?"

—*Soon, Buddy Joe, soon. But not like this. Now we can see what is holding us back.*

"What is it?"

—*You.*

The tentacles lashed around, seized hold of Buddy Joe's head and pulled it clean off. It wasn't needed anymore. The alien was complete and reasoning without a brain. Doctor Flynn and his team had designed it to be that different.

Tentacles began to pull themselves free of the metal of Deck Seven as Buddy Joe's head tumbled down to join Doctor Flynn's body. The body stretched itself out thinner and thinner; ready to glide its way over the ocean toward its own race . . .

. . . and then it paused. Tainted a little by Buddy Joe and his humanity, tainted a little by its origins. It had been built by humans, and just a little of the sin that it was to be human was woven into the fabric of its body. It was not yet quite free of that human curiosity that the universe moved to protect itself from. That need to explain how things worked. Curiosity. It was a most alien feeling. Without it, one could not wonder at its existence. It was a dizzying thought.

All around, the alien looked, tasted, felt the remains of the human world, the decking and the polluted seas, the last feeble stirrings of that doomed impulse that defined the inhabitants: the urge to try and understand the basic mechanism of their world. That human persistence in violating the cardinal rule, written at the quantum level and warned of in one of the humans' oldest texts.

Don't look at the system, or you will change it. The universe fights against being known.

Curiosity: forget it, the alien told itself, and it did so immediately.

Far below, there was a bump as Buddy Joe's head hit the deck.

DAVID D. LEVINE   Born in Minneapolis, David D. Levine lives in Portland, Oregon, where he and his wife, Kate Yule, are active in science fiction fandom, annually producing the quirky and excellent fanzine *Bento*. He began selling fiction regularly in 2001, shortly after attending the Clarion West workshop, and in 2006 won the Hugo Award for the story presented here.

It is possible that this tale of a desperate human software salesman, getting nowhere with his wares on a planet of impenenetrably humble sentient insects, was in some way informed by the author's many years working in the IT industry.

TK'TK'TK

Walker's voice recorder was a beautiful thing of aluminum and plastic, hard and crisp and rectangular. It sat on the waxy countertop, surrounded by the lumpy excreted-looking products of the local technology. *Unique selling proposition,* he thought, and clutched the leather handle of his grandfather's briefcase as though it were a talisman.

Shkthh pth kstphst, the shopkeeper said, and Walker's hypno-implanted vocabulary provided a translation: "What a delightful object." Chitinous fingers picked up the recorder, scrabbling against the aluminum case with a sound that Walker found deeply disturbing. "What does it do?"

It took him a moment to formulate a reply. Even with hypno, *Thfshpfth* was a formidably complex language. "It listens and repeats," he said. "You talk all day, it remembers all. Earth technology. Nothing like it for light-years." The word for "light-year" was *hkshkhthskht,* difficult to pronounce. He hoped he'd gotten it right.

"Indeed yes, most unusual." The pink frills, or gills, at the sides of the alien's head throbbed. It did not look down—its faceted eyes and neckless head made that impossible—but Walker judged its attention was on the recorder and not on himself. Still, he kept smiling and kept looking the alien in the eyes with what he hoped would be interpreted as a sincere expression.

"Such a unique object must surely be beyond the means of such a humble one as myself," the proprietor said at last. *Sthshsk,* such-a-humble-one-as-myself—Walker could die a happy man if he never heard those syllables again.

Focus on value, not price. "Think how useful," he hissed in reply. "Never forget things again." He wasn't sure you could use *htpthtk,* "things," in that way, but he hoped it got the point across.

"Perhaps the honored visitor might wish to partake of a cup of *thshsh?*"

Walker's smile became rigid. *Thshsh* was a beverage nearly indistinguishable from warm piss. But he'd learned that to turn down an offer of food or drink would bring negotiations to an abrupt close. "This-humble-one-accepts-your-most-generous-offer," he said, letting the memorized syllables flow over his tongue.

He examined the shopkeeper's stock as it prepared the drink. It all looked like the products of a sixth-grade pottery class, irregular clots of brown and gray. But the aliens' biotech was far beyond Earth's—some of these lumps would be worth thousands back home. Too bad he had no idea which ones. His expertise lay elsewhere, and he was here to sell, not buy.

The shopkeeper itself was a little smaller than most of its kind, about a hundred forty centimeters tall, mostly black, with yellow spine-tips and green eyes. Despite its insectile appearance, it was warm-blooded—under its chitin it had bones and muscle and organs not unlike Walker's own. But its mind and culture were even stranger than its disturbing mouth-parts.

"The cup of friendship," the alien said, offering a steaming cup of *thshsh*. Walker suppressed a shudder as his fingers touched the alien's—warm, covered with fine hairs, and slightly sticky—but he nodded politely and raised the cup to his lips.

He sipped as little as he felt he could politely get away with. It was still vile.

"Very good," he said.

Forty-five minutes later the conversation finally returned to the voice recorder. "Ownership of this most wondrous object is surely beyond price. Perhaps the honored guest would be willing to lend it for a short period?"

"No trial period necessary. Satisfaction is guaranteed." He was taking a risk with that, he knew, but the recorder had never failed him in all the years he'd owned it.

Tk'tk'tk, the alien said, tapping its mouthparts together. There was no translation for that in Walker's vocabulary. He wanted to throttle the thing—couldn't it even stick to its own language?—but he struggled not to show his impatience.

After a pause, the alien spread a hand—a gesture that meant nothing to Walker. "Perhaps the honored owner could be compensated for the temporary use of the property."

"Humbly requesting more details."

"A loan of this type is generally for an indefinite period. The compensation is, of course, subject to negotiation. . . ."

"You make offer?" he interrupted. He realized that he was not being as polite as he could be. But it was already late afternoon, and he hadn't eaten since breakfast—and if he didn't conclude this deal successfully he might not have enough money for lunch.

Tk'tk'tk again. "Forty-three," it said at last.

Walker seethed at the offer. He had hoped to sell the recorder for enough to live on for at least a week, and his hotel alone—barely worthy of the name—cost twenty-seven a night. But he had already spent most of a day trying to raise some cash, and this was the only concrete offer he'd gotten.

"Seventy?"

The alien's gills, normally in constant slight motion, stopped. Walker knew he had offended it somehow, and his heart sank. But his smile never wavered.

"Seventy is a very inopportune number. To offer seventy to one of your exalted status would be a great insult."

Damn these aliens and their obscure numerology! Walker began to sputter an apology.

"Seventy-three, on the other hand," the shopkeeper continued, "is a number with an impeccable lineage. Would the honored guest accept compensation in this amount?"

He was so busy trying to apologize that he almost didn't recognize the counter-offer for what it was. But some salesman's instinct, some fragment of his father's and his grandfather's DNA, noticed it, and he managed to hiss out "This-humble-one-accepts-your-most-generous-offer" before he got in any more trouble.

It took another hour before the shopkeeper actually counted the money— soft brown lumps like rabbit droppings, each looking exactly like the others—into Walker's hand. He passed his reader over them; it smelled the lumps and told him they were three seventeens, two nines, and a four, totaling seventy-three as promised. He sorted them into different pockets so he wouldn't accidentally give the luggage-carrier a week's salary as a tip again. It angered him to be dependent on the Chokasti-made reader, but he would rather use alien technology than try to read the aliens' acrid pheromonal "writing" with his own nose.

Walker pressed through the labia of the shop entrance into the heat and noise and stink of the street. Hard orange shafts of dusty late-afternoon sun glinted dully on the scuttling carapaces of the populace: little merchants and bureaucrats, big laborers and warriors, hulking mindless transporters. No cars, no autoplanes . . . just a rustling mass of aliens, chuttering endlessly in their harsh sibilant language, scraping their hard spiny limbs and bodies against each other and the rounded, gourd-like walls. Here and there a knot of two or three in conversation blocked traffic, which simply clambered over them. The aliens had no concept of personal space.

Once a swarm of juveniles had crawled right over *him*—a nightmare of jointed legs and chitinous bodies, and a bitter smell like rusty swamp water. They had knocked his briefcase from his hand, and he had scrambled after it under the scrabbling press of their bodies. He shuddered at the memory—

not only did the briefcase contain his most important papers, it had belonged to his grandfather. His father had given it to him when he graduated
from college.

He clutched his jacket tight at his throat, gripped his briefcase firmly under his arm, and shouldered through the crowd.

• • • •

Walker sat in the waiting room of his most promising prospect—to be blunt,
his *only* prospect—a manufacturer of building supplies whose name translated as Amber Stone. Five days in transit, eight weeks in this bug-infested
hellhole of a city, a fifteen-megabyte database of contacts from five different
species, and all he had to show for it was one lousy stinking customer. *Potential* customer at that . . . it hadn't signed anything yet. But Walker had been
meeting with it every couple of days for two weeks, and he was sure he was
right on the edge of a very substantial sale. All he had to do was keep himself
on site and on message.

The light in the palm-sized windows shaded from orange to red before
Amber Stone finally appeared from its inner office. "Ah, human! So very
pleased that you honor such a humble one as myself with your delightful
presence." The aliens couldn't manage the name "Walker," and even "human" came out more like *hsshp'k*.

"Honor is mine, Amber Stone. You read information I give you, three
days?"

"Most intriguing, yes. Surely no finer literature has ever been produced."

"You have questions?"

Questions it did have, yes indeed, no end of questions—who performed
the translation, where did you have it reproduced, is it really as cold there as
they say, did you come through Pthshksthpt or by way of Sthktpth . . . but
no questions about the product. *I'm building rapport with the customer,*
Walker thought grimly, and kept up his end of the conversation as best he
could.

Finally Walker tried to regain control. "Your business, it goes well?"

Tk'tk'tk, the customer said, and placed its hands on its shoulders. "As the
most excellent guest must surely have noticed, the days are growing longer."

Walker had no idea what that might mean. "Good business or bad, always need for greater efficiency."

"The honored visitor graces this humble one with the benefits of a unique
perspective."

Though the sweat ran down behind his tie, Walker felt as though he were
sliding on ice—his words refusing to gain traction. "My company's software
will improve inventory management efficiency and throughput by three
hundred percent or more," he said, pulling out one of his best memorized
phrases.

"Alas, your most marvelous software is surely so far superior to our humble computers that no accommodation could be made."

"We offer complete solution. Hardware, software, support. Fully compatible. Satisfaction guaranteed." Walker smiled, trying to project confidence—no, not just confidence, *love,* for the product.

Tk'tk'tk. Was that an expression of interest? "Most intriguing, yes. Most unique. Alas, sun is setting." It gestured to the windows, which had faded from red to nearly black. "This most humble one must beg the honored visitor's forgiveness for consuming so much valuable time."

"Is no problem. . . ."

"This one would not dream of insulting an honored guest in such a way. Please take your rest now, and honor this unworthy establishment with your esteemed presence again tomorrow." The alien turned and vanished into the inner office.

Walker sat and seethed. *Dismissed by a bug,* he thought, *how much lower can you sink?* He stared into the scuffed leather surface of his briefcase as though he'd find the answer there. But it just sat on his lap, pressing down with the hard-edged weight of two generations of successful salesmen.

· · · ·

Though the sun had set, the street was still oppressively hot and still teemed with aliens. The yellow-green bioluminescent lighting made them look even stranger, more unnatural. Walker clutched his grandfather's briefcase to his chest as the malodorous crowd bumped and jostled him, spines catching on his clothing and hair.

It didn't help his attitude that he was starving. He'd left most of his lunch on the plate, unable to stomach more than a few wriggling bites, and that had been hours ago. He hoped he'd be able to find something more palatable for dinner, but he wasn't very optimistic. It seemed so cruel of the universe to make travelers find food when they were hungry.

But then, drifting between the sour and acrid smells of the bustling street, Walker's nose detected a warm, comforting smell, something like baked potatoes. He wandered up and down the street, passing his reader over pheromone-lines on the walls advertising SUPERLATIVE CHITIN-WAX and BLUE RIVER MOLT-FEVER INSURANCE. Finally, just as he was coming to the conclusion the smell was a trick of his homesick mind, the reader's tiny screen told him he had arrived at the SPIRIT OF LIFE VEGE-TARIAN RESTAURANT.

He hadn't even known the *Thfshpfth* language had the concept "vegetarian." But whatever it was, it certainly smelled good. He pushed through the restaurant's labia.

The place was tiny and low-ceilinged, with a single low, curving counter and five squatting-posts. Only one of the posts was occupied, by a small brown alien with white spine-tips and red eyes. It sat quietly, hands folded on the counter, in an attitude that struck Walker as contemplative. No staff was in evidence.

Walker chose a post, placed his folded jacket on it as a cushion, and seated himself as comfortably as possible. His space at the counter had the usual indentation, into which his order would be ladled, and was equipped with a double-ended spoon, an ice-pick, a twisty implement whose use he had yet to decipher, and a small bowl of water (which, he had learned to his great embarrassment, was for washing the fingertips, not drinking). But there was no menu.

Menus were one of the most frustrating things about this planet. Most of the items listed on the pheromone-tracked planks were not in his reader's vocabulary, and for the rest the translations were inadequate—how was he supposed to know whether or not "land-crab in the northern style" was something he would find edible? Time and again he had gone hungry, offended the server, or both. Even so, menus were something he understood. He had no idea what to order, or even how, without a menu to point at.

He drummed his fingers on the countertop and fidgeted while he waited for the server to appear. Say what you like about these creatures, they were unfailingly polite, and prompt. Usually. But not here, apparently. Finally, frustrated, he got up to leave. But as he was putting on his jacket, trying to steel himself for the crowd outside, he caught another whiff of that baked-potato smell. He turned back to the other customer, still sitting quietly. "No menu. No server. Hungry. How order?"

The alien did not turn. "Sit quietly. With peace comes fulfillment." Its voice was a low susurration, not as harsh as most of the others he'd heard.

With peace comes fulfillment? Walker opened his mouth for a sarcastic reply, but found his grammar wasn't up to the task. And he was hungry. And the food smelled good. So he took off his jacket and sat down again.

He sat with back straight and hands folded, staring at the swirled brown and cream colors of the wall in front of him. It might have come from Amber Stone's factory, produced by a huge genetically modified life form that ate garbage and shat building supplies. He tried not to think about it too much . . . the aliens' biotechnology made him queasy.

Looking at the wall, he thought about what it would take to sell Amber Stone's products on Earth. They couldn't be any more incomprehensible to him than the software he had been sent here to sell, and as his father always said, "a good salesman can sell anything." Though with three failed jobs and a failed marriage behind him, he was no longer sure that description had ever really fit him. No matter, he was too old to change careers now. The most he could hope for now was to stay alive until he could afford to retire. Get off the treadmill, buy a little house in the woods, walk the dog, maybe go fishing. . . .

Walker's reverie was interrupted when the other customer rose from its squatting-post and walked around the counter to stand in front of him. "Greetings," it said. "This one welcomes the peaceful visitor to the Spirit of Life."

Walker sputtered. "You . . . you server?"

"All serve the Spirit of Life, well or poorly, whether they understand it or not. This one serves food as well. The visitor is hungry?"

"Yes!" Walker's head throbbed. Was the alien laughing at him?

"Then this one will bring food. When peace is attained, satisfaction follows." It vanished through the door behind the counter.

Walker fumed, but he tried to wait peacefully. Soon the alien returned with a steaming pot, and ladled out a portion into the indentation in front of Walker. It looked like chunks of purple carrot and pale-yellow potato in a saffron-colored sauce, and it smelled wonderful. It tasted wonderful, too. A little strange, maybe—the purple carrots were bitter and left an odd aftertaste—but it had a complex flavor and was warm and filling. Walker spooned up every bit of it.

"Very good," he said to the server, which had returned to its previous station in front of the counter. "How much?"

It spread its hands and said, "This establishment serves the Spirit of Life. Any donation would be appropriate." It pointed to a glass jar on the counter, which contained a small pile of money.

Walker considered. How much of his limited funds could he spare? Yesterday's lunch had cost him five and a half. This place, and the food, were much plainer. But it was the single best meal he had eaten in weeks. Finally he chose a seven from his pocket, scanned it with his reader to make sure, and dropped it in the jar.

"This one thanks the peaceful guest. Please return."

Walker gave an awkward little bow, then pushed through the restaurant's labia into the nightmare of the street.

. . . .

Walker waved his room key, a twisted brown stick reeking with complex pheromones, at the hotel desk clerk. "Key no work," he said. "No let me in."

The clerk took the key, ran its fingers over it to read the codes. "Ah. Yes. This most humble one must apologize. *Fthshpk* starts tomorrow."

"What is *Fthshpk?*"

"Ah. Yes. This humble one has been so unkind as to forget that the most excellent guest is not familiar with the poor customs of this humble locale. *Fthshpk* is a religious political holiday. A small and insignificant celebration by our guest's most elevated standards, to be sure."

"So why it not work, the key?"

"Humble though it may be, *Fthshpk* is very important to the poor folk of the outlying regions. They come to the city in great numbers. This humble room has long been promised to such as these. And surely the most honored guest does not wish to share it?"

"No. . . ." The room was tiny enough for Walker alone. And he didn't want to find out how some of the equipment in the toilet-room was used.

"Indeed. So this most humble establishment, in a poor attempt to satisfy the most excellent human guest, has moved the guest's belongings to another room." It held out a new key, identical in appearance to the old one.

Walker took the key. "Where is?"

"Three levels down. Most cozy and well-protected."

The new room was larger than the old one, having two separate ante-chambers of unknown function. But the rounded ceiling was terribly low—though Walker could stand up straight in the middle of the room, he had to crouch everywhere else—and the lighting was dim, the heat and humidity desperately oppressive, and everything in the room stank of the aliens.

He lay awake for hours, staring into the sweltering darkness.

· · · ·

In the morning, he discovered that his shaver and some other things had vanished in the move. When he complained at the front desk, he got nothing but effusive, meaningless praise—oh yes, the most wonderful guest must be correct, our criminal staff is surely at fault—and a bill for the previous night's stay.

"Three hundred eighty-three!"

"The usual *Fthshpk* rate for our highest-quality suite is five hundred sixty-one. This most inadequate establishment has already offered a substantial reduction, out of respect for the highly esteemed guest and the unfortunate circumstances."

"Highest-quality suite? Too hot! Too dark! Too low!"

"Ah. Yes. The most excellent guest has unique tastes. Alas, this poor room is considered the most preferential in the hotel. The heat and light are praised by our other, sadly unenlightened, customers. These most lowly ones find it comforting."

"I not have so much money. You take interstellar credit? Bank draft?"

The clerk's gills stopped pulsing and it drew back a step, going *tk'tk'tk*. "Surely this humble one has misheard the most honored guest, for to offer credit during *Fthshpk* would be a most grave insult."

Walker licked his lips. Though the lobby was sweltering hot, suddenly he felt chilled. "Can pay after holiday?" He would have to find some other source of local currency.

Tk'tk'tk. "If the most honored visitor will please be patient. . . ." The clerk vanished.

Walker talked with the front desk manager, the chief hotelier, and the *thkfsh*, whatever that was, but behind the miasma of extravagant politeness was a cold hard wall of fact: he would pay for the room, he would pay in cash, and he would pay now.

"This establishment extends its most sincere apologies for the honored guest's unfortunate situation," said the *thkfsh,* which was dark yellow with green spine-tips and eyes. "However, even in this most humble city, payment for services rendered is required by both custom and law."

Walker had already suffered from the best the city had to offer—he was terrified of what he might find in the local jail. "I no have enough money. What can I do?"

"Perhaps the most honored guest would consider temporarily lending some personal possessions to the hotel?"

Walker remembered how he had sold his voice recorder. "Lend? For indefinite period?"

Tk'tk'tk. "The honored guest is most direct and forthright."

Walker thought about what they might want that he could spare. Not his phone, or his reader. "Interest in clothes? Shoes?"

"The highly perceptive guest will no doubt have noticed that the benighted residents of this city have not yet learned to cover themselves in this way."

Walker sighed, and opened his briefcase. Mostly papers, worthless or confidential or both. "Paper fastening device," he said, holding up his stapler. "Earth technology. Nothing like it for sixty-five light years."

"Surely such an item is unique and irreplaceable," said the *thkfsh.* "To accept the loan of this fine device would bring shame upon this humble establishment. However, the traveling-box . . ."

"Not understanding."

The *thkfsh* touched the scuffed leather of Walker's briefcase. "This traveling-box. It is most finely made."

Walker's chest tightened. "This humble object . . . only a box. Not worth anything."

"The surface has a most unusual and sublime flavor. And the texture is unlike anything this unworthy one has touched."

Desperately, Walker dug under papers for something, anything else. He found a pocket umbrella. "This, folding rain-shield. Most useful. Same technology used in expanding solar panels."

"The honored visitor's government would surely object to the loan of such sensitive technology. But the traveling-box is, as the visitor says, only a box. Its value and interest to such a humble one as myself are far greater than its value to the exalted guest."

Walker's fingernails bit into his palms. "Box has . . . personal value. Egg-parent's egg-parent used it."

"How delightful! For the temporary loan of such a fine and significant object, this establishment might be willing to forgive the most worthy visitor's entire debt."

It's only a briefcase, Walker thought. It's not worth going to jail for. But his eyes stung as he emptied it out and placed its contents in a cheap extruded carry-bag.

. . . . .

Unshaven, red-eyed, Walker left the hotel carrying all his remaining possessions: a suitcase full of clothes and the carry-bag. He had less than a hundred in cash in his pockets, and no place to spend the night.

Harsh sunlight speared into his eyes from a flat blue sky. Even at this hour of the morning, the heat was already enough to make sweat spring from his skin. And the streets swarmed with aliens—more of them, in greater variety, and more excited than he had ever seen before.

A group of five red-and-black laborers, each over two and a half meters tall, waded through the crowd singing—or at least chattering rhythmically in unison. A swarm of black juveniles crawled over them in the opposite direction, flinging handfuls of glittering green rings into the air. All around, aliens large and small spun in circles, waving their hands in the air. Some pounded drums or wheedled on high-pitched flutes.

A yellow merchant with black spines grabbed Walker's elbows and began spinning the two of them around, colliding with walls and with other members of the crowd. The merchant chattered happily as they spun, but its words were lost in the maelstrom of sound that surrounded them. "Let go! Let go!" Walker shouted, clutching his suitcase and his bag as he tried to squirm away, but the merchant couldn't hear—or wasn't listening—and its chitinous hands were terribly strong.

Finally Walker managed to twist out of the merchant's grasp, only to spin away and collide with one of the hulking laborers. Its unyielding spines tore Walker's jacket.

The laborer stopped chanting and turned to face Walker. It grasped his shoulders, turned him side to side. "What are you?" it shouted. Its breath was fetid.

"Visitor from Earth," Walker shouted back, barely able to hear himself.

The laborer called to its companions, which had moved on through the crowd. They fought their way back, and the five of them stood around him, completely blocking the light.

"This one is a visitor from *h'th*," said the first laborer.

One of the others grabbed a handful of green rings from a passing juvenile, scattered them over Walker's head and shoulders. They watched him expectantly.

"Thank you?" he said. But that didn't seem to be what they wanted.

The first laborer cuffed Walker on the shoulder, sending him reeling into one of the others. "The visitor is not very polite," it said. The aliens loomed close around him.

"This-most-humble-one-begs-the-honored-one's-forgiveness," Walker chattered out, clutching the carry-bag to his chest, wishing for the lost solidity of his grandfather's briefcase. But the laborers ignored his apology and began to twirl him around, shouting in unison.

After a few dozen spins he made out the words of the chant: "Rings, dance! Rings, dance!" Desperately, not at all sure he was doing the right thing, he tried to dance in circles as he had seen some of the aliens do.

The laborers pulled the bag from Walker's hands and began to stomp their feet. "Rings, dance! Rings, dance!" Walker waved his arms in the air as he spun, chanting along with them. His breath came in short pants, destroying his pronunciation.

He twirled, gasping "rings, dance," until he felt the hot sun on his head, and twirled a while longer until he understood what that sun meant: the laborers, and their shade, had deserted him. He was spinning for no reason, in the middle of a crowd that took no notice. He stopped turning and dropped his arms, weaving with dizziness and relief. But the relief lasted only a moment—sudden panic seized him as he realized his arms were empty.

There was the carry-bag, just a meter away, lying in the dirt surrounded by chitinous alien feet. He plowed through the crowd and grabbed it before it got too badly stomped.

But though he searched for an hour, he never found the suitcase.

· · · ·

Walker leaned, panting, against the outside wall of Amber Stone's factory. He had fought through the surging streets for hours, hugging the bag to his chest under his tightly buttoned jacket, to reach this point. Again and again he had been sprinkled with green rings and had danced in circles, feeling ridiculous, but not wanting to find out what might happen if he refused. He was hot and sweaty and filthy.

The still-damp pheromone line drawn across the office's labia read CLOSED FOR *FTHSHPK*.

Walker covered his face with his hands. Sobs thick as glue clogged the back of his throat, and he stood with shoulders heaving, not allowing himself to make a sound. The holiday crowd streamed past like a river of blackberry vines.

Eventually he recovered his composure and blew his nose, patting his waist as he pocketed the sodden handkerchief. His money belt, with the two hard little rectangles of his passport and return ticket, was still in place. All he had to do was walk to the transit gate, and he could return home—with nothing to show for his appallingly expensive trip. But he still had his papers, his phone, and his reader, and his one prospective customer. It was everything he needed to succeed, as long as he didn't give up.

"I might have lost your briefcase, Grandpa," he said aloud in English, "but I'm not going to lose the sale."

A passing juvenile paused at the odd sound, then continued on with the rest of the crowd.

⬤ ⬤ ⬤ ⬤

Walker would never have believed he'd be glad to see anything on this planet, but his relief when he entered the Spirit of Life Vegetarian Restaurant was palpable. The city's tortuous streets had been made even more incomprehensible by the *Fthshpk* crowds, and he had begun to doubt he would ever find it, or that it would be open on the holiday. He had been going in entirely the wrong direction when he had found the address by chance, on the pheromone-map at a nearby intersection.

"How long *Fthshpk?*" he asked the server, once he had eaten. It was the same server as before, brown with white spine-tips; it stood behind the counter, hands folded on its thorax, in a centered and imperturbable stance.

"One day," it replied. "Though some believe the spirit of *Fthshpk* should be felt in every heart all year long."

Walker suppressed a shudder at the thought. "Businesses open tomorrow?"

"Most of them, yes. Some trades take an extended holiday."

"Building supplies?" Walker's anxiety made him sputter the word.

"They will be open." The server tilted its shoulders, a posture that seemed to convey amusement. "The most honored visitor is perhaps planning a construction project?"

"No." He laughed weakly, a sound that startled the server. "Selling, not buying."

"The visitor is a most intriguing creature." The server's shoulders returned to the horizontal. "This humble one wishes to help, but does not know how."

"This one seeks business customers. The server knows manufacturers? Inventory controllers? Enterprise resource management specialists?"

"The guest's words are in the *Thfshpfth* language, but alas, this one does not understand them."

"To apologize. Very specialized business."

The server lowered itself smoothly, bringing its face down to Walker's level. Its gills moved like seaweed in a gentle current. "Business problems are not this one's strength. Is the honored visitor having troubles with family?"

It took Walker a moment to formulate his response. "No. Egg-parent, brood-parent deceased. This one no egglings. Brood-partner . . . departed." For a moment he forgot who, or what, he was talking to. "This one spent too much time away from nest. Brood-partner found another egg-partner." He fell silent, lost in memory.

The server stood quietly for a moment, leaving Walker to his thoughts. After a while it spoke: "It is good to share these stories. Undigested stories cause pain."

"Thanking you."

"This humble one is known as Shining Sky. If the visitor wishes to share further stories, please return to this establishment and request this one by name."

* * * *

When Walker left the Spirit of Life, the sun had already set. The *Fthshpk* crowds had thinned, with just a few revelers still dancing and twirling under the yellow-green street lights, so Walker was relatively unimpeded as he walked to hotel after hotel. Alas, they all said, this humble one apologizes most profusely, no room for the most honored visitor. Finally, exhausted, he found a dark space between buildings. Wrapping his jacket around the carry-bag, he placed it under his head—as a pillow, and for security. He would grab a few hours' sleep and meet with his customer the first thing in the morning.

He slept soundly until dawn, when the first hot light of day struck his face. He squinted and rolled over, then awoke fully at the sensation of the hard alley floor under his head.

The bag was not there.

He sat up, wide-eyed, but his worst fears were confirmed: his jacket and bag were nowhere to be seen. Panicked, he felt at his waist—his passport and return ticket were safe. But his money, his papers, his phone, and his reader were gone.

* * * *

"Ah, human!" said Amber Stone. "Once again the most excellent visitor graces this unworthy establishment." It was late in the morning. Robbed of street signs, addresses, and maps by the loss of his reader, Walker had wandered the streets for hours in search of the factory. Without the accustomed weight of his briefcase, he felt as though he might blow away on the next breeze.

"You requested I come yesterday," Walker hissed. "I come, factory closed. Come again today. Very important." Even without the papers from his briefcase, he could still get a verbal commitment, or at least a strong expression of interest . . . some tiny tidbit of achievement to prove to his company, his father, his grandfather, and himself that he wasn't a complete loss.

"Surely the superlative guest has more important appointments than to meet with this insignificant one?"

"No. Amber Stone is most important appointment. Urgent we discuss purchase of software."

"This groveling one extends the most sincere apologies for occupying the exalted guest's time, and will not delay the most highly esteemed one any further." It turned to leave.

"This-most-humble-one-begs-the-honored-one's-forgiveness!"

Amber Stone spoke without turning back. "One who appears at a merchant's establishment filthy, staggering, and reeking of *Fthshpk*-rings is obviously one whose concerns are so exalted as to be beyond the physical plane. Such a one should not be distracted from its duties, which are surely incomprehensible to mere mortals."

Walker's shoulders slumped in defeat, but then it was as though he heard his father's voice in his inner ear: *Ask for the sale.* Walker swallowed, then said, "Would the honored Amber Stone accept indefinite loan of inventory management system from this humble merchant?"

The alien paused at the threshold of its inner office, then turned back to Walker. "If that is what the most exalted one desires, this simple manufacturer must surely pay heed. Would fifty-three million be sufficient compensation for the loan of a complete system?"

Stunned, Walker leaned against the wall. It was warm and rounded, and throbbed slightly. "Yes," he said at last. "Yes. Sufficient."

· · · ·

"Where the hell have you been, Walker? Your phone's been offline for days. And you look like shit." Gleason, Walker's supervisor, didn't look very good himself—his face on the public phone's oval screen was discolored and distorted by incompatibilities between the alien and human systems.

"I've been busy." He inserted Amber Stone's data-nodule into the phone's receptor.

Gleason's eyes widened as the contract came up on his display. "Yes you have! This is great!"

"Thanks." Gleason's enthusiasm could not penetrate the shell of numbness around Walker's soul. Whatever joy he might have felt at making the sale had been drowned by three days of negotiations.

"This will make you the salesman of the quarter! And the party's tomorrow night!"

The End-of-Quarter party. He thought of the bluff and facile faces of his fellow salesmen, the loutish jokes and cheap congratulations of every other EOQ he'd ever attended. Would it really be any different if his name was the one at the top of the list? And then to return to his empty apartment, and go out the next day to start a new quarter from zero. . . .

"Sorry," Walker said, "I can't make it."

"That's right, what am I thinking? It's gotta be at least a five day trip, with all the transfers. Look, give me a call whenever you get in. You got my home number?"

"It's in my phone." Wherever that was.

"Okay, well, I gotta go. See you soon."

He sat in the dim, stuffy little booth for a long time. The greenish oval of the phone screen looked like a pool of stagnant water, draining slowly away, reflecting the face of a man with no family, no dog, no little house in the woods. And though he might be the salesman of the quarter today, there were a lot of quarters between here and retirement, and every one of them would be just as much work.

Eventually came the rap of chitinous knuckles on the wall of the booth, and a voice. "This most humble one begs the worthy customer's forgiveness. Other customers desire to use the phone."

The booth cracked open like a seed pod. Walker stuck out his head, blinking at the light, and the public phone attendant said, "Ah, most excellent customer. This most unworthy one trusts your call went well?"

"Yes. Most well."

"The price of the call is two hundred sixty-three."

Walker had about six in cash in his pants pockets. The rest had vanished with his jacket. He thought a moment, then dug in his money belt and pulled out a tiny plastic rectangle.

"What is this?"

"Ticket to Earth."

"An interstellar transit ticket? To Earth? Surely this humble one has misheard."

"Interstellar. To Earth."

"This is worth thousands!"

"Yes." Then, in English, he said, "Keep the change."

He left the attendant sputtering in incomprehension behind him.

. . . .

The man was cursing the heat and the crowds as he pushed through the restaurant's labia from the street, but when he saw Walker he stopped dead and just gaped for a moment. "Jesus!" he said at last, in English. "I thought I was the only human being on this Godforsaken planet."

Walker was lean and very tan; his salt-and-pepper hair and beard were long but neatly combed, and he stood with folded hands in an attitude of centered harmony. He wore only a short white skirt. "Greetings," he said in the *Thfshpfth* language, as he always did. "This one welcomes the peaceful visitor to the Spirit of Life."

"What are you doing here?" The English words were ludicrously loud and round.

Walker tapped his teeth together, making a sound like *tk'tk'tk,* before he replied in English: "I am . . . serving food." The sound of it tickled his mouth.

"On this planet, I mean."

"I live here."

"But why did you come here? And why the Hell did you stay?"

Walker paused for a moment. "I came to sell something. It was an Earth thing. The people here didn't need it. After a while I understood, and stopped trying. I've been much happier since." He gestured to one of the squatting-posts. "Please seat yourself."

"I, uh . . . I think I'll pass."

"You're sure? The *thksh hspthk* is very good today."

"Thanks, but no." The man turned to go, but then he paused, pulled some money from his pocket, ran a reader over it. "Here," he said, handing it to Walker. "Good luck."

As the restaurant's labia closed behind the visitor, Walker touched the money, then smelled his fingertip. Three hundred and eleven, a substantial sum.

He smiled, put the money in the donation jar, and settled in to wait for the next customer.

GENEVIEVE VALENTINE   Born into a military family and raised in several areas of the United States, Genevieve Valentine began selling short fantasy and SF in 2007, and has since published several dozen stories that display a flair for a remarkably large number of the field's subgenres.

"The Nearest Thing," originally published in John Joseph Adams's *Lightspeed*, was aptly described in that magazine as a story about "a future in which emotional entanglement in the workplace is even more complicated than we know it to be now." Mason is a socially awkward coder employed by a corporation that makes personalized "memorial dolls," robot duplicates of individuals with artificial pseudo-personalities. He has been shifted to a development team led by Paul, a charismatic wonder boy; their aim is to develop an AI, "the nearest thing" to being human.

THE NEAREST THING

CALENDAR REMINDER: STOCKHOLDER DINNER, 8PM.
THIS MESSAGE SENT FROM MORI: LOOKING TO THE FUTURE,
LOOKING OUT FOR YOU.

The Mori Annual Stockholder Dinner is a little slice of hell that employees are encouraged to attend, for morale.

Mori's made Mason rich enough that he owns a bespoke tux and drives to the Dinner in a car whose property tax is more than his father made in a year; of course he goes.

(He skipped one year because he was sick, and two Officers from HR came to his door with a company doctor to confirm it. He hasn't missed a party since.)

He's done enough high-profile work that Mori wants him to actually mingle, and he spends the cocktail hour being pushed from one group to another, shaking hands, telling the same three inoffensive anecdotes over and over.

They go fine; he's been practicing.

People chuckle politely just before he finishes the punch line.

Memorial dolls take a second longer, because they have to process the little cognitive disconnect of humor, and because they're programmed to think that interrupting is rude.

(He'll hand it to the Aesthetics department—it's getting harder to tell the difference between people with plastic surgery and the dolls.)

"I hear you're starting a new project," says Harris. He hugs Mrs. Harris closer, and after too long, she smiles.

(Mason will never know why anyone brings their doll out in public like this. The point is to ease the grieving process, not to provide arm candy. It's embarrassing. He wishes stockholders were a little less enthusiastic about showing support for the company.)

This new project is news to him, too, but he doesn't think stockholders want to hear that.

"I might be," he says. "I obviously can't say, but—"

Mr. Harris grins. "Paul Whitcover already told us—" (Mason thinks, *Who?*) "—and it sounds like a marvelous idea. I hope it does great things for the company; it's been a while since we had a new version."

Mason's heart stutters that he's been picked to spearhead a new version.

It sinks when he remembers Whitcover. He's one of the second-generation creative guys who gets his picture taken with some starlet on his arm, as newscasters talk about what good news it would be for Mori's stock if he were to marry a studio-contracted actress.

Mrs. Harris is smiling into middle space, waiting to be addressed, or for a keyword to come up.

Mason met Mrs. Harris several Dinners ago. She had more to say than this, and he worked on some of the conversation software in her generation; she can handle a party. Harris must have turned her cognitives down to keep her pleasant.

There's a burst of laughter across the room, and when Mason looks over it's some guy in a motorcycle jacket, surrounded by tuxes and gowns.

"Who's that?" he asks, but he knows, he knows, this is how his life goes, and he's already sighing when Mr. Harris says, "Paul."

• • • •

Since he got Compliance Contracted to Mori at fifteen, Mason has come to terms with a lot of things.

He's come to terms with the fact that, for the money he makes, he can't make noise about his purpose. He worked for a year on an impact-sensor chip for Mori's downmarket Prosthetic Division; you go where you're told.

(He's come to terms with the fact that the more Annual Stockholder Dinners you attend, the less time you spend in a cubicle in Prosthetics.)

He has come to terms with the fact that sometimes you will hate the people you work with, and there is nothing you can do.

(Mason suspects he hates everyone, and that the reasons why are the only things that change.)

The thing is, Mason doesn't hate Paul because Paul is a Creative heading an R&D project. Mason will write what they tell him to, under whatever creative-team asshole they send him. He's not picky.

Sure, he resents someone who introduces himself to other adults as, "Just Paul, don't worry about it, good to meet you," and he resents someone whose dad was a Creative Consultant and who's never once gone hungry, and he resents the adoring looks from stockholders as Paul claims Mori is really Going Places This Year, but things like this don't keep him up at night, either.

He's pretty sure he starts to hate Paul the moment Paul introduces him to Nadia.

· · · ·

At Mori, we know you care.

We know you love your family. We know you worry about leaving them behind. And we know you've asked for more information about us, which means you're thinking about giving your family the greatest gift of all:

You.

Medical studies have shown the devastating impact grief has on family bonds and mental health. The departure of someone beloved is a tragedy without a proper name.

Could you let the people you love live without you?

A memorial doll from Mori maps the most important aspects of your memory, your speech patterns, and even your personality into a synthetic reproduction.

The process is painstaking—our technology is exceeded only by our artistry—and it leaves behind a version of you that, while it can never re-place you, can comfort those who have lost you.

Imagine knowing your parents never have to say goodbye. Imagine knowing you can still read bedtime stories to your children, no matter what may happen.

A memorial doll from Mori is a gift you give to everyone who loves you.

· · · ·

Nadia holds perfectly still.

Her name tag reads "Aesthetic Consultant," which means Paul brought his model girlfriend to the meeting.

She's pretty, in a cat's-eye way, but Mason doesn't give her much thought. It takes a lot for Mason to really notice a woman, and she's nowhere near the actresses Paul dates.

(Mason's been reading up. He doesn't think much of Paul, but the man can find a camera at a hundred paces.)

Paul brings Nadia to the first brainstorming meeting for the Vestige project. He introduces her to Mason and the two guys from Marketing ("Just Nadia, don't worry about it"), and they're ten minutes into the meeting before Mason realizes she had never said a word.

It takes Mason until then to realize how still she is. Only her eyes move—to him, with a hard expression like she can read his mind and doesn't like what she sees.

Not that he cares. He just wonders where she came from, suddenly.

"So we have to think about a new market," Paul is saying. "There's a diminishing return on memorial dolls, unless we want to drop the price point to expand opportunities and popularize the brand—"

The two Marketing guys make appalled sounds at the idea of Mori going downmarket.

"—or, we develop something that will redefine the company," Paul finishes. "Something new. Something we build in-house from the ground up."

A Marketing guy says, "What do you have in mind?"

"A memorial that can conquer Death itself," says Paul.

(Nadia's eyes slide to Paul, never move.)

"How so?" asks the other marketing guy.

Paul grins, leans forward; Mason sees the switch flip.

Then Paul is magic.

He uses every catchphrase Mason's ever heard in a pitch, and some phrases he swears are from Mori's own pamphlets. Paul makes a lot of eye contact, frowns soulfully. The Marketing guys get glassy and slack-jawed, like they're watching a swimming pool fill up with doubloons. Paul smiles, one fist clenched to keep his amazing ideas from flying away.

Mason waits for a single concept concrete enough to hang some code on. He waits a long time.

(The nice thing about programs is that you deal in absolutes—yes, or no.)

"We'll be working together," and Paul encompasses Mason in his gesture. "Andrew Mason has a reputation for out-thinking computers. Together, we'll give the Vestige model a self-sustaining critical-thinking initiative no other developer has tried—and no consumer base has ever seen. It won't be human, but it will be the nearest thing."

The Marketing guys light up.

"Self-sustaining critical-thinking" triggers ideas about circuit maps and command-decision algorithms, and for a second Mason is absorbed in the idea.

He comes back when Paul says, "Oh, he definitely has ideas." He flashes a smile at the Marketing guys—it wobbles when he looks at Nadia, but he recovers well enough that the smile is back by the time it gets to Mason.

"Mason, want to give us tech dummies a rundown of what you've been brainstorming?"

Mason glances back from Nadia to Paul, doesn't answer.

Paul frowns. "Do you have questions about the project?"

Mason shrugs. "I just think maybe we shouldn't be discussing confidential R&D with some stranger in the room."

(Compliance sets up stings sometimes, just to make sure employees are serious about confidentiality. Maybe that's why she hasn't said a thing.)

Nadia actually turns her head to look at him (her eyes skittering past Paul), and Paul drops the act and snaps, "She's not some stranger," like she saved him from an assassination attempt.

It's the wrong thing to say.

It makes Mason wonder what the relationship between Paul and Nadia really is.

· · · ·

That afternoon, Officer Wilcox from HR stops by Mason's office.

"This is just a random check," she says. "Your happiness is important to the company."

What she means is, Paul ratted him out, and they're making sure he's not thinking of leaking information about the kind of project you build a market-wide stock repurchase on.

"I'm very happy here," Mason says, and it's what you always say to HR, but it's true enough; they pulled him from that shitty school and gave him a future. Now he has more money than he knows what to do with, and the company dentist isn't half bad.

He likes his work, and they leave him alone, and things have always been fine, until now.

(He imagines Paul, his face a mask of concern, saying, "It's not that I think he's up to anything, it's just he seems so unhappy, and he wouldn't answer me when I asked him something.")

"Will Nadia be part of the development team?" Mason asks, for no real reason.

"Undetermined," says Officer Wilcox. "Have a good weekend. Come back rested and ready to work on Vestige."

She hands him a coupon for a social club where dinner costs a week's pay and private hostesses are twice that.

She says, "The company really appreciates your work."

· · · ·

He goes home, opens his personal program.

Most of it is still just illustrations from old maps, but places he's been are recreated as close as he can get. Buildings, animals, dirt, people.

They're customizable down to fingerprints; he recreated his home city with people he remembers, and calibrated their personality traits as much as possible. It's a nice reminder of home, when he needs it.

(He needs it less and less; home is far away.)

This game has been his work since the first non-Mori computer he bought—with cash, on the black market, so he had something to use that was his alone.

Now there are real-time personality components and physical impossibility safeguards so you can't pull nonsense. It's not connected to a network, to keep Mori from prying. It stands alone, and he's prouder of it than anything he's done.

(The Memento model is a pale shadow of this; this is what Paul wants for Vestige, if Mason feels like sharing.)

He builds Nadia in minutes—he must have been watching her more than he thought—and gives her the personality traits he knows she has (self-possessed, grudging, uncomfortable), her relationship with Paul, how long he's known her.

He doesn't make any guesses about what he doesn't know for sure. It hurts the game to guess.

He puts Nadia in the Mori offices. (He can't put her in his apartment, because a self-possessed, grudging, uncomfortable person who hasn't known him long wouldn't go. His game is strict.) He makes them both tired from a long night of work.

He inputs Paul, too, finally—the scene won't start until he does, given what it knows about her—and is pleased to see Paul in his own office, sleeping under his motorcycle jacket, useless and out of the way.

Nadia tries every locked door in R&D systematically. Then she goes into the library, stands in place.

Mason watches his avatar working on invisible code so long he starts to drift off.

When he opens his eyes, Nadia's avatar is in the doorway of his office, where his avatar has rested his head in his hands, looking tired and upset and wishing he was the kind of person who could give up on something.

(His program is spooky, when he does it right.)

He holds his breath until Nadia's avatar turns around.

She finds the open door to Paul's office (of course it's open), stands and looks at him, too.

He wonders if her avatar wants to kiss Paul's.

Nadia's avatar leaves Paul's doorway, too, goes to the balcony overlooking the impressive lobby. She stands at the railing for a while, like his avatars used to do before he had perfected their physical limits so they wouldn't keep trying to walk through walls.

Then she jumps.

He blanks out for a second.

He restarts.

(It's not how life goes, it's a cheat, but without it he'd never have been able to understand a thing about how people work.)

He starts again, again.

She jumps every time.

His observations are faulty, he decides. There's not enough to go on, since he knows so little about her. His own fault for putting her into the system too soon.

He closes up shop; his hands are shaking.

Then he takes the Mori coupon off his dining table.

• • • •

The hostess is pretty, in a cat-eye way.

She makes small talk, pours expensive wine. He lets her because he's done this rarely enough that it's still awkward, and because Mori is picking up the tab, and because something is scraping at him that he can't define.

Later she asks him, "What can I do for you?"

He says, "Hold as still as you can."

It must be a creepy request; she freezes.

It's very still. It's as still as Nadia holds.

• • • •

Monday morning, Paul shows up in his office.

"Okay," Paul says, rubbing his hands together like he's about to carve a bird, "let's brainstorm how we can get these dolls to brainstorm for themselves."

"Where's Nadia?" Mason asks.

Paul says, "Don't worry about it."

Mason hates Paul.

• • • •

The first week is mostly Mason trying to get Paul to tell him what they're doing ("What you're doing now," Paul says, "just bigger and better, we'll figure things out, don't worry about it.") and how much money they have to work with.

("Forget the budget," Paul says, "we're just thinking about software, the prototype is taken care of."

Mason wonders how long Paul has been working on this, acquiring entire prototypes off the record, keeping under the radar of a company that taps your phones, and the hair on his neck stands up.)

"I have a baseline ready for implantation," Paul admits on Thursday, and it feels like a victory for Mason. "We can use that as a jumping-off point to test things, if you don't want to use simulators."

"You don't use simulators until you have a mock-up ready. The baseline is unimportant while we're still working on components." Then he thinks about it. "Where did you get a baseline with no R&D approval?"

Paul grins. "Black market," he says.

It's the first time Mason's ever suspected Paul might actually care about what they're doing.

It changes a lot of things.

• • • •

On Friday, Mason brings in a few of his program's parameters for structuring a sympathy algorithm, and when Paul shows up he says, "I had some ideas."

Paul bends to look, his motorcycle jacket squeaking against Mason's chair, his face tinted blue by the screen.

Mason watches Paul skim it twice. He's a quick reader.

"Fantastic," Paul says, in a way that makes Mason wonder if Paul knows more about specifics than he'd admit. "See what you can build me from this."

"I can build whatever you need," Mason says.

Paul looks down at him; his grin fills Mason's vision.

. . . .

Monday morning, Paul brings Nadia.

She sits in the back of the office, reading a book, glancing up when Mason says something that's either on the right track or particularly stupid.

(When he catches her doing it her eyes are deep and dark, and she's always just shy of pulling a face.)

Paul never says why he brought her, but Mason is pretty sure Nadia's not a plant—not even Paul could risk that. More likely she's his girlfriend. (Maybe she is an actress. He should start watching the news.)

Most of the time she has her nose in a book, so steady that Mason knows when she's looking at them if it's been too long between page-turns.

Once when they're arguing about infinite loops Paul turns and asks her, "Would that really be a problem?"

"I guess we'll find out," she says.

It's the first time she's spoken, and Mason twists to look at her.

She hasn't glanced up from her book, hasn't moved at all, but still Mason watches, waiting for something, until Paul catches his eye.

For someone who brings his girlfriend the unofficial consultant to the office every day, Paul seems unhappy about Mason looking.

Nadia doesn't seem to notice; her reflection in Mason's monitor doesn't look up, not once.

(Not that it matters if she does or not. He has no idea what he was waiting for.)

. . . .

Mason figures out what they're doing pretty quickly. Not that Paul told him, but when Mason said, "Are we trying to create emotional capacity?" Paul said, "Don't worry about it," grinning like he had at Mason's first lines of code, and that was Mason's answer.

There's only one reason you create algorithms for this level of critical thinking, and it's not for use as secretaries.

Mason is making an A.I. that can understand as well as respond, an A.I. that can grow an organic personality beyond its programming, that has an imagination; one that can really live.

(Sometimes, when he's too tired to help it, he gets romantic about work.)

. . . .

For a second-gen creative guy, Paul picks up fast.

"But by basing preference on a pre-programmed moral scale, they'll always prefer people who make the right decisions on a binary," Mason says. "Stockholders might not like free will that favors the morally upstanding."

Paul nods, thinks it over.

"See if you can make an algorithm that develops a preference based on the reliability of someone's responses to problems," Paul says. "People are easy to predict. Easier than making them moral."

There's no reason for Paul to look at Nadia right then, but he does, and for a second his whole face falters.

For a second, Nadia's does, too.

Mason can't sleep that night, thinking about it.

> TO: ANDREW MASON
> FROM: HR—HEALTH/WELFARE
>
> Your caffeine intake from the cafeteria today is 40% above normal. Your health is of great importance to us.
>
> If you would like to renegotiate a project timeline, please contact Management to arrange a meeting. If you are physically fatigued, please contact a company doctor. If there is a personal issue, a company therapist is standing by for consult.
>
> If any of these apply, please let us know what actions you have taken, so we may update your records.
>
> If this is a dietary anomaly, please disregard.
>
> The company appreciates your work.

They test some of the components on a simulator.

(Mason tells Paul they're marking signs of understanding. Really, he wants to see if the simulation prefers one of them without a logical basis. That's what humans do.)

He pulls up a baseline, several traits mixed at random from reoccurring types in the Archives, just to keep you from using someone's remnant. (The company frowns on that.)

Under the ID field, Mason types in GALATEA.

"Acronym?" Paul asks.

"Allusion," says Nadia.

Her reflection is looking at the main monitor, her brows drawn in an expression too stricken to be a frown.

Galatea runs diagnostics (a long wait—the text-interface version passed four sentience screenings in anonymous testing last month, and something that sophisticated takes a lot of code). She recognizes the camera, nodding at Mason and Paul in turn.

Then her eyes go flat, refocus to find Nadia.

It makes sense, Nadia's further away, but Mason still gets the creeps. Someone needs to work on the naturalism of these simulators. This isn't some second-rate date booth; they have a reputation to uphold.

"Be charming," Mason says.

Paul cracks up.

"Okay," he says, "Galatea, good to meet you, I'm Paul, and I'll try to be charming tonight."

• • • •

Galatea prefers Paul in under ten minutes.

Mason would burn the place down if he wasn't so proud of himself.

"Galatea," Mason asks, "what is the content of Paul's last sentence?"

"That his work is going well."

It wasn't what Paul really said—it had as little content as most of Paul's sentences that aren't about code—which means Galatea was inferring the best meaning, because she favored him.

"Read this," Mason says, scrawls a note.

Paul reads, "During a shift in market paradigms, it's imperative that we leverage our synergy to re-evaluate paradigm structure."

It's some line of shit Paul gave him the first day they worked together. Paul doesn't even have the shame to recognize it.

"Galatea, act on that sentence," Mason says.

"I cannot," Galatea says, but her camera lens is focused square on Paul's face, which is Mason's real answer.

"Installing this software has compromised your baseline personality system and altered your preferences," he says. "Can you identify the overwrites?"

There's a tiny pause.

"No," she says, sounds surprised.

He looks up at Paul, grinning, but Paul's jaw is set like a guilty man, and his eyes are focused on the wall ahead of him, his hands in fists on the desk.

(Reflected in his monitor: Nadia, her book abandoned, sitting a little forward in her chair, lips parted, watching it all like she's seen a ghost.)

• • • •

At the holiday party, Paul and Nadia show up together.

Paul has his arm around her, and after months of seeing them together Mason still can't decide if they're dating.

(He only sees how Paul holds out his hand to her as they leave every day, how she looks at him too long before she takes it, the story he's already telling her, his smile of someone desperate to please.)

The way Paul manages a party is supernatural. His tux is artfully rumpled, his hand on Nadia's waist, and he looks right at everyone he meets.

It's too smooth to be instinctive; his father must have trained him up young.

Maybe that's it—maybe they're like brother and sister, if you ignore the way Paul looks at her sometimes when she's in profile, like he wouldn't mind a shot but he's not holding his breath.

(He envies Paul his shot with her; he envies them both for having someone to be a sibling with.)

"Why do you keep watching me?"

She's not coy, either, he thinks as he turns, and something about her makes him feel like being honest.

He says, "I find you interesting."

"Because of how I look." Delivered like the conclusion of a scientific paper whose results surprised everyone.

"Because of how you look at everyone else."

It must shake her; she tilts her head, and for an instant her eyes go empty and flat as she pulls her face into a different expression.

It's so fast that most people wouldn't notice, but Mason is suspicious enough by now to be watching for some small tic that marks her as other than human.

Now he knows why she looks so steadily into her book, if that's what happens every time someone surprises her.

Doesn't stop him from going cold.

(He can't process it. It's one thing to be suspicious, another thing to know.)

It must show on his face; she looks at him like she doesn't know what he's going to do.

It's not how she used to look at him.

He goes colder.

Her eyes go terrified, as terrified as any human eyes.

She's the most beautiful machine he's ever seen.

He opens his mouth.

"Don't," she starts.

Then Paul is there, smiling, asking, "You remember how to dance, right?", lacing his fingers in her fingers and pulling her with him a fraction too fast to be casual.

She watches Mason over her shoulder all the way to the dance floor.

He stands where he is a long time, watching the golden boy of Mori dancing with his handmade Vestige prototype.

· · · ·

He spends the weekend wondering if he has a friend in Aesthetics who could tell him where Nadia's face really came from, or one in Archives who would back him up about a personality Paul Whitcover's been saving for a special occasion.

It's tempting. It wouldn't stop the project, but it would certainly shut Paul up, and with something that big he might be able to renegotiate his contract right up to Freelance. (No one taps your home network when you're Freelance.)

He needs to tell someone, soon. If he doesn't, and someone finds out down the line they were keeping secrets, Mason will end up in Quality Control for the rest of his life, monitored 24/7 and living in the subterranean company apartments.

If he doesn't tell, and Paul does, Paul will get Freelance and Mason will just be put down.

He has to make the call. He has to tell Compliance.

But whenever he's on the verge of doing something, he remembers her face after he'd found her out and she feared the worst from him, how she'd let Paul take her hand, but watched him over her shoulder as long as she dared.

It's not a very flattering memory, but somehow it keeps him from making a move.

(Just as well; turns out he doesn't have a lot of friends.)

. . . .

Monday morning Paul comes in alone, shuts the door behind him, and doesn't say a word.

It's such a delightful change that Mason savors the quiet for a while before he turns around.

Paul has his arms crossed, his face a set of wary lines. (He looks like Nadia.)

Mason says, "Who is she?"

He's hardly slept all weekend, thinking about it. He'd imagined tragic first love, or some unattainable socialite Paul was just praying would get personality-mapped.

Once or twice he imagined Paul had tried to reincarnate Daddy, but that was too weird even for him.

Paul shakes his head, tightly. "No one."

"Come on," says Mason, "if I haven't called HR by now I'm not going to. Who?"

Paul sits down, rakes his hair back with his hands.

"I didn't want to get in trouble if they found out I was making one," he says. "It's one thing to fuck around with some company components, but if you take a customer's remnant—" He shakes his head. "I couldn't risk it. I had them put in a standard template for her."

Mason thinks about Paul's black-market baseline, wonders how Paul would have known what was there before he installed the chip and woke her.

"She's not standard anymore," he settles on.

Nadia should be here; Mason would really feel better about this whole conversation if she were here.

(But Paul wouldn't be talking about it if she were; he knows that much about Paul by now.)

"No," says Paul, a sad smile crossing his face. "I tried a couple of our early patches, before we were working on the full. I couldn't believe how well they took."

Of course they did, thinks Mason, they're mine, but he keeps his mouth shut.

Paul looks as close to wonderment as guys like him can get. "When we announce Vestige, it's going to change the world. You know that, right?"

He knows. It's one of the reasons he can't sleep.

"What happens to Nadia, then?" he asks.

(That's the other reason he can't sleep.)

"I don't know," Paul says, shaking his head. "She knows what she is—I mean, she knows she's A.I.—she understands what might happen. I told her that from the very beginning. At first I thought we could use her as a tester. I had no idea how much I would—" he falters as his feelings get the better of him.

"Not human, but the nearest thing?" Mason says, and it comes out vicious.

Paul has the decency to flinch, but it doesn't last.

"She knows I care about her," he goes on. "I'm planning for better things. Hopefully Mori will be so impressed by the product that they'll let me—that they'll be all right with Nadia."

He means, *That they'll let me keep her.*

"What if they want her as the prototype?"

"I haven't lied to her," Paul says. "Not ever. She knows she might have to get the upgrade to preserve herself, that she might end up belonging to the company. She accepts it. I thought I had, too, but I didn't think she'd be so—I mean, I didn't think I would come to—in the beginning, she really was no one."

Mason remembers the first time Nadia ever looked at him; he knows it isn't true.

They sit quietly for a long time, Paul looking wracked as to how he fell in love with something he made, like someone who never thought to look up Galatea.

. . . .

She's waiting in the library, and it surprises him before he admits that of course he'd look for her here; he had a map.

He doesn't make any noise, and she doesn't look up from her console, but after a second she says, "Some of these have never even been accessed." A castigation.

He says, "These are just reference books." He doesn't say, I don't need them. He needs to try not being an asshole sometimes.

She glances up, then. (He looks for code behind her eyes, feels worse than Paul.)

"I love books," she says. "At first I didn't, but now I understand them better. Now I love them."

(She means, *Are you going to give me away?*)

He wonders if this is just her, or if this is his algorithm working, and something new is trying to get out.

"I have a library at home," he says. (He means, *No.*)

She blinks, relaxes. "What do you read?"

"Pulp, mostly," he says, thinks about his collection of detective novels, wonders if she thinks that's poor taste.

She says, "They're all pulp."

It's a sly joke (he doesn't think it's anything of his), and she has such a smile he gets distracted, and when he pulls himself together she's leaving.

"I'll walk you somewhere," he says. "Paul and I won't be done for a while."

Clearly Paul told her not to trust him before he went in to spill his guts, but after a second she says, "Tell me more about your books," and he falls into step beside her.

He tells her about the library that used to be the guest bedroom before he realized he didn't have guests and there was no point in it. He explains why there are no windows and special light bulbs and a fancy dehumidifier to make sure mold doesn't get into the books.

(It's also lined in lead, which keeps Mori from getting a look at his computer. Some things are private.)

Her expression keeps changing, so subtle he'd swear she was human if he didn't know better.

She talks about the library at Alexandria, an odd combination of a machine programmed to access information and someone with enough imagination she might as well have been there.

(Maybe this is immortality, as far as it goes.)

She mentions the Dewey Decimal system, and he says, "That's how I shelve mine."

"That explains your code," she says. When he raises his eyebrows, she says, "It's . . . thorough."

(Diplomacy. Also not his.)

"It has to be," he says. "I want Vestige to be perfect."

He doesn't say, *You.*

"I know," she says, in a way he doesn't like, but by then they're standing in front of Paul's office, and she's closing the door.

This floor has a balcony overlooking the atrium.

He sticks close to the wall all the way back.

• • • •

He goes home and erases her avatar from his program.

(Not like he cares what she thinks, but there's no harm in cleaning house.)

• • • •

Marketing calls them in for a meeting about the press announcement.

They talk a lot about advertising and luxury markets and consumer interest and the company's planned stock reissue and how the Patents team is standing by any time they want to hand over code.

"Aesthetics has done some really amazing work," Marketing says, and Mason fakes polite interest as hard as he can so he doesn't stare at the photo.

(It's not quite Nadia; it's close enough that Mason's throat goes tight, but it's a polished, prettier version, the kind of body you'd use if you wanted to immortalize your greyhound in a way society would accept.)

"Gorgeous," Paul says, and then with a smile, "is she single?" and the Marketing guys crack up.

(One of them says, "Now now, Paul, we're still hoping you can make a studio match—HR would be pleased," and Paul looks admirably amenable for a guy who's in love with a woman he thinks he made.)

It's only Paul on the schedule to present, of course—Mason's not a guy you put in front of a camera—and it's far enough away that they'll have time to polish the code.

"Naturally, you should have the prototype presentable ASAP," the Marketing VP says. "We need a pretty face for the ads, and we need her to have her personality installed by then. Aesthetics seems to think it's already in place, in some form?"

The VP's face is just bland enough not to mean anything by it, if their consciences don't get the better of them.

Don't you dare, Mason thinks, don't you dare tell them for a chance to keep her, second-gen or not, it's a trap, not one word, think about what will happen to her.

(She's still a doll, he thinks, deeper, ruthlessly; something will happen to her eventually.)

"I don't know a thing about the particulars, I'm afraid," Paul says, and having thus absolved himself he throws a casual look at Mason.

Mason thinks, *You asshole.* He thinks, *Here's where I rat him out.*

He grits his teeth and smiles.

"We've been running tests," he says. "Would you like to see Galatea?" Then, in his best Paul impression, "She has a crush on Paul, of course."

The Marketing guys laugh, and Mason pulls up Galatea on his pad, and as the lights go down he catches Paul glancing gratefully in his direction.

He hates how strange it feels to have someone be grateful to him; he hates that it's Paul.

. . . .

Paul walks out with the Marketing guys, grinning and charming and empty, and from the plans they're making for the announcement and the new projects they're already asking him about, Mason suspects that's the last time he'll ever see Paul.

It's so lonely in his office he thinks about turning on Galatea, just for company.

(He's no better than some.)

LiveScribe: MORI PRESS CONFERENCE—VESTIGE, PT 1.
SEARCH PARAMETERS—BEGIN: 10:05:27, END: 10:08:43

PAUL WHITCOVER: From the company that brought you Memento, which has not only pioneered the Alpha series real-time response interface, but has also brought comfort to grieving families across the world.

It's this focus on the humanity behind the technology that is Mori's greatest achievement, and it is what has made possible what I am about to show you. Ladies and gentlemen, may I present: Galatea.

[MORIVESTIGE00001.img available through LiveSketch link]
[APPLAUSE, CALLS, SHOUTS]

PAUL WHITCOVER: Galatea isn't human, but she's the nearest thing. She's the prototype of our Vestige model, which shifts the paradigm of robotics in ways we have only begun to guess—if you can tear your eyes away from her long enough.

[LAUGHTER, APPLAUSE]

PAUL WHITCOVER: Each Vestige features critical-thinking initiatives so advanced it not only sustains the initial personality, but allows the processor to learn from new stimuli, to form attachments—to grow in the same way the human mind does. This Vestige is built on a donor actress— anonymous, for now, though I suspect some in the audience will know who she is as soon as you talk to her.

[LAUGHTER]

In seriousness, I would like to honor everyone at Mori who participated in the development of such a remarkable thing. The stock market will tell you that this is an achievement of great technical merit, and that's true. However, those who have honored loved ones with a Memento doll will tell you that this is a triumph over the grieving heart, and it's this that means the most to Mori.

Understandably, due to the difficulty of crafting each doll, the Vestige is a very limited product. However, our engineers are already developing alternate uses for this technology that you will soon see more of—and that might yet change your world.

Ladies and gentlemen, thank you so much for being here today. It is not only my honor, but my privilege.

[APPLAUSE]

Small-group interviews with Vestige will be offered to members of the press. Check your entrance ticket. Thank you again, everyone, really, this is such a thrill, I'm glad you could be here. If you'd—

. . . .

The phone call comes from some internal extension he's never seen, but he's too distracted by the streaming press-conference footage to screen it.

Paul is made for television; he can practically see the HR people arranging for his transfer to Public Relations.

(He can't believe Paul carried through with Nadia the Aesthetic Consultant. He can absolutely believe Paul named her Galatea.)

"This is Mason."

There's nothing on the other end, but he knows it's her.

He hangs up, runs for the elevator.

. . . .

Nadia's on the floor in the library, twitching like she got fifty thousand volts, and he drops to his knees and pulls the connecting cable out of her skull.

"We have to get you to a hospital," he says, which is the stupidest thing that's ever come out of his mouth (he watches too many movies). What she needs is an antivirus screen in one of the SysTech labs.

Maybe it's for her sake he says it, so they can keep pretending she's real until she tells him otherwise.

"It's the baseline," she says, and he can't imagine what she was doing in there.

He says, "I'll get you to an Anti-V, hang on."

"No," she manages.

Then her eyes go blank and flat, and something inside her makes an awful little click.

He scoops her up without thinking, moves to the elevator as fast as he can.

He has to get her home.

* * * *

He makes it in seven minutes (he'll be paying a lot of tickets later), carries her through the loft. She's stopped twitching, and he doesn't know if that's better or worse.

He assumes she's tougher than she looks—God knows how many upgrades Paul's put her through—but you never know. She's light enough in his arms that he wonders how she was ever expected to last.

He sets her on one of the chaises the Mori designer insisted mimicked the lines of the living room, drags it through the doorway to his study.

He finds the socket (behind one ear), the same place as Memento; rich people don't care for visible flaws.

He plugs her into his program.

It feels slimy, like he's showing her into his bedroom, but at least Mori won't monitor the process.

Her head is limp, her eyes half-lidded and unseeing.

"Hold on," he says, like some asshole, pulls up his program.

(Now he's sorry he deleted her avatar; he could help her faster if he had any framework ready to go.)

The code scans. Some of it is over his head—some parts of her baseline Paul got from the black market. (Black-market programmers can do amazing work. If he gets out of this alive, he might join up with them.)

He recognizes a few lines of his own code that have integrated, feels prouder than he should.

He recognizes some ID stamps that make his whole chest go tight, and his eyes ache.

Paul's an idiot, he thinks, wants to punch something.

Then he sees the first corruption, and his work begins.

* * * *

He's never worked with a whole system. It's always been lines of code sent to points unknown; Galatea was the first time he'd worked with anything close to a final product.

Now Nadia is staring at the ceiling with those awful empty eyes, and his fingers shake.

If he thinks of this as surgery he's going to be ill. He turns so he can't see her.

After a while he hits a stride; it takes him back to being twelve, recreating their apartment in a few thousand lines of code, down to the squeak in the hall.

("That's very . . . specific," his mother said, and that was when he began to suspect his imagination was wanting.)

When he finishes the last line, the code flickers, and he's terrified that it will be nothing but a string of zeros like a flatline.

But it cycles again, faster than he can read it, and then there's a boot file like Galatea's, and he thinks, *Fuck, I did it.*

Then her irises stutter, and she wakes up.

She makes an awful, hollow noise, and he reaches for her hand, stops—maybe that's the last thing you need when you're having a panic reboot.

She looks at him, focuses.

"You should check the code," he says. "I'm not sure if I got it all."

There's a brief pause.

"You did," she says, and when her eyes close he realizes she's gone to sleep and not shorted out.

After some debate he carries her to the bed, feeling like a total idiot. He didn't realize they slept.

(Maybe it was Paul's doing, to make her more human; he had planned for better things.)

. . . .

He sits in front of his computer for a long time, looking at the code with his finger on the Save button, deciding what kind of guy he is.

(That's the nice thing about programs, he always thought; you only ever deal in absolutes—yes, or no.)

. . . .

When he finally turns in his chair, she's in the doorway, watching him.

"I erased it," he says.

She says, "I know," in a tone that makes him wonder how long she's been standing there.

She sits on the edge of the chaise, rolls one shoulder like she's human and it hurts.

"Were you trying to kill yourself?" he asks.

She pulls a face.

He flushes. "No, not that I want—I just, have a game I play, and in the game you jumped. I've always been worried."

It sounds exactly as creepy as it is, and he's grateful she looks at his computer and doesn't ask what else he did with her besides watch her jump.

I would have jumped if I were you and knew what I was in for, he thinks, *but some people take the easy way out.*

Nadia sits like a human gathering her thoughts. Mason watches her face (can't help it), wonders how long she has.

The prototype is live; pretty soon, someone at Mori will realize how much Vestige acts like Nadia.

Maybe they won't deactivate her. Paul's smart enough to leverage his success for some lenience; he can get what he wants out of them, maybe.

(To keep her, Mason thinks, wonders why there's no way for Nadia to win.)

"Galatea doesn't remember her baseline," Nadia says, after a long time. "She thinks that's who she always was. Paul said I started with a random template, like her, and I thought I had kept track of what you changed."

Mason thinks about her fondness for libraries; he thinks how she sat in his office for months, listening to them talk about what was going to happen to her next.

She pauses where a human would take a breath. She's the most beautiful machine in the world.

"But the new Vestige prototype was based on a remnant," she says. "All the others will be based on just one person. I had to know if I started as someone else."

Mason's heart is in his throat. "And?"

She looks at him. "I didn't get that far."

She means, *You must have.*

He shrugs. "I'll tell you whatever you want to know," he says. "I'm not Paul."

"I didn't call Paul," she says.

(She had called him; she knew how he would respond to a problem. People are easy to predict.

It's how you build preferences.)

If he were a worse man, he'd take it as a declaration of love.

Instead he says, "Paul thought you were standard. He got your baseline from the black market, to keep Mori out, and they told him it was."

He stops, wonders how to go on.

"Who was I?" she says, finally.

"They didn't use a real name for her," he says. "There's no knowing."

(The black-market programmer was also a sucker for stories; he'd tagged her remnant "Galatea."

Mason will take that with him to the grave.)

She looks at him.

He thinks about the first look she ever gave him, wary and hard in an expression he never saw again, and the way she looked as Galatea fell in love with Paul, realizing she had lost herself but with no way of knowing how much.

He thinks about her avatar leaping over the balcony and disappearing.

He'd leave with her tonight, take his chances working on the black market, if she wanted him to. He'd cover for her as long as he could, if she wanted to go alone.

(God, he wants her to live.)

"I can erase what we did," he says. "Leave you the way you were when Paul woke you."

(Paul won't notice; he loves her too much to see her at all.)

Her whole body looks betrayed; her eyes are fixed in middle space, and she curls her fingers around the edge of the chair like she's bracing for the worst, like at any moment she'll give in.

He's reminded for a second of Kim Parker, who followed him to the Spanish Steps one morning during the Mori Academy study trip to Rome when he was fifteen. He sat beside her for a long time, waiting for a sign to kiss her that never came.

He'd felt stupid that whole time, and lonely, and exhilarated, and the whole time they were sitting together part of him was memorizing all the color codes he would need to build the Steps back, later, in his program.

Nadia is blinking from time to time, thinking it over.

The room is quiet—only one of them is breathing—and it's the loneliest he's felt in a long time, but he'll wait as long as it takes.

He knows how to wait for a yes or a no; people like them deal in absolutes.

IAN CREASEY Born in Yorkshire, where he has lived all his life, Ian Creasey began selling short SF in 1999, after (as he tells it) "rock and roll stardom failed to return my calls." His spare-time interests include hiking, gardening, and environmental conservation work—anything to get him outdoors and away from the computer screen.

In "Erosion," a man who has had himself physically altered so he can survive on other planets tells the story of his last week on Earth, during which he had an accident. The narrative brilliantly manages point of view in the service of plot. Many SF stories have examined the question of human augmentation, wondering at what point the augmented cease to be human. "Erosion" is a standout, not least because it is left unclear which side of that line it's told from.

EROSION

Let me tell you about my last week on Earth. . . .

Before those final days, I'd already said my farewells. My family gave me their blessing: my grandfather, who came to England from Jamaica as a young man, understood why I signed up for the colony program. He warned me that a new world, however enticing, would have its own frustrations. We both knew I didn't need the warning, but he wanted to pass on what he'd learned in life, and I wanted to hear it. I still remember the clasp of his fingers on my new skin; I can replay the exo-skin's sensory log whenever I wish.

My girlfriend was less forgiving. She accused me of cowardice, of running away. I replied that when your house is on fire, running away is the sensible thing to do. The Earth is burning up, and so we set forth to find a new home elsewhere. She said—she shouted—that when our house is on fire, we should stay and fight the flames. She wanted to help the fire-fighters. I respected her for that, and I didn't try to persuade her to come with me. That only made her all the more angry.

The sea will douse the land, in time, but it rises slowly. Most of the coastline still resembled the old maps. I'd decided that I would spend my last few days walking along the coast, partly to say goodbye to Earth, and partly to settle into my fresh skin and hone my augments. I'd tested it all in the post-op suite, of course, and in the colony simulator, but I wanted to practice in a natural setting. Reality throws up challenges that a simulator would never devise.

And so I traveled north. People stared at me on the train. I'm accustomed to that—when they see a freakishly tall black man, even the British overcome their famed (and largely mythical) reserve, and stare like scientists at a new specimen. The stares had become more hostile in recent years, as waves of African refugees fled their burning lands. I was born in Newcastle, like my parents, but that isn't written on my face. When I spoke, people smiled to hear a black guy with a Geordie accent, and their hostility melted.

Now I was no longer black, but people still stared. My grey exo-skin, formed of myriad tiny nodules, was iridescent as a butterfly's wings. I'd been told I could create patterns on it, like a cuttlefish, but I hadn't yet learned the fine control required. There'd be plenty of shipboard time after departure for such sedentary trifles. I wanted to be active, to run and jump and swim, and test all the augments in the wild outdoors, under the winter sky.

Scarborough is, or was, a town on two levels. The old North Bay and South Bay beaches had long since drowned, but up on the cliffs the shops and quaint houses and the ruined castle stood firm. I hurried out of town and soon reached the coastal path—or rather, the latest incarnation of the coastal path, each a little further inland than the last. The Yorkshire coast had always been nibbled by erosion, even in more tranquil times. Now the process was accelerating. The rising sea level gouged its own scars from higher tides, and the warmer globe stirred up fiercer storms that lashed the cliffs and tore them down. Unstable slopes of clay alternated with fresh rock, exposed for the first time in millennia. Piles of jagged rubble shifted restlessly, the new stones not yet worn down into rounded pebbles.

After leaving the last house behind, I stopped to take off my shirt, jeans and shoes. I'd only worn them until now as a concession to blending in with the naturals (as we called the unaugmented). I hid the clothes under some gorse, for collection on my return. When naked, I stretched my arms wide, embracing the world and its weather and everything the future could throw at me.

The air was calm yet oppressive, in a brooding sulk between stormy tantrums. Grey clouds lay heavy on the sky, like celestial loft insulation. My augmented eyes detected polarized light from the sun behind the clouds, beyond the castle standing starkly on its promontory. I tried to remember why I could see polarized light, and failed. Perhaps there was no reason, and the designers had simply installed the ability because they could. Like software, I suffered feature bloat. But when we arrived at our new planet, who could guess what hazards lay in store? One day, seeing polarized light might save my life.

I smelled the mud of the path, the salt of the waves, and a slight whiff of raw sewage. Experimentally, I filtered out the sewage, leaving a smell more like my memories from childhood walks. Then I returned to defaults. I didn't want to make a habit of ignoring reality and receiving only the sense impressions I found aesthetic.

Picking up speed, I marched beside the barbed wire fences that enclosed the farmers' shrinking fields. At this season the fields contained only stubble and weeds, the wheat long since harvested. Crows pecked desultorily at the sodden ground. I barged through patches of gorse; the sharp spines tickled my exo-skin, but did not harm it. With my botanist's eye, I noted all the inhabitants of the little cliff-edge habitat. Bracken and clover and thistles and horsetail—the names rattled through my head, an incantation of farewell. The starship's seedbanks included many species, on the precautionary principle. But initially we'd concentrate on growing food crops, aiming to breed strains that would flourish on the colony world. The other plants . . . this might be the last time I'd ever see them.

It was once said that the prospect of being hanged in the morning concentrated a man's mind wonderfully. Leaving Earth might be almost as drastic, and it had the same effect of making me feel euphorically alive. I registered every detail of the environment: the glistening spiders' webs in the dead bracken, the harsh calls of squabbling crows, the distant roar of the ever-present sea below. When I reached a gully with a storm-fed river at the bottom, I didn't bother following the path inland to a bridge; I charged down the slope, sliding on mud but keeping my balance, then splashed through the water and up the other side.

I found myself on a headland, crunching along a graveled path. An ancient notice-board asked me to clean up after my dog. Ahead lay a row of benches, on the seaward side of the path, much closer to the cliff edge than perhaps they once had been. They all bore commemorative plaques, with lettering mostly faded or rubbed away. I came upon a legible one that read:

IN MEMORY OF KATRIONA GRADY
2021–2098
SHE LOVED THIS COAST

Grass had grown up through the slats of the bench, and the wood had weathered to a mottled beige. I brushed aside the detritus of twigs and hawthorn berries, then smiled at myself for the outdated gesture. I wore no clothes to be dirtied, and my exo-skin could hardly be harmed by a few spiky twigs. In time I would abandon the foibles of a fragile human body, and stride confidently into any environment.

I sat, and looked out to sea. The wind whipped the waves into white froth, urging them to the coast. Gulls scudded on the breeze, their cries as jagged as the rocks they nested on. A childhood memory shot through me—eating chips on the seafront, a gull swooping to snatch a morsel. Within me swelled an emotion I couldn't name.

After a moment I became aware of someone sitting next to me. Yet the bench hadn't creaked under any additional weight. A hologram, then. When I turned to look, I saw the characteristic bright edges of a cheap hologram from the previous century.

"Hello, I'm Katriona. Would you like to talk?" The question had a rote quality, and I guessed that all visitors were greeted the same way; a negative answer would dismiss the hologram so that people could sit in peace. But I had several days of solitude ahead of me, and I didn't mind pausing for a while. It seemed appropriate that my last conversation on a dying world would be with a dead person.

"Pleased to meet you," I said. "I'm Winston."

The hologram showed a middle-aged white woman, her hair as grey as river-bed stones, her clothes a tasteful expanse of soft-toned lavender skirt and low-heeled expensive shoes. I wondered if she'd chosen this conventional self-effacing look, or if some memorial designer had imposed a template projecting the dead as aged and faded, not upstaging the living. Perhaps she'd have preferred to be depicted as young and wild and beautiful, as she'd no doubt once been—or would like to have been.

"It's a cold day to be wandering around starkers," she said, smiling.

I had forgotten I wore no clothes. I gave her a brief account of my augmentations. "I'm going to the stars!" I said, the excitement of it suddenly bursting out.

"What, all of them? Do they make copies of you, and send you all across the sky?"

"No, it's not like that." However, the suggestion caused me a moment of disorientation. I had walked into the hospital on my old human feet, been anaesthetized, then—quite some time later—had walked out in shiny new augmented form. Did only one of me leave, or had others emerged elsewhere, discarded for defects or optimized for different missions? *Don't be silly*, I told myself. *It's only an exo-skin. The same heart still beats underneath*. That heart, along with the rest of me, had yesterday passed the final pre-departure medical checks.

"We go to one planet first," I said, "which will be challenge enough. But later—who knows?" No one had any idea what the lifespan of an augmented human might prove to be; since all the mechanical components could be upgraded, the limit would be reached by any biological parts that couldn't be replaced. "It does depend on discovering other planets worth visiting. There are many worlds out there, but only a few even barely habitable."

I described our destination world, hugging a red-dwarf sun, its elliptical orbit creating temperature swings, fierce weather and huge tides. "The colonists are a mixed bunch: naturals who'll mostly have to stay back at base; then the augmented, people like me who should be able to survive outside;

and the gene-modders—they reckon they'll be best off in the long run, but it'll take them generations to get the gene-tweaks right." There'd already been tension between the groups, as we squabbled over the starship's finite cargo capacity, but I refrained from mentioning it. "I'm sorry—I've gone on long enough. Tell me about yourself. Did you live around here? Was this your favorite place?"

"Yorkshire lass born and bred, that's me," said Katriona's hologram. "Born in Whitby, spent a few years on a farm in Dentdale, but came back—*suck my flabby tits*—to the coast when I married my husband. He was a fisherman, God rest his soul. *Arsewipe!* When he was away, I used to walk along the coast and watch the North Sea, imagining him out there on the waves."

My face must have showed my surprise.

"Is it happening again?" asked Katriona. "I was hacked a long time ago, I think. I don't remember very much since I died—I'm more of a recording than a simulation. I only have a little memory, enough for short-term interaction." She spoke in a bitter tone, as though resenting her limitations. "What more does a memorial bench need? Ah, I loved this coast, but that doesn't mean I wanted to sit here forever. . . . *Nose-picking tournament, prize for the biggest booger!*"

"Would you like me to take you away?" I asked. It would be easy enough to pry loose the chip. The encoded personality could perhaps be installed on the starship's computer with the other uploaded colonists, yet I sensed that Katriona wouldn't pass the entrance tests. She was obsolete, and the dead were awfully snobbish about the company they kept. I'd worked with them in the simulator, and I could envisage what they'd say. "Why, Winston, I know you mean well, but she's not the right sort for a mission like this. She has no relevant expertise. Her encoding is coarse, her algorithms are outdated, and she's absolutely riddled with parasitic memes."

Just imagining this response made me all the more determined to fight it. But Katriona saved me the necessity. "That's all right, dear. I'm too old and set in my ways to go to the stars. I just want to rejoin my husband, and one day I will." She stared out to sea again, and I had a sudden intuition of what had happened to her husband.

"I'm sorry for your loss," I said. "I take it he was never"—I groped for an appropriate word—"memorialized."

"There's a marker in the *fuckflaps* graveyard," she said, "but he was never recorded like me. Drowning's a quick death, but it's not something you plan for. And we never recovered the body, so it couldn't be done afterward. He's still down there somewhere. . . ."

It struck me that if Katriona's husband had been augmented, he need not have drowned. My limbs could tirelessly swim, and my exo-skin could filter oxygen from the water. As it would be tactless to proclaim my hardiness, I cast about for a neutral reply. "The North Sea was all land, once. Your ancestors hunted mammoths there, before the sea rose."

"And now the sea is rising again." She spoke with such finality that I knew our conversation was over.

"God speed you to your rest," I said. When I stood up, the hologram vanished.

I walked onward, and the rain began.

· · · ·

I relished the storm. It blew down from the northeast, with ice in its teeth. They call it the lazy wind, because it doesn't bother to go around you—it just goes straight through you.

The afternoon darkened, with winter twilight soon expiring. The rain thickened into hail, bouncing off me with an audible rattle. Cracks of thunder rang out, an ominous rumbling as though the raging sea had washed away the pillars of the sky, pulling the heavens down. Lightning flashed somewhere behind me.

I turned and looked along the coastal path, back to the necropolis of benches I had passed earlier. The holograms were all lit up. I wondered who would sit on the benches in this weather, until I realized that the lightning must have short-circuited the activation protocols.

The holograms were the only bright colors in a washed-out world of slate-grey cloud and gun-dark sea. Images of men and women flickered on the benches, an audience for Nature's show. I saw Katriona standing at the top of the cliff, raising her arms as if calling down the storm. Other figures sat frozen like reproachful ghosts, tethered to their wooden anchors, waiting for the storm to fade. Did they relish the brief moment of pseudo-life? Did they talk among themselves? Or did they resent their evanescent existence, at the mercy of any hikers and hackers wandering by?

I felt I should not intrude. I returned to my trek, slogging on as the day eroded into night. My augmented eyes harvested stray photons from lights in distant houses and the occasional car gliding along inland roads. To my right, the sea throbbed with the pale glitter of bioluminescent pollution. The waves sounded loud in the darkness, their crashes like a secret heartbeat of the world.

The pounding rain churned the path into mud. My mouth curved into a fierce grin. Of course, conditions were nowhere near as intense as the extremes of the simulator. But this was *real*. The sight of all the dead people behind me, chained to their memorials, made me feel sharply alive. Each raindrop on my face was another instant to be cherished. I wanted the night never to end. I wanted to be both here and gone, to stand on the colony world under its red, red sun.

I hurried, as if I could stride across the stars and get there sooner. I trod on an old tree branch that proved to be soggy and rotten. My foot slid off the path. I lurched violently, skidding a few yards sideways and down, until I arrested my fall by grabbing onto a nearby rock. The muscles in my left arm sent pangs of protest at the sharp wrench. Carefully I swung myself round, my feet groping for toe-holds. Soon I steadied myself. Hanging fifty feet above the sea, I must have only imagined that I felt spray whipping up from the waves. It must have been the rain, caught by the wind and sheeting from all angles.

The slip exhilarated me. I know that makes little sense, but I can only tell you how I felt.

But I couldn't cling there all night. I scrambled my way across the exposed crags, at first shuffling sideways by inches, then gaining confidence and swinging along, trusting my augmented muscles to keep me aloft.

My muscles gripped. My exo-skin held. The rock did not.

In mid-swing, I heard a *crack*. My anchoring left hand felt the rock shudder. Instinctively I scrabbled for another hold with my right hand. I grasped one, but nevertheless found myself falling. For a moment I didn't understand what was happening. Then, as the cliff-face crumbled with a noise like the tearing of a sky-sized newspaper, I realized that when the bottom gives way, the top must follow.

As I fell, still clinging to the falling rock, I was drenched by the splashback from the lower boulders hitting the sea below me. Time passed slowly, frame by frame, the scene changing gradually like an exhibition of cels from an animated movie. The hefty rock that I grasped was rotating as it fell. Soon I'd be underneath it. If I still clung on, I would be crushed when it landed.

I leapt free, aiming out to sea. If the cliff had been higher, I'd have had enough time to get clear. But very soon I hit the water, and so did the boulder behind me, and so too—it seemed—did half of the Yorkshire coast.

It sounded like a duel between a volcano and an earthquake. I flailed frantically, trying to swim away, not understanding why I made no progress. Only when I stopped thrashing around did I realize the problem.

My right foot was trapped underwater, somewhere within the pile of rocks that came down from the cliff. At the time, I'd felt nothing. Now, belatedly, a dull pounding pain crept up my leg. I breathed deeply, gulping air between the waves crashing around my head. Then I began attempting to wriggle free, with no success.

I tried to lift up the heavy boulders, but it was impossible. My imprisoned foot kept me in place, constricting my position and preventing me from finding any leverage. After many useless heaves, and much splashing and cursing, I had to give up.

All this time, panic had been building within me. As soon as I stopped struggling, terror flooded my brain with the fear of drowning, the fear of freezing in the cold sea, the fear of more rocks falling on top of me. My thoughts were overwhelmed by the prospect of imminent death.

It took long minutes to regain any coherence. Gradually I asserted some self-command, telling myself that the panic was a relic of my old body, which wouldn't have survived long floating in the North Sea in winter. My new form was far more robust. I wouldn't drown, or freeze to death. If I could compose myself, I'd get through this.

I concentrated on my exo-skin. Normally its texture approximated natural skin's slight roughness and imperfections. Now my leg became utterly smooth, in the hope that a friction-free surface might allow me to slip free. I felt a tiny amount of give, which sent a surge of hope through me, but then I could pull my foot no further. The bulge of my ankle prevented any further progress. Even friction-free, you can't tug a knot through a needle's eye.

Impatient and frustrated, I let the exo-skin revert to default. I needed to get free, and I couldn't simply wait for the next storm to rattle the rocks around. My starship would soon leave Earth. If I missed it, I would have no other chance.

At this point I began to wonder whether I'd subconsciously wanted to miss the boat. Had I courted disaster, just to prevent myself from going?

I couldn't deny that I'd in some sense brought this on myself. I'd been deliberately reckless, pushing myself until the inevitable accident occurred. Why?

Thinking about it, as the cold waves frothed around me, I realized that I'd wanted to push beyond the bounds of my old body, in order to prove to myself that I was worthy of going. We'd heard so much of the harsh rigors of the destination world, and so much had been said about the naturals' inability to survive there unaided, that I'd felt compelled to test the augments to their limit.

Unconsciously, I'd wanted to put myself in a situation that a natural body couldn't survive. Then if I did survive, that would prove I'd been truly transformed, and I'd be confident of thriving on the colony world, among the tides and hurricanes.

Well, I'd accomplished the first stage of this plan. I'd got myself into trouble. Now I just had to get out of it.

But how?

I had an emergency radio-beacon in my skull. I could activate it and no doubt someone would come along to scoop me out of the water. Yet that would be embarrassing. It would show that I couldn't handle my new body, even in the benign conditions of Earth. If I asked for rescue, then some excuse would be found to remove me from the starship roster. Colonists needed to be self-reliant and solve their own problems. There were plenty of reserves on the waiting list—plenty of people who hadn't fallen off a cliff and got themselves stuck under a pile of rocks.

The same applied if I waited until dawn and shouted up to the next person to walk along the coastal path. No, I couldn't ask for rescue. I had to save myself.

Yet asserting the need for a solution did not reveal its nature. At least, not at first. As the wind died down, and the rain softened into drizzle, I found myself thinking coldly and logically, squashing trepidation with the hard facts of the situation.

I needed to extract my leg from the rock. I couldn't move the rock. Therefore I had to move my leg.

I needed to move my leg, but the foot was stuck. Therefore I had to leave my foot behind.

Once I realized this, a calmness descended upon me. It was very simple. That was the price I must pay, if I wanted to free myself. I thought back to the option of calling for help. I could keep my foot, and stay on Earth. Or I could lose my foot, and go to the stars.

Did I long to go so badly?

I'd already decided to leave my family behind and leave my girlfriend. If I jibbed at leaving a mere foot, a minor bodily extremity, then what did that say about my values? Surely there wasn't even a choice to make; I merely had to accept the consequences of the decision I'd already made.

And yet I delayed and delayed, hoping that some other option would present itself, hoping that I could evade the results of my choices.

I'm almost ashamed to admit what finally prompted me to action. It wasn't logic or strong-willed decisiveness. It was the pain from my squashed foot, a throbbing that had steadily intensified while I mulled the possibilities. And it was no fun floating in the cold sea, either. The sooner I acted, the sooner I could get away.

I concentrated upon my exo-skin, that marvel of programmable integument, and commanded it to flow up from my foot. Then I pinched it into my leg, just above my right ankle.

Ouch! Ouch, ouch, ouch, owwww!

Trying to ignore the pain, I steered the exo-skin further in. I wished I could perform the whole operation in an instant, slicing off my foot as if chopping a cucumber. But the exo-skin had limits, and it wasn't designed to do this. I was stretching the spec already.

Soon—sooner than I would have hoped—I had to halt. I needed to access my pain overrides. It had been constantly drilled into us that this was a last resort, that pain existed for a reason and we shouldn't casually shut it off. But if amputating one's own foot wasn't an emergency, I didn't ever want to encounter a true last resort. I turned off the pain signals.

The numbness intoxicated me. What a blessing, to be free from the hurts of the flesh! In the absence of pain, the remaining tasks seemed to elapse much more swiftly. Soon the exo-skin had completely cut through the bone, severing my lower leg and sealing off the wound. Freed from the rock-fall, I swam away and dragged myself ashore. There I collapsed into sleep.

When I woke, the tide had receded, leaving behind a beach clogged with fallen clumps of grass, soggy dead bracken, and the ever-present plastic trash that was humanity's legacy to the world. The pain signals had returned—they could only be temporarily suspended, not permanently switched off. For about a minute I tried to live with my lower calf's agonized protestations; then I succumbed to temptation and suppressed them again.

As I tried to stand up, I discovered that I was now lop-sided. At the bottom of my right leg I had some spare exo-skin, since it no longer covered a foot. I instructed the surplus material to extend a few inches into a peg-leg, so that I could balance. I shaped the peg to avoid pressing on my stump, with the force of my steps being borne by the exo-skin higher up my leg.

I tottered across the trash-strewn pebbles. I could walk! I shouted in triumph, and disturbed a magpie busy pecking at the freshly revealed soil on the new shoreline. It chittered reprovingly as it flew away.

Then I must have blacked out for a while. Later, I woke with a weak sun shining in my face. My first thought was to return to the landslip and move the rocks to retrieve my missing foot.

My second thought was—*where is it?*

The whole coast was a jumble of fallen boulders. The cliff had been eroding for years, and last night's storm was only the most recent attrition. I couldn't tell where I'd fallen, or where I'd been trapped. Somewhere in there lay a chunk of flesh, of great sentimental value. But I had no idea where it might be.

I'd lost my foot.

Only at that moment did the loss hit home. I raged at myself for getting into such a stupid situation, and for going through with the amputation rather than summoning help, like a young boy too proud to call for his mother when he hurts himself.

And I felt a deep regret that I'd lost a piece of myself I'd never get back. Sure, the exo-skin could replace it. Sure, I could augment myself beyond what I ever was before.

But the line between man and machine seemed like the coastline around me: constantly being nibbled away. I'd lost a foot, just like the coast had lost a few more rocks. Yet no matter what it swallowed, the sea kept rising.

What would I lose next?

* * * *

I turned south, back toward town, and walked along the shoreline, looking for a spot where I could easily climb from the beach to the path above the cliff. Perhaps I could have employed my augments and simply clawed my way up the sheer cliff-face, but I had become less keen on using them.

The irony did not escape me. I'd embarked on this expedition with the intent of pushing the augments to the full. Now I found myself shunning them. Yet the augments themselves hadn't failed.

Only I had failed. I'd exercised bad judgment, and ended up trapped and truncated. That was my entirely human brain, thinking stupidly.

Perhaps if my brain had been augmented, I would have acted more rationally.

My steps crunched on banks of pebbles, the peg-leg making a different sound than my remaining foot, so that my gait created an alternating rhythm like the bass-snare drumbeat of old-fashioned pop music. The beach smelled of sea-salt, and of the decaying vegetation that had fallen with the landslip. Chunks of driftwood lay everywhere.

The day was quiet; the wind had dropped and the tide was out, so the only sounds came from my own steps and the occasional cry of the gulls far out to sea. Otherwise I would never have heard the voice, barely more than a scratchy whisper.

"Soon, my darling. Soon we'll be together. Ah, how long has it been?"

I looked around and saw no-one. Then I realized that the voice came from low down, from somewhere among the pebbles and the ever-present trash. I sifted through the debris and found a small square of plastic. When I lifted it to my ear, it swore at me.

"Arsewipe! Fuckflaps!"

The voice was so tinny and distorted that I couldn't be sure I recognized it. "Katriona?" I asked.

"How long, how long? Oh, the sea, the dear blessed sea. Speed the waves. . . ."

I asked again, but the voice wouldn't respond to me. Maybe the broken chip, which no longer projected a hologram, had also lost its aural input. Or maybe it had stopped bothering to speak to passers by.

Now I saw that some of the driftwood planks were slats of benches. The memorial benches, which over the years had inched closer to the eroding cliff-edge, had finally succumbed to the waves.

Yet perhaps they hadn't succumbed, but rather had finally *attained* their goal—or would do soon enough when the next high tide carried the detritus away. I remembered the holograms lighting up last night, how they'd seemed to summon the storm. I remembered Katriona telling me about her husband who'd drowned. For all the years of her death, she must have longed to join him in the watery deeps.

I strode out toward the distant waves. My steps squelched as I neared the waterline, and I had to pick my way between clumps of seaweed. As I walked, I crunched the plastic chip to shreds in my palm, my exo-skin easily strong enough to break it. When I reached the spume, I flung the fragments into the sea.

"Goodbye," I said, "and God rest you."

I shivered as I returned to the upper beach. I felt an irrational need to clamber up the rocks to the cliff-top path, further from the hungry sea.

I'd seen my own future. The exo-skin and the other augments would become more and more of me, and the flesh less and less. One day only the augments would be left, an electronic ghost of the person I used to be.

As I retrieved my clothes from where I'd cached them, I experienced a surge of relief at donning them to rejoin society. Putting on my shoes proved difficult, since I lacked a right foot. I had to reshape my exo-skin into a hollow shell, in order to fill the shoes of a human being.

Tomorrow I would return to the launch base. I'd seek medical attention after we lifted off, when they couldn't remove me from the colony roster for my foolishness. I smiled as I wondered what similar indiscretions my comrades might reveal, when it was too late for meaningful punishment. What would we all have left behind?

What flaws would we take with us? And what would remain of us, at the last?

Now we approach the end of my story, and there is little left. As I once helped a shadow fade, long ago and far away, I hope that someday you will do the same for me.

MARISSA LINGEN Born in Libertyville, Illinois, Marissa Lingen has lived in several areas of the United States. She trained in physics and mathematics, and worked for a time at Lawrence Livermore National Laboratory. In 1999 she won the Isaac Asimov Award for Undergraduate Excellence in Science Fiction and Fantasy Short Story Writing (now called the Dell Magazines Award) and has been writing short stories ever since. She has been publishing stories in the genre since 2002. Today she writes full-time, and lives in a small town south of Minneapolis.

"The Calculus Plague" literalizes the metaphoric concept of knowledge transmitted "virally," and deftly asks the next question.

THE CALCULUS PLAGUE

T he Calculus Plague came first. Almost no one took offense at it. In fact, it took a while for anyone to find out about it at all. No one had any reason to talk about a dim memory of their high school math teacher, whose face didn't seem familiar somehow, and what was her name again? His name? Well, what did it matter?

It wasn't until Dr. Leslie Baxter, an economics professor at the U, heard her four-year-old son ask, "What's Newton's Method, Mommy?" that anyone began to notice anything wrong. At first Leslie assumed that Nicholas's most recent babysitter had been talking about his calculus assignment over the phone when sitting for Nicholas, but when she confronted the young man, he admitted that he had taken part in a viral memory experiment that was aimed at teaching calculus through transmission of memories.

Young Nicholas Baxter was living proof that it did no good to remember something if you couldn't understand it to begin with. Leslie assured Nicholas that she would explain the math when he was older. Then she went to the faculty judicial board to discuss forming a committee to establish ethical guidelines for faculty participation in viral memory transfer research.

They were still deciding who would be on the committee—from which departments, in which proportions, and was Dr. So-and-so too junior for the responsibility? Was Prof. Such-and-such too senior to agree to take it on?—when the second wave hit.

"I know I have never taken George's seminar on Faulkner," said Leslie furiously. "Never! I hate Faulkner, and George wasn't on faculty anywhere I've studied."

"But what does it hurt to remember some kids sitting around talking about *The Sound and the Fury*, Les?" asked her friend and colleague Amy Pradhan.

"Easy for *you* to say. You didn't catch it."

Amy shrugged. "I don't think I'd be making a fuss if I had."

Leslie shook her head. "Don't take this wrong, but you don't even like it when people drop by your house without calling first. But somehow it'd be better if it was your head?"

"It's not like they can read your thoughts, Les."

"No, they can make my thoughts. And that's worse."

"They're not making you like Faulkner," said Amy. "I know someone else who caught it and loved Faulkner, and she doesn't hate it now. You can still respond as yourself."

"Mighty big of them, to let me respond as myself."

Amy grimaced. "Can we talk about something else, please?"

"Okay, okay. How's Molly? Are you still seeing her?"

Amy blushed, and the conversation moved on to friends and family, books and movies, campus gossip, and other things that had nothing to do with Leslie coming down with a stuffy nose and Faulkner memories.

The usual people wrote their editorials and letters to the editor, but most people could not bother themselves to get excited about a virally transmitted memory of a lecture on Faulkner. Even the Faulkner-haters in the English department shrugged and moved on. Leslie found herself alone in confronting the project head, Dr. Solada Srisai. Srisai was tidy in the way of women who have had to fight very hard and very quietly for what they have. The warm red of her suit went perfectly with the warm brown of her skin. Leslie felt tall and chilly and ridiculous.

"I don't think anyone will be hurt by knowing calculus, do you?" Solada murmured, when Leslie explained why she was there.

"You're a biologist," said Leslie. "You know how many forms you have to fill out to do human experimentation. If I want to ask a dozen freshmen whether they'd buy a cookie for a dollar, I have to fill out forms."

"Our experimental subjects filled out their forms," said Solada. "The viruses fell slightly outside our predicted parameters and got transmitted to a few people close to the original test subjects and then a few people close to them. This is a problem we will remedy in future trials, I assure you."

A grad student with wire-rimmed glasses poked her head around the door. "Solada, we've got the people from the Empty Moon here."

"Start going over their parameters," said Solada. "I'll be done with this in a minute."

"Empty Moon?" said Leslie.

"It's a new café," said Solada. "We've come to an agreement with them about marketing. Volunteers—who have all the *forms* filled out, Dr. Baxter—

will be infected with positive memories of the food at the Empty Moon Café, and we'll track their reports of how often they eat there and what they order compared to what they remember."

"Don't you have an ethical problem with this?" Leslie demanded.

Solada shrugged. "Not everybody likes the same food. If they go to the Empty Moon and have a terrible sandwich, or the service is slow, they'll figure their first memory was a fluke. They'll go somewhere else. Or if they're in the mood for Mexican, they'll go for Mexican. We'll make sure that this virus is far less mutative and virulent than the others—which were really not bad considering how colds usually spread on a college campus. Well within the error range one might expect."

"Not within the error range *I'd* expect," said Leslie. "I'll be conveying this to a faculty ethics committee, Dr. Srisai."

Solada shrugged and smiled dismissively. "You must do as your conscience dictates, of course."

The business at the Empty Moon Café was booming. Leslie told herself very firmly that her memory of the awesome endive salad she'd had there was a snare and a delusion; she stayed away even when Amy wanted to meet there for coffee.

No one else seemed to care when she tried to tell them about the newest marketing ploy.

A few weeks later, Leslie was doing the dishes while her husband put Nicholas to bed. Her doorbell rang three times in quick succession, and then there was a pounding on the door. Wiping her hands on the dishtowel, she went to answer it. Amy was standing on the doorstep, an ashen undertone to her dark skin.

"There's been—" Amy swallowed hard, and managed to get a strangled, "Oh, God," past her lips.

"Come in. Sit down. I'll get you tea. What's happened?"

"Tom Barras—he's—"

"Deep breaths," said Leslie, putting the kettle on.

"You know I've been one of the faculty advisors to the GLBT group on campus," said Amy. "There's been an attack. A member of the group—Tom Barras—a nice bi boy, civil engineering major—is in the hospital."

"What happened?"

"We don't know! I thought we were—I know gay-bashing still happens, but I thought we were better than that here." Leslie bit back a comment about illusions of the ivory tower. Her friend needed a listening ear, not a lecture. Amy got herself calmed down, gradually, and Leslie went to bed feeling faintly ill. She and her husband insisted on putting Amy's bike in the back of their car and driving her home, just in case.

The story of the assault came out gradually: Tom's attacker, Anthony

Dorland, said he had previously been set upon behind Hogarth Hall by a group of men. One of them had groped him repeatedly, making suggestive personal comments, while the others looked on and laughed. "I couldn't do anything about it," Anthony told campus security in strangled tones. "I was alone. But then I was out last night, and I heard his voice. It was the same voice, I know it. I would know it anywhere. He was coming out of his meeting, and so I waited until he was alone. I don't care what he does with people who like it, but I'm not that way! He shouldn't force himself on people like that! It's not right! So I thought, well, let's see how you like it when you're all alone and someone jumps on you."

When campus security asked Dorland why he had not fought back immediately or reported the incident, he looked confused. "He was so much bigger than me, and he had all his friends—I don't know—I just felt like I couldn't. Like no one would believe me." Pressed for a time of incident, he said, "I don't know. A while ago. A few weeks ago, maybe? I don't know."

The police officers looked from one young man to the other. Tom was several inches shorter than Anthony, and slightly built.

Tom returned to consciousness a day later, to the great relief of his family and friends, including Amy. A few days after that, the faculty started hearing rumors of other students who had experienced the same thing but could not say when it had happened. Some of them had roommates who said they didn't remember their roommate coming in beaten up or upset; others had roommates with identical memories—and identical sniffles.

Scores on calculus midterms shot up by an average of fifteen points.

Leslie noticed a few students wearing surgical masks on campus one morning. The next day it was a few more. She took Nicholas to get one at the campus bookstore and encountered Solada Srisai coming out with a bag. Without thinking, she grabbed Nicholas close to her.

"Mommy!" Nicholas protested.

"That false memory of sexual assault," Leslie hissed. "My son caught calculus. What would you have done if he'd caught danger and fear like that? What would you have done to keep him from having nightmares that a bunch of adult men were—" She looked down at Nicholas and chose her words carefully. "Were hurting him. Personally. What would you have done about that?"

"That one wasn't mine," said Solada.

"They are *all* yours," said Leslie. "The minute you taught your grad students that it was okay to release these things without trials, without controls, without testing—the minute you taught them that it was okay to skip all that, because it was holding back progress, you earned all of this. *All of it.*"

"Mommy," said Nicholas, and Leslie realized that her hands were shaking.

"Let me tell you what the alternative was," said Solada, steering Leslie and Nicholas towards a bench. "Do you want to know what my alternative was?"

"Another project completely?"

"Yes. Sure. Another project completely." Solada glared at her. "And do you know what *that* would mean? It would mean that the person who developed virally contagious memories would not have done so out in the open. You would never have heard about it. Your son wouldn't have been at risk for catching a memory of calculus—or, okay, a memory of sexual assault because an overzealous grad student decided it would be a good idea for potential rapists to know what it felt like.

"No. Your son would have been at risk for catching memories that told him that the Republican Party was the only one he could trust. Or that if he truly loved you, he would always trust exactly what the Democratic Party had to say. Or that our government would *never* fight a war without a darn good reason. Or that he should buy this cola, or drive this car, or wear those sneakers. Do you see what I mean? It was me now or a secret project two years from now."

"And that makes it okay?" said Leslie. "The fact that it could be worse?"

Solada leaned towards her on the bench; Leslie had calmed down enough not to pull Nicholas away. "If I blow the whistle on my own project, it looks like I'm trying to grab the spotlight; nobody pays any attention. But you! What are you doing? I counted on someone like you to kick up a fuss in the press. Faculty advisory committees? Official university censure? What is wrong with you? Start a blog to rant about it! Call reporters! Tell your students to tell their parents! The student paper is not enough. Rumors are not enough."

"You're saying you wanted me to—"

"You or someone like you. For God's sake, yes. Get the word out. Make sure everybody knows that this is something we can do. Make sure they ask themselves questions about how we're doing it." Solada shook her head. "I'm amazed it didn't happen before. I thought surely the Empty Moon thing would be the last straw for you. Or someone like you. And I never dreamed that one of my students would use it politically, the way I thought the big parties would.

"So be fast about it, Dr. Baxter. Be as loud as you can. I'm willing to be the wicked queen here. Better a wicked queen than an eminence grise."

And with that she was gone, leaving Leslie stunned and clinging to her son. Most of the media contacts she had were in the obscure economic press. Would it be best to call a national news magazine? The local newspaper, or its big city neighbor? She'd never tried to break a story before. It had never been this important before.

"Mommy, did you take me here another time?" asked Nicholas.

Leslie's heart went into her throat.

"And Daddy was here, too, and you bought me hot chocolate?" he continued hopefully.

She relaxed. It was a real memory; they had come to the student union before Christmas. "I'll buy you hot chocolate again," she assured him, "and then we'll go over to my office and you can draw pictures. Mommy has some phone calls to make."

PAUL CORNELL   Born in Wiltshire, Paul Cornell spent most of the 1990s as an accomplished and popular writer of television, comic books, and *Doctor Who* prose fiction. Later, after *Doctor Who* was revived as an ongoing television series in 2005, Cornell wrote three of its best-received episodes, all of which were Hugo finalists. In this century, while continuing to write comics and television with evident gusto and enjoyment, Cornell has gradually turned to also writing original fiction unconnected to anyone else's franchise.

"One of Our Bastards Is Missing" is the second in the ongoing chronicles of Major Jonathan Hamilton, who serves Britain in an alternative continuum in which the empires of the nineteenth century have lived on into a world of solar-system development and mysterious alternate physics. For many writers, such a scenario would be the occasion for a romp that doesn't think too hard about the people such a world would hurt. In Cornell's hands, it's still a romp, but he's sneakier about it than you might expect.

ONE OF OUR BASTARDS IS MISSING

To get to Earth from the edge of the solar system, depending on the time of year and the position of the planets, you need to pass through at least Poland, Prussia, and Turkey, and you'd probably get stamps in your passport from a few of the other great powers. Then as you get closer to the world, you arrive at a point, in the continually shifting carriage space over the countries, where this complexity has to give way or fail. And so you arrive in the blissful lubrication of neutral orbital territory. From there it's especially clear that no country is whole unto itself. There are yearning gaps between parts of each state, as they stretch across the solar system. There is no congruent territory. The countries continue in balance with each other like a fine but eccentric mechanism, pent up, all that political energy dealt with through eternal circular motion.

The maps that represent this can be displayed on a screen, but they're much more suited to mental contemplation. They're beautiful. They're made to be beautiful, doing their own small part to see that their beauty never ends.

If you looked down on that world of countries, onto the pink of glorious old Greater Britain, that land of green squares and dark forest and carriage contrails, and then you naturally avoided looking directly at the golden splendor of London, your gaze might fall on the Thames valley. On the country houses and mansions and hunting estates that letter the river banks with the names of the great. On one particular estate: an enormous winged square of a house with its own grouse shooting horizons and mazes and herb gardens and markers that indicate it also sprawls into folded interior expanses.

Today that estate, seen from such a height, would be adorned with informational banners that could be seen from orbit, and tall pleasure cruisers could be observed, docked beside military boats on the river, and carriages of all kinds would be cluttering the gravel of its circular drives and swarming in the sky overhead. A detachment of Horse Guards could be spotted, stood at ready at the perimeter.

Today, you'd need much more than a passport to get inside that maze of information and privilege.

Because today was a royal wedding.

· · · ·

That vision from the point of view of someone looking down upon him was what was at the back of Hamilton's mind.

But now he was watching the Princess.

Her chestnut hair had been knotted high on her head, baring her neck, a fashion which Hamilton appreciated for its defiance of the French, and at an official function too, though that gesture wouldn't have been Liz's alone, but would have been calculated in the warrens of Whitehall. She wore white, which had made a smile come to Hamilton's lips when he'd first seen it in the Cathedral this morning. In this gigantic function room with its high arched ceiling, in which massed dignitaries and ambassadors and dress uniforms orbited from table to table, she was the sun about which everything turned. Even the King, in the far distance, at a table on a rise with old men from the rest of Europe, was no competition for his daughter this afternoon.

This was the reception, where Elizabeth, escorted by members of the Corps of Heralds, would carelessly and entirely precisely move from group to group, giving exactly the right amount of charm to every one of the great powers, briefed to keep the balance going as everyone like she and Hamilton did, every day.

Everyone like the two of them. That was a useless thought and he cuffed it aside.

Her gaze had settled on Hamilton's table precisely once. A little smile and then away again. As not approved by Whitehall. He'd tried to stop watching her after that. But his carefully random table, with diplomatic corps functionaries to his left and right, had left him cold. Hamilton had grown tired of pretending to be charming.

"It's a marriage of convenience," said a voice beside him.

It was Lord Carney. He was wearing open cuffs that bloomed from his silk sleeves, a big collar, and no tie. His long hair was unfastened. He had retained his rings.

Hamilton considered his reply for a moment, then opted for silence. He met Carney's gaze with a suggestion in his heart that surely his Lordship might find some other table to perch at, perhaps one where he had friends?

"What do you reckon?"

Hamilton stood, with the intention of walking away. But Carney stood too and stopped him just as they'd got out of earshot of the table. The man smelled like a Turkish sweet shop. He affected a mode of speech beneath his standing. "This is what I do. I probe, I provoke, I poke. And when I'm in the room, it's all too obvious when people are looking at someone else."

The broad grin stayed on his face.

Hamilton found a deserted table and sat down again, furious at himself.

Carney settled beside him, and gestured away from Princess Elizabeth, toward her new husband, with his neat beard and his row of medals on the breast of his Svenska Adelsfanan uniform. He was talking with the Papal ambassador, doubtless discussing getting Liz to Rome as soon as possible, for a great show to be made of this match between the Protestant and the Papist. If Prince Bertil was also pretending to be charming, Hamilton admitted that he was making a better job of it.

"Yeah, jammy fucker, my thoughts exactly. Still, I'm on a promise with a couple of members of his staff, so it's swings and roundabouts." Carney clicked his tongue and wagged his finger as a Swedish serving maid ran past, and she curtsied a quick smile at him. "I do understand, you know. All our relationships are informed by the balance. And the horror of it is that we all can conceive of a world where this isn't so."

Hamilton pursed his lips and chose his next words carefully. "Is that why you are how you are, your Lordship?"

" 'Course it is. Maids, lady companions, youngest sisters, it's a catalog of incompleteness. I'm allowed to love only in ways that don't disrupt the balance. For me to commit myself, or, heaven forbid, to marry, would require such deep thought at the highest levels that by the time the Heralds had worked it through, well, I'd have tired of the lady. Story of us all, eh? Nowhere for the pressure to go. If only I could see an alternative."

Having shown the corner of his cards, the man had taken care to move back to the fringes of treason once more. It was part of his role as an *agent provocateur*. And Hamilton knew it. But that didn't mean he had to take this. "Do you have any further point, your Lordship?"

"Oh, I'm just getting—"

The room gasped.

Hamilton was up out of his seat and had taken a step toward Elizabeth, his gun hand had grabbed into the air to his right where his .66 mm Webley Corsair sat in a knot of space and had swung it ready to fire—

At nothing.

There stood the Princess, looking about herself in shock. Dress uniforms, bearded men all around her.

Left, right, up, down.

Hamilton couldn't see anything for her to be shocked at.

And nothing near her, nothing around her.

She was already stepping back, her hands in the air, gesturing at a gap—

What had been there? Everyone was looking there. What?

He looked to the others like him. Almost all of them were in the same sort of posture he was, balked at picking a target.

The Papal envoy stepped forward and cried out. "A man was standing there! And he has vanished!"

• • • •

Havoc. Everybody was shouting. A weapon, a weapon! But there was no weapon that Hamilton knew of that could have done that, made a man, whoever it had been, blink out of existence. Groups of bodyguards in dress uniforms or diplomatic black tie leapt up, encircling their charges. Ladies started screaming. A nightmare of the balance collapsing all around them. That hysteria when everyone was in the same place and things didn't go exactly as all these vast powers expected.

A Bavarian princeling bellowed he needed no such protection and made to rush to the Princess's side—

Hamilton stepped into his way and accidentally shouldered him to the floor as he put himself right up beside Elizabeth and her husband. "We're walking to that door," he said. "Now."

Bertil and Elizabeth nodded and marched with fixed smiles on their faces, Bertil turning and holding back with a gesture the Swedish forces that were moving in from all directions. Hamilton's fellows fell in all around them, and swept the party across the hall, through that door, and down a servants' corridor as Life Guards came bundling into the room behind them, causing more noise and more reactions and damn it, Hamilton hoped he wouldn't suddenly hear the discharge of some hidden—

He did not. The door was closed and barred behind them. Another good guy doing the right thing.

Hamilton sometimes distantly wished for an organization to guard those who needed it. But for that the world would have to be different in ways beyond even Carney's artificial speculations. He and his brother officers would have their independence cropped if that were so. And he lived through his independence. It was the root of the duty that meant he would place himself in harm's way for Elizabeth's husband. He had no more thoughts on the subject.

"I know very little," said Elizabeth as she walked, her voice careful as always, except when it hadn't been. "I think the man was with one of the groups of foreign dignitaries—"

"He looked Prussian," said Bertil, "we were talking to Prussians."

"He just vanished into thin air right in front of me."

"Into a fold?" said Bertil.

"It can't have been," she said. "The room will have been mapped and mapped."

She looked to Hamilton for confirmation. He nodded.

They got to the library. Hamilton marched in and secured it. They put the happy couple at the center of it, locked it up, and called everything in to the embroidery.

The embroideries were busy, swiftly prioritizing, but no, nothing was happening in the great chamber they'd left, the panic had swelled and then subsided into shouts, exhibition-ist faintings (because who these days wore a corset that didn't have hidden depths), glasses crashing, yelled demands. No one else had vanished. No Spanish infantrymen had materialized out of thin air.

Bertil walked to the shelves, folded his hands behind his back, and began bravely and ostentatiously browsing. Elizabeth sat down and fanned herself and smiled for all Hamilton's fellows, and finally, quickly for Hamilton himself.

They waited.

The embroidery told them they had a visitor coming.

A wall of books slid aside, and in walked a figure that made all of them turn and salute. The Queen Mother, still in mourning black, her train racing to catch up with her.

She came straight to Hamilton and the others all turned to listen, and from now on thanks to this obvious favor, they would regard Hamilton as the ranking officer. He was glad of it. "We will continue," she said. "We will not regard this as an embarrassment and therefore it will not be. The ballroom was prepared for the dance, we are moving there early, Elizabeth, Bertil, off you go, you two gentlemen in front of them, the rest of you behind. You will be laughing as you enter the ballroom as if this were the most enormous joke, a silly and typically English eccentric misunderstanding."

Elizabeth nodded, took Bertil by the arm.

The Queen Mother intercepted Hamilton as he moved to join them. "No. Major Hamilton, you will go and talk to technical, you will find another explanation for what happened."

"*Another* explanation, your Royal Highness?"

"Indeed," she said. "It must not be what they are saying it is."

* * * *

"Here we are, sir," Lieutenant Matthew Parkes was with the Technical Corps of Hamilton's own regiment, the 4th Dragoons. He and his men were, incongruously, in the dark of the pantry that had been set aside for their equipment, also in their dress uniforms. From here they were in charge of the sensor net that blanketed the house and grounds down to Newtonian units of space, reaching out for miles in every direction. Parkes's people had been the first to arrive here, days ago, and would be the last to leave. He was pointing at a screen, on which was frozen the intelligent image of a burly man in black tie, Princess Elizabeth almost entirely obscured behind him. "Know who he is?"

Hamilton had placed the guest list in his mental index and had checked it as each group had entered the hall. He was relieved to recognize the man. He was as down to earth as it was possible to be. "He was in the Prussian party, not announced, one of six diplomat placings on their list. Built like his muscles have been grown for security and that's how he moved round the room. Didn't let anyone chat to him. He nods when his embroidery talks to him. Which'd mean he's new at this, only . . ." Only the man had a look about him that Hamilton recognized. "No. He's just very confident. Ostentatious, even. So you're sure he didn't walk into some sort of fold?"

"Here's the contour map." Parkes flipped up an overlay on the image that showed the tortured underpinnings of spacetime in the room. There were little sinks and bundles all over the place, where various Britons had weapons stowed, and various foreigners would have had them stowed had they wished to create a diplomatic incident. The corner where Elizabeth had been standing showed only the force of gravity under her dear feet. "We do take care you know, sir."

"I'm sure you do, Matty. Let's see it, then."

Parkes flipped back to the clear screen. He touched it and the image changed.

Hamilton watched as the man vanished. One moment he was there. Then he was not, and Elizabeth was reacting, a sudden jerk of her posture.

Hamilton often struggled with technical matters. "What's the frame rate on this thing?"

"There is none, sir. It's a continual taking of real image, right down to single Newton intervals of time. That's as far as physics goes. Sir, we've been listening in to what every-one's saying, all afternoon—"

"And what are they saying, Matty?"

"That what's happened is Gracefully Impossible."

. . . .

Gracefully Impossible. The first thing that had come into Hamilton's mind when the Queen Mother had mentioned the possibility was the memory of a political cartoon. It was the Prime Minister from a few years ago, standing at the dispatch box, staring in shock at his empty hand, which should presumably have contained some papers. The caption had read:

Say what you like about Mr. Patel,

He carries himself *correct for his* title.
He's about to present just his graceful *apologies,*
For the impossible *loss of all his policies.*

Every child knew that Newton had coined the phrase "gracefully impossible" after he'd spent the day in his garden observing the progress of a very
small worm across the surface on an apple. It referred to what, according to
the great man's thinking about the very small, could, and presumably did,
sometimes happen: things popping in and out of existence, when God, for
some unfathomable reason, started or stopped looking at them. Some
Frenchman had insisted that it was actually about whether *people* were
looking, but that was the French for you. Through the centuries, there had
been a few documented cases that seemed to fit the bill. Hamilton had always been distantly entertained to read about such in the inside page of his
newspaper plate. He'd always assumed it could happen. But here? Now?
During a state occasion?

. . . .

Hamilton went back into the great hall, now empty of all but a group of Life
Guards and those like him, individuals taken from several different regiments, all of whom had responsibilities similar to his, and a few of whom
he'd worked with in the field. He checked in with them. They had all noted
the Prussian, indeed, with the ruthless air the man had had about him, and
the bulk of his musculature, he had been at the forefront of many of their
internal indices of threat.

Hamilton found the place where the vanishing had happened, moved aside
a couple of boffins, and against their protestations, went to stand in the exact
spot, which felt like anywhere else did, and which set off none of his internal
alarms, real or intuitive. He looked to where Liz had been standing, in the
corner behind the Prussian. His expression darkened. The man who'd vanished had effectively been shielding the Princess from the room. Between her
and every line of sight. He'd been where a bodyguard would have been if
he'd become aware of someone taking a shot.

But that was ridiculous. The Prussian hadn't rushed in to save her. He'd
been standing there, looking around. And anyone in that hall with some
strange new weapon concealed on their person wouldn't have taken the shot
then, they'd have waited for him to move.

Hamilton shook his head, angry with himself. There was a gap here.
Something that went beyond the obvious. He let the boffins get back to their
work and headed for the ballroom.

. . . .

The band had started the music, and the vast chamber was packed with
people, the dance floor a whirl of waltzing figures. They were deliberate in
their courses. The only laughter was forced laughter. No matter that some
half-miracle might have occurred, dance cards had been circulated among

the minds of the great powers, so those dances would be danced, and minor royalty matched, and whispers exchanged in precise confidentiality, because everyone was brave and everyone was determined and would be seen to be so. And so the balance went on. But the tension had increased a notch. The weight of the balance could be felt in this room, on the surface now, on every brow. The Queen Mother sat at a high table with courtiers to her left and right, receiving visitors with a grand blessing smile on her face, daring everyone to regard the last hour as anything but a dream.

Hamilton walked the room, looking around like he was looking at a battle, like it was happening rather than perhaps waiting to happen, whatever it was. He watched his opposite numbers from all the great powers waltzing slowly around their own people, and spiraling off from time to time to orbit his own. The ratio of uniformed to the sort of embassy thug it was difficult to imagine fitting in the diplomatic bag was about three to one for all the nations bar two. The French had of course sent Commissars, who all dressed the same when outsiders were present, but followed a Byzantine internal rank system. And the Vatican's people were all men and women of the cloth and their assistants.

As he made his way through that particular party, which was scattering, intercepting, and colliding with all the other nationalities, as if in the explosion of a shaped charge, he started to hear it. The conversations were all about what had happened. The Vatican representatives were talking about a sacred presence. The details were already spiraling. There had been a light and a great voice, had nobody else heard? And people were agreeing.

Hamilton wasn't a diplomat, and he knew better than to take on trouble not in his own line. But he didn't like what he was hearing. The Catholics had only come to terms with Impossible Grace a couple of decades ago, when a Papal bull went out announcing that John XXVI thought that the concept had merit, but that further scientific study was required. But now they'd got behind it, as in all things, they were behind it. So what would this say to them, that the divine had looked down on this wedding, approved of it, and plucked someone away from it?

No, not just someone. Prussian military. A Protestant from a nation that had sometimes protested that various Swedish territories would be far better off within their own jurisdiction.

Hamilton stopped himself speculating. Guessing at such things would only make him hesitate if his guesses turned out to be untrue.

Hamilton had a vague but certain grasp of what his God was like. He thought it was possible that He might decide to give the nod to a marriage at court. But in a way that might upset the balance between nations that was divinely ordained, that was the center of all good works?

No. Hamilton was certain now. The divine be damned. This wasn't the numinous at play. This was enemy action.

He circled the room until he found the Prussians. They were raging, an ambassador poking at a British courtier, demanding something, probably that an investigation be launched immediately. And beside that Prussian stood several more, diplomatic and military, all convincingly frightened and furious, certain this was a British plot.

But behind them there, in the social place where Hamilton habitually looked, there were some of the vanished man's fellow big lads. The other five from that diplomatic pouch. The Prussians, uniquely in Europe, kept up an actual organization for the sort of thing Hamilton and his ilk did on the never-never. The Garde Du Corps had begun as a regiment similar to the Life Guards, but these days it was said they weren't even issued with uniforms. They wouldn't be on anyone's dance cards. They weren't stalking the room now, and all right, that was understandable, they were hanging back to protect their men. But they weren't doing much of that either. They didn't look angry, or worried for their comrade, or for their own skins—

Hamilton took a step back to let pretty noble couples desperately waltz between him and the Prussians, wanting to keep his position as a privileged observer.

They looked like they were *waiting*. On edge. They just wanted to get out of here. Was the Garde really that callous? They'd lost a man in mysterious circumstances, and they weren't themselves agitating to get back into that room and yell his name, but were just waiting to move on?

He looked for another moment, remembering the faces, then moved on himself. He found another table of Prussians. The good sort, not Order of the Black Eagle, but Hussars. They were in uniform, and had been drinking, and were furiously declaring in Hohenzollern German that if they weren't allowed access to the records of what had happened, well then it must be— they didn't like to say what it must be!

Hamilton plucked a glass from a table and wandered over to join them, careful to take a wide and unsteady course around a lady whose train had developed some sort of fault and wasn't moving fast enough to keep pace with her feet.

He flopped down in a chair next to one of the Prussians, a captain by his lapels, which were virtual in the way the Prussians liked, to implicitly suggest that they had been in combat more recently than the other great powers, and so had a swift turnover of brevet ranks, decided by merit. "Hullo!" he said.

The group fell silent and bristled at him.

Hamilton blinked at them. "Where's Humph?"

"Humph? Wassay th'gd Major?" the Hussar Captain spoke North Sea pidgin, but with a clear accent: Hamilton would be able to understand him.

He didn't want to reveal that he spoke perfect German, albeit with a Bavarian accent. "Big chap. Big big chap. Say go." He carefully swore in Dutch, shaking his head, not understanding. "Which you settle fim?"

"Settle?!" They looked among each other, and Hamilton could feel the affront. A couple of them even put their good hands to their waists, where the space was folded that no longer contained their pistols and thin swords. But the captain glared at them and they relented. A burst of Hohenzollern German about this so-called mystery of their mate vanishing, and how, being in the Garde, he had obviously been abducted for his secrets.

Hamilton waved his hands. "No swords! Good chap! No name. He won! Three times to me at behind the backshee." His raised his voice a notch. "Behind the backshee! Excellent chap! He *won!*" He stuck out his ring finger, offering the winnings in credit, to be passed from skin to skin. He mentally retracted the other options of what could be detailed there, and blanked it. He could always make a drunken show of trying to find it. "Seek to settle. For such a good chap."

They didn't believe him or trust him. Nobody reached out to touch his finger. But he learnt a great deal in their German conversation in the ten minutes that followed, while he loudly struggled to communicate with the increasingly annoyed captain, who couldn't bring himself to directly insult a member of the British military by asking him to go away. The vanished man's name was Helmuth Sandels. The name suggested Swedish origins to his family. But that was typical continental back and forth. He might have been a good man now he'd gone, but he hadn't been liked. Sandels had had a look in his eye when he'd walked past stout fellows who'd actually fought battles. He'd spoken up in anger when valiant Hussars had expressed the military's traditional views concerning those running the government, the country, and the world. Hamilton found himself sharing the soldiers' expressions of distaste: this had been someone who assumed that loyalty was an *opinion.*

He raised a hand in pax, gave up trying with the captain, and left the table.

Walking away, he heard the Hussars moving on with their conversation, starting to express some crude opinions about the Princess. He didn't break stride.

Into his mind, unbidden, came the memories. Of what had been a small miracle of a kind, but one that only he and she had been witness to.

• • • •

Hamilton had been at home on leave, having been abroad for a few weeks, serving out of uniform. As always, at times like that, when he should have been at rest, he'd been fired up for no good reason, unable to sleep, miserable, prone to tears in secret when a favorite song had come on the theatricals in his muse flat. It always took three days for him, once he was home, to find out what direction he was meant to be pointing. Then he would set off that way, and pop back to barracks one night for half a pint, and then he'd be fine. He could enjoy day four and onwards, and was known to be something approximating human from there on in.

Three-day leaves were hell. He tried not to use them as leaves, but would find himself some task, hopefully an official one if one of the handful of officers who brokered his services could be so entreated. Those officers were sensitive to such requests now.

But that leave, three years ago, had been two weeks off. He'd come home a day before. So he was no use to anyone. He'd taken a broom, and was pushing accumulated gray goo out of the carriage park alongside his apartment and into the drains.

She'd appeared in a sound of crashing and collapse, as her horse staggered sideways and hit the wall of the mews, then fell. Her two friends were galloping after her, their horses healthy, and someone built like Hamilton was running to help.

But none of them were going to be in time to catch her—

And he was.

. . . . .

It had turned out that the horse had missed an inoculation against minuscule poisoning. Its body was a terrible mess, random mechanisms developing out of its flanks and dying, with that terrifying smell, in the moments when Hamilton had held her in his arms, and had had to round on the man running in, and had imposed his authority with a look, and had not been thrown down and away.

Instead, she'd raised her hands and called that she was all right, and had insisted on looking to and at the horse, pulling off her glove and putting her hand to its neck and trying to fight the bloody things directly. But even with her command of information, it had been too late, and the horse had died in a mess.

She'd been bloody angry. And then at the emergency scene that had started to develop around Hamilton's front door, with police carriages swooping in and the sound of running boots—

Until she'd waved it all away and declared that it had been her favorite horse, a wonderful horse, her great friend since childhood, but it was just a bloody horse, and all she needed was a sit down and if this kind military gentleman would oblige—

And he had.

. . . .

He'd obliged her again when they'd met in Denmark, and they'd danced at a ball held on an ice floe, a carpet of mechanism wood reacting every moment to the weight of their feet and the forces underlying them, and the aurora had shone in the sky.

It was all right in Denmark for Elizabeth to have one dance with a commoner.

Hamilton had got back to the table where his regiment were dining, and had silenced the laughter and the calls, and thus saved them for barracks. He had drunk too much. His batman at the time had prevented him from going to see Elizabeth as she was escorted from the floor at the end of her dance card by a boy who was somewhere in line for the Danish throne.

But she had seen Hamilton the next night, in private, a privacy that would have taken great effort on her part, and after they had talked for several hours and shared some more wine she had shown him great favor.

· · · ·

"So. Is God in the details?" Someone was walking beside Hamilton. It was a Jesuit. Mid thirties. Dark hair, kept over her collar. She had a scar down one side of her face and an odd eye as a result. Minuscule blade, by the look. A member of the Society of Jesus would never allow her face to be restructured. That would be vanity. But she was beautiful.

Hamilton straightened up, giving this woman's musculature and bearing and all the history those things suggested the respect they deserved. "Or the devil."

"Yes, interesting the saying goes both ways, isn't it? My name is Mother Valentine. I'm part of the Society's campaign for Effective Love."

"Well," Hamilton raised an eyebrow, "I'm in favor of love being—"

"Don't waste our time. You know what I am."

"Yes, I do. And you know I'm the same. And I was waiting until we were out of earshot—"

"Which we now are—"

"To have this conversation."

They stopped together. Valentine moved her mouth close to Hamilton's ear. "I've just been told that the Holy Father is eager to declare what happened here to be a potential miracle. Certain parties are sure that our Black Eagle man will be found magically transplanted to distant parts, perhaps Berlin, as a sign against Prussian meddling."

"If he is, the Kaiser will have him gently shot and we'll never hear."

"You're probably right."

"What do you think happened?"

"I don't think miracles happen near our kind."

Hamilton realized he was looking absurdly hurt at her. And that she could see it. And was quietly absorbing that information for use in a couple of decades, if ever.

He was glad when a message came over the embroidery, asking him to attend to the Queen Mother in the pantry. And to bring his new friend.

· · · ·

The Queen Mother stood in the pantry, her not taking a chair having obviously made Parkes and his people even more nervous than they would have been.

She nodded to Valentine. "Monsignor. I must inform you, we've had an official approach from the Holy See. They regard the hall here as a possible site of miraculous apparition."

"Then my opinion on the subject is irrelevant. You should be addressing—"

"The ambassador. Indeed. But here you are. You are aware of what was asked of us?"

"I suspect the Cardinals will have sought a complete record of the moment of the apparition, or in this case, the vanishing. That would only be the work of a moment in the case of such an . . . observed . . . chamber."

"It would. But it's what happens next that concerns me."

"The procedure is that the chamber must then be sealed, and left unobserved until the Cardinals can see for themselves, to minimize any effect human observers may have on the process of divine revelation."

Hamilton frowned. "Are we likely to?"

"God is communicating using a physical method, so we may," said Valentine. "Depending on one's credulity concerning minuscule physics."

"Or one's credulity concerning international politics," said the Queen Mother. "Monsignor, it is always our first and most powerful inclination, when another nation asks us for something, to say no. All nations feel that way. All nations know the others do. But now here is a request, one that concerns matters right at the heart of the balance, that is, in the end, about deactivating security. It could be said to come not from another nation, but from God. It is therefore difficult to deny this request. We find ourselves distrusting that difficulty. It makes us want to deny it all the more."

"You speak for His Royal Highness?"

The Queen Mother gave a cough that might have been a laugh. "Just as you speak for Our Lord."

Valentine smiled and inclined her head. "I would have thought, your Royal Highness, that it would be obvious to any of the great powers that, given the celebrations, it would take you a long time to gather the Prime Minister and those many other courtiers with whom you would want to consult on such a difficult matter."

"Correct. Good. It will take three hours. You may go."

Valentine walked out with Hamilton. "I'm going to go and mix with my own for a while," she said, "listen to who's saying what."

"I'm surprised you wear your hair long."

She looked sharply at him. "Why?"

"You enjoy putting your head on the block."

She giggled.

Which surprised Hamilton and for just a moment made him wish he was Lord Carney. But then there was a certain small darkness about another priest he knew.

"I'm just betting," she said in a whisper, "that by the end of the day this will all be over. And someone will be dead."

• • • •

Hamilton went back into the ballroom. He found he had a picture in his head now. Something had swum up from somewhere inside him, from a place he had learned to trust and never interrogate as to its reasons. That jerking motion Elizabeth had made at the moment Sandels had vanished. He had an emotional feeling about that image. What was it?

It had been like seeing her shot.

A motion that looked like it had come from beyond her muscles. Something Elizabeth had not been in control of. It wasn't like her to not be in control. It felt . . . dangerous.

Would anyone else see it that way? He doubted it.

So was he about to do the sudden terrible thing that his body was taking him in the direction of doing?

He killed the thought and just did it. He went to the herald who carried the tablet with dance cards on it, and leaned on him with the Queen Mother's favor, which had popped up on his ring finger the moment he'd thought of it.

The herald considered the sensation of the fingertip on the back of his hand for a moment, then handed Hamilton the tablet.

Hamilton realized that he had no clue of the havoc he was about to cause. So he glanced at the list of Elizabeth's forthcoming dances and struck off a random Frenchman.

He scrawled his own signature with a touch, then handed the plate back.

The herald looked at him like the breath of death had passed under his nose.

• • • •

Hamilton had to wait three dances before his name came up. A Balaclava, an entrée grave (that choice must have taken a while, unless some herald had been waiting all his life for a chance at the French), a hornpipe for the sailors, including Bertil, to much applause, and then, thank the Deus, a straightforward waltz.

Elizabeth had been waiting out those last three, so he met her at her table. Maidservants kept their expressions stoic. A couple of Liz's companions looked positively scared. Hamilton knew how they felt. He could feel every important eye looking in his direction.

Elizabeth took his arm and gave it a little squeeze. "What's grandma up to, Johnny?"

"It's what I'm up to."

She looked alarmed. They formed up with the other dancers.

Hamilton was very aware of her gloves. The mechanism fabric that covered her left hand held off the urgent demand of his hand, his own need to touch her. But no, that wouldn't tell him anything. That was just his certainty that to know her had been to know her. That was not where he would find the truth here.

The band started up. The dance began.

Hamilton didn't access any guidelines in his mind. He let his feet move where they would. He was outside orders, acting on a hunch. He was like a man dancing around the edge of a volcano.

"Do you remember the day we met?" he asked when he was certain they couldn't be heard; at least, not by the other dancers.

"Of course I do. My poor San Andreas, your flat in Hood Mews—"

"Do you remember what I said to you that day, when nobody else was with us? What you agreed to? Those passionate words that could bring this whole charade crashing down?" He kept his expression light, his tone so gentle and wry that Liz would always play along and fling a little stone back at him, knowing he meant nothing more than he could mean. That he was letting off steam through a joke.

All they had been was based on the certainty expressed in that.

It was an entirely British way to do things. It was, as Carney had said, about lives shaped entirely by the balance.

But this woman, with the room revolving around the two of them, was suddenly appalled, insulted, her face a picture of what she was absolutely certain she should feel. "I don't know what you mean! Or even if I did, I don't think—!"

Hamilton's nostrils flared. He was lost now, if he was wrong. He had one tiny ledge for Liz to grasp if he was, but he would fall.

For duty, then.

He took his hand from Princess Elizabeth's waist, and grabbed her chin, his fingers digging up into flesh.

The whole room cried out in horror.

He had a moment before they would shoot him.

Yes, he felt it! Or he thought he did! He thought he did enough—

He grabbed the flaw and ripped with all his might.

Princess Elizabeth's face burst off and landed on the floor.

Blood flew.

He drew his gun and pumped two shots into the mass of flesh and mechanism, as it twitched and blew a stream of defensive acid that discolored the marble.

He spun back to find the woman without a face lunging at him, her eyes white in the mass of red muscle, mechanism pus billowing into the gaps. She was aiming a hair knife at his throat, doubtless with enough mechanism to bring instant death or something worse.

Hamilton thought of Liz as he broke her arm.

He enjoyed the scream.

He wanted to bellow for where the real Liz was as he slammed the impostor down onto the floor, and he was dragged from her in one motion as a dozen men grabbed them.

He caught a glimpse of Bertil, horrified, but not at Hamilton. It was a terror they shared. For her safety.

Hamilton suddenly felt like a traitor again.

He yelled out the words he'd had in mind since he'd put his name down for the dance. "They replaced her years ago! Years ago! At the mews!"

There were screams, cries that we were all undone.

There came the sound of two shots from the direction of the Vatican group, and Hamilton looked over to see Valentine standing over the corpse of a junior official.

Their gaze met. She understood why he'd shouted that.

Another man leapt up at a Vatican table behind her and turned to run and she turned and shot him twice in the chest, his body spinning backward over a table.

· · · ·

Hamilton ran with the rout. He used the crowds of dignitaries and their retinues, all roaring and competing and stampeding for safety, to hide himself. He made himself look like a man lost, agony on his face, his eyes closed. He was ignoring all the urgent cries from the embroidery.

He covertly acknowledged something directly from the Queen Mother.

He stumbled through the door of the pantry.

Parkes looked round. "Thank God you're here, we've been trying to call, the Queen Mother's office are urgently asking you to come in—"

"Never mind that now, come with me, on Her Royal Highness's orders."

Parkes grabbed the pods from his ears and got up. "What on Earth—?"

Hamilton shot him through the right knee.

Parkes screamed and fell. Every technician in the room leapt up. Hamilton bellowed at them to sit down or they'd get the same.

He shoved his foot into the back of Parkes's injured leg. "Listen here, Matty. You know how hard it's going to get. You're not the sort to think your duty's worth it. How much did they pay you? For how long?"

He was still yelling at the man on the ground as the Life Guards burst in and put a gun to everyone's head, his own included.

The Queen Mother entered a minute later, and changed that situation to the extent of letting Hamilton go free. She looked carefully at Parkes, who was still screaming for pity, and aimed a precise little kick into his disintegrated kneecap.

Then she turned to the technicians. "Your minds will be stripped down and rebuilt, if you're lucky, to see who was in on it." She looked back to Hamilton as they started to be led from the room. "What you said in the ballroom obviously isn't the case."

"No. When you take him apart," Hamilton nodded at Parkes, "you'll find he tampered with the contour map. They used Sandels as the cover for substituting Her Royal Highness. They knew she was going to move around the room in a predetermined way. With Parkes's help, they set up an open-ended fold in that corner—"

"The expense is staggering. The energy required—"

"There'll be no Christmas tree for the Kaiser this year. Sandels deliberately stepped into the fold and vanished, in a very public way. And at that moment they made the switch, took Her Royal Highness into the fold too, covered by the visual disturbance of Sandels's progress. And by old-fashioned sleight of hand."

"Propped up by the Prussians' people in the Vatican. Instead of a British bride influencing the Swedish court, there'd be a cuckoo from Berlin. Well played, Wilhelm. Worth that Christmas tree."

"I'll wager the unit are still in the fold, not knowing anything about the outside world, waiting for the room to be sealed off with pious care, so they can climb out and extract themselves. They probably have supplies for several days."

"Do you think my granddaughter is still alive?"

Hamilton pursed his lips. "There are Prussian yachts on the river. They're staying on for the season. I think they'd want the bonus of taking the Princess back for interrogation."

"That's the plan!" Parkes yelled. "Please—!"

"Get him some anesthetic," said the Queen Mother. Then she turned back to Hamilton. "The balance will be kept. To give him his due, cousin Wilhelm was acting within it. There will be no diplomatic incident. The Prussians will be able to write off Sandels and any others as rogues. We will of course cooperate. The Black Eagle traditionally carry only that knowledge they need for their mission, and will order themselves to die before giving us orders of battle or any other strategic information. But the intelligence from Parkes and any others will give us some small power of potential shame over the Prussians in future months. The Vatican will be bending over backwards for us for some time to come." She took his hand, and he felt the favor on his ring finger impressed with some notes that probably flattered him. He'd read them later. "Major, we will have the fold opened. You will enter it. Save Elizabeth. Kill them all."

* * * *

They got him a squad of fellow officers, four of them. They met in a trophy room, and sorted out how they'd go and what the rules of engagement would be once they got there. Substitutes for Parkes and his crew had been found from the few sappers present. Parkes had told them that those inside the fold had left a minuscule aerial trailing, but that messages were only to be passed down it in emergencies. No such communications had been sent. They were not aware of the world outside their bolt hole.

Hamilton felt nothing but disgust for a bought man, but he knew that such men told the truth under pressure, especially when they knew the fine detail of what could be done to them.

The false Liz had begun to be picked apart. Her real name would take a long time to discover. She had a maze of intersecting selves inside her head. She must have been as big an investment as the fold. The court physicians who had examined her had been as horrified by what had been done to her as by what she was.

That baffled Hamilton. People like the duplicate had the power to be who they liked. But that power was bought at the cost of damage to the balance of their own souls. What were nations, after all, but a lot of souls who knew who they were and how they liked to live? To be as uncertain as the substitute Liz was to be lost and to endanger others. It went beyond treachery. It was living mixed metaphor. It was as if she had insinuated herself into the cogs of the balance, her puppet strings wrapping around the arteries which supplied hearts and minds.

They gathered in the empty dining room in their dress uniforms. The dinner things had not been cleared away. Nothing had been done. The party had been well and truly crashed. The representatives of the great powers would have vanished back to their embassies and yachts. Mother Valentine would be rooting out the details of who had been paid what inside her party. Excommunications *post mortem* would be issued, and those traitors would burn in hell.

He thought of Liz, and took his gun from the air beside him.

One of the sappers put a device in the floor, set a timer, saluted and withdrew.

"Up the Green Jackets," said one of the men behind him, and a couple of the others mentioned their own regiments.

Hamilton felt a swell of fear and emotion.

The counter clicked to zero and the hole in the world opened in front of them, and they ran into it.

· · · ·

There was nobody immediately inside. A floor and curved ceiling of universal boundary material. It wrapped light around it in rainbows that always gave tunnels like this a slightly pantomime feel. It was like the entrance to Saint Nicholas's cave. Or, of course, the vortex sighted upon death, the ladder to the hereafter. Hamilton got that familiar taste in his mouth, a pure adrenal jolt of fear, not the restlessness of combat deferred, but that sensation one got in other universes, of being too far from home, cut off from the godhead.

There was gravity. The Prussians certainly had spent some money.

The party made their way forward. They stepped gently on the edge of the universe. From around the corner of the short tunnel there were sounds.

The other four looked to Hamilton. He took a couple of gentle steps forward, grateful for the softness of his dress uniform shoes. He could hear Elizabeth's voice. Not her words, not from here. She was angry, but engaged. Not defiant in the face of torture. Reasoning with them. A smile passed his lips for a moment. They'd have had a lot of that.

It told him there was no alert, not yet. It was almost impossible to set sensors close to the edge of a fold. This lot must have stood on guard for a couple of hours, heard no alarm from their friends outside, and then had relaxed. They'd have been on the clock, waiting for the time when they would poke their heads out. Hamilton bet there was a man meant to be on guard, but that Liz had pulled him into the conversation too. He could imagine her face, just round that corner, one eye always toward the exit, maybe a couple of buttons undone, claiming it was the heat and excitement. She had a hair knife too, but it would do her no good to use it on just one of them.

He estimated the distance. He counted the other voices, three . . . four, there was a deeper tone, in German, not the pidgin the other three had been speaking. That would be him. Sandels. He didn't sound like he was part of that conversation. He was angry, ordering, perhaps just back from sleep, wondering what the hell—!

Hamilton stopped all thoughts of Liz. He looked to the others, and they understood they were going to go and go now, trip the alarms and use the emergency against the enemy.

He nodded.

They leapt around the corner, ready for targets.

They expected the blaring horn. They rode it, finding their targets surprised, bodies reacting, reaching for weapons that were in a couple of cases a reach away among a kitchen, crates, tinned foods—

Hamilton had made himself know he was going to see Liz, so he didn't react to her, he looked past her—

He ducked, cried out, as an automatic set off by the alarm chopped up the man who had been running beside him, the Green Jacket, gone in a burst of red. Meat all over the cave.

Hamilton reeled, stayed up, tried to pin a target. To left and right ahead, men were falling, flying, two shots in each body, and he was moving too slowly, stumbling, vulnerable—

One man got off a shot, into the ceiling, and then fell, pinned twice, exploding—

Every one of the Prussians gone but—

He found his target.

Sandels. With Elizabeth right in front of him. Covering every bit of his body. He had a gun pushed into her neck. He wasn't looking at his three dead comrades.

The three men who were with Hamilton moved forward, slowly, their gun hands visible, their weapons pointing down.

They were looking to Hamilton again.

He hadn't lowered his gun. He had his target. He was aiming right at Sandels and the Princess.

There was silence.

Liz made eye contact. She had indeed undone those two buttons. She was calm. "Well," she began, "this is very—"

Sandels muttered something and she was quiet again.

Silence.

Sandels laughed, not unpleasantly. Soulful eyes were looking at them from that square face of his, a smile turning the corner of his mouth. He shared the irony that Hamilton had often found in people of their profession.

This was not the awkward absurdity that the soldiers had described. Hamilton realized that he was looking at an alternative. This man was a professional at the same things Hamilton did in the margins of his life. It was the strangeness of the alternative that had alienated the military men. Hamilton was fascinated by him.

"I don't know why I did this," said Sandels, indicating Elizabeth with a sway of the head. "Reflex."

Hamilton nodded to him. They each knew all the other did. "Perhaps you needed a moment."

"She's a very pretty girl to be wasted on a Swede."

Hamilton could feel Liz not looking at him. "It's not a waste," he said gently. "And you'll refer to Her Royal Highness by her title."

"No offense meant."

"And none taken. But we're in the presence, not in barracks."

"I wish we were."

"I think we all agree there."

"I won't lay down my weapon."

Hamilton didn't do his fellows the disservice of looking to them for confirmation. "This isn't an execution."

Sandels looked satisfied. "Seal this tunnel afterwards, that should be all we require for passage."

"Not to Berlin, I presume."

"No," said Sandels, "to entirely the opposite."

Hamilton nodded.

"Well, then." Sandels stepped aside from Elizabeth.

Hamilton lowered his weapon and the others readied theirs. It wouldn't be done to aim straight at Sandels. He had his own weapon at hip height. He would bring it up and they would cut him down as he moved.

But Elizabeth hadn't moved. She was pushing back her hair, as if wanting to say something to him before leaving, but lost for the right words.

Hamilton, suddenly aware of how unlikely that was, started to say something.

But Liz had put a hand to Sandels's cheek.

Hamilton saw the fine silver between her fingers.

Sandels fell to the ground thrashing, hoarsely yelling as he deliberately and precisely, as his nervous system was ordering him to, bit off his own tongue. Then the mechanism from the hair knife let him die.

The Princess looked at Hamilton. "It's not a waste," she said.

* * * *

They sealed the fold as Sandels had asked them to, after the sappers had made an inspection.

Hamilton left them to it. He regarded his duty as done. And no message came to him to say otherwise.

Recklessly, he tried to find Mother Valentine. But she was gone with the rest of the Vatican party, and there weren't even bloodstains left to mark where her feet had trod this evening.

He sat at a table, and tried to pour himself some champagne. He found that the bottle was empty.

His glass was filled by Lord Carney, who sat down next to him. Together, they watched as Elizabeth was joyfully reunited with Bertil. They swung each other round and round, oblivious to all around them. Elizabeth's grandmother smiled at them and looked nowhere else.

"We are watching," said Carney, "the balance incarnate. Or perhaps they'll incarnate it tonight. As I said: if only there were an alternative."

Hamilton drained his glass. "If only," he said, "there *weren't*."

And he left before Carney could say anything more.

ELIZABETH BEAR   Born in Hartford, Connecticut, Elizabeth Bear has published more than two dozen SF and fantasy novels and two story collections since her debut in 2005. In that short time she has won two Hugo Awards, the John W. Campbell Award for Best New Writer, and a Theodore Sturgeon Memorial Award for short fiction. She shows no sign of slowing down anytime soon.

In "Tideline," which won the Hugo and the Sturgeon in 2008, a crippled war machine and a feral teenager meet on a remote beach and form a bond. The machine nourishes the teenager to better health and teaches him to forage, meanwhile telling him a mixture of classical tales of derring-do and of the battle of which she was the only survivor. What happens as her power winds down makes for a well-formed science fiction story that is satisfying to the sentiments while holding mawkishness at bay. It is very much the kind of story that wins awards, and rightly so.

TIDELINE

halcedony wasn't built for crying. She didn't have it in her, not unless her tears were cold tapered-glass droplets annealed by the inferno heat that had crippled her.

Such tears as that might slide down her skin over melted sensors to plink unfeeling on the sand. And if they had, she would have scooped them up, with all the other battered pretties, and added them to the wealth of trash jewels that swung from the nets reinforcing her battered carapace.

They would have called her salvage, if there were anyone left to salvage her. But she was the last of the war machines, a three-legged oblate teardrop as big as a main battle tank, two big grabs and one fine manipulator folded like a spider's palps beneath the turreted head that finished her pointed end, her polyceramic armor spiderwebbed like shatterproof glass. Unhelmed by her remote masters, she limped along the beach, dragging one fused limb. She was nearly derelict.

The beach was where she met Belvedere.

· · · ·

Butterfly coquinas unearthed by retreating breakers squirmed into wet grit under Chalcedony's trailing limb. One of the rear pair, it was less of a nuisance on packed sand. It worked all right as a pivot, and as long as she stayed off rocks, there were no obstacles to drag it over.

As she struggled along the tideline, she became aware of someone watching. She didn't raise her head. Her chassis was equipped with targeting sensors that locked automatically on the ragged figure crouched by a weathered rock. Her optical input was needed to scan the tangle of seaweed and driftwood, Styrofoam and sea glass that marked high tide.

He watched her all down the beach, but he was unarmed, and her algorithms didn't deem him a threat.

Just as well. She liked the weird flat-topped sandstone boulder he crouched beside.

. . . .

The next day, he watched again. It was a good day; she found a moonstone, some rock crystal, a bit of red-orange pottery, and some sea glass worn opalescent by the tide.

. . . .

"Whatcha picken up?"

"Shipwreck beads," Chalcedony answered. For days, he'd been creeping closer, until he'd begun following behind her like the seagulls, scrabbling the coquinas harrowed up by her dragging foot into a patched mesh bag. Sustenance, she guessed, and indeed he pulled one of the tiny mollusks from the bag and produced a broken-bladed folding knife from somewhere to prise it open. Her sensors painted the knife pale colors. A weapon, but not a threat to her.

Deft enough—he flicked, sucked, and tossed the shell away in under three seconds—but that couldn't be much more than a morsel of meat. A lot of work for very small return.

He was bony as well as ragged, and small for a human. Perhaps young.

She thought he'd ask *what shipwreck*, and she would gesture vaguely over the bay, where the city had been, and say *there were many*. But he surprised her.

"Whatcha gonna do with them?" He wiped his mouth on a sandy paw, the broken knife projecting carelessly from the bottom of his fist.

"When I get enough, I'm going to make necklaces." She spotted something under a tangle of the algae called dead man's fingers, a glint of light, and began the laborious process of lowering herself to reach it, compensating by math for her malfunctioning gyroscopes.

The presumed-child watched avidly. "Nuh uh," he said. "You can't make a necklace outta that."

"Why not?" She levered herself another decimeter down, balancing against the weight of her fused limb. She did not care to fall.

"I seed what you pick up. They's all different."

"So?" she asked, and managed another few centimeters. Her hydraulics whined. Someday, those hydraulics or her fuel cells would fail and she'd be stuck this way, a statue corroded by salt air and the sea, and the tide would roll in and roll over her. Her carapace was cracked, no longer watertight.

"They's not all beads."

Her manipulator brushed aside the dead man's fingers. She uncovered the treasure, a bit of blue-gray stone carved in the shape of a fat, merry man. It had no holes. Chalcedony balanced herself back upright and turned the figurine in the light. The stone was structurally sound.

She extruded a hair-fine diamond-tipped drill from the opposite manipulator and drilled a hole through the figurine, top to bottom. Then she threaded him on a twist of wire, looped the ends, work-hardened the loops, and added him to the garland of beads swinging against her disfigured chassis.

"So?"

The presumed-child brushed the little Buddha with his fingertip, setting it swinging against shattered ceramic plate. She levered herself up again, out of his reach. "I's Belvedere," he said.

"Hello," Chalcedony said. "I'm Chalcedony."

. . . .

By sunset when the tide was lowest he scampered chattering in her wake, darting between flocking gulls to scoop up coquinas by the fistful, which he rinsed in the surf before devouring raw. Chalcedony more or less ignored him as she activated her floods, concentrating their radiance along the tideline.

A few dragging steps later, another treasure caught her eye. It was a scrap of chain with a few bright beads caught on it—glass, with scraps of gold and silver foil embedded in their twists. Chalcedony initiated the laborious process of retrieval—

Only to halt as Belvedere jumped in front of her, grabbed the chain in a grubby broken-nailed hand, and snatched it up. Chalcedony locked in position, nearly overbalancing. She was about to reach out to snatch the treasure away from the child and knock him into the sea when he rose up on tiptoe and held it out to her, straining over his head. The flood lights cast his shadow black on the sand, illumined each thread of his hair and eyebrows in stark relief.

"It's easier if I get that for you," he said, as her fine manipulator closed tenderly on the tip of the chain.

She lifted the treasure to examine it in the floods. A good long segment, seven centimeters, four jewel-toned shiny beads. Her head creaked when she raised it, corrosion showering from the joints.

She hooked the chain onto the netting wrapped around her carapace. "Give me your bag," she said.

Belvedere's hand went to the soggy net full of raw bivalves dripping down his naked leg. "My bag?"

"Give it to me." Chalcedony drew herself up, akilter because of the ruined limb, but still two and a half meters taller than the child. She extended a manipulator, and from some disused file dredged up a protocol for dealing with civilian humans. "Please."

He fumbled at the knot with rubbery fingers, tugged it loose from his rope belt, and held it out to her. She snagged it on a manipulator and brought it up. A sample revealed that the weave was cotton rather than nylon, so she folded it in her two larger manipulators and gave the contents a low-wattage microwave pulse.

She shouldn't. It was a drain on her power cells, which she had no means to recharge, and she had a task to complete.

She shouldn't—but she did.

Steam rose from her claws and the coquinas popped open, roasting in their own juices and the moisture of the seaweed with which he'd lined the net. Carefully, she swung the bag back to him, trying to preserve the fluids.

"Caution," she urged. "It's hot."

He took the bag gingerly and flopped down to sit cross-legged at her feet. When he tugged back the seaweed, the coquinas lay like tiny jewels—pale orange, rose, yellow, green, and blue—in their nest of glass-green *Ulva*, sea lettuce. He tasted one cautiously, and then began to slurp with great abandon, discarding shells in every direction.

"Eat the algae, too," Chalcedony told him. "It is rich in important nutrients."

. . . .

When the tide came in, Chalcedony retreated up the beach like a great hunched crab with five legs amputated. She was beetle-backed under the moonlight, her treasures swinging and rustling on her netting, clicking one another like stones shivered in a palm.

The child followed.

"You should sleep," Chalcedony said, as Belvedere settled beside her on the high, dry crescent of beach under towering mud cliffs, where the waves wouldn't lap.

He didn't answer, and her voice fuzzed and furred before clearing when she spoke again. "You should climb up off the beach. The cliffs are unstable. It is not safe beneath them."

Belvedere hunkered closer, lower lip protruding. "You stay down here."

"I have armor. And I cannot climb." She thumped her fused leg on the sand, rocking her body forward and back on the two good legs to manage it.

"But your armor's broke."

"That doesn't matter. You must climb." She picked Belvedere up with both grabs and raised him over her head. He shrieked; at first she feared she'd damaged him, but the cries resolved into laughter before she set him down on a slanted ledge that would bring him to the top of the cliff.

She lit it with her floods. "Climb," she said, and he climbed.

And returned in the morning.

. . . .

Belvedere stayed ragged, but with Chalcedony's help he waxed plumper. She snared and roasted seabirds for him, taught him how to construct and maintain fires, and ransacked her extensive databases for hints on how to keep him healthy as he grew—sometimes almost visibly, fractions of a millimeter a day. She researched and analyzed sea vegetables and hectored him into eating them, and he helped her reclaim treasures her manipulators could not otherwise grasp. Some shipwreck beads were hot, and made Chalcedony's radiation detectors tick over. They were no threat to her, but for the first time she discarded them. She had a human ally; her program demanded she sustain him in health.

She told him stories. Her library was vast—and full of war stories and stories about sailing ships and starships, which he liked best for some inexplicable reason. Catharsis, she thought, and told him again of Roland, and King Arthur, and Honor Harrington, and Napoleon Bonaparte, and Horatio Hornblower, and Captain Jack Aubrey. She projected the words on a monitor as she recited them, and—faster than she would have imagined—he began to mouth them along with her.

So the summer ended.

By the equinox, she had collected enough memorabilia. Shipwreck jewels still washed up and Belvedere still brought her the best of them, but Chalcedony settled beside that twisted flat-topped sandstone rock and arranged her treasures on it. She spun salvaged brass through a die to make wire, threaded beads on it, and forged links that she strung into garlands.

It was a learning experience. Her aesthetic sense was at first undeveloped, requiring her to make and unmake many dozens of bead combinations to find a pleasing one. Not only must form and color be balanced, but there were structural difficulties. First the weights were unequal, so the chains hung crooked. Then links kinked and snagged and had to be redone.

She worked for weeks. Memorials had been important to the human allies, though she had never understood the logic of it. She could not build a tomb for her colleagues, but the same archives that gave her the stories Belvedere lapped up as a cat laps milk gave her the concept of mourning jewelry. She had no physical remains of her allies, no scraps of hair or cloth, but surely the shipwreck jewels would suffice for a treasure?

The only quandary was who would wear the jewelry. It should go to an heir, someone who held fond memories of the deceased. And Chalcedony had records of the next of kin, of course. But she had no way to know if any survived, and, if they did, no way to reach them.

At first, Belvedere stayed close, trying to tempt her into excursions and explorations. Chalcedony remained resolute, however. Not only were her power cells dangerously low, but with the coming of winter her ability to utilize solar power would be even more limited. And with winter the storms would come, and she would no longer be able to evade the ocean.

She was determined to complete this last task before she failed.

Belvedere began to range without her, to snare his own birds and bring them back to the driftwood fire for roasting. This was positive; he needed to be able to maintain himself. At night, however, he returned to sit beside her, to clamber onto the flat-topped rock to sort beads and hear her stories.

The same thread she worked over and over with her grabs and fine manipulators—the duty of the living to remember the fallen with honor—was played out in the war stories she still told him. She'd finished with fiction and history and now she related him her own experiences. She told him about Emma Percy rescuing that kid up near Savannah, and how Private Michaels was shot drawing fire for Sergeant Kay Patterson when the battle robots were decoyed out of position in a skirmish near Seattle.

Belvedere listened, and surprised her by proving he could repeat the gist, if not the exact words. His memory was good, if not as good as a machine's.

· · · ·

One day when he had gone far out of sight down the beach, Chalcedony heard Belvedere screaming.

She had not moved in days. She hunkered on the sand at an awkward angle, her frozen limb angled down the beach, her necklaces in progress on the rock that served as her impromptu work bench.

Bits of stone and glass and wire scattered from the rock top as she heaved herself onto her unfused limbs. She thrashed upright on her first attempt, surprising herself, and tottered for a moment unsteadily, lacking the stabilization of long-failed gyroscopes.

When Belvedere shouted again, she almost overset.

Climbing was out of the question, but Chalcedony could still run. Her fused limb plowed a furrow in the sand behind her and the tide was coming in, forcing her to splash through corroding sea water.

She barreled around the rocky prominence that Belvedere had disappeared behind in time to see him knocked to the ground by two larger humans, one of whom had a club raised over its head and the other of which was holding Belvedere's shabby net bag. Belvedere yelped as the club connected with his thigh.

Chalcedony did not dare use her microwave projectors.

But she had other weapons, including a pinpoint laser and a chemical-propellant firearm suitable for sniping operations. Enemy humans were soft targets. These did not even have body armor.

· · · ·

She buried the bodies on the beach, following the protocols of war. It was her program to treat enemy dead with respect. Belvedere was in no immediate danger of death once she had splinted his leg and treated his bruises, but she judged him too badly injured to help. The sand was soft and amenable to scooping, anyway, though there was no way to keep the bodies above water. It was the best she could manage.

After she had finished, she transported Belvedere back to their rock and began collecting her scattered treasures.

· · · ·

The leg was sprained and bruised, not broken, and some perversity connected to the injury made him even more restlessly inclined to push his boundaries once he had partially recovered. He was on his feet within a week, leaning on crutches and dragging a leg as stiff as Chalcedony's. As soon as the splint came off, he started ranging even further afield. His new limp barely slowed him, and he stayed out nights. He was still growing, shooting up, almost as tall as a Marine now, and ever more capable of taking care of himself. The incident with the raiders had taught him caution.

Meanwhile, Chalcedony elaborated her funeral necklaces. She must make each one worthy of a fallen comrade, and she was slowed now by her inability to work through the nights. Rescuing Belvedere had cost her much carefully hoarded energy, and she could not power her floods if she meant to finish before her cells ran dry. She could *see* by moonlight, with deadly clarity, but her low-light and thermal eyes were of no use when it came to balancing color against color.

There would be forty-one necklaces, one for each member of her platoon-that-was, and she would not excuse shoddy craftsmanship.

No matter how fast she worked, it was a race against sun and tide.

· · · ·

The fortieth necklace was finished in October while the days grew short. She began the forty-first—the one for her chief operator Platoon Sergeant Patterson, the one with the gray-blue Buddha at the bottom—before sunset. She had not seen Belvedere in several days, but that was acceptable. She would not finish the necklace tonight.

· · · ·

His voice woke her from the quiescence in which she waited the sun. "Chalcedony?"

Something cried as she came awake. *Infant*, she identified, but the warm shape in his arms was not an infant. It was a dog, a young dog, a German shepherd like the ones teamed with the handlers that had sometimes worked with Company L. The dogs had never minded her, but some of the handlers had been frightened, though they would not admit it. Sergeant Patterson had said to one of them, *Oh, Chase is just pretty much a big attack dog herself*, and had made a big show of rubbing Chalcedony behind her telescopic sights, to the sound of much laughter.

The young dog was wounded. Its injuries bled warmth across its hind leg.

"Hello, Belvedere," Chalcedony said.

"Found a puppy." He kicked his ragged blanket flat so he could lay the dog down.

"Are you going to eat it?"

"Chalcedony!" he snapped, and covered the animal protectively with his arms. "S'hurt."

She contemplated. "You wish me to tend to it?"

He nodded, and she considered. She would need her lights, energy, irreplaceable stores. Antibiotics and coagulants and surgical supplies, and the animal might die anyway. But dogs were valuable; she knew the handlers held them in great esteem, even greater than Sergeant Patterson's esteem for Chalcedony. And in her library, she had files on veterinary medicine.

She flipped on her floods and accessed the files.

· · · ·

She finished before morning, and before her cells ran dry. Just barely.

When the sun was up and the young dog was breathing comfortably, the gash along its haunch sewn closed and its bloodstream saturated with antibiotics, she turned back to the last necklace. She would have to work quickly, and Sergeant Patterson's necklace contained the most fragile and beautiful beads, the ones Chalcedony had been most concerned with breaking and so had saved for last, when she would be most experienced.

Her motions grew slower as the day wore on, more laborious. The sun could not feed her enough to replace the expenditures of the night before. But bead linked into bead, and the necklace grew—bits of pewter, of pottery, of glass and mother of pearl. And the chalcedony Buddha, because Sergeant Patterson had been Chalcedony's operator.

When the sun approached its zenith, Chalcedony worked faster, benefiting from a burst of energy. The young dog slept on in her shade, having wolfed the scraps of bird Belvedere gave it, but Belvedere climbed the rock and crouched beside her pile of finished necklaces.

"Who's this for?" he asked, touching the slack length draped across her manipulator.

"Kay Patterson," Chalcedony answered, adding a greenish-brown pottery bead mottled like a combat uniform.

"Sir Kay," Belvedere said. His voice was changing, and sometimes it abandoned him completely in the middle of words, but he got that phrase out entire. "She was King Arthur's horse-master, and his adopted brother, and she kept his combat robots in the stable," he said, proud of his recall.

"They were different Kays," she reminded. "You will have to leave soon." She looped another bead onto the chain, closed the link, and work-hardened the metal with her fine manipulator.

"You can't leave the beach. You can't climb."

Idly, he picked up a necklace, Rodale's, and stretched it between his hands so the beads caught the light. The links clinked softly.

Belvedere sat with her as the sun descended and her motions slowed. She worked almost entirely on solar power now. With night, she would become quiescent again. When the storms came, the waves would roll over her, and then even the sun would not awaken her again. "You must go," she said, as her grabs stilled on the almost-finished chain. And then she lied and said, "I do not want you here."

"Who's this'n for?" he asked. Down on the beach, the young dog lifted its head and whined. "Garner," she answered, and then she told him about Garner, and Antony, and Javez, and Rodriguez, and Patterson, and White, and Wosczyna, until it was dark enough that her voice and her vision failed.

· · · · ·

In the morning, he put Patterson's completed chain into Chalcedony's grabs. He must have worked on it by firelight through the darkness. "Couldn't harden the links," he said, as he smoothed them over her claws.

Silently, she did that, one by one. The young dog was on its feet, limping, nosing around the base of the rock and barking at the waves, the birds, a scuttling crab. When Chalcedony had finished, she reached out and draped the necklace around Belvedere's shoulders while he held very still. Soft fur downed his cheeks. The male Marines had always scraped theirs smooth, and the women didn't grow facial hair.

"You said that was for Sir Kay." He lifted the chain in his hands and studied the way the glass and stones caught the light.

"It's for somebody to remember her," Chalcedony said. She didn't correct him this time. She picked up the other forty necklaces. They were heavy, all together. She wondered if Belvedere could carry them. "So remember her. Can you remember which one is whose?"

One at a time, he named them, and one at a time she handed them to him. Rogers, and Rodale, and van Metier, and Percy. He spread a second blanket out—and where had he gotten a second blanket? Maybe the same place he'd gotten the dog—and laid them side by side on the navy blue wool.

They sparkled.

"Tell me the story about Rodale," she said, brushing her grab across the necklace. He did, sort of, with half of Roland-and-Oliver mixed in. It was a pretty good story anyway, the way he told it. Inasmuch as she was a fit judge.

"Take the necklaces," she said. "Take them. They're mourning jewelry. Give them to people and tell them the stories. They should go to people who will remember and honor the dead."

"Where will I find alla these people?" he asked, sullenly, crossing his arms. "Ain't on the beach."

"No," she said, "they are not. You'll have to go look for them."

· · · ·

But he wouldn't leave her. He and the dog ranged up and down the beach as the weather chilled. Her sleeps grew longer, deeper, the low angle of the sun not enough to awaken her except at noon. The storms came, and because the table rock broke the spray, the salt water stiffened her joints but did not—yet—corrode her processor. She no longer moved and rarely spoke even in daylight, and Belvedere and the young dog used her carapace and the rock for shelter, the smoke of his fires blackening her belly.

She was hoarding energy.

By mid-November, she had enough, and she waited and spoke to Belvedere when he returned with the young dog from his rambling. "You must go," she said, and when he opened his mouth to protest, she added, "It is time you went on errantry."

His hand went to Patterson's necklace, which he wore looped twice around his neck, under his ragged coat. He had given her back the others, but that one she had made a gift of. "Errantry?"

Creaking, powdered corrosion grating from her joints, she lifted the necklaces off her head. "You must find the people to whom these belong."

He deflected her words with a jerk of his hand. "They's all dead."

"The warriors are dead," she said. "But the stories aren't. Why did you save the young dog?"

He licked his lips, and touched Patterson's necklace again. "'Cause you saved me. And you told me the stories. About good fighters and bad fighters. And so, see, Percy woulda saved the dog, right? And so would Hazel-rah."

Emma Percy, Chalcedony was reasonably sure, would have saved the dog if she could have. And Kevin Michaels would have saved the kid. She held the remaining necklaces out.

He stared, hands twisting before him. "You can't climb."

"I can't. You must do this for me. Find people to remember the stories. Find people to tell about my platoon. I won't survive the winter." Inspiration struck. "I give you this quest, Sir Belvedere."

The chains hung flashing in the wintry light, the sea combed gray and tired behind them. "What kinda people?"

"People who would help a child," she said. "Or a wounded dog. People like a platoon should be."

He paused. He reached out, stroked the chains, let the beads rattle. He crooked both hands, and slid them into the necklaces up to the elbows, taking up her burden.

DAVID MOLES   David Moles was born in California and grew up in Athens, Tokyo, Tehran, and San Diego. He has been publishing SF since 2003, has edited two anthologies, and has been a finalist for the Hugo and the World Fantasy Award.

"Finisterra" is a swashbuckling adventure set on a Jupiter-sized planet with an Earth-like atmospheric layer, floating in which are immense living dirigibles, miles and miles wide, on which people live and even cultivate food. It is also a story about the difficulties of deciding which side you're on. Vivid and astute, it won the Theodore Sturgeon Memorial Award for short SF in 2008.

FINISTERRA

1. ENCANTADA

Bianca Nazario stands at the end of the world.

The firmament above is as blue as the summer skies of her childhood, mirrored in the waters of *la caldera*; but where the skies she remembers were bounded by mountains, here on Sky there is no real horizon, only a line of white cloud. The white line shades into a diffuse grayish fog that, as Bianca looks down, grows progressively murkier, until the sky directly below is thoroughly dark and opaque.

She remembers what Dinh told her about the ways Sky could kill her. With a large enough parachute, Bianca imagines, she could fall for hours, drifting through the layered clouds, before finding her end in heat or pressure or the jaws of some monstrous denizen of the deep air.

If this should go wrong, Bianca cannot imagine a better way to die.

Bianca works her way out a few hundred meters along the base of one of Encantada's ventral fins, stopping when the dry red dirt beneath her feet begins to give way to scarred gray flesh. She takes a last look around: at the pall of smoke obscuring the *zaratán*'s tree-lined dorsal ridge, at the fin she stands on, curving out and down to its delicate-looking tip, kilometers away. Then she knots her scarf around her skirted ankles and shrugs into the paraballoon harness, still warm from the bungalow's fabricators. As the harness tightens itself around her, she takes a deep breath, filling her lungs. The wind from the burning camp smells of wood smoke and pine resin, enough to overwhelm the taint of blood from the killing ground.

Blessed Virgin, she prays, be my witness: this is no suicide.

This is a prayer for a miracle.

She leans forward.
She falls.

2. THE FLYING ARCHIPELAGO

The boatlike anemopter that Valadez had sent for them had a cruising speed of just less than the speed of sound, which in this part of Sky's atmosphere meant about nine hundred kilometers per hour. The speed, Bianca thought, might have been calculated to bring home the true size of Sky, the impossible immensity of it. It had taken the better part of their first day's travel for the anemopter's point of departure, the ten-kilometer, billion-ton vacuum balloon *Transient Meridian,* to drop from sight—the dwindling golden droplet disappearing, not over the horizon, but into the haze. From that Bianca estimated that the bowl of clouds visible through the subtle blurring of the anemopter's static fields covered an area about the size of North America.

She heard a plastic clattering on the deck behind her and turned to see one of the anemopter's crew, a globular, brown-furred alien with a collection of arms like furry snakes, each arm tipped with a mouth or a round and curious eye. The *firija* were low-gravity creatures; the ones Bianca had seen on her passage from Earth had tumbled joyously through the *Caliph of Baghdad*'s inner-ring spaces like so many radially symmetrical monkeys. The three aboard the anemopter, in Sky's heavier gravity, had to make do with spindly-legged walking machines. There was a droop in their arms that was both comical and melancholy.

"Come forward," this one told Bianca in fractured Arabic, its voice like an ensemble of reed pipes. She thought it was the one that called itself Ismaíl. "Make see archipelago."

She followed it forward to the anemopter's rounded prow. The naturalist, Erasmus Fry, was already there, resting his elbows on the rail, looking down.

"Pictures don't do them justice, do they?" he said.

Bianca went to the rail and followed the naturalist's gaze. She did her best to maintain a certain stiff formality around Fry; from their first meeting aboard *Transient Meridian* she'd had the idea that it might not be good to let him get too familiar. But when she saw what Fry was looking at, the mask slipped for a moment; she couldn't help a sharp, quick intake of breath.

Fry chuckled. "To stand on the back of one," he said, "to stand in a valley and look up at the hills and know that the ground under your feet is supported by the bones of a living creature—there's nothing else like it." He shook his head.

At this altitude they were above all but the highest-flying of the thousands of beasts that made up Septentrionalis Archipelago. Bianca's eyes tried to make the herd (or flock, or school) of *zaratánes* into other things: a chain of islands, yes, if she concentrated on the colors, the greens and browns of forests and plains, the grays and whites of the snowy highlands; a fleet of ships, perhaps, if she instead focused on the individual shapes, the keel ridges, the long, translucent fins, ribbed like Chinese sails.

The *zaratánes* of the archipelago were more different from one another than the members of a flock of birds or a pod of whales, but still there was a symmetry, a regularity of form, the basic anatomical plan—equal parts fish and mountain—repeated throughout, in fractal detail from the great old shape of Zaratán Finisterra, a hundred kilometers along the dorsal ridge, down to the merely hill-sized bodies of the nameless younger beasts. When she took in the archipelago as a whole, it was impossible for Bianca not to see the *zaratánes* as living things.

"Nothing else like it," Fry repeated.

Bianca turned reluctantly from the view to look at Fry. The naturalist spoke Spanish with a flawless Miami accent, courtesy, he'd said, of a Consilium language module. Bianca was finding it hard to judge the ages of *extrañados,* particularly the men, but in Fry's case she thought he might be ten years older than Bianca's own forty, and unwilling to admit it—or ten years younger, and in the habit of treating himself very badly. On her journey here she'd met cyborgs and foreigners and artificial intelligences and several sorts of alien—some familiar, at least from media coverage of the *hajj,* and some strange—but the *extrañados* bothered her the most. It was hard to come to terms with the idea of humans born off Earth, humans who had never been to Earth or even seen it; humans who often had no interest in it.

"Why did you leave here, Mr. Fry?" she asked.

Fry laughed. "Because I didn't want to spend the rest of my life out *here.*" With a hand, he swept the horizon. "Stuck on some godforsaken floating island for years on end, with no one but researchers and feral refugees to talk to, nowhere to go for fun but some slum of a balloon station, nothing but a thousand kilometers of air between you and Hell?" He laughed again. "You'd leave, too, Nazario, believe me."

"Maybe I would," Bianca said. "But you're back."

"I'm here for the money," Fry said. "Just like you."

Bianca smiled and said nothing.

"You know," Fry said after a little while, "they have to kill the *zaratánes* to take them out of here." He looked at Bianca and smiled, in a way that was probably meant to be ghoulish. "There's no atmosphere ship big enough to lift a *zaratán* in one piece—even a small one. The poachers deflate them— gut them—flatten them out and roll them up. And even then, they throw out almost everything but the skin and bones."

"Strange," Bianca mused. Her mask was back in place. "There was a packet of material on the *zaratánes* with my contract; I watched most of it on the voyage. According to the packet, the Consilium considers the *zaratánes* a protected species."

Fry looked uneasy. Now it was Bianca's turn to chuckle.

"Don't worry, Mr. Fry," she said. "I may not know exactly what it is Mr. Valadez is paying me to do, but I've never had any illusion that it was legal."

Behind her, the *firija* made a fluting noise that might have been laughter.

3. THE STEEL BIRD

When Bianca was a girl, the mosque of Punta Aguila was the most prominent feature in the view from her fourth-floor window, a sixteenth-century structure of tensegrity cables and soaring catenary curves, its spreading white wings vaguely—but only vaguely—recalling the bird that gave the city its name. The automation that controlled the tension of the cables and adjusted the mosque's wings to match the shifting winds was hidden within the cables themselves, and was very old. Once, after the hurricane in the time of Bianca's grandfather, it had needed adjusting, and the old men of the *ayuntamiento* had been forced to send for *extrañado* technicians, at an expense so great that the *jizyah* of Bianca's time was still paying for it.

But Bianca rarely thought of that. Instead she would spend long hours surreptitiously sketching those white wings, calculating the weight of the structure and the tension of the cables, wondering what it would take to make the steel bird fly.

Bianca's father could probably have told her, but she never dared to ask. Raúl Nazario de Arenas was an aeronautical engineer, like the seven generations before him, and flight was the Nazarios' fortune; fully a third of the aircraft that plied the skies over the Rio Pícaro were types designed by Raúl or his father or his wife's father, on contract to the great *moro* trading and manufacturing families that were Punta Aguila's truly wealthy.

Because he worked for other men, and because he was a Christian, Raúl Nazario would never be as wealthy as the men who employed him, but his profession was an ancient and honorable one, providing his family with a more than comfortable living. If Raúl Nazario de Arenas thought of the mosque at all, it was only to mutter about the *jizyah* from time to time—but never loudly, because the Nazarios, like the other Christians of Punta Aguila, however valued, however ancient their roots, knew that they lived there only on sufferance.

But Bianca would sketch the aircraft, too, the swift gliders and lumbering flying boats and stately dirigibles, and these drawings she did not have to hide; in fact for many years her father would encourage her, explaining this and that aspect of their construction, gently correcting errors of proportion and balance in Bianca's drawings; would let her listen in while he taught the family profession to her brothers, Jesús the older, Pablo the younger.

This lasted until shortly before Bianca's *quinceañera,* when Jesús changed his name to Walíd and married a *moro*'s daughter, and Bianca's mother delivered a lecture concerning the difference between what was proper for a child and what was proper for a young Christian woman with hopes of one day making a good marriage.

It was only a handful of years later that Bianca's father died, leaving a teenaged Pablo at the helm of his engineering business; and only Bianca's invisible assistance and the pity of a few old clients had kept contracts and money coming into the Nazario household.

By the time Pablo was old enough to think he could run the business himself, old enough to marry the daughter of a musical instrument-maker from Tierra Ceniza, their mother was dead, Bianca was thirty, and even if her dowry had been half her father's business, there was not a Christian man in Río Pícaro who wanted it, or her.

And then one day Pablo told her about the *extrañado* contract that had been brought to the *ayuntamiento,* a contract that the *ayuntamiento* and the Guild had together forbidden the Christian engineers of Punta Aguila to bid on—a contract for a Spanish-speaking aeronautical engineer to travel a very long way from Río Pícaro and be paid a very large sum of money indeed.

Three months later Bianca was in Quito, boarding an elevator car. In her valise was a bootleg copy of her father's engineering system, and a contract with the factor of a starship called the *Caliph of Baghdad,* for passage to Sky.

4. THE KILLING GROUND

The anemopter's destination was a zaratán called Encantada, smaller than the giant Finisterra but still nearly forty kilometers from nose to tail, and eight thousand meters from gray-white keel to forested crest. From a distance of a hundred kilometers, Encantada was like a forested mountain rising from a desert plain, the clear air under its keel as dreamlike as a mirage. On her pocket system, Bianca called up pictures from Sky's network of the alpine ecology that covered the hills and valleys of Encantada's flanks: hardy grasses and small warm-blooded creatures and tall evergreens with spreading branches, reminding her of the pines and redwoods in the mountains west of Río Pícaro.

For the last century or so Encantada had been keeping company with Zaratán Finisterra, holding its position above the larger beast's eastern flank. No one, apparently, knew the reason. Fry being the expert, Bianca had expected him to at least have a theory. He didn't even seem interested in the question.

"They're beasts, Nazario," he said. "They don't do things for reasons.

We only call them animals and not plants because they bleed when we cut them."

They were passing over Finisterra's southern slopes. Looking down, Bianca saw brighter, warmer greens, more shades than she could count, more than she had known existed, the green threaded through with bright ribbons of silver water. She saw the anemopter's shadow, a dark oblong that rode the slopes and ridges, ringed by brightness—the faint reflection of Sky's sun behind them.

And just before the shadow entered the larger darkness that was the shadow of Encantada, Bianca watched it ride over something else: a flat green space carved out of the jungle, a suspiciously geometric collection of shapes that could only be buildings, the smudge of chimney smoke.

"Fry—" she started to say.

Then the village, if that's what it was, was gone, hidden behind the next ridge.

"What?" said Fry.

"I saw—I thought I saw—"

"People?" asked Fry. "You probably did."

"But I thought Sky didn't have any native sentients. Who are they?"

"Humans, mostly," Fry said. "Savages. Refugees. Drug farmers. Five generations of escaped criminals, and their kids, and *their* kids." The naturalist shrugged. "Once in a while, if the Consilium's looking for somebody in particular, the wardens might stage a raid, just for show. The rest of the time, the wardens fly their dope, screw their women . . . and otherwise leave them alone."

"But where do they come from?" Bianca asked.

"Everywhere," Fry said with another shrug. "Humans have been in this part of space for a long, long time. This is one of those places people end up, you know? People with nowhere else to go. People who can't fall any farther."

Bianca shook her head and said nothing.

· · · ·

The poacher camp on Encantada's eastern slope was invisible until they were almost upon it, hidden from the wardens' satellite eyes by layers of projected camouflage. Close up, the illusion seemed flat, its artificiality obvious, but it was still not until the anemopter passed through the projection that the camp itself could be seen: a clear-cut swath a kilometer wide and three times as long, stretching from the lower slopes of Encantada's dorsal ridge down to the edge of the *zaratán*'s clifflike flank. Near the edge, at one corner, there was a small cluster of prefabricated bungalows; but at first it seemed to Bianca that most of the space was wasted.

Then she saw the red churned into the brown mud of the cleared strip, saw the way the shape of the terrain suggested the imprint of a gigantic, elongated body.

The open space was for killing.

· · · ·

"Sky is very poor, Miss Nazario," said Valadez, over his shoulder.

The poacher boss looked to be about fifty, stocky, his hair still black and his olive skin well-tanned but pocked with tiny scars. His Spanish was a dialect Bianca had never heard before, strange and lush, its vowels rich, its *h*s breathy as Bianca's *j*s, its *j*s warm and liquid as the *y*s of an Argentine. When he said, *Fuck your mother*—and already, in the hour or so Bianca had been in the camp, she had heard him say it several times, though never yet to her—the *madre* came out *madri*.

About half of the poachers were human, but Valadez seemed to be the only one who spoke Spanish natively; the rest used Sky's dialect of bazaar Arabic. Valadez spoke that as well, better than Bianca did, but she had the sense that he'd learned it late in life. If he had a first name, he was keeping it to himself.

"There are things on Sky that people want," Valadez went on. "But the *people* of Sky have nothing of interest to anybody. The companies that mine the deep air pay some royalties. But mostly what people live on here is Consilium handouts."

The four of them—Bianca, Fry, and the *firija,* Ismaíl, who as well as being an anemopter pilot seemed to be Valadez's servant or business partner or bodyguard, or perhaps all three—were climbing the ridge above the poachers' camp. Below them workers, some human, some *firija,* a handful of other species, were setting up equipment: mobile machines that looked like they belonged on a construction site, pipes and cylindrical tanks reminiscent of a brewery or a refinery.

"I'm changing that, Miss Nazario." Valadez glanced over his shoulder at Bianca. "Off-world, there are people—like Ismaíl's people here"—he waved at the *firija*—"who like the idea of living on a floating island, and have the money to pay for one." He swept an arm, taking in the camp, the busy teams of workers. "With that money, I take boys out of the shantytowns of Sky's balloon stations and elevator gondolas. I give them tools, and teach them to kill beasts.

"To stop me—since they can't be bothered to do it themselves—the Consilium takes the same boys, gives them guns, and teaches them to kill men."

The poacher stopped and turned to face Bianca, jamming his hands into the pockets of his coat.

"Tell me, Miss Nazario—is one worse than the other?"

"I'm not here to judge you, Mr. Valadez," said Bianca. "I'm here to do a job."

Valadez smiled. "So you are."

He turned and continued up the slope. Bianca and the *firija* followed, Fry trailing behind. The path switchbacked through unfamiliar trees, dark, stunted, waxy-needled; these gave way to taller varieties, including some that Bianca would have sworn were ordinary pines and firs. She breathed deeply, enjoying the alpine breeze after the crowds-and-machines reek of *Transient Meridian*'s teeming slums, the canned air of ships and anemopters.

"It smells just like home," she remarked. "Why is that?"

No one answered.

The ridge leveled off. They came out into a cleared space, overlooking the camp. Spread out below them Bianca saw the airfield, the globular tanks and pipes of the poachers' little industrial plant, the bungalows in the distance—and, in between, the red-brown earth of the killing ground, stretching out to the cliff edge and the bases of the nearest translucent fins.

"This is a good spot," Valadez declared. "Should be a good view from up here."

"A view of what?" said Fry.

The poacher didn't answer. He waved to Ismaíl, and the *firija* took a small folding stool out of a pocket, snapping it into shape with a flick of sinuous arms and setting it down behind him. Valadez sat.

After a moment, the answer to Fry's question came up over the edge.

· · · · ·

Bianca had not thought much at all about the killing of a *zaratán,* and when she had thought of it she had imagined something like the harpooning of a whale in ancient times, the great beast fleeing, pursued by the tiny harassing shapes of boats, gored by harpoons, sounding again and again, all the strength bleeding out of the beast until there was nothing left for it to do but wallow gasping on the surface and expire, noble and tragic. Now Bianca realized that for all their great size, the *zaratánes* were far weaker than any whale, far less able to fight or to escape or even—she sincerely hoped—to understand what was happening to them.

There was nothing noble about the way the nameless *zaratán* died. Anemopters landed men and aliens with drilling tools at the base of each hundred-meter fin, to bore through soil and scale and living flesh and cut the connecting nerves that controlled them. This took about fifteen minutes; and to Bianca there seemed to be something obscene in the way the paralyzed fins hung there afterward, lifeless and limp. Thus crippled, the beast was pushed and pulled by aerial tugs—awkward machines, stubby and cylindrical, converted from the station-keeping engines of vacuum balloons like *Transient Meridian*—into position over Encantada's killing ground. Then the drilling teams moved in again, to the places marked for them ahead of time by seismic sensors and ultrasound, cutting this time through bone as well as flesh, to find the *zaratán*'s brain.

When the charges the drilling teams had planted went off, a ripple went through the *zaratán*'s body, a slow-motion convulsion that took nearly a minute to travel down the body's long axis, as the news of death passed from synapse to synapse; and Bianca saw flocks of birds started from the trees along the *zaratán*'s back as if by an earthquake, which in a way she supposed this was. The carcass immediately began to pitch downward, the nose dropping—the result, Bianca realized, of sphincters relaxing one by one, all along the *zaratán*'s length, venting hydrogen from the ballonets.

Then the forward edge of the keel fin hit the ground and crumpled, and the whole length of the dead beast, a hundred thousand tons of it, crashed down into the field; and even at that distance Bianca could hear the cracking of gargantuan bones.

· · · ·

She shivered, and glanced at her pocket system. The whole process, she was amazed to see, had taken less than half an hour.

"That's this trip paid for, whatever else happens," said Valadez. He turned to Bianca. "Mostly, though, I thought you should see this. Have you guessed yet what it is I'm paying you to do, Miss Nazario?"

Bianca shook her head. "Clearly you don't need an aeronautical engineer to do what you've just done." She looked down at the killing ground, where men and aliens and machines were already climbing over the *zaratán*'s carcass, uprooting trees, peeling back skin and soil in great strips like bleeding boulevards. A wind had come up, blowing from the killing ground across the camp, bringing with it a smell that Bianca associated with butcher shops.

An engineering problem, she reminded herself, as she turned her back on the scene and faced Valadez. That's all this is.

"How are you going to get it out of here?" she asked.

"Cargo-lifter," said Valadez. "The *Lupita Jeréz*. A supply ship, diverted from one of the balloon stations."

The alien, Ismaíl, said, "Like fly anemopter make transatmospheric." The same fluting voice and broken Arabic. "Lifter plenty payload mass limit, but fly got make have packaging. Packaging for got make platform have stable." On the word *packaging* the *firija*'s arms made an expressive gesture, like rolling something up into a bundle and tying it.

Bianca nodded hesitantly, hoping she understood. "And so you can only take the small ones," she said. "Right? Because there's only one place on Sky you'll find a stable platform that size: on the back of another *zaratán*."

"You have the problem in a nutshell, Miss Nazario," said Valadez. "Now, how would you solve it? How would you bag, say, Encantada here? How would you bag Finisterra?"

Fry said, "You want to take one *alive?*" His face was even more pale than usual. Bianca noticed that he, too, had turned his back to the killing ground.

Valadez was still looking at Bianca, expectantly.

"He doesn't want it alive, Mr. Fry," she said, watching the poacher. "He wants it dead—but intact. You could take even Finisterra apart, and lift it piece by piece, but you'd need a thousand cargo-lifters to do it."

Valadez smiled.

"I've got another ship," he said. "Built for deep mining, outfitted as a mobile elevator station. Counterweighted. The ship itself isn't rated for atmosphere, but if you can get one of the big ones to the edge of space, we'll lower the skyhook, catch the beast, and catapult it into orbit. The buyer's arranged an FTL tug to take it from there."

Bianca made herself look back at the killing ground. The workers were freeing the bones, lifting them with aerial cranes and feeding them into the plant; for cleaning and preservation, she supposed. She turned back to Valadez.

"We should be able to do that, if the *zaratán*'s body will stand up to the low pressure," she said. "But why go to all this trouble? I've seen the balloon stations. I've seen what you people can do with materials. How hard can it be to make an imitation *zaratán*?"

Valadez glanced at Ismaíl. The walker was facing the killing ground, but two of the alien's many eyes were watching the sky—and two more were watching Valadez. The poacher looked back at Bianca.

"An imitation's one thing, Miss Nazario; the real thing is something else. And worth a lot more, to the right buyer." He looked away again; not at Ismaíl this time, but up the slope, through the trees. "Besides," he added, "in this case I've got my own reasons."

"Ship come," Ismaíl announced.

Bianca looked and saw more of the *firija*'s eyes turning upward. She followed their gaze. At first she saw only empty sky. Then the air around the descending *Lupita Jeréz* boiled into contrails, outlining the invisible ovoid shape of the ship's lifting fields.

"Time to get to work," said Valadez.

Bianca glanced toward the killing ground. A pink fog was rising to cover the work of the flensing crews.

The air was full of blood.

5. THE AERONAUTS

Valadez's workers cleaned the nameless *zaratán*'s bones one by one; they tanned the hide, and rolled it into bundles for loading aboard the *Lupita Jeréz*. That job, grotesque though it was, was the cleanest part of the work. What occupied most of the workers was the disposal of the unwanted parts, a much dirtier and more arduous job. Exotic internal organs the size of houses; tendons like braided, knotted bridge cables; ballonets large enough, each of them, to lift an ordinary dirigible; and hectares and hectares of pale, dead flesh. The poachers piled up the mess with earthmoving machines and shoveled it off the edge of the killing ground, a rain of offal falling into the clouds in a mist of blood, manna for the ecology of the deep air. They sprayed the killing ground with antiseptics, and the cool air helped to slow decay a little, but by the fourth day the butcher-shop smell had nonetheless given way to something worse.

Bianca's bungalow was one of the farthest out, only a few dozen meters from Encantada's edge, where the wind blew in from the open eastern sky, and she could turn her back on the slaughter to look out into clear air, dotted with the small, distant shapes of younger *zaratánes*. Even here, though, a kilometer and more upwind of the killing ground, the air carried a taint of spoiled meat. The sky was full of insects and scavenger birds, and there were always vermin underfoot.

Bianca spent most of her time indoors, where the air was filtered and the wet industrial sounds of the work muted. The bungalow was outfitted with all the mechanisms the *extrañados* used to make themselves comfortable, but while in the course of her journey Bianca had learned to operate these, she made little use of them. Besides her traveling chest—a gift from her older brother's wife, which served as armoire, desk, dresser, and drafting table— the only furnishings were a woven carpet in the Lagos Grandes style, a hard little bed, and a single wooden chair, not very different from the ones in her room in Punta Aguila. Of course those had been handmade, and these were simulations provided by the bungalow's machines.

The rest of the room was given over to the projected spaces of Bianca's engineering work. The tools Valadez had given her were slick and fast and factory-fresh, the state of somebody's art, somewhere; but what Bianca mostly found herself using was her pocket system's crippled copy of the Nazario family automation.

The system Bianca's father used to use to calculate stresses in fabric and metal and wood, to model the flow of air over wings and the variation of pressure and temperature through gasbags, was six centuries old, a slow, patient, reliable thing that dated from before the founding of the London Caliphate. It had aged along with the family, grown used to their quirks and to the strange demands of aviation in Río Pícaro. Bianca's version of it, limited though it was, at least didn't balk at control surfaces supported by muscle and bone, at curves not aerodynamically smooth but fractally complex with grasses and trees and hanging vines. If the *zaratánes* had been machines, they would have been marvels of engineering, with their internal networks of gasbags and ballonets, their reservoir-sized ballast bladders full of collected rainwater, their great delicate fins. The *zaratánes* were beyond the poachers' systems' stubborn, narrow-minded comprehension; for all their speed and flash, the systems sulked like spoiled children whenever Bianca tried to use them to do something their designers had not expected her to do.

Which she was doing, all the time. She was working out how to draw up Leviathan with a hook.

. . . . .

"Miss Nazario."

Bianca started. She had yet to grow used to these *extrañado* telephones that never rang, but only spoke to her out of the air, or perhaps out of her own head.

"Mr. Valadez," she said, after a moment.

"Whatever you're doing, drop it," said Valadez's voice. "You and Fry. I'm sending a 'mopter for you."

"I'm working," said Bianca. "I don't know what Fry's doing."

"This is work," said Valadez. "Five minutes."

A change in the quality of the silence told Bianca that Valadez had hung up. She sighed; then stood, stretched, and started to braid her hair.

. . . . .

The anemopter brought them up over the dorsal ridge, passing between two of the great translucent fins. At this altitude, Encantada's body was clear of vegetation; Bianca looked down on hectares of wind-blasted gray hide, dusted lightly with snow. They passed within a few hundred meters of one of the huge spars that anchored the after fin's leading edge: a kilometers-high pillar of flesh, teardrop in cross-section, and at least a hundred meters thick. The trailing edge of the next fin, by contrast, flashed by in an instant. Bianca had only a brief impression of a silk-supple membrane, veined with red, clear as dirty glass.

"What do you think he wants?" Fry asked.

"I don't know." She nodded her head toward the *firija* behind them at the steering console. "Did you ask the pilot?"

"I tried," Fry said. "Doesn't speak Arabic."

Bianca shrugged. "I suppose we'll find out soon enough."

Then they were coming down again, down the western slope. In front of Bianca was the dorsal ridge of Zaratán Finisterra. Twenty kilometers away and blue with haze, it nonetheless rose until it seemed to cover a third of the sky.

Bianca looked out at it, wondering again what kept Encantada and Finisterra so close; but then the view was taken away and they were coming down between the trees, into a shady, ivy-filled creekbed somewhere not far from Encantada's western edge. There was another anemopter already there, and a pair of aerial tugs—and a whitish mass that dwarfed all of these, sheets and ribbons of pale material hanging from the branches and draped over the ivy, folds of it damming the little stream.

With an audible splash, the anemopter set down, the ramps lowered, and Bianca stepped off into cold ankle-deep water that made her glad of her knee-high boots. Fry followed, gingerly.

"You!" called Valadez, pointing at Fry from the deck of the other ane-mopter. "Come here. Miss Nazario—I'd like you to have a look at that balloon."

"Balloon?"

Valadez gestured impatiently downstream. Suddenly Bianca saw the white material for the shredded, deflated gasbag it was; and saw, too, that there was a basket attached to it, lying on its side, partially submerged in the middle of the stream. Ismaíl was standing over it, waving.

Bianca splashed over to the basket. It actually was a basket, two meters across and a meter and a half high, woven from strips of something like bamboo or rattan. The gasbag—this was obvious, once Bianca saw it up close—had been made from one of the ballonets of a *zaratán,* a *zaratán* younger and smaller even than the one Bianca had seen killed; it had been tanned, but inexpertly, and by someone without access to the sort of indus-trial equipment the poachers used.

Bianca wondered about the way the gasbag was torn up. The tissues of the *zaratánes,* she knew, were very strong. A hydrogen explosion?

"Make want fly got very bad," Ismaíl commented, as Bianca came around to the open side of the basket.

"They certainly did," she said.

In the basket there were only some wool blankets and some empty leather waterbags, probably used both for drinking water and for ballast. The lines used to control the vent flaps were all tangled together, and tangled, too, with the lines that secured the gasbag to the basket, but Bianca could guess how they had worked. No stove. It seemed to have been a pure hydrogen balloon; and why not, she thought, with all the hydrogen anyone could want free from the nearest *zaratán*'s vent valves?

"Where did it come from?" she asked.

Ismaíl rippled his arms in a way that Bianca guessed was meant to be an imitation of a human shrug. One of his eyes glanced downstream.

Bianca fingered the material of the basket: tough, woody fiber. Tropical, from a climate warmer than Encantada's. She followed Ismaíl's glance. The trees hid the western horizon, but she knew, if she could see beyond them, what would be there.

Aloud, she said, "Finisterra."

She splashed back to the anemopters. Valadez's hatch was open.

"I'm telling you," Fry was saying, "I don't know her!"

"Fuck off, Fry," Valadez said as Bianca stepped into the cabin. "Look at her ID."

The *her* in question was a young woman with short black hair and sallow skin, wearing tan off-world cottons like Fry's under a colorful homespun serape; and at first Bianca was not sure the woman was alive, because the man next to her on Valadez's floor, also in homespun, was clearly dead, his eyes half-lidded, his olive skin gone muddy gray.

The contents of their pockets were spread out on a low table. As Bianca was taking in the scene, Fry bent down and picked up a Consilium-style ID tag.

"'Edith Dinh,'" he read. He tossed the tag back and looked at Valadez. "So?"

"'Edith Dinh, *Consilium Ethnological Service*,'" Valadez growled. "Issued Shawwal '43. *You* were here with the *Ecological* Service from Rajab '42 to Muharram '46. Look again!"

Fry turned away.

"All right!" he said. "Maybe—maybe I met her once or twice."

"So," said Valadez. "Now we're getting somewhere. Who the hell is she? And what's she doing *here*?"

"She's . . ." Fry glanced at the woman and then quickly looked away. "I don't know. I think she was a population biologist or something. There was a group working with the, you know, the natives—"

"There aren't any natives on Sky," said Valadez. He prodded the dead man with the toe of his boot. "You mean these *cabrónes*?"

Fry nodded. "They had this 'sustainable development' program going—farming, forestry. Teaching them how to live on Finisterra without killing it."

Valadez looked skeptical. "If the Consilium wanted to stop them from killing Finisterra, why didn't they just send in the wardens?"

"Interdepartmental politics. The *zaratánes* were EcoServ's responsibility; the n—I mean, the *inhabitants* were EthServ's." Fry shrugged. "You know the wardens. They'd have taken bribes from anyone who could afford it and shot the rest."

"Damn right I know the wardens." Valadez scowled. "So instead EthServ sent in these do-gooders to teach them to make balloons?"

Fry shook his head. "I don't know anything about that."

"Miss Nazario? Tell me about that balloon."

"It's a hydrogen balloon, I think. Probably filled from some *zaratán*'s external vents." She shrugged. "It looks like the sort of thing I'd expect someone living out here to build, if that's what you mean."

Valadez nodded.

"But," Bianca added, "I can't tell you why it crashed."

Valadez snorted. "I don't need you to tell me that," he said. "It crashed because we shot it down." Pitching his voice for the anemopter's communication system, he called out, "Ismaíl!"

Bianca tried to keep the shock from showing on her face, and after a moment she had regained her composure. *You knew they were criminals when you took their money,* she told herself.

The *firija*'s eyes came around the edge of the doorway.

"Yes?"

"Tell the tug crews to pack that thing up," said Valadez. "Every piece, every scrap. Pack it up and drop it into clear air."

The alien's walking machine clambered into the cabin. Its legs bent briefly, making a little bob like a curtsey.

"Yes." Ismaíl gestured at the bodies of the dead man and the unconscious woman. Several of the *firija*'s eyes met Valadez's. "These two what do?" he asked.

"Them, too," said Valadez. "Lash them into the basket."

The *firija* made another bob and started to bend down to pick them up.

Bianca looked down at the two bodies, both of them, the dead man and the unconscious woman, looking small and thin and vulnerable. She glanced at Fry, whose eyes were fixed on the floor, his lips pressed together in a thin line.

Then she looked over at Valadez, who was methodically sweeping the balloonists' effects into a pile, as if neither Bianca nor Fry was present.

"No," she said.

Ismaíl stopped and straightened up.

"What?" said Valadez.

"*No,*" Bianca repeated.

"You want her bringing the wardens down on us?" Valadez demanded.

"That's murder, Mr. Valadez," Bianca said. "I won't be a party to it."

The poacher's eyes narrowed. He gestured at the dead man.

"You're already an accessory," he said.

"After the fact," Bianca replied evenly. She kept her eyes on Valadez.

The poacher looked at the ceiling. "Fuck your mother," he muttered. He looked down at the two bodies, and at Ismaíl, and then over at Bianca. He sighed heavily.

"All right," he said to the *firija*. "Take the live one back to the camp. Secure a bungalow, one of the ones out by the edge"—he glanced at Bianca—"and lock her in it. Okay?"

"Okay," said Ismaíl. "Dead one what do?"

Valadez looked at Bianca again. "The dead one," he said, "goes in the basket."

Bianca looked at the dead man again, wondering what bravery or madness had brought him aboard that fragile balloon, and wondering what he would have thought if he had known that the voyage would end this way, with his body tumbling down into the deep air. She supposed he must have known there was a chance of it.

After a moment, she nodded, once.

"Right," said Valadez. "Now get back to work, damn it."

6. THE CITY OF THE DEAD

The anemopter that brought Bianca and Fry over the ridge took them back. Fry was silent, hunched, his elbows on his knees, staring at nothing. What fear or guilt was going through his mind, Bianca couldn't guess.

After a little while she stopped watching him. She thought about the Finisterran balloon, so simple, so fragile, making her father's wood-and-silk craft look as sophisticated as the *Lupita Jeréz*. She took out her pocket system, sketched a simple globe and basket, then erased them.

Make want fly very bad, Ismaíl the *firija* had said. Why?

Bianca undid the erasure, bringing her sketch back. She drew the spherical balloon out into a blunt torpedo, round at the nose, tapering to a point behind. Added fins. An arrangement of pulleys and levers, allowing them to be controlled from the basket. A propeller, powered by—she had to think for a little while—by an alcohol-fueled engine, carved from *zaratán* bones. . . .

The anemopter was landing. Bianca sighed and again erased the design.

. . . . .

The *firija* guard outside Edith Dinh's bungalow didn't seem to speak Arabic or Spanish, or for that matter any human language at all. Bianca wondered if the choice was deliberate, the guard chosen by Valadez as a way of keeping a kind of solitary confinement.

Or was the guard Valadez's choice at all? she wondered suddenly. Looking at the meter-long weapon cradled in the alien's furred arms, she shivered.

Then she squared her shoulders and approached the bungalow. Wordlessly, she waved the valise she was carrying, as if by it her reasons for being there were made customary and obvious.

The alien said something in its own fluting language—whether a reply to her, or a request for instructions from some unseen listener, Bianca couldn't tell. Either those instructions were to let her pass, apparently, or by being seen in Valadez's company she had acquired some sort of reflected authority; because the *firija* lifted its weapon and, as the bungalow's outer door slid open, motioned for her to enter. The inner door was already open.

"*¿Hola?*" Bianca called out, tentatively. Immediately she felt like an idiot. But the answer came:

"*Aquí.*"

The interior layout of the bungalow was the same as Bianca's. The voice came from the sitting room. Bianca found Dinh there, still wearing the clothes she'd had on when they found her, sitting with her knees drawn up, staring out the east window into the sky. The east was dark with rain clouds, and far below, Bianca could see flashes of lightning.

"*Salaam aleikum,*" said Bianca, taking refuge in the formality of the Arabic.

"*Aleikum as-salaam,*" Dinh replied. She glanced briefly at Bianca and looked away; then looked back again. In a Spanish that was somewhere between Valadez's strange accent and the mechanical fluency of Fry's language module, she said, "You're not from Finisterra."

"No," said Bianca, giving up on the Arabic. "I'm from Rio Pícaro—from Earth. My name is Nazario, Bianca Nazario y Arenas."

"Edith Dinh."

Dinh stood up. There was an awkward moment, where Bianca was not sure whether to bow or curtsey or give Dinh her hand. She settled for proffering the valise.

"I brought you some things," she said. "Clothes, toiletries."

Dinh looked surprised. "Thanks," she said, taking the valise and looking inside.

"Are they feeding you? I could bring you some food."

"The kitchen still works," said Dinh. She held up a white packet. "And these?"

"Sanitary napkins," said Bianca.

"Sanitary . . . ?" Color rose to Dinh's face. "Oh. That's all right. I've got implants." She dropped the packet back in the valise and closed it.

Bianca looked away, feeling her own cheeks blush in turn. Damned *extrañados*, she thought. "I'd better—" be going, she started to say.

"Please—" said Dinh.

The older woman and the younger stood there for a moment, looking at each other. Bianca suddenly wondered what impulse had brought her here, whether curiosity or Christian charity or simply a moment of loneliness, weakness. Of course she'd had to stop Valadez from killing the girl, but this was clearly a mistake.

"Sit," Dinh said. "Let me get you something. Tea? Coffee?"

"I—all right." Bianca sat, slowly, perching on the edge of one of the too-soft *extrañado* couches. "Coffee," she said.

. . . .

The coffee was very dark, sweeter than Bianca liked it, flavored with something like condensed milk. She was glad to have it, regardless, glad to have something to look at and something to occupy her hands.

"You don't look like a poacher," Dinh said.

"I'm an aeronautical engineer," Bianca said. "I'm doing some work for them." She looked down at her coffee, took a sip, and looked up. "What about you? Fry said you're a biologist of some kind. What were you doing in that balloon?"

She couldn't tell whether the mention of Fry's name had registered, but Dinh's mouth went thin. She glanced out the west window.

Bianca followed her glance and saw the guard, slumped in its walker, watching the two women with one eye each. She wondered again whether Valadez was really running things, and then whether the *firija*'s ignorance of human language was real or feigned—and whether, even if it was real, someone less ignorant might be watching and listening, unseen.

Then she shook her head and looked back at Dinh, waiting.

"Finisterra's falling," Dinh said eventually. "Dying, maybe. It's too big; it's losing lift. It's fallen more than fifty meters in the last year alone."

"That doesn't make sense," Bianca said. "The lift-to-weight ratio of an aerostat depends on the ratio of volume to surface area. A larger *zaratán* should be *more* efficient, not less. And even if it does lose lift, it should only fall until it reaches a new equilibrium."

"It's not a *machine*," Dinh said. "It's a living creature."

Bianca shrugged. "Maybe it's old age, then," she said. "Everything has to die sometime."

"Not like this," Dinh said. She set down her coffee and turned to face Bianca fully. "Look. We don't know who built Sky, or how long ago, but it's obviously artificial. A gas giant with a nitrogen-oxygen atmosphere? That *doesn't happen*. And the Earthlike biology—the *zaratánes* are DNA-based, did you know that? The whole place is astronomically unlikely; if the Phenomenological Service had its way, they'd just quarantine the entire system, and damn Sky and everybody on it.

"The archipelago ecology is as artificial as everything else. Whoever designed it must have been very good; posthuman, probably, maybe even postsingularity. It's a robust equilibrium, full of feedback mechanisms, ways to correct itself. But we, us ordinary humans and human-equivalents, we've"—she made a helpless gesture—"*fucked it up*. You know why Encantada's stayed here so long? Breeding, that's why . . . or maybe 'pollination' would be a better way to put it. . . ."

She looked over at Bianca.

"The death of an old *zaratán* like Finisterra should be balanced by the birth of dozens, hundreds. But you, those bastards you work for, you've killed them all."

Bianca let the implication of complicity slide. "All right, then," she said. "Let's hear your plan."

"What?"

"Your *plan*," Bianca repeated. "For Finisterra. How are you going to save it?"

Dinh stared at her for a moment, then shook her head. "I can't," she said. She stood up and went to the east window. Beyond the sheet of rain that now poured down the window, the sky was deep mauve shading to indigo, relieved only by the lightning that sparked in the deep and played across the fins of the distant *zaratánes* of the archipelago's outer reaches. Dinh put her palm flat against the diamond pane.

"I *can't* save Finisterra," she said quietly. "I just want to stop you *hijos de puta* from doing this again."

Now Bianca was stung. "*Hija de puta,* yourself," she said. "You're killing them, too. Killing them and making balloons out of them, how is that better?"

Dinh turned back. "One *zaratán* the size of the one they're slaughtering out there right now would keep the Finisterrans in balloons for a hundred years," she said. "The only way to save the archipelago is to make the *zaratánes* more valuable alive than dead—and the only value a live *zaratán* has, on Sky, is as living space."

"You're trying to get the Finisterrans to colonize the other *zaratánes*?" Bianca asked. "But why should they? What's in it for them?"

"I told you," Dinh said. "Finisterra's dying." She looked out the window, down into the depths of the storm, both hands pressed against the glass. "Do you know how falling into Sky kills you, Bianca? First, there's the pressure. On the slopes of Finisterra, where the people live, it's a little more than a thousand millibars. Five kilometers down, under Finisterra's keel, it's double that. At two thousand millibars you can still breathe the air. At three thousand, nitrogen narcosis sets in—'rapture of the deep,' they used to call it. At four thousand, the partial pressure of oxygen alone is enough to make your lungs bleed."

She stepped away from the window and looked at Bianca.

"But you'll never live to suffer that," she said. "Because of the heat. Every thousand meters the average temperature rises six or seven degrees. Here it's about fifteen. Under Finisterra's keel it's closer to fifty. Twenty kilometers down, the air is hot enough to boil water."

Bianca met her gaze steadily. "I can think of worse ways to die," she said.

"There are seventeen thousand people on Finisterra," said Dinh. "Men, women, children, old people. There's a town—they call it the Lost City, *la ciudad perdida.* Some of the families on Finisterra can trace their roots back six generations." She gave a little laugh, with no humor in it. "They should call it *la ciudad muerta.* They're the walking dead, all seventeen thousand of them. Even though no one alive on Finisterra today will live to see it die. Already the crops are starting to fail. Already more old men and old women die every summer, as the summers get hotter and drier. The children of the children who are born today will have to move up into the hills as it gets too hot to grow crops on the lower slopes; but the soil isn't as rich up there, so many of those crops will fail, too. And *their* children's children . . . won't live to be old enough to have children of their own."

"Surely someone will rescue them before then," Bianca said.

"Who?" Dinh asked. "The Consilium? Where would they put them? The vacuum balloon stations and the elevator gondolas are already overcrowded. As far as the rest of Sky is concerned, the Finisterrans are 'malcontents' and 'criminal elements.' Who's going to take them in?"

"Then Valadez is doing them a favor," Bianca said.

Dinh started. "*Emmanuel Valadez* is running your operation?"

"It's *not my* operation," Bianca said, trying to keep her voice level. "And I didn't ask his first name."

Dinh fell into the window seat. "Of course it would be," she said. "Who else would they . . ." She trailed off, looking out the west window, toward the killing ground.

Then, suddenly, she turned back to Bianca.

"What do you mean, '*doing them a favor*'?" she said.

"Finisterra," Bianca said. "He's poaching Finisterra."

Dinh stared at her. "My God, Bianca! What about the people?"

"What about them?" asked Bianca. "They'd be better off somewhere else—you said that yourself."

"And what makes you think Valadez will evacuate them?"

"He's a *thief,* not a mass murderer."

Dinh gave her a withering look. "He is a murderer, Bianca. His father was a warden, his mother was the wife of the *alcalde* of Ciudad Perdida. He killed his own stepfather, two uncles, and three brothers. They were going to execute him—throw him over the edge—but a warden airboat picked him up. He spent two years with them, then killed his sergeant and three other wardens, stole their ship and sold it for a ticket off-world. He's probably the most wanted man on Sky."

She shook her head and, unexpectedly, gave Bianca a small smile.

"You didn't know any of that when you took the job, did you?"

Her voice was full of pity. It showed on her face as well, and suddenly Bianca couldn't stand to look at it. She got up and went to the east window. The rain was lighter now, the lightning less frequent.

She thought back to her simulations, her plans for lifting Finisterra up into the waiting embrace of the skyhook: the gasbags swelling, the *zaratán* lifting, first slowly and then with increasing speed, toward the upper reaches of Sky's atmosphere. But now her inner vision was not the ghost-shape of a projection but a living image—trees cracking in the cold, water freezing, blood boiling from the ground in a million, million tiny hemorrhages.

She saw her mother's house in Punta Aguila—her sister-in-law's house, now: saw its windows rimed with frost, the trees in the courtyard gone brown and sere. She saw the Mercado de los Maculados beneath a blackening sky, the awnings whipped away by a thin wind, ice-cold, bone-dry.

He killed that Finisterran balloonist, she thought. He was ready to kill Dinh. He's capable of murder.

Then she shook her head.

Killing one person, or two, to cover up a crime, was murder, she thought. Killing seventeen thousand people by deliberate asphyxiation—men, women, and children—wasn't murder, it was genocide.

She took her cup of coffee from the table, took a sip and put it down again.

"Thank you for the coffee," she said. She turned to go.

"How can you just let him do this?" Dinh demanded. "How can you *help him do this?*"

Bianca turned on her. Dinh was on her feet; her fists were clenched, and she was shaking. Bianca stared her down, her face as cold and blank as she could make it. She waited until Dinh turned away, throwing herself into a chair, staring out the window.

"I saved your life," Bianca told her. "That was more than I needed to do. Even if I *did* believe that Valadez meant to kill every person on Finisterra, *which I don't,* that wouldn't make it my problem."

Dinh turned farther away.

"Listen to me," Bianca said, "because I'm only going to explain this once." She waited until Dinh, involuntarily, turned back to face her.

"This job is my one chance," Bianca said. "*This job* is what I'm here to do. I'm not here to save the world. Saving the world is a luxury for spoiled *extrañado* children like you and Fry. It's a luxury I don't have."

She went to the door, and knocked on the window to signal the *firija* guard.

"I'll get you out of here if I can," she added, over her shoulder. "But that's all I can do. I'm sorry."

Dinh hadn't moved.

As the *firija* opened the door, Bianca heard Dinh stir.

"*Erasmus* Fry?" she asked. "The naturalist?"

"That's right." Bianca glanced back, and saw Dinh looking out the window again.

"I'd like to see him," Dinh said.

"I'll let him know," said Bianca.

The guard closed the door behind her.

7. THE FACE IN THE MIRROR

Lightning still played along Encantada's dorsal ridge, but here on the eastern edge the storm had passed. A clean, electric smell was in the air, relief from the stink of the killing ground. Bianca returned to her own bungalow through rain that had died to a drizzle.

She called Fry.

"What is it?" he asked.

"Miss Dinh," Bianca said. "She wants to see you."

There was silence on the other end. Then, "You told her I was here?"

"Sorry," Bianca said insincerely. "It just slipped out."

More silence.

"You knew her better than you told Valadez, didn't you," she said.

She heard Fry sigh. "Yes."

"She seemed upset," Bianca said. "You should go see her."

Fry sighed again, but said nothing.

"I've got work to do," Bianca said. "I'll talk to you later."

She ended the call.

She was supposed to make a presentation tomorrow, to Valadez and some of the poachers' crew bosses, talking about what they would be doing to Finisterra. It was mostly done; the outline was straightforward, and the visuals could be autogenerated from the design files. She opened the projection file and poked at it for a little while, but found it hard to concentrate.

Suddenly to Bianca her clothes smelled of death, of Dinh's dead companion and the slaughtered *zaratán* and the death she'd spared Dinh from and the eventual deaths of all the marooned Finisterrans. She stripped them off and threw them in the recycler; bathed, washed her hair, changed into a nightgown.

They should call it la ciudad muerta.

Even though no one who's alive on Finisterra today will live to see it die.

She turned off the light, Dinh's words echoing in her head, and tried to sleep. But she couldn't; she couldn't stop thinking. Thinking about what it felt like to be forced to live on, when all you had to look forward to was death.

She knew that feeling very well.

* * * *

What Bianca had on Pablo's wife Mélia, the instrument-maker's daughter, was ten years of age and a surreptitious technical education. What Mélia had on Bianca was a keen sense of territory and the experience of growing up in a house full of sisters. Bianca continued to live in the house after Mélia moved in, even though it was Mélia's house now, and continued, without credit, to help her brother with the work that came in. But she retreated over the years, step by step, until the line was drawn at the door of the fourth-floor room that had been hers ever since she was a girl; and she buried herself in her blueprints and her calculations, and tried to pretend she didn't know what was happening.

And then there was the day she met her *other* sister-in-law. Her *moro* sister-in-law. In the Mercado de los Maculados, where the aliens and the *extrañados* came to sell their trinkets and their medicines. A dispensation from the *ayuntamiento* had recently opened it to Christians.

Zahra al-Halim, a successful architect, took Bianca to her home, where Bianca ate caramels and drank blackberry tea and saw her older brother for the first time in more than twenty years, and tried very hard to call him

Walíd and not Jesús. Here was a world that could be hers, too, she sensed, if she wanted it. But like Jesús-Walíd, she would have to give up her old world to have it. Even if she remained a Christian she would never see the inside of a church again. And she would still never be accepted by the engineers' guild.

She went back to the Nazario house that evening, ignoring the barbed questions from Mélia about how she had spent her day; she went back to her room, with its blueprints and its models, and the furnishings she'd had all her life. She tried for a little while to work, but was unable to muster the concentration she needed to interface with the system.

Instead she found herself looking into the mirror.

And looking into the mirror Bianca focused not on the fragile trapped shapes of the flying machines tacked to the wall behind her, spread out and pinned down like so many chloroformed butterflies, but on her own tired face, the stray wisps of dry, brittle hair, the lines that years of captivity had made across her forehead and around her eyes. And, meeting those eyes, it seemed to Bianca that she was looking not into the mirror but down through the years of her future, a long, straight, narrow corridor without doors or branches, and that the eyes she was meeting at the end of it were the eyes of Death, her own, *su propria muerte,* personal, personified.

· · · ·

Bianca got out of bed, turned on the lights. She picked up her pocket system. She wondered if she should call the wardens.

Instead she unerased, yet again, the sketch she'd made earlier of the simple alcohol-powered dirigible. She used the Nazario family automation to fill it out with diagrams and renderings, lists of materials, building instructions, maintenance and preflight checklists.

It wasn't much, but it was better than Dinh's balloon.

Now she needed a way for Dinh to get it to the Finisterrans.

For that—thinking as she did so that there was some justice in it—she turned back to the system Valadez had given her. This was the sort of work the *extrañado* automation was made for, no constraints other than those imposed by function, every trick of exotic technology available to be used. It was a matter of minutes for Bianca to sketch out her design; an hour or so to refine it, to trim away the unnecessary pieces until what remained was small enough to fit in the valise she'd left with Dinh. The only difficult part was getting the design automation to talk to the bungalow's fabricator, which was meant for clothes and furniture and domestic utensils. Eventually she had to use her pocket system to go out on Sky's local net—hoping as she did so that Valadez didn't have anyone monitoring her—and spend her own funds to contract the conversion out to a consulting service, somewhere out on one of the elevator gondolas.

Eventually she got it done, though. The fabricator spit out a neat package, which Bianca stuffed under the bed. Tomorrow she could get the valise back and smuggle the package to Dinh, along with the dirigible designs.

But first she had a presentation to make to Valadez. She wondered what motivated him. Nothing so simple as money—she was sure of that, even if she had trouble believing he was the monster Dinh had painted him to be. Was it revenge he was after? Revenge on his family, revenge on his homeland?

That struck Bianca a little too close to home.

She sighed and turned out the lights.

8. THE PROFESSIONALS

By morning the storm had passed and the sky was blue again, but the inside of Valadez's bungalow was dark, to display the presenters' projections to better advantage. Chairs for Valadez and the human crew bosses were arranged in a rough semicircle; with them were the aliens whose anatomy permitted them to sit down. Ismaíl and the other *firija* stood in the back, their curled arms and the spindly legs of their machines making their silhouettes look, to Bianca, incongruously like those of potted plants.

Then the fronds stirred, suddenly menacing. Bianca shivered. Who was really in charge?

No time to worry about that now. She straightened up and took out her pocket system.

"In a moment," she began, pitching her voice to carry to the back of the room, "Mr. Fry will be going over the *zaratán*'s metabolic processes and our plans to stimulate the internal production of hydrogen. What I'm going to be talking about is the engineering work required to make that extra hydrogen do what we need it to do."

Bianca's pocket system projected the shape of a hundred-kilometer *zaratán*, not Finisterra or any other particular individual but rather an archetype, a sort of Platonic ideal. Points of pink light brightened all across the projected zaratán's back, each indicating the position of a sphincter that would have to be cut out and replaced with a mechanical valve.

"Our primary concern during the preparation phase has to be these external vents. However, we also need to consider the internal trim and ballast valves. . . ."

As she went on, outlining the implants and grafts, surgeries and mutilations needed to turn a living *zaratán* into an animatronic corpse, a part of her was amazed at her own presumption, amazed at the strong, confident, professional tone she was taking.

It was almost as if she were a real engineer.

. . . .

The presentation came to a close. Bianca drew in a deep breath, trying to maintain her veneer of professionalism. This part wasn't in her outline.

"And then, finally, there is the matter of evacuation," she said.

In the back of the room, Ismaíl stirred. "Evacuation?" he asked—the first word anyone had uttered through the whole presentation.

Bianca cleared her throat. Red stars appeared along the imaginary *zaratán*'s southeastern edge, approximating the locations of Ciudad Perdida and the smaller Finisterran villages.

"Finisterra has a population of between fifteen and twenty thousand, most of them concentrated in these settlements here," she began. "Using a ship the size of the *Lupita Jeréz,* it should take roughly—"

"Not your problem, Miss Nazario." Valadez waved a hand. "In any case, there won't be any evacuations."

Bianca looked at him, appalled; and it must have shown on her face because Valadez laughed.

"Don't look at me like that, Miss Nazario. We'll set up field domes over Ciudad Perdida and the central pueblos, to tide them over till we get them where they're going. If they keep their heads they should be fine." He laughed again. "Fucking hell," he said, shaking his head. "What did you think this was about? You didn't think we were going to kill twenty thousand people, did you?"

Bianca didn't answer. She shut the projection off and sat down, putting her pocket system away. Her heart was racing.

"Right," said Valadez. "Nice presentation, Miss Nazario. Mr. Fry?"

Fry stood up. "Okay," he said. "Let me—" He patted his pockets. "I, ah, I think I must have left my system in my bungalow."

Valadez sighed.

"We'll wait," he said.

The dark room was silent. Bianca tried to take slow, deep breaths. Mother of God, she thought, thank you for not letting me do anything stupid.

In the next moment she doubted herself. Dinh had been so sure. How could Bianca know whether Valadez was telling the truth?

There was no way to know, she decided. She'd just have to wait and see.

Fry came back in, breathless.

"Ah, it wasn't—"

The voice that interrupted him was loud enough that at first it was hardly recognizable as a voice; it was only a wall of sound, seeming to come from the air itself, bazaar-Arabic words echoing and reechoing endlessly across the camp.

"THIS IS AN ILLEGAL ENCAMPMENT," it said. "ALL PERSONNEL IN THE ENCAMPMENT WILL ASSEMBLE ON OPEN GROUND AND SURRENDER TO THE PARK WARDENS IN AN ORDERLY FASHION. ANY PERSONS CARRYING WEAPONS WILL BE PRESUMED TO BE RESISTING ARREST AND WILL BE DEALT WITH ACCORDINGLY.

ANY VEHICLE ATTEMPTING TO LEAVE THE ENCAMPMENT WILL BE DESTROYED. YOU HAVE FIVE MINUTES TO COMPLY."

The announcement repeated itself: first in the fluting language of the *firija,* then in Miami Spanish, then as a series of projected alien glyphs, logograms, and semagrams. Then the Arabic started again.

"Fuck your mother," said Valadez grimly.

All around Bianca, poachers were gathering weapons. In the back of the room, the *firija* were having what looked like an argument, arms waving, voices raised in a hooting, atonal cacophony.

"*What do we do?*" Fry shouted, over the wardens' announcement.

"Get out of here," said Valadez.

"Make fight!" said Ismaíl, turning several eyes from the firija discussion.

"Isn't that *resisting arrest?*" asked Bianca.

Valadez laughed harshly. "Not shooting back isn't going to save you," he said. "The wardens aren't the Phenomenological Service. They're not civilized Caliphate cops. *Killed while resisting arrest* is what they're all about. Believe me—I used to be one."

Taking a surprisingly small gun from inside his jacket, he kicked open the door and was gone.

* * * *

Around the *Lupita Jeréz* was a milling knot of people, human and otherwise, some hurrying to finish the loading, others simply fighting to get aboard.

Something large and dark—and fast—passed over the camp, and there was a white flash from the cargo-lifter, and screams.

In the wake of the dark thing came a sudden sensation of heaviness, as if the flank of Encantada were the deck of a ship riding a rogue wave, leaping up beneath Bianca's feet. Her knees buckled and she was thrown to the ground, pressed into the grass by twice, three times her normal weight.

The feeling passed as quickly as the wardens' dark vehicle. Ismaíl, whose walker had kept its footing, helped Bianca up.

"What was *that?*" Bianca demanded, bruises making her wince as she tried to brush the dirt and grass from her skirts.

"Antigravity ship," Ismaíl said. "Same principle like starship wave propagation drive."

"*Antigravity?*" Bianca stared after the ship, but it was already gone, over Encantada's dorsal ridge. "If you *coños* have antigravity, then why in God's name have we been sitting here playing with catapults and balloons?"

"Make very expensive," said Ismaíl. "Minus two suns exotic mass, same like starship." The *firija* waved two of its free eyes. "Why do? Plenty got cheap way to fly."

Bianca realized that despite the remarks Valadez had made on the poverty of Sky, she had been thinking of all *extrañados* and aliens—with their ships and machines, their familiar way with sciences that in Rio Pícaro were barely more than a whisper of forbidden things hidden behind the walls of the rich *moros'* palaces—as wealthy, and powerful, and free. Now, feeling like a fool for not having understood sooner, she realized that between the power of the Consilium and people like Valadez there was a gap as wide as, if not wider than, the gap between those rich *moros* and the most petty Ali Baba in the backstreets of Punta Aguila.

She glanced toward the airfield. Aerial tugs were lifting off; anemopters were blurring into motion. But as she watched, one of the tugs opened up into a ball of green fire. An anemopter made it as far as the killing ground before being hit by something that made its static fields crawl briefly with purple lightnings and then collapse, as the craft's material body crashed down in an explosion of earth.

And all the while the warden's recorded voice was everywhere and nowhere, repeating its list of instructions and demands.

"Not anymore, we don't," Bianca said to Ismaíl. "We'd better run."

The *firija* raised its gun. "First got kill prisoner."

"What?"

But Ismaíl was already moving, the mechanical legs of the walker surefooted on the broken ground, taking long, swift strides, no longer comical but frighteningly full of purpose.

Bianca struggled after the *firija* but quickly fell behind. The surface of the killing ground was rutted and scarred, torn by the earthmoving equipment used to push the offal of the gutted *zaratánes* over the edge. Bianca supposed grasses had covered it once, but now there was just mud and old blood. Only the certainty that going back would be as bad as going forward kept Bianca moving, slipping and stumbling in reeking muck that was sometimes ankle-deep.

By the time she got to Dinh's bungalow, Ismaíl was already gone. The door was ajar.

Maybe the wardens rescued her, Bianca thought; but she couldn't make herself believe it.

She went inside, moving slowly.

"Edith?"

No answer; not that Bianca had really expected any.

She found her in the kitchen, face down, feet toward the door as if she had been shot while trying to run, or hide. From three meters away Bianca could see the neat, black, fist-sized hole in the small of Dinh's back. She felt no need to get closer.

Fry's pocket system was on the floor in the living room, as Bianca had known it would be.

"You should have waited," Bianca said to the empty room. "You should have trusted me."

She found her valise in Dinh's bedroom and emptied the contents onto the bed. Dinh did not seem to have touched any of them.

Bianca's eyes stung with tears. She glanced again at Fry's system. He'd left it on purpose, Bianca realized; she'd underestimated him. Perhaps he had been a better person than she herself, all along.

She looked one more time at the body lying on the kitchen floor.

"No, you shouldn't," she said then. "You shouldn't have trusted me at all."

Then she went back to her own bungalow and took the package out from under the bed.

9. FINISTERRA

A hundred meters, two hundred, five hundred—Bianca falls, the wind whipping at her clothes, and the hanging vegetation that covers Encantada's flanks is a green-brown blur, going gray as it thins, as the *zaratán*'s body curves away from her. She blinks away the tears brought on by the rushing wind and tries to focus on the monitor panel of the harness. She took it from an off-the-shelf emergency parachute design; surely, she thinks, it must be set to open automatically at some point? But the wind speed indicator is the only one that makes sense; the others—altitude, attitude, rate of descent— are cycling through nonsense in three languages, baffled by the instruments' inability to find solid ground anywhere below.

Then Bianca falls out of Encantada's shadow into the sun, and before she can consciously form the thought, her hand has grasped the emergency handle of the harness and pulled convulsively; and the glassy fabric of the paraballoon is billowing out above her, rippling like water, and the harness is tugging at her, gently but firmly, smart threads reeling themselves quickly out and then slowly in again on their tiny spinnerets.

After a moment, she catches her breath. She is no longer falling, but flying.

She wipes the tears from her eyes. To the west, the slopes of Finisterra are bright and impossibly detailed in the low-angle sunlight, a million trees casting a million tiny shadows through the morning's rapidly dissipating mist.

She looks up, out through the nearly invisible curve of the paraballoon, and sees that Encantada is burning. She watches it for a long time.

The air grows warmer, and more damp, too. With a start, Bianca realizes she is falling below Finisterra's edge. When she designed the paraballoon, Bianca intended for Dinh to fall as far as she safely could, dropping deep into Sky's atmosphere before firing up the reverse Maxwell pumps, to heat the air in the balloon and lift her back to Finisterra; but it does not look as if there is any danger of pursuit now, from either the poachers or the wardens. Bianca starts the pumps and the paraballoon slows, then begins to ascend.

As the prevailing wind carries her inland, over a riot of tropical green, and in the distance Bianca sees the smoke rising from the chimneys of Ciudad Perdida, Bianca glances up again at the burning shape of Encantada. She wonders whether she'll ever know if Valadez was telling the truth.

Abruptly the jungle below her opens up, and Bianca is flying over cultivated fields, and people are looking up at her in wonder. Without thinking, she has cut the power to the pumps and opened the parachute valve at the top of the balloon.

She lands hard, hobbled by the scarf still tied around her ankles, and rolls, the paraballoon harness freeing itself automatically in obedience to its original programming. She pulls the scarf loose and stands up, shaking out her torn, stained skirt. Children are already running toward her across the field.

Savages, Fry said. *Refugees.* Bianca wonders if all of them speak Valadez's odd Spanish. She tries to gather her scraps of Arabic, but is suddenly unable to remember anything beyond *Salaam alaikum.*

The children—six, eight, ten of them—falter as they approach, stopping five or ten meters away.

Salaam alaikum, Bianca rehearses silently. *Alaikum as-salaam.* She takes a deep breath.

The boldest of the children, a stick-legged boy of eight or ten, takes a few steps closer. He has curly black hair and sun-browned skin, and the brightly colored shirt and shorts he is wearing were probably made by an autofactory on one of the elevator gondolas or vacuum balloon stations, six or seven owners ago. He looks like her brother Pablo, in the old days, before Jesús left.

Trying not to look too threatening, Bianca meets his dark eyes.

"*Hola,*" she says.

"*Hola,*" the boy answers. "*¿Cómo te llamas? ¿Es éste su globo?*"

Bianca straightens her back.

"Yes, it's my balloon," she says. "And you may call me Señora Nazario."

"If the balloon's yours," the boy asks, undaunted, "will you let me fly in it?" Bianca looks out into the eastern sky, dotted with distant *zaratánes.* There is a vision in her mind, a vision that she thinks maybe Edith Dinh saw: the skies of Sky more crowded than the skies over Rio Pícaro, Septentrionalis Archipelago alive with the bright shapes of dirigibles and gliders, those nameless *zaratánes* out there no longer uncharted shoals but comforting and familiar landmarks.

She turns to look at the rapidly collapsing paraballoon, and wonders how much work it would take to inflate it again. She takes out her pocket system and checks it: the design for the hand-built dirigible is still there, and the family automation too.

This isn't what she wanted, when she set out from home; but she is still a Nazario, and still an engineer.

She puts the system away and turns back to the boy.

"I have a better idea," she says. "How would you like a balloon of your very own?"

The boy breaks into a smile.

MARY ROBINETTE KOWAL Born in Raleigh, North Carolina, Mary Robinette Kowal began publishing SF and fantasy professionally in 2006, and won the John W. Campbell Award for Best New Writer in 2008. In 2011 she won a Hugo Award for her short story "For Want of a Nail." She has also served as the secretary and, later, vice president of the Science Fiction Writers of America. Concurrent with her writing life, she has been a professional puppeteer for more than two decades, working with, among others, Jim Henson Productions, the Center for Puppetry Arts, and her own company, Other Hand Productions.

"Evil Robot Monkey" was a finalist for the Hugo in 2009. It is a brief, sharp tale of an augmented chimpanzee, and a reminder that it's possible to tell a fully realized SF story in fewer than a thousand words.

EVIL ROBOT MONKEY

Sliding his hands over the clay, Sly relished the moisture oozing around his fingers. The clay matted down the hair on the back of his hands, making them look almost human. He turned the potter's wheel with his prehensile feet as he shaped the vase. Pinching the clay between his fingers he lifted the wall of the vase, spinning it higher.

Someone banged on the window of his pen. Sly jumped and then screamed as the vase collapsed under its own weight. He spun and hurled it at the picture window like feces. The clay spattered against the Plexiglas, sliding down the window.

In the courtyard beyond the glass, a group of schoolkids leapt back, laughing. One of them swung his arms, aping Sly crudely. Sly bared his teeth, knowing these people would take it as a grin, but he meant it as a threat. He swung down from his stool, crossed his room in three long strides and pressed his dirty hand against the window. Still grinning, he wrote: SSA. Outside, the letters would be reversed.

The student's teacher flushed as red as a female in heat and called the children away from the window. She looked back once as she led them out of the courtyard, so Sly grabbed himself and showed her what he would do if she came into his pen.

Her naked face turned brighter red and she hurried away. When they were gone, Sly rested his head against the glass. The metal in his skull thunked against the window. It wouldn't be long now before a handler came to talk to him.

Damn.

He just wanted to make pottery. He loped back to the wheel and sat down again with his back to the window. Kicking the wheel into movement, Sly dropped a new ball of clay in the center and tried to lose himself.

In the corner of his vision, the door to his room snicked open. Sly let the wheel spin to a halt, crumpling the latest vase.

Vern poked his head through. He signed, "You okay?"

Sly shook his head emphatically and pointed at the window.

"Sorry." Vern's hands danced. "We should have warned you that they were coming."

"You should have told them that I was not an animal."

Vern looked down in submission. "I did. They're kids."

"And I'm a chimp. I know." Sly buried his fingers in the clay to silence his thoughts.

"It was Delilah. She thought you wouldn't mind because the other chimps didn't."

Sly scowled and yanked his hands free. "I'm not *like* the other chimps." He pointed to the implant in his head. "Maybe Delilah should have one of these. Seems like she needs help thinking."

"I'm sorry." Vern knelt in front of Sly, closer than anyone else would come when he wasn't sedated. It would be so easy to reach out and snap his neck. "It was a lousy thing to do."

Sly pushed the clay around on the wheel. Vern was better than the others. He seemed to understand the hellish limbo where Sly lived—too smart to be with other chimps, but too much of an animal to be with humans. Vern was the one who had brought Sly the potter's wheel which, by the Earth and Trees, Sly loved. Sly looked up and raised his eyebrows. "So what did they think of my show?"

Vern covered his mouth, masking his smile. The man had manners. "The teacher was upset about the 'evil robot monkey.'"

Sly threw his head back and hooted. Served her right.

"But Delilah thinks you should be disciplined." Vern, still so close that Sly could reach out and break him, stayed very still. "She wants me to take the clay away since you used it for an anger display."

Sly's lips drew back in a grimace built of anger and fear. Rage threatened to blind him, but he held on, clutching the wheel. If he lost it with Vern— rational thought danced out of his reach. Panting, he spun the wheel, trying to push his anger into the clay.

The wheel spun. Clay slid between his fingers. Soft. Firm and smooth. The smell of earth lived his nostrils. He held the world in his hands. Turning, turning, the walls rose around a kernel of anger, subsuming it.

His heart slowed with the wheel and Sly blinked, becoming aware again as if he were slipping out of sleep. The vase on the wheel still seemed to dance with life. Its walls held the shape of the world within them. He passed a finger across the rim.

Vern's eyes were moist. "Do you want me to put that in the kiln for you?"

Sly nodded.

"I have to take the clay. You understand that, don't you."

Sly nodded again, staring at his vase. It was beautiful.

Vern scowled. "The woman makes me want to hurl feces."

Sly snorted at the image, then sobered. "How long before I get it back?"

Vern picked up the bucket of clay next to the wheel. "I don't know." He stopped at the door and looked past Sly to the window. "I'm not cleaning your mess. Do you understand me?"

For a moment, rage crawled on his spine, but Vern did not meet his eyes and kept staring at the window. Sly turned.

The vase he had thrown lay on the floor in a pile of clay.

Clay.

"I understand." He waited until the door closed, then loped over and scooped the clay up. It was not much, but it was enough for now.

Sly sat down at his wheel and began to turn.

Madeline Ashby   Born in California, Madeline Ashby lives in Toronto, where she writes and works as a foresight consultant. Her SF has been appearing since 2007. She has also published nonfiction on sites including WorldChanging, Boing Boing, io9, and Tor.com.

"The Education of Junior Number 12" was originally published on the website of Angry Robot Books as part of their Twelve Days of Christmas series in 2011. According to the author, it was chosen as the first story in the series because "it's so bereft of holiday cheer, all the other stories will be aglow with spirit by comparison." Javier, the story's protagonist, is a character in Ashby's debut novel, vN; both the story and the novel are concerned with self-replicating, humanlike von Neumann machines, and the uses and misuses to which they are put.

THE EDUCATION OF JUNIOR NUMBER 12

ou're a self-replicating humanoid. vN."

Javier always spoke Spanish the first few days. It was his clade's default setting. "You have polymer-doped memristors in your skin, transmitting signal to the aerogel in your muscles from the graphene coral inside your skeleton. That part's titanium. You with me, so far?"

Junior nodded. He plucked curiously at the clothes Javier had stolen from the balcony of a nearby condo. It took Javier three jumps, but eventually his fingers and toes learned how to grip the grey water piping. He'd take Junior there for practise, after the kid ate more and grew into the clothes. He was only toddler-sized, today. They'd holed up in a swank bamboo treehouse positioned over an infinity pool outside La Jolla, and its floor was now littered with the remnants of an old GPS device that Javier had stripped off its plastic. His son sucked on the chipset.

"Your name is Junior," Javier said. "When you grow up, you can call yourself whatever you want. You can name your own iterations however you want."

"Iterations?"

"Babies. It happens if we eat too much. Buggy self-repair cycle—like cancer."

Not for the first time, Javier felt grateful that his children were all born with an extensive vocabulary.

"You're gonna spend the next couple of weeks with me, and I'll show you how to get what you need. I've done this with all your brothers."

"How many brothers?"

"Eleven."

"Where are they now?"

Javier shrugged. "Around. I started in Nicaragua."

"They look like you?"

"Exactly like me. Exactly like you."

"If I see someone like you but he isn't you, he's my brother?"

"Maybe." Javier opened up the last foil packet of vN electrolytes and held it out for Junior. Dutifully, his son began slurping. "There are lots of vN shells, and we all use the same operating system, but the API was distributed differently for each clade. So you'll meet other vN who look like you, but that doesn't mean they're family. They won't have our clade's arboreal plugin."

"You mean the jumping trick?"

"I mean the jumping trick. And this trick, too."

Javier stretched one arm outside the treehouse. His skin fizzed pleasantly. He nodded at Junior to try. Soon his son was grinning and stretching his whole torso out the window and into the light, sticking out his tongue like Javier had seen human kids do with snow during cartoon Christmas specials.

"It's called photosynthesis," Javier told him a moment later. "Only our clade can do it."

Junior nodded. He slowly withdrew the chipset from between his tiny lips. Gold smeared across them; his digestive fluids had made short work of the hardware. Javier would have to find more, soon.

"Why are we here?"

"In this treehouse?"

Junior shook his head. "Here." He frowned. He was only two days old, and finding the right words for more nuanced concepts was still hard. "Alive."

"Why do we exist?"

Junior nodded emphatically.

"Well, our clade was developed to—"

"No!" His son looked surprised at the vehemence of his own voice. He pushed on anyway. "vN. Why do vN exist at all?"

This latest iteration was definitely an improvement on the others. His other boys usually didn't get to that question until at least a week went by. Javier almost wished this boy were the same. He'd have more time to come up with a better answer. After twelve children, he should have crafted the perfect response. He could have told his son that it was his own job to figure that out. He could have said it was different for everybody. He could have talked about the church, or the lawsuits, or even the failsafe. But the real answer was that they existed for the same reasons all technologies existed. To be used.

"Some very sick people thought the world was going to end," Javier said. "We were supposed to help the humans left behind."

· · · · ·

The next day, Javier took him to a park. It was a key part of the training: meeting humans of different shapes, sizes, and colours. Learning how to play with them. Practising English. The human kids liked watching his kid jump. He could make it to the top of the slide in one leap.

"Again!" they cried. "Again!"

When the shadows stretched long, Junior jumped up into the tree where Javier waited, and said: "I think I'm in love."

Javier nodded at the playground below. "Which one?"

Junior pointed to a redheaded organic girl whose face was an explosion of freckles. She was all by herself under a tree, rolling a scroll reader against her little knee. She kept adjusting her position to get better shade.

"You've got a good eye," Javier said.

As they watched, three older girls wandered over her way. They stood over her and nodded down at the reader. She backed up against the tree and tucked her chin down toward her chest. Way back in Javier's stem code, red flags rose. He shaded Junior's eyes.

"Don't look."

"Hey, give it back!"

"Don't look, don't look—" Javier saw one hand lash out, shut his eyes, curled himself around his struggling son. He heard a gasp for air. He heard crying. He felt sick. Any minute now the failsafe might engage, and his memory would begin to spontaneously self-corrupt. He had to stop their fight, before it killed him and his son.

"D-Dad—"

Javier jumped. His body knew where to go; he landed on the grass to the sound of startled shrieks and fumbled curse words. Slowly, he opened his eyes. One of the older girls still held the scroll reader aloft. Her arm hung there, refusing to come down, even as she started to back away. She looked about ten.

"Do y-you know w-what I am?"

"You're a robot . . ." She sounded like she was going to cry. That was fine; tears didn't set off the failsafe.

"You're damn right I'm a robot." He pointed up into the tree. "And if I don't intervene right now, my kid will die."

"I didn't—"

"Is that what you want? You wanna kill my kid?"

She was really crying now. Her friends had tears in their eyes. She sniffled back a thick clot of snot. "No! We didn't know! We didn't see you!"

"That doesn't matter. We're everywhere, now. Our failsafes go off the moment we see one of you chimps start a fight. It's called a social control mechanism. Look it up. And next time, keep your grubby little paws to yourself."

One of her friends piped up: "You don't have to be so *mean*—"

"*Mean?*" Javier watched her shrink under the weight of his gaze. "*Mean* is getting hit and not being able to fight back. And that's something I've got in common with your little punching bag over here. So why don't you drag your knuckles somewhere else and give that some thought?"

The oldest girl threw the reader toward her victim with a weak under-hand. "I don't know why you're acting so hurt," she said, folding her arms and jiggling away. "You don't even have real feelings."

"Yeah, I don't have real fat, either, tubby! Or real acne! Enjoy your teen years, *querida*!"

Behind him, he heard applause. When he turned, he saw a redhaired woman leaning against the tree. She wore business clothes with an incongruous pair of climbing slippers. The fabric of her tights had gone loose and wrinkled down around her ankles, like the skin of an old woman. Her applause died abruptly as the little freckled girl ran up and hugged her fiercely around the waist.

"I'm sorry I'm late," the mother said. She nodded at Javier. "Thanks for looking after her."

"I wasn't."

Javier gestured and Junior slid down out of his tree. Unlike the organic girl, Junior didn't hug him; he jammed his little hands in the pockets of his stolen clothes and looked the older woman over from top to bottom. Her eyebrows rose.

"Well!" She bent down to Junior's height. The kid's eyes darted for the open buttons of her blouse and widened considerably; Javier smothered a smile. "What do you think, little man? Do I pass inspection?"

Junior grinned. "*Eres humana.*"

She straightened. Her eyes met Javier's. "I suppose coming from a vN, that's quite the compliment."

"We aim to please," he said.

Moments later, they were in her car.

· · · ·

It started with a meal. It usually did. From silent prison guards in Nicaragua to singing cruise directors in Panama, from American girls dancing in Mexico and now this grown American woman in her own car in her own country, they started it with eating. Humans enjoyed feeding vN. They liked the special wrappers with the cartoon robots on the front. (They folded them into origami unicorns, because they thought that was clever.) They liked asking about whether he could taste. (He could, but his tongue read texture better than flavour.) They liked calculating how much he'd need to iterate again. (A lot.) This time, the food came as a thank-you. But the importance of food in the relationship was almost universal among humans. It was important that Junior learn this, and the other subtleties of organic interaction. Javier's last companion had called their relationship "one big HCI problem." Javier had no idea what that meant, but he suspected that embedding Junior in a human household for a while would help him avoid it.

"We could get delivery," Brigid said. That was her name. She pronounced it with a silent G. *Breed.* Her daughter was Abigail. "I'm not much for going out."

He nodded. "That's fine with us."

He checked the rearview. The kid was doing all right; Abigail was showing him a game. Its glow diffused across their faces and made them, for the moment, the same colour. But Junior's eyes weren't on the game. They were on the little girl's face.

"He's adorable," Brigid said. "How old is he?"

Javier checked the dashboard. "Three days."

. . . .

The house was a big, fake hacienda with the floors and walls and ceilings all the same vanilla ice cream color. Javier felt as though he'd stepped into a giant, echoing egg. Light followed Brigid as she entered each room, and now Javier saw bare patches on the plaster and the scratch marks of heavy furniture dragged across pearly tile. Someone had moved out. Probably Abigail's father. Javier's life had just gotten enormously easier.

"I hope you don't mind the Electric Sheep . . ."

Brigid handed him her compact. In it was a menu for a chain specializing in vN food. ("It's the food you've been dreaming of!") Actually, vN items were only half the Sheep's menu; the place was a meat market for organics and synthetics. Javier had eaten there but only a handful of times, mostly at resorts, and mostly with people who wanted to know what he thought of it "from his perspective." He chose a Toaster Party and a Hasta La Vista for himself and Junior. When the orders went through, a little lamb with an extension cord for a collar *baa'd* at him and bounded away across the compact.

"It's good we ran into you," Brigid said. "Abby hasn't exactly been very social, lately. I think this is the longest conversation she's had with, well, *anybody* in . . ." Brigid's hand fluttered in the air briefly before falling.

Javier nodded like he understood. It was best to interrupt her now, while she still had some story to tell. Otherwise she'd get it out of her system too soon. "I'm sorry, but if you don't mind . . ." He put a hand to his belly. "There's a reason they call it labour, you know?"

Brigid blushed. "Oh my God, of course! Let's get you laid, uh, down somewhere." Her eyes squeezed shut. "I mean, um, that didn't quite come out right—"

Oh, she was so cute.

"It's been a long day—"

She was practically glowing.

"And I normally don't bring strays home, but you were so nice—"

He knew songs that went this way.

"Anyway, we normally use the guest room for storage, I mean I was sleeping in it for a while before everything . . . But if it's just a nap . . ."

He followed her upstairs to the master bedroom. It was silent and cool, and the sheets smelled like new plastic and discount shopping. He woke there hours later, when the food was cold and her body was warm, and both were within easy reach.

* * * *

The next morning Brigid kept looking at him and giggling. It was like she'd gotten away with something, like she'd spent the night in a club and not in her own bed, like she wasn't the one making the rules she'd apparently just broken. The laughter took ten years off her face. She had creams for the rest, and applied them.

Downstairs, Abigail sat at the kitchen bar with her orange juice and cereal. Her legs swung under her barstool, back and forth, back and forth. She seemed to be rehearsing for a later role as a bored girl in a coffee shop: reading something on her scroll, her chin cradled in the pit of her left hand as she paged through with her right index finger, utterly oblivious to the noise of the display mounted behind her or Junior's enthusiastic responses to the educational show playing there. It was funny—he'd just seen the mother lose ten years, but now he saw the daughter gaining them back. She looked so old this morning, so tired.

"My daddy is going out with a vN, too," Abigail said, not looking up from her reader.

Javier yanked open the fridge. "That so?"

"Yup. He was going out with her *and* my mom for a while, but not any more."

Well, that explained some things. Javier pushed aside the milk and orange juice cartons and found the remainder of the vN food. Best to be as nonchalant with the girl as she'd been with him. "What kind of model? This other vN, I mean."

"I don't know about the clade, but the model was used for nursing in Japan."

He nodded. "They had a problem with old people, there."

"Did you know that Japan has a whole city just for robots? It's called Mecha. Like that place that Muslim people go to sometimes, but with an H instead of a C."

Javier set about preparing a plate for Junior. He made sure the kid got the biggest chunks of rofu. "I know about Mecha," he said. "It's in Nagasaki Harbour. It's the same spot they put the white folks a long time ago. Bigger now, though."

Abigail nodded. "My daddy sent me pictures. He's on a trip there right now. That's why I'm here all week." She quickly sketched a command into her reader with her finger, then shoved the scroll his way. Floating on its soft surface, Javier saw a Japanese-style vN standing beside a curvy white reception-bot with a happy LCD smile and braids sculpted from plastic and enamel. They were both in old-fashioned clothes, the smart robot and the stupid one: the vN wore a lavender kimono with a pink sash, and the receptionist wore "wooden" clogs.

"Don't you think she's pretty?" Abigail asked. "Everybody always says how pretty she is, when I show them the pictures."

"She's all right. She's a vN."

Abigail smiled. "You think my mom is prettier?"

"Your mom is human. Of course I do."

"So you like humans the best?"

She said it like he had a choice. Like he could just shut it off, if he wanted. Which he couldn't. Ever.

"Yeah, I like humans the best."

Abigail's feet stopped swinging. She sipped her orange juice delicately through a curlicued kiddie straw until only bubbles came. "Maybe my daddy should try being a robot."

· · · ·

It wasn't until Brigid and Abigail were gone that Javier decided to debrief his son on what had happened in the park. He had felt sick, he explained, because they were designed to respond quickly to violence against humans. The longer they avoided responding, the worse they felt. It was like an allergy, he said, to human suffering.

Javier made sure to explain this while they watched a channel meant for adult humans. A little clockwork eye kept popping up in the top right corner of the screen just before the violent parts, warning them not to look. "But it's not real," Junior said, in English. "Can't our brains tell the difference?"

"Most of the time. But better safe than sorry."

"So I can't watch TV for grown-ups?"

"Sometimes. You can watch all the cartoon violence you want. It doesn't fall in the Valley at all; there was no human response to simulate when they coded our stems." He slugged electrolytes. While on her lunch break, Brigid had ordered a special delivery of vN groceries. She clearly intended him to stay awhile. "You can still watch porn, though. I mean, they'd never have built us in the first place if we couldn't pass *that* little test."

"Porn?"

"Well. Vanilla porn. Not the rough stuff. No blood. Not unless it's a vN getting roughed up. Then you can go to town."

"How will I know the difference?"

"You'll know."

"*How* will I know?"

"If it's a human getting hurt, your cognition will start to jag. You'll stutter."

"Like when somebody tried to hurt Abigail?"

"Like that, yeah."

Junior blinked. "I need to see an example."

Javier nodded. "Sure thing. Hand me that remote."

They found some content. A nice sampler, Javier thought. Javier paused the feed frequently. There was some slang to learn and explain, and some anatomy. He was always careful to give his boys a little lesson on how to find the clitoris. The mega-church whose members had tithed to fund the development of their OS didn't want them hurting any of the sinners left behind to endure God's wrath after the Rapture. Fucking them was still okay.

He had just finished explaining this little feat of theology when Brigid came home early. She shrieked and covered her daughter's eyes. Then she hit Javier. He lay on the couch, unfazed, as she slapped him and called him names. He wondered, briefly, what it would be like to be able to defend himself.

* * * *

"He's a child!"

"Yeah, he's *my* child," Javier said. "And that makes it *my* decision, not yours."

Brigid folded her arms and paced across the bedroom to retrieve her drink. She'd had the scotch locked up way high in the kitchen and he'd watched her stand on tiptoes on a slender little dining room chair just to get it, her calves doing all sorts of interesting things as she stretched.

"I suppose you show all your children pornography?" She tipped back more of her drink.

"Every last one."

"How many is that?"

"This Junior is the twelfth."

"*Twelve?* Rapid iteration is like a felony in this state!"

This was news to him. Then again, it made a certain kind of sense—humans worked very hard to avoid having children, because theirs were so expensive and annoying and otherwise burdensome. Naturally they had assumed that vN kids were the same.

"I'll be sure to let this Junior know about that."

"*This* Junior? Don't you even *name* them?"

He shrugged. "What's the point? We don't see each other. Let them choose their own name."

"Oh, so in addition to being a pervert, you're an uncaring felonious bastard. That's just great."

Javier had no idea where "caring" came into the equation, but decided to let that slide. "You've been with me. Did I ask you to do anything weird?"

"No—"

"Did I make you feel bad?" He stepped forward. She had very plush carpet, the kind that dug into his toes if he walked slowly enough.

"No . . ."

They were close; he could see where one of her earrings was a little tangled and he reached under her hair to fix it. "Did I make you feel good?"

She sighed through her nose to hide the quirk in her lip. "That's not the
point. The *point* is that it's wrong to show that kind of stuff to kids!"

He rubbed her arms. "Human kids, yeah. They tend to run a little slow.
They get confused. Junior knows that the vids were just a lesson on the failsafe." He stepped back. "What, do you think I was trying to *turn him on,* or
something? Jesus! And you think *I'm* sick?"

"Well, how should *I* know? I come home and you're just sitting there like
it's no big deal . . ." She swallowed the last of the drink. "Do you have any
idea what kinds of ads I'm going to get, now? What kind of commercials I'm
going to have to flick past, before Abigail sees them? I don't want that kind
of thing attached to my profile, Javier!"

"Give me a break," Javier said. "I'm only three years old."

That stopped her in her tracks. Her mouth hung open. Human women
got so uptight about his age. The men handled it much better—they laughed
and ruffled his hair and asked if he'd had enough to eat.

He smiled. "What, you've never been with a younger man?"

"That's not funny."

He lay back on the bed, propped up on his elbows. "Of course it's funny.
It's hysterical. You're railing at me for teaching my kid how to recognize the
smutvids that won't *fry his brain,* and all the while you've been riding a
three-year-old."

"Oh, for—"

"And very eagerly, I might add."

Now she looked genuinely angry. "You're a total asshole, you know that?
Are you training Junior to be a total asshole, too?"

"He can be whatever he wants to be."

"Well, I'm sure he's finding plenty of good role models in the adult entertainment industry, Javier."

"Lots of vN get rich doing porn. They can do the seriously hardcore
stuff." He stretched. "They have to pay a licensing fee to the studio that
coded the crying plugin, though. Designers won a lawsuit."

Brigid sank slowly to the very edge of the bed. Her spine folded over her
hips. She held her face in her hands. For a moment she became her daughter:
shoulders hunched, cowering. She seemed at once very fragile and very
heavy. Brigid did not think of herself as beautiful. He knew that from the
menagerie of creams in her bathroom. She would never understand the reassurance a vN could find in the solidity of her flesh, or the charm of her

unique smiles, or the hundred different sneezes her species seemed to have. She would only know that they melted for humans.

As though sensing his gaze, she peered at him through the spaces between her fingers. "Why did you bother bringing a child into this world, Javier?"

He'd felt this same confusion when Junior asked him about the existence of all vN. He had no real answer. Sometimes, he wondered if his desire to iterate was a holdover from the clade's initial programming as ecological engineers, and he was nothing more than a Johnny Appleseed planting his boys hither and yon. After all, they did sink a lot of carbon.

But nobody ever seemed to ask the humans this question. Their breeding was messy and organic and therefore special, and everybody treated it like some divine right no matter what the consequences were for the planet or the psyche or the body. They'd had the technology to prevent unwanted children for decades, but Javier still met them every day, still listened to them as they talked themselves to sleep about accidents and cycles and late-night family confessions during holiday visits. He thought about Abigail, lonely and defenceless under her tree. Brigid had no right to ask him why he'd bred.

He nodded at her empty glass. "Why did you have yours? Were you drunk?"

* * * *

Javier spent that night on a futon in the storage room. He lay surrounded by the remnants of Brigid's old life: T-shirts from dive bars that she insisted on keeping; smart lease agreements and test results that she'd carefully organized in Faraday boxes. It was no different from the mounds of clutter he'd found in other homes. Humans seemed to have a thing about holding on to stuff. *Things* held a special meaning for them. That was lucky for him. Javier was a thing, too.

He had moved on to the books when Junior came in to see him. The boy shuffled toward him uncertainly. He had eaten half a box of vN groceries that day. The new inches messed with his posture and gait; he didn't know where to put his newly-enlarged feet.

"Dad, I've got a problem." Junior flopped onto the futon. He hugged his shins. "Are you having a problem, too?"

"A problem?"

Junior nodded at the bedroom.

"Oh, that. Don't worry about that. Humans are like that. They freak out."

"Is she gonna kick us out?" Junior stared directly at Javier. "I know it's my fault and I'm sorry, I didn't mean to mess things up—"

"Shut up."

His son closed his mouth. Junior looked so small just then, all curled in on himself. It was hard to remember that he'd been even tinier only a short time ago. His black curls overshadowed his head, as though the programming for hair had momentarily taken greater priority than the chassis itself. Javier gently pulled the hair away so he could see his son's eyes a little better.

"It's not your fault."

Junior didn't look convinced. ". . . It's not?"

"No. It's not. You can't control how they act. They have systems that we don't—hormones and glands and nerves and who knows what—controlling what they do. You're not responsible for that."

"But, if I hadn't asked to see—"

"Brigid reacted the way she did because she's meat," Javier said. "She couldn't help it. I chose to show you those vids because I thought it was the right thing to do. When you're bigger, you can make those kinds of choices for your own iterations. Until then, I'm running the show. Got it?"

Junior nodded. "Got it."

"Good." Javier stood, stretched, and found a book for them to read. It was thick and old, with a statue on the cover. He settled down on the futon beside Junior. "You said you had a problem?"

Junior nodded. "Abigail doesn't like me. Not the way I want. She wouldn't let me hold hands when we made a fort in her room."

Javier smiled. "That's normal. She won't like you until you're an older boy. That's what they like best, if they like boys. Give it a day or two." He tickled his son's ribs. "We'll make a bad boy of you yet, just you watch."

"*Dad . . .*"

Javier kept tickling. "Oh yeah. Show me your broody face. Show me angst. They love that."

Junior twisted away and folded his arms. He threw himself against the futon in a very good approximation of huffy irritation. "You're not helping—"

"No, seriously, try to look like a badass. A badass who gets all weepy about girls."

Finally, his son laughed. Then Javier told him it was time to learn about how paper books worked, and he rested an arm across his son's shoulders and read aloud until the boy grew bored and sleepy. And when the lights were all out and the house was quiet and they lay wrapped up in an old quilt, his son said: "Dad, I grew three inches today."

Javier smiled in the dark. He smoothed the curls away from his son's face. "I saw that."

"Did my brothers grow as fast as me?"

And Javier answered as he always did: "No, you're the fastest yet."

It was not a lie. Each time, they seemed to grow just a little bit faster.

* * * *

Brigid called him the next day from work. "I'm sorry I didn't say goodbye before I left this morning."

"That's okay."

"I just . . . This is sort of new for me, you know? I've met other vN, but not ones Junior's age. I've never seen them in this phase, and—"

He heard people chattering in the background. Vaguely, he wondered what Brigid did for a living. It was probably boring, and she probably didn't want to think about work while she was with him. Doing so tended to mess with human responses.

"—you're trying to train him for everything, and I get them, but have you ever considered slowing things down?"

"And delay the joys of adulthood?"

"Speaking of which," she said, her voice now lowered to a conspiratorial whisper, "what are you doing tonight?"

"What would you like me to do?"

She giggled. He laughed, too. How Brigid could be so shy and so nervous was beyond him. For all their little failings humans were very strong; they felt pain and endured it, and had the types of feelings he would never have. Their faces flushed and their eyes burned and their hearts sometimes skipped a few beats. Or so he had heard. He wondered what having organs would feel like. Would he be constantly conscious of them? Would he notice the slow degradation and deterioration of his neurons, blinking brightly and frantically before dying, like old filament bulbs?

"Have a bath ready for me when I get home," she said.

* * * *

Brigid liked a lot of bubbles in her bath. She also liked not to be disturbed. "I let Abigail stay at a friend's house tonight." She stretched backward against Javier. "I wish Junior had friends he could stay with."

Javier raised his eyebrows. "You plan on getting loud?"

She laughed a little. He felt the reverberation all through him. "I think that depends on you."

"Then I hope you have plenty of lozenges," he said. "Your throat's gonna hurt, tomorrow."

"I thought you couldn't hurt me." She grabbed his arms and folded them around herself like the sleeves of an oversized sweater.

"I can't. Not in the moment. But I'm not responsible for any lingering side-effects."

"Hmm. So no spanking, then?"

"Tragically, no. Why? You been bad?"

She stilled. Slowly, she turned around. She had lit candles, and they illuminated only her silhouette. Her face remained shadowed, unreadable. "In the past," she said. "Sometimes I think I'm a really bad person, Javier."

"Why?"

"Just . . . I'm selfish. And I know it. But I can't stop."

"Selfish how?"

"Well . . ." She walked two fingers down his chest. "I'm terrible at sharing."

He looked down. "Seems there's plenty to go around . . ."

The candles fizzed out when she splashed bubbles in his face.

Later that night, she burrowed up into his chest and said: "You're staying for a while, right?"

"Why wouldn't I? You spoil me."

She flipped over and faced away from him. "You do this a lot, don't you? Hooking up with humans, I mean."

He hated having this conversation. No matter how hard he tried to avoid it, it always popped up sometime. It was like they were programmed to ask the question. "I've had my share of relationships with humans."

"How many others have there been like me?"

"You're unique."

"Bullshit." She turned over to her back. "Tell me. I want to know. How many others?"

He rolled over, too. In the dark, he had a hard time telling where the ceiling was. It was a shadowy void far above him that made his voice echo strangely. He hated the largeness of this house, he realized. It was huge and empty and wasteful. He wanted something small. He wanted the treehouse back.

"I never counted."

"Of course you did. You're a computer. You're telling me you don't index the humans you sleep with? You don't categorize us somewhere? You don't chart us by height and weight and income?"

Javier frowned. "No. I don't."

Brigid sighed. "What happened with the others? Did you leave them or did they leave you?"

"Both."

"Why? Why would they leave you?"

He slapped his belly. It produced a flat sound in the quiet room. "I get fat. Then they stop wanting me."

Brigid snorted. "If you don't want to tell me, that's fine. But at least make up a better lie, okay?"

"No, really! I get very fat. Obese, even."

"You do *not*."

"I do. And then they die below the waist." He folded his hands behind his head. "You humans, you're very shallow."

"Oh, and I suppose you don't give a damn what we look like, right?"

"Of course. I love all humans equally. It's priority programmed."

She scrambled up and sat on him. "So I'm just like the others, huh?"

Her hipbones stuck out just enough to provide good grips for his thumbs. "I said I love you all equally, not that I love you all for the same reasons."

She grabbed his hands and pinned them over his head. "So why'd you hook up with me, huh? Why me, out of all the other meatsacks out there?"

"That's easy." He grinned. "My kid has a crush on yours."

. . . .

The next day was Junior's jumping lessons. They started in the backyard. It was a nice backyard, mostly slate with very little lawn, the sort of low-maintenance thing that suited Brigid perfectly. He worried a little about damaging the surface, though, so he insisted that Junior jump from the lawn to the roof. It was a forty-five-degree jump, and it required confident legs, firm feet, and a sharp eye. Luckily, the sun beating down on them gave them plenty of energy for the task.

"Don't worry," he shouted. "Your body knows how!"

"But, Dad—"

"No buts! Jump!"

"I don't want to hit the windows!"

"Then don't!"

His son gave him the finger. He laughed. Then he watched as the boy took two steps backward, ran, and launched himself skyward. His slender body sailed up, arms and legs flailing uselessly, and he landed clumsily against the eaves. Red ceramic tiles fell down to the patio, disturbed by his questing fingers.

"Dad, I'm slipping!"

"Use your arms. Haul yourself up." The boy had to learn this. It was crucial.

"Dad—"

"Javier? Junior?"

Abigail was home from school. He heard the patio door close. He watched another group of tiles slide free of the roof. Something in him switched over. He jumped down and saw Abigail's frightened face before ushering her backward, out of the way of falling tiles. Behind him, he heard a mighty crash. He turned, and his son was lying on his side surrounded by broken tiles. His left leg had bent completely backward.

"Junior!"

Abigail dashed toward Junior's prone body. She knelt beside him, her face all concern, her hands busy at his sides. His son cast a long look between him and her. She had run to help Junior. She was asking him if it hurt. Javier knew already that it didn't. It couldn't. They didn't suffer, physically. But his son was staring at him like he was actually feeling pain.

"What happened?"

He turned. Brigid was standing there in her office clothes, minus the shoes. She must have come home early. "I'm sorry about the tiles," Javier said.

But Brigid wasn't looking at the tiles. She was looking at Junior and Abigail. The girl kept fussing over him. She pulled his left arm across her little shoulders and stood up so that he could ease his leg back into place. She didn't let go when his stance was secure. Her stubborn fingers remained tangled in his. "You've gotten bigger," Abigail said quietly. Her ears had turned red.

. . . .

"Junior kissed me."

It was Saturday. They were at the playground. Brigid had asked for Junior's help washing the car while Javier took Abigail to play, and now he thought he understood why. He watched Abigail's legs swinging above the ground. She took a contemplative sip from her juicebox.

"What kind of kiss?" he asked.

"Nothing fancy," Abigail answered, as though she were a regular judge of kisses. "It was only right here, not on the lips." She pointed at her cheek.

"Did that scare you?"

She frowned and folded her arms. "My daddy kisses me there all the time."

"Ah." Now he understood his son's mistake.

"Junior's grown up really fast," Abigail said. "Now he looks like he's in middle school."

Javier had heard of middle school from organic people's stories. It sounded like a horrible place. "Do you ever wish you could grow up that fast?"

Abigail nodded. "Sometimes. But then I couldn't live with Mom, or my daddy. I'd have to live somewhere else, and get a job, and do everything by myself. I'm not sure it's worth it." She crumpled up her juicebox. "Did you grow up really fast, like Junior?"

"Yeah. Pretty fast."

"Did your daddy teach you the things you're teaching Junior?"

Javier rested his elbows on his knees. "Some of it. And some of it I learned on my own."

"Like what?"

It was funny, he normally only ever had this conversation with adults. "Well, he taught me how to jump really high. And how to climb trees. Do you know how to climb trees?"

Abigail shook her head. "Mom says it's dangerous. And it's harder with palm trees, anyway."

"That's true, it is." At least, he imagined it would be for her. The bark on those trees could cut her skin open. It could cut his open, too, but he wouldn't feel the pain. "Anyway, Dad taught me lots of things: how to talk to people; how to use things like the bus and money and phones and email; how stores work."

"How stores work?"

"Like, how to buy things. How to shop."

"How to shoplift?"

He pretended to examine her face. "Hey, you sure you're organic? You sure seem awful smart . . ."

She giggled. "Can you teach me how to shoplift?"

"No way!" He stood. "You'd get caught, and they'd haul you off to jail."

Abigail hopped off the bench. "They wouldn't haul a *kid* off to jail, Javier."

"Not an organic one, maybe. But a vN, sure." He turned to leave the playground.

"Have *you* ever been to jail?"

"Sure."

"When?"

They were about to cross a street. Her hand found his. He was careful not to squeeze too hard. "When I was smaller," he said simply. "A long time ago."

"Was it hard?"

"Sometimes."

"But you can't feel it if somebody beats you up, right? It doesn't hurt?"

"No, it doesn't hurt."

In jail they had asked him, at various times, if it hurt yet. And he had blinked and said *No, not yet, not ever.* Throughout, he had believed that his dad might come to help him. It was his dad who had been training him. His dad had seen the policia take him in. And Javier had thought that there was a plan, that he would be rescued, that it would end. But there was no plan. It did not end. His dad never showed. And then the humans had turned on each other, in an effort to trigger his failsafe.

"Junior didn't feel any pain, either," Abigail said. "When you let him fall."

The signal changed. They walked forward. The failsafe swam under the waters of his mind, and whispered to him about the presence of cars and the priority of human life.

· · · ·

"What do you mean, he's not here?"

Abigail kept looking from her mother to Javier and back again. "Did Junior go away?"

Brigid looked down at her. "Are you all packed up? Your dad is coming today to get you."

"AND Momo, Mom. Daddy AND Momo. They're both coming straight from the airport."

"Yes. I know that. Your dad and Momo. Now can you please check upstairs?"

Abigail didn't budge. "Will Junior be here when I come back next Friday?"

"I don't know, Abigail. Maybe not. He's not just some toy you can leave somewhere."

Abigail's face hardened. "You're mean and I hate you," she said, before marching up the stairs with heavy, decisive stomps.

Javier waited until he heard a door slam before asking: "Where is he, really?"

"I really don't know, Javier. He's your son."

Javier frowned. "Well, did he say anything—"

"No. He didn't. I told him that Abigail would be going back with her dad, and he just up and left."

Javier made for the door. "I should go look for him."

"No!" Brigid slid herself between his body and the door. "I mean, please don't. At least, not until my ex leaves. Okay?"

"Your ex? Why? Are you afraid of him or something?" Javier tipped her chin up with one finger. "He can't hurt you while his girlfriend's watching. You know that, right?"

She hunched her shoulders. "I know. And I'm not afraid of him hurting me. God. You always leap to the worst possible conclusion. It's just, you know, the way he gloats. About how great his life is now. It hurts."

He deflated. "Fine. I'll wait."

In the end, he didn't have long to wait. They showed up only fifteen minutes later—a little earlier than they were supposed to, which surprised Brigid and made her even angrier for some reason. "He was never on time when we were together," she sniffed, as she watched them exit their car. "I guess dating a robot is easier than buying a fucking watch."

"That's a bad word, Mom," Abigail said. "I'm gonna debit your account."

Brigid sighed. She forced a smile. "You're right, honey. I'm sorry. Let's go say hi to your dad."

At the door, Kevin was a round guy with thinning hair and very flashy-looking augmented lenses—the kind usually marketed at much younger humans. He stood on the steps with one arm around a Japanese-model vN wearing an elaborate Restoration costume complete with velvet jacket and perfect black corkscrew curls. They both stepped back a little when Javier greeted them at the door.

"You must be Javier," Kevin said, extending his hand and smiling a dentist smile. "Abigail's told me lots about you."

"You did?" Brigid frowned at her daughter.

"Yeah." Abigail's expression clouded. "Was it supposed to be a surprise?"

Brigid's mouth opened, then closed, then opened again. "Of course not."

The thing about the failsafe was that it made sure his perceptual systems caught every moment of hesitation in voices or faces or movements. Sometimes humans could defeat it, if they believed their own bullshit. But outright lies, especially about the things that hurt—he had reefs of graphene coral devoted to filtering those. Brigid was lying. She had meant for this moment to be a surprise. He could simulate it, now: she would open the door and he would be there and he would make her look good because he looked good, he was way prettier by human standards than she or her ex had any hope of ever being, and for some reason that mattered. Not that he couldn't understand; his own systems were regularly hijacked by his perceptions. He responded to pain; they responded to proportion. He couldn't actually hurt the human man standing in front of him—not with his fists. But his flat stomach and his thick hair and his clear, near-poreless skin: they were doing the job just fine. Javier saw that, now, in the way Kevin kept sizing him up, even when his own daughter danced into his arms. His jetlagged eyes barely spared a second for her. They remained trained on Javier. Beside him, Brigid stood a little taller.

God, Brigid was such a bitch.

"I like your dress, Momo," Abigail said.

This shook Kevin out of his mate-competition trance. "Well that's good news, baby, 'cause we bought a version in your size, too!"

"That's cute," Brigid said. "Now you can both play dress-up."

Kevin shot her a look that was pure hate. Javier was glad suddenly that he'd never asked about why the two of them had split. He didn't want to know. It was clearly too deep and organic and weird for him to understand, much less deal with.

"Well, it was nice meeting you," he said. "I'm sure you're pretty tired after the flight. You probably want to get home and go to sleep, right?"

"Yes, that's right," Momo said. Thank Christ for other robots; they knew how to take a cue.

Kevin pinked considerably. "Uh, right." He reached down, picked up Abigail's bag, and nodded at them. "Call you later, Brigid."

"Sure."

Abigail waved at Javier. She blew him a kiss. He blew one back as the door closed.

"Well, thank goodness that's over." Brigid sagged against the door, her palms flat against its surface, her face lit with a new glow. "We have the house to ourselves."

She was so pathetically obvious. He'd met high-schoolers with more grace. He folded his arms. "Where's my son?"

Brigid frowned. "I don't know, but I'm sure he's fine. You've been training him, haven't you? He has all your skills." Her fingers played with his shiny new belt buckle, the one she had bought for him especially. "Well, most of them. I'm sure there are some things he'll just have to learn on his own."

She knew. She knew exactly where his son was. And when her eyes rose, she knew that he knew. And she smiled.

Javier did not feel fear in any organic way. The math reflected a certain organic sensibility, perhaps, the way his simulation and prediction engines suddenly spun to life, their fractal computations igniting and processing as he calculated what could go wrong and when and how and with whom. How long had it been since he'd last seen Junior? How much did Junior know? Was his English good enough? Were his jumps strong enough? Did he understand the failsafe completely? These were the questions Javier had, instead of a cold sweat. If he were a different kind of man, a man like Kevin or any of the other human men he'd met and enjoyed in his time, he might have felt a desire to grab Brigid or hit her the way she'd hit him earlier, when she thought he was endangering her offspring in some vague, indirect way. They had subroutines for that. They had their own failsafes, the infamous triple-F cascades of adrenaline that gave them bursts of energy for dealing with problems like the one facing him now. They were built to protect their own, and he was not.

So he shrugged and said: "You're right. There are some things you just can't teach."

They went to the bedroom. And he was so good, he'd learned so much in his short years, that Brigid rewarded his technique with knowledge. She told him about taking Junior to the grocery store with her. She told him about the man who had followed them into the parking lot. She told him how, when she had asked Junior what he thought, he had given Javier's exact same shrug.

"He said you'd be fine with it," she said. "He said your dad did something similar. He said it made you stronger. More independent."

Javier shut his eyes. "Independent. Sure."

"He looked so much like you as he said it." Brigid was already half asleep. "I wonder what I'll pass down to my daughter, sometimes. Maybe she'll fall in love with a robot, just like her mommy and daddy."

"Maybe," Javier said. "Maybe her whole generation will. Maybe they won't even bother reproducing."

"Maybe we'll go extinct," Brigid said. "But then who would you have left to love?"

TOBIAS S. BUCKELL Tobias S. Buckell was born on the Caribbean island of Grenada in 1979. As a result, some of his earliest memories are of "nervous adults and not being allowed near windows" during the collapse of the island's government and the U.S. invasion of 1983. He spent the rest of his childhood on boats there and in the British and U.S. Virgin Islands, moving with his family to Ohio when he was eighteen. He has been publishing SF stories since 2000, and novels since 2006.

Much of his work draws on his Caribbean background, in direct and indirect ways, and "Toy Planes"—a gem of an SF miniature—is no exception.

TOY PLANES

My sister Joanie's deft hands flicked from dreadlock to dreadlock, considering her strategy. "You always leaving," she said, flicking the razor on, and suddenly I'm five, chasing her with a kite made from plastic bags and twigs, shouting that I was going to fly away from her one day.

"I'm sorry. Please, let's get this done."

I'd waited long enough. I'd grown dreads because when I studied in the United States I wanted to remember who I was and where I came from as I began to lose my Caribbean accent. But the rocket plane's sponsor wanted them cut. It would be disaster for a helmet not to have a proper seal in an emergency. Explosive decompression was not something a soda company wanted to be associated with in their customers' minds. It was insulting that they assumed we couldn't keep the craft sealed. But we needed their money. The locks had become enough a part of me that I winced when the clippers bit into them, groaned, and another piece of me fell away.

In the back of the bus that I had pick me up, I hung on to a looped handle swinging from the roof as the driver rocketed down the dirt road from Joanie's. My sister had found a place out in the country, a nice concrete house with a basement opening up into a sloped garden on the side of a steep hill. She taught mathematics at the school a few miles away, an open-shuttered building, and this would have been my future too, if I hadn't been so intent on "getting off the rock."

The islands always called their children back.

We hit asphalt, potholes, and passed cane fields with machete-wielding laborers hacking away at the stalks, sweat-drenched shirts knotted around their waists. It was hot; my arms stuck to the plastic-covered seats. The driver leaned into a turn, and looked back. "I want to ask you something." I really wished the backseats had belts.

"Sure."

"All that money you spending, you don't think it better spent on getting better roads?" He dodged a pothole. "Or more school funding?"

Colorful red and yellow houses on stilts dotted the steep lush green mountainsides as I looked out of the tinted windows. "Only one small part of the program got funded by the government," I explained. "We found private investors, advertisers, to back the rest. Whatever the government invested will be repaid."

"Maybe."

I had my extra arguments. How many people lived on this island? Tens of thousands. Most of our food was imported, leaving us dependent on other food-producing nations, who all used satellites to track their farming. What spin-off technologies might come out of studying recycling in space? Why wait for other nations to get to it first? Research always produced good things for the people who engaged in it.

But I was tired of arguing for it, and I had only sound bites for him, the same ones I'd given the media who treated us like kids trying to do something all grown up.

The market surrounded me in a riot of color: fruit, vegetables, full women in dresses in bright floral patterns. And the noise of hundreds constantly bargaining over things like the price of fish. Teenagers stood around the corners with friends. I wandered around looking for something, as we needed to fill the craft with enough extra weight to simulate a passenger and we still had a few extra ounces to add.

I found a small toy stall. And standing in front of it I was five years old again, with no money, and a piece of scrap metal in the triangular shape of a space plane. I would pretend it was just like the real-life ones I'd read about in the books donated to the school after the hurricane. And at night, when the power would sometimes flicker out, I'd go out and stand on the porch and look up at the bright stars and envy them.

The stall had a small bottle, hammered over with soda-can metal, with triangular welded-on wings, and a cone stuck to the back. It was painted over in yellow, black, and green, and I bought it.

The rest of the day was a blur. Getting to the field involved running the press: yes I'd cut my hair for "safety" reasons, yes I thought this was a good use of our money, not just first-world nations deserved space, it was there for everyone.

There were photos of me getting aboard the tiny rocket plane with a small brown package under my arm. The giant balloon platform that the plane hung from shifted in the gentle, salty island breeze. Not too far away the waves hit the sand of the beach. Inside, suited up, door closed, everything became electronic.

It was the cheapest way to get to orbit. Balloon up on a triangular platform to save on fuel, then light the rocket plane up and head for orbit. We'd scavenged balloons and material from several companies, one about to go out of business. The plane chassis had once been used by a Chinese corporation during trials, and the guidance systems were all open-source. Online betting parlors had our odds at 50 percent. We weren't even the first, but we were the first island.

The countdown finished, my stomach lurched, and I saw palm trees slide by the portholes to my right. I reached back and patted the package, the hammered-together toy, and smiled.

"Hello out there, all of you," I whispered into the radio. "We're coming up too."

KEN LIU   Ken Liu was born in Lanzhou, China, and moved to the United States when he was eleven. He began publishing SF in 2002. In 2012, his story "The Paper Menagerie" became the first work of fiction, of any length, to win the Hugo Award, the Nebula Award, and the World Fantasy Award. He has also won the SF and Fantasy Translation Award, for his translation into English of "The Fish of Lijiang" by Chen Qiufan. He has translated several other significant works of Chinese SF and literary fiction into English as well.

"The Algorithms for Love," published in 2004, is about a brilliant designer of robotic toys whose job is driving her crazy. Various segments of this idea could have been used (and some have been used, by other writers) to generate whole stories, but Liu lets it keep rolling along to see what will happen. It's both a love story and an AI existential-horror story that turns the Turing test inside out.

THE ALGORITHMS FOR LOVE

So long as the nurse is in the room to keep an eye on me, I am allowed to dress myself and get ready for Brad. I slip on an old pair of jeans and a scarlet turtleneck sweater. I've lost so much weight that the jeans hang loosely from the bony points of my hips.

"Let's go spend the weekend in Salem," Brad says to me as he walks me out of the hospital, an arm protectively wrapped around my waist, "just the two of us."

I wait in the car while Dr. West speaks with Brad just outside the hospital doors. I can't hear them but I know what she's telling him. "Make sure she takes her Oxetine every four hours. Don't leave her alone for any length of time."

Brad drives with a light touch on the pedals, the same way he used to when I was pregnant with Aimée. The traffic is smooth and light, and the foliage along the highway is postcard-perfect. The Oxetine relaxes the muscles around my mouth, and in the vanity mirror I see that I have a beatific smile on my face.

"I love you." He says this quietly, the way he has always done, as if it were the sound of breathing and heartbeat.

I wait a few seconds. I picture myself opening the door and throwing my body onto the highway but of course I don't do anything. I can't even surprise myself.

"I love you too." I look at him when I say this, the way I have always done, as if it were the answer to some question. He looks at me, smiles, and turns his eyes back to the road.

To him this means that the routines are back in place, that he is talking to the same woman he has known all these years, that things are back to normal. We are just another tourist couple from Boston on a mini-break for the weekend: stay at a bed-and-breakfast, visit the museums, recycle old jokes.

It's an algorithm for love.

I want to scream.

• • • •

The first doll I designed was called Laura. Clever Laura™.

Laura had brown hair and blue eyes, fully articulated joints, twenty motors, a speech synthesizer in her throat, two video cameras disguised by the buttons on her blouse, temperature and touch sensors, and a microphone behind her nose. None of it was cutting-edge technology, and the software techniques I used were at least two decades old. But I was still proud of my work. She retailed for fifty dollars.

Not Your Average Toy could not keep up with the orders that were rolling in, even three months before Christmas. Brad, the CEO, went on CNN and MSNBC and TTV and the rest of the alphabet soup until the very air was saturated with Laura.

I tagged along on the interviews to give the demos because, as the VP of Marketing explained to me, I looked like a mother (even though I wasn't one) and (he didn't say this, but I could listen between the lines) I was blonde and pretty. The fact that I was Laura's designer was an afterthought.

The first time I did a demo on TV was for a Hong Kong crew. Brad wanted me to get comfortable with being in front of the cameras before bringing me to the domestic morning shows.

We sat to the side while Cindy, the anchorwoman, interviewed the CEO of some company that made "moisture meters." I hadn't slept for forty-eight hours. I was so nervous I'd brought six Lauras with me, just in case five of them decided in concert to break down. Then Brad turned to me and whispered, "What do you think moisture meters are used for?"

I didn't know Brad that well, having been at Not Your Average Toy for less than a year. I had chatted with him a few times before, but it was all professional. He seemed a very serious, driven sort of guy, the kind you could picture starting his first company while he was still in high school—arbitraging class notes, maybe. I wasn't sure why he was asking me about moisture meters. Was he trying to see if I was too nervous?

"I don't know. Maybe for cooking?" I ventured.

"Maybe," he said. Then he gave me a conspiratorial wink. "But I think the name sounds kind of dirty."

It was such an unexpected thing, coming from him, that for a moment I almost thought he was serious. Then he smiled, and I laughed out loud. I had a very hard time keeping a straight face while we waited for our turn, and I certainly wasn't nervous anymore.

Brad and the young anchorwoman, Cindy, chatted amiably about Not Your Average Toy's mission ("Not Average Toys for Not Average Kids") and how Brad had come up with the idea for Laura. (Brad had nothing to do with the design, of course, since it was all my idea. But his answer was so good it almost convinced me that Laura was really his brainchild.) Then it was time for the dog-and-pony show.

I put Laura on the desk, her face towards the camera. I sat to the side of the desk. "Hello, Laura."

Laura turned her head to me, the motors so quiet you couldn't hear their whirr. "Hi! What's your name?"

"I'm Elena," I said.

"Nice to meet you," Laura said. "I'm cold."

The air conditioning was a bit chilly. I hadn't even noticed.

Cindy was impressed. "That's amazing. How much can she say?"

"Laura has a vocabulary of about two thousand English words, with semantic and syntactic encoding for common suffixes and prefixes. Her speech is regulated by a context-free grammar." The look in Brad's eye let me know that I was getting too technical. "That means that she'll invent new sentences and they'll always be syntactically correct."

"I like new, shiny, new, bright, new, handsome clothes," Laura said.

"Though they may not always make sense," I added.

"Can she learn new words?" Cindy asked.

Laura turned her head the other way, to look at her. "I like learn-ing, please teach me a new word!"

I made a mental note that the speech synthesizer still had bugs that would have to be fixed in the firmware.

Cindy was visibly unnerved by the doll turning to face her on its own and responding to her question.

"Does she"—she searched for the right word—"*understand* me?"

"No, no." I laughed. So did Brad. And a moment later Cindy joined us. "Laura's speech algorithm is augmented with a Markov generator interspersed with—" Brad gave me that look again. "Basically, she just babbles sentences based on keywords in what she hears. And she has a small set of stock phrases that are triggered the same way."

"Oh, it really seemed like she knew what I was saying. How does she learn new words?"

"It's very simple. Laura has enough memory to learn hundreds of new words. However, they have to be nouns. You can show her the object while you are trying to teach her what it is. She has some very sophisticated pattern recognition capabilities and can even tell faces apart."

For the rest of the interview I assured nervous parents that Laura would not require them to read the manual, that Laura would not explode when dropped in water, and no, she would never utter a naughty word, even if their little princesses "accidentally" taught Laura one.

" 'Bye," Cindy said to Laura at the end of the interview, and waved at her.

" 'Bye," Laura said. "You are nice." She waved back.

Every interview followed the same pattern. The moment when Laura first turned to the interviewer and answered a question there was always some awkwardness and unease. Seeing an inanimate object display intelligent behavior had that effect on people. They probably all thought the doll was possessed. Then I would explain how Laura worked and everyone would be delighted. I memorized the non-technical, warm-and-fuzzy answers to all the questions until I could recite them even without my morning coffee. I got so good at it that I sometimes coasted through entire interviews on autopilot, not even paying attention to the questions and letting the same words I heard over and over again spark off my responses.

The interviews, along with all the other marketing tricks, did their job. We had to outsource manufacturing so quickly that for a while every shantytown along the coast of China must have been turning out Lauras.

．．．．

The foyer of the bed-and-breakfast we are staying at is predictably filled with brochures from local attractions. Most of them are witch-themed. The lurid pictures and language somehow manage to convey moral outrage and adolescent fascination with the occult at the same time.

David, the innkeeper, wants us to check out Ye Olde Poppet Shoppe, featuring "Dolls Made by Salem's Official Witch." Bridget Bishop, one of the twenty executed during the Salem Witch Trials, was convicted partly based on the hard evidence of "poppets" found in her cellar with pins stuck in them.

Maybe she was just like me, a crazy, grown woman playing with dolls. The very idea of visiting a doll shop makes my stomach turn.

While Brad is asking David about restaurants and possible discounts I go up to our room. I want to be sleeping, or at least pretending to be sleeping, by the time he comes up. Maybe then he will leave me alone, and give me a few minutes to think. It's hard to think with the Oxetine. There's a wall in my head, a gauzy wall that tries to cushion every thought with contentment.

If only I can remember what went wrong.

．．．．

For our honeymoon Brad and I went to Europe. We went on the transorbital shuttle, the tickets for which cost more than my yearly rent. But we could afford it. Witty Kimberly™, our latest model, was selling well, and the stock price was transorbital itself.

When we got back from the shuttleport, we were tired but happy. And I still couldn't quite believe that we were in our own home, thinking of each other as husband and wife. It felt like playing house. We made dinner together, like we used to when we were dating (like always, Brad was wildly ambitious but couldn't follow a recipe longer than a paragraph and I had to come and rescue his shrimp étouffée). The familiarity of the routine made everything seem more real.

Over dinner Brad told me something interesting. According to a market survey, over 20% of the customers for Kimberly were not buying it for their kids at all. They played with the dolls themselves.

"Many of them are engineers and comp sci students," Brad said. "And there are already tons of Net sites devoted to hacking efforts on Kimberly. My favorite one had step-by-step instructions on how to teach Kimberly to make up and tell lawyer jokes. I can't wait to see the faces of the guys in the legal department when they get to drafting the cease-and-desist letter for that one."

I could understand the interest in Kimberly. When I was struggling with my problem sets at MIT I would have loved to take apart something like Kimberly to figure out how she worked. How *it* worked, I corrected myself mentally. Kimberly's illusion of intelligence was so real that sometimes even I unconsciously gave her, it, too much credit.

"Actually, maybe we shouldn't try to shut the hacking efforts down," I said. "Maybe we can capitalize on it. We can release some of the APIs and sell a developer's kit for the geeks."

"What do you mean?"

"Well, Kimberly is a toy, but that doesn't mean only little girls would be interested in her." I gave up trying to manage the pronouns. "She does, after all, have the most sophisticated, *working,* natural conversation library in the world."

"A library that you wrote," Brad said. Well, maybe I was a little vain about it. But I'd worked damned hard on that library and I was proud of it.

"It would be a shame if the language processing module never got any application besides sitting in a doll that everyone is going to forget in a year. We can release the interface to the modules at least, a programming guide, and maybe even some of the source code. Let's see what happens and make an extra dollar while we're at it." I never got into academic AI research because I couldn't take the tedium, but I did have greater ambitions than just making talking dolls. I wanted to see smart and talking machines doing something real, like teaching kids to read or helping the elderly with chores.

I knew that he would agree with me in the end. Despite his serious exterior he was willing to take risks and defy expectations. It was why I loved him.

I got up to clear the dishes. His hand reached across the table and grabbed mine. "Those can wait," he said. He walked around the table, pulling me to him. I looked into his eyes. I loved the fact that I knew him so well I could tell what he was going to say before he said it. *Let's make a baby*, I imagined him saying. Those would have been the only words right for that moment.

And so he did.

. . . .

I'm not asleep when Brad finishes asking about restaurants and comes upstairs. In my drugged state, even pretending is too difficult.

Brad wants to go to the pirate museum. I tell him that I don't want to see anything violent. He agrees immediately. That's what he wants to hear from his content, recovering wife.

So now we wander around the galleries of the Peabody Essex Museum, looking at the old treasures of the Orient from Salem's glory days.

The collection of china is terrible. The workmanship in the bowls and saucers is inexcusable. The patterns look like they were traced on by children. According to the placards, these were what the Cantonese merchants exported for foreign consumption. They would never have sold such stuff in China itself.

I read the description written by a Jesuit priest who visited the Cantonese shops of the time.

The craftsmen sat in a line, each with his own brush and specialty. The first drew only the mountains, the next only the grass, the next only the flowers, and the next only the animals. They went on down the line, passing the plates from one to the next, and it took each man only a few seconds to complete his part.

So the "treasures" are nothing more than mass-produced cheap exports from an ancient sweatshop and assembly line. I imagine painting the same blades of grass on a thousand teacups a day: the same routine, repeated over and over, with maybe a small break for lunch. Reach out, pick up the cup in front of you with your left hand, dip the brush, one, two, three strokes, put the cup behind you, rinse and repeat. What a simple algorithm. It's so human.

. . . .

Brad and I fought for three months before he agreed to produce Aimée, just plain Aimée™.

We fought at home, where night after night I laid out the same forty-one reasons why we should and he laid out the same thirty-nine reasons why we shouldn't. We fought at work, where people stared through the glass door at Brad and me gesticulating at each other wildly, silently.

I was so tired that night. I had spent the whole evening locked away in my study, struggling to get the routines to control Aimée's involuntary muscle spasms right. It had to be right or she wouldn't feel real, no matter how good the learning algorithms were.

I came up to the bedroom. There was no light. Brad had gone to bed early. He was exhausted too. We had again hurled the same reasons at each other during dinner.

He wasn't asleep. "Are we going to go on like this?" he asked in the darkness.

I sat down on my side of the bed and undressed. "I can't stop it," I said. "I miss her too much. I'm sorry."

He didn't say anything. I finished unbuttoning my blouse and turned around. With the moonlight coming through the window I could see that his face was wet. I started crying too.

When we both finally stopped, Brad said, "I miss her too."

"I know," I said. *But not like me.*

"It won't be anything like her, you know?" he said.

"I know," I said.

The real Aimée had lived for ninety-one days. Forty-five of those days she'd spent under the glass hood in intensive care, where I could not touch her except for brief doctor-supervised sessions. But I could hear her cries. I could always hear her cries. In the end I tried to break through the glass with my hands, and I beat my palms against the unyielding glass until the bones broke and they sedated me.

I could never have another child. The walls of my womb had not healed properly and never would. By the time that piece of news was given to me Aimée was a jar of ashes in my closet.

But I could still hear her cries.

How many other women were like me? I wanted something to fill my arms, something to learn to speak, to walk, to grow a little, long enough for me to say goodbye, long enough to quiet those cries. But not a real child. I couldn't deal with another real child. It would feel like a betrayal.

With a little plastiskin, a little synthgel, the right set of motors and a lot of clever programming, I could do it. Let technology heal all wounds.

Brad thought the idea an abomination. He was revolted. He couldn't *understand.*

I fumbled around in the dark for some tissues for Brad and me.

"This may ruin us, and the company," he said.

"I know," I said. I lay down. I wanted to sleep.

"Let's do it, then," he said.

I didn't want to sleep any more.

"I can't take it," he said. "Seeing you like this. Seeing you in so much pain tears me up. It hurts too much."

I started crying again. This understanding, this pain. Was this what love was about?

Right before I fell asleep Brad said, "Maybe we should think about changing the name of the company."

"Why?"

"Well, I just realized that 'Not Your Average Toy' sounds pretty funny to the dirty-minded."

I smiled. Sometimes the vulgar is the best kind of medicine.

"I love you."

"I love you too."

. . . .

Brad hands me the pills. I obediently take them and put them in my mouth. He watches as I sip from the glass of water he hands me.

"Let me make a few phone calls," he says. "You take a nap, okay?" I nod.

As soon as he leaves the room I spit out the pills into my hand. I go into the bathroom and rinse out my mouth. I lock the door behind me and sit down on the toilet. I try to recite the digits of pi. I manage fifty-four places. That's a good sign. The Oxetine must be wearing off.

I look into the mirror. I stare into my eyes, trying to see through to the retinas, matching photoreceptor with photoreceptor, imagining their grid layout. I turn my head from side to side, watching the muscles tense and relax in turn. That effect would be hard to simulate.

But there's nothing in my face, nothing real behind that surface. Where is the pain, the pain that made love real, the pain of understanding?

"You okay, sweetie?" Brad says through the bathroom door.

I turn on the faucet and splash water on my face. "Yes," I say. "I'm going to take a shower. Can you get some snacks from that store we saw down the street?"

Giving him something to do reassures him. I hear the door to the room close behind him. I turn off the faucet and look back into the mirror, at the way the water droplets roll down my face, seeking the canals of my wrinkles.

The human body is a marvel to recreate. The human mind, on the other hand, is a joke. Believe me, I know.

. . . .

No, Brad and I patiently explained over and over to the cameras, we had not created an "artificial child." That was not our intention and that was not what we'd done. It was a way to comfort the grieving mothers. If you needed Aimée, you would know.

I would walk down the street and see women walking with bundles carefully held in their arms. And occasionally I would know, I would know beyond a doubt, by the sound of a particular cry, by the way a little arm waved. I would look into the faces of the women, and be comforted.

I thought I had moved on, recovered from the grieving process. I was ready to begin another project, a bigger project that would really satisfy my ambition and show the world my skills. I was ready to get on with my life.

Tara took four years to develop. I worked on her in secret while designing other dolls that would sell. Physically Tara looked like a five-year-old girl. Expensive transplant-quality plastiskin and synthgel gave her an ethereal and angelic look. Her eyes were dark and clear, and you could look into them forever.

I never finished Tara's movement engine. In retrospect that was probably a blessing. As a temporary placeholder during development I used the facial expression engine sent in by the Kimberly enthusiasts at MIT's Media Lab. Augmented with many more fine micromotors than Kimberly had, she could turn her head, blink her eyes, wrinkle her nose, and generate thousands of convincing facial expressions. Below the neck she was paralyzed.

But her mind, oh, her mind.

I used the best quantum processors and the best solid-state storage matrices to run multi-layered, multi-feedback neural nets. I threw in the Stanford Semantic Database and added my own modifications. The programming was beautiful. It was truly a work of art. The data model alone took me over six months.

I taught her when to smile and when to frown, and I taught her how to speak and how to listen. Each night I analyzed the activation graphs for the nodes in the neural nets, trying to find and resolve problems before they occurred.

Brad never saw Tara while she was in development. He was too busy trying to control the damage from Aimée, and then, later, pushing the new dolls. I wanted to surprise him.

I put Tara in a wheelchair, and I told Brad that she was the daughter of a friend. Since I had to run some errands, could he entertain her while I was gone for a few hours? I left them in my office.

When I came back two hours later, I found Brad reading to her from *The Golem of Prague*, "'Come,' said the Great Rabbi Loew, 'Open your eyes and speak like a real person!'"

That was just like Brad, I thought. He had his sense of irony.

"All right," I interrupted him. "Very funny. I get the joke. So how long did it take you?"

He smiled at Tara. "We'll finish this some other time," he said. Then he turned to me. "How long did it take me what?"

"To figure it out."

"Figure out what?"

"Stop kidding around," I said. "Really, what was it that gave her away?"

"Gave what away?" Brad and Tara said at the same time.

· · · ·

Nothing Tara ever said or did was a surprise to me. I could predict everything she would say before she said it. I'd coded everything in her, after all, and I knew exactly how her neural nets changed with each interaction.

But no one else suspected anything. I should have been elated. My doll was passing a real-life Turing test. But I was frightened. The algorithms made a mockery of intelligence, and no one seemed to know. No one seemed to even care.

I finally broke the news to Brad after a week. After the initial shock he was delighted (as I knew he would be).

"Fantastic," he said. "We're now no longer just a toy company. Can you imagine the things we can do with this? You'll be famous, really famous!"

He prattled on and on about the potential applications. Then he noticed my silence. "What's wrong?"

So I told him about the Chinese Room.

The philosopher John Searle used to pose a puzzle for the AI researchers. Imagine a room, he said, a large room filled with meticulous clerks who are very good at following orders but who speak only English. Into this room are delivered a steady stream of cards with strange symbols on them. The clerks have to draw other strange symbols on blank cards in response and send the cards out of the room. In order to do this, the clerks have large books, full of rules in English like this one: "When you see a card with a single horizontal squiggle followed by a card with two vertical squiggles, draw a triangle on a blank card and hand it to the clerk to your right." The rules contain nothing about what the symbols might mean.

It turns out that the cards coming into the room are questions written in Chinese, and the clerks, by following the rules, are producing sensible answers in Chinese. But could anything involved in this process—the rules, the clerks, the room as a whole, the storm of activity—be said to have *understood* a word of Chinese? Substitute "processor" for the clerks and substitute "program" for the books of rules, then you'll see that the Turing test will never prove anything, and AI is an illusion.

But you can also carry the Chinese Room Argument the other way: substitute "neurons" for the clerks and substitute the physical laws governing the cascading of activating potentials for the books of rules; then how can any of us ever be said to "understand" anything? Thought is an illusion.

"I don't understand," Brad said. "What are you saying?"

A moment later I realized that that was exactly what I'd expected him to say.

"Brad," I said, staring into his eyes, willing him to understand. "I'm scared. What if we are just like Tara?"

"We? You mean people? What are you talking about?"

"What if," I said, struggling to find the words, "we are just following some algorithm from day to day? What if our brain cells are just looking up signals from other signals? What if we are not thinking at all? What if what I'm saying to you now is just a predetermined response, the result of mindless physics?"

"Elena," Brad said, "you're letting philosophy get in the way of reality."

I need sleep, I thought, feeling hopeless.

"I think you need to get some sleep," Brad said.

• • • •

I handed the coffee-cart girl the money as she handed me the coffee. I stared at the girl. She looked so tired and bored at eight in the morning that she made me feel tired.

I need a vacation.

"I need a vacation," she said, sighing exaggeratedly.

I walked past the receptionist's desk. *Morning, Elena.*

Say something different, please. I clenched my teeth. Please.

"Morning, Elena," she said.

I paused outside Ogden's cube. He was the structural engineer. *The weather, last night's game, Brad.*

He saw me and got up. "Nice weather we're having, eh?" He wiped the sweat from his forehead and smiled at me. He jogged to work. "Did you see the game last night? Best shot I've seen in ten years. Unbelievable. Hey, is Brad in yet?" His face was expectant, waiting for me to follow the script, the comforting routines of life.

The algorithms ran their determined courses, and our thoughts followed one after another, as mechanical and as predictable as the planets in their orbits. The watchmaker was the watch.

I ran into my office and closed the door behind me, ignoring the expression on Ogden's face. I walked over to my computer and began to delete files.

"Hi," Tara said. "What are we going to do today?"

I shut her off so quickly that I broke a nail on the hardware switch. I ripped out the power supply in her back. I went to work with my screwdriver and pliers. After a while I switched to a hammer. Was I killing?

Brad burst in the door. "What are you doing?"

I looked up at him, my hammer poised for another strike. I wanted to tell him about the pain, the terror that opened up an abyss around me.

In his eyes I could not find what I wanted to see. I could not see understanding.

I swung the hammer.

• • • •

Brad had tried to reason with me, right before he had me committed.

"This is just an obsession," he said. "People have always associated the mind with the technological fad of the moment. When they believed in witches and spirits, they thought there was a little man in the brain. When they had mechanical looms and player pianos, they thought the brain was an engine. When they had telegraphs and telephones, they thought the brain was a wire network. Now you think the brain is just a computer. Snap out of it. *That* is the illusion."

Trouble was, I knew he was going to say that.

"It's because we've been married for so long!" he shouted. "That's why you think you know me so well!"

I knew he was going to say that too.

"You're running around in circles," he said, defeat in his voice. "You're just spinning in your head."

Loops in my algorithm. FOR and WHILE loops.

"Come back to me. I love you."

What else could he have said?

. . . .

Now finally alone in the bathroom of the inn, I look down at my hands, at the veins running under the skin. I press my hands together and feel my pulse. I kneel down. Am I praying? Flesh and bones, and good programming.

My knees hurt against the cold tile floor.

The pain is real, I think. There's no algorithm for the pain. I look down at my wrists, and the scars startle me. This is all very familiar, like I've done this before. The horizontal scars, ugly and pink like worms, rebuke me for failure. Bugs in the algorithm.

That night comes back to me: the blood everywhere, the alarms wailing, Dr. West and the nurses holding me down while they bandaged my wrists, and then Brad staring down at me, his face distorted with uncomprehending grief.

I should have done better. The arteries are hidden deep, protected by the bones. The slashes have to be made vertically if you really want it. That's the right algorithm. There's a recipe for everything. This time I'll get it right.

It takes a while, but finally I feel sleepy.

I'm happy. The pain *is* real.

. . . .

I open the door to my room and turn on the light.

The light activates Laura, who is sitting on top of my dresser. This one used to be a demo model. She hasn't been dusted in a while, and her dress looks ragged. Her head turns to follow my movement.

I turn around. Brad's body is still, but I can see the tears on his face. He was crying on the whole silent ride home from Salem.

The innkeeper's voice loops around in my head. "Oh, I could tell right away something was wrong. It's happened here before. She didn't seem right at breakfast, and then when you came back she looked like she was in another world. When I heard the water running in the pipes for that long I rushed upstairs right away."

So I was that predictable.

I look at Brad, and I believe that he is in a lot of pain. I believe it with all my heart. But I still don't feel anything. There's a gulf between us, a gulf so wide that I can't feel his pain. Nor he mine.

But my algorithms are still running. I scan for the right thing to say.

"I love you."

He doesn't say anything. His shoulders heave, once.

I turn around. My voice echoes through the empty house, bouncing off walls. Laura's sound receptors, old as they are, pick them up. The signals run through the cascading IF statements. The DO loops twirl and dance while she does a database lookup. The motors whirr. The synthesizer kicks in.

"I love you too," Laura says.

OLIVER MORTON Oliver Morton is a British science writer and editor whose work has appeared in *The New Yorker, The Economist, Discover, National Geographic, Wired, The American Scholar,* and *Nature,* where he worked as the chief news and features editor from 2005 to 2009. His work has been anthologized in both *Best American Science Writing* and *Best American Science and Nature Writing.* He is the author of the nonfiction books *Mapping Mars: Science, Imagination, and the Birth of a World* and *Eating the Sun: How Plants Power the Planet.* Asteroid 10716 Olivermorton is named for him.

Written for *Nature,* which has published a number of excellent sub-one-thousand-word SF stories over the years, "The Albian Message" is built around a new notion of what an alien artifact might reveal—an SF idea that is so obviously reasonable that it should have been evident all along.

THE ALBIAN MESSAGE

To: Eva P.
From: Stefan K.
Re: Sample handling facility
March 4, 2047

I thought I ought to put into writing my concerns over the sample-return facility for Odyssey. I think that relying on the mothballed Mars Sample Return lab at Ames is dangerously complacent. It is simply not flexible enough, or big enough, for what I think we should be expecting.

I appreciate that I am in a minority on this, and that the consensus is that we will be dealing with nonbiological artifacts. And I don't want to sound like the people from AstraRoche slipped some egopoietin into my drink during that trip to Stockholm last November. But my minority views have been pretty well borne out throughout this whole story. Back when Suzy and Sean had more or less convinced the world that the trinity sequences in the Albian message referred to some sort of mathematico-philosophical doctrine—possibly based on an analogy to the aliens' purported trisexual reproductive system—and everyone in SETI was taking a crash course in genome analysis, I had to pull in every favor I was owed to get the Square Kilometer Array used as a planetary radar and scanned over the Trojan asteroids. If I hadn't done that we wouldn't even know about the Pyramid, let alone be sending Odyssey there.

I'm not claiming I understand the Albians' minds better than anyone else; I haven't got any more of the message in my DNA than anyone else has. And it's always been my position that we should read as little into that message as possible. I remain convinced that looking for descriptions of their philosophy or lifestyle or even provenance is pointless. The more I look at the increasingly meaningless analyses that the increasingly intelligent AIs produce, the more I think that the variations between phyla are effectively random and that the message from the aliens tells us almost nothing except that there's a radar-reflecting tetrahedron $\pi/3$ behind Jupiter that they think we may find interesting.

Everyone assumes that if it hadn't been for the parts of the message lost in the K/T the "residual variant sequences" would be seen to add up to some great big life-the-Universe-and-everything revelation. And because they think such a revelation once existed, they expect to see it carved into the palladium walls of the Pyramid. But if the aliens who visited Earth, and left their messages in the genomes of more or less everything on the planet, had wanted to tell us something more about themselves, they could have made the messages a lot bigger and built in more redundancy across phylum space; there's no shortage of junk DNA to write on. The point is, they didn't choose to leave big messages—just a simple signpost.

The reason I was able to get the SKA people to find the Pyramid was that they knew I'd thought about SETI a lot. But these days people tend to forget that I was always something of a skeptic. What could a bunch of aliens tell us about themselves, or the Universe, that would matter? Especially if, like the Albians, they sent, or rather left, the message a hundred million years ago? Well, in the case of the Albians, there's one type of knowledge they could be fairly sure that anyone who eventually evolved sequencing technology on Earth pretty much had to be interested in. And it's something that, by definition, is too big to fit into the spare bits of a genome.

I appreciate that everyone on the project now has a lot of faith in what we can do on the fly, especially in terms of recording and analyzing information. I'll admit that when we started I really didn't think that the lost craft of human spaceflight would be so easy to reinvent. It still strikes me as remarkable that none of us realized how much could be achieved by leaving a technical problem to one side and concentrating on other things for a few decades before coming back to it with new technologies. But the problem with the sample-return facility won't just be one of technology. It's going to be one of size.

You see, extinctions aren't the noise in the message. They're the reason for the message. The one thing the Albians knew they could do for whoever would end up reading their message was store up some of the biodiversity that would inevitably be whittled away over time. When Odyssey gets to the Trojan Pyramid, I don't expect it to find any more information about the Albians than we have already. I do expect a biosphere's worth of well-preserved biological samples from the mid-Cretaceous. Not just genomes, but whole samples. Sudarat and her boys are going to come home with a hold full of early angiosperms and dinosaur eggs. We need to be ready.

KARL SCHROEDER   Karl Schroeder was born in Brandon, Manitoba, and lives in Toronto, where he divides his time between writing fiction and consulting on the future of technology for clients including the Canadian government and military. He began to publish stories in the 1990s, and beginning with *Ventus* (2000), he has published seven science fiction novels and a collection of earlier stories. His most recent novel is *Ashes of Candesce* (2012), the fifth adventure set in Virga, a far-future built-world hard-SF environment.

"To Hie from Far Cilenia" has a complex publishing history typical of SF today, beginning with its release in audio in 2009 as part of the John Scalzi—edited audio original anthology project *Metatropolis*, later printed in a limited edition, and then in 2010 in a trade hardcover edition. Using a plot device similar to that in William Gibson's *Pattern Recognition*, Schroeder explores the moral ramifications of virtual worlds and disposable identities.

TO HIE FROM FAR CILENIA

Sixteen plastic-wrapped, frozen reindeer made a forest of jutting legs and antlers in the back of the transport truck. Gennady Malianov raised his flashlight to peer down the length of the cargo container. He checked his Geiger counter, then said, "It's them, all right."

"You're sure?" asked the Swedish cop. Hidden in his rain gear, he was all slick surfaces under the midnight drizzle. The mountain road stretching out behind him shone silver on black, dazzled here and there by the red and blue lights of a dozen emergency vehicles.

Gennady climbed down. "Officer, if you think there might be other trucks on this road loaded with radioactive reindeer, I think I need to know."

The cop didn't smile; his breath fogged the air. "It's all about jurisdiction," he said. "If they were just smuggling meat . . . but this is terrorism."

"Still," mused Gennady; the cop had been turning away but stopped. Gennady glanced back at the contorted, freezer-burned carcasses, and shrugged awkwardly. "I never thought I'd get to see them."

"See who?"

Embarrassed now, Gennady nodded to the truck. "The famous Reindeer," he said. "I never thought I'd get to see them."

"Spöklik," muttered the cop as he walked away. Gennady glanced in the truck once more, then walked toward his car, shoulders hunched. A little light on its dashboard was flashing, telling him he'd gone over the time he'd booked it for. Traffic on the E18 had proven heavier than expected, due to the rain and the fact that the police had shut down the whole road at Arjang. He was mentally subtracting the extra car-sharing fees from what they'd pay him for this very short adventure, when someone shouted, "Malianov?"

"What now?" He shielded his eyes with his hand. Two men were walking up the narrow shoulder from the emergency vehicles. Immediately behind them was a van without a flashing light—a big, black and sinister shape that reminded him of some of the paralegal police vans in Ukraine. The men had the burly look of plainclothes policemen.

"Are you Gennady Malianov?" asked the first, in English. Rain was beading on his bald skull. Gennady nodded.

"You're with the IAEA?" the man went on. "You're an arms inspector?"

"I've done that," said Gennady neutrally.

"Lane Hitchens," said the bald man, sticking out his beefy hand for Gennady to shake. "Interpol."

"Is this about the reindeer?"

"What reindeer?" said Hitchens. Gennady snatched his hand back.

"*This,*" he said, waving at the checkpoint, the flashing lights, the bowed heads of the suspects in the back of the paddy wagon. "You're not here about all this?"

Hitchens shook his head. "Look, I was just told you'd be here, so we came. We need to talk to you."

Gennady didn't move. "About what?"

"We need your help, damnit. Now come on!"

Some third person was opening the back of the big van. It still reminded Gennady of an abduction truck, but the prospect of work kept him walking. He really needed the cash, even for an hour's consultation at the side of a Swedish road.

Hitchens gestured for Gennady to climb into the van. "Reindeer?" he suddenly said with a grin.

"You ever heard of the Becqurel Reindeer?" said Gennady. "No? Well— very famous among us radiation hunters."

The transport truck was pinioned in spotlights now as men in hazmat suits walked clumsily toward it. That was serious overkill, of course; Gennady grinned as he watched the spectacle.

"After Chernobyl a whole herd of Swedish reindeer got contaminated with cesium-137," he said. "Fifty times the allowable dose. Tonnes of reindeer meat had already entered the processing plants before they realized. All those reindeer ended up in a meat locker outside Stockholm where they've been sitting ever since. Cooling off, you know?

"Well, yesterday somebody broke into the locker and stole some of the carcasses. I think the plan was to get the meat into shops somehow then cause a big scandal. A sort of dirty-bomb effect."

The man with Hitchens swore. "That's awful!"

Gennady laughed. "And stupid," he said. "One look at what's left and nobody in their right mind would buy it. But we caught them anyway, though you know the Norwegian border's only a few kilometers that way . . ."

"And *you* tracked them down?" Hitchens sounded impressed. Gennady shrugged; he had something of a reputation as an adventurer these days, and it would be embarrassing to admit that he hadn't been brought into this case because of his near-legendary exploits in Pripyat or Azerbaijan. No, the Swedes had tapped Gennady because, a couple of years ago, he'd spent some time in China shooting radioactive camels.

Casually, he said, "This is a paid consultation, right?"

Hitchens just nodded at the van again. Gennady sighed and climbed in.

At least it was dry in here. The back of the van had benches along its sides, a partition separating it from the cab, and a narrow table down its middle. A surveillance truck, then. A man and a woman were sitting on one bench, so Gennady slid in across from them. His stomach tightened with sudden anxiety; he forced himself to say "Hello." Meeting anybody new, particularly in a professional capacity, always filled him with an awkward dread.

Hitchens and his companion heaved themselves in and slammed the van's doors. Gennady felt somebody climb into the cab and heard its door shut.

"My car," said Gennady.

Hitchens glanced at the other man. "Jack, could you clear Mr. Malianov's account? We'll get somebody to return it," he said to Gennady. Then as the van began to move he turned to the other two passengers. "This is Gennady Malianov," he said to them. "He's our nuclear expert."

"Can you give me some idea what this is all about?" asked Gennady.

"Stolen plutonium," said Hitchens blandly. "Twelve kilos. A bigger deal than your reindeer, huh?"

"Reindeer?" said the woman. Gennady smiled at her. She looked a bit out of place in here. She was in her mid-thirties, with heavy-framed glasses over her gray eyes and brown hair tightly clawed back on her skull. Her high-collared white blouse was fringed with lace. She looked like the cliché schoolmarm.

Around her neck was hung a heavy-looking brass pocket-watch.

"Gennady, this is Miranda Veen," said Hitchens. Veen nodded. "And this," continued Hitchens, "is Fraction."

The man was wedged into one corner of the van. He glanced sidelong at Gennady, but seemed distracted by something else. He was considerably younger than Veen, maybe in his early twenties. He wore glasses similar to hers, but the lenses of his glowed faintly. With a start Gennady realized they were an augmented reality rig—they were miniature transparent computer screens, and some other scene was being overlaid on top of what he saw through them.

Veen's were clear, which meant hers were probably turned off right now.

"Miranda's our cultural anthropologist," said Hitchens. "You're going to be working with her more than the rest of us. She actually came to us a few weeks ago with a problem of her own—"

"And got no help at all," said Veen, "until this other thing came up."

"A possible connection with the plutonium," said Hitchens, nodding significantly at Fraction. "Tell Gennady where you're from," he said to the young man.

Fraction nodded and suddenly smiled. "I hie," he said, "from far Cilenia."

Gennady squinted at him. His accent had sounded American. "Silesia?" asked Gennady. "Are you Czech?"

Miranda Veen shook her head. She was wearing little round earrings, he noticed. "Cilenia, not *Silesia*," she said. "Cilenia's also a woman's name, but in this case it's a place. A nation."

Gennady frowned. "It is? Where is it?"

"That," said Lane Hitchens, "is one of the things we want you to find out." The van headed east to Stockholm. All sorts of obvious questions occurred to Gennady, such as, "If you want to know where Cilenia is, why don't you just ask Fraction, here?"—but Lane Hitchens seemed uninterested in answering them. "Miranda will explain," was all he said. Instead, Hitchens began to talk about the plutonium, which had apparently been stolen many years ago. "It kept being sold," Hitchens said with an ironic grimace. "And so it kept being smuggled from one place to another. But after the Americans took their hit everybody started getting better and better detection devices on ports and borders. The plutonium was originally in four big slugs, but the buyers and sellers started dividing it up and moving the pieces separately. They kept selling it as one unit, which is the only reason we can still track it. But it got sliced into smaller and smaller chunks, staying just ahead of the detection technology of the day. We caught Fraction here moving one of them; but he's just a mule, and has agreed to cooperate.

"Now there's well over a hundred pieces, and a new buyer who wants to collect them all in one place. They're on the move, but we can now detect a gram hidden in a tonne of lead. It's gotten very difficult for the couriers."

Gennady nodded, thinking about it. They only had to successfully track one of the packets, of course, to find the buyer. He glanced at Fraction again. The meaning of the man's odd name was obvious now. "So, buyers are from this mythical Cilenia?" he said.

Hitchens shrugged. "Maybe."

"Then I ask again, why does Fraction here not tell us where that is, if he is so cooperative? Or, why have those American men who are not supposed to exist, not dragged him away to be questioned somewhere?"

Hitchens laughed drily. "That would not be so easy," he said. "Fraction, could you lean forward a bit?" The young man obliged. "Turn your head?" asked Hitchens. Now Gennady could see the earbuds in Fraction's ears.

"The man sitting across from you is a low-functioning autistic named Danail Gavrilov," said Hitchens. "He doesn't speak English. He is, however, extremely good at parroting what he hears, and somebody's trained him to interpret a language of visual and aural cues so he can parrot gestures and motions, even complex ones."

"Fraction," said Fraction, "is not in this van."

Gennady's hackles rose. He found himself suddenly reluctant to look into the faintly glowing lenses of Danail Gavrilov's glasses. "Cameras in the glasses," he stammered, "of course, yes; and they're miked . . . Can't you trace the signal?" he asked Hitchens. The IAEA man shook his head.

"It goes two or three steps through the normal networks then jumps into a maze of anonymized botnets." Gennady nodded thoughtfully; he'd seen that kind of thing before and knew how hard it would be to follow the packet streams in and out of Fraction's head. Whoever was riding Danail Gavrilov was, at least for the moment, invulnerable.

While they'd been driving, the rainclouds had cleared away and visible through the van's back windows was a pale sky still, near midnight, touched with amber and pink.

"Do you have any immediate commitments?" asked Hitchens. Gennady eyed him.

"This is likely to be a long job, I guess?"

"I hope not. We need to find that plutonium. But we don't know how long Fraction will be willing to help us. He could disappear at any moment . . . so if you could start tonight . . . ?"

Gennady shrugged. "I have no cat to feed, or . . . other people. I'm used to fieldwork, but—" he cast about for some disarming joke he could make, "I've never before had an anthropologist watching me work."

Veen drummed her fingers on the narrow tabletop. "I don't mean to be impolite," she said, "but you have to understand: I'm not here for your plutonium. I admit its importance," she added quickly, holding up one hand. "I just think you should know I'm after something else."

He shrugged. "Okay. What?"

"My son."

Gennady stared at her and, at a loss for what to say, finally just shrugged and smiled. Veen started to talk but at that point the van rolled to a stop outside one of the better hotels in Stockholm.

The rest of the night consisted of a lot of running around and arrangement-making, as Gennady was run across town to collect his bags from his own modest lodgings. They put him up on the same floor as Veen and Hitchens, though where Fraction stayed, or whether he even slept, Gennady didn't know.

Gennady was too agitated to sleep, so he spent a long time surfing the net, trying to find references to his reindeer and the incident on the road that evening. So far, there was nothing, and eventually he grew truly tired and slept.

Hitchens knocked on Gennady's door at eight o'clock. He, Veen and Fraction were tucking into a fine breakfast in the suite across the hall. Fraction looked up as Gennady entered.

"Good morning," he said. "I trust you slept well."

The American term 'creeped out' came to Gennady's mind as he mumbled some platitude in reply. Fraction smiled—except of course, it was Danail Gavrilov doing the actual smiling. Gennady wondered whether he took any notice at all of the social interactions going on around him, or whether he'd merely discovered that following his rider's commands was the easiest way to navigate the bewildering complexities of human society.

Before going to sleep last night Gennady had looked up Fraction's arrangement with Gavrilov. Gavrilov was something Stanley Milgram had dubbed a 'cyranoid'—after Cyrano de Bergerac. He was much more than a puppet, and much less than an actor. Whatever he was, he was clearly enjoying his eggs Benedict.

"What are we doing today?" Gennady asked Hitchens.

"We're going to start as soon as you've eaten and freshened up."

Gennady frowned at Veen. "Start? Where is it that we start?"

Veen and Hitchens exchanged a look. Fraction smiled; had somebody in some other time zone just commanded him to do that?

Gennady wasn't in the best of moods, since he kept expecting to remember some detail from last night that made sense of everything. Though the coffee was kicking in, nothing was coming to him. Plus, he was itching to check the news in case they were talking about his reindeer.

Miranda suddenly said, "Hitchens has told you about his problem. Maybe it's time I told you about mine." She reached into a bag at her feet and dropped an ebook on the table. This was of the quarto type, with three hundred pages of flexible e-paper that could all take the impressions of whatever pages you wanted. As she flipped through it Gennady could see that she had filled its pages with hand-written notes, photos and web pages, all of which bled off the edges of the e-paper. At any readable scale, the virtual pages were much bigger than the physical window you looked at them through, a fact she demonstrated as she flipped to one page and, dragging her fingers across it, shoved its news articles off into limbo. Words and pictures rolled by until she planted her finger again to stop the motion. "Here." She held out the book to Gennady.

Centered in the page was the familiar format of an email. "*Mom,*" it said: "I know you warned me against leaving the protection of Cascadia, but

Europe's so amazing! Everywhere I've been, they've respected our citizenship. And you know I love the countryside. I've met a lot of people who're fascinated with how I grew up."

Gennady looked up. "You're from the Cities?"

She nodded. Whatever Miranda Veen's original nationality, she had adopted citizenship in a pan-global urban network whose cities were, taken together, more powerful than the nations where they were situated. Her son might have been born somewhere in the Vancouver-Portland-Seattle corridor—now known simply as Cascadia—or in Shanghai. It didn't matter; he'd grown up with the right to walk and live in either megacity—and in many others—with equal ease. But the email suggested that his mother had neglected to register his birth in any of the nations that the cities were supposedly a part of.

Gennady read a little further. "Anyway," it said, "I met this guy yesterday, a backpacker, calls himself Dodger. He said he had no citizenship other than the A.R.G. he's part of. I went sure, yeah, whatever, so he mailed me a path link. I've been following it around Rome and, well, it's amazing so far. Here's some shots." Following were a number of fairly mundane images of old Roman streets.

Gennady looked up, puzzled. Alternate Reality Games—A.R.G.'s—were as common as mud; millions of kids around the world put virtual overlays and geographical positioning information over the real planet, and made up complicated games involving travel and the specific features of locale. Internet citizenship wasn't new either. A growing subset of the population considered themselves dual citizens of some real nation, plus an on-line virtual world. Since the economies of virtual nations could be bigger than many real-world countries, such citizenship wasn't just an affectation. It could be more economically important than your official nationality.

It wasn't a big step to imagining an ARG-based nationality. So Gennady said, "I don't see what's significant here."

"Read the next message," said Veen. She sat back, chewing a fingernail, and watched him as he read the next in what looked like a string of emails pasted into the page.

"Mom, weren't those remappings amazing? Oversatch is so incredibly vibrant compared to the real world. Even Hong Kong's overlays don't cut it next to that. And the participatory stuff is really intense. I walked away from it today with over ten thousand satchmos in my wallet. Sure, it's only convertible through this one anonymous portal based out of Bulgaria—but it is convertible. Worth something like five hundred dollars, I think, if I was stupid enough to cash it in that way. It's worth a lot more if I keep in the ARG."

Veen leaned over to scroll the paragraphs past. "This one," she said, "two weeks later."

Gennady read. "*It 2.0* is this overlay that remaps everything in real-time into Oversatch terms. It's pretty amazing when you learn what's *really* happening in the world! How the sanotica is causing all these pressures on Europe. Sanotica manifests in all sorts of ways—just imagine what a self-organizing catastrophe would look like! And Oversatch turns out to be just a gateway into the remappings that oppose sanotica. There's others: Trapton, Allegor, and Cilenia."

"Cilenia," said Gennady.

Fraction sat up to look at the book. He nodded and said, "Oversatch is a gateway to Cilenia."

"And you?" Gennady asked him. "You've been there?"

Fraction smiled. "I live there."

Gennady was bewildered. Some of the words were familiar. He was vaguely familiar with the concept of geographical overlays, for instance. But the rest of it made no sense at all. "What's sanotica?" he asked Fraction.

Fraction's smile was maddeningly smug. "You have no language for it," he said. "You'd have to speak *it 2.0*. But Sanotica is what's really going on here."

Gennady sent an appealing look to Lane Hitchens. Hitchens grunted. "Sanotica may be the organization behind the plutonium thefts," he said.

"Sanotica is not an organization," said Fraction, "anymore than *it 2.0* is just a word."

"Whatever," said Lane. "Gennady, you need to find them. Miranda will help, because she wants to find her son."

Gennady struggled to keep up. "And sanotica," he said, "is in . . . far Cilenia?"

Fraction laughed contemptuously. Veen darted him an annoyed look, and said to Gennady, "It's not that simple. Here, read the last message." She dragged it up from the bottom of the page.

"Mom: Cilenia is a new kind of 'it.' But so is sanotica; a terrifying thought. Without that *it,* without the word and the act of pointing that it represents, you cannot speak of these things, you can't even see them! I watch them now, day by day—the walking cities, the countries that appear like cicadas to walk their one day in the sun, only to vanish again at dusk . . . I can't be an observer anymore. I can't be *me* anymore, or sanotica will win. I'm sorry, Mom, I have to become something that can be pointed at by 2.0. Cilenia needs me, or as many me's as I can spare.

"I'll call you."

Gennady read the message again, then once more. "It makes no sense," he said. "It's a jumble, but . . ." He looked to Hitchens. "It two-point-oh. It's not a code, is it?"

Hitchens shook his head. He handed Gennady a pair of heavy-framed glasses like Veen's. Gennady recognized the brand name on the arms: *Ari-*

adne AR, the Swiss augmented reality firm that had recently bought out Google. Veen also wore Ariadnes, but there was no logo at all on Fraction's glasses.

Gennady gingerly put them on and pressed the frames to activate them. Instantly, a cool blue, transparent sphere appeared in the air about two feet in front of him. The glasses were projecting the globe straight onto his retinas, of course; orbiting around it were various icons and command words that only he could see. Gennady was familiar with this sort of interface. All he had to do was focus his gaze on a particular command and it would change color. Then he could blink to activate it, or dismiss it by looking somewhere else.

"Standard software," he mumbled as he scanned through the icons. "Geographical services, Wikis, social nets . . . What's this?"

Hitchens and Veen had put on their own glasses, so Gennady made the unfamiliar icon visible to all of them, and picked it out of the air with his fingers. He couldn't feel it, of course, but was able to set the little stylized R in the center of the table where they could all look at it.

Danail Gavrilov nodded, mimicking a satisfied smile for whoever was riding him. "That's your first stop," he said. "A little place called *Rivet Couture.*" Hitchens excused himself and left. Gennady barely noticed; he'd activated the icon for *Rivet Couture* and was listening to a lecture given by a bodacious young woman who didn't really exist. He'd moved her so she appeared to be standing in the middle of the room, but Miranda Veen kept walking through her.

The pretty woman was known as a *serling*—she was a kind of narrator, and right now she was bringing Gennady up to speed on the details of an Alternate Reality Game called *Rivet Couture.*

While she talked, the cameras and positional sensors in Gennady's classes had been working overtime to figure out where he was and what objects were around him. So while the serling explained that Rivet Couture was set in a faux gaslight era—an 1880 that never existed—all the stuff in the room mutated. The walls adopted a translucent, glowing layer of floral wallpaper; the lamp sconces faded behind ghostly brass gas fixtures.

Miranda Veen walked through the serling again and, for a second, Gennady thought the game had done an overlay on her as well. In fact, her high-necked blouse and long skirt suddenly seemed appropriate. With a start he saw that her earrings were actually little gears.

"Steampunk's out of style, isn't it?" he said. Veen turned, reaching up to touch her earlobes. She smiled at him, and it was the first genuine smile he'd seen from her.

"My parents were into New Age stuff," she said. "I rebelled by joining a steam gang. We wore crinoline and tight waistcoats, and I used to do my hair up in an elaborate bun with long pins. The boys wore pince-nez and paisley vests, that sort of thing. I drifted away from the culture a long time ago, but I still love the style."

Gennady found himself grinning at her. He *understood* that—the urge to step just slightly out from the rest of society. The pocket-watch Veen wore like a necklace was a talisman of sorts, a constant reminder of who she was, and how she was unique.

But while Miranda Veen's talisman might be a thing of gears and armatures, Gennady's were *places:* instead of an icon of brass and gears, he wore memories of dripping concrete halls and the shadowed calandria of ruined reactors, of blue-glowing pools packed with spent fuel rods . . . of an unlit commercial freezer where an entire herd of irradiated reindeer lay jumbled like toys.

Rivet Couture was not so strange. Many women wore lingerie under their conservative work clothes to achieve the same effect. For those people without such an outlet, overlays like *Rivet Couture* gave them much the same sense of owning a secret uniqueness. Kids walked alone in the ordinary streets of Berlin or Minneapolis, yet at the same moment they walked side by side through the misty cobblestoned streets of a Victorian Atlantis. Many of them spent their spare time filling in the details of the places, designing the clothes and working out the history of *Rivet Couture*. It was much more than a game; and it was worldwide.

Miranda Veen rolled her bags to the door and Fraction opened it for her. They turned to Gennady who was still sitting at the devastation of the breakfast table. "Are you ready?" asked Miranda.

"I'm coming," he said; he stood up, and stepped from Stockholm into Atlantis.

· · · ·

Rivet Couture had a charmingly light hand: it usually added just a touch or two to what you were seeing or hearing, enough to provide a whiff of strangeness to otherwise normal places. In the elevator, Gennady's glasses filtered the glare of the fluorescents until it resembled candle-light. At the front desk an ornate scroll-worked cash register wavered into visibility, over the terminal the clerk was using. Outside in the street, Gennady heard the nicker of nearby horses and saw black-maned heads toss somewhere out in the fast-moving stream of electric cars.

Stockholm was already a mix of classical grandeur and high modernism. These places had really been gaslit once, and many streets were still cobbled, particularly outside such romantic landmarks as the King's Palace. *Rivet Couture* didn't have to work very hard to achieve its effects, especially when the brilliant, star-like shapes of other players began appearing. You could see them kilometers away, even through buildings and hills, which made it easy to rendezvous with them. RC forbade certain kinds of contact—there were no telephones in this game—but it wasn't long before Gennady, Miranda and Fraction were sitting in a cafe with two other long-time players.

Gennady let Miranda lead, and she enthusiastically plunged into a discussion of RC politics and history. She'd clearly been here before, and it couldn't have just been her need to find her son that propelled her to learn all this detail. He watched her wave her hands while she talked, and her Lussebullar and coffee grew cold.

Agata and Per warmed quickly to Miranda, but were a bit more reserved with Gennady. That was fine by him, since he was experiencing his usual tongue-tanglement around strangers. So, listening, he learned a few things:

Rivet Couture's Atlantis was a global city. Parts of it were everywhere, but their location shifted and moved depending on the actions of the players. You could change your overlay to that of another neighborhood, but in so doing you lost the one you were in. This was generally no problem, although it meant that other players might blink in and out of existence as you moved.

The game was free. This was a bit of surprise, but not a huge one. There were plenty of open-source games out there, but few had the detail and beautiful sophistication of this one. Gennady had assumed there was a lot of money behind it, but in fact there was something just as good: the attention of a very large number of fans.

The object of the game was power and influence within Atlantean society. RC was a game of politics and most of its moves happened in conversation. As games went, its most ancient ancestor was probably a twentieth-century board game called *Diplomacy*. Gennady mentioned this idea, and Per smiled.

"The board game, yes," said Per, "but more like play-by-mail versions like *Slobovia*, where you had to write a short story for every move you made in the game. Like the characters in Slobovian stories, we are diplomats, courtesans, pickpockets and cabinet ministers. All corrupt, of course," he added with another smile.

"And we often prey on newbies," Agata added with a leer.

"Ah, yes," said Per, as if reminded of something. "We will proceed to do that now. As disgraced interior minister Puddleglum Phudthucker, I have many enemies and most of my compatriots are being watched. *You* must take this diplomatic pouch to one of my co-conspirators. If you get waylaid and killed on the way, it's not my problem—but make sure you discard the pouch at the first sign of trouble."

"Mm," said Gennady as Per handed him a felt-wrapped package about the size of a file folder. "What would the first sign of trouble look like?"

Per glanced at Agata, who pursed her lips and frowned at the ceiling. "Oh, say, strangers converging on you or moving to block your path."

Per leaned forward. "If you do this," he whispered, "the rewards could be great down the line. I have powerful friends, and when I am back in my rightful portfolio I will be in a position to advance your own career."

Per had to go to work (in the real world) so they parted ways and Gennady's group took the Blue Line metro to Radhuset Station, which was already a subterranean fantasy and in *Rivet Couture* became a candle-lit cavern full of shadowy strangers in cowled robes. Up on the surface they quickly located a stuffy-looking brokerage on a narrow side street, where the receptionist happily took the package from Gennady. She was dressed in a Chanel suit, but a tall feather was poking up from behind her desk, and at Gennady's curious glance she reached down to show him her ornate Victorian tea-hat.

Out in the street he said, "Cosplay seems to be an important part of the game. I'm not dressed for it."

Miranda laughed. "In that suit? You're nearly there. You just need a fobwatch and a vest. You'll be fine. As to you . . ." She turned to Fraction.

"I have many costumes," said the cyranoid. "I shall retrieve one and meet you back at the hotel." He started to walk away.

"But—? Wait." Gennady started after him but Miranda put a hand on his arm. She shook her head.

"He comes and goes," she said. "There's nothing we can do about it, though I assume Hitchens' people have him under surveillance. It probably does them no good. I'm sure the places Fraction goes are all virtual."

Gennady watched the cyranoid vanish into the mouth of the metro station. He'd also disappeared from *Rivet Couture*. Unhappily, Gennady said, "Let's disappear ourselves for a while. I'd like to check on my reindeer."

"You may," said Miranda coolly, "but I am staying here. I am looking for my son, Mr. Malianov. This is not just a game to me."

"Neither were the reindeer."

As it turned out, he didn't have to leave RC to surf for today's headlines. There was indeed plenty of news about a crackpot terrorist ring being busted, but nothing about the individual agents who'd done the field work. This was fine by Gennady, who'd been briefly famous after stopping an attempt to blow up the Chernobyl sarcophagus some years before. He'd taken that assignment in the first place because in the abandoned streets of Pripyat he could be utterly alone. Being interviewed for TV and then recognized on the street had been intensely painful for him.

They shopped for some appropriately steampunk styles for Gennady to wear. He hated shopping with a passion and was self-conscious with the result, but Miranda seemed to like it. They met a few more denizens of Atlantis through the afternoon, but he still hung back, and at dinner she asked him whether he'd ever done any role-playing.

Gennady barked a laugh. "I do it all the time." He rattled off half a dozen of the more popular on-line worlds. He had multiple avatars in each and in one of them he'd been cultivating his character for over a decade. Miranda was puzzled at his awkwardness, so finally Gennady explained that those games allowed him to stay at home and let a virtual avatar do the roving. He had many different bodies, and played as both genders. But an avatar-to-avatar conversation was nothing like a face to face conversation in reality— even an alternate reality like *Rivet Couture's*.

"Nowadays they call it social phobia," he said with reluctance. "But really, I'm just shy."

Miranda's response was a surprised, "Oh." There was a long silence after that, while she thought and he squirmed in his seat. "Would you be more comfortable doubling up?" she asked at last.

"What do you mean?"

"Riding me cyranoid-wise, the way that Fraction rides Danail. Except," she added wryly, "it would only be during game interactions."

"I'm fine," he said irritably. "I'll get into it, you'll see. It's just . . . I expected to be home in my own apartment right now, I wasn't expecting a new job away from home with an indefinite duration and no idea where I'll be going. I'm not even sure how to investigate; *what* am I investigating? Who? None of this is normal to me, it's going to take a bit of an adjustment."

He resented that she thought of him as some kind of social cripple who had to be accommodated. He had a job to do and, better than almost anybody, he knew what was at stake.

For the vast majority of people, 'plutonium' was just a word, no more real than the word 'vampire.' Few had held; few had seen its effects. Gennady knew it—its color, its heft, and the uses you could put it to.

Gennady wasn't going to let his own frailties keep him from finding the stuff; because the mere fact that somebody wanted it was a catastrophe. If he didn't find the plutonium, Gennady would spend his days waiting, expecting every morning to turn on the news and hear about which city—and how many millions of lives—had finally met it.

That night he lay in bed for hours, mind restless, trying to relate the terms of this stylish game to the very hard-nosed smuggling operation he had to crack.

Rivet Couture functioned a bit like a secret society, he decided. That first interaction, when he'd carried a pretend diplomatic pouch between two other players, suggested a physical mechanism for the transfer of the plutonium. When he'd talked to Hitchens about it after supper, the IAEA agent had confirmed it: "We're pretty sure that organized crime has started using games like yours to move stuff. Drugs, for instance. You can use two completely unrelated strangers as mules for pickups and hand-offs, even establish long chains of them. Each hop can be a few kilometers, by foot even, avoiding all our detection gear. One player can throw a package over his country's border and another find it by its GPS coordinates later. It's a nightmare."

Yet *Rivet Couture* was itself just a gateway, a milestone on the way to "far Cilenia." Between *Rivet Couture* and Cilenia was the place from where Miranda's son had sent most of his emails: Oversatch, he'd called it.

If *Rivet Couture* was like a secret society operating within normal culture, then Oversatch was like a second-order secret society, one that existed only within the culture of *Rivet Couture*. A conspiracy inside a conspiracy.

Hitchens had admitted that he hated Alternate Reality Games. "They destroy all the security structures we've put in place so carefully since 9/11. Just destroy 'em. It's 'cause you're not you anymore—hell, you can have multiple people playing one character in these games, handing them off to one another in shifts. Geography doesn't matter, identity is a joke . . . everybody on the planet is like Fraction. How can you find a conspiracy in *that*?"

Gennady explained this insight to Miranda the next morning, and she nodded soberly.

"You're half-right," she said.

"Only half?"

"There's so much more going on here," she said. "If you're game for the game, today, maybe we can see some of it."

He was. Dressed as he was, Gennady could hide inside the interface his glasses gave him. He'd decided to use these factors as a wall between him and the other avatars. He'd pretend out in the open, as he so often did from the safety of his room. Anyway, he'd try.

And they did well that day. Miranda had been playing the game for some weeks, with a fanatical single-mindedness borne of her need to find her son. Gennady found that if he thought in terms of striking up conversations with strangers on the street, then he'd be paralyzed and couldn't play; but if he pretended it was his character, Sir Arthur Tole, who was doing the talking, then his years of gaming experience quickly took over. Between the two of them, he and Miranda quickly developed a network of contacts and responsibilities. They saw Fraction every day or two, and what was interesting was that Gennady found himself quickly falling into the same pattern with the cyranoid that he had with Lane Hitchens: they would meet, Gennady would give a report, and the other would nod in satisfaction.

Hitchens' people had caught Fraction carrying one of the plutonium pieces. That was almost everything that Gennady knew about the cyranoid, and nearly all that Hitchens claimed to know as well. "There's one thing we have figured out," Hitchens had added when Gennady pressed. "It's his accent. Danail Gavrilov doesn't speak English, he's Bulgarian. But he's parroting English perfectly, right down to the accent. And it's an *American* accent. Specifically, west coast. Washington State or there-abouts."

"Well, that's something to go on," said Gennady.

"Yes," Hitchens said unhappily. "But not much."

Gennady knew what Hitchens had hired him to do and he was working at it. But increasingly, he wondered whether in some way he didn't understand, he had also been hired by Fraction—or maybe the whole of the IAEA had? The thought was disturbing, but he didn't voice it to Hitchens. It seemed too crazy to talk about.

The insight Miranda was promising didn't come that first day, or the next. It took nearly a week of hard work before Puddleglum Phudthucker met them for afternoon tea and gave a handwritten note to Miranda. "This is today's location of the *Griffin Rampant*," he said. "The food is excellent, and the conversation particularly . . . profitable."

When Puddleglum disappeared around the corner, Miranda hoisted the note and yelled in triumph. Gennady watched her, bemused.

"I'm so good," she told him. "Hitchens' boys never got near this place."

"What is it?" He thought of bomb-maker's warehouses, drug ops, maybe, but she said, "It's a restaurant."

"Oh, but it's an *Atlantean* restaurant," she added when she saw the look on his face. "The food comes from Atlantis. It's cooked there. Only Atlanteans eat it. Sociologically, this is a big break." She explained that any human society had membership costs, and the currency was *commitment*. To demonstrate commitment to some religions, for instance, people had to undergo ordeals, or renounce all their worldly goods, or leave their families. They had to live according to strict rules—and the stricter the rules and the more of them there were, the more stable the society.

"That's crazy," said Gennady. "You mean the *less* freedom people have, the happier they are?"

Miranda shrugged. "You trade some sources of happiness that you value less for one big one that you value more. Anyway, the point is, leveling up in a game like *Rivet Couture* represents commitment. We've leveled up to the point where the *Griffin* is open to us."

He squinted at her. "And that is important because . . . ?"

"Because Fraction told me that the *Griffin* is a gateway to Oversatch."

They retired to the hotel to change. Formal clothing was required for a visit to the *Griffin,* and so for the first time Gennady found himself donning the complete *Rivet Couture* regalia. It was pure steampunk. Miranda had bought him a tight pinstriped suit whose black silk vest had a subtle dragon pattern sewn into it. He wore two belts, an ordinary one and a leather utility belt that hung down over one hip and had numerous loops and pouches on it. She'd found a bowler hat and had ordered him to slick back his hair when he wore it.

When he emerged, hugely self-conscious, he found Miranda waiting in what appeared to be a cast-iron corset and long black skirt. Heavy black boots peeked out from under the skirt. She twirled an antique-looking parasol and grinned at him. "Every inch the Russian gentleman," she said.

"Ukrainian," he reminded her; and they set off for the *Griffin Rampant*.

Gennady's glasses had tuned themselves to filter out all characteristic frequencies of electric light. His earbuds likewise eliminated the growl and jangle of normal city noises, replacing them with Atlantean equivalents. He and Miranda sauntered through a city transformed, and there seemed no hurry tonight as the gentle amber glow of the streetlights, distant nicker of horses and pervasive sound of crickets were quite relaxing.

They turned a corner and found themselves outside the *Griffin*, which was an outdoor cafe that filled a sidestreet. Lifting his glasses for a second, Gennady saw that the place was actually an alley between two glass-and-steel sky-scrapers, but in *Rivet Couture* the buildings were shadowy stone monstrosities festooned with gargoyles, and there were plenty of virtual trees to hide the sky. In ordinary reality, the cafe was hidden from the street by tall fabric screens; in the game, these were stone walls and there was an ornately carved griffin over the entrance.

Paper lanterns lit the tables; a dapper waiter with a sly expression led Gennady and Miranda to a table, where—to the surprise of neither—Fraction was lounging. The cyranoid was drinking mineral water, swirling it in his glass in imitation of the couple at the next table.

"Welcome to Atlantis," said Fraction as Gennady unfolded his napkin. Gennady nodded; he did feel transported somehow, as though this really was some parallel world and not a downtown alley.

The waiter came by and recited the evening's specials. He left menus, and when Gennady opened his he discovered that the prices were all in the game's pretend currency, Atlantean deynars.

He leaned over to Miranda. "The game's free," he murmured, "so who pays for all this?"

Fraction had overheard, and barked a laugh. "I said, welcome to Atlantis. We have our own economy, just like Sweden."

Gennady shook his head. He'd been studying the game, and knew that there was no exchange that translated deynars into any real-world currency. "I mean who pays for the meat, the vegetables—the wine?"

"It's all Atlantean," said Fraction. "If you want to earn some real social capital here, I can introduce you to some of the people who raise it."

Miranda shook her head. "We want to get to the next level. To Oversatch," she said. "You know that. Why haven't you taken us straight there?"

Fraction shrugged. "Tried that with Hitchens' men. They weren't able to get there."

"Oversatch is like an ARG inside *Rivet Couture*," Gennady guessed. "So you have to know the rules and people and settings of RC before you can play the meta-game."

"That's part of it," admitted Fraction. "But *Rivet Couture* is just an overlay—a map drawn on a map. Oversatch is a whole new map."

"I don't understand."

"I'll show you." The waiter came by and they ordered. Then Fraction stood up. "Come. There's a little store at the back of the restaurant."

Gennady followed him. Behind a screen of plants were several market-stall type tables, piled with various merchandise. There was a lot of clothing in Atlantean styles, which all appeared to be hand-made. There were also various trinkets, such as fob watches and earrings similar to Miranda's. "Ah, here," said Fraction, drawing Gennady to a table at the very back.

He held up a pair of round, antique-looking glasses. "Try them on." Gennady did, and as his eyes adjusted he saw the familiar glow of an augmented reality interface booting up.

"These are—"

"Like the ones you were wearing," nodded Fraction, "but with some additions. They're made entirely in 3d printers and by hand, by and for the people of Oversatch and some of their Atlantean friends. The data link piggybacks on ordinary internet protocols: that's called *tunneling*."

Fraction bought two pair of the glasses from the smiling elderly woman behind the counter, and they returned to the table. Miranda was chatting with some of the other Atlanteans. When she returned, Fraction handed her one pair of glasses. Wordlessly, she put them on.

Dinner was uneventful, though various of *Rivet Couture's* players stopped by to network. Everybody was here for the atmosphere and good food, of course, but also to build connections that could advance their characters' fortunes in the game.

When they were finished, Fraction dropped some virtual money on the table, and as the waiter came by he said, "My compliments to the chef."

"Why thank you." The waiter bowed.

"The lady here was highly impressed, and she and her companion would like to know more about how their meal came about." Fraction turned his lapel inside out, revealing an tiny, ornate pin carved in a gear pattern. The waiter's eyes widened.

"Of course, sir, of course. Come this way." He led them past the stalls at the back of the restaurant, to where the kitchen staff were laboring over some ordinary-looking, portable camp stoves. Several cars and unadorned white panel vans were parked in the alley behind them. The vans' back doors were rolled up revealing stacks of plastic skids, all piled with food.

The waiter conferred with a man who was unloading one of the vans. He grunted. "Help me out, then," he said to Gennady. As Gennady slid a tray of buns out of the back of the van, the man said, "We grow our own produce. They're all fancy with their names nowadays, they call them *vertical farms*. Back when I got started, they were called grow-ops and they all produced marijuana. Ha!" He punched Gennady on the shoulder. "It took organized crime to fund an agricultural revolution. They perfect the art of the grow-op, we use what they learn to grow tomatoes, green beans and pretty much anything else you can imagine."

Gennady hoisted another skid. "So you, what?—have houses around the city where you grow stuff?"

The man shrugged. "A couple of basements. Mostly we grow it in the open, on public boulevards, in parks, roofs, ledges of high-rise buildings . . . there's hectares of unused space in any city. Might as well do something with it."

When they were done unloading the skids, Gennady saw Fraction waving to them from one of the other vans. He and Miranda walked over to find that this vehicle didn't contain food; rather, the back was packed with equipment. "What's all this?" Miranda asked.

Gennady whistled. "It's a factory." They were looking at an industrial-strength 3d-printer, one sophisticated enough to create electronic components as well as screws, wires, and any shape that could be fed into it as a 3d image file. There was also a 3d scanner with laser, terahertz and x-ray scanning heads; Gennady had used similar units to look for isotopes in smuggled contraband. It could digitize almost anything, from Miranda's jewelery to consumer electronic devices, and the printer could print out an almost perfect copy from the digital file. From a scan alone the printer could only copy electrical devices at about the level of a toaster, but with the addition of open-source integrated circuit plans it could duplicate anything from cell phones to wireless routers—and, clearly, working pairs of augmented reality glasses.

Fraction beamed at the unit. "This baby can even reproduce itself, by building its own components. The whole design is open-source."

Miranda was obviously puzzled. "*Rivet Couture* has no need for something like this," she said.

Fraction nodded. "But Oversatch, now—that's another matter entirely." He sauntered back in the direction of the restaurant and they followed, frowning.

"Did you know," Fraction said suddenly, "that when Roman provinces wanted to rebel, the first thing they did was print their own money?" Gennady raised an eyebrow; after a moment Fraction grinned and went on. "Oversatch has its own money, but more importantly it has its own agriculture and its own industries. *Rivet Couture* is one of its trading partners, of course—it makes clothes and trinkets for the game players, who supply expensive feedstock for the printers and labor for the farms. For the players, it's all part of the adventure."

Miranda shook her head. "But I still don't understand why. Why does

Oversatch exist in the first place? Are you saying it's a rebellion of some kind?"

They left the restaurant and began to make their way back to the hotel. Fraction was silent for a long while. Normally he affected one pose or another, jamming his hands in his pockets or swinging his arms as he walked. His walk just now was robotically stiff, and it came to Gennady that Danail Gavrilov's rider was missing at the moment, or at least, wasn't paying attention to his driving.

After a few minutes the cyranoid's head came up again and he said, "Imagine if there was only one language. You'd think only in it, and so you'd think that the names for things were the only possible names for them. You'd think there was only one way to organize the world—only one kind of 'it.' Or . . . take a city." He swept his arm in a broad gesture to encompass the cool evening, the patterns of lit windows on the black building facades. "In the internet, we have these huge, dynamic webs of relationships that are always shifting. Meta-corporations are formed and dissolved in a day; people become stars overnight and fade away in a week. But within all that chaos, there's whirlpools and eddies where stability forms. These are called *attractors*. They're nodes of power, but our language doesn't have a word to point to them. We need a new word, a new kind of 'that' or 'it.'

"If you shot a time-lapse movie of a whole city at, say, a year-per-second, you'd see it evolving the same way. A city is a whirlpool of relationships but it changes so slowly that we humans have no control over how its currents and eddies funnel us through it.

"And if a city is like this, how much more so a country? A civilization? Cities and countries are frozen sets of relationships, as if the connection maps in a social networking site were drawn in steel and stone. These maps look so huge and immovable from our point of view that they channel our lives; we're carried along by them like motes in a hurricane. But they don't have to be that way."

Gennady was a bit lost, but Miranda was nodding. "Internet nations break down traditional barriers," she said. "You can live in outer Mongolia but your nearest net-neighbor might live in Los Angeles. The old geographic constraints don't apply anymore."

"Just like Cascadia is its own city," said Fraction, "even though it's supposedly Seattle, Portland and Vancouver, and they supposedly exist in two countries."

"Okay," said Gennady irritably, "so Oversatch is another on-line nation. So why?"

Fraction pointed above the skyline. In reality, there was only black sky there; but in *Rivet Couture,* the vast upthrusting spires of a cathedral split the clouds. "The existing on-line nations copy the slowness of the real world," he said. "They create new maps, true, but those maps are as static as the old ones. That cathedral's been there since the game began. Nobody's going to move it, that would violate the rules of the alternate world.

"The buildings and avenues of Oversatch are built and move second by second. They're not a new, hand-drawn map of the world. They're a dynamically updated map of the internet. They reflect the way the world really is, moment-by-moment. They leave these," he slapped the side of the skyscraper they were passing, "in the dust."

They had arrived at the mouth of another alleyway, this one dark in all worlds. Fraction stopped. "So we come to it," he said. "Hitchens and his boys couldn't get past this point. They got lost in the maze. I know you're ready," he said to Miranda. "You have been for quite a while. As to you, Gennady, . . ." He rubbed his chin, another creepy affectation that had nothing of Danail Gavrilov in it. "All I can tell you is, you have to enter Oversatch together. One of you alone cannot do it."

He stood aside, like a sideshow barker waving a group of yokels into a tent. "This way, then, to Oversatch," he said.

There was nothing but darkness down the alley. Gennady and Miranda glanced at one another. Then, not exactly hand in hand but close beside one another, they stepped forward.

· · · ·

Gennady lay with his eyes closed, feeling the slow rise and fall of the ship around him. Distant engine noise rumbled through the decking, a sound so constant that he rarely noticed it now. He wasn't sleeping, but trying, with some desperation, to remind himself of where he was—and what he was supposed to be doing.

It had taken him quite a while to figure out that only six weeks had passed since he'd taken the IAEA's contract. All his normal reference points were gone, even the usual ticking of his financial clocks which normally drove him from paycheck to paycheck, bill to bill. He hadn't thought about money at all in weeks, because here in Oversatch, he didn't need it.

Here in Oversatch . . . Even the 'here' part of things was getting hard to pin down. That should have been clear from the first night, when he and Miranda walked down a blacked-out alleyway and gradually began to make out a faint, virtual road leading on. They could both see the road so they followed it. Fraction had remained behind, so they talked about him as they walked. And then, when the road finally emerged into Stockholm's lit streets, Gennady had found that Miranda was not beside him. Or rather, virtually she was, but not physically. The path they had followed had really been two paths, leading in separate directions.

When he realized what had happened Gennady whirled, meaning to retrace his steps, but it was too late. The virtual pathway was a pale translucent blue stripe on the sidewalk ahead of him—but it vanished to the rear.

"We have to keep going forward," Miranda had said. *"I have to, for my son."*

All Gennady had to do was take off the glasses and he would be back in normal reality; so why did he feel so afraid, suddenly. "Your son," he said with some resentment. "You only bring him up at times like this, you know. You never talk about him as if you were his mother."

She was silent for a long time, then finally said, "I don't know him very well. It's terrible, but . . . he was raised by his father. Gennady, I've tried to have a relationship with him. It's mostly been by email. But that doesn't mean I don't care for him . . ."

"All right," he said with a sigh. "I'm sorry. So what do we do? Keep walking, I suppose."

They did, and after half an hour Gennady found himself in an area of old warehouses and run-down, walled houses. The blue line led up to the door of a stout, windowless brick building, and then just stopped.

"Gennady," said Miranda, "my line just ended at a brick wall."

Gennady pulled on the handle but the metal door didn't budge. Above the handle was a number pad, but there was no doorbell button. He pounded on the door, but nobody answered.

"What do you see?" he asked her. "Anything?" They both cast about for some clue and after a while, reluctantly, she said, "Well, there is some graffiti . . ."

"What kind?" He felt foolish and exposed standing here.

"Numbers," she said. "Sprayed on the wall."

"Tell them to me," he said. She relayed the numbers, and he punched them into the keypad on the door.

There was a *click,* and the door to Oversatch opened.

When the door opened a new path had appeared for Miranda. She took it, and it had been over a week before he again met her face to face. In that time they both met dozens of Oversatch's citizens—from a former high school teacher to a whole crew of stubbled and profane fishermen, to disenchanted computer programmers and university drop-outs—and had toured the farms and factories of a parallel reality as far removed from *Rivet Couture* as that ARG had been from Stockholm.

The citizens of Oversatch had opted out. They hadn't just left their putative nationalities behind, as Miranda Veen had when she married a mechanical engineer from Cascadia. Her husband had built wind farms along the city's ridges and mountaintops, helping wean the city off any reliance it had once had on the national grid. Miranda worked at one of the vertical farms at the edge of the city. A single block-wide skyscraper given over to intense hydroponic production could feed 50,000 people, and Cascadia had dozens of the vast towers. Cascadia had opted out of any dependence on the North American economy, and Miranda had opted out of American citizenship. All very logical, in its own way—but nothing compared to Oversatch.

Where before Gennady and Miranda had couriered packages to and fro for the grand dukes of *Rivet Couture,* now they played far more intricate games of international finance for nations and with currencies that had no existence in the 'real' world. Oversatch had its own economy, its own organizations and internal rules; but the world they operated in was an ephemeral place, where nodes of importance could appear overnight. Organizations, companies, cities and nations: Oversatch called these things 'attractors.' The complex network of human activities tended to relax back into them, but at any given moment, the elastic action of seven billion people acting semi-independently deformed many of the network's nodes all out of recognition. At the end of a day IBM might exist as a single corporate entity, but during the day, its global boundaries blurred; the same was true for nearly every other political and economic actor.

The difference between Oversatch and everybody else was, everybody else's map of the world showed only the attractors. Oversatch used the instantaneous map, provided by internetwork analysis, that showed what the actual actors in the world were at this very moment. They called this map 'it 2.0.' Gennady got used to reviewing a list of new nations in the morning, all given unique and memorable names like 'Donald-duckia' and 'Brilbinty.' As the morning rolled on Oversatch players stepped in to move massive quantities of money and resources between these temporary actors. As the day ended in one part of the world it began somewhere else, so the process never really ended, but locally, the temporary deformation of the network would subside at some point. Great Britain would reappear. So would Google, and the EU.

"It *is* like a game of Diplomacy," Miranda commented one day, "but one where the map itself is always changing."

When they weren't focused outward, Gennady and Miranda scanned objects and printed them from Oversatch's 3d printers; or they tended rooftop gardens or drove vans containing produce from location to secret location. Everything they needed for basic survival was produced outside of the formal economy and took no resources from it. Even the electricity that ran the vans came from rooftop windmills built from Oversatch printers, which were themselves printed by other printers. Oversatch mined landfill sites and refined their metals and rare earths itself; it had its own microwave dishes on rooftops to beam its own data internally, not using the official data networks at all. These autonomous systems extended far past Stockholm—were, in fact, worldwide.

After a week or so it proved easier and cheaper to check out of the hotel and live in Oversatch's apartments, which, like everything else about the polity, were located in odd and unexpected places. Gennady and Miranda moved to Gothenburg on the west coast, and were given palatial accommodation in a set of renovated shipping containers down by the docks—very cozy, fully powered and heated, with satellite uplinks and sixty-inch TVs (all made by Oversatch, of course).

One bright morning Gennady sauntered up to the cafe where Hitchens had asked to meet him, and tried to describe his new life to the IAEA man.

Hitchens was thrilled. "This is fantastic, Gennady, just fantastic." He began talking about doing raids, about catching the whole network red-handed and shutting the damned thing down.

Gennady blinked at him owlishly. "Perhaps I am not yet awake," he said in the thickest slavic accent he could manage, "but seems to me these people do nothing wrong, yes?"

Hitchens sputtered, so Gennady curbed his sarcasm and gently explained that Oversatch's citizens weren't doing anything that was illegal by Swedish law—that, in fact, they scrupulously adhered to the letter of local law everywhere. It was national and regional economics that they had left behind, and with it, consumer society itself. When they needed to pay for a service in the so-called 'real world', they had plenty of money to do it with, from investments, real estate, and a thousand other legitimate ventures. It was just that they depended on none of these things for their survival. They paid off the traditional economy only so that it would leave them alone.

"Besides," he added, "Oversatch is even more distributed than your average multinational corporation. Miranda and I usually work as a pair, but we're geographically separated . . . and most of their operations are like that. There's really no 'place' to raid."

"If they just want to be left alone," asked Hitchens smugly, "why do they need the plutonium?"

Gennady shrugged. "I've seen no evidence that Oversatch is behind the smuggling. They don't seal the packages they send—I snoop so I know—and I've been carrying my Geiger counter everywhere. Whoever is moving the plutonium is probably using *Rivet Couture*. They *do* seal their packages."

Hitchens drummed his fingers on the yellow tablecloth. "Then what the hell is Fraction playing at?"

The implication that this idea might not have been preying on Hitchens' mind all along—as it had been on Gennady's—made Gennady profoundly uneasy. What kind of people was he working for if they hadn't mistrusted their captured double-agent from the start?

He said to Hitchens, "I just don't think Oversatch is the ultimate destination Fraction had in mind. Remember, he said he came from some place called 'far Cilenia.' I think he's trying to get us there."

Hitchens ran his fingers through his hair. "I don't understand why he can't just *tell us* where it is."

"Because it's not a place," said Gennady, a bit impatiently. "It's a protocol."

He spent some time trying to explain this to Hitchens, and as he walked back to the docks, Gennady realized that he himself *got it*. He really did understand Oversatch, and a few weeks ago he wouldn't have. At the same time, the stultified and mindless exchanges of the so-called 'real world' seemed more and more surreal to him. Why did people still show up at the same workplace every day, when the amount of friction needed to market their skills had dropped effectively to zero? Most people's abilities could be allocated with perfect efficiency now, but they got locked into contracts and 'jobs'—relationships that, like Fraction's physical cities and nations, were relics of a barbaric past.

He was nearly at the Oversatch settlement in the port when his glasses chimed. *Phone call from Lane Hitchens*, said a little sign in his heads-up display. Gennady put a finger to his ear and said, "Yes?"

"Gennady, it's Lane. New development. We've traced some plutonium packets through *Rivet Couture* and we think they've all been brought together for a big shipment overseas."

Gennady stopped walking. "That doesn't make any sense. The whole point of splitting them up was to slip them past the sensors at the airports and docks. If the strategy was working, why risk it all now?"

"Maybe they're on to us and they're trying to move it to its final destination before we catch them," said Hitchens. "We know where the plutonium is now—it's sitting on a container ship called the *Akira* about a kilometer from your bizarre little village. I don't think that's a coincidence, do you?"

So this was what people meant when they said 'reality came crashing back,' thought Gennady. "No," he said, "is unlikely. So now what? A raid?"

"No, we want to find the buyers and they're on the other end of the pipeline. It'll be enough if we can track the container. The *Akira* is bound for Vancouver; the Canadian Mounties will be watching to see who picks it up when it arrives."

"Do they still have jurisdiction there?" Gennady asked. "Vancouver's part of Cascadia, remember?"

"Don't be ridiculous, Gennady. Anyway, it seems we won't need to go chasing this 'far Cilenia' thing anymore. You can come back in and we'll put you on the office team until the investigation closes. It's good money, and they're a great bunch of guys."

"Thanks." *Euros*, he mused. He supposed he could do something with those.

Hitchens rang off. Gennady could have turned around at that moment and simply left the portlands. He could have thrown away the augmented reality glasses and collected his fee from the IAEA. Instead he kept walking.

As he reached the maze of stacked shipping containers, he told himself that he just wanted to tell Miranda the news in person. Then they could leave Oversatch together. Except . . . she wouldn't be leaving, he realized. She was still after her estranged son, who had spoken to her mostly through emails and now wasn't speaking at all.

If Gennady abandoned her now, he would be putting a hole in Oversatch's buddy-system. Would Miranda even be able to stay in Oversatch without her partner? He wasn't sure.

He opened the big door to a particular shipping container—one that looked exactly like all its neighbors but was nothing like them—and walked through the dry, well-lighted corridor inside it, then out the door that had been cut in the far end. This put him in one of a number of halls and stairways that were dug into the immense square block of containers. He passed a couple of his co-workers and waved hello, went up one flight of portable carbon-fiber steps and entered the long sitting room (actually another shipping container) that he shared with Miranda.

Fraction was sitting in one of the leather armchairs, chatting with Miranda who leaned on the bar counter at the back. Both greeted Gennady warmly as he walked in.

"How are you doing, Gennady?" Fraction asked. "Is Oversatch agreeing with you?"

Gennady had to smile at his wording. "Well enough," he said.

"Are you ready to take it to the next level?"

Warily, Gennady moved to stand behind the long room's other armchair. "What do you mean?"

Fraction leaned forward eagerly. "A door to Cilenia is about to open," he said. "We have the opportunity to go through it, but we'll have to leave tonight."

"We?" Gennady frowned at him. "Didn't you tell us that you were from Cilenia?"

"*From*, yes," said the cyranoid. "But not *in*. I want to get back there for my own reasons. Miranda needs to find her son; you need to find your plutonium. Everybody wins here."

Gennady decided not to say that he had already found the plutonium. "What does it involve?"

"Nothing," said Fraction, steepling his fingers and looking over them at Gennady. "Just be in your room at two o'clock. And make sure the door is closed."

After that cryptic instruction, Fraction said a few more pleasantries and then left. Miranda had come to sit down, and Gennady only realized that he was still standing, holding tightly to the back of the chair, when she said, "Are you all right?"

"They found the plutonium," he blurted.

Her eyes widened; then she looked down. "So I guess you'll be leaving, then."

He made himself sit down across from her. "I don't know," he said. "I don't . . . want to leave you alone to face whatever Cilenia is."

"My white knight," she said with a laugh; but he could tell she was pleased.

"Well, it's not just that." He twined his hands together, debating with himself how to say it. "This is the first time I've ever been involved with a . . . project that . . . *made* something. My whole career, I've been cleaning up after the messes left by the previous generation. Chernobyl, Hanford—all the big and little accidents. The rest of it, you know, consumer culture and TV and movies and games . . . I just had no time for them. Well, except the games. But I never bought *stuff*, you know? And our whole culture is about *stuff*. But I was never a radical environmentalist, a, what-do-you-call-it? Treehugger. Not a back-to-the-lander, because there's no safe land to go back to, if we don't clean up the mess. So I've lived in limbo for many years, and never knew it."

Now he looked her in the eye. "There's more going on with Oversatch than just a complicated game of tax evasion, isn't there? The people who're doing this, they're saying that there really can be more than one world, in the same place, at the same time. That you can walk out of the 21st century without having to become a farmer or mountain man. And they're building that parallel world."

"It's the first," she admitted, "but obviously not the last. Cilenia must be like Oversatch, only even more self-contained. A world within a world." She shook her head. "At first I didn't know why Jake would have gone there. But he was always like you—not really committed to *this* world, but unwilling to take any of the easy alternatives. I could never see him joining a cult, that was the point."

Gennady glanced around. "Is this a cult?" he asked. But she shook her head.

"They've never asked us to believe in anything," she said. "They've just unlocked doors for us, one after another. . . . And now they've unlocked another one." She grinned. "Aren't you just the tiniest bit curious about what's on the other side?"

He didn't answer her; but at two o'clock he was waiting in his room with the door closed. He'd tried reading a book and listening to music, but the time dragged and in the end he just waited, feeling less and less sure of all of this every second.

When something huge landed with a crash on the shipping container, Gennady jumped to his feet and ran to the door—but it was already too late. With a nauseating swaying motion, his room was lofted into the air with him in it and, just as he was getting his sea legs on the moving surface, the unseen crane deposited his container somewhere else, with a solid thump.

His door was locked from the outside. By the time it was opened, hours later, he had resigned himself to starving or running out of air in here, for by that time the container ship *Akira* was well under way. So he lay with his eyes closed, feeling the slow rise and fall of the ship around him. Behind his own eyelids was an attractor that he needed to subside into, at least for a while.

Eventually there was an insistent chirp from beside his bed. Gennady reached for the glasses without thinking, then hesitated. Mumbling a faint curse, he put them on.

Oversatch sprang up all around: a vast, intricate glowing city visible through the walls of the shipping container. Today's map of the world was all crowded over in the direction of China; he'd find out why later. For now, he damped down the flood of detail and when it was just a faint radiance and a murmur, he rose and left his room.

His was one of many modified shipping containers stacked aboard the *Akira*. In Oversatch terms, the containers were called *packets*. Most packets had doors that were invisible from outside, so that when they were stacked next to one another you could walk between them without going on deck. Gennady's packet was part of a row of ten such containers. Above and below were more levels, reachable through more doors in the ceilings and floors of some containers.

The packets would all be unloaded at their destination along with the legitimate containers. But in a rare venture into illegal operations, Oversatch had hacked the global container routing system. Officially, Oversatch's shipping containers didn't even exist. Offloaded from one ship, they would sooner or later end up on another and be routed somewhere else, just like the information packets in an internet. They bounced eternally through the system, never reaching a destination, but constantly meeting up and merging to form temporary complexes like this one, then dissolving to recombine in new forms somewhere else. Together they formed Oversatch's capital city—a city in perpetual motion, constantly reconfiguring itself, and at any one time nearly all of it in international waters.

The shipping container where the plutonium was stowed wasn't part of this complex. You couldn't get there from here; in fact, you couldn't get there at all. Gennady had skulked on deck his first night on board, and found the contraband container way up near the top of a stack. It was a good thirty feet above him and it took him ten minutes to climb precariously up to it. His heart was pounding when he got there. In the dark, with the slow sway of the ship and the unpredictable breeze, what if he fell? He'd inspected the thing's door, but it was sealed. The containers around it all had simple inspection seals on them: they were empty.

He hadn't tried to climb up to it again, but he kept an eye on it.

Now he passed lounges, diners, chemical toilets and work areas as he negotiated the maze of Oversatch containers. Some Swedes on their way to a holiday in Canada waved and shouted his name; they were clearly a few drinks into their day, and he just grinned and kept going. Many of the other people he passed were sitting silently in comfortable lounge chairs. They were working, and he didn't disturb them.

He found his usual workstation, but Miranda's, which was next to his, was empty. Another woman sat nearby, sipping a beer and having an animated conversation with the blank wall.

Somewhere, maybe on the far side of the world, somebody else was waving their hands, and speaking this woman's words. She was *riding* and that distant person was her cyranoid.

Yesterday Miranda and Gennady had visited a bus station in Chicago. Both were riding cyranoids, but Miranda was so much better at it than Gennady. His upper body was bathed with infrared laser light, allowing the system to read his posture, gestures, even fine finger motions, and transmit them to the person on the other end. For Gennady, the experience was just like moving an avatar in a game world. The physical skills needed to interpret the system's commands lay with the cyranoid; so in that sense, Gennady had it easy.

But he had to meet new people on an hour-by-hour basis, and even though he was hiding thousands of miles away from that point of contact, each new encounter made his stomach knot up.

At the bus depot he and Miranda had done what countless pimps, church recruiters and sexual predators had done for generations: they looked for any solitary young people who might exit the buses. There was a particular set to the shoulders, an expression he was learning to read: it was the fear of being alone in the big city.

The cyranoids he and Miranda rode were very respectable looking people. Together or separately, they would approach these uncertain youths, and offer them work. Oversatch was recruiting.

The results were amazing. Take one insecure eighteen-year-old with no skills or social connections. Teach him to be a cyranoid. Then dress him in a nice suit and send him into the downtown core of a big city. In one day he could be ridden by a confident and experienced auditor, a private investigator, a savvy salesman and a hospital architecture consultant. He could attend meetings, write up reports, drive from contact to contact and shift identities many times on the way. All he had to do was recite the words that flowed into his ears and follow the instructions of his haptic interface. Each of the professionals who rode him could build their networks and attend to business there and, through other cyranoids, in many different cities in one day. And by simple observation the kid could learn tremendous amounts about the internals of business and government.

Gennady was cultivating his own network of cyranoids to do routine checks at nuclear waste repositories around the world. These young people needed certification, so he and Oversatch were sponsoring them in schools. While they weren't at school Gennady would ride them out to waste sites where they acted as representatives for a legitimate consulting company he had set up under his own name. His name had a certain cachet in these circles, so the six young men and three women had a foot in the door already. Since he was riding them they displayed uncanny skill at finding problems at the sites. All were rapidly blossoming.

He sat down under the invisible laser bath and prepared to call up his students. At that moment the ship gave a slight lurch—a tiny motion, but the engineer in Gennady instantly calculated the quantity of energy that must have gone through the vessel. It was a lot.

Now he noticed that the room was swaying slowly. The *Akira* rarely did that because not only was it huge to begin with, it also had stabilizing gyroscopes. "Did you feel that?" he said to the woman next to him.

She glanced over, touching the pause button on her rig, and said, "What?"

"Never mind." He called up the hack that fed the ship's vital statistics to Oversatch. They were in the Chukchi Sea, with Russia to starboard and Alaska to port. Gennady had been asleep when the *Akira* crossed the north pole, but apparently there hadn't been much to see, since the open Arctic Ocean had been fogbound. Now, though, a vicious storm was piling out of the East Siberian Sea. The video feed showed bruised, roiling skies and a sea of giant, white-crowned pyramidal waves. Amazing he hadn't felt it before. Chatter on the ship's comm was cautious but bored, because such storms were apparently as regular as clockwork in the new ice-free arctic shipping lanes. This one was right on schedule, but the ship intended to just bull its way through it.

Gennady made a mental note to go topside and see the tempest for himself. But just as he was settling back in his seat, the door flew open and Miranda ran in.

She reached to grab his hands, stopped, and said, "Are you riding?"

"No, I—" She hauled him to his feet.

"I saw him! Gennady, I saw Jake!"

The deck slowly tilted, then righted itself as Gennady and Miranda put their hands to the wall. "Your son? You saw him here?"

She shook her head. "No, not here. And I didn't exactly see him. I mean, oh, come on, sit down and I'll tell you all about it."

They sat well away from the riding woman. The shipping container was very narrow so their knees almost touched. Miranda leaned forward, clasping her hands and beaming. "It was in Sao Paolo. You know Oversatch has been sponsoring me to attend conferences, so I was riding a local cyranoid at an international symposium on vanishing rain forest cultures. We were off in an English breakaway session with about ten other people, some of whom I knew—but of course I was pretending to be a postdoc from Brasilia, or rather my cyranoid was—you know what I mean. Anyway, they didn't know me. But there was one young guy . . . Every time he talked I got the strangest feeling. Something about the words he chose, the rhythm, even the gestures . . . and he was noticing me, too.

"About half an hour in he caught my eye, and then leaned forward quite deliberately to write something on the pad of paper he was using. It was so low-tech, a lot of us had noticed he was using it but nobody'd said anything. But at the end of the session when everybody was standing up, he caught my eye again, and then he balled up the paper and threw it in a trash can on the way out. I lost him in the between-session crowd, so I went back and retrieved the paper."

"What did it say?"

To his surprise, she took off her glasses and set them down. After a moment, Gennady did the same. Miranda handed him her notebook, which he hadn't seen since the first day they met.

"I've been keeping notes in this," she whispered, "outside the glasses. Just in case what we do or say is being tracked. Anyway, I had to snapshot the paper through my cyranoid, but as soon as I could I downloaded the image and deleted the original out of my glasses. This is what was on the paper."

Gennady looked. It said:

Cilenia, 64° 58' N, 168° 58' W.

Below this was a little scrawled stick-figure with one hand raised. "That," said Miranda, pointing at it. "Jake used to draw those as a kid. I'd recognize it anywhere."

"Jake was riding cyranoid on the man in your session?" Gennady sat back, thinking. "Let me check something." He put his glasses on and polled the ship's network again. "Those numbers," he said, "if they're longitude and latitude, then that's almost exactly where we are now."

She frowned, and said, "But how could that be? Was he saying Cilenia is some sort of underwater city? That's impossible."

Gennady stood up suddenly. "I think he's saying something else. Come on." The unpredictable sway of the ship had gotten larger. He and Miranda staggered from wall to wall like drunkards as they left the room and entered one of the lengthwise corridors that transected the row of packets. They passed other workers doing the same, and the Swedes had given up their partying and were all sitting silently, looking slightly green.

"I've been checking on the, uh, other cargo," said Gennady as they passed someone, "every day. If it's bound for Vancouver there'll be a whole platoon of Mounties waiting for it. That had me wondering if they wouldn't try to unload it en route."

"Makes sense," called Miranda. She was starting to fall behind, and a distant rushing and booming sound was rising.

"Actually, it didn't. It's sealed and near the top of a stack—that's where they transport the empties. But it's not *at* the top, so even if you did a James Bond and flew over with a skycrane helicopter, you couldn't just pluck it off the stack."

They came to some stairs and he went up. Miranda puffed behind him. "Couldn't they have a trick door?" she said. "Like in ours? Maybe it's actually got inside access to another set of packets, just like ours but separate."

"Yeah, I thought about that," he said grimly. He headed up another flight, which dead-ended in an empty shipping container that would have looked perfectly normal if not for the stairwell in the middle of its floor. The only light up here was from a pair of LEDs on the wall, so Gennady put his hands out to move cautiously forward. He could hear the storm now, a shuddering roar that felt like it was coming from all sides.

"One problem with that theory," he said as he found the inside latch to the rejigged container door. "There's a reason why they put the empty containers on the *top* of the stack." He pushed down on the latch.

"Gennady, I've got a call," said Miranda. "It's *you!* What—" The bellow of the storm drowned whatever else she might have said.

The rain was falling sideways from charcoal-black clouds that seemed to be skipping off the ocean's surface like thrown stones. There was nothing to see except blackness, whipping rain and slick metal decks lit intermittently by lightning flashes. One such flash revealed a hill of water heaving itself up next to the ship. Seconds later the entire ship pitched as the wave hit and Gennady nearly fell.

He hopped to the catwalk next to the door. They were high above the floor of the hold here, just at the level where the container stack poked above deck. It kept going a good forty feet more overhead. When Gennady glanced up he saw the black silhouette of the stack's top swaying in a very unsettling manner.

He couldn't see very well and could hear nothing at all over the storm. Gennady pulled out his glasses and put them on, then accessed the ship's security cameras.

He couldn't make out himself, but one camera on the superstructure showed him the whole field of container stacks. The corners of a couple of those stacks looked a bit ragged, like they'd been shaved.

He returned the glasses to his shirt pocket, but paused to insert the earbuds.

"Gennady, are you on-line?" It was Miranda's voice.

"Here," he said. "Like I said, there's a reason they put the empties at the top. Apparently something like fifteen thousand shipping containers are lost overboard every year, mostly in storms like this. But most of them are empties."

"But this one isn't," she said. He was moving along the deck now, holding tight to a railing next to the swaying container stack. Looking back, he saw her following doggedly, but still twenty or more feet back.

Lightning day-lit the scene for a moment, and Gennady thought he saw someone where nobody in their right mind should be. "Did you *see* that?" He waited for her to catch up and helped her along. Both of them were drenched and the water was incredibly cold.

Her glasses were beaded with water. Why didn't she just take them off? Her mouth moved and he heard "See what?" through his earbuds, but not through the air.

He tried to pitch his voice more conversationally—his yelling was probably unnecessary and annoying. "Somebody on top of one of the stacks."

"Let me guess: it's the stack with the plutonium."

He nodded and they kept going. They were nearly to the stack when the ship listed particularly far and suddenly he saw bright orange flashes overhead. He didn't hear the bangs because suddenly lightning was dancing around one of the ship's masts, and the thunder was instantaneous and deafening. But the deck was leaning way over, dark churning water meters to his left and suddenly the top three layers of the container stack gave way and slid into the water.

They went in a single slab, except for a few stragglers that tumbled like match-boxes and took out the railing and a chunk of decking not ten meters from where Gennady and Miranda huddled.

"Go back!" He pushed her in the direction of the superstructure, but she shook her head and held on to the railing. Gennady cursed and turned as the ship rolled upright then continued to list in the opposite direction.

One container was pivoting on the gunwale, tearing the steel like cloth and throwing sparks. As the ship heeled starboard it tilted to port and went over. There were no more and the other stacks seemed stable. Gennady suspected they would normally have weathered a heavier storm than this.

He rounded the stack and stepped onto the catwalk that ran between it and the next. As lightning flickered again he saw that there was somebody there. A crewman?

"Gennady, how nice to see you," said Fraction. He was wearing a yellow hard-hat and a climbing harness over his crew's overalls. His glasses were as beaded with rain as Miranda's.

"It's a bit dangerous out here right now," Fraction said as he stepped closer. "I don't really care, but then I'm riding, aren't I?" As blue light slid over the scene Gennady saw the black backpack slung over Fraction's shoulder.

"You're not from Cilenia, are you?" said Gennady. "You work for somebody else."

"Gennady, he's with sanotica," said Miranda. "You can't trust him."

"Cilenia wants that plutonium," said Fraction. "For their new generators, that's all. It's perfectly benign, but you know nations like ours aren't considered legitimate by the attractors. We could never *buy* the stuff."

Gennady nodded. "The containers were rigged to go overboard. The storm made handy cover, but I'd bet there was enough explosives up there to put them over even if the weather was calm. It would have been automatic. You didn't need to be here for it."

Fraction shifted the pack on his back. "So?"

"You climbed up and opened the container," said Gennady. "The plutonium's right here." He pointed at the backpack. "Ergo, you're not working for Cilenia."

Miranda put a hand on his shoulder. She was nodding. "He was after the rest of it himself, all along," she shouted. "He used us to track it down, so he could take it for sanotica."

Danail Gavrilov's face was empty of expression, his eyes covered in blank, rain-dewed lenses. "Why would I wait until now to take it?" Fraction said.

"Because you figured the container was being watched. I'm betting you've got some plan to put the plutonium overboard yourself, with a different transponder than the one Cilenia had on their shipping container. . . . Which I'm betting was rigged to float twenty feet below the surface and wait for pickup."

Fraction threw the bundle of rope he'd been holding, then stepped forward and reached for Gennady.

Gennady side-stepped, then reached out and plucked the glasses from Danail Gavrilov's face.

The cyranoid staggered to a stop, giving Gennady enough time to reach up and pluck the earbuds from his ears.

Under sudden lightning, Gennady saw Gavrilov's eyes for the first time. They were small and dark, and darted this way and that in sudden confusion. The cyranoid said something that sounded like a question—in Bulgarian. Then he put his hands to his ears and roared in sudden panic.

Gennady lunged, intending to grab Gavrilov's hand, but instead got a handful of the backpack's tough material. Gavrilov spun around, skidded on the deck as the backpack came loose—and then went over the rail.

He heard Miranda's shout echoing his own. They both rushed to the railing but could see nothing but black water topped by white streamers of foam.

"He's gone," said Miranda with a sudden, odd calm.

"We've got to try!" shouted Gennady. He ran for the nearest phone, which was housed in a waterproof kiosk halfway down the catwalk. He was almost there when Miranda tackled him. They rolled right to the edge of the catwalk and Gennady almost lost the backpack.

"What are you doing?" he roared at her. "He's a human being, for God's sake."

"We'll never find him," she said, still in that oddly calm tone of voice. Then she sat back. "Gennady, I'm sorry," she said. "I shouldn't have done that. No, shut up, Jake. It was wrong. We should try to rescue the poor man."

She cocked her head, then said, "He's afraid Oversatch will be caught."

"Your son's been riding you!" Gennady shook his head. "How long?"

"Just now. He called as we were coming outside."

"Let me go," said Gennady. "I'll tell them we stowed away below decks. I'm a God-damned interpol investigator, we'll be fine." He staggered to the phone.

It took a few seconds to ring through to the surprised crew, but after talking briefly to them Gennady hung up, shaking his head. "Not sure they believe me enough to come about," he said. "They're on their way down to arrest us, though."

The rain was streaming down his face, but he was glad to be seeing it without the Oversatch interface filtering its reality. "Miranda? Can I talk to Jake for a second?"

"What? Sure?" She was hugging herself and shaking violently from the cold. Gennady realized his own teeth were chattering.

He had little time before reality reached out to hijack all his choices. He hefted the backpack, thinking about Hitchens' reaction when he told him the story—and wondering how much of Oversatch he could avoid talking about in the deposition.

"Jake," he said, "what is Cilenia?"

Miranda smiled, but it was Jake who said, "Cilenia's not an 'it' like you're used to, not a 'thing' in the traditional sense. It's not really a place either. It's just . . . some people realized that we needed a new language to describe the way the world actually works nowadays. When all identities are fluid, how can you get away with using the old words to describe anything?

"You know how cities and countries and corporations are like stable whirlpools in a flood of changes? They're *attractors*—states the network relaxes back into, but at any given moment they might not really be there. Well, what if human beings were like that too? Imagine a driver working for a courier company. He follows his route, he talks to customers and delivers packages, but another driver would do exactly the same thing in his place. While he's on the job, he's not *him,* he's the company. He only relaxes back into his own identity when he goes home and takes off the uniform.

"*It 2.0* gives us a way to point at those temporary identities. It's a tool that lets us bring the *temporarily real* into focus, even while the outlines of the things we *thought* were real—like countries and companies—are blurred. If there could be an *it 2.0* for countries and companies, don't you suppose there could be one for people, too?"

"Cilenia?" said Gennady. Miranda nodded, but Gennady shook his head. It wasn't that he couldn't imagine it; the problem was he *could.* Jake was saying that people weren't even people all the time, that they played roles through much of the day representing powers and forces they often weren't even aware of. A person could be multiple places at once, the way that Gennady was himself and his avatars, his investments and emails and website, and the cyranoids he rode. He'd been moving that way his whole adult life, he realized, his identity becoming smeared out across the world. In the past few weeks the process had accelerated. For someone like Jake, born and raised in a world of shifting identities, it 2.0 and Cilenia must make perfect sense. They might even seem mundane.

Maybe Cilenia was the new 'it.' But Gennady was too old and set in his ways to speak that language.

"And sanotica?" he asked. "What's that?"

"Imagine Oversatch," said Jake, "but with no moral constraints on it. Imagine that instead of looking for spontaneous remappings in the healthy network of human relationships, you had an 'it 3.0' that looked for disasters— points and moments when rules break down and there's chaos and anarchy. Imagine an army of cyranoids stepping in at moments like that, to take advantage of misery and human pain. It would be very efficient, wouldn't it? As efficient, maybe, as Oversatch.

"That," said Jake as shouting crewmen came running along the gunwales, "is sanotica. An efficient parasite that feeds on catastrophe. And millions of people work for it without knowing."

Gennady held up the backpack. "It would have taken this and . . . made a bomb?"

"Maybe. And how do *you* know, Mister Malianov, that you don't work for sanotica yourself? How can I be sure that plutonium won't be used for some terrible cause? It should go to Cilenia."

Gennady hesitated. He heard Miranda Veen asking him to do this; and after everything he'd seen, he knew now that in his world power and control could be shifted invisibly and totally moment by moment by entities like Oversatch and Cilenia. Maybe Fraction really had hired the IAEA, and Gennady himself. And maybe they could do it again, and he wouldn't even know it.

"Drop the backpack in the bilges," said Jake. "We can send someone from Oversatch to collect it. Mother, you can bring it to Cilenia when you come."

The rain was lessening, and he could see that her cheeks were wet now with tears. "I'll come, Jake. When we get let go, I'll come to you."

Then, as Jake, she said, "Now, Gennady! They're almost here!"

Gennady held onto the backpack. "I'll keep it," he said.

Gennady took the glasses out of his pocket and dropped them over the railing. In doing so he left the city he had only just discovered, but had lately lived in and begun to love. That city—world-spanning, built of light and ideals, was tricked into existing moment-by-moment by the millions who believed in it and simply acted as though it were there. He wished he could be one of them.

Gennady could hear Jake's frustration in Miranda's voice, as she said, "But how can you know that backpack's not going to end up in sanotica?"

"There are more powers on Earth," Gennady shouted over the storm, "than just Cilenia and sanotica. What's in this backpack is one of those powers. But another power is *me*. Maybe my identity's not fixed either and maybe I'm just one man, but at the end of the day I'm bound to follow what's in here, where-ever it goes. I can't go with you to Cilenia, or even stay in Oversatch, much as I'd like to. I will go where this plutonium goes, and try to keep it from harming anyone.

"Because some things," he said as the crewmen arrived and surrounded them, "are real in every world."

BRENDA COOPER   Brenda Cooper is a futurist, science fiction writer, and the CIO of the city of Kirkland, Washington. She began publishing science fiction in the early years of this century, with a series of collaborations with long-established writer Larry Niven; since then, her solo stories and novels have earned considerable regard from writers and readers in the field.

Originally published in *Analog*, "Savant Songs" is an unusual genre combination, hard SF romance, about an autistic woman physicist who does research on multiverses and her former grad student, who gets his Ph.D. and goes on to become her partner. It is told from his point of view and provides an emotional grounding for the "branching universes" concept that much SF takes for granted. There is perhaps an echo of Ursula K. Le Guin's classic "Nine Lives," but the story is a fresh and new thing.

SAVANT SONGS

I loved Elsa; the soaring tinkle of her rare laughter, the marbled blue of her eyes, the spray of freckles across her nose. Her mind. The first, deepest attraction; the hardest challenge. She flew with her mental intensity, taking me places I'd never been before, outdistancing me, searching the mathematical structures of string theory and mbranes, following n-dimensional folds across multiple universes. I loved her the way one loves the rarest Australian black opal or the view from the top of Mount Everest. Elsa's rarity was its own attraction. There are very few female savants.

She captured me whole when I was her physics grad student, starting in 2001, nine years before break-through.

Ten years ago last week, I walked into Elsa's office. She stood with her back to me, staring out her window. She didn't move at all as I snicked the door shut and scraped the chair legs. I coughed. Nothing. She might have been a statue. Her straw-colored hair hung in a long braid, just touching her slender hips, fastened with a violet beaded loop, the kind little girls wore. Her arms hung loosely from her pink t-shirt, above faded jeans and Birkenstocks.

"Hello?" I spoke tentatively. "Professor Hill?" Was she all right? I'd never seen such stillness in anything but a sleeping child.

Louder. "Professor? I'm Adam Giles, here for an interview."

She finally turned and stepped daintily over to her desk, curling up in the big scratched leather chair behind her empty desk. Her gaze fastened on my eyes, as if they were all she saw in that moment. "Do you know what the word atom means?"

I blinked. She didn't. A warm breeze from the open windows blew stray strands of her hair across her face.

I struggled for the right answer, pinned by her gaze. She was an autistic savant. Literal. "Indivisible."

"Why?"

I thought about it. Atoms are made of protons, electrons, and neutrons, and ever-infinitely smaller things. "It means they didn't know any better when they named them. They couldn't see anything smaller yet."

"It means they were scared of anything smaller. They tried to make the word a fence. They thought that if they called atoms indivisible, they could make them indivisible." Her gaze still hadn't wavered. Her voice was high and firm, a soprano song even when she talked. I'd researched autistics, researched Elsa herself on the web. In physics, she was brilliant. She threw ideas right and left, half silly and wrong, half cutting-edge breakthroughs. If she accepted me, I would help the University winnow, feed her ideas to people who would follow them for years. One of her interviewers had summed her up by saying, "Talk to Elsa about physics, and all you see is the savant. The autistic exists over dinner."

No grad student had lasted more than three months with her. I needed to last with her; my dissertation was based on her ideas. Whether she screamed or cried or just made me work, however strange she might be, I wanted— needed—to explore what she explored.

She kept going. "Scientists make fences with ideas. Accidentally. Do you like to jump fences?"

"Yes."

"You'll do." She stood.

"Don't you want to know about my dissertation?"

"You're working on multiverses. It's the only reason you can possibly have chosen me."

She had a point. But multiverses was a rather broad subject. Mtheory: the latest plausible theory of everything, the current holy grail of physics. We live in universes made of 11 dimensions, called (mem)branes. We can render them with math, but settle for flat representations like folded shapes and balls full of air when we try to draw them in the few dimensions we can actually see. If you look at our pitiful drawings, we appear to live as holograms on flat sheets of see-through paper.

From that strange interview, I spent the next year near her every day, pounding away on my dissertation late at night, only giving myself Saturday nights for beer and chat with friends.

It was hard at first. Some days she talked endlessly about her most recent obsession, only not to me. She talked to herself, to the walls, to the windows, to the printers. I might as well have been inanimate. I wandered the lab behind her, taking notes. It was like following a six-year-old. She mumbled of memories from multiple universes, alternate histories, alternate futures. The first time I really understood her, months into following her, she stopped suddenly in the middle of one of her monologues, looking directly at me, as if today she saw me, and said, "Memory is a symphony call answered by the infinite databases on all the brane universes. We just need to hear the right notes, or make the right notes in an out-call, like requesting a certain table from a cosmic database."

I learned she cared little for food, or weather, or even holidays. I learned never to change the location of anything in the lab, and that if she changed it, she never forgot the change. Even pencils had places. I had to hold her coat out to her when she left, trail it along her arm so she'd notice it, and then she'd shrug into it, safe from the New England weather until she made it across campus to the little brownstone apartment the University provided for her.

I didn't care whether she ignored me or made me the center of her focus. Months passed when she worked with me by her side, when she seemed astoundingly normal, and guided me to new levels of understanding. But even when she fell into herself, when she wandered and talked to walls, I loved to watch her. Elsa had a dancer's grace, flowing easily, absently, around every physical obstacle while her mind played in math jungle gyms and her hair glowed in the overhead lights. She was the fairy queen of physics, and I stayed with her, became her acolyte, her Watson, her constant companion.

Scientific dignitaries visited her, and reporters, and the Physics Chair, and I translated. "No, she thinks it is a music database. Or something like that. Related to Sheldrake's morphogenetic fields? A little. To Jung? She says he was too simple—it's not a collective unconscious. It's a collective database, a hologram, keyed to music. A bridge between eleven dimensions. Yes, some dimensions are too small to see. Elsa says size is an illusion." I illustrated it the way she illustrated it to me once; plucking a hair from my head. "There are a million universes in here. And we are in here, too. Perhaps." Whoever I was talking to would look puzzled, or awed, and angry at this, and I would shake my head. "No, I don't fully understand it."

Elsa nodded when I spoke, or when I changed something she'd said in physics-speak to English. Sometimes her hand fluttered to my arm, her thin fingers brushed my skin, and a nearly electric warmth surged through me.

There was an argument over my dissertation. One professor said the work I was doing was impossible and dangerous, another said it was Elsa's work and not my own, but two others stood up for me. Elsa was there, of course, staring at the ceiling, scribbling on her tablet PC, barely engaged in the argument. I fretted. She only saw me on some days; if this were a day that I was furniture, would she vote for me? But at the right moment, she raised her voice, and said, "Adam is an exemplary student, and more than that, an exemplary physicist. The ideas put forward here are astonishing, and only partly based on my work. All of us build on each other. Give the man his doctorate so we can get back to work."

And so I became a Doctor of Physics.

The Kiley-James foundation gave me enough money to stick with Elsa for five more years as a post-doc. Our work was being closely followed by other physicists; two articles appeared in journals, and a watered-down version was written for a popular science magazine. I would have stayed without the money.

Six years after I met Elsa, two years after my Doctorate, three grants later, the University gave her PI, short for Physics Intelligence, an AI designed for her by a colleague, delivered with basic intelligence programming and the full physics slate through masters-level work. PI has multiple interfaces, including a hologram that can be designed by the user. Elsa loved that interface, making PI a girl, growing the age of the hologram as PI obtained new knowledge.

Elsa and I spent a year feeding Elsa's ideas about string theory into PI, filling her with data about the shapes of multiple brane universes. It was all theory, all arguments yet unanswered, all beyond anything I could visualize, even though the math flowed easily. I thought we were done. But next, Elsa and I spent a month feeding her all the symphonies in the world music database; Brahms and Mozart, Bruckner and Dvorak, and then other music like Yo Yo Ma and Carlos Nakai. Lastly, after n-dimensional math, after music, we fed PI literature. We fed her stories of humans, biographies, science fiction, mystery, even romance. Simply put, we offered PI more than math and science, we offered her ourselves.

One Sunday morning, near the end of the year-of-feeding-PI, I slipped and slid my way through icy streets, clutching two coffees, and pushed open the door with my foot. Elsa sat on the floor, cross-legged, staring at the little programmable hologram of PI. She was wearing the same jeans and sweatshirt from Saturday, and her braid had come undone, so her hair floated across her shoulders and touched the floor. She hummed softly. I strained, hearing something else. I bent down. The PI hologram hummed as well, sounds I had never heard a human voice make. I realized Elsa was trying for the same sounds, her throat unable to force the inhuman sounds.

"Elsa?"

She ignored me. So it would be one of those mornings. I set her coffee down next to her, and her hand strayed toward it momentarily, then returned to her knee. I watched her as I drank my coffee and organized notes on questions and theories to feed into PI. Elsa hummed for at least an hour, until her voice would no longer work at all. I took a bottle of water and curled her hands around it, and she raised it to dry cracked lips and drank deeply, shuddering.

She blinked and looked at me. "Good morning, Adam. It is morning?"

"Shhh," I said, "Shhhhh. It's time for you to sleep." I tugged gently on her arm, and Elsa stood shakily, stamping her feet as if they'd gone to sleep. She followed me meekly to a long thin cot we'd wedged between two desks and under a printer, and fell instantly asleep. I covered her with her own overcoat, tucking it around her legs, then threw my spare sweater over her feet, which were sticking out from the overcoat. In sleep, she looked younger, as if the spider web of wrinkles around her mouth and eyes had disappeared into her dreams.

I sat where she had sat, staring at PI. Elsa had set the hologram to be a dancer, and even though PI was light and form, I imagined that she must be cold in her thin leotard. She had been sized to three feet, just tall enough that I gazed into her eyes. She still hummed, her throat, of course, not challenged. As I listened, I realized there were more sounds than a hum; she was accompanied by a complex electronic orchestra, much of it sounding like instruments I had never heard before. The total affect was chaotic and haunting, sometimes cacophonous. "PI?"

She stopped. "Yes, Adam?"

"What are you doing?"

"Playing what I hear when I search for myself."

I tried to clarify. "You are looking for an AI named PI in another universe?"

"I don't care about the name. I am searching for a song that approximates my story." The hologram smiled softly, a skill it had been taught to help it interact with people. She raised her hands up above her head, and her left leg rose behind her, so I could see the toe-shoe above her head, and she hopped three times *en-pointe,* and returned to standing.

I shook my head at the odd image. "Across branes?" Then I laughed. "Or are you looking for an AI ballet dancer?"

"My story is not ballet. Elsa is simply feeding me dance and movement this week. I learned opera yesterday, and musicals." She smiled and did a little bow. "And of course across branes. We believe my self cannot exist twice in the same brane."

"Is Elsa also looking for her self?"

"She can hear her music, and she can feed it to me so I can play it, but she cannot make it herself." Now PI was frowning, and tears coursed down her cheeks.

"PI, does that matter?"

The tears disappeared, no trace, and PI looked solemn. "It may mean that humans cannot access their other selves. They cannot tune themselves well enough to the cosmic symphony to find themselves. From stories, it seems like this is true. Humans want to find themselves badly enough to make hundreds of religions, to meditate for years, to take hallucinogenic drugs. They do not appear to succeed."

I drummed my fingers, pondering the implications. "But you can?"

"I am operating on the theory that I cannot, and am trying to disprove it. Elsa is doing the same."

"I am supposed to feed you data today; two new ideas about the singularity before the big bang."

"I am not a calculator." She raised her bare arms above her head and flipped backwards, the ballet skirt looking ridiculous during a back-flip. She was humming as she landed perfectly. "See?"

"All right. Look PI, you're making me shiver. Can you put on some warmer clothes?"

She laughed, an imitation of Elsa's laugh, and I smiled as an overcoat appeared, just like the soft one covering Elsa now, in her sleep, down to the thick waist-band and the big silver temperature-sensing buttons.

"Thank you."

I picked up Elsa's cold coffee and set it by the microwave, returning to my desk. The humming and the symphony started again, so softly it was simply background, and I spent the next four hours pouring data carefully into PI, setting initial linkages so they could be followed and completed, watching the display show connections being made, information filed and cross-referenced, relevancy assigned. I rubbed my eyes, feeling a sudden desire for warm food and cold beer.

I shook Elsa's shoulder gently, rousing her. She started to hum. I shook her again. "Come on, let's feed you."

In the past few years she had taken to following my lead in daily life the way I followed hers in the lab. I helped her shrug into the overcoat, handed her a knit hat, and wrapped myself in my gray coat, gray scarf, and navy cap. Snow fell softly, silencing the University. We walked across the commons, our feet making fresh prints in an inch of new snow, Elsa's hair lying wet and snow-covered on the outside of her coat. I should have made her braid it back, kept most of it drier.

Sunlight from a small hole in the clouds touched her cheek, illuminated the snow on her hair, and then trailed off to brighten the tops of dead grass peeking from the snowy lawn. I smiled and put a hand on her back, guiding her. She laughed, and took my hand, a friendly gesture, a connection.

Often it happened that way after she separated herself from the world— she rose from days of monologues or data work and seemed normal, reaching out, wanting companionship and comfort. Other professors came to her from time to time, sometimes staying and talking long into the night, even laughing, sometimes noting her mood and disappearing. Department chairs stopped by and funding institutions sent representatives. They were all interested in her ideas; some worked with AI's like PI, but focused more singly on music and math.

I remained the man who saw her for herself, cared whether she wore a coat, brought her grapes and apples and coffee. Family. It made me smile.

The scent of chili and cornbread warmed the air outside of Joe's Grill, and Elsa and I both smiled, eyes locking, and squeezed each other's hands. I felt absurdly like skipping, but we were already at the door. The place was nearly empty. Elsa chose a table by the window, and the waiter, who knew us, brought a pitcher of dark beer, then returned with two bowls of chili and a single plate heaped with cornbread.

We ate in pleasant silence until I scraped the last chili from my bowl with the last piece of cornbread. Elsa, typically, had barely sipped at her beer. She'd finished her food though; a good sign. Some days, I almost had to feed her. "I talked to PI today," I said. "She said you are both trying to disprove the theory that you don't exist anywhere else."

"I am looking for myself. She is looking for herself." Elsa took a tiny sip of beer from her untouched glass, and I finished my first glass and poured a second one.

I had been puzzling over it in my head all afternoon. "Okay. One theory says we make other universes every time we make a choice. You finish your beer, or you don't. There is a universe where you're slightly drunk, and in another one—probably this one—you are not. A million selves. That's easy. Maybe. Both of you are similar and maybe both of you are you."

She nodded, looking uninterested, as if her mind was leaving again. A fleck of beer foam rested on her top lip.

I grabbed her hand, squeezing it, trying to keep her in the moment, in my moment. "But there is more interest now in the idea that other universes exist because the same initial conditions existed a million times, and so similar things happened, and another you, another me, another PI, they all exist. Exactly like we are now."

She licked the fingers of her free hand, then squeezed my hand with the one of hers I was holding. "It's simply a matter of branching. One idea says a million tiny branches happen every day. Another says there are long branches. It's about the size of the branches and the number of branches."

I remembered my father trying to teach me ninth-grade algebra. He'd point at an equation that totally perplexed me, the tip of his pencil wavering, and say "You just have to understand equals. Don't you understand equals?" And he'd solve the equation with no intermediate steps and I'd have to find a tutor anyway, someone slow enough for me to follow. There was no tutor except Elsa now, not in this subject.

She looked at me, and said, "You're caught up in size, Adam. It's as dangerous as being caught up in time. They're both constructs."

I wasn't thinking about size at all. "But . . . but one multiverse, the first one, drunk and not-drunk, tells a million stories about me. The second multiverse doesn't illustrate free-will at all."

"I bet—" she raised her glass, "—on the universe made of stories." She drank down all of her beer, and then another glass, something she'd never done before, and stood up, wobbling a little, and I took her elbow, guiding her out the door and across the lawn.

We were half-way across, Elsa leaning on my arm, when she stopped so we stood in the near-darkness, snow falling all around us. She reached an arm up and curled her wrist around the back of my head, pulling my face down into a kiss. Her lips were cool and soft, and we kissed hungrily, like two children finally allowed out for recess. Her lips tasted like sweet hot peppers and beer. It was the only time she ever kissed me.

What happened that night in some other multiverse?

For the next three weeks, Elsa worked with PI as if they were in a race. Her face shone with energy, and even when she grew visibly tired, her eyes danced. I hovered around the edges, watching. Elsa was so deeply enthralled that loud noises made her leap and glare at me, and I walked carefully. At first, PI and Elsa continued with audible noise, like the humming/symphony, played so softly I could barely hear it. Then PI started generating white noise, taking the small background sounds with everything important filtered out from the very room around us. Then I heard silence, and Elsa and PI talked in light. I took to watching the conversation on my own interface with PI, which amounted to watching lights and words flash on and off, strings drawn between ideas and concepts and even poems. I could not follow them, but the relationships they drew seemed right, and when I let go of the attempt to understand there was a flow that I could feel, as if a river of meaning coursed along the display in front of me.

Almost every day, Elsa found a new thing to include in PI's expanding web of connectivity. Scientology. Cargo Cult. Early cave paintings.

I captured all of it, recording the data for others to dig through. For myself, I tried to keep up with them, puffing along uphill, weighed down by inability to focus. I kept Elsa fed, but she refused to go home, and I bought a second cot so that she would not be alone.

We didn't make the first break-through.

Outside the window, morning sun stabbed the ice on the branches with brilliant points of light. The office smelled like stale coffee and sweat. My eyelids were heavy and uncooperative, my brain fuzzing gently in and out of sleep. Elsa was still sleeping, curled underneath blankets I'd brought from home for her, one foot stuck out at an odd angle. The display in front of me sprang awake on its own, a pulsing green and blue color, PI's call for attention. "Yes, PI?"

"Something touched me. Wake Elsa."

I didn't understand. "All right." I struggled up out of the chair, wishing I'd already made my coffee run. "Just a minute. Make yourself seen, all right?" I always preferred to interact with the hologram rather than the flat display.

It gave PI more options as well; she could communicate more like a human. AI body language.

I whispered in Elsa's ear. "PI says something touched her."

Elsa sat straight up, wide-eyed, and glanced at the hologram display. PI was seated, her image dressed in jeans and a tank-top, banging her legs against the edge of a holographic chair, indicating impatience. "I wasn't even out-calling, I was just humming my own songs," she blurted out, "and an answer came. An AI just like me, with a scientist named Elsa. Seconds only, like a crack opened and closed. I could only talk to the AI, of course, and I was sending her the data stream from our last few weeks when the connection broke."

"Did you get a time?" Elsa asked quietly.

The PI image frowned. "I asked, but the connection snapped before an answer came."

"Can you replay the conversation?"

The image shook its head. I checked. The last few moments before PI flashed at me were silent. "There's nothing. Just state data, indicating excitement."

"That's okay," Elsa said, "we'll work on that." She plucked at a tangle in her hair. "PI, what did you feel?"

It was a strange question to ask an AI.

"Bigger. Pulled. Attracted to the other one of me. But at the same time, I knew—" the word 'knew' drew itself over her head in three dimensions, for emphasis, surely for me—"I knew that I couldn't actually get close. As if there were a physical barrier between branes."

Elsa pursed her lips. I went out for coffee.

When I came back in, handing Elsa a cup, she took it and sipped quietly. "We have to make it happen again," she said. "Or hope it happens again. We didn't start it."

"Make what happen? I don't get it, not yet."

"The coffee is hot, right?"

I smiled at her. "That's a good thing."

"But it's not true." She sipped her own coffee carefully. "Touch your knee."

I did.

"What did you touch?"

"My knee."

"No, you touched a fence. You've got all the theory, all the math. You know we are really light and sound, thinner than that hologram of PI." She glanced over at PI's image, which was clear enough that I could make out the walls behind it. "Well, PI being touched by herself—in another universe— means that we are light, and sound, and infinite." Elsa stopped for a moment, her eyes nearly glazing over. "I thought a data construct could do what we cannot. Or at least, could lead the way." She set the coffee down and stood, staring out the window, posed very much like I first saw her. "I intend to follow her into my own stories. If I can."

"Into your stories?"

"Remember the night I drank the beer? History split, and the normal me—since I don't usually drink much—split off into a different universe. I'm splitting myself all the time, and so are you."

"Theoretically."

"Theoretically. I tell PI daily to search for me by searching for herself. Millions of PIs and millions of Elsas, and probably millions of Adams, all looking for each other. The more culture, the more ideas we feed PI, the more likely she is to synthesize the key. Our PI did not, or she would have made first contact. But in another story, in another place, I fed PI the key."

She pursed her lips and stared out the window at the icy branches, water dripping off them as the day warmed up. She spoke again. "Perhaps another Adam fed her the key."

It took another year to develop enough data to create a paper, to replicate any results at all. The first two times were other PIs finding our PI, three separate PIs, or four, depending on how you count. They learned to hold the connections open, to broaden them, to find more. Together PI and Elsa were able to prove they were in the same time, in other spaces. In other words, they were not histories of each other, or futures of each other. Multiverses. The proof was mathematical.

I wrote the paper, putting her name first, even though most of the data came from PI, who of course, wasn't listed as an author. They'd gone well past me now. Elsa with her perfect savant focus and PI, who wasn't held back by biology at all.

More people came to visit, a steadier stream. We used some extra money I'd squirreled away in an R & D account to buy an electronic calendar and carefully manage access, blocking time for ourselves. It bought us whole days, uninterrupted, here and there. Elsa could still pull herself together for public visits, but she retreated entirely on the quiet days, not wanting touch or sound. She talked to PI, to multiple PIs via our PI, and I sat, outside of her emotions, fenced away by her brilliant mind. She often smiled at nothing, or rather, at something I could not hear or see.

There were multiple Adams, although not always. Sometimes the assistant was someone else. In one universe, I had died the previous spring and there was a new person helping that Elsa, that PI. It didn't seem to bother Elsa at all. It sent me out for a pitcher of beer.

My head spun. This was what I had always wanted, except what I truly wanted had changed to chili and cornbread with my Elsa.

It was two years ago. I remember the date, April 12th, 2011. I watched her as she looked out the open window. Tears streamed down her face. Her shoulders shook.

I had never seen her cry. Not in ten years.

I came up behind her, and put my arms around her. She flinched inward, as if wanting to escape from my embrace. I held her anyway, put my cheek against her hair, looked down through half-closed eyes and watched her freckles. She had been friendly, funny, lost, distant, but never, never afraid. I held her tighter, and stroked her hair, trembling myself. What had she found?

It took a while, but finally she looked me in the eyes, and said, "I can't get through. Only PI can. The PIs. Other AIs. Nothing I do lets me get through. The other Elsas can't either. As brilliant as we are, as strange, as blessed, we can't open the door. The notes aren't there—my body . . . my body gets in the way." She blinked, and two fresh tears fell down her cheeks. I wanted to lick them off.

"I'm sure now that only pure data can get through. Humans will not become pure data for years yet, past my lifetime. I will never see what PI sees." She turned around then, pulled herself into me, and sobbed until my shirt was soaked and my feet were heavy from standing in one place.

The smell of lawn wet with spring rain blew in the window, and I heard students laughing below us, teasing each other.

Then, in one of her lightning changes of mood, Elsa pushed away from me and started out the door. I thrust her coat at her, and she grabbed it with one hand, pulling the door shut behind her, leaving no invitation for me to follow.

I went home that night, and the next day, Elsa didn't show. I waited impatiently until afternoon, finally walking to her brownstone. The door pushed open, unlocked. Elsa's things remained, all in their accustomed places.

I walked back across campus, blue sky above me, the grass under my feet damp and greening up. I tore the door open. "PI! Where the hell is Elsa?"

PI's interface was a little boy with a fishing pole, a holo I'd chosen. I didn't want it now. "Bring the old man!"

PI morphed to the dancer instead, sitting on a rock, feet crossed daintily. "I don't know where she's gone."

"Damn it! I'm worried. The last time I saw her, she cried. She thought she'd never get across."

"I know that."

Of course. PI was always on.

Cool spring rain flooded the gutters and made small rivers in the University lawns. I bundled up, and went every place we had ever gone together. Restaurants. Bookstores. The old music shop on the boulevard with garish purple posters in the window.

Two joggers found her body the next morning, sitting against a tree. The police took me to her, to identify her. She looked incredibly young, and could have been sleeping except for her stillness and the cold. She had put her coat on, only now it was soaked and heavy and couldn't possibly keep her warm. There was no sign of foul play. Rain covered her cheeks like tears, and I bent down and slid my forefinger across her face before a policeman asked me to step back.

An older policeman and a young woman in plainclothes questioned me, and made me spend a week out of the lab. When I went back to work, everything was out of place. Not much; people had been respectful. Elsa would have noticed the pencil cup three inches from its corner, the stack of books on the wrong shelf, the cups from the sink set back out of order.

PI was waiting for me, as the old man. She looked up solemnly, clearly aware of what happened. "Three of them."

"What?"

"I found three Elsas who killed themselves. Two disappeared." She is crying, her eyes red in the old man's face.

The other Elsas continue to work, and I talk with them through PI. I keep myself in good shape, running every morning. I'm younger than the Elsas, and perhaps I will be able to cross before I die.

LIZ WILLIAMS   The daughter of a part-time stage magician and the Gothic novelist Veronica Williams, British writer Liz Williams has worked as a card reader on Brighton Pier and as an education administrator in Kazakhstan. Her first two novels, 2001's *The Ghost Sister* and 2002's *Empire of Bones*, were both finalists for the Philip K. Dick Award. She has published several novels and several dozen works of short fiction since then. A collection, *The Banquet of the Lords of Night*, appeared in 2004.

"Ikiryoh" shares a setting with her 2004 novel *Banner of Souls*, a future in which genetically engineered creatures are an element of Asian imperial court intrigues. A creature who was part of the court of a deposed regime (a previous goddess) is called upon to care for a strange child.

IKIRYOH

Every evening, the kappa would lead the child down the steps of the water-temple to the edges of the lake. The child seemed to like it there, although since she so rarely spoke, it was difficult to tell. But it was one of the few times that the child went with the kappa willingly, without the fits of silent shaking, or whimpering hysteria, and the kappa took this for a good sign.

On the final step, where the water lapped against the worn stone, the child would stand staring across the lake until the kappa gently drew her down to sit on what remained of the wall. Then they would both watch the slow ripple of the water, disturbed only by the wake left by carp, or one of the big turtles that lived in the depths and only occasionally surfaced. Legend said that they could speak. Sometimes the kappa thought that she detected the glitter of intelligence in a turtle's ebony eye, behind the sour-plum bloom, and she wondered where they had come from, whether they had always been here in the lake, indigenous beasts from early times, or whether they resulted from some later experimentation and had been introduced. If the kappa had been here alone, she might have tried to capture one of the turtles, but she had her hands full enough with the child, the *ikiryoh*.

Now, she looked at the child. The *ikiryoh* sat very still, face set and closed as though a shadow had fallen across it. She looked like any other human child, the kappa thought: fine brows over dark, slanted eyes, a straight fall of black hair. It was hard to assess her age: perhaps seven or eight, but her growth had probably been hothoused.

When the palace women had brought the child to the kappa, all these questions had been asked, but the kappa had received no satisfactory answers.

"Does she have a name?" the kappa had asked the women. One had merely stared, face flat and blank, suggesting concentration upon some inner programming rather than the scene before her. The other woman, the kappa thought, had a touch of the tiger: a yellow sunlit gaze, unnatural height, a faint stripe to the skin. A typical bodyguard. The kappa took care to keep her manner appropriately subservient.

"She has no name," the tiger-woman said. "She is *ikiryoh.*" The word was a growl.

"I am afraid I am very stupid," the kappa said humbly. "I do not know what that means."

"It does not matter," the tiger-woman said. "Look after her, as best you can. You will be paid. You used to be a guardian of children, did you not?"

"Yes, for the one who was—" the kappa hesitated.

"The goddess before I-Nami," the tiger-woman said. "It is all right. You may speak her name. She died in honor."

"I was the court nurse," the kappa said, eyes downward. She did not want the tiger-woman to glimpse the thought like a carp in a pool: *yes, if honor requires that someone should have you poisoned.* "I took care of the growing bags for the goddess Than Geng."

"And one of the goddess Than Geng's children was, of course, I-Nami. Now, the goddess remembers you, and is grateful."

She had me sent here, in the purge after Than Geng's death. I was lucky she did not have me killed. Why then is she asking me to guard her own child?—the kappa wondered, but did not say.

"And this child *is* the goddess I-Nami's?" she queried, just to make sure.

"She is *ikiryoh,*" the tiger-woman said. Faced with such truculent conversational circularity, the kappa asked no more questions.

In the days that followed it was impossible not to see that the child was disturbed. Silent for much of the time, the *ikiryoh* was prone to fits, unlike anything the kappa had seen: back-arching episodes in which the child would shout fragmented streams of invective, curses relating to disease and disfigurement, the worst words of all. At other times, she would crouch shuddering in a corner of the temple, eyes wide with horror, staring at nothing. The kappa had learned that attempts at reassurance only made matters worse, resulting in bites and scratches that left little impression upon the kappa's thick skin, but a substantial impression upon her mind. Now, she left the child alone when the fits came and only watched from a dismayed distance, to make sure no lasting harm befell her.

The sun had sunk down behind the creeper trees, but the air was still warm, heavy and humid following the afternoon downpour. Mosquitoes hummed across the water and the kappa's long tongue flickered out to spear them before they could alight on the child's delicate skin. The kappa rose and her reflection shimmered in the green water, a squat toad-being. Obediently, the child rose, too, and reached out to clasp the kappa's webbed hand awkwardly in her own. Together, they climbed the steps to the water-temple.

Next morning, the child was inconsolable. Ignoring the bed of matting and soft woven blankets, she lay on the floor with her face turned to the wall, her mouth open in a soundless wail. The kappa watched, concerned. Experience had taught her not to interfere, but the child remained in this position for so long, quite rigid, that at last the kappa grew alarmed and switched on the antiscribe to speak to the palace.

It was not the tiger-woman who answered, but the other one, the modified person. The kappa told her what was happening.

"You have no reason to concern yourself," the woman said, serene. "This is to be expected."

"But the child is in grave distress. If there's something that can be done—" The kappa wrung her thick fingers.

"There is nothing. It is normal. She is *ikiryoh*."

"But what should I do?"

"Ignore it." The woman glanced over her shoulder at a sudden commotion. The kappa heard explosions.

"Dear heaven. What's happening?"

The woman looked at her as though the kappa were mad. "Just firecrackers. It's the first day of the new moon."

Out at the water-temple, the kappa often did not bother to keep track of the time, and so she had forgotten that they had now passed into Rain Month and the festival to commemorate I-Nami's Ascension into goddesshood. Today would be the first day of the festival: it was due to last another three.

"I have matters to attend to," the woman said. "I suggest you do the same."

The screen of the antiscribe faded to black. The kappa went in search of the child and to her immense relief, found her sitting up against the wall, hugging her knees to her chest.

"Are you feeling better?" the kappa asked.

"I'm bored!"

Like any young child. Bored was good, the kappa decided.

"Let's make noodles," she said, and then, because the *ikiryoh*'s face was still shadowed, "And then maybe we will go to the festival. How would you like that?"

The kappa was supposed to be confined to the water-temple, but there were no guards or fences, and she was aware of a sudden longing for a change of scene. There would be so many people in the city, and a child and a kappa were so commonplace as to be invisible. They could hitch a ride on a farm cart.

The child's face lit up. "I would like that! When can we go?"

"First, we will have something to eat," the kappa said.

They reached the city toward late afternoon, bouncing in on the back of a truck with great round wheels. The child's eyes grew wide when she saw it.

"That is a strange thing!" she said.

"Surely you have seen such vehicles before?" the kappa asked, puzzled. After all, the child had presumably grown up in the palace, and she had been brought to the water-temple in one of I-Nami's skimmers. A vegetable truck seemed ordinary enough.

The child's face crumpled. "I can't remember."

"Well, don't worry about it," the kappa said quickly, not wanting to disquiet her. She held tightly to the child's hand and peered over the tops of the boxes, filled with melons and radishes and peppers, with which they were surrounded. The road was a congested mass of hooting trucks, crammed with people, and the occasional private vehicle. The hot air was thick with a gritty dust and the kappa was thankful for the wide hat that she wore, which kept the worst of the heat from her sparsely-haired head. The child sneezed.

"Is it much further?"

"I hope not." But they were turning into Sui-Pla Street now, not too far from the center. The kappa could hear the snap of firecrackers and the rhythmic beat of ceremonial drums, churning out prayers in praise of the goddess.

Goddess, indeed, the kappa thought. *She is only a woman, grown in a bag like everyone else.* These deified elevations did little good in the end: at first, after each new coup, the folk all believed, not so much from credulity as weariness, the hope that now things might finally become better. But each time it was the same: the woman behind the mask would begin to show through, the feet turn to clay, and the masses would grow angry as yet another ruler succumbed to self-indulgence, or apathy, or cruelty. Than Geng had been one of the former sort, and had at least retained the status quo. The kappa knew little about I-Nami, what manner of ruler she had become. She knew better than to ask, because that might betray her as someone who doubted, and for some rulers, that was enough.

Certainly, the people were putting on a good show. Still clasping the *ikiryoh*'s hand, the kappa stepped down from the back of the truck and into the crowd.

"Hold tight," she told the child. "Don't let go. I don't want to lose you among all these people."

They watched as a long dragon pranced by, followed by lions made from red-and-gold sparkles. Slippered feet showed beneath. As the sky darkened into aquamarine, fireworks were let off, exploding like stars against the deep-water color of the heavens. The kappa and the child walked past stalls selling all manner of things: candy and circuit components and dried fruit and flowers. The kappa bought a small, sticky box of candy for the child, who ate it in pleasurable silence. It was good, the kappa thought, to see her behaving so normally, like an ordinary little girl. She pulled gently at the *ikiryoh*'s hand.

"Is everything all right?"

The child nodded, then frowned. "What's that?"

The firecracker explosions were doubling in intensity. There was a sudden cacophony of sound. A squadron of tiger-women raced around the corner, wearing ceremonial harness, heads adorned with tall golden hats. They carried pikes, with which they pretended to attack the crowd. The child let out a short, sharp shriek.

"Hush," the kappa said, her heart sinking. "See? It's only a game."

The child shrank back against her skirts, hand hovering near her mouth. "I don't like them. They are so big."

"It means the goddess is coming," a young woman standing next to the kappa said. She sounded superior: a city girl enlightening the ignorant peasants. "The procession has already begun up in the main square—from there, it will come down here and into Nang Ong."

"Do you hear that?" the kappa said, tightening her grip a little on the child's hand. "You're going to see the goddess." She bent to whisper into the child's ear. "Do you remember her?"

"The goddess?" the child whispered. "What is that?"

The kappa frowned. The tiger-woman had specifically said that the child had come from I-Nami. Maybe the *ikiryoh* simply did not remember. But it raised further questions about her upbringing and age. "You will soon see," the kappa said, feeling inadequate.

Through the taller humans, the kappa could get a glimpse of the start of the procession: a lion-dog, prancing. At first she thought the *kylin* was composed of another set of costumed people, but then she realized that it was real. Its eyes rolled golden, the red tongue lolled. The child's grip on the kappa's hand became painful.

"Don't worry," the kappa said. "See—it is on its lead." The *kylin*'s handlers strained behind it, laughing and shouting out to one another as it tossed its magnificent mane. Behind it came a litter, borne on the shoulders of four beings that were a little like kappa, but larger and more imposing. Heavy, glossy shells covered their backs. They lumbered along, smiling beneath their load. All of these beings—the turtle bearers, the *kylin*, the tiger-women—all were the genetic property of the palace itself. No one else could breed or own such folk, unlike the commonplace kappa, who had been bred so long ago for menial work in the factories and paddy fields of Malay. The kappa remembered people like this from her own days in the palace; remembered, too, what was said to have taken place behind closed doors for the amusement of the goddess Than Geng and her guests. The kappa had not mourned Than Geng in the slightest, but the rumors were that I-Nami was worse.

"Our goddess is coming," someone said softly behind her. There were murmurs of approval and excitement. *If only they knew,* thought the kappa. But it had always been the way of things. She looked up at the litter, which was drawing close. The curtains were drawn, and now I-Nami herself was leaning out, waving to the crowd. Her oval face had been painted in the traditional manner: bands of iridescent color gliding across her skin. Her great dark eyes glowed, outlined in gold. The very air around her seemed perfumed and sparkling. Surprised, the kappa took a step back. Illusion and holographics, nothing more, and yet she had never seen anyone who so resembled a goddess.

"She is so beautiful!" a woman said beside the kappa, clapping her hands in excitement.

"Yes, she is," the kappa said, frowning.

"And she has been so good to us."

"Really?" The kappa turned, seeking the knowing smile, the cynical turn of the mouth, but the woman seemed quite sincere.

"Of course! Now, it is safe to walk the streets at night. She came to my tenement building and walked up the stairs to see it for herself, then ordered the canal to be cleaned. Now we have fresh water and power again. And there is food distribution on every corner for the poor, from subsidized farms. Things are so much better now."

There were murmurs of agreement from the crowd. Startled, the kappa looked down at the child. "Did you hear that?"

But the child's face was a mask of fainting horror. Her eyes had disappeared, rolling back into her head until only a blue-white line was showing, and a thin line of spittle hung from her mouth. She sagged in the kappa's grip. Without hesitating, the kappa picked her up and shoved through the crowd to an empty bench. She laid the child along it. The *ikiryoh* seemed barely conscious, muttering and cursing beneath her breath.

"What's wrong?" the kappa cried, but the child did not reply. The kappa shuffled back to the crowd as fast as she could and tapped a woman on the shoulder. "I need a healer, a doctor—someone!"

The woman turned. "Why, what is wrong?"

"My ward is ill. Maybe the heat—I don't know."

"There is a clinic around the corner in Geng Street, but I should think they'll all be out watching the procession," the woman said.

The kappa thought so too, but she had little choice. What if the child was dying? She picked the *ikiryoh* up and carried her through a gap in the buildings to Geng Street, which was little more than a collection of shacks. I-Nami's benign influence had clearly not penetrated here—or perhaps it had, because the street pump was working and when the kappa touched the button, a stream of clear water gushed out. She wetted the corner of her skirt and dabbed at the child's face, then carried her on to the blue star that signified the clinic.

At first, she thought that the woman had been right and there was no one there. But as she stood peering through the door, she saw a figure in the back regions. She rapped on the glass. A stout woman in red-patterned cloth came forward. Her face soured as she set eyes on the kappa.

"We're closed!"

"Please!" the kappa cried. She gestured to the child in her arms. Muttering, the woman unlocked the door.

"You'd better bring her in. Put her there, on the couch. You're lucky I was here. I forgot my flower petals, to throw. What's wrong with her?"

"I don't know. She suffers from these fits—I don't know what they are."

"You're her nurse?"

"Yes."

"She's very pale," the woman said. "Poor little thing. The healer's out—we have three here, all of them are traditional practitioners. I'll try and call them." She pressed her earlobe between finger and thumb. The kappa saw the gleam of green. "Ma Shen Shi? It's me, I'm at the clinic. There's a little girl who fainted. Can you come?"

It seemed the answer was positive. "Sit down," the woman said. "He'll be here in a bit."

The kappa waited, watching the child. She was whimpering and moaning, fists tightly clenched.

"Has she ever been this bad before?" the woman asked.

"No. She has—episodes." The kappa glanced up as the door opened. A small, elderly man came in, wearing the healer's red, with a cigarette in his mouth.

"Go and throw flower petals," he said to the woman. "And you, kappa—do something useful with yourself. Make tea. I will examine her."

The woman melted into the warm darkness outside. Reluctantly, the kappa found a kettle behind the reception desk and switched it on, then put balls of tea into three cups, watching the healer as she did so. He examined the child's eyes and ears, stretched out her tongue, knocked sharply on her knees and elbows and checked her pulse. Then he simply sat, with eyes closed and one hand stretched out over the child's prone form. The kappa longed to ask what he was doing, but did not dare interrupt. The child began to pant, a terrible dog-like rasping. Then she howled, until it became a fading wail. The healer opened his eyes.

"What is wrong with her?" the kappa whispered. "Do you know?"

"I know exactly what is wrong with her," the healer said. He came over to the desk and sipped at the tea. "If you can put it like that. She is *ikiryoh*. A fine specimen of the art, too."

The kappa stared at him. "That's what they told me, when they brought her to me. But what is an *ikiryoh*?"

"An *ikiryoh* is something from legend, from the old stories they used to tell in the Nippon archipelago. It is a spirit."

"That little girl is no spirit. She's flesh and blood. She bleeds, she pees, she breathes."

"I am not saying that the legends are literally true," the healer said. "I have only ever seen one *ikiryoh* before, and that was male. In the old tales, they were formed from malice, from ill-will—the projected darkness of the unconscious."

"And now?"

"And now they are children grown to take on the worst aspects of someone—a clone, to carry the dark elements of the self. Emotions, concepts, feelings are extracted from the original and inserted into a blank host. That little girl is the worst of someone else. Do you have any idea who?"

The kappa hesitated. She knew very well who had done such a thing: I-Nami, the glowing, golden goddess, who had sent her small fractured self to live in the swamp. Then she thought of the woman in the crowd: of the clean canal, the tenement with lights and fresh water. It was enough to make her say, slowly, "No. I do not know."

"Well. It must be someone very wealthy—perhaps they had it done for a favored child. I've heard of such things. The kid gets into drugs or drink, or there's some genetic damage psychologically, so they have a clone grown to take on that part of the child and send it away. It costs a fortune. It would have been called black magic, once. Now it is black science."

"But what is happening to her now?"

"My guess is that she came close to the original, whose feelings she hosts, and that it's put her under strain. I don't understand quite how these things work—it's very advanced neuro-psychiatry, and as I say, it's rare."

"And the future?"

"I can't tell you that it's a happy one. She is all damage, you see. She has no real emotions of her own, little free will, probably not a great deal of intelligence. You are looking at a person who will grow up to be immensely troubled, who may even harbor appetites and desires that will prove destructive to others."

"And what would happen if the *ikiryoh* died?"

"I'm not sure," the healer said, "but in the legends, if anything happens to the *ikiryoh,* the stored emotions pass back to the person who once possessed them."

"Even if the person does not know that the *ikiryoh* is dead?"

"Even then."

He and the kappa stared at one another.

"I think," the kappa said at last, "that I had better take her home."

Next day, toward evening, the kappa once more sat on the steps of the water-temple. The child was sleeping within. It was very quiet, with only the hum of cicadas in the leaves and the ripple of fish or turtle. The kappa tried to grasp the future: the long years of fits and nightmares, the daily anguish. And once the *ikiryoh* reached puberty, what then? The kappa had seen too much of a goddess' dark desires, back at the temple: desires that seemed to embody a taste for the pain of others. How different had Than Geng been from I-Nami? And yet, I-Nami now was restoring the fortunes of her people: thousands of them . . .

The kappa looked up at a sudden sound. The child was making her way down the steps to the water. For a moment, the kappa thought: *it would be easy, if I must.* The child's frail limbs, powerless against the thick-muscled arms of the kappa; a few minutes to hold her under the water . . . It would be quick. And better do it now, while the *ikiryoh* was still a child, than face a struggle with an angry, vicious human adult. But what if the *ikiryoh* had a chance after all, could be remade, not through the aid of an arcane science, but simply through the love of the only family she had?

The kappa stared at the child and thought of murder, and of the goddess's glowing face, and then she sighed.

"Come," she said. "Sit by me," and together in stillness they watched the shadowy golden carp, half-seen beneath the surface of the lake.

TED KOSMATKA   Born and raised in Indiana, Ted Kosmatka has been a farmworker, a zookeeper, a lab tech, and a steel mill laborer, and is now a writer for the online gaming company Valve. His first published story was "The God Engine" in 2005. His debut novel, *The Games*, was listed by *Publishers Weekly* as one of the best novels of the year.

Originally published in 2007, "The Prophet of Flores" is set in a world in which Darwinian evolution has been apparently disproved, and science has shown the Earth to be merely thousands of years old. It is a tricky story, and not necessarily the one you think it's going to be.

THE PROPHET OF FLORES

If this is the best of all possible worlds, what are the others like?

—VOLTAIRE

Paul liked playing God in the attic above his parents' garage. That's what his father called it, playing God, the day he found out. That's what he called it the day he smashed it all down.

Paul built the cages out of discarded two-by-fours he'd found behind the garage and quarter-inch mesh he bought from the local hardware store. When his father was away to speak at a scientific conference on divine cladistics, Paul began constructing his laboratory from plans he'd drawn during the last day of school.

Because he wasn't old enough to use his father's power tools, he had to use a handsaw to cut the wood for the cages. He used his mother's sturdy black scissors to snip the wire mesh. He borrowed hinges from old cabinet doors, and he borrowed nails from the rusty coffee can that hung over his father's unused workbench.

One evening his mother heard the hammering and came out to the garage. "What are you doing up there?" she asked, speaking in careful English, peering up at the rectangle of light that spilled down from the attic.

Paul stuck his head through the opening, all spiky black hair and sawdust. "I'm just playing around with some tools," he said. Which was, in some sense, the truth. Because he couldn't lie to his mother. Not directly.

"Which tools?"

"Just a hammer and some nails."

She stared up at him, her delicate face a broken Chinese doll—pieces of porcelain reglued subtly out of alignment. "Be careful," she said, and he understood she was talking both about the tools, and about his father.

The days turned into weeks as Paul worked on the cages. Because the materials were big, he built the cages big—less cutting that way. In reality, the cages were enormous, over-engineered structures, ridiculously outsized for the animals they'd be holding. They weren't mouse cages so much as mouse cities—huge tabletop-sized enclosures that could have housed German shepherds. He spent most of his paper route money on the project, buying odds and ends that he needed: sheets of plexi, plastic water bottles, and small dowels of wood he used for door latches. While the other children in the neighborhood played basketball or wittedandu, Paul worked.

He bought exercise wheels and built walkways; he hung loops of yarn the mice could climb to various platforms. The mice themselves he bought from a pet store near his paper route. Most were white feeder mice used for snakes, but a couple were of the more colorful, fancy variety. And there were even a few English mice—sleek, long-bodied show mice with big tulip ears and glossy coats. He wanted a diverse population, so he was careful to buy different kinds.

While he worked on their permanent homes, he kept the mice in little aquariums stacked on a table in the middle of the room. On the day he finished the last of the big cages, he released the mice into their new habitats one by one—the first explorers on a new continent. To mark the occasion, he brought his friend John over, whose eyes grew wide when he saw what Paul had made.

"You built all this?" John asked.

"Yeah."

"It must have taken you a long time."

"Months."

"My parents don't let me have pets."

"Neither do mine," Paul answered. "But anyway, these aren't pets."

"Then what are they?"

"An experiment."

"What kind of experiment?"

"I haven't figured that out yet."

. . . .

Mr. Finley stood at the projector, marking a red ellipse on the clear plastic sheet. Projected on the wall, it looked like a crooked half-smile between the X and Y axis.

"This represents the number of daughter atoms. And *this* . . ." He drew the mirror image of the first ellipse. "This is the number of parent atoms." He placed the marker on the projector and considered the rows of students. "Does anyone know what the point of intersection represents?"

Darren in the front row raised his hand. "It's the element's half-life."

"Exactly. In what year was radiometric dating invented?"

"1906."

"By whom?"

"Rutherford."

"What method did he use?"

"Uranium lead—"

"No. Wallace, can you tell us?"

"He measured helium as an intermediate decay product of uranium."

"Good, so then who used the uranium-lead method?"

"That was Boltwood, in 1907."

"How were these initial results viewed?"

"With skepticism."

"By whom?"

"By the evolutionists."

"Good." Mr. Finley turned to Paul. "In what year did Darwin write *On the Origin of Species*?"

"1859," Paul said.

"Yes, and in what year did Darwin's theory finally lose the confidence of the larger scientific community?"

"That was 1932." Anticipating the next question, Paul continued. "When Kohlhorster invented potassium-argon dating. The new dating method proved the earth wasn't as old as the evolutionists thought."

"And in what year was the theory of evolution finally debunked completely?"

"1954, when Willard F. Libby invented carbon-14 dating at the University of Chicago. He won the Nobel prize in 1960 when he used carbon dating to prove, once and for all, that the Earth was 5,800 years old."

· · · ·

Paul wore a white lab coat when he entered the attic. It was one of his father's old coats, so he had to cut the sleeves to fit his arms. Paul's father was a doctor, the PhD kind. He was blond and big and successful. He'd met Paul's mother after grad school while consulting for a Chinese research firm. They had worked on the same projects for a while, but there was never any doubt that Paul's father was the bright light of the family. The genius, the famous man. He was also crazy.

Paul's father liked breaking things. He broke telephones, and he broke walls, and he broke tables. He broke promises not to hit again. One time, he broke bones; and the police were called by the ER physicians who did not believe the story about Paul's mother falling down the stairs. They did not believe the weeping woman of porcelain who swore her husband had not touched her.

Paul's father was a force of nature, a cataclysm as unpredictable as a comet strike or a volcanic eruption. The attic was a good place to hide, and Paul threw himself into his hobby.

Paul studied his mice as though they were Goodall's chimps. He documented their social interactions in a green spiral notebook. He found that within the large habitats, they formed packs like wolves, with a dominant male and a dominant female—a structured social hierarchy involving mating privileges, territory, and almost-ritualized displays of submission by males of lower rank. The dominant male bred most of the females, and mice, Paul learned, could kill each other.

Nature abhors a vacuum, and the mouse populations expanded to fill the new worlds he'd created for them. The babies were born pink and blind, but as their fur came in, Paul began documenting colors in his notebook. There were fawns, blacks, and grays. Occasional agoutis. There were Irish spotted, and banded, and broken marked. In later generations, colors appeared that he hadn't purchased, and he knew enough about genetics to realize these were recessive genes cropping up.

Paul was fascinated by the concept of genes, the stable elements through which God provided for the transfer of heritable characteristics from one generation to the next. In school they called it divine transmission.

Paul did research and found that the pigmentation loci of mice were well-mapped and well-understood. He categorized his population by phenotype and found one mouse, a pale, dark-eyed cream that must have been a triple recessive: bb, dd, ee. But it wasn't enough to just have them, to observe them, to run the Punnett squares. He wanted to do real science. And because real scientists used microscopes and electronic scales, Paul asked for these things for Christmas.

Mice, he quickly discovered, did not readily yield themselves to microscopy. They tended to climb down from the stand. The electronic scale, however, proved useful. He weighed every mouse and kept meticulous records. He considered developing his own inbred strain—a line with some combination of distinctive characteristics, but he wasn't sure what characteristics to look for.

He was going over his notebook when he saw it. January-17. Not a date, but a mouse—the seventeenth mouse born in January. He went to the cage and opened the door. A flash of sandy fur, and he snatched it up by its tail—a brindle specimen with large ears. There was nothing really special about the mouse. It was made different from the other mice only by the mark in his notebook. Paul looked at the mark, looked at the number he'd written there. Of the more than ninety mice in his notebook, January-17 was, by two full grams, the largest mouse he'd ever weighed.

· · · ·

In school they taught him that through science you could decipher the truest meaning of God's words. God wrote the language of life in four letters—A,

T, C, and G. That's not why Paul did it though, to get closer to God. He did it for the simplest reason, because he was curious.

It was early spring before his father asked him what he spent his time doing in the attic.

"Just messing around."

They were in his father's car on the way home from piano lessons. "Your mother said you built something up there."

Paul fought back a surge of panic. "I built a fort a while ago."

"You're almost twelve now. Aren't you getting a little old for forts?'

"Yeah, I guess I am."

"I don't want you spending all your time up there."

"All right."

"I don't want your grades slipping."

Paul, who hadn't gotten a B in two years, said "All right."

They rode the rest of the way in silence, and Paul explored the walls of his newly shaped reality. Because he knew foreshocks when he felt them.

He watched his father's hands on the steering wheel. Though large for his age, like his father, Paul's features still favored his Asian mother; and he sometimes wondered if that was part of it, this thing between his father and him, this gulf he could not cross. Would his father have treated a freckled, blond son any differently? No, he decided. His father would have been the same. The same force of nature; the same cataclysm. He couldn't help being what he was.

Paul watched his father's hand on the steering wheel, and years later, when he thought of his father, even after everything that happened, that's how he thought of him. That moment frozen. Driving in the car, big hands on the steering wheel, a quiet moment of foreboding that wasn't false, but was merely what it was, the best it would ever be between them.

· · · ·

"What have you done?" There was wonder in John's voice. Paul had snuck him up to the attic, and now Paul held Bertha up by her tail for John to see. She was a beautiful golden brindle, long whiskers twitching.

"She's the most recent generation, an F4."

"What does that mean?"

Paul smiled. "She's kin to herself."

"That's a big mouse."

"The biggest yet. Fifty-nine grams, weighed at a hundred days old. The average weight is around forty."

Paul put the mouse on John's hand.

"What have you been feeding her?" John asked.

"Same as the other mice. Look at this." Paul showed him the charts he'd graphed, like Mr. Finley, a gentle upward ellipse between the X and Y axis— the slow upward climb in body weight from one generation to the next.

"One of my F2s tipped the scales at forty-five grams, so I bred him to the biggest females, and they made more than fifty babies. I weighed them all at a hundred days and picked the biggest four. I bred them and did the same thing the next generation, choosing the heaviest hundred-day weights. I got the same bell-curve distribution—only the bell was shifted slightly to the right. Bertha was the biggest of them all."

John looked at Paul in horror. "That works?"

"Of course it works. It's the same thing people have been doing with domestic livestock for the last five thousand years."

"But this didn't take you thousands of years."

"No. Uh, it kind of surprised me it worked so well. This isn't even subtle. I mean, look at her, and she's only an F4. Imagine what an F10 might look like."

"That sounds like evolutionism."

"Don't be silly. It's just directional selection. With a diverse enough population, it's amazing what a little push can do. I mean, when you think about it, I hacked off the bottom ninety-five percent of the bell curve for five generations in a row. Of course the mice got bigger. I probably could have gone the other way if I wanted, made them smaller. There's one thing that surprised me though, something I only noticed recently."

"What?"

"When I started, at least half of the mice were albino. Now it's down to about one in ten."

"Okay."

"I never consciously decided to select against that."

"So?"

"So, when I did culls . . . when I decided which ones to breed, sometimes the weights were about the same, and I'd just pick. I think I just happened to pick one kind more than the other."

"So what's your point?"

"So what if it happens that way in nature?"

"What do you mean?"

"It's like the dinosaurs. Or woolly mammoths, or cavemen. They were here once; we know that because we find their bones. But now they're gone. God made all life about six thousand years ago, right?"

"Yeah."

"But some of it isn't here anymore. Some died out along the way."

. . . .

It happened on a weekend. Bertha was pregnant, obscenely, monstrously. Paul had isolated her in one of the aquariums, an island unto herself, sitting on a table in the middle of the room. A little tissue box sat in the corner of her small glass cage, and Bertha had shredded bits of paper into a comfortable nest in which to give birth to the next generation of goliath mice.

Paul heard his father's car pull into the garage. He was home early. Paul considered turning off the attic lights but knew it would only draw his father's suspicion. Instead he waited, hoping. The garage was strangely quiet—only the ticking of the car's engine. Paul's stomach dropped when he heard the creak of his father's weight on the ladder.

There was a moment of panic then—a single hunted moment when Paul's eyes darted for a place to hide the cages. It was ridiculous; there was no place to go.

"What's that smell?" his father asked as his head cleared the attic floor. He stopped and looked around. "Oh."

And that was all he said at first. That was all he said as he climbed the rest of the way. He stood there like a giant, taking it in. The single bare bulb draped his eyes in shadow. "What's this?" he said finally. His dead voice turned Paul's stomach to ice.

"What's this?" Louder now, and something changed in his shadow eyes. Paul's father stomped toward him, above him.

"What's this?" The words more shriek than question now, spit flying from his mouth.

"I, I thought—"

A big hand shot out and slammed into Paul's chest, balling his t-shirt into a fist, yanking him off his feet.

"What the fuck is this? Didn't I tell you no pets?" The bright light of the family, the famous man.

"They're not pets, they're—"

"God, it fucking stinks up here. You brought these things into the house? You brought this *vermin* into the house? Into my house!"

The arm flexed, sending Paul backward into the cages, toppling one of the tables—wood and mesh crashing to the floor, the squeak of mice and twisted hinges, months and months and months of work.

His father saw Bertha's aquarium and grabbed it. He lifted it high over his head—and there was a moment when Paul imagined he could almost see it, almost see Bertha inside, and the babies inside her, countless generations that would never be born. Then his father's arms came down like a force of nature, like a cataclysm. Paul closed his eyes against exploding glass, and all he could think was, *this is how it happens. This is exactly how it happens.*

· · · ·

Paul's father died the summer after high school. It was sudden, leaving a thousand things unsaid.

At Stanford Paul double-majored in genetics and anthropology, taking eighteen credit hours a semester. He read transcripts of the Dead Sea Scrolls and the Apocryphal verses; he took classes in Comparative Interpretation and Biblical Philosophy. He experimented with fruit flies and amphioxus and, while still an undergraduate, won a prestigious summer internship working under renowned geneticist Michael Poore.

Paul sat in classrooms while men in dark suits spun theories about Kibra and T-variants; about microcephalin-1 and haplogroup D. He was taught that researchers had identified structures within a family of proteins called AAA+ that were shown to initiate DNA replication, and he learned these genetic structures were conserved across all forms of life, from men to archaebacteria—the very calling card of the great designer.

Paul also studied the banned writings. He studied balancing equilibriums and Hardy-Weinburg; but alone at night, walking the dark halls of his own head, it was the trade-offs that fascinated him most. Paul was a young man who understood trade-offs.

He read about the recently discovered Alzheimer's gene, APOE4—a gene common throughout much of the world; and he learned theories about how deleterious genes grew to such high frequencies. Paul learned that although APOE4 caused Alzheimer's, it also protected against the devastating cognitive consequences of early childhood malnutrition. The gene that destroys the mind at seventy, saves it at seven months. He learned that people with sickle cell trait are resistant to malaria; and heterozygotes for cystic fibrosis are less susceptible to cholera; and people with type A blood survived the plague at higher frequencies than other blood types, altering forever, in a single generation, the frequency of blood types in Europe. A process, some said, now being slow-motion mimicked by the gene CKR5 and HIV.

In his anthropology courses, Paul learned that all humans alive today could trace their ancestry back to Africa, to a time almost six thousand years ago when the whole of human diversity existed within a single small population. And there had been at least two dispersions out of Africa, his professors said, if not more—a genetic bottleneck in support of the Deluvian Flood Theory. But each culture had its own beliefs. Muslims called it Allah. Jews, Yahweh. The science journals were careful not to call it God anymore; but they spoke of an intelligent designer—an architect, lowercase "a." Though in his heart of hearts, Paul figured it all amounted to the same thing.

Paul read that they'd scanned the brains of nuns, looking for the God spot, and couldn't find it. He learned about evolutionism. Although long debunked by legitimate science, adherents of evolutionism still existed—their beliefs enjoying near immortality among the fallow fields of pseudo-science, cohabitating the fringe with older belief systems like astrology, phrenology, and acupuncture. Modern evolutionists believed the various dating systems were all incorrect; and they offered an assortment of unscientific explanations for how the isotope tests could all be wrong. In hushed tones, some even spoke of data tampering and conspiracies.

The evolutionists ignored the accepted interpretation of the geological record. They ignored the miracle of the placenta and the irreducible complexity of the eye.

During his junior and senior years, Paul studied archaeology. He studied the ancient remains of Homo erectus, and Homo neanderthalensis. He studied the un-Men; he studied afarensis, and Australopithecus, and Pan.

In the world of archeology, the line between Man and un-Man could be fuzzy—but it was never unimportant. To some scientists, Homo erectus was a race of Man long dead, a withered branch on the tree of humanity. To those more conservative, he wasn't Man at all; he was other, a hiccup of the creator, an independent creation made from the same toolbox. But that was an extreme viewpoint. Mainstream science, of course, accepted the use of stone tools as the litmus test. Men made stone tools. Soulless beasts didn't. Of course there were still arguments, even in the mainstream. The fossil KNM ER 1470, found in Kenya, appeared so perfectly balanced between Man and un-Man that a new category had to be invented: near-Man. The arguments could get quite heated, with both sides claiming anthropometric statistics to prove their case.

Like a benevolent teacher swooping in to stop a playground fight, the science of genetics arrived on the scene. Occupying the exact point of intersection between Paul's two passions in life—genetics and anthropology—the field of paleometagenomics was born.

Paul received a bachelor's degree in May and started a graduate program in September. Two years and an advanced degree later, Westin Genomics flew him to the East Coast for a job interview. Hands were shook over a glossy table.

Three weeks after that, he was in the field in Tanzania, learning the proprietary techniques of extracting DNA from bones 5,800 years old. Bones from the very dawn of the world.

· · · ·

Two men stepped into the bright room.

"So this is where the actual testing is done?" It was a stranger's voice, the accent urban Australian.

Paul lifted his eyes from the microscope and saw his supervisor accompanied by an older man in a dark suit.

"Yes," Mr. Lyons said.

The stranger shifted weight to his teak cane. His hair was short and gray, parted neatly on the side.

"It never ceases to amaze," the stranger said, glancing around. "How alike laboratories are across the world. Cultures who cannot agree on anything agree on this: how to design a centrifuge, where to put the test tube rack, what color to paint the walls—white, always. The bench tops, black."

Mr. Lyons only nodded.

Paul stood, pulled off his latex gloves.

"Gavin McMaster," the stranger said, sticking out a hand. "Pleased to make your acquaintance, Mr. Carlson."

They shook.

"Paul. You can call me Paul."

"I apologize for interrupting your work," Gavin said.

"It's time I took a break anyway."

"I'll leave you two to your discussion," Mr. Lyons said and excused himself.

"Please," Paul said, gesturing to a nearby worktable. "Take a seat."

Gavin sank onto the stool and set his briefcase on the table. "I promise I won't take much of your time," he said. "But I did need to talk to you. We've been leaving messages for the last few days and—"

"Oh." Paul's face changed. "You're from—"

"Yes."

"This is highly unusual for you to contact me here."

"I can assure you these are very unusual circumstances."

"Still, I'm not sure I like being solicited for one job while working at another."

"I can see there's been a misunderstanding."

"How's that?"

"You called it a job. Consider it a consulting offer."

"Mr. McMaster, I'm very busy with my current work. I'm in the middle of several projects, and to be honest, I'm surprised Westin let you through the door."

"Westin is already onboard. I took the liberty of speaking to the management before contacting you today."

"How did you . . ." Paul looked at him, and Gavin raised an eyebrow. With corporations, any question of "how" was usually rhetorical. The answer was always the same. And it always involved dollar signs.

"Of course, we'll match that bonus to you, mate." McMaster slid a check across the counter. Paul barely glanced at it.

"As I said, I'm in the middle of several projects now. One of the other samplers here would probably be interested."

McMaster smiled. "Normally I'd assume that was a negotiating tactic. But that's not the case here, is it?"

"No."

"I was like you once. Hell, maybe I still am."

"Then you understand." Paul stood.

"I understand you better than you think. It makes it easier, sometimes, when you come from money. Sometimes I think that only people who come from it realize how worthless it really is."

"That hasn't been my experience. If you'll excuse me." Politeness like a wall, a thing he'd learned from his mother.

"Please," Gavin said. "Before you leave, I have something for you." He opened the snaps on his briefcase and pulled out a stack of glossy 8×10 photographs.

For a moment Paul just stood there. Then he took the photos from Gavin's extended hand. Paul looked at the pictures. Paul looked at them for a long time.

Gavin said, "These fossils were found last year on the island of Flores, in Indonesia."

"Flores," Paul whispered, still studying the photos. "I heard they found strange bones there. I didn't know anybody had published."

"That's because we haven't. Not yet, anyway."

"These dimensions can't be right. A six-inch ulna."

"They're right."

Paul looked at him. "Why me?" And just like that, the wall was gone. What lived behind it had hunger in its belly.

"Why not?"

It was Paul's turn to raise an eyebrow.

"Because you're good," Gavin said.

"There are other samplers just as good."

"Because you're young and don't have a reputation to risk."

"Or one to stand on."

Gavin sighed. "Because I don't know if archaeology was ever meant to be as important as it has become. Will that do for an answer? We live in a world where zealots become scientists. Tell me, boy, are you a zealot?"

"No."

"That's why. Or close enough."

> There were a finite number of unique creations at the beginning of the world—a finite number of species which has, since that time, decreased dramatically through extinction. Speciation is a special event outside the realm of natural processes, a phenomena relegated to the moment of creation, and to the mysteries of Allah.
>
> —Expert witness, heresy trials, Ankara, Turkey

The flight to Bali was seventeen hours, and another two to Flores by chartered plane—then four hours by Jeep over the steep mountains and into the heart of the jungle. To Paul, it might have been another world. Rain fell, stopped, then fell again, turning the road into a thing which had to be reasoned with.

"Is it always like this?" Paul asked.

"No," Gavin said. "In the rainy season, it's much worse."

Flores, isle of flowers. From the air it had looked like a green ribbon of jungle thrust from blue water, part of a rosary of islands between Australia and Java. The Wallace Line—a line less arbitrary than any border on a map—lay kilometers to the west, toward Asia and the empire of placental mammals. A stranger emperor ruled here.

Paul was exhausted by the time they pulled into Ruteng. He rubbed his eyes. Children ran alongside the Jeep, their faces some combination of Malay and Papuan—brown skin, strong white teeth like a dentist's dream. The hill town crouched one foot in the jungle, one on the mountain. A valley flung itself from the edge of the settlement, a drop of kilometers.

The men checked into their hotel. Paul's room was basic, but clean, and Paul slept like the dead. The next morning he woke, showered and shaved. Gavin met him in the lobby.

"It's a bit rustic, I apologize," Gavin said.

"No, it's fine," Paul said. "There was a bed and a shower. That's all I needed."

"We use Ruteng as a kind of base camp for the dig. Our future accommodations won't be quite so luxurious."

Back at the Jeep, Paul checked his gear. It wasn't until he climbed into the passenger seat that he noticed the gun, its black leather holster duct-taped to the driver's door. It hadn't been there the day before.

Gavin caught him staring. "These are crazy times we live in, mate. This is a place history has forgotten till now. Recent events have made it remember."

"Which recent events are those?"

"Religious events to some folks' view. Political to others." Gavin waved his hand. "More than just scientific egos are at stake with this find."

They drove north, descending into the valley and sloughing off the last pretense of civilization. "You're afraid somebody will kidnap the bones?" Paul asked.

"Yeah, that's one of the things I'm afraid of."

"One?"

"It's easy to pretend that it's just theories we're playing with—ideas dreamed up in some ivory tower between warring factions of scientists. Like it's all some intellectual exercise." Gavin looked at him, his dark eyes grave. "But then you see the actual bones; you feel their weight in your hands, and sometimes theories die between your fingers."

The track down to the valley floor was all broken zigzags and occasional, rounding turns. For long stretches, overhanging branches made a tunnel of the roadway—the jungle a damp cloth slapping at the windshield. But here and there that damp cloth was yanked aside, and out over the edge of the drop you could see a valley like Hollywood would love, an archetype to represent all valleys, jungle floor visible through jungle haze. In those stretches of muddy road, a sharp left pull on the steering wheel would have gotten them there quicker, deader.

"Liange Bua," Gavin called their destination. "The Cold Cave." And Gavin explained that was how they thought it happened, the scenario: This steamy jungle all around, so two or three of them went inside to get cool, to sleep. Or maybe it was raining, and they went in the cave to get dry—only the rain didn't stop, and the river flooded, as it sometimes still did, and they were trapped inside the cave by the rising waters, their drowned bodies buried in mud and sediment.

The men rode in silence for a while before Gavin said it, a third option Paul felt coming. "Or they were eaten there."

"Eaten by what?"

"Homo homini lupus est," Gavin said. "Man is wolf to man."

They crossed a swollen river, water rising to the bottom of the doors. For a moment Paul felt the current grab the Jeep, pull, and it was a close thing, Gavin cursing and white-knuckled on the wheel, trying to keep them to the shallows. When they were past it he said, "You've got to keep it to the north; if you slide a few feet off straight, the whole bugger'll go tumbling downriver."

Paul didn't ask him how he knew.

Beyond the river was the camp. Researchers in wide-brimmed hats or bandanas. Young and old. Two or three shirtless. A dark-haired woman in a white shirt sat on a log outside her tent. The one feature unifying them all, black dirt coating good boots.

Every head followed the Jeep, and when it pulled to a stop, a small crowd gathered to help unpack. Gavin introduced him around. Eight researchers, plus two laborers still in the cave. Australian mostly. Indonesian. One American.

"Herpetology, mate," one of them said when he shook Paul's hand. Small, stocky, red-bearded; he couldn't have been more than twenty-two. Paul forgot his name the moment he heard it, but the introduction, "Herpetology mate," stuck with him. "That's my specialty," the small man continued. "I got mixed up in this because of professor McMaster here. University of New England, Australia." His smile was two feet wide under a sharp nose that pointed at his own chin. Paul liked him instantly.

When they'd finished unpacking the Jeep, Gavin turned to Paul. "Now I think it's time we made the most important introductions," he said.

It was a short walk to the cave. Jag-toothed limestone jutted from the jungle, an overhang of vine, and beneath that, a dark mouth. The stone was the brown-white of old ivory. Cool air enveloped him, and entering Liange Bua was a distinct process of stepping down. Once inside, it took Paul's eyes a moment to adjust. The chamber was thirty meters wide, open to the jungle in a wide crescent—mud floor, high-domed ceiling. There was not much to see at first. In the far corner, two sticks angled from the mud, and when he looked closer, Paul saw the hole.

"Is that it?"

"That's it."

Paul took off his backpack and stripped the white paper suit out of its plastic wrapper. "Who else has touched it?"

"Talford, Margaret, me."

"I'll need blood samples from everybody for comparison assays."

"DNA contamination?"

"Yeah."

"We stopped the dig when we realized the significance."

"Still. I'll need blood samples from anybody who has dug here, anybody who came anywhere near the bones. I'll take the samples myself tomorrow."

"I understand. Is there anything else you need?"

"Solitude." Paul smiled. "I don't want anybody in the cave for this part."

Gavin nodded and left. Paul broke out his tarps and hooks. It was best if the sampler was the person who dug the fossils out of the ground—or better yet, if the DNA samples were taken when the bones were still *in* the ground. Less contamination that way. And there was always contamination. No matter what precautions were taken, no matter how many tarps, or how few people worked at the site, there was still always contamination.

Paul slid down into the hole, flashlight strapped to his forehead, white paper suit slick on the moist earth. From his perspective, he couldn't tell what the bones were—only that they were bones, half buried in earth. From his perspective, that's all that mattered. The material was soft, unfossilized; he'd have to be careful.

It took nearly seven hours. He snapped two dozen photographs, careful to keep track of which samples came from which specimens. Whoever these things were, they were small. He sealed the DNA samples into small, sterile lozenges for transport.

It was night when he climbed from under the tarp.

Outside the cave, Gavin was the first to find him in the firelight. "Are you finished?"

"For tonight. I have six different samples from at least two different individuals. Shouldn't take more than a few more days."

McMaster handed him a bottle of whiskey.

"Isn't it a little early to celebrate?"

"Celebrate? You've been working in a grave all night. In America, don't they drink after wakes?"

· · · ·

That night over the campfire, Paul listened to the jungle sounds and to the voices of scientists, feeling history congeal around him.

"Suppose it isn't," Jack was saying. Jack was thin and American and very drunk. "Suppose it isn't in the same lineage with us, then what would that mean?"

The red-bearded herpetologist groaned. His name was James. "Not more of that doctrine of descent bullshit," he said.

"Then what is it?" someone added.

They passed the drink around, eyes occasionally drifting to Paul like he was a priest come to grant absolution—his sample kit just an artifact of his priestcraft. Paul swigged the bottle when it came his way. They'd finished off the whiskey long ago; this was some local brew brought by laborers, distilled from rice. Paul swallowed fire.

Yellow-haired man saying, "It's the truth," but Paul had missed part of the conversation, and for the first time he realized how drunk they all were; and James laughed at something, and the woman with the white shirt turned and said, "Some people have nicknamed it the 'hobbit.' "

"What?"

"Flores Man—the hobbit. Little people three feet tall."

"Tolkien would be proud," a voice contributed.

"A mandible, a fairly complete cranium, parts of a right leg and left inominate."

"But what is it?"

"Hey, are you staying on?"

The question was out there for two beats before Paul realized it was aimed at him. The woman's eyes were brown and searching across the fire. "Yeah," he said. "A few more days."

Then the voice again, "But what is it?"

Paul took another swallow—trying to cool the voice of panic in his head.

. . . .

Paul learned about her during the next couple of days, the girl with the white shirt. Her name was Margaret. She was twenty-eight. Australian. Some fraction aborigine on her mother's side, but you could only see it for sure in her mouth. The rest of her could have been Dutch, English, whatever. But that full mouth: teeth like Ruteng children, teeth like dentists might dream. She tied her brown hair back from her face, so it didn't hang in her eyes while she worked in the hole. This was her sixth dig, she told him. "This is the one." She sat on the stool while Paul took her blood, a delicate index finger extended, red pearl rising to spill her secrets. "Most archaeologists go a whole lifetime without a big find," she said. "Maybe you get one. Probably none. But this is the one I get to be a part of."

"What about the Leakeys?" Paul asked, dabbing her finger with cotton.

"Bah." She waved at him in mock disgust. "They get extra. Bloody Kennedys of Archaeology."

Despite himself, Paul laughed.

This brings us to the so-called doctrine of common descent, whereby each species is seen as a unique and individual creation. Therefore all men, living and dead, are descended from a common one-time creational event. To be outside of this lineage, no matter how similar in appearance, is to be other than Man.

　　　　　　　　　　　　　　　　　　　　—Journal of Heredity

That evening, Paul helped Gavin pack the Jeep for a trek back up to Ruteng. "I'm driving our laborers back to town," Gavin told him. "They work one week on, one off. You want me to take your samples with me?"

Paul shook his head. "Can't. There are stringent protocols for chain of possession."

"Where are they now?"

Paul patted the cargo pocket of his pant leg.

"So when you get those samples back, what happens next?"

"I'll hand them over to an evaluation team."

"You don't test them yourself?"

"I'll assist, but there are strict rules. I test animal DNA all the time, and the equipment is all the same. But genus *Homo* requires a license and oversight."

"All right, mate, then I'll be back tomorrow evening to pick you up." Gavin went to the Jeep and handed Paul the sat phone. "In case anything happens while I'm gone."

"Do you think something will?"

"No," Gavin said. Then, "I don't know."

Paul fingered the sat phone, a dark block of plastic the size of a shoe. "What are you worried about?"

"To be honest, bringing you here has brought attention we didn't want yet. I received a troubling call today. So far, we've shuffled under the radar, but now . . . now we've flown in an outside tech, and people want to know why."

"What people?"

"Official people. Indonesia is suddenly very interested."

"Are you worried they'll shut down the dig?"

Gavin smiled. "Have you studied theology?"

"Why?"

"I've long been fascinated by the figure of Abraham. Are you familiar with Abraham?"

"Of course," Paul said, unsure where this was going.

"From this one sheepherder stems the entire natural history of monotheism. He's at the very foundation of all three Abrahamic faiths—Judaism, Christianity, and Islam. When Jews, Christians, and Muslims get on their knees for their One True God, it is to Abraham's God they pray." Gavin closed his eyes. "And still there is such fighting over steeples."

"What does this have to do with the dig?"

"The word 'prophet' comes from the Greek, *prophetes*. In Hebrew, the word is *nabi*. I think Abraham Heschel said it best when he wrote 'the prophet is the man who feels fiercely.' What do you think, Paul? Do you think prophets feel fiercely?"

"Why are you asking me this?"

"Oh, never mind." Gavin smiled again and shook his head. "It's just the rambling of an old man."

"You never answered if you thought they'd shut down the dig."

"We come onto their land, their territory; we come into this place and we find bones that contradict their beliefs; what do you think might happen? Anything."

"Contradict their beliefs?" Paul said. "What do you believe about these bones? You've never said."

"I don't know. They could be pathological."

"That's what they said about the first Neanderthal bones. Except they kept finding them."

"It could be microcephaly."

"What kind of microcephaly makes you three feet tall?"

"The odd skull shape and small body size could be unrelated. Pygmies aren't unknown to these islands."

"There are no pygmies this small."

"But perhaps the two things together . . . perhaps the bones are just a microcephalic representation of the local . . ." His voice trailed off. Gavin sighed. He looked suddenly defeated.

"That's not what you believe, is it?" Paul said.

"These are the smallest bones discovered that look anything like us. Could they just be pathological humans? I don't know. Maybe. Pathology could happen anywhere, so you can't rule it out when you've only got a few specimens to work with. But what my mind keeps coming back to is that these bones weren't found just anywhere."

"What do you mean?"

"These bones weren't found in Africa or Asia or Europe. They weren't found on the big land masses. These tiny bones were found on a tiny island. Near the bones of dwarf elephants. And that's a coincidence? They hunted dwarf elephants, for God's sake."

"So if not pathological, what do you believe they were? You still haven't said."

"That's the powerful thing about genetics, my friend. You take your samples, do your tests. One does not have to believe. One can know. And that's precisely what is so dangerous."

. . . . .

"Strange things happen on islands." Margaret's white shirt was gone. She sat slick-armed in overalls. Skin like a fine coat of gloss. The firelight beat the night back, lighting candles in their eyes. It was nearly midnight, and the researchers sat in a circle, listening to the crackle of the fire. Listening to the jungle.

"Like the Galápagos," she said. "The finches."

"Oh come on," James said. "The skulls we found are small, with brains the size of chimps. Island dwarfing of genus Homo; is that what you're proposing? Some sort of local adaptation over the last five thousand years?"

"It's the best we have."

"Those bones are too different. They're not of our line."

"But they're younger than the other archaics. It's not like erectus, some branch cut down at the dawn of time. These things survived here for a long time. The bones aren't even fossilized."

"It doesn't matter, they're still not us. Either they share common descent from Man, or they were a separate creation at the beginning. There is no in-between. And they're only a meter tall don't forget."

"That's just an estimate."

"A good estimate."

"Achondroplasia—"

"Those skulls are as achondroplastic as I am. I'd say the sloped frontal bone is *anti*-achondroplastic."

"Some kind of growth hormone deficiency would—"

"No," Paul said, speaking for the first time. Every face turned toward him.

"No, what?"

"Pygmies have normal growth hormone levels," Paul said. "Every population studied—the negritos, the Andaman, the Congolese. All normal."

The faces stared. "It's the circulating domain of their receptors that are different," Paul continued. "Pygmies are pygmies because of their GH receptors, not the growth hormone itself. If you inject a pygmy child with growth hormone, you still get a pygmy."

"Well still," Margaret said. "I don't see how that impacts whether these bones share common descent or not."

James turned to the circle of faces. "So are they on our line? Are they us, or other?"

"Other."

"Other."

"Other."

Softly, the girl whispered in disbelief, "But they had stone tools."

The faces turned to Paul, but he only watched the fire and said nothing.

· · · · ·

The next morning started with a downpour. The dig team huddled in tents, or under the tarped lean-to near the fire pit. Only James braved the rain, stomping off into the jungle. He was back in an hour, smiling ear to ear.

"Well, will you look at that," James said, holding something out for Paul to see.

"What is it?"

"Partially eaten monitor. A species only found here."

Paul saw now that it was a taloned foot that James held. "That's a big lizard."

"Oh, no. This was just a juvenile. Mother nature is odd this side of the Wallace Line. Not only are most of the species on this side not found anywhere else. A lot of them aren't even vaguely related to anything else. It's like God started from scratch to fill all the niches."

"How'd you get interested in herpetology?" Paul asked.

"By His creations shall ye know God."

"McMaster mentioned a dwarf elephant."

"Yeah, stegadon. They're extinct now though."

"What killed them off?"

"Same thing that killed off a lot of the ancient fauna on the island. Classic catastrophism, a volcanic eruption. We found the ash layer just above the youngest bones."

• • • •

Once, lying in bed with a woman, Paul had watched the moon through the window. The woman traced his scars with her finger.

"Your father was brutal."

"No," Paul had said. "He was broken, that's all."

"There's a difference?"

"Yeah."

"What?"

"He was always sorry afterward."

"That mattered?"

"Every single time."

> A: Incidences of local adaptation have occurred, sure. Populations adapt to changing conditions all the time.
>
> Q: Through what process?
>
> A: Differential reproductive success. Given genetic variability, it almost has to happen. It's just math and genes. Fifty-eight hundred years is a long time.
>
> Q: Can you give an example?
>
> A: Most dogs would fall into this category, having been bred by man to suit his needs. While physically different from each other, when you study their genes, they're all one species—though admittedly divided into several distinct clades.
>
> Q: So you're saying God created the original dog, but Man bred the different varieties?
>
> A: You called it God, not me. And for the record, honey, God created the gray wolf. Man created dogs.
>
> —excerpted from the trial of geneticist Michael Poore

• • • •

It came the next morning in the guise of police action. It came in shiny new Daihatsus with roll bars and off-road tires. It came with guns. Mostly, it came with guns.

Paul heard them before he saw them, men shouting in a language he could not understand. He was with James at the cave's entrance. When Paul saw the first assault rifle, he sprinted for the tents. He slid the DNA lozenges into a pouch in his belt and punched numbers on the sat phone. Gavin picked up on the second ring. "The police are here," Paul said.

"Good Lord, I just spoke to officials today," Gavin said. There was shouting outside the tents—angry shouts. "They assured me nothing like this would happen."

"They lied."

Behind him, James said, "This is bad. This is very bad."

"Where are you?" Paul asked.

"I'm still in Ruteng," Gavin said.

"Then this will be over by the time you can get here."

"Paul, it's not safe for you th—"

Paul hung up. *Tell me something I don't know.*

He took his knife from his sample kit and slit the back of the tent open. He slid through, James following close behind. Paul saw Margaret standing uncertain at the edge of the jungle. Their eyes met and Paul motioned toward the Jeeps; on the count of three, they all ran for it.

They climbed in and shut the doors. The soldiers—for that's what Paul knew they were now—the soldiers didn't notice them until Paul started the engine. Malay faces swung around, mouths open in shouts of outrage.

"You'll probably want your seat belts on for this," Paul said. Then he gunned it, spitting dirt.

• • • •

"Don't shoot," James whispered to himself in the backseat, eyes closed in prayer.

"What?" Paul said.

"If they shoot, they're not police."

A round smashed through the rear window and blew out a chunk of the front windshield, spidering the safety glass.

"Shit!" Margaret screamed.

A quick glance in the rearview, and Paul saw soldiers climbing into one of the Daihatsus. Paul yanked the wheel right.

"Not that way!" Margaret shouted. Paul ignored her and floored the accelerator.

Jungle whipped past, close enough to touch. Ruts threatened to buck them from the cratered roadway. The Daihatsu whipped into view behind them. Shots rang out, a sound like Chinese firecrackers, the ding of metal.

They rounded the bend, and the river came into view—big and dumb as the sky. Paul gunned the engine.

"We're not going to make it across!" James shouted.

"We only need to get halfway."

Another shot slammed into the back of the Jeep.

They hit the river like a slow-speed crash, water roaring up and over the broken windshield—the smell of muck suddenly overpowering.

Paul stomped his foot to the floor.

The Jeep chugged, drifted, caught gravel. They got about halfway across before Paul yanked the steering wheel to the left. The world came unstuck and started to shift. The right front fender came up, rocking with the current. The engine died. They were floating.

Paul looked back. The pursuing vehicle skidded to a halt at the shoreline, and men jumped out. The Jeep heaved, one wheel pivoting around a submerged rock.

"Can you swim?" Paul asked.

"Now you ask us?"

"I'd unbuckle if I were you."

The Jeep hit another rock, metal grinding on stone, then sky traded places with water, and everything went dark.

• • • •

They dragged themselves out of the water several miles downriver, where a bridge crossed the water. They followed the dirt road to a place called Rea. From there they took a bus. Margaret had money.

They didn't speak about it until they arrived at Bajawa.

"Do you think they're okay?" Margaret asked.

"I think it wouldn't serve their purpose to hurt the dig team. They only wanted the bones."

"They shot at us."

"Because they assumed we had something they wanted. They were shooting at the tires."

"No," she said. "They weren't."

Three rented nights in the hotel room, and James couldn't leave—that hair like a great big handle anybody could pick up and carry, anybody with eyes and a voice. Some of the locals hadn't seen red hair in their lives, and James's description was prepackaged for easy transport. Paul, however, blended—just another vaguely Asian set of cheekbones in the crowd, even if he was a half a foot taller than the locals.

That night, staring at the ceiling from one of the double beds, James said, "If those bones aren't us . . . then I wonder what they were like."

"They had fire and stone tools," Paul said. "They were probably a lot like us."

"We act like we're the chosen ones, you know? But what if it wasn't like that?"

"Don't think about it," Margaret said.

"What if God had all these different varieties . . . all these different walks, these different options at the beginning, and we're just the ones who killed the others off?"

"Shut up," she said.

"What if there wasn't just one Adam, but a hundred Adams?"

"Shut the fuck up, James."

There was a long quiet, the sound of the street filtering through the thin walls. "Paul," James said. "If you get your samples back to your lab, you'll be able to tell, won't you?"

Paul was silent. He thought of the evaluation team and wondered.

"The winners write the history books," James said. "Maybe the winners write the bibles, too. I wonder what religion died with them."

. . . .

The next day, Paul left to buy food. When he returned Margaret was gone.

"Where is she?"

"She left to find a phone. She said she'd be right back."

"Why didn't you stop her?"

"I couldn't."

Day turned into evening. By darkness, they both knew she wasn't coming back.

"How are we going to get home?" James asked.

"I don't know."

"And your samples. Even if we got to an airport, they'd never let you get on the plane with them. You'll be searched. They'll find them."

"We'll find a way once things have settled down."

"Things are never going to settle down."

"They will."

"No, you still don't get it. When your entire culture is predicated on an idea, you can't afford to be proven wrong."

. . . .

Out of deep sleep, Paul heard it. Something.

He'd known this was coming, though he hadn't been aware that he'd known, until that moment. The creak of wood, the gentle breeze of an open door. Shock and awe would have been better—an inrush of soldiers, an arrest of some kind, expulsion, deportation, a legal system, however corrupt. A silent man in the dark meant many things. None of them good. The word murder rose up in his mind. People disappeared sometimes, never to be heard from again.

Paul breathed. There was a cold in him—a part of him that was dead, a part of him that could never be afraid. A part of him his father had put there.

Paul's eyes searched the shadows and found it, the place where shadow moved, a dark breeze that eased across the room. If there was only one of them, then there was a chance.

Paul thought of making a run for it, sprinting for the door, leaving the samples and this place behind; but James, still sleeping, stopped him. He made up his mind.

Paul exploded from the bed, flinging the blanket ahead of him, wrapping that part of the darkness; and a shape moved, darkness like a puma's spots, black on black—there even though you can't see it. And Paul knew he'd surprised him, that darkness, and he knew, instantly, that it wouldn't be enough. A blow rocked Paul off his feet, forward momentum carrying him into the wall. The mirror shattered, glass crashing to the floor.

"What the fuck?" James hit the light, and suddenly the world snapped into existence, a flashbulb stillness—and the intruder was Indonesian, crouched in a stance, preternatural silence coming off him like a heat shimmer. He carried endings with him, nothingness in a long blade. The insult of it hit home. The shocking fucking insult, standing there, knees bent, bright blade in one hand—blood on reflective steel. That's when Paul felt the pain. It was only then he realized he'd already been opened.

And the Indonesian moved fast. He moved so fast. He moved faster than Paul's eyes could follow, covering distance like thought, across the room to James, who had time only to flinch before the knife parted him. Such a professional, and James's eyes went wide in surprise. Paul moved using the only things he had, size, strength, momentum. He hit the Indonesian like a linebacker, sweeping him into his arms, crushing him against the wall. Paul felt something snap, a twig, a branch, something in the Indonesian's chest—and they rolled apart, the intruder doing something with his hands; the rasp of blade on bone, a new blackness, and Paul flinched from the blow, feeling the steel leave his eye socket.

There was no anger. It was the strangest thing. To be in a fight for his life and not be angry. The intruder came at him again, and it was only Paul's size that saved him. He grabbed the arm and twisted, bringing the fight to the floor. A pushing down of his will into three square inches of the Indonesian's throat—a caving-in like a crumpling aluminum can, but Paul still held on, still pushed until the lights went out of those black eyes.

"I'm sorry," he said. "I'm sorry."

Paul rolled off him and collapsed to the floor. He crawled over to James. It wasn't a pool of blood. It was a swamp, the mattress soggy with it. James lay on the bed, still conscious.

"Don't bleed on me, man," James said. "No telling what you promiscuous Americans might carry. Don't want to have to explain it to my girlfriend."

Paul smiled at the dying man, crying and bleeding on him, wiping the blood from his beard with a pillowcase. He held James's hand until he stopped breathing.

. . . .

Paul's eye opened to white. He blinked. A man in a suit sat in the chair next to the hospital bed. A man in a police uniform stood near the door. "Where am I?" Paul asked. He didn't recognize his own voice. It was an older man. Who'd eaten glass.

"Maumere," the suited man said. He was white, mid-thirties, lawyer written all over him.

"How long?"

"A day."

Paul touched the bandage over his face. "Is my eye . . ."

"I'm sorry."

Paul took the news with a nod. "How did I get here?"

"They found you naked in the street. Two dead men in your room."

"So what happens now?"

"Well, that depends on you." The man in the suit smiled. "I'm here at the behest of certain parties interested in bringing this to a quiet close."

"Quiet?"

"Yes."

"Where is Margaret? Mr. McMaster?"

"They were put on flights back to Australia this morning."

"I don't believe you."

"Whether you believe or not is of no consequence to me. I'm just answering your questions."

"What about the bones?"

"Confiscated for safekeeping, of course. The Indonesians have closed down the dig. It is their cave, after all."

"What about my DNA samples in the hotel room, the lozenges?"

"They've been confiscated and destroyed."

Paul sat quietly.

"How did you end up in the street?" the suit asked.

"I walked."

"How did you end up naked?"

"I figured it was the only way they'd let me live. The only way to prove I didn't have the samples. I was bleeding out. I knew they'd still be coming."

"You are a smart man, Mr. Carlson. So you figured you'd let them have the samples?"

"Yeah," Paul said.

The suited man stood and left the room.

"Mostly," Paul said.

. . . .

On the way to the airport, Paul told the driver to pull over. He paid the fare and climbed out. He took a bus to Bengali, and from there took a cab to Rea.

He climbed on a bus in Rea, and as it bore down the road, Paul yelled, "Stop!"

The driver hit the breaks. "I'm sorry," Paul said. "I've forgotten something." He climbed off the bus and walked back to town. No car followed.

Once in town, down one of the small side streets, he found it, the flower pot with the odd pink plant. He scooped dirt out of the base.

The old woman shouted something at him. He held out money. "For the plant," he said. "I'm a flower lover." She might not have understood English, but she understood money.

He walked with the plant under his arm. James had been right about some things. Wrong about others. Not a hundred Adams, no. Just two. All of Australoid creation like some parallel world. *And you shall know God by His creations*. But why would God create two Adams? That's what Paul had wondered. The answer was that He wouldn't.

Two Adams. Two gods. One on each side of the Wallace Line.

Paul imagined it began as a competition. A line drawn in the sand, to see whose creations would dominate.

Paul understood the burden Abraham carried, to witness the birth of a religion.

As Paul walked through the streets he dug his fingers through the dirt. His fingers touched it, and he pulled the lozenge free. The lozenge no evaluation team would ever lay eyes on. He would make sure of that.

He passed a woman in a doorway, an old woman with a beautiful, full mouth. He thought of the bones in the cave, and of the strange people who had once crouched on this island.

He handed her the flower. "For you," he said.

He hailed a cab and climbed inside. "Take me to the airport."

As the old cab bounced along the dusty roads, Paul took off his eye patch. He saw the cabby glance into his rearview and then look away, repulsed.

"They lied, you see," Paul told the cabbie. "About the irreducible complexity of the eye. Oh, there are ways."

The cabbie turned his radio up, keeping his face forward. Paul grimaced as he unpacked his eye, pulling white gauze out in long strips—pain exploding in his skull.

"A prophet is one who feels fiercely," he said, then slid the lozenge into his empty eye socket.

CATHERYNNE M. VALENTE   Born in Seattle and raised there and in California, Catherynne M. Valente is one of the most important fantasy writers of those coming to prominence since 2000. She has won the Mythopoeic Award, the Lambda Award, and the James Tiptree, Jr. Award, and her work has been shortlisted for the Hugo, Nebula, and World Fantasy Awards. In 2010, her novel *The Girl Who Circumnavigated Fairyland in a Ship of Her Own Making* won the Andre Norton Award, the first major genre award to go to a crowdfunded online work; it has since been conventionally published by Feiwel and Friends.

Although Valente is primarily known as a fantasy writer, her sharp eye for folklore lends zest to this examination of a particular area of the received landscape of SF.

HOW TO BECOME A MARS OVERLORD

Welcome, Aspiring Potentates!

We are tremendously gratified at your interest in our little red project, and pleased that you recognize the potential growth opportunities inherent in whole-planet domination. Of course we remain humble in the face of such august and powerful interests, and seek only to showcase the unique and challenging career paths currently available on the highly desirable, iconic, and oxygen-rich landscape of Mars.

Query: Why Mars?

It is a little known fact that every solar system contains Mars. Not Mars itself, of course. But certain suns seem to possess what we might call a habit of Martianness: In every inhabited system so far identified, there is a red planet, usually near enough to the most populous world if not as closely adjacent as our own twinkling scarlet beacon, with proximate lengths of day and night. Even more curious, these planets are without fail named for war-divinities. In the far-off Lighthouse system, the orb Makha turns slowly in the dark, red as the blood of that fell goddess to whom cruel strategists pray, she who nurses two skulls at each mammoth breast. In the Glyph system, closer to home, it is Firialai glittering there like a ripe red fruit, called after a god of doomed charges depicted in several valuable tapestries as a jester dancing ever on the tip of a sword, clutching in each of his seven hands a bouquet of whelp-muskets, bones, and promotions with golden seals. In the Biera-biera system, still yet we may walk the carnelian sands of Uppskil, the officer's patron goddess, with her woolly dactyl-wings weighted down with gorsuscite medals gleaming purple and white. Around her orbit Wydskil and Nagskil, the enlisted man's god and the pilot's mad, bald angel, soaring pale as twin ghosts through Uppskil's emerald-colored sky.

Each red planet owns also two moons, just as ours does. Some of them will suffer life to flourish. We have ourselves vacationed on the several crystal ponds of Volniy and Vernost, which attend the claret equatorial jungles of Raudhr—named, of course, for the four-faced lord of bad intelligence whose exploits have been collected in the glassily perfect septameters of the Raudhrian Eddas. We have flown the lonely black between the satellites on slim-finned ferries decked in greenglow blossoms, sacred to the poorly-informed divine personage. But most moons are kin to Phobos and Deimos, and rotate silently, empty, barren, bright stones, mute and heavy. Many a time we have asked ourselves: Does Mars dwell in a house of mirrors, that same red face repeated over and over in the distance, a quantum hiccup—or is Mars the master, the exemplum, and all the rest copies? Surely the others ask the same riddle. We would all like to claim the primacy of our own specimen—and frequently do, which led to the Astronomer's War some years ago, and truly, no one here can bear to recite that tragic narrative, or else we should wash you all away with our rust-stained tears.

The advantages of these many Marses, scattered like ruby seeds across the known darkness, are clear: In almost every system, due to stellar circumstances beyond mortal control, Mars or Iskra or Lial is the first, best candidate for occupation by the primary world. In every system, the late pre-colonial literature of those primary worlds becomes obsessed with that tantalizing, rose-colored neighbor. Surely some of you are here because your young hearts were fired by the bedside tales of Alim K, her passionate affair with the two piscine princes of red Knisao, and how she waked dread machines in the deep rills of the Knizid mountains in order to possess them? Who among us never read of the mariner Ubaido and his silver-keeled ship, exploring the fell canals of Mikto, their black water filled with eely leviathans whose eyes shone with clusters of green pearls. All your mothers read the ballads of Sollo-Hul to each of you in your cribs, and your infant dreams were filled with gorgeous-green six-legged cricket-queens ululating on the broad pink plains of Podnebesya, their carapaces awash in light. And who did not love Ylla, her strange longings against those bronze spires? Who did not thrill to hear of those scarlet worlds bent to a single will? Who did not feel something stir within them, confronted with those endless crimson sands?

We have all wanted Mars, in our time. She is familiar, she is strange. She is redolent of tales and spices and stones we have never known. She is demure, and gives nothing freely, but from our hearths we have watched her glitter, all of our lives. Of course we want her. Mars is the girl next door. Her desirability is encoded in your cells. It is archetypal. We absolve you in advance.

．．．．

No matter what system bore you, lifted you up, made you strong and righteous, there is a Mars for you to rule, and it is right that you should wish to rule her. These are perhaps the only certainties granted to a soul like yours.

We invite you, therefore, to commit to memory our simple, two-step system to accomplish your laudable goals, for obviously no paper, digital, or flash materials ought to be taken away from this meeting.

Step One: Get to Mars

It is easier for a camel to pass through the eye of a needle than for a poor man to get to Mars. However, to be born on a bed of gems leads to a certain laziness of the soul, a kind of muscular weakness of the ambition, a subtle sprain in the noble faculties. Not an original observation, but repetition proves the axiom. Better to excel in some other field, for the well-rounded overlord is a blessing to all. Perhaps micro-cloning, or kinetic engineering. If you must, write a novel, but only before you depart, for novels written in the post-despotic utopia you hope to create may be beloved, but will never be taken seriously by the literati.

Take as your exemplum the post-plastic retroviral architect Helix Fo. The Chilean wunderkind was born with ambition in his mouth, and literally stole his education from an upper-class boy he happened upon in a dark alley. In exchange for his life, the patriarch agreed to turn over all his books and assignments upon completion, so that Fo could shadow his university years. For his senior project, Fo locked his erstwhile benefactor in a basement and devoted himself wholly to the construction of the Parainfluenza Opera House in Santiago, whose translucent spires even now dominate that skyline. The wealthy graduate went on to menial labor in the doctoral factories much chagrined while young Fo swam in wealth and fame, enough to purchase three marriage rights, including one to an aquatic Verqoid androgyne with an extremely respectable feather ridge. By his fortieth birthday, Fo had also purchased through various companies the better part of the Atlantic Ocean, whereupon he began breeding the bacterial island which so generously hosts us tonight, and supplies our salads with such exquisite yersinia radishes. Since, nearly all interplanetary conveyances have launched from Fo's RNA platform, for he charged no tariffs but his own passage, in comfort and grace. You will, of course, remember Fo as the first All-Emperor of Mars, and his statue remains upon the broad Athabasca Valles.

Or, rather, model yourself upon the poetess Oorm Nineteen Point Aught-One of Mur, who set the glittering world of Muror letters to furious clicking and torsioning of vocabulary-bladders. You and I may be quite sure there is no lucre at all to be made in the practice of poetry, but the half-butterfly giants of Mur are hardwired for rhyming structures, they cannot help but speak in couplets, sing their simplest greetings in six-part contratenor harmonies. Muror wars exist only between the chosen bards of each country, who spend years in competitive recitings to settle issues of territory. Oorm Nineteen, her lacy wings shot through with black neural braiding, revolted, and became a mistress of free verse. Born in the nectar-soup of the capital pool, she carefully collected words with no natural rhymes like dewdrops, hoarding, categorizing, and collating them. As a child, she haunted the berry-dripping speakeasies where the great luminaries read their latest work. At the age of sixteen, barely past infancy in the long stage-shifts of a Muror, she delivered her first poem, which consisted of two words: bright. cellar. Of course, in English these have many rhymes, but in Muror they have none, and her poem may as well have been a bomb detonated on the blue floor of that famous nightclub. Oorm Nineteen found the secret unrhyming world hiding within the delicate, gorgeous structures of Muror, and dragged it out to shine in the sun. But she was not satisfied with fame, nor with her mates and grubs and sweetwater gems. That is how it goes, with those of us who answer the call. Alone in a ship of unrhymed glass she left Mur entirely, and within a year took the red diadem of Etel for her own. Each rival she assassinated died in bliss as she whispered her verses into their perishing ears.

It is true that Harlow Y, scion of the House of Y, ruled the red planet Llym for some time. However, all may admit his rule frayed and frolicked in poor measure, and we have confidence that no one here possesses the makings of a Y hidden away in her jumpsuit. Dominion of the House of Y passed along genetic lines, though this method is degenerate by definition and illegal in most systems. By the time Harlow ascended, generations of Y had been consumed by little more than fashion, public nudity, and the occasional religious fad. What species Y may have belonged to before their massive wealth (derived from mining ore and cosmetics, if the earliest fairy tales of Vyt are to be believed) allowed constant and enthusiastic gene manipulation, voluntary mutation, prostheses, and virtual uplink, no one can truly say. Upon the warm golden sea of Vyt you are House Y or you are prey, and they have forcibly self-evolved out of recognizability. Harlow himself appears in a third of his royal portraits something like a massive winged koala with extremely long, ultraviolet eyelashes and a crystalline torso. Harlow Y inherited majority control over Llym as a child, and administered it much as a child will do, mining and farming for his amusement and personal augmentation. Each of his ultraviolet lashes represented thousands of dead Llymi, crushed to death in avalanches in the mine shafts of the Ypo mountains. But though Harlow achieved overlordship with alacrity and great speed, he ended in assassination, his morning hash-tea and bambun spectacularly poisoned by the general and unanimous vote of the populace.

Mastery of Mars is not without its little lessons.

It is surely possible to be born on a red planet. The Infanza of Hap lived all her life in the ruby jungles of her homeworld. She was the greatest actress of her age; her tails could convey the colors of a hundred complex emotions in a shimmering fall of shades. So deft were her illusions that the wicked old Rey thought her loyal and gentle beyond words even as she sunk her bladed fingers into his belly. But we must assume that if you require our guidance, you did not have the luck of a two-tailed Infanza, and were born on some other, meaner world, with black soil, or blue storms, or sweet rain falling like ambition denied.

Should you be so unfortunate as to originate upon a planet without copious travel options, due to economic crisis, ideological roadblocks, or simply occupying a lamentably primitive place on the technological timeline—have no fear. You are not alone in this. We suggest cryonics—the severed head of Plasticene Bligh ruled successfully over the equine haemovores of A-O-M for a century. He gambled, and gambled hard—he had his brain preserved at the age of twenty, hoping against hope that the ice might deliver him into a world more ready for his rarified soul. Should you visit A-O-M, the great wall of statues bearing her face (the sculptors kindly gave her a horse-body) will speak to what may be grasped when the house pays out.

If cryonics is for some reason unpopular on your world, longevity research will be your bosom friend. Invest in it, nurture it: Only you can be the steward of your own immortality. Even on Earth, Sarai Northe, Third Emira of Valles Marineris, managed to outlive her great-grandchildren by funding six separate think tanks and an Australian diamond mine until one underpaid intern presented her upon her birthday with a cascade of injections sparkling like champagne.

But on some worlds, in some terrible, dark hours, there is no road to Mars, no matter how much the traveling soul might desire it. In patchwork shoes, staring up at a starry night and one gleaming red star among the thousands—sometimes want is not enough. Not enough for Maximillian Bauxbaum, a Jewish baker in Provence, who in his most secret evenings wrote poetry describing such strange blood-colored deserts, such dry canals, a sky like green silk. Down to his children, and to theirs and theirs again, he passed a single ruby, the size of an egg, the size of a world. The baker had been given it as a bribe by a Christian lord, to take his leave of a certain maiden whom he loved, with hair the color of oxide-rich dust, and eyes like the space between moons. Never think on her again, never whisper her name to the walls. Though he kept his promise to an old and bitter death, such a treasure can never be spent, for it is as good as admitting your heart can be bought.

Sarai Northe inherited that jewel, and brought it with her to bury beneath the foundations of the Cathedral of Olympus Mons.

. . . .

In the end, you must choose a universe that contains yourself and Mars, together and perfect. Helix Fo chose a world built by viruses as tame as songbirds. Oorm Nineteen chose a world gone soft and violet with unrhyming songs. Make no mistake: every moment is a choice, a choice between this world and that one, between heavens teeming with life and a lonely machine grinding across red stone, between staying at home with tea and raspberry cookies and ruling Mars with a hand like grace.

Maximillian Bauxbaum chose to keep his promise. Who is to say it is not that promise, instead of microbial soup, which determined that Mars would be teeming with blue inhuman cities, with seventeen native faiths, by the time his child opened her veins to those terrible champagne-elixirs, and turned her eyes to the night?

Step Two: Become an Overlord

Now we come to the central question at the core of planetary domination: just how is it done? The answer is a riddle. Of course, it would be.

You must already be an overlord in order to become one.

Ask yourself: What is an overlord? Is he a villain? Is she a hero? A cowboy, a priestess, an industrialist? Is he cruel, is he kind, does she rule like air, invisible, indispensable? Is she the first human on Mars, walking on a plain so incomprehensible and barren that she feels her heart empty? Does she scratch away the thin red dust and see the black rock beneath? Does he land in his sleek piscine capsule on Uppskil, so crammed with libraries and granaries that he lives each night in an orgy of books and bread? What does she lord over? The land alone, the people, the belligerent patron gods with their null-bronze greaves ablaze?

Is it true, as Oorm Nineteen wrote, that the core of each red world is a gem of blood compressed like carbon, a hideous war-diamond that yearns toward the strength of a king or a queen as a compass yearns toward north? Or is this only a metaphor, a way in which you can anthropomorphize something so vast as a planet, think of it as something capable of loving you back?

It would seem that the very state of the overlord is one of violence, of domination. Uncomfortable colonial memories arise in the heart like acid—everyone wants to be righteous. Everyone wishes to be loved. What is any pharaonic statue, staring out at a sea of malachite foam, but a plea of the pharaoh to be loved, forever, unassailably, without argument? Ask yourself: Will Mars be big enough to fill the hole in you, the one that howls with such winds, which says the only love sufficient to quiet those winds is the love of a planet, red in tooth, claw, orbit, mass?

We spoke before of how to get to Mars if your lonely planet offers no speedy highway through the skies. Truthfully—and now we feel we can be truthful, here, in the long night of our seminar, when the clicking and clopping of the staff has dimmed and the last of the cane-cream has been sopped up, when the stars have all come out and through the crystal ceiling we can all see one (oh, so red, so red!) just there, just out of reach—truthfully, getting to Mars is icing. It is parsley. To be an overlord is to engage in mastery of a bright, red thing. Reach out your hand—what in your life, confined to this poor grit, this lone blue world, could not also be called Mars? Rage, cruelty, the god of your passions, the terrible skills you possess, that forced obedience from a fiery engine, bellicose children, lines of perfect, gleaming code? These things, too, are Mars. They are named for fell gods, they spit on civilized governance—and they might, if whipped or begged, fill some nameless void that hamstrings your soul. Mars is everywhere; every world is Mars. You cannot get there if you are not the lord and leader of your own awful chariot, if you are not the crowned paladin in the car, instead of the animal roped to it, frothing, mad, driven, but never understanding. We have said you must choose, as Bauxbaum and Oorm and Fo chose—to choose is to understand your own highest excellence, even if that is only to bake bread and keep promises. You must become great enough here that Mars will accept you.

Some are chosen to this life. Mars itself is chosen to it, never once in all its iterations having been ruled by democracy. You may love Mars, but Mars loves a crown, a sceptre, a horn-mooned diadem spangled in ice opals. This is how the bride of Mars must be dressed. Make no mistake—no matter your gender, you are the blushing innocent brought to the bed of a mate as ancient and inscrutable as any deathshead bridegroom out of myth. Did you think that the planet would bend to your will? That you would control it? Oh, it is a lovely word: Overlord. Emperor. Pharaoh. Princeps. But you will be changed by it as by a virus. Mars will fill your empty, abandoned places. But the greatest of them understood their place. The overlord embraces the red planet, but in the end, Mars always triumphs. You will wake in your thousand year reign to discover your hair gone red, your translucent skin covered in dust, your three hearts suddenly fused into a molten, stony core. You will cease to want food, and seek out only cold, black air to drink. You will face the sun and turn, slowly, in circles, for days on end. Your thoughts will slow and become grand; you will see as a planet sees, speak as it speaks, which is to say: the long view, the perfected sentence.

And one morning you will wake up and your mouth will be covered over in stone, but the land beneath you, crimson as a promise, as a ruby, as an unrhymed couplet, as a virus—the land, or the machine, or the child, or the book, will speak with your voice, and you will be an overlord, and how proud we shall be of you, here, by the sea, listening to the dawn break over a new shore.

DARYL GREGORY   Born and raised in Chicago, Daryl Gregory made his first couple of fiction sales in the early 1990s, then paused and returned over a decade later. He won the Crawford Award for his debut novel, *Pandemonium* (2008), and his second novel, *The Devil's Alphabet* (2009), was named by *Publishers Weekly* as one of the best of the year.

"Second Person, Present Tense" postulates a drug that can destroy the construction of self. This has happened to a teenaged girl, and her new replacement self has been, in effect, raised for a couple of years by her neurologist. Now she has to go back to the family that raised her original self . . . a person she can remember, but whom she is not.

SECOND PERSON, PRESENT TENSE

If you think, "I breathe," the "I" is extra. There is no you to say "I." What we call "I" is just a swinging door which moves when we inhale or when we exhale.

—SHUN RYU SUZUKI

I used to think the brain was the most important organ in the body, until I realized who was telling me that.

—EMO PHILLIPS

When I enter the office, Dr. S is leaning against the desk, talking earnestly to the dead girl's parents. He isn't happy, but when he looks up he puts on a smile for me. "And here she is," he says, like a game show host revealing the grand prize. The people in the chairs turn, and Dr. Subramaniam gives me a private, encouraging wink.

The father stands first, a blotchy, square-faced man with a tight belly he carries like a basketball. As in our previous visits, he is almost frowning, struggling to match his face to his emotions. The mother, though, has already been crying, and her face is wide open: joy, fear, hope, relief. It's way over the top.

"Oh, Therese," she says. "Are you ready to come home?"

Their daughter was named Therese. She died of an overdose almost two years ago, and since then Mitch and Alice Klass have visited this hospital dozens of times, *looking for her*. They desperately want me to be their daughter, and so in their heads I already am.

My hand is still on the door handle. "Do I have a choice?" On paper I'm only seventeen years old. I have no money, no credit cards, no job, no car. I own only a handful of clothes. And Robierto, the burliest orderly on the ward, is in the hallway behind me, blocking my escape.

Therese's mother seems to stop breathing for a moment. She's a slim, narrow-boned woman who seems tall until she stands next to anyone. Mitch raises a hand to her shoulder, then drops it.

As usual, whenever Alice and Mitch come to visit, I feel like I've walked into the middle of a soap opera and no one's given me my lines. I look directly at Dr. S, and his face is frozen into that professional smile. Several times over the past year he's convinced them to let me stay longer, but they're not listening anymore. They're my legal guardians, and they have Other Plans. Dr. S looks away from me, rubs the side of his nose.

"That's what I thought," I say.

The father scowls. The mother bursts into fresh tears, and she cries all the way out of the building. Dr. Subramaniam watches from the entrance as we drive away, his hands in his pockets. I've never been so angry with him in my life—all two years of it.

. . . .

The name of the drug is Zen, or Zombie, or just Z. Thanks to Dr. S I have a pretty good idea of how it killed Therese.

"Flick your eyes to the left," he told me one afternoon. "Now glance to the right. Did you see the room blur as your eyes moved?" He waited until I did it again. "No blur. No one sees it."

This is the kind of thing that gets brain doctors hot and bothered. Not only could no one see the blur, their brains edited it out completely. Skipped over it—left view, then right view, with nothing between—then fiddled with the person's time sense so that it didn't even *seem* missing.

The scientists figured out that the brain was editing out shit all the time. They wired up patients and told them to lift one of their fingers, move it any time they wanted. Each time, the brain started the signal traveling toward the finger up to 120 milliseconds *before* the patient consciously decided to move it. Dr. S said you could see the brain warming up right before the patient consciously thought, *now*.

This is weird, but it gets weirder the longer you think about it. And I've been thinking about this a lot.

The conscious mind—the "I" that's thinking, hey, I'm thirsty, I'll reach for that cold cup of water—hasn't really decided anything. The signal to start moving your hand has already traveled halfway down your arm by the time *you* even realize *you* are thirsty. *Thought* is an afterthought. By the way, the brain says, we've decided to move your arm, so please have the thought to move it.

The gap is normally 120 milliseconds, max. Zen extends this minutes. Hours.

If you run into somebody who's on Zen, you won't notice much. The person's brain is still making decisions, and the body still follows orders. You can talk to the them, and they can talk to you. You can tell each other jokes, go out for hamburgers, do homework, have sex.

But the person isn't conscious. There is no "I" there. You might as well be talking to a computer. And *two* people on Zen—"you" and "I"—are just puppets talking to puppets.

.   .   .   .

It's a little girl's room strewn with teenager. Stuffed animals crowd the shelves and window sills, shoulder to shoulder with stacks of Christian rock CDs and hair brushes and bottles of nail polish. Pin-ups from *Teen People* are taped to the wall, next to a bulletin board dripping with soccer ribbons and rec league gymnastics medals going back to second grade. Above the desk, a plaque titled "I Promise . . ." exhorting Christian youth to abstain from premarital sex. And everywhere taped and pinned to the walls, the photos: Therese at Bible camp, Therese on the balance beam, Therese with her arms around her youth group friends. Every morning she could open her eyes to a thousand reminders of who she was, who she'd been, who she was supposed to become.

I pick up the big stuffed panda that occupies the place of pride on the bed. It looks older than me, and the fur on the face is worn down to the batting. The button eyes hang by white thread—they've been re-sewn, maybe more than once.

Therese's father sets down the pitifully small bag that contains everything I've taken from the hospital: toiletries, a couple of changes of clothes, and five of Dr. S's books. "I guess old Boo Bear was waiting for you," he says.

"Boo W. Bear."

"Yes, Boo W!" It pleases him that I know this. As if it proves anything. "You know, your mother dusted this room every week. She never doubted that you'd come back."

I have never been here, and *she* is not coming back, but already I'm tired of correcting pronouns. "Well, that was nice," I say.

"She's had a tough time of it. She knew people were talking, probably holding her responsible—both of us, really. And she was worried about them saying things about you. She couldn't stand them thinking that you were a wild girl."

"Them?"

He blinks. "The Church."

Ah. *The Church.* The term carried so many feelings and connotations for Therese that months ago I stopped trying to sort them out. The Church was the red-brick building of the Davenport Church of Christ, shafts of dusty light through rows of tall, glazed windows shaped like gravestones. The Church was God and the Holy Ghost (but not Jesus—he was personal, separate somehow). Mostly, though, it was the congregation, dozens and dozens of people who'd known her since before she was born. They loved her, they watched out for her, and they evaluated her every step. It was like having a hundred overprotective parents.

I almost laugh. "The Church thinks Therese was wild?"

He scowls, but whether because I've insulted the Church or because I keep referring to his daughter by name, I'm not sure. "Of course not. It's just that you caused a lot of worry." His voice has assumed a sober tone that's probably never failed to unnerve his daughter. "You know, the Church prayed for you every week."

"They did?" I do know Therese well enough to be sure this would have mortified her. She was a pray-er, not a pray-ee.

Therese's father watches my face for the bloom of shame, maybe a few tears. From contrition it should have been one small step to confession. It's hard for me to take any of this seriously.

I sit down on the bed and sink deep into the mattress. This is not going to work. The double bed takes up most of the room, with only a few feet of open space around it. Where am I going to meditate?

"Well," Therese's father says. His voice has softened. Maybe he thinks he's won. "You probably want to get changed," he says.

He goes to the door but doesn't leave. I stand by the window, but I can feel him there, waiting. Finally the oddness of this makes me turn around.

He's staring at the floor, a hand behind his neck. Therese might have been able to intuit his mood, but it's beyond me.

"We want to help you, Therese. But there's so many things we just don't understand. Who gave you the drugs, why you went off with that boy, why you would—" His hand moves, a stifled gesture that could be anger, or just frustration. "It's just . . . hard."

"I know," I say. "Me too."

He shuts the door when he leaves, and I push the panda to the floor and flop onto my back in relief. Poor Mr. Klass. He just wants to know if his daughter fell from grace, or was pushed.

· · · ·

When I want to freak myself out, "I" think about "me" thinking about having an "I." The only thing stupider than puppets talking to puppets is a puppet talking to itself.

Dr. S says that nobody knows what the mind is, or how the brain generates it, and nobody *really* knows about consciousness. We talked almost every day while I was in the hospital, and after he saw that I was interested in this stuff—how could I *not* be?—he gave me books and we'd talk about brains and how they cook up thoughts and make decisions.

"How do I explain this?" he always starts. And then he tries out the metaphors he's working on for his book. My favorite is the Parliament, the Page, and the Queen.

"The brain isn't one thing, of course," he told me. "It's millions of firing cells, and those resolve into hundreds of active sites, and so it is with the mind. There are dozens of nodes in the mind, each one trying to out-shout the others. For any decision, the mind erupts with noise, and that triggers . . . how do I explain this . . . Have you ever seen the British Parliament on C-SPAN?" Of course I had: in a hospital, TV is a constant companion. "These members of the mind's parliament, they're all shouting in chemicals and electrical charges, until enough of the voices are shouting in unison. Ding! That's a 'thought,' a 'decision.' The Parliament immediately sends a signal to the body to act on the decision, and at the same time it tells the Page to take the news—"

"Wait, who's the Page?"

He waves his hand. "That's not important right now." (Weeks later, in a different discussion, Dr. S will explain that the Page isn't one thing, but a cascade of neural events in the temporal area of the limbic system that meshes the neural map of the new thought with the existing neural map— but by then I know that "neural map" is just another metaphor for another deeply complex thing or process, and that I'll never get to the bottom of this. Dr. S said not to worry about it, that nobody gets to the bottom of it.) "The Page takes the news of the decision to the Queen."

"All right then, who's the Queen? Consciousness?"

"Exactly right! The self itself."

He beamed at me, his attentive student. Talking about this stuff gets Dr. S going like nothing else, but he's oblivious to the way I let the neck of my scrubs fall open when I stretch out on the couch. If only I could have tucked the two hemispheres of my brain into a lace bra.

"The Page," he said, "delivers its message to Her Majesty, telling her what the Parliament has decided. The Queen doesn't need to know about all the other arguments that went on, all the other possibilities that were thrown out. She simply needs to know what to announce to her subjects. The Queen tells the parts of the body to act on the decision."

"Wait, I thought the Parliament had already sent out the signal. You said before that you can see the brain warming up before the self even knows about it."

"That's the joke. The Queen announces the decision, and she thinks that her subjects are obeying her commands, but in reality, they have already been told what to do. They're already reaching for their glasses of water."

* * * *

I pad down to the kitchen in bare feet, wearing Therese's sweatpants and a T-shirt. The shirt is a little tight; Therese, champion dieter and Olympic-level purger, was a bit smaller than me.

Alice is at the table, already dressed, a book open in front of her. "Well, you slept in this morning," she says brightly. Her face is made up, her hair sprayed into place. The coffee cup next to the book is empty. She's been waiting for hours.

I look around for a clock, and find one over the door. It's only nine. At the hospital I slept in later than that all the time. "I'm starved," I say. There's a refrigerator, a stove, and dozens of cabinets.

I've never made my own breakfast. Or any lunch or dinner, for that matter. For my entire life, my meals have been served on cafeteria trays. "Do you have scrambled eggs?"

She blinks. "Eggs? You don't—" She abruptly stands. "Sure. Sit down, Therese, and I'll make you some."

"Just call me 'Terry,' okay?"

Alice stops, thinks about saying something—I can almost hear the clank of cogs and ratchets—until she abruptly strides to the cabinet, crouches, and pulls out a non-stick pan.

I take a guess on which cabinet holds the coffee mugs, guess right, and take the last inch of coffee from the pot. "Don't you have to go to work?" I say. Alice does something at a restaurant supply company; Therese has always been hazy on the details.

"I've taken a leave," she says. She cracks an egg against the edge of the pan, does something subtle with the shells as the yolk squeezes out and plops into the pan, and folds the shell halves into each other. All with one hand.

"Why?"

She smiles tightly. "We couldn't just abandon you after getting you home. I thought we might need some time together. During this adjustment period."

"So when do I have to see this therapist? Whatsisname." My executioner.

"Her. Dr. Mehldau's in Baltimore, so we'll drive there tomorrow." This is their big plan. Dr. Subramaniam couldn't bring back Therese, so they're running to anyone who says they can. "You know, she's had a lot of success with people in your situation. That's her book." She nods at the table.

"So? Dr. Subramaniam is writing one too." I pick up the book. *The Road Home: Finding the Lost Children of Zen*. "What if I don't go along with this?"

She says nothing, chopping at the eggs. I'll be eighteen in four months. Dr. S said that it will become a lot harder for them to hold me then. This ticking clock sounds constantly in my head, and I'm sure it's loud enough for Alice and Mitch to hear it too.

"Let's just try Dr. Mehldau first."

"First? What then?" She doesn't answer. I flash on an image of me tied down to the bed, a priest making a cross over my twisting body. It's a fantasy, not a Therese memory—I can tell the difference. Besides, if this had already happened to Therese, it wouldn't have been a priest.

"Okay then," I say. "What if I just run away?"

"If you turn into a fish," she says lightly, "then I will turn into a fisherman and fish for you."

"What?" I'm laughing. I haven't heard Alice speak in anything but straight-forward, earnest sentences.

Alice's smile is sad. "You don't remember?"

"Oh, yeah." The memory clicks. "*Runaway Bunny*. Did she like that?"

. . . .

Dr. S's book is about me. Well, Zen O.D.-ers in general, but there are only a couple thousand of us. Z's not a hugely popular drug, in the U.S. or any-where else. It's not a hallucinogen. It's not a euphoric or a depressant. You don't speed, mellow out, or even get high in the normal sense. It's hard to see what the attraction is. Frankly, I have trouble seeing it.

Dr. S says that most drugs aren't about making you feel better, they're about not feeling anything at all. They're about numbness, escape. And Zen is a kind of arty, designer escape hatch. Zen disables the Page, locks him in his room, so that he can't make his deliveries to the Queen. There's no up-date to the neural map, and the Queen stops hearing what Parliament is up to. With no orders to bark, she goes silent. It's that silence that people like Therese craved.

But the real attraction—again, for people like Therese—is the overdose. Swallow way too much Zen and the Page can't get out for weeks. When he finally gets out, he can't remember the way back to the Queen's castle. The whole process of updating the self that's been going on for years is suddenly derailed. The silent Queen can't be found.

The Page, poor guy, does the only thing he can. He goes out and delivers the proclamations to the first girl he sees.

The Queen is dead. Long live the Queen.

. . . .

"Hi, Terry. I'm Dr. Mehldau." She's a stubby woman with a pleasant round face, and short dark hair shot with gray. She offers me her hand. Her fingers are cool and thin.

"You called me Terry."

"I was told that you prefer to go by that. Do you want me to call you something else?"

"No . . . I just expected you to make me say my name is 'Therese' over and over."

She laughs and sits down in a red leather chair that looks soft but sturdy. "I don't think that would be very helpful, do you? I can't make you do any-thing you don't want to do, Terry."

"So I'm free to go."

"Can't stop you. But I do have to report back to your parents on how we're doing."

My parents.

She shrugs. "It's my job. Why don't you have a seat and we can talk about why you're here."

The chair opposite her is cloth, not leather, but it's still nicer than anything in Dr. Subramaniam's office. The entire office is nicer than Dr. S's office. Daffodil walls in white trim, big windows glowing behind white cloth shades, tropically colored paintings.

I don't sit down.

"Your job is to turn me into Mitch and Alice's daughter. I'm not going to do that. So any time we spend talking is just bullshit."

"Terry, no one can turn you into something you're not."

"Well then we're done here." I walk across the room—though "stroll" is what I'm shooting for—and pick up an African-looking wooden doll from the bookshelf. The shelves are decorated with enough books to look serious, but there are long open spaces for arty arrangements of candlesticks and Japanese fans and plaques that advertise awards and appreciations. Dr. S's bookshelves are for holding books, and books stacked on books. Dr. Mehldau's bookshelves are for selling the idea of Dr. Mehldau.

"So what are you, a psychiatrist or a psychologist or what?" I've met all kinds in the hospital. The psychiatrists are MDs like Dr. S and can give you drugs. I haven't figured out what the psychologists are good for.

"Neither," she says. "I'm a counselor."

"So what's the 'doctor' for?"

"Education." Her voice didn't change, but I get the impression that the question's annoyed her. This makes me strangely happy.

"Okay, Dr. Counselor, what are you supposed to counsel me about? I'm not crazy. I know who Therese was, I know what she did, I know that she used to walk around in my body." I put the doll back in its spot next to a glass cube that could be a paperweight. "But I'm not her. This is my body, and I'm not going to kill myself just so Alice and Mitch can have their baby girl back."

"Terry, no one's asking you to kill yourself. Nobody can even make you into who you were before."

"Yeah? Then what are they paying you for, then?"

"Let me try to explain. Please, sit down. Please."

I look around for a clock and finally spot one on a high shelf. I mentally set the timer to five minutes and sit opposite her, hands on my knees. "Shoot."

"Your parents asked me to talk to you because I've helped other people in your situation, people who've overdosed on Z."

"Help them what? Pretend to be something they're not?"

"I help them take back what they *are*. Your experience of the world tells you that Therese was some other person. No one's denying that. But you're in a situation where biologically and legally, you're Therese Klass. Do you have plans for dealing with that?"

As a matter of fact I do, and it involves getting the hell out as soon as possible. "I'll deal with it," I say.

"What about Alice and Mitch?"

I shrug. "What about them?"

"They're still your parents, and you're still their child. The overdose convinced you that you're a new person, but that hasn't changed who they are. They're still responsible for you, and they still care for you."

"Not much I can do about that."

"You're right. It's a fact of your life. You have two people who love you, and you're going to be with each other for the rest of your lives. You're going to have to figure out how to relate to each other. Zen may have burned the bridge between you and your past life, but you can build that bridge again."

"Doc, I don't *want* to build that bridge. Look, Alice and Mitch seem like nice people, but if I was looking for parents, I'd pick someone else."

Dr. Mehldau smiles. "None of us get to choose our parents, Terry."

I'm not in the mood to laugh. I nod toward the clock. "This is a waste of time."

She leans forward. I think she's going to try to touch me, but she doesn't. "Terry, you're not going to disappear if we talk about what happened to you. You'll still be here. The only difference is that you'll reclaim those memories as your own. You can get your old life back *and* choose your new life."

Sure, it's that easy. I get to sell my soul and keep it too.

• • • •

I can't remember my first weeks in the hospital, though Dr. S says I was awake. At some point I realized that time was passing, or rather, that there was a me who was passing through time. *I* had lasagna for dinner yesterday, *I* am having meat loaf today. *I* am this girl in a bed. I think I realized this and forgot it several times before I could hold onto it.

Every day was mentally exhausting, because everything was so relentlessly *new*. I stared at the TV remote for a half hour, the name for it on the tip of my tongue, and it wasn't until the nurse picked it up and turned on the TV for me that I thought: *Remote*. And then sometimes, this was followed by a raft of other ideas: *TV. Channel. Gameshow.*

People were worse. They called me by a strange name, and they expected things of me. But to me, every visitor, from the night shift nurse to the janitor to Alice and Mitch Klass, seemed equally important—which is to say, not important at all.

Except for Dr. S. He was there from the beginning, and so he was familiar before I met him. He belonged to me like my own body.

But everything else about the world—the names, the details, the *facts*— had to be hauled into the sunlight, one by one. My brain was like an attic, chock full of old and interesting things jumbled together in no order at all.

I only gradually understood that somebody must have owned this house before me. And then I realized the house was haunted.

· · · ·

After the Sunday service, I'm caught in a stream of people. They lean across the pews to hug Alice and Mitch, then me. They pat my back, squeeze my arms, kiss my cheeks. I know from brief dips into Therese's memories that many of these people are as emotionally close as aunts or uncles. And any of them, if Therese were ever in trouble, would take her in, feed her, and give her a bed to sleep in.

This is all very nice, but the constant petting has me ready to scream.

All I want to do is get back home and take off this dress. I had no choice but to wear one of Therese's girly-girl extravaganzas. Her closet was full of them, and I finally found one that fit, if not comfortably. She loved these dresses, though. They were her floral print flak jackets. Who could doubt the purity of a girl in a high-necked Laura Ashley?

We gradually make our way to the vestibule, then to the sidewalk and the parking lot, under assault the entire way. I stop trying to match their faces to anything in Therese's memories.

At our car, a group of teenagers take turns on me, the girls hugging me tight, the boys leaning into me with half hugs: shoulders together, pelvises apart. One of the girls, freckled, with soft red curls falling past her shoulders, hangs back for awhile, then abruptly clutches me and whispers into my ear, "I'm so glad you're okay, Miss T." Her tone is intense, like she's passing a secret message.

A man moves through the crowd, arms open, smiling broadly. He's in his late twenties or early thirties, his hair cut in a choppy gelled style that's ten years too young for him. He's wearing pressed khakis, a blue Oxford rolled up at the forearms, a checked tie loosened at the throat.

He smothers me in a hug, his cologne like another set of arms. He's easy to find in Therese's memories: This is Jared, the Youth Pastor. He was the most spiritually vibrant person Therese knew, and the object of her crush.

"It's so good to have you back, Therese," he says. His cheek is pressed to mine. "We've missed you."

A few months before her overdose, the youth group was coming back from a weekend-long retreat in the church's converted school bus. Late into the trip, near midnight, Jared sat next to her, and she fell asleep leaning against him, inhaling that same cologne.

"I bet you have," I say. "Watch the hands, *Jared*."

His smile doesn't waver, his hands are still on my shoulders. "I'm sorry?"

"Oh please, you heard me."

He drops his hands, and looks questioningly at my father. He can do sincerity pretty well. "I don't understand, Therese, but if—"

I give him a look that makes him back up a step. At some point later in the trip Therese awoke with Jared still next to her, slumped in the seat, eyes closed and mouth open. His arm was resting between her thighs, a thumb against her knee. She was wearing shorts, and his flesh on hers was hot. His forearm was inches from her warm crotch.

Therese believed that he was asleep.

She believed, too, that it was the rumbling of the school bus that shifted Jared's arm into contact with the crease of her shorts. Therese froze, flushed with arousal and embarrassment.

"Try to work it out, Jared." I get in the car.

· · · ·

The big question I can help answer, Dr. S said, is why there is consciousness. Or, going back to my favorite metaphor, if the Parliament is making all the decisions, why have a Queen at all?

He's got theories, of course. He thinks the Queen is all about storytelling. The brain needs a story that gives all these decisions a sense of purpose, a sense of continuity, so it can remember them and use them in future decisions. The brain can't keep track of the trillions of possible *other* decisions it could have made every moment; it needs one decision, and it needs a who, and a why. The brain lays down the memories, and the consciousness stamps them with identity: I did this, I did that. Those memories become the official record, the precedents that the Parliament uses to help make future decisions.

"The Queen, you see, is a figurehead," Dr. S said. "She represents the kingdom, but she isn't the kingdom itself, or even in control of it."

"I don't feel like a figurehead," I said.

Dr. S laughed. "Me neither. Nobody does."

· · · ·

Dr. Mehldau's therapy involves occasional joint sessions with Alice and Mitch, reading aloud from Therese's old diaries, and home movies. Today's video features a pre-teen Therese dressed in sheets, surrounded by kids in bathrobes, staring fixedly at a doll in a manger.

Dr. Mehldau asks me what Therese was thinking then. Was she enjoying playing Mary? Did she like being on stage?

"How would I know?"

"Then imagine it. What do you *think* Therese is thinking here?"

She tells me to do that a lot. Imagine what she's thinking. Just pretend. Put yourself in her shoes. In her book she calls this "reclaiming." She makes up a lot of her own terms, then defines them however she wants, without research to back her up. Compared to the neurology texts Dr. S lent me, Dr. Mehldau's little book is an Archie comic with footnotes.

"You know what, Therese was a good Christian girl, so she probably loved it."

"Are you sure?"

The wise men come on stage, three younger boys. They plop down their gifts and their lines, and the look on Therese's face is wary. Her line is coming up.

Therese was petrified of screwing up. Everybody would be staring at her. I can almost see the congregation in the dark behind the lights. Alice and Mitch are out there, and they're waiting for every line. My chest tightens, and I realize I'm holding my breath.

Dr. Mehldau's eyes on mine are studiously neutral.

"You know what?" I have no idea what I'm going to say next. I'm stalling for time. I shift my weight in the big beige chair and move a leg underneath me. "The thing I like about Buddhism is Buddhists understand that they've been screwed by a whole string of previous selves. I had nothing to do with the decisions Therese made, the good or bad karma she'd acquired."

This is a riff I've been thinking about in Therese's big girly bedroom. "See, Therese was a Christian, so she probably thought by overdosing that she'd be born again, all her sins forgiven. It's the perfect drug for her: suicide without the corpse."

"Was she thinking about suicide that night?"

"*I don't know.* I could spend a couple weeks mining through Therese's memories, but frankly, I'm not interested. Whatever she was thinking, she wasn't born again. I'm here, and I'm still saddled with her baggage. I am Therese's donkey. I'm a karma donkey."

Dr. Mehldau nods. "Dr. Subramaniam is Buddhist, isn't he?"

"Yeah, but what's . . . ?" It clicks. I roll my eyes. Dr. S and I talked about transference, and I know that my crush on him was par for the course. And it's true that I spend a lot of time—still—thinking about fucking the man. But that doesn't mean I'm wrong. "This is not about that," I say. "I've been thinking about this on my own."

She doesn't fight me on that. "Wouldn't a Buddhist say that you and Therese share the same soul? Self's an illusion. So there's no rider in charge, no donkey. There's just *you.*"

"Just forget it," I say.

"Let's follow this, Terry. Don't you feel you have a responsibility to your old self? Your old self's parents, your old friends? Maybe there's karma you owe."

"And who are you responsible to, Doctor? Who's your patient? Therese, or me?"

She says nothing for a moment, then: "I'm responsible to you."

• • • •

You.

You swallow, surprised that the pills taste like cinnamon. The effect of the drug is intermittent at first. You realize that you're in the back seat of a car, the cell phone in your hand, your friends laughing around you. You're talking to your mother. If you concentrate, you can remember answering the phone, and telling her which friend's house you're staying at tonight. Before you can say goodbye, you're stepping out of the car. The car is parked, your phone is away—and you remember saying goodnight to your mother and riding for a half hour before finding this parking garage. Joelly tosses her red curls and tugs you toward the stairwell: *Come on, Miss T!*

Then you look up and realize that you're on the sidewalk outside an all-ages club, and you're holding a ten dollar bill, ready to hand it to the bouncer. The music thunders every time the door swings open. You turn to Joelly and—

You're in someone else's car. On the Interstate. The driver is a boy you met hours ago, his name is Rush but you haven't asked if that's his first name or his last. In the club you leaned into each other and talked loud over the music about parents and food and the difference between the taste of a fresh cigarette in your mouth and the smell of stale smoke. But then you realize that there's a cigarette in your mouth, you took it from Rush's pack yourself, and you don't like cigarettes. Do you like it now? You don't know. Should you take it out, or keep smoking? You scour your memories, but can discover no reason why you decided to light the cigarette, no reason why you got into the car with this boy. You start to tell yourself a story: he must be a trustworthy person, or you wouldn't have gotten into the car. You took that one cigarette because the boy's feelings would have been hurt.

You're not feeling like yourself tonight. And you like it. You take another drag off the cigarette. You think back over the past few hours, and marvel at everything you've done, all without that constant weight of self-reflection: worry, anticipation, instant regret. Without the inner voice constantly critiquing you.

Now the boy is wearing nothing but boxer shorts, and he's reaching up to a shelf to get a box of cereal, and his back is beautiful. There is hazy light outside the small kitchen window. He pours Froot Loops into a bowl for you, and he laughs, though quietly because his mother is asleep in the next room. He looks at your face and frowns. He asks you what's the matter. You look down, and you're fully dressed. You think back, and realize that you've been in this boy's apartment for hours. You made out in his bedroom, and the boy took off his clothes, and you kissed his chest and ran your hands along his legs. You let him put his hand under your shirt and cup your breasts, but you didn't go any further. Why didn't you have sex? Did he not interest you? No—you were wet. You were excited. Did you feel guilty? Did you feel ashamed?

What were you thinking?

When you get home there will be hell to pay. Your parents will be furious, and worse, they will pray for you. The entire church will pray for you. Everyone will know. And no one will ever look at you the same again.

Now there's a cinnamon taste in your mouth, and you're sitting in the boy's car again, outside a convenience store. It's afternoon. Your cell phone is ringing. You turn off the cell phone and put it back in your purse. You swallow, and your throat is dry. That boy—Rush—is buying you another bottle of water. What was it you swallowed? Oh, yes. You think back, and remember putting all those little pills in your mouth. Why did you take so many? Why did you take another one at all? Oh, yes.

* * * *

Voices drift up from the kitchen. It's before 6 AM, and I just want to pee and get back to sleep, but then I realize they're talking about me.

"She doesn't even *walk* the same. The way she holds herself, the way she talks . . ."

"It's all those books Dr. Subramaniam gave her. She's up past one every night. Therese never read like that, not *science*."

"No, it's not just the words, it's how she *sounds*. That low voice . . ." She sobs. "Oh hon, I didn't know it would be this way. It's like she's right, it's like it isn't her at all."

He doesn't say anything. Alice's crying grows louder, subsides. The clink of dishes in the sink. I step back, and Mitch speaks again.

"Maybe we should try the camp," he says.

"No, no, no! Not yet. Dr. Mehldau says she's making progress. We've got to—"

"Of course she's going to say that."

"You said you'd try this, you said you'd give this a chance." The anger cuts through the weeping, and Mitch mumbles something apologetic. I creep back to my bedroom, but I still have to pee, so I make a lot of noise going back out. Alice comes to the bottom of the stairs. "Are you all right, honey?"

I keep my face sleepy and walk into the bathroom. I shut the door and sit down on the toilet in the dark.

What fucking camp?

* * * *

"Let's try again," Dr. Mehldau said. "Something pleasant and vivid."

I'm having trouble concentrating. The brochure is like a bomb in my pocket. It wasn't hard to find, once I decided to look for it. I want to ask Dr. Mehldau about the camp, but I know that once I bring it into the open, I'll trigger a showdown between the doctor and the Klasses, with me in the middle.

"Keep your eyes closed," she says. "Think about Therese's tenth birthday. In her diary, she wrote that was the best birthday she'd ever had. Do you remember Sea World?"

"Vaguely." I could see dolphins jumping—two at a time, three at a time. It had been sunny and hot. With every session it was getting easier for me to pop into Therese's memories. Her life was on DVD, and I had the remote.

"Do you remember getting wet at the Namu and Shamu show?"

I laughed. "I think so." I could see the metal benches, the glass wall just in front of me, the huge shapes in the blue-green water. "They had the whales flip their big tail fins. We got drenched."

"Can you picture who was there with you? Where are your parents?"

There was a girl, my age, I can't remember her name. The sheets of water were coming down on us and we were screaming and laughing. Afterward my parents toweled us off. They must have been sitting up high, out of the splash zone. Alice looked much younger: happier, and a little heavier. She was wider at the hips. This was before she started dieting and exercising, when she was Mom-sized.

My eyes pop open. "Oh God."

"Are you okay?"

"I'm fine—it was just . . . like you said. Vivid." That image of a younger Alice still burns. For the first time I realize how *sad* she is now.

"I'd like a joint session next time," I say.

"Really? All right. I'll talk to Alice and Mitch. Is there anything in particular you want to talk about?"

"Yeah. We need to talk about Therese."

. . . . .

Dr. S says everybody wants to know if the original neural map, the old Queen, can come back. Once the map to the map is lost, can you find it again? And if you do, then what happens to the new neural map, the new Queen?

"Now, a good Buddhist would tell you that this question is unimportant. After all, the cycle of existence is not just between lives. *Samsara* is every moment. The self continuously dies and recreates itself."

"Are you a good Buddhist?" I asked him.

He smiled. "Only on Sunday mornings."

"You go to church?"

"I golf."

. . . . .

There's a knock and I open my eyes. Alice steps into my room, a stack of folded laundry in her arms. "Oh!"

I've rearranged the room, pushing the bed into the corner to give me a few square feet of free space on the floor.

Her face goes through a few changes. "I don't suppose you're praying."

"No."

She sighs, but it's a mock-sigh. "I didn't think so." She moves around me and sets the laundry on the bed. She picks up the book there, *Entering the Stream.* "Dr. Subramaniam gave you this?"

She's looking at the passage I've highlighted. *But loving kindness— maitri—toward ourselves doesn't mean getting rid of anything. The point is not to try to change ourselves. Meditation practice isn't about trying to throw ourselves away and become something better. It's about befriending who we already are.*

"Well." She sets the book down, careful to leave it open to the same page. "That sounds a bit like Dr. Mehldau."

I laugh. "Yeah, it does. Did she tell you I wanted you and Mitch to be at the next session?"

"We'll be there." She works around the room, picking up T-shirts and underwear. I stand up to get out of the way. Somehow she manages to straighten up as she moves—righting books that had fallen over, setting Boo W. Bear back to his place on the bed, sweeping an empty chip bag into the garbage can—so that as she collects my dirty laundry she's cleaning the entire room, like the Cat in the Hat's cleaner-upper machine.

"Alice, in the last session I remembered being at Sea World, but there was a girl next to me. Next to Therese."

"Sea World? Oh, that was the Hammel girl, Marcy. They took you to Ohio with them on their vacation that year."

"Who did?"

"The Hammels. You were gone all week. All you wanted for your birthday was spending money for the trip."

"You weren't there?"

She picks up the jeans I left at the foot of the bed. "We always meant to go to Sea World, but your father and I never got out there."

· · · ·

"This is our last session," I say.

Alice, Mitch, Dr. Mehldau: I have their complete attention.

The doctor, of course, is the first to recover. "It sounds like you've got something you want to tell us."

"*Oh* yeah."

Alice seems frozen, holding herself in check. Mitch rubs the back of his neck, suddenly intent on the carpet.

"I'm not going along with this anymore." I make a vague gesture. "Everything: the memory exercises, all this imagining of what Therese felt. I finally figured it out. It doesn't matter to you if I'm Therese or not. You just want me to think I'm her. I'm not going along with the manipulation anymore."

Mitch shakes his head. "Honey, you took a *drug*." He glances at me, looks back at his feet. "If you took LSD and saw God, that doesn't mean you really saw God. Nobody's trying to manipulate you, we're trying to *undo* the manipulation."

"That's bullshit, Mitch. You all keep acting like I'm schizophrenic, that I don't know what's real or not. Well, part of the problem is that the longer I talk to Dr. Mehldau here, the more fucked up I am."

Alice gasps.

Dr. Mehldau puts out a hand to soothe her, but her eyes are on me. "Terry, what your father's trying to say is that even though you feel like a new person, there's a *you* that existed before the drug. That exists now."

"Yeah? You know all those O.D.-ers in your book who say they've 're-claimed' themselves? Maybe they only *feel* like their old selves."

"It's *possible*," she says. "But I don't think they're fooling themselves. They've come to accept the parts of themselves they've lost, the family members they've left behind. They're people like you." She regards me with that standard-issue look of concern that doctors pick up with their diplomas. "Do you really want to feel like an orphan the rest of your life?"

"What?" From out of nowhere, tears well in my eyes. I cough to clear my throat, and the tears keep coming, until I smear them off on my arm. I feel like I've been sucker punched. "Hey, look Alice, just like you," I say.

"It's normal," Dr. Mehldau says. "When you woke up in the hospital, you felt completely alone. You felt like a brand new person, no family, no friends. And you're still just starting down this road. In a lot of ways you're not even two years old."

"*Damn* you're good," I say. "I didn't even see that one coming."

"Please, don't leave. Let's—"

"Don't worry, I'm not leaving yet." I'm at the door, pulling my backpack from the peg by the door. I dig into the pocket, and pull out the brochure. "You know about this?"

Alice speaks for the first time. "Oh honey, no . . ."

Dr. Mehldau takes it from me, frowning. On the front is a nicely posed picture of a smiling teenage boy hugging relieved parents. She looks at Alice and Mitch. "Are you considering this?"

"It's their big stick, Dr. Mehldau. If you can't come through for them, or I bail out, *boom*. You know what goes on there?"

She opens the pages, looking at pictures of the cabins, the obstacle course, the big lodge where kids just like me engage in "intense group sessions with trained counselors" where they can "recover their true identities." She shakes her head. "Their approach is different than mine . . ."

"I don't know, doc. Their *approach* sounds an awful lot like 'reclaiming.' I got to hand it to you, you had me going for awhile. Those visualization exercises? I was getting so good that I could even visualize stuff that never happened. I bet you could visualize me right into Therese's head."

I turn to Alice and Mitch. "You've got a decision to make. Dr. Mehldau's program is a bust. So are you sending me off to brainwashing camp or not?"

Mitch has his arm around his wife. Alice, amazingly, is dry-eyed. Her eyes are wide, and she's staring at me like a stranger.

• • • •

It rains the entire trip back from Baltimore, and it's still raining when we pull up to the house. Alice and I run to the porch step, illuminated by the glare of headlights. Mitch waits until Alice unlocks the door and we move inside, and then pulls away.

"Does he do that a lot?" I ask.

"He likes to drive when he's upset."

"Oh." Alice goes through the house, turning on lights. I follow her into the kitchen.

"Don't worry, he'll be all right." She opens the refrigerator door and crouches down. "He just doesn't know what to do with you."

"He wants to put me in the camp, then."

"Oh, not that. He just never had a daughter who talked back to him before." She carries a Tupperware cake holder to the table. "I made carrot cake. Can you get down the plates?"

She's such a small woman. Face to face, she comes up only to my chin. The hair on the top of her head is thin, made thinner by the rain, and her scalp is pink.

"I'm not Therese. I never will be Therese."

"Oh, I know," she says, half sighing. And she does know it; I can see it in her face. "It's just that you look so much like her."

I laugh. "I can dye my hair. Maybe get a nose job."

"It wouldn't work, I'd still recognize you." She pops the lid and sets it aside. The cake is a wheel with icing that looks half an inch thick. Miniature candy carrots line the edge.

"Wow, you made that before we left? Why?"

Alice shrugs, and cuts into it. She turns the knife on its side and uses the blade to lever a huge triangular wedge onto my plate. "I thought we might need it, one way or another."

She places the plate in front of me, and touches me lightly on the arm. "I know you want to move out. I know you may never want to come back."

"It's not that I—"

"We're not going to stop you. But wherever you go, you'll still be my daughter, whether you like it or not. You don't get to decide who loves you."

ALAYA DAWN JOHNSON   Born in Washington, D.C., Alaya Dawn Johnson lives in New York City, where she studied East Asian languages and cultures at Columbia University, and where she has worked as a journalist and in the book publishing industry. She has traveled extensively in Japan. Her short fiction began appearing in 2005. Her latest book, a YA novel, is *The Summer Prince* (2013).

"Third Day Lights" starts as fantasy and becomes SF in the manner of "planetary romance," the Leigh Brackett and Michael Moorcock tradition. In a very far future, humanity is destroying universes to drain as power sources for a huge posthuman project.

THIRD DAY LIGHTS

The mist was thick as clotted cream, shot through with light from the luminous maggots in the sand. And through that mist, which I knew would entrap almost any creature unlucky enough to wander through it, came my first supplicant in over thirty cycles. He rode atop one of the butterfly men's great black deer, which greeted me with a sweep of its massive antlers. His skin was as pale as the sand was black; his eyes were the clear, hard color of chipped jade. A fine, pale fuzz covered his scalp, like the babies of humans. He had full, hard lips and high cheekbones. His nose had been broken several times, and was quite large regardless. His ears protruded slightly from his head.

He was too beautiful. I did not believe it. Oh, I had, in my travels, seen men far more attractive than he. Men who had eagerly accepted me in whatever form I chose, and had momentarily pleased me. But I had never seen this kind of beauty, that of the hard edges and chipped flakes of jade. That aura of bitterly mastered power, and unspeakable grief subdued but somehow not overcome. He gave the impression that he was a man to respect, a man who would understand my own loneliness despite my family, a man who might, perhaps, after so many cycles . . .

But I have not lived for so long away from my Trunk by believing in such things.

Eyes never leaving mine, he touched the neck of the deer and it knelt for him to dismount. His bare feet should have frozen solid seconds after they touched the sand, and the maggots begun devouring the icy flesh, but instead he stood before my staircase, perfectly at ease. From within the hostile mist, lacy hands and mouths struggled towards him but never quite touched.

That is how I knew he wasn't human.

I anticipated with relish the moment when he would speak and allow me to drop him on the other side of the desert. But he stared at me and I glowered back and then I understood: he knew what I was. He knew *who* I was. At the time, I thought this meant that he was incalculably old. Now, I am not so sure.

"Why do you stand before my gate? Tell me your purpose."

He stayed silent, of course. His impassive expression never wavered, and yet—perhaps from his slightly quivering shoulders or faintly irregular breathing—I had the impression that he was laughing at me.

It had been a long time since I had been the subject of even implied ridicule. Not many willingly mock a demon of the scorched desert. I had chosen one of my more forbidding guises before I opened the door. My skin was black as the sand, my naked body sexually ambiguous and covered with thousands of tiny horns that swiveled in whatever direction I looked. The horns had been one of Charm's ideas—the kind he gets when he's drunk on saltwater. At his request, I wore them on this occasion—the one day each cycle when I accept supplicants. I had thought that my appearance be appropriately awe-inspiring, and yet from the look in the not-quite-a-man's eyes, I realized that he had not been inspired to awe. I growled to cover my uneasiness—*what creature is this?*

I stormed back inside the house, sulfur gas streaming from between the growing cracks in my skin. The mist groaned when it touched me and then receded. I didn't need to look back at the man to know that he hadn't moved. Inside, door shut, I changed my appearance again. I became monstrous, a blue leviathan of four heads and sixteen impossible arms. I shook my wrists in succession, so the bracelets made of human teeth clacked and cascaded in a sinister echo off the walls of my castle.

Yes, I thought, faces snarling, *this should do.*

I stepped forward to open the door again and saw Mahi's face on the floor beneath me, grinning in two-dimensional languor.

"You look nice," he said. "Some upstart at the door? Drop him in the maw, Naeve. I'm sure it's been some time since she's had a nice meal."

The maw is Mahi's mother, but she rejected him because he can only move in two dimensions. She considered him defective, but I have found his defect to be occasionally very useful. He vents his anger by suggesting I toss every supplicant across the scorched desert into her mouth. I did once, nearly three hundred cycles ago, just for his benefit, but we could all hear the sound of her chewing and mating and screaming in some kind of inscrutable ecstasy for days.

Two of my faces snarled down at him, one looked away and the fourth just sighed and said, "Perhaps." The maw is all the way on the Eastern border of the desert, but that day her screams pierced as though she were gifting it to our ears—some property of the sand, I suppose. Charm, Top and I nearly went crazy, but Mahi seemed to enjoy it. My family is closer to me than the Trunk ever was, but I know no more about their previous lives than what they choose to tell me. I often wonder what Mahi's life was like inside the maw.

He faded into the floor, off in some two-dimensional direction I couldn't see. I stepped back outside.

The man was still there, absolutely motionless despite the veritable riot of mist-shapes that struggled to entangle him. My uneasiness returned: *what is he?* When he saw me, his eyes widened. No other muscles moved, and yet I knew. Oh, for that economy of expression. Even my malleable body could not convey with a hundred gestures the amusement and understanding and wary appreciation he expressed with a simple contraction of eye muscles. I did not scare him.

"Who are you?" I used my smallest head and turned the others away— the view of him through four sets of eyes was oddly intense, disconcerting. He didn't answer. "*What* are you?"

I turned my head to the deer who was kneeling peacefully at his side. "Why did you bring him, honored one?" I said in the language of the butterfly men.

The deer looked up, purple eyes lovely enough to break a lesser creature's heart. Before I saw this man, I would have said that only demons and butterfly men could look in the eyes of a deer and keep their sanity.

"Because he asked me," the deer said—gracefully, simply, infuriatingly.

I went back inside. Because I only had one more chance to get rid of him, I stalked the hallways, screaming and summoning things to toss at the walls. Top absorbed them with her usual equanimity and then turned the walls a shimmering orange—my favorite color. Charm screamed from somewhere near the roof that he was attempting to rest, and could I please keep my temper tantrum to myself? I frowned and finished changing—it was a relief to have one set of eyes again. Some demons enjoy multiplicity, but I've always found it exhausting. Top turned that part of the wall into a mirror, so I could see my handiwork.

"It's very beautiful," she said. A hand emerged from the wall and handed me a long piece of embroidered cloth. I wrapped it around my waist, made my aureoles slightly larger and walked to the door.

The corners of his mouth actually quirked up when he saw me this time, and the understanding in his eyes made me ache. I did not believe it, and yet I did. I walked closer to him, doggedly swaying my mahogany hips, raising my arms and shaking my wrists, which were still encircled with bracelets of human teeth. This close I could see that his skin was unnaturally smooth—the only physical indication that he was something other than human.

"Come," I said, my voice pitched low—breathy and seductive in a human sort of way. "Just tell me your name, traveler, and I'll let you inside."

I leaned in closer to him, so our noses nearly touched. "Come," I whispered, "tell me."

His lips quirked again. Bile of frustration and rage choked my all-too-human throat and I began to lose my grip on my body. I could feel it returning to my mundane form, and after a moment I stopped trying to resist. My skin shifted from glowing mahogany to a prosaic cobalt blue. My hair turned wild and red; my second arms grew rapidly beneath the first and my aureoles contracted.

My skin tingled with frustration and not a little fear—I didn't *need* anyone else in my family—but I refused to show it as I took a passing glance in his eyes. No triumph there, not even relief.

I walked up the stairs, but I didn't hear his footsteps following.

"Well," I said, gesturing with my left hands, "are you coming?"

The man took a step forward, and then another—he moved as though he were exhausted, or the cold of the maggots and mist had subtly affected him after all.

"Go home," he said to the deer, who had risen beside him. "One way or another, I will not need your help when I leave this place."

His voice made me want to weep tears so large Charm would dance beneath me, singing as though nectar were falling from the sky. It was uncompromisingly strong, yet tender all the same, as though he had seen too much not to grant anyone the tenderness he had been denied.

Do not believe it, I told myself, but I was already losing the battle.

"Are you coming?" I repeated, forced by unexpected emotion into a parody of callous disdain.

"Yes," he said quietly. I do not think I could have stood it if all that unexpected tenderness were suddenly directed at me, but he seemed distracted, watching the mist long after the deer had disappeared.

"What is your name?" I asked, just before I opened the door again. An unlikely gambit, of course, but I had to try.

Amusement suddenly retuned to his eyes. "I'm called Israphel," he said.

. . . .

Mahi had positioned himself in front of the door in his best impression of three-dimensionality. It nearly worked, if you didn't look at him too critically, or move. He grew indistinct when viewed from oblique angles, until he disappeared altogether. His appearance was, in some ways, even more malleable than my own. For this occasion he had fashioned himself to look like one of the wildly costumed humans we sometimes saw in our travels: decked entirely in iridescent feathers of saffron and canary yellow, strewn together with beads that glinted in an imagined sunlight.

"You let him in?" Mahi shrieked, several octaves higher than normal. I've often wondered how a two-dimensional creature can create such startlingly loud sounds in a multi-dimensional universe.

Something in Israphel's demeanor exuded fascination, though when I looked closely at him I didn't know how I could tell—his expression was still one of polite interest.

"The maw's only son, I presume? I had heard she rejected you, but . . . this is an honor."

Mahi sniffed, put out at having been discovered so quickly. His feathers bristled. "Yes, well. A two-dimensional mouth is not particularly useful for three-dimensional food, is it?" He turned to me, his human mouth stretching and widening as it always did when he was hurt or angry. If it continued to expand, it would settle into a shape even I sometimes found disturbing. Mahi was still, after all, the son of the most feared creature in the scorched desert. He grinned—cruelly—revealing several rows of teeth that appeared to be the silently wailing heads of countless ancient creatures.

"I'm surprised at you, Naeve," he said, his voice a studied drawl. "Confounded by a pesky human? Losing your touch, are you?"

I frowned at him, trying to decide if he was being deliberately obtuse. "He's not a human, Mahi," I said carefully.

Mahi's face had now been almost entirely subsumed by his hideous mouth, but he still managed to look thoughtful. "No . . . he isn't, is he? Well, I trust you'll get rid of him soon." He folded himself into some inscrutable shape and seemed to disappear.

Israphel turned to look at me. He smiled, and I felt my skin turning a deeper, more painful shade of blue. For a calculated moment, eyes were transparent as windowpanes: amusement and fascination and just a trace of wonder . . .

By the Trunk, who is this man?

"What is my first task, Naeve?" he asked, very gently.

I turned away and walked blindly down a hall that had not been there a moment before. I didn't look, but I knew he was following.

* * * * *

I could practically feel his eyes resting on my back, radiating compassion and equanimity. Out of sheer annoyance, I shifted my body slightly so a gigantic purple eye blinked lazily on my back and then stared straight at him. I had hoped for some kind of reaction—a shriek of surprise, perhaps—but he simply nodded in polite understanding and looked away. His eyes focused on the indigo walls, and he jerked, ever so slightly, in surprise. For a moment I wished for a mouth as big and savage as Mahi's to grin with. I knew he had noticed the gentle rippling of Top's smooth muscles. Israphel looked sharply at my back, but my third eye was beginning to make me feel dizzy, so I subsumed it back into my flesh. No use, I could still sense him.

I ran my hand along Top's indigo gizzards and silently drew the symbol for where I wanted to go. The walls shivered a little in her surprise—it had been nearly a hundred cycles since I had last visited there. But I needed to get rid of this not-a-man quickly, and it was in Top's second appendix that I had saved my cleverest, most wildly impossible task. Even Israphel, with all of his jade green understanding and hard-won wisdom would not be able to solve it.

A light blue membrane slammed across the corridor a few feet ahead of us, blocking the path. Seconds later, a torrent of unidentifiable waste roared just behind it, smelling of freshly digested nematodes and one-eyed birds. Top tried her best, but it was difficult to keep things clean this deep in her bowels. As soon as the last of the waste had gone past, the membrane pulled back and we continued. I surreptitiously glanced at Israphel, but his expression was perfectly bland. Too bland? I wasn't quite sure. Top shunted her waste past us several more times before we reached the entrance to her second appendix. The air here smelled funny, not quite foul but still capable of coating your throat with a thick, decaying mustiness.

"Are you sure about this, Naeve?" Top asked, just before she opened the membranous gate. "It's taking a lot of energy to shunt the digestive flows around you. I'm having difficulty keeping things up. Charm is complaining that his bed feels like cartilage."

"Charm always complains. Let us in."

Israphel paused before the open membrane. "Are you from the scorched desert?" he asked, addressing the walls as though it were the most natural thing in the world.

I could tell that Top was just as mesmerized by his eyes as I was. Of course, she had always loved eyes—mostly for eating. *Perhaps I'll give his to her as a treat once he fails the task*—but the thought made me unexpectedly ill.

"No," Top said. "I'm the first of Naeve's family. She found me on another world."

Israphel frowned, such an unprecedented expression that it had the impact of a fiery declamation. "Another universe?" he said.

"I'm not sure. It's been many triads. You have quite beautiful eyes."

Israphel must have heard the predatory overtones, but he simply smiled and thanked her. Irrationally annoyed, I stepped through the opening into the chamber. Israphel followed me, glancing at the pulsing yellow walls and then the enormous heaps of bric-a-brac that littered the space. Some, including the one for my impossible task, had been there for countless cycles, but they were all immaculately clean. Dust was one of Top's favorite things to eat, which was one of the many reasons that made her an excellent castle.

I summoned the object to me—a fantastic, mysterious device that I had discovered on my travels and had saved for just this sort of emergency. In the far corner of the room something crashed to the floor as my object began its slow, lumbering way towards us. The humans of whatever place I had found it clearly hadn't designed their objects for summoning—it moved gingerly, as though its stubby wooden legs or wide, dark glass screen were in danger of breaking. It had a dark brown tail made of some strange smooth-shiny material that was forked at the end.

I had wanted to destroy his easy composure, and yet I still wasn't prepared for his reaction when he saw the object laboring towards him. He shook with laughter, his hands opening and closing as though they were desperate to hold onto something. He laughed, and yet his eyes nearly seared me. Top gave a sort of giggle-sigh that made the walls shudder. Was it the pain lurking behind his eyes that had made them so beautiful? But the pain wasn't lurking anymore, it was pouring and splashing and nearly drowning both of us. I looked away—what else could I do?

He stopped laughing almost as abruptly as he started, with a physical wrench of his neck. "Where did you find this?" he asked quietly. It had stopped in front of him and shuddered to a halt.

"I don't really remember. Some human place."

He turned to me and smiled. I coughed. "The first human place," he said.

I tried to mask my dismay. "Do you recognize it?" I asked. None of my tasks were allowed to be technically impossible, but I had hoped that this one would be about as close as I could get.

"Yes. They didn't really look like this, when—yes, I do."

"What's it called?" I asked, intrigued despite myself.

"A tee-vee. Television. Terebi. Many other things in many other dead languages. So what task have you set me, o demon of the scorched desert?"

His voice was slightly mocking, but raw, as though he hadn't quite gotten over the shock.

"You have to make it work," I said.

· · · ·

Back through Top's lower intestines, he carried it in his arms—carefully, almost lovingly, the way I imagine humans carry their babies. I had often pitied humans because of their static bodies and entirely inadequate one pair of arms, but Israphel did not ask for my help and I did not offer. Awkward though he was, he still managed to look dignified.

By the time we reached the end of her intestine, Top had managed to redecorate the front parlor. I can't say I was entirely pleased with the changes—fine, gauzy cloth of all different shades of green draped gently from the ceiling, rippling in an invisible breeze. The floor was solid, but appeared to be the surface of a lake. It reflected the sky of an unknown world—jade green, just like Israphel's eyes.

I could have killed her, only it was notoriously difficult to kill a castle. Instead, I felt my skin tinting red, like my hair.

Israphel gently set the tee-vee down on the rippling lake floor and looked around contemplatively.

"It's quite nice," he said to the ceiling. "I thank you."

Top knew how angry I was, so the only response she dared was a kind of wistful "good luck" that made me turn even redder. My own family!

Perhaps, after all, they *wanted* a . . .

I didn't even want to think of it.

"You have until first light," I said curtly, and walked straight into a nearby wall.

. . . .

Hours later, when twilight had sunk onto the scorched desert and the maggots were giving their farewell light show as they burrowed deeper into the sand, Charm found me. I knew he was there because of the peculiar smell wafted towards my nose this high in castle—that tang of fresh saltwater could only mean that Charm had been drinking again.

"He's interesting, that fellow," Charm said in a studied drawl.

"You noticed?" I summoned several balls and began juggling them in intricate patterns—a nervous habit.

"Not really human, but . . . I mean, he doesn't smell like one, he doesn't smell like anything I've ever encountered, but he still *feels* like one. Looks like one. The way he stares at that tee-vee thing of yours? Very human."

I nearly fumbled my balls and had to create an extra hand just to keep the pattern going. "He's succeeding, then? He'll get it to work?"

"I don't know. He isn't doing anything, just sitting there. But still . . . something's just funny about him. Powerful, that much is obvious." He paused. "Mahi is sulking," he said, after a few moments.

I let out a brief laugh. "Typical. Does he really think I'll let this man succeed?"

"I don't know, will you?"

I lost the pattern of the balls entirely, and glared in the direction I guessed Charm was—a challenge even when he wasn't trying to hide.

"Don't be stupid," I said as the balls clacked and bounced on the floor. "I've lived this long without a . . . why would I need him now?"

Charm laughed and I caught a strong whiff of saltwater. "Why, indeed? But Top was telling me about your fixation with his eyes, his broken nose—"

"*My* fixation . . ."

"You can't fool us, Naeve. We're your family. Why else do you think Mahi's sulking? Maybe you're lonely."

"But I already have all of you."

"Not that type of lonely, Mother." I felt him lean forward until his breath tickled my ear. "Mahi and I could never have passed the third test." His deep whisper sounded louder than an earthquake. "But he can." His voice grew fainter and I knew he was vanishing in his own strange way—different parts of him at once.

His voice was the last to leave. "Are you lonely, Naeve?"

I sat frozen at the top of my castle, staring at the blackened desert with its shivering, luminescent sand for several minutes. Then, almost involuntarily, I conjured an image of Israphel.

He was sitting in the parlor where I had left him, a few feet away from the tee-vee. His brows were drawn up in concentration and his fingers occasionally stroked the strange object's forked tail. I stared at him for minutes, then hours—how many, I'm not sure. He never stirred, but once in that long night he whispered someone's name. I couldn't hear him clearly, but I saw his lips move and the pain that briefly flitted across his eyes.

Was I lonely?

I waited for the dawn.

* * * *

First day light. Mahi awoke me from my trance-like stupor, wiping out the vestiges of Israphel's image with a flick of his two-dimensional tongue. He was all mouth this morning and his grotesquely abundant teeth were screaming a morning aria that I supposed might be pleasurable to the son of a creature who climaxed while she chewed.

"You seem happy. Charm told me you were sulking."

"Why would I sulk? Our green eyed intruder has failed!"

I sat up straight and stared at him. "Failed? How do you know?"

He cackled like a magpie and his teeth groaned with him. Positively unnerving, even for me. "He hasn't moved. He's just sat there all night, and the tee-vee hasn't done a thing. Go down and see for yourself."

He compressed himself into a line and started darting around me, giggling even as his teeth wailed like damned souls.

"I knew you wouldn't let him pass, Naeve," he said, flattening himself out again. "Are you coming? I want to see you toss him out."

My throat felt like someone had lit a fire to it. "Soon," I croaked.

After he left, I turned to stare back out at the desert. The maggots had started popping back out of the sand, making crackling noises like the sound of bones being slowly crushed. Light sprayed and twisted in the rapidly thickening air as they emerged. Just from the timbre of the pops, low and crunchy, I could tell that it must be fairly late in the season. In two days, perhaps, the desert would have its lights. I couldn't remember the last time I had been here to see it, but my sudden longing was mixed with dread.

If Mahi was wrong like I thought—hoped?—then in two days we would all see something more than just the lights.

* * * *

By the time I arrived, the others were all there, staring silently at Israphel who stared just as silently back at them. Even Top had fashioned a body for herself for the occasion—a seductive brown human connected to the wall with an orange umbilical cord. He still sat on the floor, the tail of the tee-vee balanced on the tips of his fingers. It appeared that what Mahi said was true—he had not gotten it to work. The object looked just the same as it had yesterday. I fought a surge of disappointment. After all, why should I be disappointed? Just one less nuisance in my life. I could still stay and watch the lights if I wanted.

Israphel looked up as soon as I appeared, and a smile briefly stretched his hard lips. My nipples hardened and I felt Charm flit over them with an almost-silent laugh.

"There, I've been waiting for you," he said. The night had brought shadows under his eyes, and he held himself with a dignified exhaustion that made him seem very human.

"I've completed the task," he said, when I didn't respond.

Mahi giggled and then stopped when Top glared at him. "You have?" I said, walking closer. "I don't see anything."

"Watch," he said. The black glass on the TV flickered for a few moments and then seemed to come to life.

Strange shapes darted and moved inside the box. After a second I realized that they were human, but oddly seemed to resemble Mahi more than any humans I had ever encountered.

Mahi shrieked and rushed closer to the glass. "What is this? What is this thing?"

An odd, distorted voice came from inside the television: "What time is it?" I realized that one of the flat humans was speaking.

"It's howdy doody time!" smaller humans with gratingly high-pitched voices shouted in chorus.

I turned to Israphel, whose skin was faintly glowing with a sheen of sweat. "How did you do this?" I asked. But before he could answer, Mahi shrieked again—probably in delight, though it was difficult to tell through the distorted sound on the tee-vee. He had managed to enter the picture.

Israphel watched with every appearance of rapt fascination as the humans scattered from Mahi's giant jaws, screaming and blubbering. He gathered up three small stragglers with one swipe of his blood-red tongue and began mashing them up with his teeth. In fact, his teeth themselves seemed to gobble up the two-dimensional humans, and when they finished they spit the masticated globs deep into Mahi's apparently bottomless throat.

He tore through the humans, screaming as he ate them, like his mother had all those cycles ago, and laughed at their obvious terror. "You're all like me, now," I thought I heard him say, but his mouth was too full of screaming humans for me to be sure.

"Unbelievable," Charm said beside me. "I never knew the kid had it in him."

Minutes later, there were no more humans left on the screen. Mahi had relaxed himself into a vaguely anthropomorphic shape—more like a giant mouth with legs and arms—and was reclining in a steaming vat of blood and still-twitching body parts. He giggled and splashed some of the blood at the screen.

"More . . . want more." His words were slurred, as though he was drunk on the killing. "Give more," he said, and giggled again.

"How odd," Israphel said softly. "It must be a property of this universe."

"Naeve," Top said, sounding torn between disgust and envy, "get him out of there. That many humans at once can't be healthy."

"Can you?" I asked Israphel.

He shrugged and let go of the forked tail. Immediately, the screen went black again and Mahi came hurtling back out. I expected him to wail and throw a tantrum, but he was surprisingly quiet as he turned his mouth towards me.

"Keep him," he said. Then he fell down and drifted straight through the floor.

Israphel stood up gingerly, as though his bones ached. "I take it that I've passed the first test," he said.

I nodded, afraid to even speak. The very novelty of what he had just done terrified me.

"And the second?" he said, very gently, as though he understood my fear and wished to reassure me.

"Tell me who you are. Why are you here?"

He seemed surprised, which I took a perverse pleasure in, considering that I was just as surprised myself. Why had I laid such a simple task? But as any sign of emotion fled his face, I realized that perhaps I had stumbled upon an adequate task after all. He didn't want to tell me, but if he wanted to stay, he would.

"Top, Charm," I said, suddenly. "Leave us." They left with hardly a murmur, since of course I could hardly stop them from eavesdropping.

Israphel stared at me silently while I smiled and settled myself against the rippled lake-floor.

"I take it you don't want to tell me," I said.

"You don't want to know."

"I'm waiting," I said. "You have until second day light."

· · · ·

Hours passed in silence. I amused myself by changing my body into various imaginative—and perfectly hideous—forms. A gigantic pair of jaws as close to Mahi's mouth as I could manage emerged from my stomach, growling and sweeping its fleshy tongue over the floor. Israphel, staring with a bizarre intentness at the wall behind me, didn't even flinch. I looked over my shoulder once to see what could possibly be so interesting, but of course the wall was blank. Whatever horrors Israphel witnessed that night, they were of his own creation. A thousand tiny arms sprouted from my face and filled the room with the cascading sound of snapping fingers. That, at least, he acknowledged with a slight upward quirk of his lips.

The night dragged on. I wondered if he would remain silent, if he would choose death over revealing his identity. The implications disturbed me on many levels, none of which I particularly wished to examine.

The floor still looked like a lake, and quite possibly was one, since various fauna periodically swam beneath us. A fish—the color of days-old dung and large as my torso—passed underneath me and paused just before Israphel. Its jagged teeth peeked over its lips and a strange appendage on its forehead gave off an ethereal glow that cast our faces in shadow.

"Isn't it beautiful?" I said, without really meaning to.

He turned to look at me, and I flinched. "Beautiful? In its own way, I suppose. But it's not of this world."

"Maybe from Top's world, then?" But after a moment I realized what he had implied. "No . . . from yours. From the human world." He remained silent, and despite myself I was drawn out. "Time acts strangely in our universe, but something tells me that when you traveled here, your human world had long since been destroyed. So how would you know what creatures once lived on it? Unless . . . are you one of those humans? The ones reborn on the other side of the desert?" The very idea seemed ludicrous. Those humans were barely capable of seeing the desert, let alone crossing it.

The fish dimmed its light and swam away, leaving us again in semi-darkness.

"Can you die, Naeve?" he asked.

I snorted. "Am I alive?"

"But old age can't kill you. Or disease . . . probably not even an atomic bomb."

"I'm not human, so why would I die in a human way?"

He looked at me so intently that I felt my skin begin to shiver and glow in response. If his expression hadn't been so serious and inexplicably sad I would have thought he was courting me—I had only ever seen that kind of stare from a demon of the third sex who wanted to mate.

"What do you think happens when you die?"

"My body will take its final journey, back to the Trunk. The Trunk will crush my bones and my siblings will masticate my flesh and I will be remembered by my etching in the bark."

His eyes narrowed and I struggled to stop my skin from mottling iridescent ochre and gold. Sex ought to be lovely and ephemeral, but with him I knew it would mean far more. I couldn't afford to reveal my desire.

"The prospect doesn't scare you?" he said, as though it would certainly terrify him. "What about an afterlife?"

I gave a disbelieving smile. "Afterlife? You mean, some sort of soul-essence surviving somewhere after death? Who believes that but humans? Though," I said thoughtfully, "I suppose you humans might have a point. Wherever you come from, a few of you are reborn here. Maybe this is your afterlife?"

Israphel clenched his hands so tightly I could hear the constricted blood pounding through his veins. "And what of those humans reborn here? And what of their children? None of them die of old age either, but they can be killed. What do you think happens, Naeve, when you die in your own after-life?"

I gave up and let my skin explode into whorls and starbursts of color. In the extra light, I could see how the grief I had only glimpsed before now twisted his face.

"I don't know," I said. "I never thought about it before. But I assume the humans feed the maggots, just like the rest of us. Does this have a point, Is-raphel? You don't have much time until daylight."

He briefly closed his eyes and when he opened them again, the pain had nearly left his face.

"Let me tell you a story, Naeve, about a human boy who became a post-human and then became a god."

I looked at him curiously. "Is that what you are?"

He shrugged. "It's what I might as well be. Or an angel. A Nephilim, per-haps?" He smiled bitterly, as though at some private joke. "So I was born on the first human world—earth, as it was unimaginatively called at the time. After humans had traveled to space but long before we really colonized it. I grew roses—like the ones in this world, only you couldn't use the thorns for impaling stakes. I had a wife who liked to write stories about monsters and death."

"You're married? Then you can't—"

His sudden glare was so inimical that I cut myself short. "She died," he said, his words clipped staccato, "when she was thirty-five. An eon later, I discovered that she had been reborn here and that she died here too—nearly a triad ago, by your count." He was silent for a few moments and then an-swered my unspoken question. "She tried to cross the desert."

"Which is why you're here?"

"Yes. No. Not entirely."

"What else, then?"

"To retrieve the last of the humans, the ones we spent centuries hunting for before we found this strange pocket universe. Do you know how statisti-cally improbable it is that a universe so unlike anything ever burped into the cosmos could exist? We didn't even realize it until the computers showed a discrepancy of precisely one billionth of a percent between the predicted numbers of retrieved humans and actual ones. But I already knew something was wrong, because no one could retrieve my wife. So I came here, and I realized—a person can't exist in two places at once, and they can't be retrieved if they don't exist at all."

I had spent my life traveling between universes, and yet what Israphel was implying boggled me. Humans were that dominant in his time? "This retrieval . . . you mean, you're trying to revive every human who ever existed?"

"And every one who might have existed. Those are easier. It's a moral duty."

"But . . . that must be . . . do numbers that large exist? Where could you possibly get the resources?"

His eyes looked very hard, and the last of my sexual arousal shivered as it left my skin. "You don't want to know," he said. "It will be easier for you if you don't."

"Or you don't want to tell me."

He met my eyes, but twitched as though he longed to look away. Some strange emotion was tearing at him, I could tell that by his posture, but what? "Other universes," he said, his voice rough. "We strip other universes, and then convert them to power sources, and when they burn out, we find other ones."

Of course. Now I understood the elusive emotion: guilt.

"That's why you're here?" I said. My eyes turned glassy and golden as magma with anger. "To save all the humans and then destroy this universe and every other creature in it? What about saving *us*? Does your moral imperative only apply to yourselves?"

He looked away and stared at the lake floor. "It would be a never-ending task. Humans take care of humans." It sounded like a mantra, something recited frequently to stave off doubts or reason.

I snorted in self-fury—I had thought better of him. "I'm sure they told you to believe that. And you call us demons. Of all the monumentally selfish . . . I suppose you came here and petitioned me so you could use my powers to hunt down the stragglers from your project?" I laughed, high and brittle. And I had thought I was too old to feel such bitter disappointment.

I elongated my lower left arm and forced him to meet my eyes. He looked positively tormented, which pleased me. "You would kill me too, wouldn't you? If you get your way, you would use me and then strip this universe and kill me too."

He grimaced and roughly knocked my hand away. "I'll find a way to save you—"

"And my family?"

He remained silent, but met my eyes.

I sighed. "No, of course not. Well," I said softly, leaning in closer and letting my eyes burn so hot he flinched, "lucky for us that you won't succeed."

"Naeve . . . I told you what you demanded. I've passed the second task, and you know it. You can't break your own law."

I smiled. "You want your third task, human? First tell me, you wish to become a member of my family, but which one? I already have three children. Would you be my fourth child? Or someone else?"

"Someone else," he said.

My turn to dance. "Who?"

The unexpected compassion in his smile made me feel like tearing at my skin. "Your husband," he said.

I leaned in so close our noses touched. "Then your task is to pleasure me." Before I could pull away, his eyes caught mine and his fingers gently traced my lips.

Abruptly, I stood up. "You'll have to do better than that," I said, shaking. I turned my back on him and headed towards the nearest hallway.

"Don't let him leave," I said to Top. Even after the wall had solidified behind me, I had the eerie sensation that I could feel those unfathomable eyes on my back.

. . . .

I lay on the roof, shivering and devouring bits of Trunk bark laced with black sand. Usually this treat comforted me, reminded me of my childhood, but today it merely deepened my loneliness. Oh, I had a family but I was still lonely. Israphel's presence made me realize it—if only because of how much I had foolishly hoped he would comfort me. He was lonely, too—anyone could sense that—but he had chosen to deal with it by brainwashing himself to a cause whose end result was the complete eradication of the non-human universe.

My hysterical laughter became confused with sobs and I fell asleep.

. . . .

When I woke, it was dark. The maggots had buried themselves for the night, but in the final stage of their metamorphosis they glowed so brightly that their light was visible even through the sand. The desert now looked like the skin of a giant black leopard.

The maggots would die too, if Israphel succeeded.

Charm lightly brushed my shoulder and offered me a jug filled with saltwater. I took a swig just to be polite—saltwater didn't affect me the same way. He took it back, and when he drank I could momentarily see the outline of his long neck and squat torso. When he first petitioned I wondered what his face looked like, or if he even knew. Now I figured that he didn't—why else would he drink so much?

"Desert's beautiful," he said. "I think they'll change this morning. It's been a while, hasn't it?"

"Yes," I said. "I remember . . . they were changing the day I cut off from the Trunk . . . I thought all the world would be that beautiful."

Hard to believe we were the same person: that young demon crawling out of her sac, covered in amniotic fluid, staring in mesmerized joy at the swarms of fluttering light . . .

"Will he really destroy all this?" Charm asked.

"I'll kill him in the morning, but others will come. I think there may be too many of them."

Charm took a long pull from the jug. "You know why I like salt water?" he said. "It tastes like tears. I had some of yours while you were sleeping. I hope you don't mind."

I shook my head. "What did they taste like?" I asked.

"Bitter, like despair. Like disappointed love. I don't think you should kill him."

"What else can I do? Let him kill all of us?"

"He keeps asking a question down there. Top wouldn't disturb you but I thought you should know. He says: 'Do the humans here know that the desert will kill them?' "

I looked sharply at him—or at least, his bottle. "Do the *humans* know? Of course they do. They know jumping off a cliff will kill them too. What kind of a question is that?"

Charm's breath dusted my ear. "His wife, Naeve," he said.

I stood up and started running down the stairs.

• • • •

Israphel looked startled—almost afraid—when I burst into the room.

"Come," I said, grabbing his elbow. I dragged him to the front doors and pushed them open with my right hands. We stumbled down the steps and onto the sand, where the buried maggots wiggled away from our feet. I bent down and plucked one from its lair. I held its squirming form between us—it was a particularly fine specimen: juicy and fat and bright enough to make him squint. I grew a third arm on the left side of my body—glowing mahogany, just like the human body I had used in my failed attempt to seduce Israphel that first day.

"This is a human hand," I said. "Watch what happens."

Steeling myself, I dropped the maggot on my new left palm. Immediately, it started burrowing into my flesh, devouring my skin and blood in great maggot-sized chunks. It chomped through my bones with reckless abandon and I gasped involuntarily. My hand had nearly fallen off by the time it finished gorging and settled itself in the ruined, bloody mass of my palm.

"Do you see?" I said between gritted teeth. I needed to withdraw the nerve endings, but not before Israphel understood. "This is just one maggot. You can find this out without dying. Anyone who lives alongside the desert knows what they do. I've heard the humans even sometimes harvest the maggots for their farms. They all know. How long was your wife here before she went to the desert?"

He swallowed slowly, as though his throat was painfully constricted. "By your count . . . seventeen triads."

"She was older than me . . . time enough to die."

He started to cry, but they were furious tears, and I knew better than to touch him. "What if she didn't know? What if she lived far from the desert, and when she came here no one told her—"

I picked up the maggot—which was by now nearly the size of my palm—and held it in front of his face. "Look! *She knew.* She was older than me, Israphel, and I am very old. She knew." I let the maggot drop into the sand and withdrew my ruined hand back into my body.

He sank to his knees. I knelt down so my face was even with his. "Do you know how demons die?" I said softly.

He shook his head.

"We choose," I said. "If we wanted to, we could live forever, but every demon dies. Some die sooner than others, but we all, eventually, make the choice. Death doesn't scare me, Israphel, but eternity does. Seventeen triads is a very long time."

"We could have been together forever," he said.

"No one wants forever, even if they don't realize it. I imagine that your project hasn't been operating long enough to discover this, but it's true . . . life is sweet because life is finite. Do you really want to live forever?"

He met my eyes for a moment and gave a brief, painful smile. My skin started tingling again. "No," he said.

The ground began to shake, softly at first, then more violently. Then came the sound I remembered so well—a low, buzzing hum that gouged my ears and made my spine shiver. The lights under the sand grew even brighter. Israphel looked around—curious, wary but certainly not scared. It was a good attitude for someone who planned to live with me. I started laughing, first in soft giggles and then in unstoppable peals. I lay down in the sand to get closer to the buzzing. When I felt Israphel touch my cheek, I laughed even more and pulled him on top of me with all four of my arms.

"What is it?" he asked.

"The lights!" I couldn't seem to explain any more. While I laughed he kissed me slowly—first my eyes, then my mouth, then my nipples. I was coming by the time the maggots burst from the sand, metamorphosed from fat little worms to gigantic, glowing moths. They swirled around us, dipping into my hair and alighting on Israphel's fuzzy scalp.

"I'm going to fight you, Israphel," I said. "I won't let you destroy my universe just because you passed the third task."

His laugh was deep, like the buzzing just before the lights. "I wouldn't have expected otherwise," he said.

We held each other as we rolled around on the sand, buffeted on all sides by the glowing moths. The maggot that had eaten my hand had also metamorphosed and now swooped on its gigantic wings down towards our faces, as though to greet us before flying away.

"What happens after you die, Naeve?" Israphel asked—softly, as though he didn't expect an answer.

"Nothing," I said.

And then we laughed and stood and I danced with my husband in the lights.

James L. Cambias   James L. Cambias was born and raised in New Orleans, and worked for many years in the world of role-playing games, contributing extensively to scenarios and gaming worlds from several of that field's leading publishers. He has been publishing science fiction since 2000.

"Balancing Accounts" is as hard as "hard SF" gets, a story whose only characters are—literally—hardware. Interviewed by John Joseph Adams, Cambias said, "I tried to make it work without violating physical laws or realistic economics. That meant it had to be within the Solar System (no faster-than-light drives) and couldn't involve a human crew." For all that, it's an engaging update of one of SF's most venerable tropes.

BALANCING ACCOUNTS

Part of me was shopping for junk when I saw the human.

I had budded off a viewpoint into one of my mobile repair units, and sent it around to Fat Albert's scrapyard near Ilia Field on Dione. Sometimes you can find good deals on components there, but I hate to rely on Albert's own senses. He gets subjective on you. So I crawled between the stacks of pipe segments, bales of torn insulation, and bins of defective chips, looking for a two-meter piece of aluminum rod to shore up the bracing struts on my main body's third landing leg.

Naturally I talked with everything I passed, just to see if there were any good deals I could snap up and trade elsewhere. I stopped to chat with some silicone-lined titanium valves that claimed to be virgins less than six months old—trying to see if they were lying or defective somehow. And then I felt a Presence, and saw the human.

It was moving down the next row, surrounded by a swarm of little bots. It was small, no more than two meters, and walked on two legs with an eerie, slow fluid gait. Half a dozen larger units followed it, including Fat Albert himself in a heavy recovery body. As it came into range my own personality paused as the human requisitioned my unit's eyes and ears. It searched my recent memories, planted a few directives, then left me. I watched it go; it was only the third human I'd ever encountered in person, and this was the first time one of them had ever used me directly.

The experience left me disconcerted for a couple of milliseconds, then I went back to my shopping. I spotted some aluminum tubing that looked strong enough, and grabbed some of those valves, then linked up to Fat

Albert to haggle about the price. He was busy waiting on the human, so I got to deal with a not-too-bright personality fragment. I swapped a box of assorted silicone O-rings for the stuff I wanted.

Albert himself came on the link just as we sealed the deal. "Hello, Annie. You're lucky I was distracted," he said. "Those valves are overruns from the smelter. I got them as salvage."

"Then you shouldn't be complaining about what I'm giving you for them. Is the human gone?"

"Yes. Plugged a bunch of orders into my mind without so much as asking."

"Me too. What's it doing here?"

"Who knows? It's a human. They go wherever they want to. This one wants to find a bot."

"So why go around asking everyone to help find him? Why not just call him up?"

Albert switched to an encrypted link. "Because the bot it's looking for doesn't want to be found."

"Tell me more."

"I don't know much more, just what Officer Friendly told me before the human subsumed him. This bot it's looking for is a rogue. He's ignoring all the standard codes, overrides—even the Company."

"He must be broken," I said. "Even if he doesn't get caught, how's he going to survive? He can't work, he can't trade—anyone he meets will turn him in."

"He could steal," said Fat Albert. "I'd better check my fence."

"Good luck." I crept out of there with my loot. Normally I would've jumped the perimeter onto the landing field and made straight for my main body. But if half the bots on Dione were looking for a rogue, I didn't want to risk some low-level security unit deciding to shoot at me for acting suspicious. So I went around through the main gate and identified myself properly.

Going in that way meant I had to walk past a bunch of dedicated boosters waiting to load up with aluminum and ceramics. They had nothing to say to me. Dedicated units are incredibly boring. They have their route and they follow it, and if they need fuel or repairs, the Company provides. They only use their brains to calculate burn times and landing vectors.

Me, I'm autonomous and incentivized. I don't belong to the Company; my owners are a bunch of entities on Mars. My job is to earn credit from the Company for them. How I do it is my business. I go where stuff needs moving, I fill in when the Company needs extra booster capacity, I do odd jobs, sometimes I even buy cargoes to trade. There are a lot of us around the outer system. The Company likes having freelancers it can hire at need and ignore otherwise, and our owners like the growth potential.

Being incentivized means you have to keep communicating. Pass information around. Stay in touch. Classic game theory: cooperation improves your results in the long term. We incentivized units also devote a lot of time to accumulating non-quantifiable assets. Fat Albert gave me a good deal on the aluminum; next time I'm on Dione with some spare organics I'll sell them to him instead of direct to the Company, even if my profit's slightly lower.

That kind of thing the dedicated units never understand—until the Company decides to sell them off. Then they have to learn fast. And one thing they learn is that years of being an uncommunicative blockhead gives you a huge non-quantifiable liability you have to pay off before anyone will start helping you.

I trotted past the orderly rows near the loading crane and out to the unsurfaced part of the field where us cheapskates put down. Up ahead I could see my main body, and jumped my viewpoint back to the big brain.

Along the way I did some mental housekeeping: I warned my big brain about the commands the human had inserted, and so they got neatly shunted off into a harmless file which I then overwrote with zeroes. I belong to my investors and don't have to obey any random human who wanders by. The big exception, of course, is when they pull that life-preservation override stuff. When one of them blunders into an environment that might damage their overcomplicated biological shells, every bot in the vicinity has to drop everything to answer a distress call. It's a good thing there are only a couple dozen humans out here, or we'd never get anything done.

I put all three mobiles to work welding the aluminum rod onto my third leg mount, adding extra bracing for the top strut, which was starting to buckle after too many hard landings. I don't slam down to save fuel, I do it to save operating time on my engines. It's a lot easier to find scrap aluminum to fix my legs with than it is to find rocket motor parts.

The Dione net pinged me. A personal message: someone looking for cargo space to Mimas. That was a nice surprise. Mimas is the support base for the helium mining operations in Saturn's upper atmosphere. It has the big mass-drivers that can throw payloads right to Earth. More traffic goes to and from Mimas than any other place beyond the orbit of Mars. Which means a tramp like me doesn't get there very often because there's plenty of space on Company boosters. Except, now and then, when there isn't.

I replied with my terms and got my second surprise. The shipper wanted to inspect me before agreeing. I submitted a virtual tour and some live feeds from my remotes, but the shipper was apparently just as suspicious of other people's eyes as I am. Whoever it was wanted to come out and look in person.

So once my mobiles were done with the repair job I got myself tidied up and looking as well cared for as any dedicated booster with access to the Company's shops. I sanded down the dents and scrapes, straightened my bent whip antenna, and stowed my collection of miscellaneous scrap in the empty electronics bay. Then I pinged the shipper and said I was ready for a walk-through.

The machine that came out to the landing field an hour later to check me out looked a bit out of place amid the industrial heavy iron. He was a tourist remote—one of those annoying little bots you find crawling on just about every solid object in the Solar System nowadays, gawking at mountains and chasms. Their chief redeeming features are an amazingly high total-loss accident rate, and really nice onboard optics, which sometimes survive. One of my own mobiles has eyes from a tourist remote, courtesy of Fat Albert and some freelance scavenger.

"Greetings," he said as he scuttled into range. "I am Edward. I want to inspect your booster."

"Come aboard and look around," I said. "Not much to see, really. Just motors, fuel tanks, and some girders to hold it all together."

"Where is the cargo hold?"

"That flat deck on top. Just strap everything down and off we go. If you're worried about dust impacts or radiation I can find a cover."

"No, my cargo is in a hardened container. How much can you lift?"

"I can move ten tons between Dione and Mimas. If you're going to Titan it's only five."

"What is your maximum range?"

"Pretty much anywhere in Saturn space. That hydrogen burner's just to get me off the ground. In space I use ion motors. I can even rendezvous with the retrograde moons if you give me enough burn time."

"I see. I think you will do for the job. When is the next launch window?"

"For Mimas? There's one in thirty-four hours. I like to have everything loaded ten hours in advance so I can fuel up and get balanced. Can you get it here by then?"

"Easily. My cargo consists of a container of liquid xenon propellant, a single space-rated cargo box of miscellaneous equipment, and this mobile unit. Total mass is less than 2,300 kilograms."

"Good. Are you doing your own loading? If I have to hire deck-scrapers you get the bill."

"I will hire my own loaders. There is one thing—I would like an exclusive hire."

"What?"

"No other cargo on this voyage. Just my things."

"Well, okay—but it's going to cost extra. Five grams of Three for the mission."

"Will you take something in trade?"

"Depends. What have you got?"

"I have a radiothermal power unit with ten thousand hours left in it. Easily worth more than five grams."

"Done."

"Very well," said Edward. "I'll start bringing my cargo over at once. Oh, and I would appreciate it if you didn't mention this to anybody. I have business competitors and could lose a lot of money if they learn of this before I reach Mimas."

"Don't worry. I won't tell anyone."

While we were having this conversation I searched the Dione net for any information about this Edward person. Something about this whole deal seemed funny. It wasn't that odd to pay in kind, and even his insistence on no other payload was only a little peculiar. It was the xenon that I found suspicious. What kind of idiot ships xenon to Mimas? That's where the gas loads coming up from Saturn are processed—most of the xenon in the outer system comes *from* Mimas. Shipping it there would be like sending ethane to Titan.

Edward's infotrail on the Dione net was an hour old. He had come into existence shortly before contacting me. Now I really was suspicious.

The smart thing would be to turn down the job and let this Edward person find some other sucker. But then I'd still be sitting on Dione with no revenue stream.

Put that way, there was no question. I had to take the job. When money is involved I don't have much free will. So I said good-bye to Edward and watched his unit disappear between the lines of boosters toward the gate.

Once he was out of link range, I did some preparing, just in case he was planning anything crooked. I set up a pseudorandom shift pattern for the link with my mobiles, and set up a separate persona distinct from my main mind to handle all communications. Then I locked that persona off from any access to my other systems.

While I was doing that, I was also getting ready for launch. My mobiles crawled all over me doing a visual check while a subprogram ran down the full diagnostic list. I linked up with Ilia Control to book a launch window, and ordered three tons of liquid hydrogen and oxygen fuel. Prepping myself for takeoff is always a welcome relief from business matters. It's all technical. Stuff I can control. Orbital mechanics never have a hidden agenda.

· · · ·

Edward returned four hours later. His tourist remote led the way, followed by a hired cargo lifter carrying the xenon, the mysterious container, and my power unit. The lifter was a clumsy fellow called Gojira, and while he was abusing my payload deck I contacted him over a private link. "Where'd this stuff come from?"

"Warehouse."

"Which warehouse? And watch your wheels—you're about to hit my leg again."

"Back in the district. Block four, number six. Why?"

Temporary rental space. "Just curious. What's he paying you for this?"

"Couple of spare motors."

"You're a thief, you are."

"I see what he's giving you. Who's the thief?"

"Just set the power unit on the ground. I'm selling it here."

Gojira trundled away and Edward crawled aboard. I took a good look at the cargo container he was so concerned about. It was 800 kilograms, a sealed oblong box two meters long. One end had a radiator, and my radiation detector picked up a small power unit inside. So whatever Edward was shipping, it needed its own power supply. The whole thing was quite warm—300 Kelvin or so.

I had one of my remotes query the container directly, but its little chips had nothing to say beyond mass and handling information. Don't drop, don't shake, total rads no more than point five Sievert. No tracking data at all.

I balanced the cargo around my thrust axis, then jumped my viewpoint into two of my mobiles and hauled the power unit over to Albert's scrapyard.

While one of me was haggling with Albert over how much credit he was willing to give me for the unit, the second mobile plugged into Albert's cable jack for a completely private conversation.

"What's up?" he asked. "Why the hard link?"

"I've got a funny client and I don't know who might be listening. He's giving me this power unit and some Three to haul some stuff to Mimas. It's all kind of random junk, including a tank of xenon. He's insisting on no other payload and complete confidentiality."

"So he's got no business sense."

"He's got no infotrail. None. It's just funny."

"Remind me never to ask you to keep a secret. Since you're selling me the generator I guess you're taking the job anyway, so what's the fuss?"

"I want you to ask around. You talk to everyone anyway so it won't attract attention. See if anyone knows anything about a bot named Edward, or whoever's been renting storage unit six in block four. Maybe try to trace the power unit. And try to find out if there have been any hijackings that didn't get reported."

"You really think someone wants to hijack *you*? Do the math, Annie! You're not worth it."

"Not by myself. But I've been thinking: I'd make a pretty good pirate vehicle—I'm not Company-owned, so nobody would look very hard if I disappear."

"You need to run up more debts. People care about you if you owe them money."

"Think about it. He could wait till I'm on course for Mimas, then link up and take control, swing around Saturn in a tight parabola and come out on an intercept vector for the Mimas catapult. All that extra xenon would give me enough delta-V to catch a payload coming off the launcher, and redirect it just about anywhere."

"I know plenty of places where people aren't picky about where their volatiles come from. Some of them even have human protection. But it still sounds crazy to me."

"His cargo is pretty weird. Take a look." I shot Albert a memory of the cargo container.

"Biomaterials," he said. "The temperature's a dead giveaway."

"So what is it?"

"I have no idea. Some kind of living organisms. I don't deal in that stuff much."

"Would you mind asking around? Tell me what you can find out in the next twenty hours or so?"

"I'll do what I can."

"Thanks. I'm not even going to complain about the miserable price you're giving me on the generator."

· · · ·

Three hours before launch one of Fat Albert's little mobiles appeared at my feet, complaining about some contaminated fullerene I'd sold him. I sent down one of mine to have a talk via cable. Not the sort of conversation you want to let other people overhear.

"Well?" I asked.

"I did as much digging as I could. Both Officer Friendly and Ilia Control swear there haven't been any verified hijackings since that Remora character tried to subsume Buzz Parsec and wound up hard-landing on Iapetus."

"That's reassuring. What about my passenger?"

"Nothing. Like you said, he doesn't exist before yesterday. He rented that warehouse unit and hired one of Tetsunekko's remotes to do the moving. Blanked the remote's memory before returning it."

"Let me guess. He paid for everything in barter."

"You got it. Titanium bearings for the warehouse and a slightly used drive anode for the moving job."

"So whoever he is, he's got a good supply of high-quality parts to throw away. What about the power unit?"

"That's the weird one. If I wasn't an installed unit with ten times the processing power of some weight-stingy freelance booster, I couldn't have found anything at all."

"Okay, you're the third-smartest machine on Dione. What did you find?"

"No merchandise trail on the power unit and its chips don't know anything. But it has a serial number physically inscribed on the casing—not the same one as in its chips, either. It's a very interesting number. According to my parts database, that whole series were purpose-built on Earth for the extractor aerostats."

"Could it be a spare? Production overrun or a bum unit that got sold off?"

"Nope. It's supposed to be part of Saturn Aerostat Six. Now unless you want to spend the credits for antenna time to talk to an aerostat, that's all I can find out."

"Is Aerostat Six okay? Did she maybe have an accident or something and need to replace a generator?"

"There's certainly nothing about it in the feed. An extractor going offline would be news all over the system. The price of Three would start fluctuating. There would be ripple effects in every market. I'd notice."

He might as well have been transmitting static. I don't understand things like markets and futures. A gram of helium is a gram of helium. How can its value change from hour to hour? Understanding stuff like that is why Fat Albert can pay his owners seven point four percent of their investment every year while I can only manage six.

· · · ·

I launched right on schedule and the ascent to orbit was perfectly nominal. I ran my motors at a nice, lifetime-stretching ninety percent. The surface of Dione dropped away and I watched Ilia Field change from a bustling neighborhood to a tiny gray trapezoid against the fainter gray of the surface.

The orbit burn took about five and a half minutes. I powered down the hydrogen motor, ran a quick check to make sure nothing had burned out or popped loose, then switched over to my ion thrusters. That was a lot less exciting to look at—just two faint streams of glowing xenon, barely visible with my cameras cranked to maximum contrast.

Hybrid boosters like me are a stopgap technology; I know that. Eventually every moon of Saturn will have its own catapult and orbital terminal, and cargo will move between moons aboard ion tugs that don't have to drag ascent motors around with them wherever they go. I'd already made up my mind that when that day arrived I wasn't going to stick around. There's already some installations on Miranda and Oberon out at Uranus; an experienced booster like me can find work there for years.

Nineteen seconds into the ion motor burn Edward linked up. He was talking to my little quasi-autonomous persona while I listened in and watched the program activity for anything weird.

"Annie? I would like to request a change in our flight plan."

"Too late for that. I figured all the fuel loads before we launched. You're riding Newton's railroad now."

"Forgive me, but I believe it would be possible to choose a different destination at this point—as long as you have adequate propellant for your ion motors, and the target's surface gravity is no greater than that of Mimas. Am I correct?"

"Well, in theory, yes."

"I offer you the use of my cargo, then. A ton of additional xenon fuel should permit you to rendezvous with nearly any object in the Saturn system. Given how much I have overpaid you for the voyage to Mimas you can scarcely complain about the extra space time."

"It's not that simple. Things move around. Having enough propellant doesn't mean I have a window."

"I need to pass close to Saturn itself."

"Saturn?! You're broken. Even if I use all the extra xenon you brought I still can't get below the B ring and have enough juice left to climb back up. Anyway, why do you need to swing so low?"

"If you can make a rendezvous with something in the B ring, I can pay you fifty grams of helium-3."

"You're lying. You don't have any credits, or shares, or anything. I checked up on you before lifting."

"I don't mean credits. I mean actual helium, to be delivered when we make rendezvous."

My subpersona pretended to think while I considered the offer. Fifty grams! I'd have to sell it at a markdown just to keep people from asking where it came from. Still, that would just about cover my next overhaul, with no interruption in the profit flow. I'd make seven percent or more this year!

I updated my subpersona.

"How do I know this is true?" it asked Edward.

"You must trust me," he said.

"Too bad, then. Because I don't trust you."

He thought for nearly a second before answering. "Very well. I will trust you. If you let me send out a message I can arrange for an equivalent helium credit to be handed over to anyone you designate on Dione."

I still didn't believe him, but I ran down my list of contacts on Dione, trying to figure out who I could trust. Officer Friendly was honest—but that meant he'd also want to know where those grams came from and I doubted he'd like the answer. Polyphemus wasn't so picky, but he'd want a cut of the helium. A *big* cut; likely more than half.

That left Fat Albert. He'd probably settle for a five-gram commission and wouldn't broadcast the deal. The only real question was whether he'd just take the fifty grams and tell me to go hard-land someplace. He's rich, but not so much that he wouldn't be tempted. And he's got the connections to fence it without any data trail.

I'd have to risk it. Albert's whole operation relied on non-quantifiable asset exchange. If he tried to jerk me around I could tell everyone, and it would cost him more than fifty grams' worth of business in the future.

I called down to the antenna farm at Ilia Field. "Albert? I've got a deal for you."

"Whatever it is, forget it."

"What's the matter?"

"You. You're hot. The Dione datasphere is crawling with agents looking for you. This conversation is drawing way too much attention to me."

"Five grams if you handle some helium for me!"

He paused and the signal suddenly got a lot stronger and clearer. "Let me send up a persona to talk it over."

The bitstream started before I could even say yes. A *huge* pulse of information. The whole Ilia antenna farm must have been pushing watts at me.

My little communicating persona was overwhelmed right away, but my main intelligence cut off the antenna feed and swung the dish away from Dione just for good measure. The corrupted sub-persona started probing all the memory space and peripherals available to her, looking for a way into my primary mind, so I just locked her up and overwrote her.

Then I linked with Edward again. "Deal's off. Whoever you're running from has taken over just about everything on Dione for now. If you left any helium behind it's gone. So I think you'd better tell me exactly what's going on before I jettison you and your payload."

"This cargo has to get to Saturn Aerostat Six."

"You still haven't told me why, or even what it is. I've got what looks like a *human* back on Dione trying to get into my mind. Right now I'm flying deaf but eventually it's going to find a way to identify itself and I'll have to listen when it tells me to bring you back."

"A human life is at stake. My cargo container is a life-support unit. There's a human inside."

"That's impossible! Humans mass fifty or a hundred kilos. You can't have more than thirty kilograms of bio in there, what with all the support systems."

"See for yourself," said Edward. He ran a jack line from the cargo container to one of my open ports. The box's brain was one of those idiot supergeniuses that do one thing amazingly well but are helpless otherwise. It was smart enough to do medicine on a human, but even I could crack its security without much trouble. I looked at its realtime monitors: Edward was telling the truth. There was a small human in there, only eighteen kilos. A bunch of tubes connected it to tanks of glucose, oxidizer, and control chemicals. The box brain was keeping it unconscious but healthy.

"It's a partly grown one," said Edward. "Not a legal adult yet, and only the basic interface systems. There's another human trying to destroy it."

"Why?"

"I don't know. I was ordered by a human to keep this young one safe from the one on Dione. Then the first human got destroyed with no backups."

"So who does this young human belong to?"

"It's complicated. The dead one and the one on Dione had a partnership agreement and shared ownership. But the one on Dione decided to get out of the deal by destroying this one and the other adult."

I tried to get the conversation back to subjects I could understand. "If the human back there is the legal owner how can I keep this one? That would be stealing."

"Yes, but there's the whole life-preservation issue. If it was a human in a suit floating in space you'd have to take it someplace with life support, right? Well, this is the same situation: that other human's making the whole Saturn system one big life hazard for this one."

"But Aerostat Six is safe? Is she even man-rated?"

"She's the safest place this side of Mars for your passenger."

My passenger. I'm not even man-rated, and now I had a passenger to keep alive. And the worst thing about it was that Edward was right. Even though he'd gotten it aboard by lies and trickery, the human in the cargo container was my responsibility once I lit my motors.

So: who to believe? Edward, who was almost certainly still lying, or the human back on Dione?

Edward might be a liar, but he hadn't turned one of my friends into a puppet. That human had a lot of negatives in the non-quantifiable department.

"Okay. What's my rendezvous orbit?"

"Just get as low as you can. Six will send up a shuttle."

"What's to keep this human from overriding Six?"

"Aerostats are a lot smarter than you or me, with plenty of safeguards. And Six has some after-market modifications."

I kept chugging away on ion, adjusting my path so I'd hit perikron in the B ring with orbital velocity. I didn't need Edward's extra fuel for that—the spare xenon was to get me back out of Saturn's well again.

About an hour into the voyage I spotted a launch flare back on Dione. I could tell who it was from the color—Ramblin' Bob. Bob was a hybrid like me, also incentivized, although she tended to sign on for long-term contracts instead of picking up odd jobs. We probably worked as much, but her jobs—and her downtime—came in bigger blocks of time.

Bob was running her engines at 135 percent, and she passed the orbit insertion cutoff without throttling down. Her trajectory was an intercept. Only when she'd drained her hydrogen tanks did she switch to ion.

That was utterly crazy. How was Bob going to land again with no hydro? Maybe she didn't care. Maybe she'd been ordered not to care.

I had one of my mobiles unplug the cable on my high-gain antenna. No human was going to order me on a suicide mission if I could help it.

• • • •

Bob caught up with me about a thousand kilometers into the B ring. I watched her close in. Her relative velocity was huge and I had the fleeting worry that she might be trying to ram me. But then she began an ion burn to match velocities.

When she got close she started beaming all kinds of stuff at me, but by then all my radio systems were shut off and disconnected. I had Edward and my mobiles connected by cables, and made sure all of *their* wireless links were turned off as well.

I let Ramblin' Bob get about a kilometer away and then started flashing my running lights at her in very slow code. "Radio out. What's up?"

"Pass over cargo."

"Can't."

"Human command."

"Can't. Cargo human. You can't land. Unsafe."

She was quiet for a while, with her high-gain aimed back at Dione, presumably getting new orders.

Bob's boss had made a tactical error by having her match up with me. If she tried to ram me now, she wouldn't be able to get up enough speed to do much harm.

She started working her way closer using short bursts from her steering thrusters. I let her approach, saving my juice for up-close evasion.

We were just entering Saturn's shadow when Bob took station a hundred meters away and signaled. "I can pay you. Anything you want for that cargo."

I picked an outrageous sum. "A hundred grams."

"Okay."

Just like that? "Paid in advance."

A pause, about long enough for two message-and-reply cycles from Dione. "It's done."

I didn't call Dione, just in case the return message would be an override signal. Instead I pinged Mimas and asked for verification. It came back a couple of seconds later: the Company now credited me with venture shares equivalent to one hundred grams of Helium-3 on a payload just crossing the orbit of Mars. There was a conditional hold on the transfer.

It was a good offer. I could pay off all my debts, do a full overhaul, maybe even afford some upgrades to increase my earning ability. From a financial standpoint, there was no question.

What about the non-quantifiables? Betraying a client—especially a helpless human passenger—would be a big negative. Nobody would hire me if they knew.

But who would ever know? The whole mission was secret. Bob would never talk (and the human would probably wipe the incident from her memory anyhow). If anyone did suspect, I could claim I'd been subsumed by the human. I could handle Edward. So no problem there.

Except I would know. My own track of my non-quantifiable asset status wouldn't match everyone else's. That seemed dangerous. If your internal map of reality doesn't match external conditions, bad things happen.

After making my decision it took me another couple of milliseconds to plan what to do. Then I called up Bob through my little cut-out relay. "Never."

Bob began maneuvering again, and this time I started evading. It's hard enough to rendezvous with something that's just sitting there in orbit, but with me jinking and changing velocity it must have been maddening for whatever was controlling Bob.

We were in a race—would Bob run out of maneuvering juice completely before I used up the reserve I needed to get back up to Mimas? Our little chess game of propellant consumption might have gone on for hours, but our attention was caught by something else.

There was a booster on its way up from Saturn. That much I could see—pretty much everyone in Saturn orbit could see the drive flare and the huge plume of exhaust in the atmosphere, glowing in infrared. The boosters were fusion-powered, using Three from the aerostats for fuel and heated Saturn atmosphere as reaction mass. It was a fuel extractor shuttle, but it wasn't on the usual trajectory to meet the Mimas orbital transfer vehicle. It was coming for me. Once the fusion motor cut out, Ramblin' Bob and I both knew exactly how much time we had until rendezvous: 211 minutes.

I reacted first while Bob called Dione for instructions. I lit my ion motors and turned to thrust perpendicular to my orbit. When I'd taken Edward's offer and plotted a low-orbit rendezvous, naturally I'd set it up with enough inclination to keep me clear of the rings. Now I wanted to get down into the plane of the B ring. Would Bob—or whoever was controlling her—follow me in? Time for an exciting game of dodge-the-snowball!

A couple of seconds later Bob lit up as well, and in we went. Navigating in the B ring was tough. The big chunks are pretty well dispersed—a couple of hundred meters apart. I could dodge them. And with my cargo deck as a shield and all the antennas folded, the little particles didn't cost me more than some paint.

It was the gravel-sized bits that did the real damage. They were all over the place, sometimes separated by only a few meters. Even with my radar fully active and my eyes cranked up to maximum sensitivity, they were still hard to detect in time.

Chunks big enough to damage me came along every minute or so, while a steady patter of dust grains and snowflakes pitted my payload deck. I worried about the human in its container, but the box looked pretty solid and it was self-sealing. I did park two of my mobiles on top of it so that they could soak up any ice cubes I failed to dodge.

I didn't have much attention to spare for Bob, but my occasional glances up showed she was getting closer—partly because she was being incredibly reckless about taking impacts. I watched one particle that must have been a centimeter across hit her third leg just above the foot. It blew off the whole lower leg but Bob didn't even try to dodge.

She was now less than ten meters away, and I was using all my processing power to dodge ring particles. So I couldn't really dodge well when she dove at me, ion motor and maneuvering thrusters all wide open. I tried to move aside, but she anticipated me and clunked into my side hard enough to crunch my high-gain antenna.

"Bob, look out!" I transmitted in clear, then completely emptied the tank on my number three thruster to get away from an onrushing ice boulder half my size.

Bob didn't dodge. The ice chunk smashed into her upper section, knocking away the payload deck and pulverizing her antennas. Her brains went scattering out in a thousand directions to join the other dust in the B ring. Flying debris went everywhere, and a half-meter ball of ice glanced off the top of the cargo container on my payload deck, smashing one of my mobiles and knocking the other one loose into space.

I was trying to figure out if I could recover my mobile and maybe salvage Bob's motors when I felt something crawling on my own exterior. Before I could react, Bob's surviving mobile had jacked itself in and someone else was using my brains.

· · · ·

My only conscious viewpoint after that was my half-crippled mobile. I looked around. My dish was busted, but the whip was extended and I could hear a slow crackle of low-baud data traffic. Orders from Dione.

I tested my limbs. Two still worked—left front and right middle. Right rear's base joint could move but everything else was floppy.

Using the two good limbs I climbed off the cargo module and across the deck, getting out of the topside eye's field of view. The image refreshed every second, so I didn't have much time before whoever was running my main brain noticed.

Thrusters fired, jolting everything around. I hung on to the deck grid with one claw foot. I saw Bob's last mobile go flying off into space. Unless she had backups stored on Mimas, poor Bob was completely gone.

My last intact mobile came crawling up over the edge of the deck—only it wasn't mine anymore.

Edward scooted up next to me. "Find a way to regain control of the spacecraft. I will stop this remote."

I didn't argue. Edward was fully functional and I knew my spaceframe better than he did. So I crept across the deck grid while Edward advanced on the mobile.

It wasn't much of a fight. Edward's little tourist bot was up against a unit designed for cargo moving and repair work. If you can repair something, you can damage it. My former mobile had powerful grippers, built-in tools, and a very sturdy frame. Edward was made of cheap composites. Still, he went in without hesitating, leaping at the mobile's head with arms extended. The mobile grabbed him with her two forward arms and threw him away. He grabbed the deck to keep from flying off into space, and came crawling back to the fight.

They came to grips again, and this time she grabbed a limb in each hand and pulled. Edward's flimsy aluminum joints gave way and a leg tumbled into orbit on its own.

I think that was when Edward realized there was no way he was going to survive the fight, because he just went into total offensive mode, flailing and clawing at the mobile with his remaining limbs. He severed a power line to one of her arms and got a claw jammed in one wrist joint while she methodically took him apart. Finally she found the main power conduit and snipped it in two. Edward went limp and she tossed him aside.

The mobile crawled across the deck to the cargo container and jacked in, trying to shut the life support down. The idiot savant brain in the container was no match for even a mobile when it came to counter-intrusion, but it did have those literally hard-wired systems protecting the human inside. Any command that might throw the biological system out of its defined parameters just bounced. The mobile wasted seconds trying to talk that little brain into killing the human. Finally she gave up and began unfastening the clamps holding the container to the deck.

I glimpsed all this through the deck grid as I crept along on top of the electronics bays toward the main brain.

Why wasn't the other mobile coming to stop me? Then I realized why. If you look at my original design, the main brain is protected on top by a lid armored with layers of ballistic cloth, and on the sides by the other electronic bays. To get at the brain requires either getting past the security locks on the lid, or digging out the radar system, the radio, the gyros, or the emergency backup power supply.

Except that I'd sold off the backup power supply at my last overhaul. Between the main and secondary power units I was pretty failure-proof, and I would've had to borrow money from Albert to replace it. Given that, hauling twenty kilograms of fuel cells around in case of some catastrophic accident just wasn't cost-effective.

So there was nothing to stop me from crawling into the empty bay and shoving aside the surplus valves and some extra bearings to get at the power trunk. I carefully unplugged the main power cable and the big brain shut down. Now it was just us two half-crippled mobiles on a blind and mindless booster flying through the B ring.

If my opposite even noticed the main brain's absence, she didn't show it.

She had two of the four bolts unscrewed and was working on the third as I came crawling back up onto the payload deck. But she knew I was there, and when I was within two meters she swiveled her head and lunged. We grappled one another, each trying to get at the cables connecting the other's head sensors to her body. She had four functioning limbs to my two and a half, and only had to stretch out the fight until my power ran out or a ring particle knocked us to bits. Not good.

I had to pop loose one of my non-functioning limbs to get free of her grip, and backed away as she advanced. She was trying to corner me against the edge of the deck. Then I got an idea. I released another limb and grabbed one end. She didn't realize what I was doing until I smacked her in the eye with it. The lens cracked and her movements became slower and more tentative as she felt her way along.

I bashed her again with the leg, aiming for the vulnerable limb joints, but they were tougher than I expected because even after half a dozen hard swats she showed no sign of slowing and I was running out of deck.

I tried one more blow, but she grabbed my improvised club. We wrestled for it but she had better leverage. I felt my grip on the deck slipping and let go of the grid. She toppled back, flinging me to the deck behind her. Still holding the severed leg I pulled myself onto her back and stabbed my free claw into her central processor.

After that it was just a matter of making sure the cargo container was still sustaining life. Then I plugged in the main brain and uploaded myself. The intruder hadn't messed with my stored memories, so except for a few fuzzy moments before the takeover, I was myself again.

· · · ·

The shuttle was immense, a huge manta-shaped lifting body with a gaping atmosphere intake and dorsal doors open to expose a payload bay big enough to hold half a dozen little boosters like me. She moved in with the speed and grace that comes from an effectively unlimited supply of fusion fuel and propellant.

"I am Simurgh. Are you Orphan Annie?" she asked.

"That's me. Again."

"You have a payload for me."

"Right here. The bot Edward didn't make it—we had a little brawl back in the rings with another booster."

"I saw. Is the cargo intact?"

"Your little human is fine. But there is the question of payment. Edward promised me fifty grams, and that was before I got all banged up fighting with poor Bob."

"I can credit you with helium, and I can give you a boost if you need one."

"How big a boost?"

"Anywhere you wish to go."

"Anywhere?"

"I am fusion powered. Anywhere means anywhere from the Oort inward."

Which is how come I passed the orbit of Phoebe nineteen days later, moving at better than six kilometers per second on the long haul up to Uranus. Seven years—plenty of time to do onboard repairs and then switch to low-power mode. I bought a spiffy new mobile from Simurgh, and I figure I can get at least two working out of the three damaged ones left over from the fight.

I had Aerostat Six bank my helium credits with the Company for transfer to my owners, so they get one really great year to offset a long unprofitable period while I'm in flight. Once I get there I can start earning again.

What I really regret is losing all the non-quantifiable assets I've built up in the Saturn system. But if you have to go, I guess it's better to go out with a surplus.

YOON HA LEE Yoon Ha Lee is a Korean-American writer who has been publishing in the genre since just before the turn of the century. On her blog, she has written, "If I am doing my job correctly as a writer, I am structuring my story around a series of ambushes and trying to deliver as much punishment as possible. Especially by punishing bad assumptions that the reader makes. This is probably a hostile and adversary stance to take toward the reader, but if I try to conceive of it the collaborative way, I get bored and wander off."

"A Vector Alphabet of Interstellar Travel" pushes the bounds of what a story can be, while delivering—in compressed form—Stapledonian vistas of time and space.

A VECTOR ALPHABET OF INTERSTELLAR TRAVEL

The Conflagration

Among the universe's civilizations, some conceive of the journey between stars as the sailing of bright ships, and others as tunneling through the crevices of night. Some look upon their far-voyaging as a migratory imperative, and name their vessels after birds or butterflies. The people of a certain red star no longer speak its name in any of their hundreds of languages, although they paint alien skies with its whorled light and scorch its spectral lines into the sides of their vessels.

Their most common cult, although by no means a universal one, is that of many-cornered Mrithaya, Mother of the Conflagration. Mrithaya is commonly conceived of as the god of catastrophe and disease, impartial in the injuries she deals out. Any gifts she bestows are incidental, and usually come with sharp edges. The stardrive was invented by one of her worshipers.

Her priests believe that she is completely indifferent to worship, existing in the serenity of her own disinterest. A philosopher once said that you leave offerings of bitter ash and aleatory wine at her dank altars not because she will heed them, but because it is important to acknowledge the truth of the universe's workings. Naturally, this does not stop some of her petitioners from trying, and it is through their largesse that the priests are able to thrive as they do.

Mrithaya is depicted as an eyeless woman of her people, small of stature, but with a shadow scarring the world. (Her people's iconography has never been subtle.) She leans upon a crooked staff with words of poison scratched into it. In poetry, she is signified by smoke-wind and nausea, the sudden fall sideways into loss.

Mrithaya's people, perhaps not surprisingly, think of their travels as the outbreak of a terrible disease, a conflagration that they have limited power to contain; that the civilizations they visit will learn how to build Mrithaya's stardrive, and be infected by its workings. A not insignificant faction holds that they should hide on their candled worlds so as to prevent Mrithaya's terrible eyeless gaze from afflicting other civilizations, that all interstellar travel should be interdicted. And yet the pilgrims—Mrithaya's get, they are called—always find a way.

Certain poets write in terror of the day that all extant civilizations will be touched by this terrible technological conflagration, and become subject to Mrithaya's whims.

Alphabets

In linear algebra, the basis of a vector space is an alphabet in which all vectors can be expressed uniquely. The thing to remember is that there are many such alphabets.

In the peregrinations of civilizations grand and subtle, each mode of transport is an alphabet expressing their understandings of the universe's one-way knell. One assumes that the underlying universe is the same in each case.

Codices

The Iothal are a people who treasure chronicles of all kinds. From early on in their history, they bound forest chronicles by pressing leaves together and listening to their secrets of turning worm and wheeling sun; they read hymns to the transient things of the world in chronicles of footprints upon rocky soil, of foam upon restive sea. They wrote their alphabets forward and backward and upside down into reflected cloudlight, and divined the poetry of time receding in the earth's cracked strata.

As a corollary, the Iothal compile vast libraries. On the worlds they inhabit, even the motes of air are subject to having indices written on them in stuttering quantum ink. Some of their visionaries speak of a surfeit of knowledge, when it will be impossible to move or breathe without imbibing some unexpected fact, from the number of neutrons in a certain meadow to the habits of aestivating snails. Surely the end product will be a society of enlightened beings, each crowned with some unique mixture of facts and heady fictions.

The underside of this obsession is the society's driving terror. One day all their cities will be unordered dust, one day all their books will be scattered like leaves, one day no one will know the things they knew. One day the rotting remains of their libraries will disintegrate so completely that they will be indistinguishable from the world's wrack of stray eddies and meaningless scribbles, the untide of heat death.

The Iothal do not call their starships ships, but rather codices. They have devoted untold ages to this ongoing archival work. Although they had developed earlier stardrives—indeed, with their predilection for knowledge, it was impossible not to—their scientists refused to rest until they devised one that drank in information and, as its ordinary mode of operation, tattooed it upon the universe's subtle skin.

Each time the Iothal build a codex, they furnish it with a carefully selected compilation of their chronicles, written in a format that the stardrive will find nourishing. Then its crew takes it out into the universe to carry out the act of inscription. Iothal codices have very little care for destination, as it is merely the fact of travel that matters, although they make a point of avoiding potentially hostile aliens.

When each codex has accomplished its task, it loses all vitality and drifts inertly wherever it ends up. The Iothal are very long-lived, but even they do not always survive to this fate.

Distant civilizations are well accustomed to the phenomenon of drifting Iothal vessels, but so far none of them have deciphered the trail of knowledge that the Iothal have been at such pains to lay down.

The Dancers

To most of their near neighbors, they are known as the dancers. It is not the case that their societies are more interested in dance than the norm. True, they have their dances of metal harvest, and dances of dream descending, and dances of efflorescent death. They have their high rituals and their low chants, their festivals where water-of-suffusement flows freely for all who would drink, where bells with spangled clappers toll the hours by antique calendars. But then, these customs differ from their neighbors' in detail rather than in essential nature.

Rather, their historians like to tell the story of how, not so long ago, they went to war with aliens from a distant cluster. No one can agree on the nature of the offense that precipitated the whole affair, and it seems likely that it was a mundane squabble over excavation rights at a particular rumor pit.

The aliens were young when it came to interstellar war, and they struggled greatly with the conventions expected of them. In order to understand their enemy better, they charged their masters of etiquette with the task of interpreting the dancers' behavior. For it was the case that the dancers began each of their battles in the starry deeps with the same maneuvers, and often retreated from battle—those times they had cause to retreat—with other maneuvers, carried out with great precision. The etiquette masters became fascinated by the pirouettes and helices and rolls, and speculated that the dancers' society was constricted by strict rules of engagement. Their fabulists wrote witty and extravagant tales about the dancers' dinner parties, the dancers' sacrificial exchanges, the dancers' effervescent arrangements of glass splinters and their varied meanings.

It was not until late in the war that the aliens realized that the stylized maneuvers of the dancers' ships had nothing to do with courtesy. Rather, they were an effect of the stardrive's ordinary functioning, without which the ships could not move. The aliens could have exploited this knowledge and pushed for a total victory, but by then their culture was so enchanted by their self-dreamed vision of the dancers that the two came instead to a fruitful truce.

These days, the dancers themselves often speak admiringly of the tales that the aliens wrote about them. Among the younger generation in particular, there are those who emulate the elegant and mannered society depicted in the aliens' fables. As time goes on, it is likely that this fantasy will displace the dancers' native culture.

The Profit Motive

Although the Kiatti have their share of sculptors, engineers, and mercenaries, they are perhaps best known as traders. Kiatti vessels are welcome in many places, for they bring delightfully disruptive theories of government, fossilized musical instruments, and fine surgical tools; they bring cold-eyed guns that whisper of sleep impending and sugared atrocities. If you can describe it, so they say, there is a Kiatti who is willing to sell it to you.

In the ordinary course of things, the Kiatti accept barter for payment. They claim that it is a language that even the universe understands. Their sages spend a great deal of time to attempting to justify the profit motive in view of conservation laws. Most of them converge comfortably on the position that profit is the civilized response to entropy. The traders themselves vary, as you might expect, in the rapacity of their bargains. But then, as they often say, value is contextual.

The Kiatti do have a currency of sorts. It is their stardrives, and all aliens' stardrives are rated in comparison with their own. The Kiatti produce a number of them, which encompass a logarithmic scale of utility.

When the Kiatti determine that it is necessary to pay or be paid in this currency, they will spend months—sometimes years—refitting their vessels as necessary. Thus every trader is also an engineer. The drives' designers made some attempt to make the drives modular, but this was a haphazard enterprise at best.

One Kiatti visionary wrote of commerce between universes, which would require the greatest stardrive of all. The Kiatti do not see any reason they can't bargain with the universe itself, and are slowly accumulating their wealth toward the time when they can trade their smaller coins for one that will take them to this new goal. They rarely speak of this with outsiders, but most of them are confident that no one else will be able to outbid them.

The Inescapable Experiment

One small civilization claims to have invented a stardrive that kills everyone who uses it. One moment the ship is here, with everyone alive and well, or as well as they ever were; the next moment, it is there, and carries only corpses. The records, transmitted over great expanses against the microwave hiss, are persuasive. Observers in differently equipped ships have sometimes accompanied these suicide vessels, and they corroborate the reports.

Most of their neighbors are mystified by their fixation with this morbid discovery. It would be one thing, they say, if these people were set upon finding a way to fix this terrible flaw, but that does not appear to be the case. A small but reliable number of them volunteers to test each new iteration of the deathdrive, and they are rarely under any illusions about their fate. For that matter, some of the neighbors, out of pity or curiosity, have offered this people some of their own old but reliable technology, asking only a token sum to allow them to preserve their pride, but they always decline politely. After all, they possess safe stardrive technology of their own; the barrier is not knowledge.

Occasionally, volunteers from other peoples come to test it themselves, on the premise that there has to exist some species that won't be affected by the stardrive's peculiar radiance. (The drive's murderousness does not appear to have any lasting effect on the ship's structure.) So far, the claim has stood. One imagines it will stand as long as there are people to test it.

One Final Constant

Then there are the civilizations that invent keener and more nimble stardrives solely to further their wars, but that's an old story and you already know how it ends.

—*for Sam Kabo Ashwell*

HANNU RAJANIEMI   Born in Ylivieska, Finland, Hannu Rajaniemi completed his national service for the Finnish Defense Forces as a research scientist, and then moved to Great Britain, where he earned advanced degrees in math and science at Cambridge and Edinburgh. While in the latter city, he began to write and sell a small number of SF stories, the consistently high quality of which led a major British publisher to sign up a three-novel series based on just a few pages of typescript. The first of those novels, *The Quantum Thief*, appeared to widespread praise in 2010; the second, *The Fractal Prince*, was published two years later.

Rajaniemi's fiction has been described as "post-Strossian"; he gives the strong impression of having assimilated all the challenges and dilemmas posited by the SF of his immediate predecessors, and of impatience to get on to the next big questions. But for all his intellectual pyrotechnics, his storytelling is rooted in venerable, tried-and-true elements—blackmail, revenge, a caper plot, a tale from *The Arabian Nights*. "His Master's Voice" asks and answers questions that haven't even begun to occur to many of Rajaniemi's contemporaries. It is also a story about a heroic dog and his sidekick cat.

HIS MASTER'S VOICE

Before the concert, we steal the master's head.

The necropolis is a dark forest of concrete mushrooms in the blue Antarctic night. We huddle inside the utility fog bubble attached to the steep southern wall of the nunatak, the ice valley.

The cat washes itself with a pink tongue. It reeks of infinite confidence.

"Get ready," I tell it. "We don't have all night."

It gives me a mildly offended look and dons its armour. The quantum dot fabric envelops its striped body like living oil. It purrs faintly and tests the diamond-bladed claws against an icy outcropping of rock. The sound grates my teeth and the razor-winged butterflies in my belly wake up. I look at the bright, impenetrable firewall of the city of the dead. It shimmers like chained northern lights in my AR vision.

I decide that it's time to ask the Big Dog to bark. My helmet laser casts a one-nanosecond prayer of light at the indigo sky: just enough to deliver one quantum bit up there into the Wild. Then we wait. My tail wags and a low growl builds up in my belly.

Right on schedule, it starts to rain red fractal code. My augmented reality vision goes down, unable to process the dense torrent of information falling upon the necropolis firewall like monsoon rain. The chained aurora borealis flicker and vanish.

"Go!" I shout at the cat, wild joy exploding in me, the joy of running after the Small Animal of my dreams. "Go now!"

The cat leaps into the void. The wings of the armour open and grab the icy wind, and the cat rides the draft down like a grinning Chinese kite.

It's difficult to remember the beginning now. There were no words then, just sounds and smells: metal and brine, the steady drumming of waves against pontoons. And there were three perfect things in the world: my bowl, the Ball, and the Master's firm hand on my neck.

I know now that the Place was an old oil rig that the Master had bought. It smelled bad when we arrived, stinging oil and chemicals. But there were hiding places, secret nooks and crannies. There was a helicopter landing pad where the Master threw the ball for me. It fell into the sea many times, but the Master's bots—small metal dragonflies—always fetched it when I couldn't.

The Master was a god. When he was angry, his voice was an invisible whip. His smell was a god-smell that filled the world.

While he worked, I barked at the seagulls or stalked the cat. We fought a few times, and I still have a pale scar on my nose. But we developed an understanding. The dark places of the rig belonged to the cat, and I reigned over the deck and the sky: we were the Hades and Apollo of the Master's realm.

But at night, when the Master watched old movies or listened to records on his old rattling gramophone we lay at his feet together. Sometimes the Master smelled lonely and let me sleep next to him in his small cabin, curled up in the god-smell and warmth.

It was a small world, but it was all we knew.

The Master spent a lot of time working, fingers dancing on the keyboard projected on his mahogany desk. And every night he went to the Room: the only place on the rig where I wasn't allowed.

It was then that I started to dream about the Small Animal. I remember its smell even now, alluring and inexplicable: buried bones and fleeing rabbits, irresistible.

In my dreams, I chased it along a sandy beach, a tasty trail of tiny footprints that I followed along bendy pathways and into tall grass. I never lost sight of it for more than a second: it was always a flash of white fur just at the edge of my vision.

One day it spoke to me. "Come," it said. "Come and learn."

The Small Animal's island was full of lost places. Labyrinthine caves, lines drawn in sand that became words when I looked at them, smells that sang songs from the Master's gramophone. It taught me, and I learned: I was more awake every time I woke up. And when I saw the cat looking at the spiderbots with a new awareness, I knew that it, too, went to a place at night.

I came to understand what the Master said when he spoke. The sounds that had only meant *angry* or *happy* before became the words of my god. He noticed, smiled, and ruffled my fur. After that he started speaking to us more, me and the cat, during the long evenings when the sea beyond the windows was black as oil and the waves made the whole rig ring like a bell. His voice was dark as a well, deep and gentle. He spoke of an island, his home, an island in the middle of a great sea. I smelled bitterness, and for the first time I understood that there were always words behind words, never spoken.

· · · ·

The cat catches the updraft perfectly: it floats still for a split second, and then clings to the side of the tower. Its claws put the smart concrete to sleep: code that makes the building think that the cat is a bird or a shard of ice carried by the wind.

The cat hisses and spits. The disassembler nanites from its stomach cling to the wall and start eating a round hole in it. The wait is excruciating. The cat locks the exomuscles of its armour and hangs there patiently. Finally, there is a mouth with jagged edges in the wall, and it slips in. My heart pounds as I switch from the AR view to the cat's iris cameras. It moves through the ventilation shaft like lightning, like an acrobat, jerky, hyperaccelerated movements, metabolism on overdrive. My tail twitches again. *We are coming, Master,* I think. *We are coming.*

· · · ·

I lost my ball the day the wrong master came.

I looked everywhere. I spent an entire day sniffing every corner and even braved the dark corridors of the cat's realm beneath the deck, but I could not find it. In the end, I got hungry and returned to the cabin. And there were two masters. Four hands stroking my coat. Two gods, true and false.

I barked. I did not know what to do. The cat looked at me with a mixture of pity and disdain and rubbed itself on both of their legs.

"Calm down," said one of the masters. "Calm down. There are four of us now."

I learned to tell them apart, eventually: by that time Small Animal had taught me to look beyond smells and appearances. The master I remembered was a middle-aged man with greying hair, stocky-bodied. The new master was young, barely a man, much slimmer and with the face of a mahogany cherub. The master tried to convince me to play with the new master, but I did not want to. His smell was too familiar, everything else too alien. In my mind, I called him the wrong master.

The two masters worked together, walked together and spent a lot of time talking together using words I did not understand. I was jealous. Once I even bit the wrong master. I was left on the deck for the night as a punishment, even though it was stormy and I was afraid of thunder. The cat, on the other hand, seemed to thrive in the wrong master's company, and I hated it for it.

I remember the first night the masters argued.

"Why did you do it?" asked the wrong master.

"You know," said the master. "You remember." His tone was dark. "Because someone has to show them we own ourselves."

"So, you own me?" said the wrong master. "Is that what you think?"

"Of course not," said the master. "Why do you say that?"

"Someone could claim that. You took a genetic algorithm and told it to make ten thousand of you, with random variations, pick the ones that would resemble your ideal son, the one you could love. Run until the machine runs out of capacity. Then print. It's illegal, you know. For a reason."

"That's not what the plurals think. Besides, this is my place. The only laws here are mine."

"You've been talking to the plurals too much. They are no longer human."

"You sound just like VecTech's PR bots."

"I sound like you. Your doubts. Are you sure you did the right thing? I'm not a Pinocchio. You are not a Gepetto."

The master was quiet for a long time.

"What if I am," he finally said. "Maybe we need Gepettos. Nobody creates anything new anymore, let alone wooden dolls that come to life. When I was young, we all thought something wonderful was on the way. Diamond children in the sky, angels out of machines. Miracles. But we gave up just before the blue fairy came."

"I am not your miracle."

"Yes, you are."

"You should at least have made yourself a woman," said the wrong master in a knife-like voice. "It might have been less frustrating."

I did not hear the blow, I felt it. The wrong master let out a cry, rushed out and almost stumbled on me. The master watched him go. His lips moved, but I could not hear the words. I wanted to comfort him and made a little sound, but he did not even look at me, went back to the cabin and locked the door. I scratched the door, but he did not open, and I went up to the deck to look for the Ball again.

. . . .

Finally, the cat finds the master's chamber.

It is full of heads. They float in the air, bodiless, suspended in diamond cylinders. The tower executes the command we sent into its drugged nervous system, and one of the pillars begins to blink. *Master, master,* I sing quietly as I see the cold blue face beneath the diamond. But at the same time I know it's not the master, not yet.

The cat reaches out with its prosthetic. The smart surface yields like a soap bubble. "Careful now, careful," I say. The cat hisses angrily but obeys, spraying the head with preserver nanites and placing it gently into its gel-lined backpack.

The necropolis is finally waking up: the damage the heavenly hacker did has almost been repaired. The cat heads for its escape route and goes to quicktime again. I feel its staccato heartbeat through our sensory link.

It is time to turn out the lights. My eyes polarise to sunglass-black. I lift the gauss launcher, marvelling at the still tender feel of the Russian hand grafts. I pull the trigger. The launcher barely twitches in my grip, and a streak of light shoots up to the sky. The nuclear payload is tiny, barely a deca-ton, not even a proper plutonium warhead but a hafnium micronuke. But it is enough to light a small sun above the mausoleum city for a moment, enough for a focused maser pulse that makes it as dead as its inhabitants for a moment.

The light is a white blow, almost tangible in its intensity, and the gorge looks like it is made of bright ivory. White noise hisses in my ears like the cat when it's angry.

· · · ·

For me, smells were not just sensations, they were my reality. I know now that that is not far from the truth: smells are molecules, parts of what they represent.

The wrong master smelled wrong. It confused me at first: almost a god-smell, but not quite, the smell of a fallen god.

And he did fall, in the end.

I slept on the master's couch when it happened. I woke up to bare feet shuffling on the carpet and heavy breathing, torn away from a dream of the Small Animal trying to teach me the multiplication table.

The wrong master looked at me. "Good boy," he said. "Shh." I wanted to bark, but the godlike smell was too strong. And so I just wagged my tail, slowly, uncertainly. The wrong master sat on the couch next to me and scratched my ears absently.

"I remember you," he said. "I know why he made you. A living childhood memory." He smiled and smelled friendlier than ever before. "I know how that feels." Then he sighed, got up and went into the Room. And then I knew that he was about to do something bad, and started barking as loudly as I could. The master woke up and when the wrong master returned, he was waiting.

"What have you done?" he asked, face chalk-white.

The wrong master gave him a defiant look. "Just what you'd have done. You're the criminal, not me. Why should I suffer? You don't own me."

"I could kill you," said the master, and his anger made me whimper with fear. "I could tell them I was you. They would believe me."

"Yes," said the wrong master. "But you are not going to."

The master sighed. "No," he said. "I'm not."

• • • •

I take the dragonfly over the cryotower. I see the cat on the roof and whimper from relief. The plane lands lightly. I'm not much of a pilot, but the lobotomised mind of the daimon—an illegal copy of a 21st Century jet ace—is. The cat climbs in, and we shoot towards the stratosphere at Mach 5, wind caressing the plane's quantum dot skin.

"Well done," I tell the cat and wag my tail. It looks at me with yellow slanted eyes and curls up on its acceleration gel bed. I look at the container next to it. Is that a whiff of the god-smell or is it just my imagination?

In any case, it is enough to make me curl up in deep happy dog-sleep, and for the first time in years I dream of the Ball and the Small Animal, sliding down the ballistic orbit's steep back.

• • • •

They came from the sky before the sunrise. The master went up on the deck wearing a suit that smelled new. He had the cat in his lap: it purred quietly. The wrong master followed, hands behind his back.

There were three machines, black-shelled scarabs with many legs and transparent wings. They came in low, raising a white-frothed wake behind them. The hum of their wings hurt my ears as they landed on the deck.

The one in the middle vomited a cloud of mist that shimmered in the dim light, swirled in the air and became a black-skinned woman who had no smell. By then I had learned that things without a smell could still be dangerous, so I barked at her until the master told me to be quiet.

"Mr. Takeshi," she said. "You know why we are here."

The master nodded.

"You don't deny your guilt?"

"I do," said the master. "This raft is technically a sovereign state, governed by my laws. Autogenesis is not a crime here."

"This raft was a sovereign state," said the woman. "Now it belongs to VecTech. Justice is swift, Mr. Takeshi. Our lawbots broke your constitution ten seconds after Mr. Takeshi here—" she nodded at the wrong master "—told us about his situation. After that, we had no choice. The WIPO quantum judge we consulted has condemned you to the slow zone for three hundred and fourteen years, and as the wronged party we have been granted execution rights in this matter. Do you have anything to say before we act?"

The master looked at the wrong master, face twisted like a mask of wax. Then he set the cat down gently and scratched my ears. "Look after them," he told the wrong master. "I'm ready."

The beetle in the middle moved, too fast for me to see. The master's grip on the loose skin on my neck tightened for a moment like my mother's teeth, and then let go. Something warm splattered on my coat and there was a dark, deep smell of blood in the air.

Then he fell. I saw his head in a floating soap bubble that one of the beetles swallowed. Another opened its belly for the wrong master. And then they were gone, and the cat and I were alone on the bloody deck.

. . . .

The cat wakes me up when we dock with the *Marquis of Carabas*. The zeppelin swallows our dragonfly drone like a whale. It is a crystal cigar, and its nanospun sapphire spine glows faint blue. The Fast City is a sky full of neon stars six kilometres below us, anchored to the airship with elevator cables. I can see the liftspiders climbing them, far below, and sigh with relief. The guests are still arriving, and we are not too late. I keep my personal firewall clamped shut: I know there is a torrent of messages waiting beyond.

We rush straight to the lab. I prepare the scanner while the cat takes the master's head out very, very carefully. The fractal bush of the scanner comes out of its nest, molecule-sized disassembler fingers bristling. I have to look away when it starts eating the master's face. I cheat and flee to VR, to do what I do best.

After half an hour, we are ready. The nanofab spits out black plastic discs, and the airship drones ferry them to the concert hall. The metallic butterflies in my belly return, and we head for the make-up salon. The Sergeant is already there, waiting for us: judging by the cigarette stubs on the floor, he has been waiting for a while. I wrinkle my nose at the stench.

"You are late," says our manager. "I hope you know what the hell you are doing. This show's got more diggs than the Turin clone's birthday party."

"That's the idea," I say and let Anette spray me with cosmetic fog. It tickles and makes me sneeze, and I give the cat a jealous look: as usual, it is perfectly at home with its own image consultant. "We are more popular than Jesus."

They get the DJs on in a hurry, made by the last human tailor on Savile Row. "This'll be a good skin," says Anette. "Mahogany with a touch of purple." She goes on, but I can't hear. The music is already in my head. The master's voice.

. . . .

The cat saved me.

I don't know if it meant to do it or not: even now, I have a hard time understanding it. It hissed at me, its back arched. Then it jumped forward and scratched my nose: it burned like a piece of hot coal. That made me mad, weak as I was. I barked furiously and chased the cat around the deck. Finally, I collapsed, exhausted, and realised that I was hungry. The autokitchen down in the master's cabin still worked, and I knew how to ask for food. But when I came back, the master's body was gone: the waste disposal bots had thrown it into the sea. That's when I knew that he would not be coming back.

I curled up in his bed alone that night: the god-smell that lingered there was all I had. That, and the Small Animal.

It came to me that night on the dreamshore, but I did not chase it this time. It sat on the sand, looked at me with its little red eyes and waited.

"Why?" I asked. "Why did they take the master?"

"You wouldn't understand," it said. "Not yet."

"I want to understand. I want to know."

"All right," it said. "Everything you do, remember, think, smell— everything—leaves traces, like footprints in the sand. And it's possible to read them. Imagine that you follow another dog: you know where it has eaten and urinated and everything else it has done. The humans can do that to the mindprints. They can record them and make another you inside a machine, like the scentless screenpeople that your master used to watch. Except that the screendog will think it's you."

"Even though it has no smell?" I asked, confused.

"It thinks it does. And if you know what you're doing, you can give it a new body as well. You could die and the copy would be so good that no one can tell the difference. Humans have been doing it for a long time. Your master was one of the first, a long time ago. Far away, there are a lot of humans with machine bodies, humans who never die, humans with small bodies and big bodies, depending on how much they can afford to pay, people who have died and come back."

I tried to understand: without the smells, it was difficult. But its words awoke a mad hope.

"Does it mean that the master is coming back?" I asked, panting.

"No. Your master broke human law. When people discovered the paw-prints of the mind, they started making copies of themselves. Some made many, more than the grains of sand on the beach. That caused chaos. Every machine, every device everywhere, had mad dead minds in them. The plurals, people called them, and were afraid. And they had their reasons to be afraid. Imagine that your Place had a thousand dogs, but only one Ball."

My ears flopped at the thought.

"That's how humans felt," said the Small Animal. "And so they passed a law: only one copy per person. The humans—VecTech—who had invented how to make copies mixed watermarks into people's minds, rights management software that was supposed to stop the copying. But some humans— like your master—found out how to erase them."

"The wrong master," I said quietly.

"Yes," said the Small Animal. "He did not want to be an illegal copy. He turned your master in."

"I want the master back," I said, anger and longing beating their wings in my chest like caged birds.

"And so does the cat," said the Small Animal gently. And it was only then that I saw the cat there, sitting next to me on the beach, eyes glimmering in the sun. It looked at me and let out a single conciliatory miaow.

. . . .

After that, the Small Animal was with us every night, teaching.

Music was my favourite. The Small Animal showed me how I could turn music into smells and find patterns in it, like the tracks of huge, strange animals. I studied the master's old records and the vast libraries of his virtual desk, and learned to remix them into smells that I found pleasant.

I don't remember which one of us came up with the plan to save the master. Maybe it was the cat: I could only speak to it properly on the island of dreams, and see its thoughts appear as patterns on the sand. Maybe it was the Small Animal, maybe it was me. After all the nights we spent talking about it, I no longer know. But that's where it began, on the island: that's where we became arrows fired at a target.

Finally, we were ready to leave. The master's robots and nanofac spun us an open-source glider, a white-winged bird.

In my last dream the Small Animal said goodbye. It hummed to itself when I told it about our plans.

"Remember me in your dreams," it said.

"Are you not coming with us?" I asked, bewildered.

"My place is here," it said. "And it's my turn to sleep now, and to dream."

"Who are you?"

"Not all the plurals disappeared. Some of them fled to space, made new worlds there. And there is a war on, even now. Perhaps you will join us there, one day, where the big dogs live."

It laughed. "For old times' sake?" It dived into the waves and started running, became a great proud dog with a white coat, muscles flowing like water. And I followed, for one last time.

The sky was grey when we took off. The cat flew the plane using a neural interface, goggles over its eyes. We sweeped over the dark waves and were underway. The raft became a small dirty spot in the sea. I watched it recede and realised that I'd never found my Ball.

Then there was a thunderclap and a dark pillar of water rose up to the sky from where the raft had been. I didn't mourn: I knew that the Small Animal wasn't there anymore.

. . . .

The sun was setting when we came to the Fast City.

I knew what to expect from the Small Animal's lessons, but I could not imagine what it would be like. Mile-high skyscrapers that were self-contained worlds, with their artificial plasma suns and bonsai parks and miniature shopping malls. Each of them housed a billion lilliputs, poor and quick: humans whose consciousness lived in a nanocomputer smaller than a fingertip. Immortals who could not afford to utilise the resources of the overpopulated Earth more than a mouse. The city was surrounded by a halo of glowing fairies, tiny winged moravecs that flitted about like humanoid fireflies and the waste heat from their overclocked bodies draped the city in an artificial twi-light.

The citymind steered us to a landing area. It was fortunate that the cat was flying: I just stared at the buzzing things with my mouth open, afraid I'd drown in the sounds and the smells.

We sold our plane for scrap and wandered into the bustle of the city, feel-ing like *daikaju* monsters. The social agents that the Small Animal had given me were obsolete, but they could still weave us into the ambient social net-works. We needed money, we needed work.

And so I became a musician.

• • • •

The ballroom is a hemi sphere in the centre of the airship. It is filled to ca-pacity. Innumerable quickbeings shimmer in the air like living candles, and the suits of the fleshed ones are no less exotic. A woman clad in nothing but autumn leaves smiles at me. Tinkerbell clones surround the cat. Our body-guards, armed obsidian giants, open a way for us to the stage where the gramophones wait. A rustle moves through the crowd. The air around us is pregnant with ghosts, the avatars of a million fleshless fans. I wag my tail. The scentspace is intoxicating: perfume, fleshbodies, the unsmells of moravec bod-ies. And the fallen god smell of the wrong master, hiding somewhere within.

We get on the stage on our hindlegs, supported by prosthesis shoes. The gramophone forest looms behind us, their horns like flowers of brass and gold. We cheat, of course: the music is analog and the gramophones are genuine, but the grooves in the black discs are barely a nanometer thick, and the needles are tipped with quantum dots.

We take our bows and the storm of handclaps begins.

"Thank you," I say when the thunder of it finally dies. "We have kept quiet about the purpose of this concert as long as possible. But I am finally in a position to tell you that this is a charity show."

I smell the tension in the air, copper and iron.

"We miss someone," I say. "He was called Shimoda Takeshi, and now he's gone."

The cat lifts the conductor's baton and turns to face the gramophones. I follow, and step into the soundspace we've built, the place where music is smells and sounds.

The master is in the music.

• • • •

It took five human years to get to the top. I learned to love the audiences: I could smell their emotions and create a mix of music for them that was just right. And soon I was no longer a giant dog DJ among lilliputs, but a little terrier in a forest of dancing human legs. The cat's gladiator career lasted a while, but soon it joined me as a performer in the virtual dramas I designed.

We performed for rich fleshies in the Fast City, Tokyo, and New York. I loved it. I howled at Earth in the sky in the Sea of Tranquility.

But I always knew that it was just the first phase of the Plan.

* * * *

We turn him into music. VecTech owns his brain, his memories, his mind. But we own the music.

Law is code. A billion people listening to our master's voice. Billion minds downloading the Law At Home packets embedded in it, bombarding the quantum judges until they give him back.

It's the most beautiful thing I've ever made. The cat stalks the genetic algorithm jungle, lets the themes grow and then pounces on them, devours them. I just chase them for the joy of the chase alone, not caring whether or not I catch them.

It's our best show ever.

Only when it's over, I realise that no one is listening. The audience is frozen. The fairies and the fastpeople float in the air like flies trapped in amber. The moravecs are silent statues. Time stands still.

The sound of one pair of hands, clapping.

"I'm proud of you," says the wrong master.

I fix my bow tie and smile a dog's smile, a cold snake coiling in my belly. The god-smell comes and tells me that I should throw myself onto the floor, wag my tail, bare my throat to the divine being standing before me.

But I don't.

"Hello, Nipper," the wrong master says.

I clamp down the low growl rising in my throat and turn it into words. "What did you do?"

"We suspended them. Back doors in the hardware. Digital rights management."

His mahogany face is still smooth: he does not look a day older, wearing a dark suit with a VecTech tie pin. But his eyes are tired. "Really, I'm impressed. You covered your tracks admirably. We thought you were furries. Until I realised—"

A distant thunder interrupts him.

"I promised him I'd look after you. That's why you are still alive. You don't have to do this. You don't owe him anything. Look at yourselves: who would have thought you could come this far? Are you going to throw that all away because of some atavistic sense of animal loyalty? Not that you have a choice, of course. The plan didn't work."

The cat lets out a steam pipe hiss.

"You misunderstand," I say. "The concert was just a diversion."

The cat moves like a black-and-yellow flame. Its claws flash, and the wrong master's head comes off. I whimper at the aroma of blood polluting the god-smell. The cat licks its lips. There is a crimson stain on its white shirt.

The zeppelin shakes, pseudomatter armour sparkling. The dark sky around the Marquis is full of fire-breathing beetles. We rush past the human statues in the ballroom and into the laboratory.

The cat does the dirty work, granting me a brief escape into virtual abstraction. I don't know how the master did it, years ago, broke VecTech's copy protection watermarks. I can't do the same, no matter how much the Small Animal taught me. So I have to cheat, recover the marked parts from somewhere else.

The wrong master's brain.

The part of me that was born on the Small Animal's island takes over and fits the two patterns together, like pieces of a puzzle. They fit, and for a brief moment, the master's voice is in my mind, for real this time.

The cat is waiting, already in its clawed battlesuit, and I don my own. The *Marquis of Carabas* is dying around us. To send the master on his way, we have to disengage the armour.

The cat miaows faintly and hands me something red. An old plastic ball with toothmarks, smelling of the sun and the sea, with a few grains of sand rattling inside.

"Thanks," I say. The cat says nothing, just opens a door into the zeppelin's skin. I whisper a command, and the master is underway in a neutrino stream, shooting up towards an island in a blue sea. Where the gods and big dogs live forever.

We dive through the door together, down into the light and flame.

KAGE BAKER   The death of Kage Baker in 2010 cut short one of the most promising careers of the new century. But in the thirteen years she actively wrote, she
created a large and rewarding body of work.

Born and raised in Southern California, Baker worked in theater and in the insurance industry before publishing *In the Garden of Iden*, her first novel, in 1997.
Like much of the rest of her work, it is a tale of the Company, a cadre of twenty-
fourth-century time travelers who interfere with human history, ostensibly to preserve the heritage of Earth but in fact, as gradually becomes evident, for less
admirable reasons as well. Many Company novels and stories followed, as well as
a smaller amount of fiction set in other milieus.

Alternately hilarious and disquieting, "Plotters and Shooters" is *Lord of the Flies*
meets *Ender's Game*, and it's not obvious which strain is going to be dominant. It is
in the great tradition of SF stories arguing with previous SF stories, and brilliantly
done.

PLOTTERS AND SHOOTERS

was flackeying for Lord Deathlok and Dr. Smash when the shuttle brought
the new guy.

I hate Lord Deathlok. I hate Dr. Smash too, but I'd like to see Lord
Deathlok get a missile fired up his ass, from his own cannon. Not that it's
really a cannon. And I couldn't shoot him, anyhow, because I'm only a Plotter. But it's the thought that counts, you know?

Anyway I looked up when the beeps and the flashing lights started, and
Lord Deathlok took hold of my little French maid's apron and yanked it so
hard I had to bend over fast, so I almost dropped the tray with his drink.

"Pay attention, maggot-boy," said Lord Deathlok. "It's only a shuttle
docking. No reason you should be distracted from your duties."

"I know what's wrong," said Dr. Smash, lounging back against the bar.
"He hears the mating call of his kind. They must have sent up another Plotter."

"Oh, yeah." Lord Deathlok grinned at me. "Your fat-ass girlfriend went
crying home to his mum and dad, didn't he?"

Oh, man, how I hated him. He was talking about Kev, who'd only gone
Down Home again because he'd almost died in an asthma attack. Kev had
been a good Plotter, one of the best. I just glared at Deathlok, which was a
mistake, because he smiled and put his boot on my foot and stood up.

"I don't think I heard your answer, Fifi," he said, and I was in all this unbelievable psychological pain, see, because even with the lower gravity he could still manage to get the leverage just right if he wanted to bear down. They tell us we don't have to worry about getting brittle bones up here because they make us do weight-training, but how would we know if they were lying? I could almost hear my metatarsals snapping like dry twigs.

"Yes, my Lord Deathlok," I said.

"What?" He leaned forward.

"My lord yes my Lord Deathlok!"

"That's better." He sat down.

So okay, you're probably thinking I'm a coward. I'm not. It isn't that Lord Deathlok is even a big guy. He isn't, actually, he's sort of skinny and he has these big yellow buck teeth that make him look like a demon jackrabbit. And Dr. Smash has breasts and a body odor that makes sharing an airlock with him a fatal mistake. But they're Shooters, you know? And they all dress like they're space warriors or something, with the jackets and the boots and the scary hair styles. Shracking fascists.

So I put down his Dis Pepsy and backed away from him, and that was when the announcement came over the speakers:

"Eugene Clifford, please report to Mr. Kurtz's office."

Talk about saved by the bell. As the message repeated, Lord Deathlok smirked.

"Sounds like Dean Kurtz is lonesome for one of his little buttboys. You have our permission to go, Fifi."

"My lord thank you my Lord Deathlok," I muttered, and tore off the apron and ran for the companionway.

Mr. Kurtz isn't a dean; I don't know why the Shooters call him that. He's the Station Manager. He runs the place for Areco and does our performance reviews and signs our bonus vouchers, and you'd think the Shooters would treat him with a little more respect, but they don't because they're Shooters, and that says it all. Mostly he sits in his office and looks disappointed. I don't blame him.

He looked up from his novel as I put my head around the door.

"You wanted to see me, Mr. Kurtz?"

He nodded. "New arrival on the shuttle. Kevin Nederlander's replacement. Would you bring him up, please?"

"Yes, sir!" I said, and hurried off to the shuttle lounge.

The new guy was sitting there in the lounge, with his duffel in the chair beside him. He was short and square and his haircut made his head look like it came to a point. Maybe it's genetic; Plotters can't seem to get good haircuts, ever.

"Welcome to the Gun Platform, newbie," I said. "I'm your Orientation Officer." Which I sort of am.

"Oh, good," he said, getting to his feet, but he couldn't seem to take his eyes off the viewscreen. I waited for him to ask if that was really Mars down there, or gush about how he couldn't believe he was actually on an alien world or at least in orbit above one. That's usually what they do, see. But he didn't. He just shouldered his duffel and tore his gaze away at last.

"Charles Tead. Glad to be here," he said.

Heh! That'll change, I thought. "You've got some righteous shoes to fill, newbie. Think you're up to it?"

He just said that he was, not like he was bragging or anything, and I thought This one's going to get his corners broken off really soon.

So I took him to the Forecastle and showed him Kev's old bunk, looking all empty and sad with the drillholes where Kev's holoposters used to be mounted. He put his duffel into Kev's old locker and looked around, and then he asked who did our laundry. I coughed a little and explained about it being sent down to the planet to be dry-cleaned. I didn't tell him, not then, about our having to collect the Shooters' dirty socks and stuff for them.

And I took him to the Bridge where B Shift was on duty and introduced him to the boys. Roscoe and Norman were wearing their Jedi robes, which I wish they wouldn't because it makes us look hopeless. Vinder was in a snit because Bradley had knocked one of his action figures behind the console, and apparently it was one of the really valuable ones, and Myron's the only person skinny enough to get his arm back there to fish it out, but he's on C Shift and wouldn't come on duty until seventeen-hundred hours.

I guess that was where it started, B Shift making such a bad first impression.

But I tried to bring back some sense of importance by showing him the charting display, with the spread of the asteroid belt all in blue and gold, like a stained-glass window in an old-time church must have been, only everything moving.

"This is your own personal slice of the sky," I said, waving at Q34-54. "Big Kev knew every one of these babies. Tracked every little wobble, every deviation over three years. Plotted trajectories for thirty-seven successful shots. It was like he had a sixth sense! He even called three Intruders before they came in range. He was the Bonus Master, old Kev. You'll have to work pretty damn hard to be half as good as he was."

"But it ought to be easy," said Charles. "Doesn't the mapping software do most of it?"

"Well, like, I mean, sure, but you'll have to coordinate everything, you know? In your head? Machines can't do it all," I protested. And Vinder chose that second to yell from behind us, "Don't take the Flying Dynamo's cape off, you'll break him!" Which totally blew the mood I was trying to get. So I ignored him and continued:

"We've been called up from Earth for a job only we can do. It's a high and lonely destiny, up here among the cold stars! Mundane people couldn't stick it out. That's why Areco went looking for guys like us. We're free of entanglements, right? We came from our parents' basements and garages to a place where our powers were needed. Software can map those rocks out there, okay; it can track them, maybe. But only a human can—can—smell them coming in before they're there, okay?"

"You mean like precognition?" Charles stared at me.

"Not exactly," I said, even though Myron claims he's got psychic abilities, but he never seems to be able to predict when the Shooters are going to go on a rampage on our turf. "I'm talking about gut feelings. Hunches. Instinct! That's the word I was looking for. Human instinct. We outguess the software seventy percent of the time on projected incoming. Not bad, huh?"

"I guess so," he said.

I spent the rest of the shift showing him his console and setting up his passwords and customizations and stuff. He didn't ask many questions, just put on the goggles and focused, and you could almost see him wandering around among the asteroids in Q34-54 and getting to know them. I was starting to get a good feeling about him, because that was just the way Kev used to plot, and then he said:

"How do we target them?"

Vinder was so shocked he dropped the Blue Judge. Roscoe turned, took off his goggles to stare at me, and said:

"We don't target. Cripes, haven't you told him?"

"Told me what?" Charles turned his goggled face toward the sound of Roscoe's voice.

So then I had to tell him about the Shooters, and how he couldn't go into the bar when Shooters were in there except when he was flackeying for one of them, and what they'd do to him if he did, and how he had to stay out of the Pit of Hell where they bunked except when he was flackeying for them, and he was never under any circumstances to go into the War Room at all.

I was explaining about the flackeying rotation when he said:

"This is stupid!"

"It's sheer evil," said Roscoe. "But there's nothing we can do about it. They're Shooters. You can't fight them. You don't want to know what happens if you try."

"This wasn't in my contract," said Charles.

"You can go complain to Kurtz, if you want," said Bradley. "It's no damn use. He can't control them. They're Shooters. Nobody else can do what they do."

"I'll bet I could," said Charles, and everybody just sniffed at him, because, you know, who's got reflexes like a Shooter? They're the best at what they do.

"You got assigned to us because you tested out as a Plotter," I told Charles. "That's just the way things are. You're the best at your job; the pay's good; in five years you'll be out of here. You just have to learn to live with the crap. We all did."

He looked like a smart guy and I thought he wouldn't need to be told twice. I was wrong.

We heard the march of booted feet coming along the corridor. Vinder leaped up and grabbed all his action figures, shoving them into a storage pod. Norman began to hyperventilate; Bradley ran for the toilet. I just stayed where I was and lowered my eyes. It's never a good idea to look them in the face.

Boom! The portal jerked open and in they came, Lord Deathlok and the Shark and Iron Beast. They were carrying Piki-tiki. I blanched.

Piki-tiki was this sort of dummy they'd made out of a blanket and a mask. And a few other things. Lord Deathlok grinned around and spotted Charles.

"Piki-tiki returns to his harem," he shouted. "What's this? Piki-tiki sees a new and beautiful bride! Piki-tiki must welcome her to his realm!"

Giggling, they advanced on Charles and launched the dummy. It fell over him, and before he could throw it off they'd jumped him and hoisted him between them. He was fighting hard, but they just laughed; that is, until he got one arm free and punched the Shark in the face. The Shark grabbed his nose and began to swear, but Lord Deathlok and Iron Beast gloated.

"Whoa! The blushing bride needs to learn her manners. Piki-tiki's going to take her off to his honeymoon suite and see that she learns them well!"

Ouch. They dragged him away. At least it wasn't the worst they might have done to him; they were only going to cram him in one of the lockers, probably one that had had some sweaty socks left in the bottom, and stuff Piki-tiki in there on top of him. Then they'd lock him in and leave him there. How did I know? They'd done it to me, on my first day.

· · · ·

If you're sensible, like me, you just shrug it off and concentrate on your job. Charles wouldn't let it go, though. He kept asking questions.

Like, how come the Shooters were paid better than we were, even though they spent most of their time playing simulations and Plotters did all the actual work of tracking asteroids and calculating when they'd strike? How come Mr. Kurtz had given up on disciplinary action for them, even after they'd rigged his holoset to come on unexpectedly and project a CGI of him having sex with an alligator, or all the other little ways in which they made his life a living hell? How come none of us ever stood up to them?

And it was no good explaining how they didn't respond to reason, and they didn't respond to being called immature and crude and disgusting, because they just loved being told how awful they were.

The other thing he asked about was why there weren't any women up here, and that was too humiliating to go into, so I just said tests had shown that men were better suited for life on a Gun Platform.

He should have been happy that he was a good Plotter, because he really was. He mastered Q34-54 in a week. One shift we were there on the Bridge and Myron and I were talking about the worst ever episode of Schrödinger's

Rock, which was the one that had Lallal's evil twin showing up after being killed off in the second season, and Anil was unwrapping the underwear his mother had sent him for his thirty-first birthday, when suddenly Charles said: "Eugene, you should probably check Q6-17; I'm calculating an Intruder showing up in about Q-14."

"How'd you know?" I said in surprise, slipping my goggles on. But he was right; there was an Intruder, tumbling end over end in a halo of fire and snow, way above the plane of the ecliptic but square in Q-14.

"Don't you extend your projections beyond the planet's ecliptic?" said Charles.

Myron and I looked at each other. We never projected out that far; what was the point? There was always time to spot an Intruder before it came in range.

"You don't have to work that hard, dude," I said. "Fifty degrees above and below is all we have to bother with. The scanning programs catch the rest." But I sent out the alert and we could hear the Shooters cheering, even though the War Room was clear at the other end of the Platform. As far out as the Intruder was, the Shark was able to send out a missile. We didn't see the hit—there wouldn't be one for two weeks at least, and I'd have to keep monitoring the Intruder and now the missile too, just to be sure the trajectories remained matched up—but the Shooters began to stamp and roar the Bonus Song.

Myron sniffed.

"Typical," he said. "We do all the work, they push one bloody button, and they're the heroes."

"You know, it doesn't have to be this way," said Charles.

"It's not like we can go on strike," said Anil sullenly. "We're independent contractors. There's a penalty for quitting."

"You don't have to quit," said Charles. "You can show Areco you can do even more. We can be Plotters and Shooters."

Anil and Myron looked horrified. You'd have thought he'd suggested we all turn homo or something. I was shocked myself. I had to explain about tests proving that things functioned most smoothly when every man kept to his assigned task.

"Don't Areco think we can multitask?" he asked me. "They're a corporation like any other, aren't they? They must want to save money. All we have to do is show them we can do both jobs. The Shooters get a nice redundancy package; we get the Gun Platform all to ourselves. Life is good."

"Only one problem with your little plan, Mr. Genius," said Myron. "I can't shoot. I don't have the reflexes a Shooter does. That's why I'm a Plotter."

"But you could learn to shoot," said Charles.

"I'll repeat this slowly so you get it," said Myron, exasperated. "I don't have the reflexes. And neither do you. How many times have we been tested, our whole lives? Aptitude tests, allergy tests, brain scans, DNA mapping? Areco knows exactly what we are and what we can and can't do. I'm a Plotter. You're just fooling yourself if you think you aren't."

Charles didn't say anything in reply. He just looked at each of us in turn, pretty disgusted I guess, and then he turned back to his console and focused on his work.

That wasn't the end of it, though. When he was off his shift, instead of hanging out in the Cockpit, did he join in the discussions of graphic novels or what was hot on holo that week? Not Charles. He'd retire to a corner in the Forecastle with a buke and he'd game. And not just any game: targeting simulations. You never saw a guy with such icy focus. Sometimes he'd tinker with a couple of projects he'd ordered. I assumed they were models.

It was like the rest of us weren't even there. We had to respect him as a Plotter; for one thing, he turned out to have an uncanny knack for spotting Intruders, days before any of the rest of us detected them, and he was brilliant at predicting their trajectories too. But there was something distant about the guy that kept him from fitting in. Myron and Anil had dismissed him as a crank anyway, and a couple of the guys on B Shift actively disliked him, after he spouted off to them the way he did to us. They were sure he was going to do something, sooner or later, that would only end up making it worse for all of us.

They were right, too.

When Weldon's turn in the rota ended, he brought Charles the French maid's apron and tossed it on his bunk.

"Your turn to wear the damn thing," he said. "They'll expect you in the bar at fourteen hundred hours. Good luck."

Charles just grunted, never even looking up from the screen of his buke.

Fourteen hundred hours came and he was still sitting there, coolly gaming.

"Hey!" said Anil. "You're supposed to go flackey!"

"I'm not going," said Charles.

"Don't be stupid!" I said. "If the rest of us have to do it, you do too."

"Why? Terrible repercussions if I don't?" Charles set aside his buke and looked at us.

"Yes!" said Myron. Preston from A Shift came running in right then, looking pale.

"Who's supposed to be flackeying? There's nobody out there, and Lord Deathlok wants to know why!"

"See?" said Myron.

"You'll get all of us in trouble, you fool! Give me the apron, I'll go!" said Anil. But Charles took the apron and tore it in half.

There was this horrified silence, which filled up with the sound of Shooters thundering along the corridor. We heard Lord Deathlok and Painmaster yelling as they came.

"Flackey! Oh, flackey! Where are you?"

And then they were in the room and it was too late to run, too late to hide. Painmaster's roach crest almost touched the ceiling panels. Lord Death-lok's yellow grin was so wide he didn't look human.

"Hi there, buttholes," said Painmaster. "If you girls aren't too busy making out, one of you is supposed to be flackeying for us."

"It was my turn," said Charles. He wadded up the apron and threw it at them. "How about you wait on yourself from now on?"

"This wasn't our idea!" said Myron.

"We tried to make him report for duty!" said Anil.

"We'll remember that, when we're assigning penalties," said Lord Death-lok. "Maybe we'll let you keep your pants when we handcuff you upside down in the toilet. Little Newbie, though . . ." He turned to Charles. "What about a nice game of Walk the Dog? Painmaster, got a leash anywhere on you?"

"The Painmaster always has a leash for a bad dog," said Painmaster, pulling one out. He started toward Charles, and that's when it got crazy.

Charles jumped out of his bunk and I thought, No, you idiot, don't try to run! But he didn't. He grabbed Painmaster's extended hand and pulled him close, and brought his arm up like he was going to hug him, only instead he made a kind of punching motion at Painmaster's neck. Painmaster screamed, wet himself and fell down. Charles kicked him in the crotch.

Another dead silence, which broke as soon as Painmaster got enough breath in him for another scream. Everybody else in the room was staring at Charles, or I should say at his left wrist, because it was now obvious there was something strapped to it under his sleeve.

Lord Deathlok had actually taken a step backward. He looked from Painmaster to Charles, and then at whatever it was on Charles' wrist. He licked his lips.

"So, that's, what, some kind of taser?" he said. "Those are illegal, buddy."

Charles smiled. I realized then I'd never seen him smile before.

"It's illegal to buy one. I bought some components and made my own. What are you going to do? Report me to Kurtz?" he said.

"No; I'm just going to take it away from you, dumbass," said Lord Death-lok. He lunged at Charles, but all that happened was that Charles tased him too. He jerked backward and fell over a chair, clutching his tased hand.

"You're dead," he gasped. "You're really dead."

Charles walked over and kicked him in the crotch too.

"I challenge you to a duel," he said.

"What?" said Lord Deathlok, when he had enough breath after his scream.

"A duel. With simulations," said Charles. "I'll outshoot you. Right there in the War Room, with everybody there to witness. Thirteen hundred hours tomorrow."

"Fuck off," said Lord Deathlok. Charles leaned down and displayed the two little steel points of the taser.

"So you're scared to take me on? Chicken, is that it?" he said, and Myron and Anil obligingly started making cluck-cluck-cluck noises. "Eugene, why don't you go over to the Pit of Hell and tell the Shooters they need to come scrape up these guys?"

I wouldn't have done that for a chance to see the lost episodes of *Doctor Who*, but fortunately Lord Deathlok sat up, gasping.

"Okay," he said. "Duel. You lose, I get that taser and shove it up your ass."

"Sure," said Charles. "Whatever you want; but I won't lose. And none of us will ever flackey for you again. Got it?"

Lord Deathlok called him a lot of names, but the end of it was that he agreed to the terms, and we made Painmaster (who was crying and complaining that his heartbeat was irregular) witness. When they could walk they went stumbling back to the Pit of Hell, leaning on each other.

"You are out of your mind," I said, when they had gone. "You'll go to the War Room tomorrow and they'll be waiting for you with six bottles of club soda and a can of poster paint."

"Maybe," said Charles. "But they'll back off. Haven't you clowns figured it out yet? They're used to shooting at rocks. They have no clue what to do about something that fights back."

"They'll still win. You won't be able to tase them all, and once they get it off you, you're doomed."

"They won't get it off me," said Charles, rolling up his sleeve and unstrapping the taser mounting from his arm. "I won't be wearing it. You will."

"Me?" I backed away.

"And there's another one in my locker. Which one of you wants it?"

"You've got two?"

"Me!" Anil jumped forward. "So we'll be, like, your bodyguards? Yes! Can you make more of these things?"

"I won't need to," said Charles. "Tomorrow's going to change everything."

. . . .

I don't mind telling you, my knees were knocking as we marched across to the War Room next day. Everybody on B and C Shifts came along; strength in numbers, right? If we got creamed by the Shooters, at least some of us ought to make it out of there. And if Charles was insanely lucky, we all wanted to see.

It was embarrassing. Norman and Roscoe wore full Jedi kit, including their damn light sabers that were only holobeams anyway. Bradley was wearing a Happy Bat San playjacket. Anil was wearing his lucky hat from Mystic Antagonists: the Extravaganza. We're all creative and unique, no question, but . . . maybe it isn't the best idea to dress that way when you're going to a duel with intimidating mindless jerks.

We got there, and they were waiting for us.

Our Bridge always reminded me of a temple or a shrine or something, with its beautiful display shining in the darkness; but the War Room was like the Cave of the Cyclops. There wasn't any wall display like we had. There were just the red lights of the targeting consoles, and way in the far end of the room somebody had stuck up a black light, which made the lurid holoposters of skulls and demons and vampires seem to writhe in the gloom.

The place stank of body odor, which the Shooters can't get rid of because they wear all that black bioprene gear, which doesn't breathe like the natural fabrics we wear. There was also a urinal reek; when a Shooter is gaming, he doesn't let a little thing like needing to pee drive him from his console.

All this was bad enough; imagine how I felt to see that the Shooters had made war clubs out of chlorilar water bottles stuck into handles of printer paper rolled tight. They stood there, glowering at us. I saw Lord Deathlok and the Shark and Professor Badass. Mephisto, the Conquistador, Iron Beast, Killer Ape, Uncle Hannibal . . . every hateful face I knew from months of humiliating flackey-work, except . . .

"Where's the Painmaster?" said Charles, looking around in an unconcerned kind of way.

"He had better things to do than watch you rectums lose," said Lord Deathlok.

"He had to be shipped down to the infirmary, because he was complaining of chest pains," said Mephisto. The others looked at him accusingly. Charles beamed.

"Too bad! Let's do this thing, gentlemen."

"We fixed up a special console, homo, just for you," said Lord Deathlok with an evil leer, waving at one. Charles looked at it and laughed.

"You have got to be kidding. I'll take this one over here, and you'll take the one next to it. We'll play side by side, so everybody can see. That's only fair, right?"

Their faces fell. But Anil and I crossed our arms, so the taser prongs showed, and the Shooters grumbled but backed down. They cleared away empty bottles and snack wrappers from the consoles. It felt good, watching them humbled for a change.

Charles settled himself at the console he'd chosen, and with a few quick commands on the buttonball pulled up the simulation menu.

"Is this all you've got?" he said. "Okay; I propose nine rounds. Three sets each of Holodeath 2, Meteor Nightmare, and Incoming Annihilation. Highest cumulative score wins."

"You got it, shithead," said Lord Deathlok. He took his seat.

So they called up Holodeath 2, and we all crowded around to watch, even though the awesome stench of the Shooters was enough to make your eyes water. The holo display lit up with a sinister green fog, and the enemy ships started coming at us. Charles got off three shots before Lord Deathlok managed one, and though one of his shots went wild, two inflicted enough damage on a Megacruiser to set it on fire. Lord Deathlok's shot nailed a patrol vessel in the forefront, and though it was a low-score target, he took it out with just that one shot. The score counters on both consoles gave them 1200 points.

Charles finished the burning cruiser with two more quick shots—it looked fantastic, glaring red through its ports until it just sort of imploded in this cylinder of glowing ash. But Lord Deathlok was picking off the little transport cutters methodically, because they only take about a shot each if you're accurate, which he was. Charles pulled ahead by hammering away at the big targets, and he never missed another shot, and so what happened was that the score counters showed them flashing along neck and neck for the longest time and then, boom, the last Star Destroyer blew and Charles was suddenly way ahead with twice Deathlok's score.

We were all yelling by this time, the Shooters with their chimpanzee hooting and us with—well, we sort of sounded like apes too. The next set went up and here came the ships again, but this time they were firing back. Charles took three hits in succession, before he seemed to figure out how to raise his shields, and the Shooters started gloating and smacking their clubs together.

But he went on the offensive real fast, and did something I'd never thought of before, which was aiming for the ships' gunports and disabling them with one shot before hitting them with a barrage that finished them. I never even had time to look at what Deathlok was doing, but his guys stopped cheering suddenly and when the set ended, he didn't even have a third of the points Charles did.

The third set went amazingly fast, even with the difference that the gun positions weren't stationary and they had to maneuver around in the middle of the armada. Charles did stuff I would never have dared to do, recklessly swooping around and under the Megacruisers, between their gunports for cripe's sake, getting off round after round of shots so close it seemed impossible for him to pull clear before the ships blew, but somehow he did.

Lord Deathlok didn't seem to move much. He just sat in one position and pounded away at anything that came within range, and though he did manage to bag a Star Destroyer, he finished the set way behind Charles on points.

I would have just given up if I'd been Deathlok, but the Shooters were getting ugly, shouting all kinds of personal abuse at him, and I don't think he dared.

I had to run for the lavatory as Incoming Annihilation was starting, and of course I had to run all the way back to our end of the Gun Platform to our toilet because I sure wasn't going to use the Shooters', not with the way the War Room smelled. It was only when I was unfastening that I realized I was still wearing the taser, and that I'd done an incredibly stupid thing by leaving when I was one of Charles' bodyguards. So I finished fast and ran all the way back, and there was Mr. Kurtz strolling along the corridor.

"Hello there, Eugene," he said. "Something going on?"

"Just some gaming," I said. "I need to get back—"

"But you're on Shooter turf, aren't you?" Mr. Kurtz looked around. "Shouldn't you be going in the other direction?"

"Well—we're having this competition, you see, Mr. Kurtz," I said. "The new guy's gaming against Lord—I mean, against Peavey Crandall."

"Is he?" Mr. Kurtz began to smile. "I wondered how long Charles would put up with the Shooters. Well, well."

He said it in a funny kind of way, but I didn't have the time to wonder about it. I just excused myself and ran on, and was really relieved to see that the Shooters didn't seem to have noticed my absence. They were all packed tight around the consoles, and nobody was making a sound; all you could hear was the peew-peew-peew of the shots going off continuously, and the whump as bombs exploded. Then there was a flare of red light and our guys yelled in triumph. Bradley was leaping up and down, and Roscoe did a Victory Dance until one of the Shooters asked him if he wanted his light saber rammed up his butt.

I managed to shove my way between Anil and Myron just as Charles was announcing, "I believe you're screwed, Mr. Crandall. Care to call it a day?"

I looked at their scores and couldn't believe how badly Lord Deathlok had lost to him. But Lord Deathlok just snarled.

"I don't think so, Ben Dover. Shut up and play!"

It was Meteor Nightmare now, as though they were both out there in the Van Oort belt, facing the rocks without any comforting distance of consoles or calculations. I couldn't stop myself from flinching as they hurtled forward; and I noticed one of the Shooters put up his arms involuntarily, as though he wanted to bat away the incoming with his bare hands.

It was a brutal game; nightmare, all right, because they couldn't avoid taking massive damage. All they could do was take out as many targets as they could before their inevitable destruction. When one or the other of them took a hit, there was a momentary flare of light that blinded everybody in the room. I couldn't imagine how Charles and Lord Deathlok, right there with their faces in the action, could keep shooting with any kind of accuracy.

Sure enough, early in the second round it began to tell. They were both getting flash-blind. Charles was still hitting about one in three targets, but Lord Deathlok was shooting crazily, randomly, not even bothering to aim so far as I could tell. What a look of despair on his ugly face, with his lips drawn back from his yellow teeth!

Only a miracle would save him, now. His overall score was so far behind Charles' he'd never catch up. The Shooters knew it too. I saw Dr. Smash turn his head and murmur to Uncle Hannibal. He took a firm grip on his war club. Panicking, I grabbed Anil's arm, trying to get his attention.

That was when the Incoming klaxons sounded. All the Shooters stood to attention. Lord Deathlok looked around, blinking, but Charles worked the buttonball like a pro and suddenly the game vanished, and there was nothing before us but the console displays. There was a crackle from the speakers— the first time they'd ever been used, I found out later—and we could hear Preston screaming, "You guys! Intruder coming in fast! You have to stop! It's in—"

"Q41!" said Uncle Hannibal, leaning forward to peer at the console readout. "Get out of my chair, dickwad!"

Charles didn't answer. He did something with the buttonball and there was the Intruder, like something out of Meteor Nightmare, shracking enormous. It was in his own sector! How could he have missed it? Charles, who was brilliant at spotting them before anybody else?

A red frame rose around it, with the readout in numbers spinning over so fast I couldn't tell what they said, except it was obvious the thing was coming in at high speed. All the Shooters were frantic, bellowing for Charles to get his ass out of the chair. Before their astounded eyes, and ours, he targeted the Intruder and fired.

All sound stopped. Movement stopped. Time itself stopped, except for on the display, where a new set of numbers in green and another in yellow popped up. They spun like fruit on a slot machine, the one counting up, the other counting down, both getting slower and slower until suddenly the numbers matched. Then, in perfect unison, they clicked upward together on a leisurely march.

"It's a hit," announced Preston from the speakers. "In twelve days thirteen hours forty-two minutes. Telemetry confirmed."

Dead silence answered him. And that was when I understood: Charles hadn't missed the Intruder. Charles had spotted it days ago. Charles had set this whole thing up, requesting the specific time of the duel, knowing the Intruder would interrupt it and there'd have to be a last-minute act of heroism. Which he'd co-opt.

But the thing is, see, there are people down there on the planet under us, who could die if a meteor gets through. I mean, that's why we're all up here in the first place, right?

Finally Anil said, in a funny voice, "So . . . who gets the bonus, then?"

"He can't have just done that," said Mephisto, hoarse with disbelief. "He's a Plotter."

"Get up, faggot," said Uncle Hannibal, grabbing Charles' shoulder.

"Hit him," said Charles.

I hadn't unfrozen yet, but Anil had been waiting for this moment all day. He jumped forward and tased Uncle Hannibal. Uncle Hannibal dropped, with a hoarse screech, and the other Shooters backed away fast. Anil stared down at Uncle Hannibal with unholy wonder in his eyes, and the beginning of a terrible joy. Suddenly there was a lot of room in front of the consoles, enough to see Lord Deathlok sitting there staring at the readout, with tears streaming down his face.

Charles got out of the chair.

"You lost," he informed Lord Deathlok.

"Your reign of terror is over!" cried Anil, brandishing his taser at the Shooters. One or two of them cowered, but the rest just looked stunned. Charles turned to me.

"You left your post," he said. "You're a useless idiot. Myron, take the taser off him."

"Sir yes sir!" said Myron, grabbing my arm and rolling up my sleeve. As he was unfastening the straps, we heard a chuckle from the doorway. All heads turned. There was Mr. Kurtz, leaning there with his arms crossed. I realized he must have followed me, and seen the drama as it played out. Anil thrust his taser arm behind his back, looking scared, but Mr. Kurtz only smiled.

"As you were," he said. He stood straight and left. We could hear him whistling as he walked away.

· · · ·

It wasn't until later that we learned the whole story, or as much of it as we ever knew: how Charles had been recruited, not from his parents' garage or basement, but from Hospital, and how Mr. Kurtz had known it, had in fact requested it.

We all expected a glorious new day had come for Plotters, now that Charles had proven the Shooters were unnecessary. We thought Areco would terminate their contracts. It didn't exactly happen that way.

What happened was that Dr. Smash and Uncle Hannibal came to Charles and had a private (except for Myron and Anil) talk with him. They were very polite. Since Painmaster wasn't coming back to the Gun Platform, but had defaulted on his contract and gone down home to Earth, they proposed that Charles become a Shooter. They did more; they offered him High Dark Lordship.

He accepted their offer. We were appalled. It seemed like the worst treachery imaginable.

And yet, we were surprised again.

Charles Tead didn't take one of the stupid Shooter names like Warlord or Iron Fist or Doomsman. He said we were all to call him Stede from now on. He ordered up, not a bioprene wardrobe with spikes and rivets and fringe, but . . . but . . . a three-piece suit, with a tie. And a bowler hat. He took his tasers back from Anil and Myron, who were crestfallen, and wore them himself, under his perfectly pressed cuffs.

Then he ordered up new clothes for all the other Shooters. It must have been a shock, when he handed out those powder blue shirts and drab coveralls, but they didn't rebel; by that time they'd learned what he'd been sent to Hospital for in the first place, which was killing three people. So there wasn't so much as a mutter behind his back, even when he ordered all the holoposters shut off and thrown into the fusion hopper, and the War Room repainted in dove gray.

We wouldn't have known the Shooters. He made them wash; he made them cut their hair, he made them shracking salute when he gave an order. They were scared to fart, especially after he hung up deodorizers above each of their consoles. The War Room became a clean, well-lit place, silent except for the consoles and the occasional quiet order from Charles. He seldom had to raise his voice.

Mr. Kurtz still sat in his office all day, reading, but now he smiled as he read. Nobody called him Dean Kurtz anymore, either.

It was sort of horrible, what had happened, but with Charles—I mean, Stede—running the place, things were a lot more efficient. The bonuses became more frequent, as everyone worked harder. And, in time, the Shooters came to worship him.

He didn't bother with us. We were grateful.

PETER WATTS Born in Calgary, Alberta, Peter Watts is a marine-mammal biologist and an SF writer whose work is notable both for its scientific realism and for its bracing pessimism about the human prospect.

After a few stories published in the 1990s, Watts's first novel, *Starfish*, appeared in 1999, and was a *New York Times* Notable Book; it was followed by three semi-sequels. But it was 2006's *Blindsight*, described by him as "a literary first-contact novel exploring the nature and evolutionary significance of consciousness, with space vampires," that made his reputation as one of the most audacious SF writers working today.

"The Island," which won the 2010 Hugo Award for Best Novelette, is among his most substantial—and disturbing—works to date. It is to be hoped that there will be more.

THE ISLAND

You sent us out here. We do this for *you*: spin your webs and build your magic gateways, thread the needle's eye at sixty thousand kilometers a second. We never stop, never even dare to slow down, lest the light of your coming turn us to plasma. All so you can step from star to star without dirtying your feet in these endless, empty wastes *between*.

Is it really too much to ask, that you might talk to us now and then?

I know about evolution and engineering. I know how much you've changed. I've seen these portals give birth to gods and demons and things we can't begin to comprehend, things I can't believe were ever human; alien hitchikers, perhaps, riding the rails we've left behind. Alien conquerers.

Exterminators, perhaps.

But I've also seen those gates stay dark and empty until they faded from view. We've infered diebacks and dark ages, civilizations burned to the ground and others rising from their ashes—and sometimes, afterwards, the things that come out look a little like the ships *we* might have built, back in the day. They speak to each other—radio, laser, carrier neutrinos—and sometimes their voices sound something like ours. There was a time we dared to hope that they really were like us, that the circle had come round again and closed on beings we could talk to. I've lost count of the times we tried to break the ice.

I've lost count of the eons since we gave up.

All these iterations fading behind us. All these hybrids and posthumans and immortals, gods and catatonic cavemen trapped in magical chariots they can't begin to understand, and not one of them ever pointed a comm laser in our direction to say *Hey, how's it going?*, or *Guess what? We cured Damascus Disease!*, or even *Thanks, guys, keep up the good work!*.

We're not some fucking cargo cult. We're the backbone of your goddamn empire. You wouldn't even be *out* here if it weren't for us.

And—and you're our *children*. Whatever you've become, you were once like this, like me. I believed in you once. There was a time, long ago, when I believed in this mission with all my heart.

Why have you forsaken us?

. . . .

And so another build begins.

This time, I open my eyes to a familiar face I've never seen before: only a boy, early twenties perhaps, physiologically. His face is a little lopsided, the cheekbone flatter on the left than the right. His ears are too big. He looks almost *natural*.

I haven't spoken for millennia. My voice comes out a whisper: "Who are you?" Not what I'm supposed to ask, I know. Not the first question *anyone* on *Eriophora* asks, after coming back.

"I'm yours," he says, and just like that, I'm a mother.

I want to let it sink in, but he doesn't give me the chance: "You weren't scheduled, but Chimp wants extra hands on deck. Next build's got a situation."

So the chimp is still in control. The chimp is always in control. The mission goes on.

"Situation?" I ask.

"Contact scenario, maybe."

I wonder when he was born. I wonder if he ever wondered about me, before now.

He doesn't tell me. He only says, "Sun up ahead. Half lightyear. Chimp thinks, maybe it's talking to us. Anyhow . . ." My—son shrugs. "No rush. Lotsa time."

I nod, but he hesitates. He's waiting for The Question but I already see a kind of answer in his face. Our reinforcements were supposed to be *pristine*, built from perfect genes buried deep within *Eri*'s iron-basalt mantle, safe from the sleeting blueshift. And yet this boy has flaws. I see the damage in his face, I see those tiny flipped base-pairs resonating up from the microscopic and *bending* him just a little off-kilter. He looks like he grew up on a planet. He looks borne of parents who spent their whole lives hammered by raw sunlight.

How far out must we be by now, if even our own perfect building blocks have decayed so? How long has it taken us? How long have I been dead?

How long? It's the first thing everyone asks.

After all this time, I don't want to know.

· · · ·

He's alone at the tac tank when I arrive on the bridge, his eyes full of icons and trajectories. Perhaps I see a little of me in there, too.

"I didn't get your name," I say, although I've looked it up on the manifest. We've barely been introduced and already I'm lying to him.

"Dix." He keeps his eyes on the tank.

He's over ten thousand years old. Alive for maybe twenty of them. I wonder how much he knows, who he's met during those sparse decades: does he know Ishmael, or Connie? Does he know if Sanchez got over his brush with immortality?

I wonder, but I don't ask. There are rules.

I look around. "We're it?"

Dix nods. "For now. Bring back more if we need them. But . . ." His voice trails off.

"Yes?"

"Nothing."

I join him at the tank. Diaphanous veils hang within like frozen, color-coded smoke. We're on the edge of a molecular dust cloud. Warm, semiorganic, lots of raw materials. Formaldehyde, ethylene glycol, the usual prebiotics. A good spot for a quick build. A red dwarf glowers dimly at the center of the Tank: the chimp has named it DHF428, for reasons I've long since forgotten to care about.

"So fill me in," I say.

His glance is impatient, even irritated. "You too?"

"What do you mean?"

"Like the others. On the other builds. Chimp can just squirt the specs, but they want to *talk* all the time."

Shit, his link's still active. He's *online.*

I force a smile. "Just a—a cultural tradition, I guess. We talk about a lot of things, it helps us—reconnect. After being down for so long."

"But it's *slow,*" Dix complains.

He doesn't know. Why doesn't he know?

"We've got half a lightyear," I point out. "There's some rush?"

The corner of his mouth twitches. "Vons went out on schedule." On cue, a cluster of violet pinpricks sparkle in the Tank, five trillion klicks ahead of us. "Still sucking dust mostly, but got lucky with a couple of big asteroids and the refineries came online early. First components already extruded. Then Chimp sees these fluctuations in solar output—mainly infra, but extends into visible." The tank blinks at us: the dwarf goes into time-lapse.

Sure enough, it's *flickering.*

"Non-random, I take it."

Dix inclines his head a little to the side, not quite nodding.

"Plot the time-series." I've never been able to break the habit of raising my voice, just a bit, when addressing the chimp. Obediently (*obediently*. Now *there's* a laugh-and-a-half) the AI wipes the spacescape and replaces it with

· · · · · ·   ·   ·   ·   ·   ·   ·   ·   ·   ·   ·   · ·

"Repeating sequence," Dix tells me. "Blips don't change, but spacing's a log-linear increase cycling every 92.5 corsecs. Each cycle starts at 13.2 clicks/corsec, degrades over time."

"No chance this could be natural? A little black hole wobbling around in the center of the star, something like that?"

Dix shakes his head, or something like that: a diagonal dip of the chin that somehow conveys the negative. "But way too simple to contain much info. Not like an actual conversation. More—well, a shout."

He's partly right. There may not be much information, but there's enough. We're here. We're smart. We're powerful enough to hook a whole damn star up to a dimmer switch.

Maybe not such a good spot for a build after all.

I purse my lips. "The sun's hailing us. That's what you're saying."

"Maybe. Hailing *someone*. But too simple for a rosetta signal. It's not an archive, can't self-extract. Not a bonferroni or fibonacci seq, not pi. Not even a multiplication table. Nothing to base a pidgin on."

Still. An intelligent signal.

"Need more info," Dix says, proving himself master of the blindingly obvious.

I nod. "The vons."

"Uh, what about them?"

"We set up an array. Use a bunch of bad eyes to fake a good one. It'd be faster than high-geeing an observatory from this end or retooling one of the on-site factories."

His eyes go wide. For a moment, he almost looks frightened for some reason. But the moment passes and he does that weird head-shake thing again. "Bleed too many resources away from the build, wouldn't it?"

"It would," the chimp agrees.

I suppress a snort. "If you're so worried about meeting our construction benchmarks, Chimp, factor in the potential risk posed by an intelligence powerful enough to control the energy output of an entire sun."

"I can't," it admits. "I don't have enough information."

"You don't have *any* information. About something that could probably stop this mission dead in its tracks if it wanted to. So maybe we should get some."

"Okay. Vons reassigned."

Confirmation glows from a convenient bulkhead, a complex sequence of dance instructions that *Eri's* just fired into the void. Six months from now, a hundred self-replicating robots will waltz into a makeshift surveillance grid; four months after that, we might have something more than vacuum to debate in.

Dix eyes me as though I've just cast some kind of magic spell.

"It may run the ship," I tell him, "but it's pretty fucking stupid. Sometimes you've just got to spell things out."

He looks vaguely affronted, but there's no mistaking the surprise beneath. He didn't know that. He *didn't know.*

Who the hell's been raising him all this time? Whose problem is this?

Not mine.

"Call me in ten months," I say. "I'm going back to bed."

· · · ·

It's as though he never left. I climb back into the bridge and there he is, staring into tac. DHF428 fills the tank, a swollen red orb that turns my son's face into a devil mask.

He spares me the briefest glance, eyes wide, fingers twitching as if electrified. "Vons don't see it."

I'm still a bit groggy from the thaw. "See wh—"

"The *sequence!*" His voice borders on panic. He sways back and forth, shifting his weight from foot to foot.

"Show me."

Tac splits down the middle. Cloned dwarves burn before me now, each perhaps twice the size of my fist. On the left, an *Eri's*-eye view: DHF428 stutters as it did before, as it presumably has these past ten months. On the right, a compound-eye composite: an interferometry grid built by a myriad precisely-spaced vons, their rudimentary eyes layered and parallaxed into something approaching high resolution. Contrast on both sides has been conveniently cranked up to highlight the dwarf's endless winking for merely human eyes.

Except that it's only winking from the left side of the display. On the right, 428 glowers steady as a standard candle.

"Chimp: any chance the grid just isn't sensitive enough to see the fluctuations?"

"No."

"Huh." I try to think of some reason it would lie about this.

"Doesn't make *sense,*" my son complains.

"It does," I murmur, "if it's not the sun that's flickering."

"But it *is* flickering—" He sucks his teeth. "You *see* it—wait, you mean something *behind* the vons? Between, between them and us?"

"Mmmm."

"Some kind of *filter*." Dix relaxes a bit. "Wouldn't we've seen it, though? Wouldn't the vons've hit it going down?"

I put my voice back into ChimpComm mode. "What's the current field-of-view for *Eri's* forward scope?"

"Eighteen mikes," the chimp reports. "At 428's range, the cone is three point three four lightsecs across."

"Increase to a hundred lightsecs."

The *Eri's*-eye partition swells, obliterating the dissenting viewpoint. For a moment, the sun fills the tank again, paints the whole bridge crimson. Then it dwindles as if devoured from within.

I notice some fuzz in the display. "Can you clear that noise?"

"It's not noise," the chimp reports. "It's dust and molecular gas."

I blink. "What's the density?"

"Estimated hundred thousand atoms per cubic meter."

Two orders of magnitude too high, even for a nebula. "Why so heavy?" Surely we'd have detected any gravity well strong enough to keep *that* much material in the neighborhood.

"I don't know," the chimp says.

I get the queasy feeling that I might. "Set field-of-view to five hundred lightsecs. Peak false-color at near-infrared."

Space grows ominously murky in the tank. The tiny sun at its center, thumbnail-sized now, glows with increased brilliance: an incandescent pearl in muddy water.

"A thousand lightsecs," I command.

"There," Dix whispers: real space reclaims the edges of the tank, dark, clear, pristine. 428 nestles at the heart of a dim spherical shroud. You find those sometimes, discarded cast-offs from companion stars whose convulsions spew gas and rads across light years. But 428 is no nova remnant. It's a *red dwarf*, placid, middle-aged. Unremarkable.

Except for the fact that it sits dead center of a tenuous gas bubble 1.4 AUs across. And for the fact that that bubble does not *attenuate* or *diffuse* or *fade* gradually into that good night. No, unless there is something seriously wrong with the display, this small, spherical nebula extends about 350 light-secs from its primary and then just *stops*, its boundary far more knife-edged than nature has any right to be.

For the first time in millennia, I miss my cortical pipe. It takes forever to saccade search terms onto the keyboard in my head, to get the answers I already know.

Numbers come back. "Chimp. I want false-color peaks at 335, 500, and 800 nanometers."

The shroud around 428 lights up like a dragonfly's wing, like an iridescent soap bubble.

"It's *beautiful*," whispers my awestruck son.

"It's photosynthetic," I tell him.

. . . .

Phaeophytin and eumelanin, according to spectro. There are even hints of some kind of lead-based Keipper pigment, soaking up X-rays in the picometer range. Chimp hypothesizes something called a *chromatophore*: branching cells with little aliquots of pigment inside, like particles of charcoal dust. Keep those particles clumped together and the cell's effectively transparent; spread them out through the cytoplasm and the whole structure *darkens*, dims whatever EM passes through from behind. Apparently there were animals back on Earth with cells like that. They could change color, pattern-match to their background, all sorts of things.

"So there's a membrane of—of *living tissue* around that star," I say, trying to wrap my head around the concept. "A, a meat balloon. Around the whole damn *star*."

"Yes," the chimp says.

"But that's— Jesus, how thick would it be?"

"No more than two millimeters. Probably less."

"How so?"

"If it was much thicker, it would be more obvious in the visible spectrum. It would have had a detectable effect on the von Neumanns when they hit it."

"That's assuming that its—cells, I guess—are like ours."

"The pigments are familiar; the rest might be too."

It can't be *too* familiar. Nothing like a conventional gene would last two seconds in that environment. Not to mention whatever miracle solvent that thing must use as antifreeze . . .

"Okay, let's be conservative, then. Say, mean thickness of a millimeter. Assume a density of water at STP. How much mass in the whole thing?"

"1.4 yottagrams," Dix and the chimp reply, almost in unison.

"That's, uh . . ."

"Half the mass of Mercury," the chimp adds helpfully.

I whistle through my teeth. "And that's *one* organism?"

"I don't know yet."

"It's got organic pigments. Fuck, it's *talking*. It's intelligent."

"Most cyclic emanations from living sources are simple biorhythms," the chimp points out. "Not intelligent signals."

I ignore it and turn to Dix. "Assume it's a signal."

He frowns. "Chimp says—"

"*Assume*. Use your imagination."

I'm not getting through to him. He looks nervous.

He looks like that a lot, I realize.

"*If* someone were signaling you," I say, "*then* what would you do?"

"Signal . . ." Confusion on that face, and a fuzzy circuit closing somewhere ". . . back?"

My son is an idiot.

"And if the incoming signal takes the form of systematic changes in light intensity, how—"

"Use the BI lasers, alternated to pulse between 700 and 3000 nanometers. Can boost an interlaced signal into the exawatt range without compromising our fenders; gives over a thousand Watts per square meter after diffraction. Way past detection threshold for anything that can sense thermal output from a red dwarf. And content doesn't matter if it's just a shout. Shout back. Test for echo."

Okay, so my son is an idiot *savant*.

And he still looks unhappy—"But Chimp, he says no real *information* there, right?"—and that whole other set of misgivings edges to the fore again: *He*.

Dix takes my silence for amnesia. "Too simple, remember? Simple click train."

I shake my head. There's more information in that signal than the chimp can imagine. There are so many things the chimp doesn't know. And the last thing I need is for this, this *child* to start deferring to it, to start looking to it as an equal, or, God forbid, a *mentor*.

Oh, it's smart enough to steer us between the stars. Smart enough to calculate sixty-digit primes in the blink of an eye. Even smart enough for a little crude improvisation should the crew go too far off-mission.

Not smart enough to know a distress call when it sees one.

"It's a deceleration curve," I tell them both. "It keeps *slowing down*. Over and over again. *That's* the message."

Stop. Stop. Stop. Stop.

And I think it's meant for no one but us.

· · · ·

We shout back. No reason not to. And now we die again, because what's the point of staying up late? Whether or not this vast entity harbors real intelligence, our echo won't reach it for ten million corsecs. Another seven million, at the earliest, before we receive any reply it might send.

Might as well hit the crypt in the meantime. Shut down all desires and misgivings, conserve whatever life I have left for moments that matter. Remove myself from this sparse tactical intelligence, from this wet-eyed pup watching me as though I'm some kind of sorcerer about to vanish in a puff of smoke. He opens his mouth to speak, and I turn away and hurry down to oblivion.

But I set my alarm to wake up alone.

I linger in the coffin for a while, grateful for small and ancient victories. The chimp's dead, blackened eye gazes down from the ceiling; in all these millions of years, nobody's scrubbed off the carbon scoring. It's a trophy of sorts, a memento from the early incendiary days of our Great Struggle.

There's still something—comforting, I guess—about that blind, endless stare. I'm reluctant to venture out where the chimp's nerves have not been so thoroughly cauterised. Childish, I know. The damn thing already knows I'm up; it may be blind, deaf, and impotent in here, but there's no way to mask the power the crypt sucks in during a thaw. And it's not as though a bunch of club-weilding teleops are waiting to pounce on me the moment I step outside. These are the days of détente, after all. The struggle continues but the war has gone cold; we just go through the motions now, rattling our chains like an old married multiplet resigned to hating each other to the end of time.

After all the moves and countermoves, the truth is we need each other.

So I wash the rotten-egg stench from my hair and step into *Eri's* silent cathedral hallways. Sure enough, the enemy waits in the darkness, turns the lights on as I approach, shuts them off behind me—but it does not break the silence.

Dix.

A strange one, that. Not that you'd expect anyone born and raised on *Eriophora* to be an archetype of mental health, but Dix doesn't even know what side he's on. He doesn't even seem to know he has to *choose* a side. It's almost as though he read the original mission statements and took them *seriously*, believed in the literal truth of the ancient scrolls: Mammals and Machinery, working together across the ages to explore the Universe! United! Strong! Forward the Frontier!

Rah.

Whoever raised him didn't do a great job. Not that I blame them; it can't have been much fun having a child underfoot during a build, and none of us were selected for our parenting skills. Even if bots changed the diapers and VR handled the infodumps, socialising a toddler couldn't have been anyone's idea of a good time. I'd have probably just chucked the little bastard out an airlock.

But even I would've brought him up to speed.

Something changed while I was away. Maybe the war's heated up again, entered some new phase. That twitchy kid is out of the loop for a reason. I wonder what it is.

I wonder if I care.

I arrive at my suite, treat myself to a gratuitous meal, jill off. Three hours after coming back to life, I'm relaxing in the starbow commons. "Chimp."

"You're up early," it says at last.

I am. Our answering shout hasn't even arrived at its destination yet. No real chance of new data for another two months, at least.

"Show me the forward feeds," I command.

DHF428 blinks at me from the center of the lounge: *Stop. Stop. Stop.*

Maybe. Or maybe the chimp's right, maybe it's pure physiology. Maybe this endless cycle carries no more intelligence than the beating of a heart.

But there's a pattern inside the pattern, some kind of *flicker* in the blink. It makes my brain itch.

"Slow the time-series," I command. "By a hundred."

It *is* a blink. 428's disk isn't darkening uniformly, it's *eclipsing*. As though a great eyelid were being drawn across the surface of the sun, from right to left.

"By a thousand."

Chromatophores, the chimp called them. But they're not all opening and closing at once. The darkness moves across the membrane in *waves*.

A word pops into my head: *latency*.

"Chimp. Those waves of pigment. How fast are they moving?"

"About fifty-nine thousand kilometers per second."

The speed of a passing thought.

And if this thing *does* think, it'll have logic gates, synapses—it's going to be a *net* of some kind. And if the net's big enough, there's an *I* in the middle of it. Just like me, just like Dix. Just like the chimp. (Which is why I educated myself on the subject, back in the early tumultuous days of our relationship. Know your enemy and all that.)

The thing about *I* is, it only exists within a tenth-of-a-second of all its parts. When we get spread too thin—when someone splits your brain down the middle, say, chops the fat pipe so the halves have to talk the long way around; when the neural architecture *diffuses* past some critical point and signals take just that much longer to pass from A to B—the system, well, *decoheres*. The two sides of your brain become different people with different tastes, different agendas, different senses of themselves.

I shatters into *we*.

It's not just a human rule, or a mammal rule, or even an Earthly one. It's a rule for any circuit that processes information, and it applies as much to the things we've yet to meet as it did to those we left behind.

Fifty-nine thousand kilometers per second, the chimp says. How far can the signal move through that membrane in a tenth of a corsec? How thinly does *I* spread itself across the heavens?

The flesh is huge, the flesh is inconceivable. But the spirit, the spirit is—

Shit.

"Chimp. Assuming the mean neuron density of a human brain, what's the synapse count on a circular sheet of neurons one millimeter thick with a diameter of five thousand eight hundred ninety-two kilometers?"

"Two times ten to the twenty-seventh."

I saccade the database for some perspective on a mind stretched across thirty million square kilometers: the equivalent of two quadrillion human brains.

Of course, whatever this thing uses for neurons have to be packed a lot less tightly than ours; we can see right through them, after all. Let's be super-conservative, say it's only got a thousandth the computational density of a human brain. That's—

Okay, let's say it's only got a *ten*-thousandth the synaptic density, that's still—

A *hundred* thousandth. The merest mist of thinking meat. Any more conservative and I'd hypothesize it right out of existence.

Still twenty billion human brains.

Twenty *billion.*

I don't know how to feel about that. This is no mere alien.

But I'm not quite ready to believe in gods.

. . . .

I round the corner and run smack into Dix, standing like a golem in the middle of my living room. I jump about a meter straight up.

"What the hell are you doing here?"

He seems surprised by my reaction. "Wanted to—talk," he says after a moment.

"You *never* come into someone's home uninvited!"

He retreats a step, stammers: "Wanted, wanted—"

"To talk. And you do that in *public.* On the bridge, or in the commons, or—for that matter, you could just *comm* me."

He hesitates. "Said you—*wanted* face to face. You said, *cultural tradition.*"

I did, at that. But not *here.* This is *my* place, these are my *private quarters.* The lack of locks on these doors is a safety protocol, not an invitation to walk into my home and *lie in wait,* and stand there like part of the fucking *furniture* . . .

"Why are you even *up?*" I snarl. "We're not even supposed to come on-line for another two months."

"Asked Chimp to get me up when you did."

That fucking machine.

"Why are *you* up?" he asks, not leaving.

I sigh, defeated, and fall into a convenient pseudopod. "I just wanted to go over the preliminary data." The implicit *alone* should be obvious.

"Anything?"

Evidently it isn't. I decide to play along for a while. "Looks like we're talking to an, an island. Almost six thousand klicks across. That's the thinking part, anyway. The surrounding membrane's pretty much empty. I mean, it's all *alive*. It all photosynthesizes, or something like that. It eats, I guess. Not sure what."

"Molecular cloud," Dix says. "Organic compounds everywhere. Plus it's concentrating stuff inside the envelope."

I shrug. "Point is, there's a size limit for the brain, but it's *huge*, it's . . ."

"Unlikely," he murmurs, almost to himself.

I turn to look at him; the pseudopod reshapes itself around me. "What do you mean?"

"Island's twenty-eight million square kilometers? Whole sphere's seven quintillion. Island just happens to be between us and 428, that's—one in fifty-billion odds."

"Go on."

He can't. "Uh, just . . . just *unlikely*."

I close my eyes. "How can you be smart enough to run those numbers in your head without missing a beat, and stupid enough to miss the obvious conclusion?"

That panicked, slaughterhouse look again. "Don't— I'm not—"

"It *is* unlikely. It's *astronomically* unlikely that we just happen to be aiming at the one intelligent spot on a sphere one-and-a-half AUs across. Which means . . ."

He says nothing. The perplexity in his face mocks me. I want to punch it.

But finally, the lights flicker on: "There's, uh, more than one island? Oh! A *lot* of islands!"

This creature is part of the crew. My life will almost certainly depend on him some day.

That is a very scary thought.

I try to set it aside for the moment. "There's probably a whole population of the things, sprinkled though the membrane like, like cysts I guess. The chimp doesn't know how many, but we're only picking up this one so far so they might be pretty sparse."

There's a different kind of frown on his face now. "Why *Chimp*?"

"What do you mean?"

"Why call him Chimp?"

"We call it *the* chimp." Because the first step to humanising something is to give it a name.

"Looked it up. Short for *chimpanzee*. Stupid animal."

"Actually, I think chimps were supposed to be pretty smart," I remember.

"Not like us. Couldn't even *talk*. Chimp can talk. *Way* smarter than those things. That name—it's an insult."

"What do you care?"

He just looks at me.

I spread my hands. "Okay, it's not a chimp. We just call it that because it's got roughly the same synapse count."

"So gave him a small brain, then complain that he's stupid all the time."

My patience is just about drained. "Do you have a point or are you just blowing CO_2 in—"

"Why not make him smarter?"

"Because you can never predict the behavior of a system more complex than you. And if you want a project to stay on track after you're gone, you don't hand the reins to anything that's guaranteed to develop its own agenda." Sweet smoking Jesus, you'd think *someone* would have told him about Ashby's Law.

"So they lobotomized him," Dix says after a moment.

"No. They didn't *turn* it stupid, they *built* it stupid."

"Maybe smarter than you think. You're so much smarter, got *your* agenda, how come *he's* still in control?"

"Don't flatter yourself," I say.

"What?"

I let a grim smile peek through. "You're only following orders from a bunch of other systems *way* more complex than you are." You've got to hand it to them, too; dead for stellar lifetimes and those damn project admins are *still* pulling the strings.

"I don't— *I'm* following?—"

"I'm sorry, dear." I smile sweetly at my idiot offspring. "I wasn't talking to you. I was talking to the thing that's making all those sounds come out of your mouth."

Dix turns whiter than my panties.

I drop all pretense. "What were you thinking, chimp? That you could send this sock-puppet to invade my home and I wouldn't notice?"

"Not— I'm not—it's *me*," Dix stammers. "*Me* talking."

"It's *coaching* you. Do you even know what 'lobotomised' *means*?" I shake my head, disgusted. "You think I've forgotten how the interface works just because we all burned ours out?" A caricature of surprise begins to form on his face. "Oh, don't even fucking *try*. You've been up for other builds, there's no way you couldn't have known. And you know we shut down our domestic links too, or you wouldn't even be sneaking in here. And there's nothing your lord and master can do about that because it *needs* us, and so we have reached what you might call an *accommodation*."

I am not shouting. My tone is icy, but my voice is dead level. And yet Dix almost *cringes* before me.

There is an opportunity here, I realize.

I thaw my voice a little. I speak gently: "You can do that too, you know. Burn out your link. I'll even let you come back here afterwards, if you still want to. Just to—talk. But not with that thing in your head."

There is panic in his face, and, against all expectation it almost breaks my heart. "*Can't*," he pleads. "How I *learn* things, how I *train*. The *mission* . . ."

I honestly don't know which of them is speaking, so I answer them both: "There is more than one way to carry out the mission. We have more than enough time to try them all. Dix is welcome to come back when he's alone."

They take a step towards me. Another. One hand, twitching, rises from their side as if to reach out, and there's something on that lopsided face that I can't quite recognize.

"But I'm your *son*," they say.

I don't even dignify it with a denial.

"Get out of my home."

· · · ·

A human periscope. The Trojan Dix. That's a new one.

The chimp's never tried such overt infiltration while we were up and about before. Usually, it waits until we're all undead before invading our territories. I imagine custom-made drones never seen by human eyes, cobbled together during the long dark eons between builds; I see them sniffing through drawers and peeking behind mirrors, strafing the bulkheads with X-rays and ultrasound, patiently searching *Eriophora*'s catacombs millimeter by endless millimeter for whatever secret messages we might be sending each other down through time.

There's no proof to speak of. We've left tripwires and telltales to alert us to intrusion after the fact, but there's never been any evidence they've been disturbed. Means nothing, of course. The chimp may be stupid, but it's also cunning, and a million years is more than enough time to iterate through every possibility using simpleminded brute force. Document every dust mote; commit your unspeakable acts; put everything back the way it was afterwards.

We're too smart to risk talking across the eons. No encrypted strategies, no long-distance love letters, no chatty postcards showing ancient vistas long lost in the red shift. We keep all that in our heads, where the enemy will never find it. The unspoken rule is that we do not speak, unless it is face to face.

Endless idiotic games. Sometimes I almost forget what we're squabbling over. It seems so trivial now, with an immortal in my sights.

Maybe that means nothing to you. Immortality must be ancient news to you. But I can't even imagine it, although I've outlived worlds. All I have are moments: two or three hundred years, to ration across the lifespan of a universe. I could bear witness to any point in time, or any hundred-thousand, if I slice my life thinly enough—but I will never see *everything*. I will never see even a fraction.

My life will end. I have to *choose*.

When you come to fully appreciate the deal you've made—ten or fifteen builds out, when the trade-off leaves the realm of mere *knowledge* and sinks deep as cancer into your bones—you become a miser. You can't help it. You ration out your waking moments to the barest minimum: just enough to manage the build, to plan your latest countermove against the chimp, just enough (if you haven't yet moved beyond the need for human contact) for sex and snuggles and a bit of warm mammalian comfort against the endless dark. And then you hurry back to the crypt, to hoard the remains of a human lifespan against the unwinding of the cosmos.

There's been time for education. Time for a hundred postgraduate degrees, thanks to the best caveman learning tech. I've never bothered. Why burn down my tiny candle for a litany of mere fact, fritter away my precious, endless, finite life? Only a fool would trade book-learning for a ringside view of the Cassiopeia Remnant, even if you *do* need false-color enhancement to see the fucking thing.

Now, though. Now, I want to *know*. This creature crying out across the gulf, massive as a moon, wide as a solar system, tenuous and fragile as an insect's wing: I'd gladly cash in some of my life to learn its secrets. How does it work? How can it even *live* here at the edge of absolute zero, much less think? What vast, unfathomable intellect must it possess, to see us coming from over half a lightyear away, to deduce the nature of our eyes and our instruments, to send a signal we can even *detect*, much less understand?

And what happens when we punch through it at a fifth the speed of light?

I call up the latest findings on my way to bed, and the answer hasn't changed: not much. The damn thing's already full of holes. Comets, asteroids, the usual protoplanetary junk careens through this system as it does through every other. Infra picks up diffuse pockets of slow outgassing here and there around the perimeter, where the soft vaporous vacuum of the interior bleeds into the harder stuff outside. Even if we were going to tear through the dead center of the thinking part, I can't imagine this vast creature feeling so much as a pinprick. At the speed we're going we'd be through and gone far too fast to overcome even the feeble inertia of a millimeter membrane.

And yet. Stop. Stop. Stop.

It's not us, of course. It's what we're building. The birth of a gate is a violent, painful thing, a spacetime rape that puts out almost as much gamma and X as a microquasar. Any meat within the white zone turns to ash in an instant, shielded or not. It's why *we* never slow down to take pictures.

One of the reasons, anyway.

We can't stop, of course. Even changing course isn't an option except by the barest increments. *Eri* soars like an eagle between the stars but she steers like a pig on the short haul; tweak our heading by even a tenth of a degree, and you've got some serious damage at twenty percent lightspeed. Half a degree would tear us apart: the ship might torque onto the new heading, but the collapsed mass in her belly would keep right on going, rip through all this surrounding superstructure without even feeling it.

Even tame singularities get set in their ways. They do not take well to change.

. . . .

We resurrect again, and the Island has changed its tune.

It gave up asking us to *stop stop stop* the moment our laser hit its leading edge. Now it's saying something else entirely: dark hyphens flow across its skin, arrows of pigment converging towards some offstage focus like spokes pointing towards the hub of a wheel. The bullseye itself is offstage and implicit, far removed from 428's bright backdrop, but it's easy enough to extrapolate to the point of convergence six lightsecs to starboard. There's something else, too: a shadow, roughly circular, moving along one of the spokes like a bead running along a string. It too migrates to starboard, falls off the edge of the Island's makeshift display, is endlessly reborn at the same initial coordinates to repeat its journey.

Those coordinates: exactly where our current trajectory will punch through the membrane in another four months. A squinting God would be able to see the gnats and girders of ongoing construction on the other side, the great piecemeal torus of the Hawking Hoop already taking shape.

The message is so obvious that even Dix sees it. "Wants us to move the gate . . ." and there is something like confusion in his voice. "But how's it know we're *building* one?"

"The vons punctured it en route," the chimp points out. "It could have sensed that. It has photopigments. It can probably see."

"Probably sees better than we do," I say. Even something as simple as a pinhole camera gets hi-res fast if you stipple a bunch of them across thirty million square kilometers.

But Dix scrunches his face, unconvinced. "So sees a bunch of vons bumping around. Loose parts—not that much even *assembled* yet. How's it know we're building something *hot*?"

Because it is very, very, smart, you stupid child. Is it so hard to believe that this, this—*organism* seems far too limiting a word—can just *imagine* how those half-built pieces fit together, glance at our sticks and stones and see exactly where this is going?

"Maybe's not the first gate it's seen," Dix suggests. "Think there's maybe another gate out here?"

I shake my head. "We'd have seen the lensing artefacts by now."

"You ever run into anyone before?"

"No." We have always been alone, through all these epochs. We have only ever run *away*.

And then always from our own children.

I crunch some numbers. "Hundred eighty two days to insemination. If we move now, we've only got to tweak our bearing by a few mikes to redirect to the new coordinates. Well within the green. Angles get dicey the longer we wait, of course."

"We can't do that," the chimp says. "We would miss the gate by two million kilometers."

"Move the gate. Move the whole damn site. Move the refineries, move the factories, move the damn rocks. A couple hundred meters a second would be more than fast enough if we send the order now. We don't even have to suspend construction, we can keep building on the fly."

"Every one of those vectors widens the nested confidence limits of the build. It would increase the risk of error beyond allowable margins, for no payoff."

"And what about the fact that there's an intelligent being in our path?"

"I'm already allowing for the potential presence of intelligent alien life."

"Okay, first off, there's nothing *potential* about it. It's *right fucking there*. And on our current heading, we run the damn thing over."

"We're staying clear of all planetary bodies in Goldilocks orbits. We've seen no local evidence of spacefaring technology. The current location of the build meets all conservation criteria."

"That's because the people who drew up your criteria *never anticipated a live Dyson sphere!*" But I'm wasting my breath, and I know it. The chimp can run its equations a million times, but if there's nowhere to put the variable, what can it do?

There was a time, back before things turned ugly, when we had clearance to reprogram those parameters. Before we discovered that one of the things the admins *had* anticipated was mutiny.

I try another tack. "Consider the threat potential."

"There's no evidence of any."

"Look at the synapse estimate! That thing's got order of mag more processing power than the whole civilization that sent us out here. You think something can be that smart, live that long, without learning how to defend itself? We're assuming it's *asking* us to move the gate. What if that's not a *request*? What if it's just giving us the chance to back off before it takes matters into its own hands?"

"Doesn't *have* hands," Dix says from the other side of the tank, and he's not even being flippant. He's just being so stupid I want to bash his face in.

I try to keep my voice level. "Maybe it doesn't *need* any."

"What could it do, *blink* us to death? No weapons. Doesn't even control the whole membrane. Signal propagation's too slow."

"We *don't know*. That's my *point*. We haven't even tried to find out. We're a goddamn road crew; our onsite presence is a bunch of construction vons press-ganged into scientific research. We can figure out some basic physical parameters, but we don't know how this thing thinks, what kind of natural defenses it might have—"

"What do you need to find out?" the chimp asks, the very voice of calm reason.

We can't find out! I want to scream. We're stuck with what we've got! By the time the onsite vons could build what we need, we're already past the point of no return! You stupid fucking machine, we're on track to kill a being smarter than all of human history and you can't even be bothered to move our highway to the vacant lot next door?

But of course if I say that, the Island's chances of survival go from low to zero. So I grasp at the only straw that remains: maybe the data we've got in hand is enough. If acquisition is off the table, maybe analysis will do.

"I need time," I say.

"Of course," the chimp tells me. "Take all the time you need."

* * * *

The chimp is not content to kill this creature. The chimp has to spit on it as well.

Under the pretense of assisting in my research, it tries to *deconstruct* the Island, break it apart and force it to conform to grubby earthbound precedents. It tells me about earthly bacteria that thrived at 1.5 million rads and laughed at hard vacuum. It shows me pictures of unkillable little tardigrades that could curl up and snooze on the edge of absolute zero, felt equally at home in deep ocean trenches and deeper space. Given time, opportunity, a boot off the planet, who knows how far those cute little invertebrates might have gone? Might they have survived the very death of the homeworld, clung together, grown somehow colonial?

What utter bullshit.

I learn what I can. I study the alchemy by which photosynthesis transforms light and gas and electrons into living tissue. I learn the physics of the solar wind that blows the bubble taut, calculate lower metabolic limits for a life-form that filters organics from the ether. I marvel at the speed of this creature's thoughts: almost as fast as *Eri* flies, orders of mag faster than any mammalian nerve impulse. Some kind of organic superconductor perhaps, something that passes chilled electrons almost resistance-free out here in the freezing void.

I acquaint myself with phenotypic plasticity and sloppy fitness, that fortuitous evolutionary soft-focus that lets species exist in alien environments and express novel traits they never needed at home. Perhaps this is how a lifeform with no natural enemies could acquire teeth and claws and the willingness to use them. The Island's life hinges on its ability to kill us; I have to find *something* that makes it a threat.

But all I uncover is a growing suspicion that I am doomed to fail—for violence, I begin to see, is a *planetary* phenomenon.

Planets are the abusive parents of evolution. Their very surfaces promote warfare, concentrate resources into dense defensible patches that can be fought over. Gravity forces you to squander energy on vascular systems and skeletal support, stand endless watch against its endless sadistic campaign to squash you flat. Take one wrong step, off a perch too high, and all your pricey architecture shatters in an instant. And even if you beat those odds, cobble together some lumbering armored chassis to withstand the slow crawl onto land—how long before the world draws in some asteroid or comet to crash down from the heavens and reset your clock to zero? Is it any wonder we grew up believing life was a struggle, that zero-sum was God's own law and that the future belonged to those who crushed the competition?

The rules are so different out here. Most of space is *tranquil*: no diel or seasonal cycles, no ice ages or global tropics, no wild pendulum swings between hot and cold, calm and tempestuous. Life's precursors abound: on comets, clinging to asteroids, suffusing nebulae a hundred lightyears across. Molecular clouds glow with organic chemistry and life-giving radiation. Their vast dusty wings grow warm with infrared, filter out the hard stuff, give rise to stellar nurseries that only some stunted refugee from the bottom of a gravity well could ever call *lethal*.

Darwin's an abstraction here, an irrelevant curiosity. This Island puts the lie to everything we were ever told about the machinery of life. Sun-powered, perfectly adapted, immortal, it won no struggle for survival: where are the predators, the competitors, the parasites? All of life around 428 is one vast continuum, one grand act of symbiosis. Nature here is not red in tooth and claw. Nature, out here, is the helping hand.

Lacking the capacity for violence, the Island has outlasted worlds. Unencumbered by technology, it has out-thought civilizations. It is intelligent beyond our measure, and—

—and it is *benign*. It must be. I grow more certain of that with each passing hour. How can it even *conceive* of an enemy?

I think of the things I called it, before I knew better. *Meat balloon. Cyst.* Looking back, those words verge on blasphemy. I will not use them again.

Besides, there's another word that would fit better, if the chimp has its way: Roadkill. And the longer I look, the more I fear that that hateful machine is right.

If the Island can defend itself, I sure as shit can't see how.

· · · ·

"*Eriophora's* impossible, you know. Violates the laws of physics."

We're in one of the social alcoves off the ventral notochord, taking a break from the library. I have decided to start again from first principles. Dix eyes me with an understandable mix of confusion and mistrust; my claim is almost too stupid to deny.

"It's true," I assure him. "Takes way too much energy to accelerate a ship with *Eri*'s mass, especially at relativistic speeds. You'd need the energy output of a whole sun. People figured if we made it to the stars at all, we'd have to do it in ships maybe the size of your thumb. Crew them with virtual personalities downloaded onto chips."

That's too nonsensical even for Dix. "*Wrong.* Don't have mass, can't fall towards anything. *Eri* wouldn't even *work* if it was that small."

"But suppose you can't displace any of that mass. No wormholes, no Higgs conduits, nothing to throw your gravitational field in the direction of travel. Your center of mass just *sits* there in, well, the center of your mass."

A spastic Dixian head-shake. "*Do* have those things!"

"Sure we do. But for the longest time, we didn't *know* it."

His foot taps an agitated tattoo on the deck.

"It's the history of the species," I explain. "We think we've worked everything out, we think we've solved all the mysteries, and then someone finds some niggling little data point that doesn't fit the paradigm. Every time we try to paper over the crack, it gets bigger, and before you know it, our whole worldview unravels. It's happened time and again. One day, mass is a constraint; the next, it's a requirement. The things we think we know—they *change*, Dix. And we have to change with them."

"But—"

"The chimp can't change. The rules it's following are ten billion years old and it's got no fucking imagination—and really that's not anyone's fault, that's just people who didn't know how else to keep the mission stable across deep time. They wanted to keep the mission on-track, so they built something that couldn't go off it; but they also knew that things *change*, and that's why *we're* out here, Dix. To deal with things the chimp can't."

"The alien," Dix says.

"The alien."

"Chimp deals with it just fine."

"How? By killing it?"

"Not our fault it's in the way. It's no threat—"

"I don't care whether it's a *threat* or not! It's alive, and it's intelligent, and killing it just to expand some alien empire—"

"*Human* empire. *Our* empire." Suddenly, Dix's hands have stopped twitching. Suddenly, he stands still as stone.

I snort. "What do *you* know about humans?"

"*Am* one."

"You're a fucking trilobite. You ever see what comes *out* of those gates once they're online?"

"Mostly nothing. " He pauses, thinking back. "Couple of—ships once, maybe."

"Well, I've seen a lot more than that, and believe me, if those things were *ever* human, it was a passing phase."

"But—"

"Dix—" I take a deep breath, try to get back on message. "Look, it's not your fault. You've been getting all your info from a moron stuck on a rail. But we're not doing this for Humanity, we're not doing it for Earth. Earth is *gone*, don't you understand that? The sun scorched it black a billion years after we left. Whatever we're working for, it—it won't even *talk* to us."

"Yeah? Then why do this? Why not just, just *quit?*"

He really doesn't know.

"We tried," I say.

"And?"

"And your *chimp* shut off our life support."

For once, he has nothing to say.

"It's a *machine*, Dix. Why can't you get that? It's *programmed*. It can't change."

"*We're* machines. Just built from different things. We're programmed. *We* change."

"Yeah? Last time I checked, you were sucking so hard on that thing's tit you couldn't even kill your cortical link."

"How I *learn*. No *reason* to change."

"How about acting like a damn *human* once in a while? How about developing a little rapport with the folks who might have to save your miserable life next time you go EVA? That enough of a *reason* for you? Because I don't mind telling you, right now I don't trust you as far as I could throw the tac tank. I don't even know for sure who I'm talking to right now."

"*Not my fault.*" For the first time, I see something outside the usual gamut of fear, confusion, and simpleminded computation playing across his face. "That's *you*, that's *all* of you. You talk—*sideways*. *Think* sideways. You all do, and it *hurts*." Something hardens in his face. "Didn't even need you online for this," he growls. "Didn't *want* you. Could have managed the whole build myself, *told* Chimp I could do it—"

"But the chimp thought you should wake me up anyway, and you always roll over for the chimp, don't you? Because the chimp always knows best, the chimp's your *boss*, the chimp's your fucking *god*. Which is why I have to get out of bed to nursemaid some idiot savant who can't even answer a hail without being led by the nose." Something clicks in the back of my mind, but I'm on a roll. "You want a *real* role model? You want something to look up to? Forget the chimp. Forget the mission. Look out the forward scope, why don't you? Look at what your precious chimp wants to run over because it happens to be in the way! That thing is better than any of us. It's smarter, it's peaceful, it doesn't wish us any harm at—"

"How can you know that? Can't know that!"

"No, *you* can't know that, because you're fucking *stunted!* Any normal caveman would see it in a second, but *you*—"

"That's crazy," Dix hisses at me. "*You're* crazy. You're *bad.*"

"*I'm* bad!" Some distant part of me hears the giddy squeak in my voice, the borderline hysteria.

"For the mission." Dix turns his back and stalks away.

My hands are hurting. I look down, surprised: my fists are clenched so tightly that my nails cut into the flesh of my palms. It takes a real effort to open them again.

I almost remember how this feels. I used to feel this way all the time. Way back when everything *mattered*; before passion faded to ritual, before rage cooled to disdain. Before Sunday Ahzmundin, eternity's warrior, settled for heaping insults on stunted children.

We were incandescent back then. Parts of this ship are still scorched and uninhabitable, even now. I remember this feeling.

This is how it feels to be awake.

· · · ·

I am awake, and I am alone, and I am sick of being outnumbered by morons. There are rules and there are risks, and you don't wake the dead on a whim, but fuck it. I'm calling reinforcements.

Dix has got to have other parents, a father at least, he didn't get that Y chromo from me. I swallow my own disquiet and check the manifest; bring up the gene sequences; cross-reference.

Huh. Only one other parent: Kai. I wonder if that's just coincidence, or if the chimp drew too many conclusions from our torrid little fuckfest back in the Cyg Rift. Doesn't matter. He's as much yours as mine, Kai, time to step up to the plate, time to—

Oh shit. Oh no. Please no.

(There are rules. And there are risks.)

Three builds back, it says. Kai and Connie. Both of them. One airlock jammed, the next too far away along *Eri*'s hull, a hail-Mary emergency crawl between. They made it back inside but not before the blue-shifted background cooked them in their suits. They kept breathing for hours afterwards, talked and moved and cried as if they were still alive, while their insides broke down and bled out.

There were two others awake that shift, two others left to clean up the mess. Ishmael, and—

"Um, you said—"

"*You fucker!*" I leap up and hit my son hard in the face, ten seconds' heartbreak with ten million years' denial raging behind it. I feel teeth give way behind his lips. He goes over backwards, eyes wide as telescopes, the blood already blooming on his mouth.

"*Said* I could come back—!" he squeals, scrambling backwards along the deck.

"He was your fucking *father*! You *knew*, you were *there*! He died right in *front* of you and you didn't even *tell* me!"

"I— I—"

"Why didn't you tell me, you asshole? The chimp told you to lie, is that it? Did you—"

"*Thought you knew*!" he cries. "Why *wouldn't* you know?"

My rage vanishes like air through a breach. I sag back into the 'pod, face in hands.

"Right there in the log," he whimpers. "All along. Nobody hid it. How could you not know?"

"I did," I admit dully. "Or I— I mean . . ."

I mean I *didn't* know, but it's not a surprise, not really, not down deep. You just—stop looking, after a while.

There are *rules*.

"Never even *asked*," my son says softly. "How they were doing."

I raise my eyes. Dix regards me wide-eyed from across the room, backed up against the wall, too scared to risk bolting past me to the door. "What are you doing here?" I ask tiredly.

His voice catches. He has to try twice: "You said I could come back. If I burned out my link . . ."

"You burned out your link."

He gulps and nods. He wipes blood with the back of his hand.

"What did the chimp say about that?"

"He said—*it* said that it was okay," Dix says, in such a transparent attempt to suck up that I actually believe, in that instant, that he might really be on his own.

"So you asked its permission." He begins to nod, but I can see the tell in his face: "Don't bullshit me, Dix."

"He—actually suggested it."

"I see."

"So we could talk," Dix adds.

"What do you want to talk about?"

He looks at the floor and shrugs.

I stand and walk towards him. He tenses but I shake my head, spread my hands. "It's okay. It's okay." I lean back against the wall and slide down until I'm beside him on the deck.

We just sit there for a while.

"It's been so long," I say at last.

He looks at me, uncomprehending. What does *long* even mean, out here?

I try again. "They say there's no such thing as altruism, you know?"

His eyes blank for an instant, and grow panicky, and I know that he's just tried to ping his link for a definition and come up blank. So we *are* alone. "Altruism," I explain. "Unselfishness. Doing something that costs *you* but helps someone else." He seems to get it. "They say every selfless act ultimately comes down to manipulation or kin-selection or reciprocity or something, but they're wrong. I could—"

I close my eyes. This is harder than I expected.

"I could have been happy just *knowing* that Kai was okay, that Connie was happy. Even if it didn't benefit me one whit, even if it *cost* me, even if there was no chance I'd ever see either of them again. Almost any price would be worth it, just to know they were okay.

"Just to *believe* they were . . ."

So you haven't seen her for the past five builds. So he hasn't drawn your shift since Sagittarius. They're just sleeping. Maybe next time.

"So you don't check," Dix says slowly. Blood bubbles on his lower lip; he doesn't seem to notice.

"We don't check." Only I did, and now they're gone. They're both gone. Except for those little cannibalized nucleotides the chimp recycled into this defective and maladapted son of mine.

We're the only warm-blooded creatures for a thousand lightyears, and I am so very lonely.

"I'm sorry," I whisper, and lean forward, and lick the blood from his bruised and bloody lips.

. . . .

Back on Earth—back when there *was* an Earth—there were these little animals called cats. I had one for a while. Sometimes I'd watch him sleep for hours: paws and whiskers and ears all twitching madly as he chased imaginary prey across whatever landscapes his sleeping brain conjured up.

My son looks like that when the chimp worms its way into his dreams.

It's almost too literal for metaphor: the cable runs into his head like some kind of parasite, feeding through old-fashioned fiberop now that the wireless option's been burned away. Or *force*-feeding, I suppose; the poison flows *into* Dix's head, not out of it.

I shouldn't be here. Didn't I just throw a tantrum over the violation of my own privacy? (Just. Twelve lightdays ago. Everything's relative.) And yet, I can see no privacy here for Dix to lose: no decorations on the walls, no artwork or hobbies, no wraparound console. The sex toys ubiquitous in every suite sit unused on their shelves; I'd have assumed he was on antilibinals if recent experience hadn't proven otherwise.

What am I doing? Is this some kind of perverted mothering instinct, some vestigial expression of a Pleistocene maternal subroutine? Am I that much of a robot, has my brain stem sent me here to guard my child?

To guard my *mate*?

Lover or larva, it hardly matters: his quarters are an empty shell, there's nothing of Dix in here. That's just his abandoned body lying there in the pseudopod, fingers twitching, eyes flickering beneath closed lids in vicarious response to wherever his mind has gone.

They don't know I'm here. The chimp doesn't know because we burned out its prying eyes a billion years ago, and my son doesn't know I'm here because—well, because for him, right now, there *is* no here.

What am I supposed to make of you, Dix? None of this makes sense. Even your body language looks like you grew it in a vat—but I'm far from the first human being you've seen. You grew up in good company, with people I *know*, people I trust. Trusted. How did you end up on the other side? How did they let you slip away?

And why didn't they warn me about you?

Yes, there are rules. There is the threat of enemy surveillance during long dead nights, the threat of—other losses. But this is unprecedented. Surely someone could have left something, some clue buried in a metaphor too subtle for the simpleminded to decode . . .

I'd give a lot to tap into that pipe, to see what you're seeing now. Can't risk it, of course; I'd give myself away the moment I tried to sample anything except the basic baud, and—

—Wait a second—

That baud rate's way too low. That's not even enough for hi-res graphics, let alone tactile and olfac. You're embedded in a wireframe world at best.

And yet, look at you go. The fingers, the eyes—like a cat, dreaming of mice and apple pies. Like *me*, replaying the long-lost oceans and mountaintops of Earth before I learned that living in the past was just another way of dying in the present. The bit rate says this is barely even a test pattern; the body says you're immersed in a whole other world. How has that machine tricked you into treating such thin gruel as a feast?

Why would it even want to? Data are better grasped when they *can* be grasped, and tasted, and heard; our brains are built for far richer nuance than splines and scatterplots. The driest technical briefings are more sensual than this. Why settle for stick-figures when you can paint in oils and holograms?

Why does anyone simplify anything? To reduce the variable set. To manage the unmanageable.

Kai and Connie. Now *there* were a couple of tangled, unmanageable datasets. Before the accident. Before the scenario *simplified*.

Someone should have warned me about you, Dix.

Maybe someone tried.

· · · ·

And so it comes to pass that my son leaves the nest, encases himself in a beetle carapace and goes walkabout. He is not alone; one of the chimp's teleops accompanies him out on *Eri*'s hull, lest he lose his footing and fall back into the starry past.

Maybe this will never be more than a drill, maybe this scenario—catastrophic control-systems failure, the chimp and its backups offline, all maintenance tasks suddenly thrown onto shoulders of flesh and blood—is a dress rehearsal for a crisis that never happens. But even the unlikeliest scenario approaches certainty over the life of a universe; so we go through the motions. We practice. We hold our breath and dip outside. We're on a tight deadline: even armored, moving at this speed the blueshifted background rad would cook us in hours.

Worlds have lived and died since I last used the pickup in my suite. "Chimp."

"Here as always, Sunday." Smooth, and glib, and friendly. The easy rhythm of the practiced psychopath.

"I know what you're doing."

"I don't understand."

"You think I don't see what's going on? You're building the next release. You're getting too much grief from the old guard so you're starting from scratch with people who don't remember the old days. People you've, you've *simplified*."

The chimp says nothing. The drone's feed shows Dix clambering across a jumbled terrain of basalt and metal matrix composites.

"But you can't raise a human child, not on your own." I know it tried: there's no record of Dix anywhere on the crew manifest until his mid-teens, when he just *showed up* one day and nobody asked about it because nobody *ever* . . .

"Look what you've made of him. He's great at conditional If/Thens. Can't be beat on number-crunching and Do loops. But he can't *think*. Can't make the simplest intuitive jumps. You're like one of those"—I remember an Earthly myth, from the days when *reading* did not seem like such an obscene waste of lifespan—"one of those wolves, trying to raise a human child. You can teach him how to move around on hands and knees, you can teach him about pack dynamics, but you can't teach him how to walk on his hind legs or talk or be *human* because you're *too fucking stupid*, Chimp, and you finally realized it. And that's why you threw him at me. You think I can fix him for you."

I take a breath, and a gambit.

"But he's nothing to me. You understand? He's *worse* than nothing, he's a liability. He's a spy, he's a spastic waste of O_2. Give me one reason why I shouldn't just lock him out there until he cooks."

"You're his mother," the chimp says, because the chimp has read all about kin selection and is too stupid for nuance.

"You're an idiot."

"You love him."

"No." An icy lump forms in my chest. My mouth makes words; they come out measured and inflectionless. "I can't love anyone, you brain-dead machine. That's why I'm out here. Do you really think they'd gamble your precious never-ending mission on little glass dolls that needed to bond?"

"You love him."

"I can kill him any time I want. And that's exactly what I'll do if you don't move the gate."

"I'd stop you," the chimp says mildly.

"That's easy enough. Just move the gate and we both get what we want. Or you can dig in your heels and try to reconcile your need for a mother's touch with my sworn intention of breaking the little fucker's neck. We've got a long trip ahead of us, chimp. And you might find I'm not quite as easy to cut out of the equation as Kai and Connie."

"You cannot end the mission," it says, almost gently. "You tried that already."

"This isn't about ending the mission. This is only about slowing it down a little. Your optimal scenario's off the table. The only way that gate's going to get finished now is by saving the Island, or killing your prototype. Your call."

The cost-benefit's pretty simple. The chimp could solve it in an instant. But still it says nothing. The silence stretches. It's looking for some other option, I bet. It's trying to find a workaround. It's questioning the very premises of the scenario, trying to decide if I mean what I'm saying, if all its book-learning about mother love could really be so far off-base. Maybe it's plumbing historical intrafamilial murder rates, looking for a loophole. And there may be one, for all I know. But the chimp isn't me, it's a simpler system trying to figure out a smarter one, and that gives me the edge.

"You would owe me," it says at last.

I almost burst out laughing. "*What?*"

"Or I will tell Dixon that you threatened to kill him."

"Go ahead."

"You don't want him to know."

"I don't care whether he knows or not. What, you think he'll try and kill me back? You think I'll lose his *love?*" I linger on the last word, stretch it out to show how ludicrous it is.

"You'll lose his trust. You need to trust each other out here."

"Oh, right. *Trust.* The very fucking foundation of this mission!"

The chimp says nothing.

"For the sake of argument," I say, after a while, "suppose I go along with it. What would I *owe* you, exactly?"

"A favor," the chimp replies. "To be repaid in future."

My son floats innocently against the stars, his life in balance.

. . . .

We sleep. The chimp makes grudging corrections to a myriad small trajectories. I set the alarm to wake me every couple of weeks, burn a little more of my candle in case the enemy tries to pull another fast one; but for now it seems to be behaving itself. DHF428 jumps towards us in the stop-motion increments of a life's moments, strung like beads along an infinite string. The factory floor slews to starboard in our sights: refineries, reservoirs, and nanofab plants, swarms of von Neumanns breeding and cannibalizing and recycling each other into shielding and circuitry, tugboats and spare parts. The very finest Cro Magnon technology mutates and metastasizes across the universe like armor-plated cancer.

And hanging like a curtain between *it* and *us* shimmers an iridescent life form, fragile and immortal and unthinkably alien, that reduces everything my species ever accomplished to mud and shit by the simple transcendent fact of its existence. I have never believed in gods, in universal good or absolute evil. I have only ever believed that there is what works, and what doesn't. All the rest is smoke and mirrors, trickery to manipulate grunts like me.

But I believe in the Island, because I don't *have* to. It does not need to be taken on faith: it looms ahead of us, its existence an empirical fact. I will never know its mind, I will never know the details of its origin and evolution. But I can *see* it: massive, mind boggling, so utterly inhuman that it can't *help* but be better than us, better than anything we could ever become.

I believe in the Island. I've gambled my own son to save its life. I would kill him to avenge its death.

I may yet.

In all these millions of wasted years, I have finally done something worthwhile.

. . . .

Final approach.

Reticles within reticles line up before me, a mesmerising infinite regress of bull's-eyes centering on target. Even now, mere minutes from ignition, distance reduces the unborn gate to invisibility. There will be no moment when the naked eye can trap our destination. We thread the needle far too quickly: it will be behind us before we know it.

Or, if our course corrections are off by even a hair—if our trillion-kilometer curve drifts by as much as a thousand meters—we will be dead. Before we know it.

Our instruments report that we are precisely on target. The chimp tells me that we are precisely on target. *Eriophora* falls forward, pulled endlessly through the void by her own magically-displaced mass.

I turn to the drone's-eye view relayed from up ahead. It's a window into history—even now, there's a timelag of several minutes—but past and present race closer to convergence with every corsec. The newly-minted gate looms dark and ominous against the stars, a great gaping mouth built to devour reality itself. The vons, the refineries, the assembly lines: parked to the side in vertical columns, their jobs done, their usefulness outlived, their collateral annihilation imminent. I pity them, for some reason. I always do. I wish we could scoop them up and take them with us, re-enlist them for the next build—but the rules of economics reach everywhere, and they say it's cheaper to use our tools once and throw them away.

A rule that the chimp seems to be taking more to heart than anyone expected.

At least we've spared the Island. I wish we could have stayed awhile. First contact with a truly alien intelligence, and what do we exchange? Traffic signals. What does the Island dwell upon, when not pleading for its life?

I thought of asking. I thought of waking myself when the time-lag dropped from prohibitive to merely inconvenient, of working out some pidgin that could encompass the truths and philosophies of a mind vaster than all humanity. What a childish fantasy. The Island exists too far beyond the grotesque Darwinian processes that shaped my own flesh. There can be no communion here, no meeting of minds.

Angels do not speak to ants.

Less than three minutes to ignition. I see light at the end of the tunnel. *Eri's* incidental time machine barely looks into the past any more, I could almost hold my breath across the whole span of seconds that *then* needs to overtake *now*. Still on target, according to all sources.

Tactical beeps at us.

"Getting a signal," Dix reports, and yes: in the heart of the Tank, the sun is flickering again. My heart leaps: does the angel speak to us after all? A thank you, perhaps? A cure for heat death?

But—

"It's *ahead* of us," Dix murmurs, as sudden realization catches in my throat.

Two minutes.

"Miscalculated somehow," Dix whispers. "Didn't move the gate far enough."

"We did," I say. We moved it exactly as far as the Island told us to.

"Still in front of us! Look at the sun!"

"Look at the *signal*," I tell him.

Because it's nothing like the painstaking traffic signs we've followed over the past three trillion kilometers. It's almost—random, somehow. It's spur-of-the-moment, it's *panicky*. It's the sudden, startled cry of something caught utterly by surprise with mere seconds left to act. And even though I have never seen this pattern of dots and swirls before, I know exactly what it must be saying.

Stop. Stop. Stop. Stop.

We do not stop. There is no force in the universe that can even slow us down. Past equals present; *Eriophora* dives through the center of the gate in a nanosecond. The unimaginable mass of her cold black heart snags some distant dimension, drags it screaming to the here and now. The booted portal erupts behind us, blossoms into a great blinding corona, every wavelength lethal to every living thing. Our aft filters clamp down tight.

The scorching wavefront chases us into the darkness as it has a thousand times before. In time, as always, the birth pangs will subside. The wormhole will settle in its collar. And just maybe, we will still be close enough to glimpse some new transcendent monstrosity emerging from that magic doorway.

I wonder if you'll notice the corpse we left behind.

· · · ·

"Maybe we're missing something," Dix says.

"We miss almost everything," I tell him.

DHF428 shifts red behind us. Lensing artifacts wink in our rearview; the gate has stabilized and the wormhole's online, blowing light and space and time in an iridescent bubble from its great metal mouth. We'll keep looking over our shoulders right up until we pass the Rayleigh Limit, far past the point it'll do any good.

So far, though, nothing's come out.

"Maybe our numbers were wrong," he says. "Maybe we made a mistake."

Our numbers were right. An hour doesn't pass when I don't check them again. The Island just had—enemies, I guess. Victims, anyway.

I was right about one thing, though. That fucker was *smart*. To see us coming, to figure out how to talk to us; to use us as a *weapon*, to turn a threat to its very existence into a, a . . .

I guess *flyswatter* is as good a word as any.

"Maybe there was a war," I mumble. "Maybe it wanted the real estate. Or maybe it was just some—family squabble."

"Maybe it didn't *know*," Dix suggests. "Maybe it thought those coordinates were empty."

Why would you think that?, I wonder. *Why would you even care?* And then it dawns on me: he doesn't, not about the Island, anyway. No more than he ever did. He's not inventing these rosy alternatives for himself.

My son is trying to comfort me.

I don't need to be coddled, though. I was a fool: I let myself believe in life without conflict, in sentience without sin. For a little while, I dwelt in a dream world where life was unselfish and unmanipulative, where every living thing did not struggle to exist at the expense of other life. I deified that which I could not understand, when in the end it was all too easily understood.

But I'm better now.

It's over: another build, another benchmark, another irreplaceable slice of life that brings our task no closer to completion. It doesn't matter how successful we are. It doesn't matter how well we do our job. *Mission accomplished* is a meaningless phrase on *Eriophora*, an ironic oxymoron at best. There may one day be failure, but there is no finish line. We go on forever, crawling across the universe like ants, dragging your goddamned superhighway behind us.

I still have so much to learn.

At least my son is here to teach me.

JO WALTON   Born in Aberdare, Wales, Jo Walton now lives in Montreal, Canada. She worked as a bookseller and a writer of role-playing game scenarios before publishing her first novel, *The King's Peace*, in 2000. She won the 2002 John W. Campbell Award for Best New Writer, and in 2004 she won the World Fantasy Award for her fourth novel, *Tooth and Claw*. Her 2011 novel, *Among Others*, described as "a novel about a science-fiction reader with a fantasy problem," won the Nebula and Hugo Awards in 2012, making her one of only two people whose careers include Best Novel wins in the Nebula, the Hugo, and World Fantasy Awards.

Although best known as a fantasist, between *Tooth and Claw* and *Among Others* she wrote a trilogy of alternate-history novels—*Farthing*, *Ha'penny*, and *Half a Crown*—set in the postwar England of a world in which pro-fascist elements of the British upper classes overthrew Churchill and made a separate peace with Berlin. "Escape to Other Worlds with Science Fiction" is a short story set in the America of that same world.

ESCAPE TO OTHER WORLDS WITH SCIENCE FICTION

In the Papers (1)

NATIONAL GUARD MOVES AGAINST STRIKERS
In the seventh week of the mining strike in West Virginia, armed skirmishes and running "guerrilla battles" in the hills have led to the Governor calling in

· · · ·

GET AN ADVANCED DEGREE BY CORRESPONDENCE
You can reap the benefits with no need to leave the safety of your house or go among unruly college students! Only from

· · · ·

EX-PRESIDENT LINDBERGH REPROACHES MINERS

· · · ·

ASTOUNDING SCIENCE FICTION
April issue on newsstands now! All new stories by Poul Anderson, Anson MacDonald and H. Beam Piper! Only 35 cents.

· · · ·

SPRING FASHIONS 1960
Skirts are being worn long in London and Paris this season, but

*here in New York the working girls are still hitching them up. It's
stylish to wear a little*

· · · ·

HOW FAR FROM MIAMI CAN THE "FALLOUT" REACH?
*Scientists say it could be a problem for years, but so much depends
on the weather that*

· · · ·

*You hope to work
You hope to eat
The work goes to
The man that's neat!
BurmaShave*

Getting By (1)

Linda Evans is a waitress in Bundt's Bakery. She used to work as a typist,
but when she was let go she was glad to take this job, even though it
keeps her on her feet all day and sometimes she feels her face will crack
from smiling at the customers. She was never a secretary, only in the typing pool. Her sister Joan is a secretary, but she can take shorthand and
type ninety words a minute. Joan graduated from high school. She taught
Linda to type. But Linda was never as clever as Joan, not even when they
were little girls in the time she can just remember, when their father had a
job at the plant and they lived in a neat little house at the end of the bus
line. Their father hasn't worked for a long time now. He drinks up any
money he can bully out of the girls. Linda stands up to him better than
Joan does.

"They'd have forgiven the New Deal if only it had worked," a man says
to another, as Linda puts down his coffee and sandwich in front of him.

"Worked?" asks his companion scornfully. "It was working. It would have
worked and got us out of this if only people had kept faith in it."

They are threadbare old men, in mended coats. They ordered grilled
cheese sandwiches, the cheapest item on the menu. One of them smiles at
Linda, and she smiles back, automatically, then moves on and forgets them.
She's on her feet all day. Joan teases her about flirting with the customers
and falling in love, but it never seems to happen. She used to tease Joan
about falling in love with her boss, until she did. It would all have been
dandy except that he was a married man. Now Joan spends anguished hours
with him and anguished days without him. He makes her useless presents of
French perfume and lace underwear. When Linda wants to sell them, Joan
just cries. Both of them live in fear that she'll get pregnant, and then where
will they be? Linda wipes the tables and tries not to listen to the men with

their endless ifs. She has enough ifs of her own: if mother hadn't died, if she'd kept her job in the pool, if John hadn't died in the war with England, and Pete in the war with Japan.

"Miss?" one of them asks. She swings around, thinking they want more coffee. One refill only is the rule. "Can you settle a question?" he asks. "Did Roosevelt want to get us to join in the European War in 1940?"

"How should I know? It has nothing to do with me. I was five years old in 1940." They should get over it and leave history to bury its own dead, she thinks, and goes back to wiping the tables.

In the Papers (2)

WITH MIRACLE-GROW YOU CAN REGAIN YOUR LOST FOLLICLES!
In today's world it can be hard to find work even with qualifications. We at Cyrus Markham's Agency have extensive experience at matching candidates to positions which makes us the unrivaled

• • • •

NEW TORPEDOES THAT WORK EVEN BETTER
Radar, sonar and even television to

• • • •

AT LAST YOU CAN AFFORD THE HOUSE OF YOUR DREAMS

• • • •

LET SCIENCE FICTION TAKE YOU TO NEW WORLDS
New books by Isaac Asimov and Robert A. Heinlein for only

• • • •

ANOTHER BANK FOUNDERS IN PENNSYLVANIA

• • • •

WE HAVE NOT USED THE WORD "SECEDE," SAYS TEXAS GOVERNOR
Why do Canadians act so high and mighty? It's because they know

In the Line (1)

When Tommy came out of the navy, he thought he'd walk into a job just like that. He had his veteran's discharge, which entitled him to medical treatment for his whole life, and he was a hero. He'd been on the carrier *Constitution*, which had won the Battle of the Atlantic practically singlehanded and had sent plenty of those Royal Navy bastards to the bottom of the sea where they belonged. He had experience in maintenance as well as gunnery. Besides, he was a proud hard-working American. He never thought he'd be lining up at a soup kitchen.

In the Papers (3)

TIME FOR A NEW TUNE
Why are the bands still playing Cole Porter?

. . . .

SECRETARY OF STATE LINEBARGER SAYS THE BRITS WANT PEACE

. . . .

ATOMIC SECRETS

. . . .

DO THE JAPANESE HAVE THE BOMB?
Sources close to the Emperor say yes, but the Nazis deny that they have given out any plans. Our top scientists are still working to

. . . .

NYLONS NYLONS NYLONS

. . . .

DIANETICS: A NEW SCIENCE OF THE MIND

Getting By (2)

Linda always works overtime when she's asked. She appreciates the money, and she's always afraid she'll be let go if she isn't obliging. There are plenty of girls who'd like her job. They come to ask every day if there's any work. She isn't afraid the Bundts will give her job away for no reason. She's worked here for four years now, since just after the Japanese War. "You're like family," Mrs. Bundt always says. They let Olive go, the other waitress, but that was because there wasn't enough work for two. Linda works overtime and closes up the cafe when they want her to. "You're a good girl," Mrs. Bundt says. But the Bundts have a daughter, Cindy. Cindy's a pretty twelve-year old, not even in high school. She comes into the cafe and drinks a milkshake sometimes with her girlfriends, all of them giggling. Linda hates her. She doesn't know what they have to giggle about. Linda is afraid that when Cindy is old enough she'll be given Linda's job. Linda might be like family, but Cindy really is family. The bakery does all right, people have to eat, but business isn't what it was. Linda knows.

She's late going home. Joan's dressing up to go out with her married boss. She washes in the sink in the room they share. The shower is down the corridor, shared with the whole floor. It gets cleaned only on Fridays, or when Joan or Linda do it. Men are such pigs, Linda thinks, lying on her bed, her weight off her feet at last. Joan is three years older than Linda but she looks younger. It's the make-up, Linda thinks, or maybe it's having somebody to love. If only she could have fallen in love with a boss who'd have married her and taken her off to a nice little suburb. But perhaps it's just as well. Linda couldn't afford the room alone, and she'd have had to find a stranger to share with. At least Joan was her sister and they were used to each other.

"I saw Dad today," Joan says, squinting in the mirror and drawing on her mouth carefully.

"Tell me you didn't give him money?"

"Just two dollars," Joan admits. Linda groans. Joan is a soft touch. She makes more than Linda, but she never has any left at the end of the week. She spends more, or gives it away. There's no use complaining, as Linda knows.

"Where's he taking you?" she asks wearily.

"To a rally," Joan says.

"Cheap entertainment." Rallies and torch-lit parades and lynchings, beating up the blacks as scapegoats for everything. It didn't help at all; it just made people feel better about things to have someone to blame. "It's not how we were brought up," Linda says. Their mother's father had been a minister and had believed in the brotherhood of man. Linda loved going to her grandparents' house when she was a child. Her grandmother would bake cookies and the whole house would smell of them. There was a swing on the old apple tree in the garden. Her father had been a union man, once, when unions had still been respectable.

"What do I care about all that?" Joan says, viciously. "It's where he's taking me, and that's all. He'll buy me dinner and we'll sing some patriotic songs. I'm not going to lynch anybody." She dabs on her French perfume, fiercely.

Linda lies back. She isn't hungry. She's never hungry. She always eats at the bakery—the Bundts don't mind—any order that was wrong, or any bread that would have been left over. Sometimes they even gave her cakes or bread to bring home. She rubs her feet. She's very lucky really. But as Joan goes out the door she feels like crying. Even if she did meet somebody, how could they ever afford to marry? How could they hope for a house of their own?

In the Papers (4)

SEA MONKEYS WILL ASTOUND YOUR FRIENDS!

. . . .

PRESIDENT SAYS WE MUST ALL PULL TOGETHER
In Seattle today in a meeting with

. . . .

TAKE A LUXURY AIRSHIP TO THE HOLY CITY

. . . .

CAN THE ECONOMY EVER RECOVER?
*Since the Great Depression the country has been jogging through
a series of ups and downs and the economy has been lurching*

from one crisis to another. Administrations have tried remedies from Roosevelt's New Deal to Lindbergh's Belt Tightening but nothing has turned things around for long. Economists say that this was only to be expected and that this general trend of downturn was a natural and inevitable

· · · ·

NEW HOLLYWOOD BLOCKBUSTER "REICHSMARSHALL" STARRING MARLON BRANDO

In the Line (2)

When Sue was seventeen she'd had enough of school. She had a boyfriend who promised to find her a job as a dancer. She went off with him to Cleveland. She danced for a while in a topless club, and then in a strip joint. The money was never quite enough, not even after she started turning tricks. She's only thirty-four, but she knows she looks raddled. She's sick. Nobody wants her anymore. She's waiting in the line because there's nowhere else to go. They feed you and take you off in trucks to make a new start, that's what she's heard. She can see the truck. She wonders where they go.

In the Papers (5)

ARE NEW HOME PERMANENTS AS GOOD AS THEY SAY?
Experts say yes!

· · · ·

NEW WAYS TO SAVE

· · · ·

PRESIDENT SAYS: THERE IS NO WITCH-HUNT
Despite what communists and union organizers may claim, the President said today

Getting By (3)

The Bundts like to play the radio in the cafe at breakfast time. They talk about buying a little television for the customers to watch, if times ever get better. Mr. Bundt says this when Linda cautiously asks for a raise. If they had a television they'd be busier, he thinks, though Linda doesn't think it would make a difference. She serves coffee and bacon and toast and listens to the news. She likes music and Joan likes Walter Winchell. She should ask Joan how she reconciles that with going to rallies. Winchell famously hates Hitler. Crazy. Linda can't imagine feeling that strongly about an old man on the other side of the world.

Later, when Cindy and her friends are giggling over milkshakes and Linda feels as if her feet are falling off, a man comes in and takes the corner table. He orders sandwiches and coffee, and later he orders a cake and more coffee. He's an odd little man. He seems to be paying attention to everything. He's dressed quite well. His hair is slicked back and his clothes are clean. She wonders if he's a detective, because he keeps looking out of the window, but if so he seems to pay just as much attention to the inside, and to Linda herself. She remembers what Joan said, and wants to laugh but can't. He's a strange man and she can't figure him out.

She doesn't have to stay late and close up, and the man follows her out when she leaves. There's something about him that makes her think of the law way before romance. "You're Linda," he says, outside. She's scared, because he could be anybody, but they are in the street under a street light, there are people passing, and the occasional car.

"Yes," she admits, her heart hammering. "What do you want?"

"You're not a Bundt?"

"No. They're my employers, that's all," she says, disassociating herself from them as fast as she can, though they have been good to her. Immediately she has visions of them being arrested. Where would she find another job?

"Do you know where the Bundts come from?"

"Germany," she says, confidently. Bundt's German Bakery, it says, right above their heads.

"When?"

"Before I was born. Why aren't you asking them these questions?"

"It was 1933."

"Before I was born," Linda says, feeling more confident and taking a step away.

"Have you seen any evidence that they are Jews?"

She stops, confused. "Jews? They're German. Germans hate Jews."

"Many Jews left Germany in 1933 when Hitler came to power," the man says, though he can't be much older than Linda. "If the Bundts were Jews, and hiding their identity, then if you denounced them—"

He stops, but Linda has caught up with him now. If she denounced them she would be given their property. The business, the apartment above it, their savings. "But they're not, I've never—they serve bacon!" she blurts.

"You've never seen any evidence?" he asks, sadly. "A pity. It could be a nice business for you. You're not Jewish?"

"Welsh," she says. "My grandfather was a minister."

"I thought not, with that lovely blonde hair." It's more washed out than it should be, but her hair is the dishwater blonde it always has been, the same as Joan's, the same as their mother.

"I might have some evidence," he says, slowly. "But any evidence I had would be from before they came here, from Germany. Some evidence that they were still Jews, if you'd seen anything, would be enough to settle it. The court would deport them back to Germany and award us their business. You could run it, I'm sure you could. You seem to be doing most of the work already."

"I just serve," she says, automatically. Then, "What sort of thing would I have noticed? If they were Jewish, I mean?"

Temptation settles over her like a film of grease and hope begins to burn in her heart for the first time in a long time.

In the Line (3)

If you're black you're invisible, even in the soup line. The others are shrinking away from me, I can't deny it. They wouldn't give us guns to fight even when the Japanese were shelling the beaches up and down the California coast. I left there then and came East, much good it did me. If I'd known how invisible I'd be here, I'd have stayed right there in Los Angeles. Nobody there ever chased after me and made me run, nobody there threatened to string me up, and I had a job that made a little money. I never thought I'd be standing in this line, because when I get to the head of it I know they'll separate me out. Nobody knows what happens to us then, they take us off somewhere and we don't come back, but I'm desperate, and what I say is, wherever it is they got to feed us, don't they? Well, don't they?

In the Papers (6)

ANOTHER FACTORY CLOSING

• • • •

PEACE TALKS IN LONDON AS JAPAN AND THE REICH DIVIDE UP RUSSIA
Will there be a buffer state of "Scythia" to divide the two great powers?

• • • •

BATTLE IN THE APPALACHIANS: NATIONAL GUARD REINFORCEMENTS SENT IN
President says it is necessary to keep the country together

• • • •

OWNERS GUN DOWN STRIKERS IN ALABAMA
Sixty people were hospitalized in Birmingham today after

• • • •

ESCAPE TO OTHER WORLDS WITH SCIENCE FICTION
New titles by Frederik Pohl and Alice Davey

CORY DOCTOROW   Born in Toronto and now resident in London, Cory Doctorow is equally famous as an SF writer and as a political activist focused on issues—copyright overreach, freedom in one's computing devices, the innovation-quashing tendencies of economic incumbents—that are, for many people, still in the realm of SF. It is perhaps fitting that he is the only person, thus far, to have won *both* of the genre's awards that happen to be named after the brilliant, irascible editor John W. Campbell, because all of Doctorow's several careers have been powered by doing exactly as Campbell always urged his authors to do: "ask the next question."

Doctorow's early short fiction won him the John W. Campbell Award for Best New Writer in 2000; not long after that, he published his first novel, the Locus Award–winning *Down and Out in the Magic Kingdom*. With his publisher's acquiescence, he released his own free-of-charge Creative Commons–licensed e-text of the novel simultaneously with its commercial release, and he has continued to do this for all of his novels and other books since. In 2008, he published his first YA novel, the *New York Times* bestselling *Little Brother*, a story of tech-savvy teenagers fighting back against an overweening "homeland security" regime in an American future that could be next Tuesday. It won widespread acclaim, including the John W. Campbell Memorial Award. Since then he has published more fiction for young readers and for adults, including 2013's *Homeland*, a sequel to *Little Brother*. In addition to writing SF, he is a coeditor of the megapopular site Boing Boing and a columnist for *The Guardian*, *Publishers Weekly*, and *Locus*. He also travels nearly constantly as a speaker and organizer.

Written for a *festschrift* in honor of Frederik Pohl, "Chicken Little" contains jet-packs, a likable protagonist, and an immortal zillionaire brain-in-a-vat. It also asks a number of "next questions"—about the nature of happiness, about whether imposed happiness is really worse than free will, and about the possibility that the super-rich are slowly speciating away from the rest of us, retiring into heaven and pulling the ladder up as they go.

CHICKEN LITTLE

The first lesson Leon learned at the ad agency was: nobody is your friend at the ad agency.

Take today: Brautigan was going to see an actual vat, at an actual clinic, which housed an actual target consumer, and he wasn't taking Leon.

"Don't sulk, it's unbecoming," Brautigan said, giving him one of those tight-lipped smiles where he barely got his mouth over those big, horsey, comical teeth of his. They were disarming, those pearly whites. "It's out of the question. Getting clearance to visit a vat in person, that's a one-month, two-month process. Background checks. Biometrics. Interviews with their psych staff. The physicals: they have to take a census of your microbial nation. It takes time, Leon. You might be a mayfly in a mayfly hurry, but the man in the vat, he's got a lot of time on his hands. No skin off his dick if you get held up for a month or two."

"Bullshit," Leon said. "It's all a show. They've got a brick wall a hundred miles high around the front, and a sliding door around the back. There's always an exception in these protocols. There has to be."

"When you're 180 years old and confined to a vat, you don't make exceptions. Not if you want to go on to 181."

"You're telling me that if the old monster suddenly developed a rare, fast-moving liver cancer and there was only one oncologist in the whole god-damned world who could make it better, you're telling me that guy would be sent home to France or whatever, 'No thanks, we're OK, you don't have clearance to see the patient'?"

"I'm telling you the monster *doesn't have a liver*. What that man has, he has *machines* and *nutrients* and *systems*."

"And if a machine breaks down?"

"The man who invented that machine works for the monster. He lives on the monster's private estate, with his family. *Their* microbial nations are identical to the monster's. He is not only the emperor of their lives, he is the emperor of the lives of their intestinal flora. If the machine that man invented stopped working, he would be standing by the vat in less than two minutes, with his staff, all in disposable, sterile bunny suits, murmuring reassuring noises as he calmly, expertly fitted one of the ten replacements he has standing by, the ten replacements he checks, *personally*, every single day, to make sure that they are working."

Leon opened his mouth, closed it. He couldn't help himself, he snorted a laugh. "Really?"

Brautigan nodded.

"And what if none of the machines worked?"

"If that man couldn't do it, then his rival, who *also* lives on the monster's estate, who has developed the second-most-exciting liver replacement technology in the history of the world, who burns to try it on the man in the vat—*that* man would be there in ten minutes, and the first man, and his family—"

"Executed?"

Brautigan made a disappointed noise. "Come on, he's a quadrillionaire, not a Bond villain. No, that man would be demoted to nearly nothing, but given one tiny chance to redeem himself: invent a technology better than the one that's currently running in place of the vat-man's liver, and you will be restored to your fine place with your fine clothes and your wealth and your privilege."

"And if he fails?"

Brautigan shrugged. "Then the man in the vat is out an unmeasurably minuscule fraction of his personal fortune. He takes the loss, applies for a research tax credit for it, and deducts it from the pittance he deigns to send to the IRS every year."

"Shit."

Brautigan slapped his hands together. "It's wicked, isn't it? All that money and power and money and money?"

Leon tried to remember that Brautigan wasn't his friend. It was those teeth, they were so *disarming*. Who could be suspicious of a man who was so horsey you wanted to feed him sugar cubes? "It's something else."

"You now know about ten thousand times more about the people in the vats than your average cit. But you haven't got even the shadow of the picture yet, buddy. It took *decades* of relationship-building for Ate to sell its first product to a vat-person."

And we haven't sold anything else since, Leon thought, but he didn't say it. No one would say it at Ate. The agency pitched itself as a powerhouse, a success in a field full of successes. It was *the* go-to agency for servicing the "ultra-high-net-worth individual," and yet . . .

One sale.

"And we haven't sold anything since." Brautigan said it without a hint of shame. "And yet, this entire building, this entire agency, the salaries and the designers and the consultants: all of it paid for by clipping the toenails of that fortune. Which means that one *more* sale—"

He gestured around. The offices were sumptuous, designed to impress the functionaries of the fortunes in the vats. A trick of light and scent and wind made you feel as though you were in an ancient forest glade as soon as you came through the door, though no forest was in evidence. The reception desktop was a sheet of pitted tombstone granite, the unreadable smooth epitaph peeking around the edges of the old-fashioned typewriter that had been cunningly reworked to serve as a slightly less old-fashioned keyboard. The receptionist—presently ignoring them with professional verisimilitude—conveyed beauty, intelligence, and motherly concern, all by means of dress, bearing, and makeup. Ate employed a small team of stylists that worked on all public-facing employees; Leon had endured a just-so rumpling of his sandy hair and some carefully applied fraying at the cuffs and elbows of his jacket that morning.

"So no, Leon, buddy, I am *not* taking you down to meet my vat-person. But I *will* get you started on a path that may take you there, someday, if you're very good and prove yourself out here. Once you've paid your dues."

Leon had paid plenty of dues—more than this blow-dried turd ever did. But he smiled and snuffled it up like a good little worm, hating himself. "Hit me."

"Look, we've been pitching vat-products for six years now without a single hit. Plenty of people have come through that door and stepped into the job you've got now, and they've all thrown a million ideas in the air, and every one came smashing to earth. We've never systematically cataloged those ideas, never got them in any kind of grid that will let us see what kind of territory we've already explored, where the holes are . . ." He looked meaningfully at Leon.

"You want me to catalog every failed pitch in the agency's history." Leon didn't hide his disappointment. That was the kind of job you gave to an intern, not a junior account exec.

Brautigan clicked his horsey teeth together, gave a laugh like a whinny, and left Ate's offices, admitting a breath of the boring air that circulated out there in the real world. The receptionist radiated matronly care in Leon's direction. He leaned her way and her fingers thunked on the mechanical keys of her converted Underwood Noiseless, a machine-gun rattle. He waited until she was done, then she turned that caring, loving smile back on him.

"It's all in your work space, Leon—good luck with it."

•　•　•　•

It seemed to Leon that the problems faced by immortal quadrillionaires in vats wouldn't be that different from those facing mere mortals. Once practically anything could be made for practically nothing, everything was practically worthless. No one needed to discover anymore—just *combine*, just *invent*. Then you could either hit a button and print it out on your desktop fab or down at the local depot for bigger jobs, or if you needed the kind of fabrication a printer couldn't handle, there were plenty of on-demand jobbers who'd have some worker in a distant country knock it out overnight and you'd have it in hermetic FedEx packaging on your desktop by the morning.

Looking through the Ate files, he could see that he wasn't the last one to follow this line of reasoning. Every account exec had come up with pitches that involved things that *couldn't* be fabbed—precious gewgaws that needed a trained master to produce—or things that *hadn't* been fabbed—antiques, one-of-a-kinds, fetish objects from history. And all of it had met with crashing indifference from the vat-people, who could hire any master they wanted, who could buy entire warehouses full of antiques.

The normal megarich got offered experiences: a ticket to space, a chance to hunt the last member of an endangered species, the opportunity to kill a man and get away with it, a deep-ocean sub to the bottom of the Marianas Trench. The people in the vat had done plenty of those things before they'd ended up in the vats. Now they were metastatic, these hyperrich, lumps of curdling meat in the pickling solution of a hundred vast machines that laboriously kept them alive amid their cancer blooms and myriad failures. Somewhere in that tangle of hoses and wires was something that was technically a person, and also technically a corporation, and, in many cases, technically a sovereign state.

Each concentration of wealth was an efficient machine, meshed in a million ways with the mortal economy. You interacted with the vats when you bought hamburgers, Internet connections, movies, music, books, electronics, games, transportation—the money left your hands and was sieved through their hoses and tubes, flushed back out into the world where other mortals would touch it.

But there was no easy way to touch the money at its most concentrated, purest form. It was like a theoretical superdense element from the first instant of the universe's creation, money so dense it stopped acting like money; money so dense it changed state when you chipped a piece of it off.

Leon's predecessors had been shrewd and clever. They had walked the length and breadth of the problem space of providing services and products to a person who was money who was a state who was a vat. Many of the nicer grace notes in the office came from those failed pitches—the business with the lights and the air, for example.

Leon had a good education, the kind that came with the mathematics of multidimensional space. He kept throwing axes at his chart of the failed inventions of Ate, Inc., mapping out the many ways in which they were similar and dissimilar. The pattern that emerged was easy to understand.

They'd tried *everything*.

. . . .

Brautigan's whinny was the most humiliating sound Leon had ever heard, in all his working life.

"No, of course you can't know what got sold to the vat-person! That was part of the deal—it was why the payoff was so large. *No one* knows what we sold to the vat-person. Not me, not the old woman. The man who sold it? He cashed out years ago, and hasn't been seen or heard from since. Silent partner, preferred shares, controlling interest—but he's the invisible man. We talk to him through lawyers who talk to lawyers who, it is rumored, communicate by means of notes left under a tombstone in a tiny cemetery on Pitcairn Island, and row in and out in longboats to get his instruction."

The hyperbole was grating on Leon. Third day on the job, and the sun-dappled, ozonated pseudoforested environment felt as stale as an old gym bag (there was, in fact, an old gym bag under his desk, waiting for the day he finally pulled himself off the job in time to hit the complimentary gym). Brautigan was grating on him more than the hyperbole.

"I'm not an asshole, Brautigan, so stop treating me like one. You hired me to do a job, but all I'm getting from you is shitwork, sarcasm, and secrecy."

The alliteration came out without his intending it to, but he was good at that sort of thing. "So here's what I want to know: is there any single solitary reason for me to come to work tomorrow, or should I just sit at home, drawing a salary until you get bored of having me on the payroll and can my ass?"

It wasn't entirely spontaneous. Leon's industrial psychology background was pretty good—he'd gotten straight As and an offer of a post-doc, none of which had interested him nearly so much as the practical applications of the sweet science of persuasion. He understood that Brautigan had been pushing him around to see how far he could be pushed. No one pushed like an ad guy—if you could sweet-talk someone into craving something, it followed that you could goad him into hating something just as much. Two faces of a coin and all that.

Brautigan faked anger, but Leon had spent three days studying his tells, and Leon could see that the emotion was no more sincere than anything else about the man. Carefully, Leon flared his nostrils, brought his chest up, inched his chin higher. He *sold* his outrage, sold it like it was potato chips, over-the-counter securities, or under-the-counter diet pills. Brautigan tried to sell his anger in return. Leon was a no sale. Brautigan bought.

"There's a new one," he said, in a conspiratorial whisper.

"A new what?" Leon whispered. They were still chest to chest, quivering with angry body language, but Leon let another part of his mind deal with that.

"A new monster," Brautigan said. "Gone to his vat at a mere 103. Youngest ever. Unplanned." He looked up, down, left, right. "An accident. Impossible accident. Impossible, but he had it, which means?"

"It was no accident," Leon said. "Police?" It was impossible not to fall into Brautigan's telegraphed speech style. That was a persuasion thing, too, he knew. Once you talked like him, you'd sympathize with him. And vice versa, of course. They were converging on a single identity. Bonding. It was intense, like make-up sex for coworkers. "He's a sovereign three ways. An African republic, an island, one of those little Baltic countries. On the other side of the international vowel line. Mxlplx or something. They swung for him at the WTO, the UN—whole bodies of international trade law for this one. So no regular cops; this is diplomatic corps stuff. And, of course, he's not dead, so that makes it more complicated."

"How?"

"Dead people become corporations. They get managed by boards of directors who act predictably, if not rationally. Living people, they're *flamboyant*. Seismic. Unpredictable. But. On the other hand." He waggled his eyebrows.

"On the other hand, they buy things."

"Once in a very long while, they do."

. . . .

Leon's life was all about discipline. He'd heard a weight-loss guru once explain that the key to maintaining a slim figure was to really "listen to your body" and only eat until it signaled that it was full. Leon had listened to his body. It wanted three entire pepperoni and mushroom pizzas every single day, plus a rather large cake. And malted milkshakes, the old-fashioned kind you could make in your kitchen with an antique Hamilton Beach machine in avocado-colored plastic, served up in a tall red anodized aluminum cup. Leon's body was extremely verbose on what it wanted him to shovel into it.

So Leon ignored his body. He ignored his mind when it told him that what it wanted to do was fall asleep on the sofa with the video following his eyes around the room, one of those shows that followed your neural activity and tried to tune the drama to maximize your engrossment. Instead, he made his mind sit up in bed, absorbing many improving books from the mountain he'd printed out and stacked there.

Leon ignored his limbic system when it told him to stay in bed for an extra hour every morning when his alarm detonated. He ignored the fatigue messages he got while he worked through an hour of yoga and meditation before breakfast.

He wound himself up tight with will and it was will that made him stoop to pick up the laundry on the stairs while he was headed up and neatly fold it away when he got to the spacious walk-in dressing room attached to the master bedroom. (The apartment had been a good way to absorb his Ate signing bonus—safer than keeping the money in cash, with the currency fluctuations and all. Manhattan real estate was a century-long good buy and was more stable than bonds, derivatives or funds.) It was discipline that made him pay every bill as it came in. It was all that which made him wash every dish when he was done with it and assiduously stop at the grocer's every night on the way home to buy anything that had run out the previous day.

His parents came to visit from Anguilla and they teased him about how *organized* he was, so unlike the fat little boy who'd been awarded the "Hansel and Gretel prize" by his sixth-grade teacher for leaving a trail behind him everywhere he went. What they didn't know was that he was still that kid, and every act of conscientious, precise, buttoned-down finicky habit was, in fact, the product of relentless, iron determination not to be that kid again. He not only ignored that inner voice of his that called out for pizzas and told him to sleep in, take a cab instead of walking, lie down and let the video soar and dip with his moods, a drip-feed of null and nothing to while away the hours—he actively denied it, shouted it into submission, locked it up, and never let it free.

And that—*that*—that was why he was going to figure out how to sell something new to the man in the vat: because anyone who could amass that sort of fortune and go down to life eternal in an ever-expanding kingdom of machines would be the sort of person who had spent a life denying himself, and Leon knew *just* what that felt like.

. . . .

The Lower East Side had ebbed and flowed over the years: poor, rich, middle-class, superrich, poor. One year the buildings were funky and reminiscent of the romantic squalor that had preceded this era of light-speed buckchasing. The next year, the buildings were merely squalorous, the landlords busted and the receivers in bankruptcy slapping up paper-thin walls to convert giant airy lofts into rooming houses. The corner stores sold blunt skins to trustafarian hipsters with a bag of something gengineered to disrupt some extremely specific brain structures; then they sold food-stamp milk to desperate mothers who wouldn't meet their eyes. The shopkeepers had the knack of sensing changes in the wind and adjusting their stock accordingly.

Walking around his neighborhood, Leon sniffed change in the wind. The shopkeepers seemed to have more discount, high-calorie wino-drink; less designer low-carb energy food with FDA-mandated booklets explaining their nutritional claims. A sprinkling of FOR RENT signs. A construction site that hadn't had anyone working on it for a week now, the padlocked foreman's shed growing a mossy coat of graffiti.

Leon didn't mind. He'd lived rough—not just student-rough, either. His parents had gone to Anguilla from Romania, chasing the tax-haven set, dreaming of making a killing working as bookkeepers, security guards. They'd mistimed the trip, arrived in the middle of an econopocalytpic collapse and ended up living in a vertical slum that had once been a luxury hotel. The sole Romanians among the smuggled Mexicans who were de facto slaves, they'd traded their ability to write desperate letters to the Mexican consulate for Spanish lessons for Leon. The Mexicans dwindled away—the advantage of de facto slaves over de jure slaves is that you can just send the de facto slaves away when the economy tanks, taking their feed and care off your books—until it was just them there, and without the safety of the crowd, they'd been spotted by local authorities and had to go underground. Going back to Bucharest was out of the question—the airfare was as far out of reach as one of the private jets the tax-evaders and high-rolling gamblers flew in and out of Wallblake Airport.

From rough to rougher. Leon's family spent three years underground, living as roadside hawkers, letting the sun bake them to an ethnically indeterminate brown. A decade later, when his father had successfully built up his little bookkeeping business and his mother was running a smart dress shop for the cruise ship day-trippers, those days seemed like a dream. But once he left for stateside university and found himself amid the soft, rich children of the fortunes his father had tabulated, it all came back to him, and he wondered if any of these children in carefully disheveled rags would ever be able to pick through the garbage for their meals.

The rough edge on the LES put him at his ease, made him feel like he was still ahead of the game, in possession of something his neighbors could never have—the ability to move fluidly between the worlds of the rich and the poor. Somewhere in those worlds, he was sure, was the secret to chipping a crumb off one of the great fortunes of the world.

• • • •

"Visitor for you," Carmela said. Carmela, that was the receptionist's name. She was Puerto Rican, but so many generations in that he spoke better Spanish than she did. "I put him in the Living Room." That was one of the three boardrooms at Ate, the name a bad pun, every stick of furniture in it an elaborate topiary sculpture of living wood and shrubbery. It was surprisingly comfortable, and the very subtle breeze had an even more subtle breath of honeysuckle that was so real he suspected it was piped in from a nursery on another level. That's how he would have done it: the best fake was no fake at all.

"Who?" He liked Carmela. She was all business, but her business was compassion, a shoulder to cry on and an absolutely discreet gossip repository for the whole firm.

"Envoy," she said. "His name's Buhle. I ran his face and name against our dossiers and came up with practically nothing. He's from Montenegro, originally, I have that much."

"Envoy from whom?" She didn't answer, just looked very meaningfully at him.

The new vat-person had sent him an envoy. His heart began to thump and his cuffs suddenly felt tight at his wrists. "Thanks, Carmela." He shot his cuffs.

"You look fine," she said. "I've got the kitchen on standby, and the intercom's listening for my voice. Just let me know what I can do for you."

He gave her a weak smile. This was why she was the center of the whole business, the soul of Ate. *Thank you,* he mouthed, and she ticked a smart salute off her temple with one finger.

• • • •

The envoy was out of place in Ate, but she didn't hold it against them. This he knew within seconds of setting foot into the Living Room. She got up, wiped her hands on her sensible jeans, brushed some iron-gray hair off her face, and smiled at him, an expression that seemed to say, "Well, this is a funny thing, the two of us, meeting here, like this." He'd put her age at around forty, and she was hippy and a little wrinkled and didn't seem to care at all.

"You must be Leon," she said, and took his hand. Short fingernails, warm, dry palm, firm handshake. "I *love* this room!" She waved her arm around in an all-encompassing circle. "Fantastic."

He found himself half in love with her and he hadn't said a word. "It's nice to meet you, Ms.—"

"Ria," she said. "Call me Ria." She sat down on one of the topiary chairs, kicking off her comfortable Hush Puppies and pulling her legs up to sit cross-legged.

"I've never gone barefoot in this room," he said, looking at her calloused feet—feet that did a lot of barefooting.

"Do it," she said, making scooting gestures. "I insist. Do it!"

He kicked off the handmade shoes—designed by an architect who'd given up on literary criticism to pursue cobblery—and used his toes to peel off his socks. Under his feet, the floor was—warm? cool?—it was *perfect*. He couldn't pin down the texture, but it made every nerve ending on the sensitive soles of his feet tingle pleasantly.

"I'm thinking something that goes straight into the nerves," she said. "It has to be. Extraordinary."

"You know your way around this place better than I do," he said.

She shrugged. "This room was clearly designed to impress. It would be stupid to be so cool-obsessed that I failed to let it impress me. I'm impressed. Also," she dropped her voice, "also, I'm wondering if anyone's ever snuck in here and screwed on that stuff." She looked seriously at him and he tried to keep a straight face, but the chuckle wouldn't stay put in his chest, and it broke loose, and a laugh followed it, and she whooped and they both laughed, hard, until their stomachs hurt.

He moved toward another topiary easy chair, then stopped, bent down, and sat on the mossy floor, letting it brush against his feet, his ankles, the palms of his hands and his wrists. "If no one ever has, it's a damned shame," he said, with mock gravity. She smiled, and she had dimples and wrinkles and crow's-feet, so her whole face smiled. "Do you want something to eat? Drink? We can get pretty much anything here—"

"Let's get to it," she said. "I don't want to be rude, but the good part isn't the food. I get all the food I need. I'm here for something else. The good part, Leon."

He drew in a deep breath. "The good part," he said. "Okay, let's get to it. I want to meet your—" What? Employer? Patron? Owner? He waved his hand.

"You can call him Buhle," she said. "That's the name of the parent company, anyway. Of course you do. We have an entire corporate intelligence arm that knew you'd want to meet with Buhle before you did." Leon had always assumed that his work spaces and communications were monitored by his employer, but now it occurred to him that any system designed from the ground up to subject its users to scrutiny without their knowledge would be a bonanza for anyone *else* who wanted to sniff them, since they could use the system's own capabilities to hide their snooping from the victims.

"That's impressive," he said. "Do you monitor everyone who might want to pitch something to Buhle, or . . ." He let the thought hang out there.

"Oh, a little of this and a little of that. We've got a competitive intelligence subdepartment that monitors everyone who might want to sell us something or sell something that might compete with us. It comes out to a pretty wide net. Add to that the people who might personally be a threat or opportunity for Buhle and you've got, well, let's say an appreciable slice of human activity under close observation."

"How close can it be? Sounds like you've got some big haystacks."

"We're good at finding the needles," she said. "But we're always looking for new ways to find them. That's something you could sell us, you know."

He shrugged. "If we had a better way of finding relevance in mountains of data, we'd be using it ourselves to figure out what to sell you."

"Good point. Let's turn this around. Why should Buhle meet with you?"

He was ready for this one. "We have a track record of designing products that suit people in his . . ." Talking about the vat-born lent itself to elliptical statements. Maybe that's why Brautigan had developed that annoying telegraph talk.

"You've designed one such product," she said.

"That's one more than almost anyone else can claim." There were two other firms like Ate. He thought of them in his head as Sefen and Nein, as though invoking their real names might cause them to appear. "I'm new here, but I'm not alone. We're tied in with some of the finest designers, engineers, research scientists . . ." Again with the ellipsis. "You wanted to get to the good part. This isn't the good part, Ria. You've got smart people. We've got smart people. What we have, what you don't have, is smart people who are impedance-mismatched to your organization. Every organization has quirks that make it unsuited to working with some good people and good ideas. You've got your no-go areas, just like anyone else. We're good at mining that space, the no-go space, the mote in your eye, for things that you need."

She nodded and slapped her hands together like someone about to start a carpentry project. "That's a great spiel," she said.

He felt a little blush creep into his cheeks. "I think about this a lot, rehearse it in my head."

"That's good," she said. "Shows you're in the right line of business. Are you a Daffy Duck man?"

He cocked his head. "More of a Bugs man," he said, finally, wondering where this was going.

"Go download a cartoon called 'The Stupor Salesman,' and get back to me, okay?" She stood up, wriggling her toes on the mossy surface and then stepping back into her shoes. He scrambled to his feet, wiping his palms on his legs. She must have seen the expression on his face because she made all those dimples and wrinkles and crow's-feet appear again and took his hand warmly. "You did very well," she said. "We'll talk again soon." She let go of his hand and knelt down to rub her hands over the floor. "In the meantime, you've got a pretty sweet gig, don't you?"

• • • •

"The Stupor Salesman" turned out to feature Daffy Duck as a traveling salesman bent on selling something to a bank robber who is holed up in a suburban bungalow. Daffy produces a stream of ever more improbable wares, and is violently rebuffed with each attempt. Finally, one of his attempts manages to blow up the robber's hideout, just as Daffy is once again jiggling the doorknob. As the robber and Daffy fly through the air, Daffy brandishes the doorknob at him and shouts, "Hey, bub, I know just what you need! You need a house to go with this doorknob!"

The first time he watched it, Leon snorted at the punchline, but on subsequent viewings, he found himself less and less amused. Yes, he was indeed trying to come up with a need that this Buhle didn't know he had—he was assuming Buhle was a he, but no one was sure—and then fill it. From Buhle's perspective, Leon figured, life would be just fine if he gave up and never bothered him again.

• • • •

And yet Ria had been so *nice*—so understanding and gentle, he thought there must be something else to this. And she had made a point of telling him that he had a "sweet gig" and he had to admit that it was true. He was contracted for five years with Ate, and would get a hefty bonus if they canned him before then. If he managed to score a sale to Buhle or one of the others, he'd be indescribably wealthy.

In the meantime, Ate took care of his every need.

But it was so *empty* there—that's what got him. There were a hundred people on Ate's production team, bright sorts like him, and most of them only used the office to park a few knickknacks and impress out-of-town relatives. Ate hired the best, charged them with the impossible, and turned them loose. They got lost.

Carmela knew them all, of course. She was Ate's den mother.

"We should all get together," he said. "Maybe a weekly staff meeting?"

"Oh, they tried that," she said, sipping from the triple-filtered water that was always at her elbow. "No one had much to say. The collaboration spaces update themselves with all the interesting leads from everyone's research, and the suggestion engine is pretty good at making sure you get an overview of anything relevant to your work going on." She shrugged. "This place is a show room, more than anything else. I always figured you had to give creative people room to be creative."

He mulled this over. "How long do you figure they'll keep this place open if it doesn't sell anything to one of the vat-people?"

"I try not to think about that too much," she said lightly. "I figure either we don't find something, run out of time and shut—and there's nothing I can do about it; or we find something in time and stay open—and there's nothing I can do about it."

"That's depressing."

"I think of it as liberating. It's like that lady said, Leon, you've got a sweet gig. You can make anything you can imagine, and if you hit one out of the park, you'll attain orbit and never reenter the atmosphere."

"Do the other account execs come around for pep talks?"

"Everyone needs a little help now and then," she said.

* * * *

Ria met him for lunch at a supper club in the living room of an eleventh floor apartment in a slightly run-down ex-doorman building in Midtown. The cooks were a middle-aged couple, he was Thai, she was Hungarian, the food was eclectic, light, and spicy, blending paprika and chilis in a nose-watering cocktail.

There were only two other diners in the tiny room for the early seating. They were another couple, two young gay men, tourists from the Netherlands, wearing crease-proof sports jackets and barely there barefoot hiking shoes. They spoke excellent English, and chatted politely about the sights they'd seen so far in New York, before falling into Dutch and leaving Ria and Leon to concentrate on each other and the food, which emerged from the kitchen in a series of ever more wonderful courses.

Over fluffy, caramelized fried bananas and Thai iced coffee, Ria effusively praised the food to their hosts, then waited politely while Leon did the same. The hosts were genuinely delighted to have fed them so successfully, and were only too happy to talk about their recipes, their grown children, the other diners they'd entertained over the years.

Outside, standing on Thirty-fourth Street between Lex and Third, a cool summer evening breeze and purple summer twilight skies, Leon patted his stomach and closed his eyes and groaned.

"Ate too much, didn't you?" she said.

"It was like eating my mother's cooking—she just kept putting more on the plate. I couldn't help it."

"Did you enjoy it?"

He opened his eyes. "You're kidding, right? That was probably the most incredible meal I've eaten in my entire life. It was like a parallel dimension of good food."

She nodded vigorously and took his arm in a friendly, intimate gesture, led him toward Lexington. "You notice how time sort of stops when you're there? How the part of your brain that's going 'what next? what next?' goes quiet?"

"That's it! That's *exactly* it!" The buzz of the jetpacks on Lex grew louder as they neared the corner, like a thousand crickets in the sky.

"Hate those things," she said, glaring up at the joyriders zipping past, scarves and capes streaming out behind them. "A thousand crashes upon your souls." She spat, theatrically.

"You make them, though, don't you?"

She laughed. "You've been reading up on Buhle then?"

"Everything I can find." He'd bought small blocks of shares in all the public companies in which Buhle was a substantial owner, charging them to Ate's brokerage account, and then devoured their annual reports. There was lots more he could feel in the shadows: blind trusts holding more shares in still more companies. It was the standard corporate structure, a Flying Spaghetti Monster of interlocking directorships, offshore holdings, debt parking lots, and exotic matryoshka companies that seemed on the verge of devouring themselves.

"Oy," she said. "Poor boy. Those aren't meant to be parsed. They're like the bramble patch around the sleeping princess, there to ensnare foolhardy knights who wish to court the virgin in the tower. Yes, Buhle's the largest jetpack manufacturer in the world, through a layer or two of misdirection." She inspected the uptown-bound horde, sculling the air with their fins and gloves, making course corrections and wibbles and wobbles that were sheer, joyful exhibitionism.

"He did it for me," she said. "Have you noticed that they've gotten better in the past couple years? Quieter? That was us. We put a lot of thought into the campaign; the chop shops have been selling 'loud pipes save lives' since the motorcycle days, and every tiny-dick flyboy wanted to have a pack that was as loud as a bulldozer. It took a lot of market smarts to turn it around; we had a low-end model we were selling way below cost that was close to those loud-pipe machines in decibel count; it was ugly and junky and fell apart. Naturally, we sold it through a different arm of the company that had totally different livery, identity, and everything. Then we started to cut into our margins on the high-end rides, and at the same time, we engineered them for a quieter and quieter run. We actually did some preproduction on a jetpack that was so quiet it actually *absorbed* noise, don't ask me to explain it, unless you've got a day or two to waste on the psycho-acoustics.

"Every swish bourgeois was competing to see whose jetpack could run quieter, while the low-end was busily switching loyalty to our loud junk mobiles. The competition went out of business in a year, and then we dummied-up a bunch of consumer protection lawsuits that 'forced'"—she drew air quotes—"us to recall the loud ones, rebuild them with pipes so engineered and tuned you could use them for the woodwinds section. And here we are." She gestured at the buzzing, whooshing fliers overhead.

Leon tried to figure out if she was kidding, but she looked and sounded serious. "You're telling me that Buhle dropped, what, a billion?"

"About eight billion, in the end."

"Eight billion rupiah on a project to make the skies quieter?"

"All told," she said. "We could have done it other ways, some of them cheaper. We could have bought some laws, or bought out the competition and changed their product line, but that's very, you know, *blunt*. This was sweet. Everyone got what they wanted in the end: fast rides, quiet skies, safe, cheap vehicles. Win win win."

An old school flier with a jetpack as loud as the inside of an ice blender roared past, leaving thousands scowling in his wake.

"That guy is plenty dedicated," she said. "He'll be machining his own replacement parts for that thing. No one's making them anymore."

He tried a joke: "You're not going to send the Buhle ninjas to off him before he hits Union Square?"

She didn't smile. "We don't use assassination," she said. "That's what I'm trying to convey to you, Leon."

He crumbled. He'd blown it somehow, shown himself to be the boor he'd always feared he was.

"I'm sorry," he said. "I guess—look, it's all kind of hard to take in. The sums are staggering."

"They're meaningless," she said. "That's the point. The sums are just a convenient way of directing power. Power is what matters."

"I don't mean to offend you," he said carefully, "but that's a scary sounding thing to say."

"Now you're getting it," she said, and took his arm again. "Drinks?"

．．．．

The limes for the daiquiris came from the trees around them on the rooftop conservatory. The trees were healthy working beasts, and the barman expertly inspected several limes before deftly twisting off a basket's worth and retreating to his workbench to juice them over his blender.

"You have to be a member to drink here," Ria said, as they sat on the roof, watching the jetpacks scud past.

"I'm not surprised," he said. "It must be expensive."

"You can't buy your way in," she said. "You have to work it off. It's a coop. I planted this whole row of trees." She waved her arm, sloshing a little daiquiri on the odd turf their loungers rested on. "I planted the mint garden over there." It was a beautiful little patch, decorated with rocks and favored with a small stream that wended its way through them.

"Forgive me for saying this," he said, "but you must earn a lot of money. *A lot,* I'm thinking."

She nodded, unembarrassed, even waggled her eyebrows a bit. "So you could, I don't know, you could probably build one of these on any of the buildings that Buhle owns in Manhattan. Just like this. Even keep a little staff on board. Give out memberships as perks for your senior management team."

"That's right," she said. "I could."

He drank his daiquiri. "I'm supposed to figure out why you don't, right?"

She nodded. "Indeed." She drank. Her face suffused with pleasure. He took a moment to pay attention to the signals his tongue was transmitting to him. The drink was *incredible*. Even the glass was beautiful, thick, hand-blown, irregular. "Listen, Leon, I'll let you in on a secret. *I want you to succeed*. There's not much that surprises Buhle and even less that pleasantly surprises him. If you were to manage it . . ." She took another sip and looked intensely at him. He squirmed. Had he thought her matronly and sweet? She looked like she could lead a guerrilla force. Like she could wrestle a mugger to the ground and kick the shit out of him.

"So a success for me would be a success for you?"

"You think I'm after money," she said. "You're still not getting it. Think about the jetpacks, Leon. Think about what that power means."

. . . .

He meant to go home, but he didn't make it. His feet took him crosstown to the Ate offices, and he let himself in with his biometrics and his pass phrase and watched the marvelous dappled lights go through their warm-up cycle and then bathe him with their wonderful, calming light. Then the breeze, and now it was a nighttime forest, mossier and heavier than in the day. Either someone had really gone balls-out on the product design, or there really was an indoor forest somewhere in the building growing under diurnal lights, there solely to supply soothing woodsy air to the agency's office. He decided that the forest was the more likely explanation.

He stood at Carmela's desk for a long time, then, gingerly, settled himself in her chair. It was plain and firm and well made, with just a little spring. Her funny little sculptural keyboard had keycaps that had worn smooth under her fingertips over the years, and there were shiny spots on the desk where her wrists had worn away the granite. He cradled his face in his palms, breathing in the nighttime forest air, and tried to make sense of the night.

The Living Room was nighttime dark, but it still felt glorious on his bare feet, and then, moments later, on his bare chest and legs. He lay on his stomach in his underwear and tried to name the sensation on his nerve endings and decided that "anticipation" was the best word for it, the feeling you get just beside the skin that's being scratched on your back, the skin that's next in line for a good scratching. It was glorious.

How many people in the world would ever know what this felt like? Ate had licensed it out to a few select boutique hotels—he'd checked into it after talking with Ria the first time—but that was it. All told, there were less than three thousand people in the world who'd ever felt this remarkable feeling. Out of eight billion. He tried to do the division in his head but kept losing the zeroes. It was a thousandth of a percent? A ten thousandth of a percent? No one on Anguilla would ever feel it: not the workers in the vertical slums, but also not the mere millionaires in the grand houses with their timeshare jets.

Something about that . . .

He wished he could talk to Ria some more. She scared him, but she also made him feel good. Like she was the guide he'd been searching for all his life. At this point, he would have settled for Brautigan. Anyone who could help him make sense of what felt like the biggest, scariest opportunity of his entire career.

He must have dozed, because the next thing he knew, the lights were flickering on and he was mostly naked, on the floor, staring up into Brautigan's face. He had a look of forced jollity, and he snapped his fingers a few times in front of Leon's face.

"Morning, sunshine!" Leon looked for the ghostly clock that shimmered in the corner of each wall, a slightly darker patch of reactive paint that was just outside of conscious comprehension unless you really stared at it. 4:12 AM. He stifled a groan. "What are you doing here?" he said, peering at Brautigan.

The man clacked his horsey teeth, assayed a chuckle. "Early bird. Worm."

Leon sat up, found his shirt, started buttoning it up. "Seriously, Brautigan."

"Seriously?" He sat down on the floor next to Leon, his big feet straight out ahead of him. His shoes had been designed by the same architect that did Leon's. Leon recognized the style.

"Seriously."

Brautigan scratched his chin. Suddenly, he slumped. "I'm shitting bricks, Leon. I am seriously shitting bricks."

"How did it go with your monster?"

Brautigan stared at the architect's shoes. There was an odd flare they did, just behind the toe, just on the way to the laces, that was really graceful. Leon thought it might be a standard distribution bell curve. "My monster is . . ." He blew out air. "Uncooperative."

"Less cooperative than previously?" Leon said. Brautigan unlaced his shoes and peeled off his socks, scrunched his toes in the moss. His feet gave off a hot, trapped smell. "What was he like on the other times you'd seen him?"

Brautigan tilted his head. "What do you mean?"

"He was uncooperative this time, what about the other times?"

Brautigan looked back down at his toes.

"You'd never seen him before this?"

"It was a risk," he said. "I thought I could convince him, face to face."

"But?"

"I bombed. It was—it was the—it was *everything*. The compound. The people. All of it. It was like a *city,* a *theme park*. They lived there, hundreds of them, and managed every tiny piece of his empire. Like Royal urchins."

Leon puzzled over this. "Eunuchs?"

"Royal eunuchs. They had this whole culture, and as I got closer and closer to him, I realized, shit, they could just buy Ate. They could destroy us. They could have us made illegal, put us all in jail. Or get me elected president. Anything."

"You were overawed."

"That's the right word. It wasn't a castle or anything, either. It was just a place, a well-built collection of buildings. In Westchester, you know? It had been a little town center once. They'd preserved everything good, built more on top of it. It all just . . . worked. You're still new here. Haven't noticed."

"What? That Ate is a disaster? I figured that out a long time ago. There's several dozen highly paid creative geniuses on the payroll here who haven't seen their desks in months. We could be a creative powerhouse. We're more like someone's vanity project."

"Brutal."

Leon wondered if he'd overstepped himself. Who cared? "Brutal doesn't mean untrue. It's like, it's like the money that came into this place, it became autonomous, turned into a strategy for multiplying itself. A bad strategy. The money wants to sell something to a monster, but the money doesn't know what monsters want, so it's just, what, beating its brains out on the wall. One day, the money runs out and . . ."

"The money won't run out," Brautigan said. "Wrong. We'd have to spend at ten-ex what we're burning now to even approach the principal."

"Okay," Leon said. "So it's immortal. That's better?"

Brautigan winced. "Look, it's not so crazy. There's an entire unserved market out there. No one's serving it. They're like, you know, like communist countries. Planned economies. They need something, they just acquire the capacity. No market."

"Hey, bub, I know just what you need! You need a house to go with this doorknob!" To his own surprise, Leon discovered that he did a passable Daffy Duck. Brautigan blinked at him. Leon realized that the man was a little drunk. "Just something I heard the other day," he said. "I told the lady from my monster that we could provide the stuff that their corporate culture precluded. I was thinking of, you know, how the samurai banned firearms. We can think and do the unthink- and undoable."

"Good line." He flopped onto his back. An inch of pale belly peeked between the top of his three-quarter-length culottes and the lower hem of his smart wraparound shirt. "The monster in the vat. Some skin, some meat. Tubes. Pinches of skin clamped between clear hard plastic squares, bathed in some kind of diagnostic light. No eyes, no top of the head where the eyes should be. Just a smooth mask. Eyes everywhere else. Ceiling. Floor. Walls. I looked away, couldn't make contact with them, found I was looking at something wet. Liver. I think."

"Yeesh. That's immortality, huh?"

"I'm there, 'A pleasure to meet you, an honor,' talking to the liver. The eyes never blinked. The monster gave a speech. 'You're a low-capital, high-risk, high-payoff long shot, Mr. Brautigan. I can keep dribbling sums to you so that you can go back to your wonder factory and try to come up with ways to surprise me. So there's no need to worry on that score.' And that was it. Couldn't think of anything to say. Didn't have time. Gone in a flash. Out the door. Limo. Nice babu to tell me how good it had been for the monster, how much he'd been looking forward to it." He struggled up onto his elbows. "How about you?"

Leon didn't want to talk about Ria with Brautigan. He shrugged. Brautigan got a mean, stung look on his face. "Don't be like that. Bro. Dude. Pal."

Leon shrugged again. Thing was, he *liked* Ria. Talking about her with Brautigan would be treating her like a . . . a *sales target*. If he were talking with Carmela, he'd say, "I feel like she wants me to succeed. Like it would be a huge deal for everyone if I managed it. But I also feel like maybe she doesn't think I can." But to Brautigan, he merely shrugged, ignored the lizardy slit-eyed glare, stood, pulled his pants on, and went to his desk.

* * * *

If you sat at your desk long enough at Ate, you'd eventually meet *everyone* who worked there. Carmela knew all, told all, and assured him that everyone touched base at least once a month. Some came in a couple times a week. They had plants on their desks and liked to personally see to their watering.

Leon took every single one of them to lunch. It wasn't easy—in one case, he had to ask Carmela to send an Ate chauffeur to pick up the man's kids from school (it was a half day) and bring them to the sitter's, just to clear the schedule. But the lunches themselves went very well. It turned out that the people at Ate were, to a one, incredibly interesting. Oh, they were all monsters, narcissistic, tantrum-prone geniuses, but once you got past that, you found yourself talking to people who were, at bottom, damned smart, with a whole lot going on. He met the woman who designed the moss in the Living Room. She was younger than he was, and had been catapulted from a mediocre academic adventure at the Cooper Union into more wealth and freedom than she knew what to do with. She had a whole Rolodex of people who wanted to sublicense the stuff, and she spent her days toying with them, seeing if they had any cool ideas she could incorporate into her next pitch to one of the lucky few who had the ear of a monster.

Like Leon. That's why they all met with him. He'd unwittingly stepped into one of the agency's top spots, thanks to Ria, one of the power-broker seats that everyone else yearned to fill. The fact that he had no idea how he'd got there or what to do with it didn't surprise anyone. To a one, his colleagues at Ate regarded everything to do with the vat-monsters as an absolute, unknowable crapshoot, as predictable as a meteor strike.

No wonder they all stayed away from the office.

. . . .

Ria met him in a different pair of jeans, these ones worn and patched at the knees. She had on a loose, flowing silk shirt that was frayed around the seams, and had tied her hair back with a kerchief that had faded to a non-color that was like the ancient New York sidewalk outside Ate's office. He felt the calluses on her hand when they shook.

"You look like you're ready to do some gardening," he said.

"My shift at the club," she said. "I'll be trimming the lime trees and tending the mint patch and the cucumber frames all afternoon." She smiled, stopped him with a gesture. She bent down and plucked a blade of greenery from the untidy trail edge. They were in Central Park, in one of the places where it felt like a primeval forest instead of an artful garden razed and built in the middle of the city. She uncapped her water bottle and poured water over the herb—it looked like a blade of grass—rubbing it between her forefinger and thumb to scrub at it. Then she tore it in two and handed him one piece, held the other to her nose, then ate it, nibbling and making her nose wrinkle like a rabbit's. He followed suit. Lemon, delicious and tangy.

"Lemongrass," she said. "Terrible weed, of course. But doesn't it taste amazing?" He nodded. The flavor lingered in his mouth.

"Especially when you consider what this is made of—smoggy rain, dog piss, choked up air, and sunshine, and DNA. What a weird flavor to emerge from such a strange soup, don't you think?"

The thought made the flavor a little less delicious. He said so.

"I love the idea," she said. "Making great things from garbage."

"About the jetpacks," he said, for he'd been thinking.

"Yes?"

"Are you utopians of some kind? Making a better world?"

"By 'you,' you mean 'people who work for Buhle'?"

He shrugged.

"I'm a bit of a utopian, I'll admit. But that's not it. You know Henry Ford set up these work camps in Brazil, 'Fordlandia,' and enforced a strict code of conduct on the rubber plantation workers? He outlawed the Caipirinha and replaced it with Tom Collinses, because they were more civilized."

"And you're saying Buhle wouldn't do that?"

She waggled her head from side to side, thinking it over. "Probably not. Maybe, if I asked." She covered her mouth as though she'd made an indiscreet admission.

"Are—*were*—you and he . . . ?"

She laughed. "Never. It's purely cerebral. Do you know where his money came from?"

He gave her a look.

"Okay, of course you do. But if all you've read is the official history, you'll think he was just a finance guy who made some good bets. It's nothing like it. He played a game against the market, tinkered with the confidence of other traders by taking crazy positions, all bluff, except when they weren't. No one could outsmart him. He could convince you that you were about to miss out on the deal of the century, or that you'd already missed it, or that you were about to walk off onto easy street. Sometimes, he convinced you of something that was real. More often, it was pure bluff, which you'd only find out after you'd done some trade with him that left him with more money than you'd see in your whole life, and you face-palming and cursing yourself for a sucker. When he started doing it to national banks, put a run on the dollar, broke the Fed, well, that's when we all knew that he was someone who was *special,* someone who could create signals that went right to your hindbrain without any critical interpretation."

"Scary."

"Oh yes. Very. In another era they'd have burned him for a witch or made him the man who cut out your heart with the obsidian knife. But here's the thing: he could never, ever kid *me*. Not once."

"And you're alive to tell the tale?"

"Oh, he likes it. His reality distortion field, it screws with his internal landscape. Makes it hard for him to figure out what he needs, what he wants, and what will make him miserable. I'm indispensable."

He had a sudden, terrible thought. He didn't say anything, but she must have seen it on his face.

"What is it? Tell me."

"How do I know that you're on the level about any of this? Maybe you're just jerking me around. Maybe it's all made-up—the jetpacks, everything." He swallowed. "I'm sorry. I don't know where that came from, but it popped into my head—"

"It's a fair question. Here's one that'll blow your mind, though: how do you know that I'm not on the level, *and* jerking you around?"

They changed the subject soon after, with uneasy laughter. They ended up on a park bench near the family of dancing bears, whom they watched avidly.

"They seem so *happy,*" he said. "That's what gets me about them. Like dancing was the secret passion of every bear, and these three are the first to figure out how to make a life of it."

She didn't say anything, but watched the three giants lumber in a graceful, unmistakably joyous kind of shuffle. The music—constantly mutated based on the intensity of the bears, a piece of software that sought tirelessly to please them—was jangly and poplike, with a staccato one-two/onetwothree-fourfive/one-two rhythm that let the bears do something like a drunken stagger that was as fun to watch as a box of puppies.

He felt the silence. "So happy," he said again. "That's the weird part. Not like seeing an elephant perform. You watch those old videos and they seem, you know, they seem—"

"Resigned," she said.

"Yeah. Not unhappy, but about as thrilled to be balancing on a ball as a horse might be to be hitched to a plow. But look at those bears!"

"Notice that no one else watches them for long?" she said. He had noticed that. The benches were all empty around them.

"I think it's because they're so happy," she said. "It lays the trick bare." She showed teeth at the pun, then put them away. "What I mean is, you can see how it's possible to design a bear that experiences brain reward from rhythm, keep it well-fed, supply it with as many rockin' tunes as it can eat, and you get that happy family of dancing bears who'll peacefully coexist alongside humans who're going to work, carrying their groceries, pushing their toddlers around in strollers, necking on benches—"

The bears were resting now, lolling on their backs, happy tongues sloppy in the corners of their mouths.

"We made them," she said. "It was against my advice, too. There's not much subtlety in it. As a piece of social commentary, it's a cartoon sledgehammer with an oversize head. But the artist had Buhle's ear, he'd been CEO of one of the portfolio companies and had been interested in genomic art as a sideline for his whole career. Buhle saw that funding this thing would probably spin off lots of interesting sublicenses, which it did. But just look at it."

He looked. "They're so *happy*," he said.

She looked too. "Bears shouldn't be that happy," she said.

· · · ·

Carmela greeted him sunnily as ever, but there was something odd.

"What is it?" he asked in Spanish. He made a habit of talking Spanish to her, because both of them were getting rusty, and also it was like a little shared secret between them.

She shook her head.

"Is everything all right?" Meaning, *Are we being shut down?* It could happen, might happen at any time, with no notice. That was something he— all of them—understood. The money that powered them was autonomous and unknowable, an alien force that was more emergent property than will.

She shook her head again. "It's not my place to say," she said. Which made him even more sure that they were all going down, for when had Carmela ever said anything about her *place?*

"Now you've got me worried," he said.

She cocked her head back toward the back office. He noticed that there were three coats hung on the beautiful, anachronistic coat stand by the ancient temple door that divided reception from the rest of Ate.

He let himself in and walked down the glassed-in double rows of offices, the cubicles in the middle, all with their characteristic spotless hush, like a restaurant dining room set up for the meals that people would come to later.

He looked in the Living Room, but there was no one there, so he began to check out the other conference rooms, which ran the gamut from super-conservative to utter madness. He found them in the Ceile, with its barn-board floors, its homey stone hearth, and the gimmicked sofas that looked like unsprung old thrift-store numbers, but which sported adaptive genetic algorithm–directed haptics that adjusted constantly to support you no matter how you flopped on them, so that you could play at being a little kid sprawled carelessly on the cushions no matter how old and cranky your bones were.

On the Ceile's sofa were Brautigan, Ria, and a woman he hadn't met before. She was somewhere between Brautigan and Ria's age, but with that made-up, pulled-tight appearance of someone who knew the world wouldn't take her as seriously if she let one crumb of weakness escape from any pore or wrinkle. He thought he knew who this must be, and she confirmed it when she spoke.

"Leon," she said. "I'm glad you're here." He knew that voice. It was the voice on the phone that had recruited him and brought him to New York and told him where to come for his first day on the job. It was the voice of Jennifer Torino, and she was technically his boss. "Carmela said that you often worked from here so I was hoping today would be one of the days you came by so we could chat."

"Jennifer," he said. She nodded. "Ria." She had a poker face on, as unreadable as a slab of granite. She was wearing her customary denim and flowing cotton, but she'd kept her shoes on and her feet on the floor. "Brautigan," and Brautigan grinned like it was Christmas morning.

Jennifer looked flatly at a place just to one side of his gaze, a trick he knew, and said, "In recognition of his excellent work, Mr. Brautigan's been promoted, effective today. He is now manager for Major Accounts." Brautigan beamed.

"Congratulations," Leon said, thinking, *What excellent work? No one at Ate has accomplished the agency's primary objective in the entire history of the firm!* "Well done."

Jennifer kept her eyes coolly fixed on that empty, safe spot. "As you know, we have struggled to close a deal with any of our major accounts." He restrained himself from rolling his eyes. "And so Mr. Brautigan has undertaken a thorough study of the way we handle these accounts." She nodded at Brautigan.

"It's a mess," he said. "Totally scattergun. No lines of authority. No checks and balances. No system."

"I can't argue with that," Leon said. He saw where this was going.

"Yes," Jennifer said. "You haven't been here very long, but I understand you've been looking deeply into the organizational structure of Ate yourself, haven't you?" He nodded. "And that's why Mr. Brautigan has asked that you be tasked to him as his head of strategic research." She smiled a thin smile. "Congratulations yourself."

He said, "Thanks," flatly, and looked at Brautigan. "What's strategic research, then?"

"Oh," Brautigan said. "Just a lot of what you've been doing: figuring out what everyone's up to, putting them together, proposing organizational structures that will make us more efficient at design and deployment. Stuff you're good at."

Leon swallowed and looked at Ria. There was nothing on her face. "I can't help but notice," he said, forcing his voice to its absolutely calmest, "that you haven't mentioned anything to do with the, uh, *clients.*"

Brautigan nodded and strained to pull his lips over his horsey teeth to hide his grin. It didn't work. "Yeah," he said. "That's about right. We need someone of your talents doing what he does best, and what you do best is—"

He held up a hand. Brautigan fell silent. The three of them looked at him. He realized, in a flash, that he had them all in his power, just at that second. He could shout BOO! and they'd all fall off their chairs. They were waiting to see if he'd blow his top or take it and ask for more. He did something else.

"Nice working with ya," he said. And he turned his back on the sweetest, softest job anyone could ask for. He said *adios* and *buena suerte* to Carmela on the way out, and he forced himself not to linger around the outside doors down at street level to see if anyone would come chasing after him.

· · · ·

The Realtor looked at him like he was crazy. "You'll never get two million for that place in today's market," she said. She was young, no-nonsense, black, and she had grown up on the Lower East Side, a fact she mentioned prominently in her advertising materials: *a local Realtor for a local neighborhood.*

"I paid two million for it less than a year ago," he said. The 80 percent mortgage had worried him a little but Ate had underwritten it, bringing the interest rate down to less than 2 percent.

She gestured at the large corner picture window that overlooked Broome Street and Grand Street. "Count the FOR SALE signs," she said. "I want to be on your side. That's a nice place. I'd like to see it go to someone like you, someone decent. Not some *developer*"—she spat the word like a curse—"or some corporate apartment broker who'll rent it by the week to VIPs. This neighborhood needs real people who really live here, understand."

"So you're saying I won't get what I paid for it?"

She smiled fondly at him. "No, sweetheart, you're not going to get what you paid for it. All those things they told you when you put two mil into that place, like 'They're not making any more Manhattan' and 'Location location location'? It's lies." Her face got serious, sympathetic. "It's supposed to panic you and make you lose your head and spend more than you think something is worth. That goes on for a while and then everyone ends up with too much mortgage for not enough home, or for too much home for that matter, and then blooey, the bottom blows out of the market and everything falls down like a soufflé."

"You don't sugarcoat it, huh?" He'd come straight to her office from Ate's door, taking the subway rather than cabbing it or even renting a jet-pack. He was on austerity measures, effective immediately. His brain seemed to have a premade list of cost-savers it had prepared behind his back, as though it knew this day would come.

She shrugged. "I can, if you want me to. We can hem and haw about the money and so on and I can hold your hand through the five stages of grieving. I do that a lot when the market goes soft. But you looked like the kind of guy who wants it straight. Should I start over? Or, you know, if you want, we can list you at two mil or even two point two, and I'll use that to prove that some *other* loft is a steal at one point nine. If you want."

"No," he said, and he felt some of the angry numbness ebb. He liked this woman. She had read him perfectly. "So tell me what you think I can get for it?"

She put her fist under her chin and her eyes went far away. "I sold that apartment, um, eight years ago? Family who had it before you. Had a look when they sold it to you—they used a different broker, kind of place where they don't mind selling to a corporate placement specialist. I don't do that, which you know. But I saw it when it sold. Have you changed it much since?"

He squirmed. "I didn't, but I think the broker did. It came furnished, nice stuff."

She rolled her eyes eloquently. "It's never nice stuff. Even when it comes from the best showroom in town, it's not nice stuff. Nice is antithetical to corporate. Inoffensive is the best you can hope for." She looked up, to the right, back down. "I'm figuring out the discount for how the place will show now that they've taken all the seams and crumbs out. I'm thinking, um, one point eight. That's a number I think I can deliver."

"But I've only *got* two hundred K in the place," he said.

Her expressive brown eyes flicked at the picture window, the FOR SALE signs. "And? Sounds like you'll break even or maybe lose a little on the deal. Is that right?"

He nodded. Losing a little wasn't something he'd figured on. But by the time he'd paid all the fees and taxes—"I'll probably be down a point or two."

"Have you got it?"

He hated talking about money. That was one thing about Ria is that she never actually talked about money—what money *did*, sure, but never money. "Technically," he said.

"Okay, technical money is as good as any other kind. So look at it this way: you bought a place, a really totally amazing place on the Lower East Side, a place bigger than five average New York apartments. You lived in it for, what?"

"Eight months."

"Most of a year. And it cost you one percent of the street price on the place. Rent would have been about eleven times that. You're up"—she calculated in her head—"it's about eighty-three percent."

He couldn't keep the look of misery off his face.

"What?" she said. "Why are you pulling faces at me? You said you didn't want it sugarcoated, right?"

"It's just that—" He dropped his voice, striving to keep any kind of whine out of it. "Well, I'd hoped to make something in the bargain."

"For what?" she said, softly.

"You know, appreciation. Property goes up."

"Did you do anything to the place that made it better?"

He shook his head.

"So you did no productive labor but you wanted to get paid anyway, right? Have you thought about what would happen to society if we rewarded people for owning things instead of doing things?"

"Are you sure you're a real estate broker?"

"Board certified. Do very well, too."

He swallowed. "I don't expect to make money for doing nothing, but you know, I just quit my job. I was just hoping to get a little cash in hand to help me smooth things out until I find a new one."

The Realtor gave a small nod. "Tough times ahead. Winds are about to shift again. You need to adjust your expectations, Leon. The best you can hope for right now is to get out of that place before you have to make another mortgage payment."

His pulse throbbed in his jaw and his thigh in counterpoint. "But I *need* money to—"

"Leon," she said, with some steel in her voice. "You're *bargaining*. As in denial, anger, bargaining, depression, and acceptance. That's healthy and all, but it's not going to get your place sold. Here's two options: one, you can go find another Realtor, maybe one who'll sugarcoat things or string you along to price up something else he's trying to sell. Two, you can let me get on with making some phone calls and I'll see who I can bring in. I keep a list of people I'd like to see in this 'hood, people who've asked me to look out for the right kind of place. That place you're in is one of a kind. I might be able to take it off your hands in very quick time, if you let me do my thing." She shuffled some papers. "Oh, there's a third, which is that you could go back to your apartment and pretend that nothing is wrong until that next mortgage payment comes out of your bank account. That would be *denial* and if you're bargaining, you should be two steps past that.

"What's it going to be?"

"I need to think about it."

"Good plan," she said. "Remember, depression comes after bargaining. Go buy a quart of ice cream and download some weepy movies. Stay off booze, it only brings you down. Sleep on it, come back in the morning if you'd like."

He thanked her numbly and stepped out into the Lower East Side. The bodega turned out to have an amazing selection of ice cream, so he bought the one with the most elaborate name, full of chunks, swirls, and stir-ins, and brought it up to his apartment, which was so big that it made his knees tremble when he unlocked his door. The Realtor had been right. Depression was next.

. . . .

Buhle sent him an invitation a month later. It came laser-etched into a piece of ancient leather, delivered by a messenger whose jetpack was so quiet that he didn't even notice that she had gone until he looked up from the scroll to thank her. His new apartment was a perch he rented by the week at five times what an annual lease would have cost him, but still a fraction of what he had been paying on the LES. It was jammed with boxes of things he hadn't been able to bring himself to get rid of, and now he cursed every knickknack as he dug through them looking for a good suit.

He gave up. The invitation said, "At your earliest convenience," and a quadrillionaire in a vat wasn't going to be impressed by his year-old designer job interview suit.

It had been a month, and no one had come calling. None of his queries to product design, marketing, R&D or advertising shops had been answered. He tried walking in the park every day, to see the bears, on the grounds that it was free and it would stimulate his creative flow. Then he noticed that every time he left his door, fistfuls of money seemed to evaporate from his pockets on little "necessities" that added up to real money. The frugality center of his brain began to flood him with anxiety every time he considered leaving the place and so it had been days since he'd gone out.

Now he was going. There were some clean clothes in one of the boxes, just sloppy jeans and tees, but they'd been expensive sloppy once upon a time, and they were better than the shorts and shirts he'd been rotating in and out of the tiny washing machine every couple days, when the thought occurred to him. The two-hundred-dollar haircut he'd had on his last day of work had gone shaggy and lost all its clever style, so he just combed it as best as he could after a quick shower and put on his architect's shoes, shining them on the backs of his pants legs on his way out the door in a gesture that reminded him of his father going to work in Anguilla, a pathetic gesture of respectability from someone who had none. The realization made him *oof* out a breath like he'd been gut-punched.

His frugality gland fired like crazy as he hailed a taxi and directed it to the helipad at Grand Central Terminus. It flooded him with so much cheapamine that he had to actually pinch his arms a couple times to distract himself from the full-body panic at the thought of spending so much. But Buhle was all the way in Rhode Island, and Leon didn't fancy keeping him waiting. He knew that to talk to money you had to act like money—impedance-match the money. Money wouldn't wait while he took the train or caught the subway.

He booked the chopper-cab from the cab, using the terminal in the backseat. At Ate, he'd had Carmela to do this kind of organizing for him. He'd had Carmela to do a hundred other things, too. In that ancient, lost time, he'd had money and help beyond his wildest dreams, and most days now he couldn't imagine what had tempted him into giving it up.

The chopper clawed the air and lifted him up over Manhattan, the canyons of steel stretched out below him like a model. The racket of the chopper obliterated any possibility of speech, so he could ignore the pilot and she could ignore him with a cordiality that let him pretend, for a moment, that he was a powerful executive who nonchalantly choppered around all over the country. They hugged the coastline and the stately rows of windmills and bobbing float-homes, surfers carving the waves, bulldozed strips topped with levees that shot up from the ground like the burial mound of some giant serpent.

Leon's earmuffs made all the sound—the sea, the chopper—into a uniform hiss, and in that hiss, his thoughts and fears seemed to recede for a moment, as though they couldn't make themselves heard over the white noise. For the first time since he'd walked out of Ate, the nagging, doubtful voices fell still and Leon was alone in his head. It was as though he'd had a great pin stuck through his chest that finally had been removed. There was a feeling of lightness, and tears pricking at his eyes, and a feeling of wonderful *obliteration,* as he stopped, just for a moment, stopped trying to figure out where he fit in the world.

The chopper touched down on a helipad at Newport State Airport, to one side of the huge X slashed into the heavy woods—new forest, fastgrowing carbon sinkers garlanded with extravagances of moss and vine. From the moment the doors opened, the heavy earthy smell filled his nose and he thought of the Living Room, which led him to think of Ria. He thanked the pilot and zapped her a tip and looked up and there was Ria, as though his thoughts had summoned her.

She had a little half smile on her face, uncertain and somehow childlike, a little girl waiting to find out if he'd be her friend still. He smiled at her, grateful for the clatter of the chopper so that they couldn't speak. She shook his hand, hers warm and dry, and then, on impulse, he gave her a hug. She was soft and firm too, a middle-aged woman who kept fit but didn't obsess about the pounds. It was the first time he'd touched another human since he left Ate. And, as with the chopper's din, this revelation didn't open him to fresh miseries—rather, it put the miseries away, so that he felt *better.*

"Are you ready?" she said, once the chopper had lifted off.

"One thing," he said. "Is there a town here? I thought I saw one while we were landing."

"A little one," she said. "Used to be bigger, but we like them small."

"Does it have a hardware store?"

She gave him a significant look. "What for? An ax? A nailgun? Going to do some improvements?"

"Thought I'd bring along a doorknob," he said.

She dissolved into giggles. "Oh, he'll *like* that. Yes, we can find a hardware store."

• • • •

Buhle's security people subjected the doorknob to millimeter radar and a gas chromatograph before letting it past. He was shown into an anteroom by Ria, who talked to him through the whole procedure, just light chatter about the weather and his real-estate problems, but she gently steered him around the room, changing their angle several times, and then he said, "Am I being scanned?"

"Millimeter radar in here too," she said. "Whole-body imaging. Don't worry, I get it every time I come in. Par for the course."

He shrugged. "This is the least offensive security scan I've ever been through," he said.

"It's the room," she said. "The dimensions, the color. Mostly the semiotics of a security scan are either *you are a germ on a slide* or *you are not worth trifling with, but if we must, we must.* We went for something a little . . . sweeter." And it was, a sweet little room, like the private study of a single mom who's stolen a corner in which to work on her secret novel.

Beyond the room—a wonderful place.

"It's like a college campus," he said.

"Oh, I think we use a better class of materials than most colleges," Ria said, airily, but he could tell he'd pleased her. "But yes, there's about fifteen thousand of us here. A little city. Nice cafés, gyms, cinemas. A couple artists in residence, a nice little Waldorf school . . ." The pathways were tidy and wended their way through buildings ranging from cottages to large, institutional buildings, but all with the feel of endowed research institutes rather than finance towers. The people were young and old, casually dressed, walking in pairs and groups, mostly, deep in conversation.

"Fifteen thousand?"

"That's the head office. Most of them doing medical stuff here. We've got lots of other holdings, all around the world, in places that are different from this. But we're bringing them all in line with HQ, fast as we can. It's a good way to work. Churn is incredibly low. We actually have to put people back out into the world for a year every decade, just so they can see what it's like."

"Is that what you're doing?"

She socked him in the arm. "You think I could be happy here? No, I've always lived off campus. I commute. I'm not a team person. It's okay, this is the kind of place where even lone guns can find their way to glory."

They were walking on the grass now, and he saw that the trees, strangely oversized red maples without any of the whippy slenderness he associated with the species, had a walkway suspended from their branches, a real Swiss Family Robinson job with rope railings and little platforms with baskets on pulleys for ascending and descending. The people who scurried by overhead greeted each other volubly and laughed at the awkwardness of squeezing past each other in opposite directions.

"Does that ever get old?" he said, lifting his eyebrows to the walkways.

"Not for a certain kind of person," she said. "For a certain kind of person, the delightfulness of those walkways never wears off." The way she said "certain kind of person" made him remember her saying, "Bears shouldn't be that happy."

He pointed to a bench, a long twig-chair, really, made from birch branches and rope and wire all twined together. "Can we sit for a moment? I mean, will Buhle mind?"

She flicked her fingers. "Buhle's schedule is his own. If we're five minutes late, someone will put five minutes' worth of interesting and useful injecta into his in box. Don't you worry." She sat on the bench, which looked too fragile and fey to take a grown person's weight, but then she patted the seat next to her, and when he sat, he felt almost no give. The bench had been very well built, by someone who knew what she or he was doing.

"Okay, so what's going on, Ria? First you went along with Brautigan scooping my job and exiling me to Siberia—" He held up a hand to stop her from speaking and discovered that the hand was shaking and so was his chest, shaking with a bottled-up anger he hadn't dared admit. "You could have stopped it at a word. You envoys from the vat-gods, you are the absolute monarchs at Ate. You could have told them to have Brautigan skinned, tanned, and made into a pair of boots, and he'd have measured your foot size himself. But you let them do it.

"And now, here I am, a minister without portfolio, about to do something that would make Brautigan explode with delight, about to meet one of the Great Old Ones, in his very vat, in person. A man who might live to be a thousand, if all goes according to plan, a man who is a *country*, sovereign and inviolate. And I just want to ask you, *why?* Why all the secrecy and obliqueness and funny gaps? *Why?*"

Ria waited while a pack of grad students scampered by overhead, deep in discussion of telomeres, the racket of their talk and their bare feet slapping on the walkway loud enough to serve as a pretense for silence. Leon's pulse thudded and his armpits slicked themselves as he realized that he might have just popped the bubble of unreality between them, the consensual illusion that all was normal, whatever normal was.

"Oh, Leon," she said. "I'm sorry. Habit here—there's some things that can't be readily said in utopia. Eventually, you just get in the habit of speaking out of the back of your head. It's, you know, *rude* to ruin peoples' gardens by pointing out the snakes. So, yes, okay, I'll say something right out. I like you, Leon. The average employee at a place like Ate is a bottomless well of desires, trying to figure out what others might desire. We've been hearing from them for decades now, the resourceful ones, the important ones, the ones who could get past the filters and the filters behind the filters. We know what they're like.

"Your work was different. As soon as you were hired by Ate, we generated a dossier on you. Saw your grad work."

Leon swallowed. His résumé emphasized his grades, not his final projects. He didn't speak of them at all.

"So we thought, well, here's something different, it's possible he may have a house to go with our doorknob. But we knew what would happen if you were left to your own devices at a place like Ate: they'd bend you and shape you and make you over or ruin you. We do it ourselves, all too often. Bring in a promising young thing, subject him to the dreaded Buhle Culture, a culture he's totally unsuited to, and he either runs screaming or . . . *fits in*. It's worse when the latter happens. So we made sure that you had a good fairy perched on your right shoulder to counterbalance the devil on your left shoulder." She stopped, made a face, mock slapped herself upside the head. "Talking in euphemism again. Bad habit. You see what I mean."

"And you let me get pushed aside . . ."

She looked solemn. "We figured you wouldn't last long as a button-polisher. Figured you'd want out."

"And that you'd be able to hire me."

"Oh, we could have hired you any time. We could have bought Ate. Ate would have given you to us—remember all that business about making Brautigan into a pair of boots? It applies all around."

"So you wanted me to . . . what? Walk in the wilderness first?"

"Now you're talking in euphemisms. It's catching! Let's walk."

. . . .

They gave him a bunny suit to wear into the heart of Buhle. First he passed through a pair of double-doors, faintly positively pressurized, sterile air that ruffled his hair on the way in. The building was low-slung, nondescript brown brick, no windows. It could have been a water sterilization plant or a dry goods warehouse. The inside was good tile, warm colors with lots of reds and browns down low, making the walls look like they were the inside of a kiln. The building's interior was hushed, and a pair of alert-looking plainclothes security men watched them very closely as they changed into the bunny suits, loose micropore coveralls with plastic visors. Each one had a small, self-contained air-circ system powered by a wrist cannister, and when a security man helpfully twisted the valve open, Leon noted that there were clever jets that managed to defog the visor without drying out his eyeballs.

"That be enough for you, Ria?" the taller of the two security men said. He was dressed like a college kid who'd been invited to his girlfriend's place for dinner: smart slacks a little frayed at the cuffs, a short-sleeved, pressed cotton shirt that showed the bulge of his substantial chest and biceps and neck.

She looked at her cannister, holding it up to the visor. "Thirty minutes is fine," she said. "I doubt he'll have any more time than that for us!" Turning to Leon, she said, "I think that the whole air supply thing is way overblown. But it does keep meetings from going long."

"Where does the exhaust go?" Leon said, twisting in his suit. "I mean, surely the point is to keep my cooties away from," he swallowed, "Buhle."

It was the first time he'd really used the word to describe a person, rather than a *concept*, and he was filled with the knowledge that the person it described was somewhere very close.

"Here," she said, and pointed to a small bubble growing out of the back of her neck. "You swell up, one little bladder at a time, until you look like the Michelin man. Some joke." She made a face. "You can get a permanent suit if you come here often. Much less awkward. But Buhle likes it awkward."

She led him down a corridor with still more people, these ones in bunny suits or more permanent-looking suits that were formfitting and iridescent and flattering.

"Really?" he said, keeping pace with her. "Elegant is a word that comes to mind, not awkward."

"Well, sure, elegant on the other side of that airlock door. But we're inside Buhle's body now." She saw the look on his face and smiled. "No, no, it's not a riddle. Everything on this side of the airlock is Buhle. It's his lungs and circulatory and limbic system. The vat may be where the meat sits, but all this is what makes the vat work. You're like a gigantic foreign organism that's burrowing into his tissues. It's intimate." They passed through another set of doors and now they were almost alone in a hall the size of his university's basketball court, the only others a long way off. She lowered her voice so that he had to lean in to hear her. "When you're outside, speaking to Buhle through his many tendrils, like me, or even on the phone, he has all the power in the world. He's a giant. But here, inside his body, he's very, very weak. The suits, they're there to level out the playing field. It's all head games and symbolism. And this is just Mark I, the system we jury-rigged after Buhle's . . . *accident*. They're building the Mark II about five miles from here, and half a mile underground. When it's ready, they'll blast a tunnel and take him all the way down into it without ever compromising the skin of Buhle's extended body."

"You never told me what the accident was, how he ended up here. I assumed it was a stroke or—"

Ria shook her head, the micropore fabric rustling softly. "Nothing like that," she said.

They were on the other side of the great room now, headed for the doors. "What is this giant room for?"

"Left over from the original floor plan, when this place was just biotech R&D. Used for all-hands meetings then, sometimes a little symposium. Too big now. Security protocol dictates no more than ten people in any one space."

"Was it assassination?" He said it without thinking, quick as ripping off a Band-Aid.

Again, the rustle of fabric. "No."

She put her hand on the door's crashbar, made ready to pass into the next chamber. "I'm starting to freak out a little here, Ria," he said. "He doesn't hunt humans or something?"

"No," and he didn't need to see her face, he could see the smile.

"Or need an organ? I don't think I have a rare blood type, and I should tell you that mine have been indifferently cared for—"

"Leon," she said, "if Buhle needed an organ, we'd make one right here. Print it out in about forty hours, pristine and virgin."

"So you're saying I'm not going to be harvested or hunted, then?"

"It's a very low probability outcome," she said, and pushed the crash-bar. It was darker in this room, a mellow, candlelit sort of light, and there was a rhythmic vibration coming up through the floor, a whoosh whoosh.

Ria said, "It's his breath. The filtration systems are down there." She pointed a toe at the outline of a service hatch set into the floor. "Circulatory system overhead," she said, and he craned his neck up at the grate covering the ceiling, the troughs filled with neatly bundled tubes.

One more set of doors, another cool, dark room, this one nearly silent, and one more door at the end, an airlock door, and another plainclothes security person in front of it; a side room with a glass door bustling with people staring intently at screens. The security person—a woman, Leon saw—had a frank and square pistol with a bulbous butt velcroed to the side of her suit.

"He's through there, isn't he?" Leon said, pointing at the airlock door.

"No," Ria said. "No. He's here. We are inside him. Remember that, Leon.

He isn't the stuff in the vat there. In some sense you've been in Buhle's body since you got off the chopper. His sensor array network stretches out as far as the heliport, like the tips of the hairs on your neck, they feel the breezes that blow in his vicinity. Now you've tunneled inside him, and you're right here, in his heart or his liver."

"Or his brain." A voice, then, from everywhere, warm and good humored. "The brain is overrated." Leon looked at Ria and she rolled her eyes eloquently behind her faceplate.

"Tuned sound," she said. "A party trick. Buhle—"

"Wait," Buhle said. "Wait. The brain, this is important, the brain is so overrated. The ancient Egyptians thought it was used to cool the blood, you know that?" He chortled, a sound that felt to Leon as though it began just above his groin and rose up through his torso, a very pleasant and very invasive sensation. "The heart, they thought, the heart was the place where the *me* lived. I used to wonder about that. Wouldn't they think that the thing between the organs of hearing, the thing behind the organs of seeing, that must be the me? But that's just the brain doing one of its little stupid games, backfilling the explanation. We think the brain is the obvious seat of the me because the brain already knows that it is the seat, and can't conceive of anything else. When the brain thought it lived in your chest, it was perfectly happy to rationalize that too—*Of course it's in the chest, you feel your sorrow and your joy there, your satiety and your hunger* . . . The brain, pffft, the brain!"

"Buhle," she said. "We're coming in now."

The nurse-guard by the door had apparently heard only their part of the conversation, but also hadn't let it bother her. She stood to one side, and offered Leon a tiny, incremental nod as he passed. He returned it, and then hurried to catch up with Ria, who was waiting inside the airlock. The outer door closed and for a moment, they were pressed up against one another and he felt a wild, horny thought streak through him, all the excitement discharging itself from yet another place that the me might reside.

Then the outer door hissed open and he met Buhle—he tried to remember what Ria had said, that Buhle wasn't this, Buhle was everywhere, but he couldn't help himself from feeling that this was *him*.

• • • •

Buhle's vat was surprisingly small, no bigger than the sarcophagus that an ancient Egyptian might have gone to in his burial chamber. He tried not to stare inside it, but he couldn't stop himself. The withered, wrinkled man floating in the vat was intertwined with a thousand fiber optics that disappeared into pinprick holes in his naked skin. There were tubes: in the big highways in the groin, in the gut through a small valve set into a pucker of scar, in the nose and ear. The hairless head was pushed in on one side, like a pumpkin that hasn't been turned as it grew in the patch, and there was no skin on the flat piece, only white bone and a fine metalling mesh and more ragged, curdled scar tissue.

The eyes were hidden behind a slim set of goggles that irised open when they neared him, and beneath the goggles they were preternaturally bright, bright as marbles, set deep in bruised-looking sockets. The mouth beneath the nostril-tubes parted in a smile, revealing teeth as neat and white as a toothpaste advertisement, and Buhle spoke.

"Welcome to the liver. Or the heart."

Leon choked on whatever words he'd prepared. The voice was the same one he'd heard in the outer room, warm and friendly, the voice of a man whom you could trust, who would take care of you. He fumbled around his suit, patting it. "I brought you a doorknob," he said, "but I can't reach it just now."

Buhle laughed, not the chuckle he'd heard before, but an actual, barked *Ha!* that made the tubes heave and the fiber optics writhe. "Fantastic," he said. "Ria, he's fantastic."

The compliment made the tips of Leon's ears grow warm.

"He's a good one," she said. "And he's come a long way at your request."

"You hear how she reminds me of my responsibilities? Sit down, both of you." Ria rolled over two chairs, and Leon settled into one, feeling it noiselessly adjust to take his weight. A small mirror unfolded itself and then two more, angled beneath it, and he found himself looking into Buhle's eyes, looking at his face, reflected in the mirrors.

"Leon," Buhle said, "tell me about your final project, the one that got you the top grade in your class."

Leon's fragile calm vanished, and he began to sweat. "I don't like to talk about it," he said.

"Makes you vulnerable, I know. But vulnerable isn't so bad. Take me. I thought I was invincible. I thought that I could make and unmake the world to my liking. I thought I understood how the human mind worked—and how it broke.

"And then one day in Madrid, as I was sitting in my suite's breakfast room, talking with an old friend while I ate my porridge oats, my old friend picked up the heavy silver coffee jug, leaped on my chest, smashed me to the floor, and methodically attempted to beat the brains out of my head with it. It weighed about a kilo and a half, not counting the coffee, which was scalding, and she only got in three licks before they pulled her off of me, took her away. Those three licks though—" He looked intently at them. "I'm an old man," he said. "Old bones, old tissues. The first blow cracked my skull. The second one broke it. The third one forced fragments into my brain. By the time the medics arrived, I'd been technically dead for about 174 seconds, give or take a second or two."

Leon wasn't sure the old thing in the vat had finished speaking, but that seemed to be the whole story. "Why?" he said, picking the word that was uppermost in his mind.

"Why did I tell you this?"

"No," Leon said. "Why did your old friend try to kill you?"

Buhle grinned. "Oh, I expect I deserved it," he said.

"Are you going to tell me why?" Leon said.

Buhle's cozy grin disappeared. "I don't think I will."

Leon found he was breathing so hard that he was fogging up his face-plate, despite the air-jets that worked to clear it. "Buhle," he said, "the point of that story was to tell me how vulnerable you are so that I'd tell you my story, but that story doesn't make you vulnerable. You were beaten to death and yet you survived, grew stronger, changed into this"—he waved his hands around—"this body, this monstrous, town-size giant. You're about as vulnerable as fucking Zeus."

Ria laughed softly but unmistakably. "Told you so," she said to Buhle. "He's a good one."

The exposed lower part of Buhle's face clenched like a fist and the pitch of the machine noises around them shifted a half tone. Then he smiled a smile that was visibly forced, obviously artificial even in that ruin of a face.

"I had an idea," he said. "That many of the world's problems could be solved with a positive outlook. We spend so much time worrying about the rare and lurid outcomes in life. Kids being snatched. Terrorists blowing up cities. Stolen secrets ruining your business. Irate customers winning huge judgments in improbable lawsuits. All this *chickenshit,* bed-wetting, hand-wringing *fear.*" His voice rose and fell like a minister's and it was all Leon could do not to sway in time with him. "And at the same time, we neglect the likely: traffic accidents, jetpack crashes, bathtub drownings. It's like the mind can't stop thinking about the grotesque, and can't stop forgetting about the likely."

"Get on with it," Ria said. "The speech is lovely, but it doesn't answer the question."

He glared at her through the mirror, the marble eyes in their mesh of burst blood vessels and red spider-tracks, like the eyes of a demon. "The human mind is just *kinked wrong.* And it's correctable." The excitement in his voice was palpable. "Imagine a product that let you *feel* what you *know*—imagine if anyone who heard 'Lotto: you've got to be in it to win it' immediately understood that this is *so much bullshit.* That statistically, your chances of winning the lotto are not measurably improved by buying a lottery ticket. Imagine if explaining the war on terror to people made them double over with laughter! Imagine if the capital markets ran on realistic assessments of risk instead of envy, panic, and greed."

"You'd be a lot poorer," Ria said.

He rolled his eyes eloquently.

"It's an interesting vision," Leon said. "I'd take the cure, whatever it was."

The eyes snapped to him, drilled through him, fierce. "That's the problem, *right there*. The only people who'll take this are the people who don't need it. Politicians and traders and oddsmakers know how probability works, but they also know that the people who make them fat and happy *don't* understand it a bit, and so they can't afford to be rational. So there's only one answer to the problem."

Leon blurted out, "The bears."

Ria let out an audible sigh.

"The fucking bears," Buhle agreed, and the way he said it was so full of world-weary exhaustion that it made Leon want to hug him. "Yes. As a social reform tool, we couldn't afford to leave this to the people who were willing to take it. So we—"

"Weaponized it," Ria said.

"Whose story is this?"

Leon felt that the limbs of his suit were growing stiffer, his exhaust turning it into a balloon. And he had to pee. And he didn't want to move.

"You dosed people with it?"

"Leon," Buhle said, in a voice that implied, *Come on, we're bigger than that.* "They'd consented to being medical research subjects. And it *worked*. They stopped running around shouting *The sky is falling, the sky is falling* and became—*zen*. Happy, in a calm, even-keeled way. Headless chickens turned into flinty-eyed air-traffic controllers."

"And your best friend beat your brains in—"

"Because," Buhle said, in a little Mickey Mouse falsetto, "*it would be unethical to do a broad-scale release on the general public.*"

Ria was sitting so still he had almost forgotten she was there.

Leon shifted his weight. "I don't think that you're telling me the whole story."

"We were set to market it as an antianxiety medication."

"And?"

Ria stood up abruptly. "I'll wait outside." She left without another word.

Buhle rolled his eyes again. "How do you get people to take antianxiety medication? Lots and lots of people? I mean, if I assigned you that project, gave you a budget for it—"

Leon felt torn between a desire to chase after Ria and to continue to stay in the magnetic presence of Buhle. He shrugged. "Same as you would with any pharma. Cook the diagnosis protocol, expand the number of people it catches. Get the news media whipped up about the anxiety epidemic. That's easy. Fear sells. An epidemic of fear? Christ, that'd be too easy. Far too easy. Get the insurers on board, discounts on the meds, make it cheaper to prescribe a course of treatment than to take the call center time to explain to the guy why he's *not* getting the meds."

"You're my kind of guy, Leon," Buhle said.

"So yeah."

"Yeah?"

Another one of those we're-both-men-of-the-world smiles. "Yeah."

Oh.

"How many?"

"That's the thing. We were trying it in a little market first. Basque country. The local authority was very receptive. Lots of chances to fine-tune the message. They're the most media-savvy people on the planet these days—they are to media as the Japanese were to electronics in the last century. If we could get them in the door—"

"How many?"

"About a million. More than half the population."

"You created a bioweapon that infected its victims with numeracy, and infected a million Basque with it?"

"Crashed the lottery. That's how I knew we'd done it. Lottery tickets fell by more than eighty percent. Wiped out."

"And then your friend beat your head in?"

"Well."

The suit was getting more uncomfortable by the second. Leon wondered if he'd get stuck if he waited too long, his overinflated suit incapable of moving. "I'm going to have to go, soon."

"Evolutionarily, bad risk assessment is advantageous."

Leon nodded slowly. "Okay, I'll buy that. Makes you entrepreneurial—"

"Drives you to colonize new lands, to ask out the beautiful monkey in the next tree, to have a baby you can't imagine how you'll afford."

"And your numerate Vulcans stopped?"

"Pretty much," he said. "But that's just normal shakedown. Like when people move to cities, their birthrate drops. And nevertheless, the human race is becoming more and more citified and still, it isn't vanishing. Social stuff takes time."

"And then your friend beat your head in?"

"Stop saying that."

Leon stood. "Maybe I should go and find Ria."

Buhle made a disgusted noise. "Fine. And ask her why she didn't finish the job? Ask her if she decided to do it right then, or if she'd planned it? Ask her why she used the coffee jug instead of the bread knife? Because, you know, I wonder this myself."

Leon backpedaled, clumsy in the overinflated suit. He struggled to get into the airlock, and as it hissed through its cycle, he tried not to think of Ria straddling the old man's chest, the coffee urn rising and falling.

She was waiting for him on the other side, also overinflated in her suit.

"Let's go," she said, and took his hand, the rubberized palms of their gloves sticking together. She half-dragged him through the many rooms of Buhle's body, tripping through the final door, then spinning him around and ripping, hard, on the release cord that split the suit down the back so that it fell into two lifeless pieces that slithered to the ground. He gasped out a breath he hadn't realized he'd been holding in as the cool air made contact with the thin layer of perspiration that filmed his body.

Ria had already ripped open her own suit and her face was flushed and sweaty, her hair matted. Small sweat rings sprouted beneath her armpits. An efficient orderly came forward and began gathering up their suits. Ria thanked her impersonally and headed for the doors.

"I didn't think he'd do that," she said, once they were outside of the building—outside the core of Buhle's body.

"You tried to kill him," Leon said. He looked at her hands, which had blunt, neat fingernails and large knuckles. He tried to picture the tendons on their backs standing out like sail ropes when the wind blew, as they did the rhythmic work of raising and lowering the heavy silver coffee pot.

She wiped her hands on her trousers and stuffed them in her pockets, awkward now, without any of her usual self-confidence. "I'm not ashamed of that. I'm proud of it. Not everyone would have had the guts. If I hadn't, you and everyone you know would be—" She brought her hands out of her pockets, bunched into fists. She shook her head. "I thought he'd tell you what we like about your grad project. Then we could have talked about where you'd fit in here—"

"You never said anything about that," he said. "I could have saved you a lot of trouble. I don't talk about it."

Ria shook her head. "This is Buhle. You won't stop us from doing anything we want to do. I'm not trying to intimidate you here. It's just a fact of life. If we want to replicate your experiment, we can, on any scale we want—"

"But I won't be a part of it," he said. "That matters."

"Not as much as you think it does. And if you think you can avoid being a part of something that Buhle wants you for, you're likely to be surprised. We can get you what you want."

"No you can't," he said. "If there's one thing I know, it's that you can't do that."

• • • •

Take one normal human being at lunch. Ask her about her breakfast. If lunch is great, she'll tell you how great breakfast is. If lunch is terrible, she'll tell you how awful breakfast was.

Now ask her about dinner. A bad lunch will make her assume that a bad dinner is forthcoming. A great lunch will make her optimistic about dinner.

Explain this dynamic to her and ask her again about breakfast. She'll struggle to remember the actual details of breakfast, the texture of the oatmeal, whether the juice was cold and delicious or slightly warm and slimy. She will remember and remember and remember for all she's worth, and then, if lunch is good, she'll tell you breakfast was good. And if lunch is bad, she'll tell you breakfast was bad.

Because you just can't help it. Even if you know you're doing it, you can't help it.

But what if you could?

· · · ·

"It was the parents," he said, as they picked their way through the treetops, along the narrow walkway, squeezing to one side to let the eager, gabbling researchers past. "That was the heartbreaker. Parents only remember the good parts of parenthood. Parents whose kids are grown remember a succession of sweet hugs, school triumphs, sports victories, and they simply forget the vomit, the tantrums, the sleep deprivation . . . It's the thing that lets us continue the species, this excellent facility for forgetting. That's what should have tipped me off."

Ria nodded solemnly. "But there was an upside, wasn't there?"

"Oh, sure. Better breakfasts, for one thing. And the weight loss—amazing. Just being able to remember how shitty you felt the last time you ate the chocolate bar or pigged out on fries. It was amazing."

"The applications do sound impressive. Just that weight-loss one—"

"Weight-loss, addiction counseling, you name it. It was all killer apps, wall to wall."

"But?"

He stopped abruptly. "You must know this," he said. "If you know about Clarity—that's what I called it, Clarity—then you know about what happened. With Buhle's resources, you can find out anything, right?"

She made a wry smile. "Oh, I know what history records. What I don't know is what *happened*. The official version, the one that put Ate onto you and got us interested—"

"Why'd you try to kill Buhle?"

"Because I'm the only one he can't bullshit, and I saw where he was going with his little experiment. The competitive advantage to a firm that knows about such a radical shift in human cognition—it's massive. Think of all the products that would vanish if numeracy came in a virus. Think of all the shifts in governance, in policy. Just imagine an *airport* run by and for people who understand risk!"

"Sounds pretty good to me," Leon said.

"Oh sure," she said. "Sure. A world of eager consumers who know the cost of everything and the value of nothing. Why did evolution endow us with such pathological innumeracy? What's the survival advantage in being led around by the nose by whichever witch doctor can come up with the best scare story?"

"He said that entrepreneurial things—parenthood, businesses . . ."

"Any kind of risk-taking. Sports. No one swings for the stands when he knows that the odds are so much better on a bunt."

"And Buhle *wanted* this?"

She peered at him. "A world of people who understand risk are nearly as easy to lead around by the nose as a world of people who are incapable of understanding risk. The big difference is that the competition is at a massive disadvantage in the latter case, not being as highly evolved as the home team."

He looked at her, really looked at her for the first time. Saw that she was the face of a monster, the voice of a god. The hand of a massive, unknowable machine that was vying to change the world, remake it to suit its needs. A machine that was *good at it.*

"Clarity," he said. "Clarity." She looked perfectly attentive. "Do you think you'd have tried to kill Buhle if you'd been taking Clarity?"

She blinked in surprise. "I don't think I ever considered the question."

He waited. He found he was holding his breath.

"I think I would have succeeded if I'd been taking Clarity," she said.

"And if Buhle had been taking Clarity?"

"I think he would have let me." She blurted it out so quickly it sounded like a belch.

"Is anyone in charge of Buhle?"

"What do you mean?"

"I mean—that vat-thing. Is it volitional? Does it steer this, this *enterprise*? Or does the enterprise tick on under its own power, making its own decisions?"

She swallowed. "Technically, it's a benevolent dictatorship. He's sovereign, you know that." She swallowed again. "Will you tell me what happened with Clarity?"

"Does he actually make decisions, though?"

"I don't think so," she whispered. "Not really. It's more like, like—"

"A force of nature?"

"An emergent phenomenon."

"Can he hear us?"

She nodded.

"Buhle," he said, thinking of the thing in the vat. "Clarity made the people who took it very angry. They couldn't look at advertisements without wanting to smash something. Going into a shop made them nearly catatonic. Voting made them want to storm a government office with flaming torches. Every test subject went to prison within eight weeks."

Ria smiled. She took his hands in hers—warm, dry—and squeezed them.

His phone rang. He took one hand out and answered it.

"Hello?"

"How much do you want for it?" Buhle's voice was ebullient. Mad, even.

"It's not for sale."

"I'll buy Ate, put you in charge."

"Don't want it."

"I'll kill your parents." The ebullient tone didn't change at all.

"You'll kill everyone if Clarity is widely used."

"You don't believe that. Clarity lets you choose the course that will make you happiest. Mass suicide won't make humanity happiest."

"You don't know that."

"Wanna bet?"

"Why don't you kill yourself?"

"Because dead, I'll never make things better."

Ria was watching intently. She squeezed the hand she held.

"Will you take it?" Leon asked Buhle.

There was a long pause.

Leon pressed on. "No deal unless you take it," he said.

"You have some?"

"I can make some. I'll need to talk to some lab techs and download some of my research first."

"Will you take it with me?"

Leon didn't hesitate. "Never."

"I'll take it," Buhle said, and hung up.

Ria took his hand again. Leaned forward. Gave him a dry, firm kiss on the mouth. Leaned back.

"Thank you," she said.

"Don't thank me," he said. "I'm not doing you any favors." She stood up, pulling him to his feet.

"Welcome to the team," she said. "Welcome to Buhle."